THE LAND GOD MADE IN ANGER

JOHN GORDON DAVIS was born in Zimbabwe, then called Rhodesia, of English parents, and was educated in South Africa. He became a member of the Seamen's Union, spending his university vacations at sea with the Dutch whaling fleet in the Antarctic, and on British merchantmen. He took degrees in political science and law, and joined the Rhodesian Civil Service as a public prosecutor, before becoming Crown Counsel. He was then appointed to the same position in Hong Kong. The success of *Hold My Hand I'm Dying*, his first novel, allowed him to take up writing full time. He and his wife Rosemary live in southern Spain.

JOHN GORDON DAVIS

The Land God Made in Anger

FONTANA/Collins

The extract from *The Encyclopaedia of the Third Reich* by
L. L. Snyder is reproduced by kind permission of Robert Hale Ltd.
The extract from *Who's Who in Nazi Germany* by Robert Wistrich
is reproduced by kind permission of Weidenfeld and Nicolson.
The extract from *The History of the Gestapo* by Jacques Delarue
is reproduced by kind permission of Macdonald & Co Ltd.

First published in Great Britain by Collins 1990
First issued in Fontana Paperbacks 1990

Copyright © Westminster NV 1990

Printed and bound in Great Britain by
William Collins Sons & Co. Ltd, Glasgow

To my dear sister, Jill Gordon-Davis Roomans

Acknowledgements

The authors to whom I am much indebted for allowing me to quote or paraphrase their work are identified in the story that follows.

I am further deeply indebted to the following people who unstintingly helped me with aspects of this book. (However any technical errors — and I don't believe there are any — are my own responsibility.) This list reflects my indebtedness in the order it arose.

Buck Buchanan and Ian McKerron of Anglo American Corporation, for opening many doors; Ken Stone, geologist, for lending me his house and showing me the desert; Paul van der Byl, former Information Officer of South West Africa-Namibia, for much history and folklore; Rudi Latuit and Steven Brain of the Department of Wildlife for permitting me access to prohibited areas of the Skeleton Coast; Commander Ian Manning of the South African Navy, for nautical wisdom; Herr Horst Bredow of the U-Boat Archive in Germany, for his expertise on submarines; Karl-Heinz Wahnig, former submariner, for more advice; Dr Simon Wiesenthal of the Documentation Centre, Vienna, for telling me about his extraordinary life-work hunting Nazi war-criminals; Jan van der Merwe, Chief Reporter of the Pretoria News, for political wisdom (and for many happy hours); Marichen Waldner, political correspondent for *Rapport* newspaper, for more wisdom on that subject; Professor Simon Bekker and Janis Grobbelaar of the University of South Africa for much elaboration on the same; Hans Strydom, former Political Editor of the *Sunday Times*, for further elaboration; Cyril Wilkinson, until recently head of BBC TV, Western Region, for a host of material and encouragement; Kirby McIntosh, of Walvis Bay, for showing me round town; Mr Coghill and Mr Swanepoel, also of Walvis Bay, for their instruction on the fishing industry of the Skeleton Coast; Alan Louw, also of Walvis Bay, professional diver, and Andrew Baynes of the British Sub-Aqua Club, for expert advice on that subject, James W. W. Thompson, Esq., FRCS (Ed), for advice on medical matters. And I am deeply indebted to David and Tana Hilton-Barber and to Colin and Dafni Wright for putting me up from time to time (putting up with me). But my greatest indebtedness is to my wife, Rosemary, for so much that cannot even be adumbrated.

Southern Africa is real. The characters, with obvious exceptions, are fictitious.

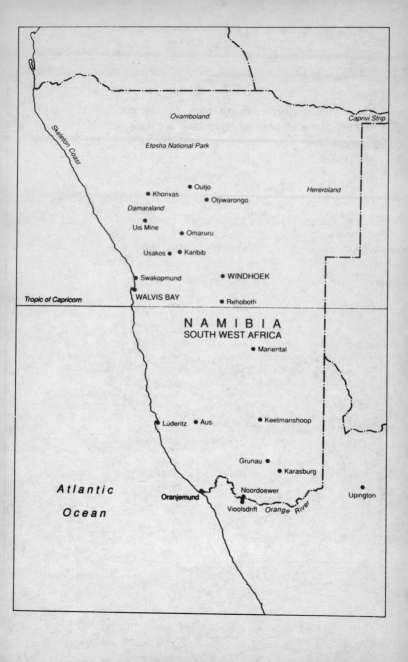

1

On these harsh shores it hardly ever rains. The sun beats down onto the desert coast, blinding white and yellow and brown and apricot and pink on the sand dunes that stretch on and on to the east. To the west the cold Atlantic seethes and crashes, stretching for thousands of miles to the Americas; this land is called the Skeleton Coast, for so many ships have wrecked themselves on its treacherous expanse, and so many shipwrecked men have perished. If they survived the savage sea, they died of thirst and starvation after they came crawling ashore. Here nobody lives. The only people who sometimes pass through this land are the strandlopers, hardy people from the hot hard hinterland of Namibia, who journey out of the vast desert to catch seals and shellfish.

This blinding day in June, 1945, two Damara strandlopers sat on the hot shore, resting. Before them, the vast Atlantic ocean was empty. Suddenly, something extraordinary happened.

Less than a thousand metres away, a man came out of the sea, like a demon. One moment there was nothing but the seething sea; the next there was a man, his arms thrashing. He started swimming frantically towards them. The two Damaras stared; then, to their further astonishment, another man erupted out. The two Damaras scrambled up and ran over the sand dune. They peered over the top.

The two demons were rearing up in the swells, disappearing in the white crashing thunder of the breakers. The man in front was the slower. He looked frantically behind him. He came labouring and gasping closer, then suddenly his feet found the bottom. He staggered upright and then collapsed as

1

another wave hit him. He staggered up again, then came stumbling up onto the beach, the waves crashing about his exhausted legs. He looked back, his chest heaving, clutching a small package to his chest. Then he pulled a pistol out of his pocket. He pointed it wildly at the other man, and pulled the trigger. Nothing happened. He turned and staggered off down the beach, trying to run, his legs buckling.

The second man came floundering towards the beach, wild-eyed. The two Damaras could see that blood was flowing from his head, flooding red into the crashing sea. He wrenched off a life-jacket; then he started trying to run after the other man.

The first man was fifty yards ahead, but he was slower. He staggered along, looking back wildly; then he could run no more. He reeled to face his adversary, and pointed the gun at him again. Again nothing happened. Then he hurled the gun. It hit the man a savage blow in the face, which caused him to lurch; and the first man pulled out a knife, and came at him. The second man recovered, and then went into a circle, crouched, his bare hands bunched, the blood streaming down his face. The first man circled after him, his face contorted, the knife in front, his other hand clutching his package; then suddenly he dropped it, picked up a handful of sand, and threw it. The second man staggered backwards, clawing the sand off his bloody face, blinded, and the first man lunged at him.

He came wildly, his killer knife on high, and plunged it deep into the man's breast. He lurched backwards, one arm up to ward off another stab, but the knife flashed again, and sank into his shoulder. He sprawled onto his back, blood spurting, and tried to scramble up, and the first man crashed on top of him, and the knife lunged down again. He pulled it out, and stabbed and stabbed the man four more times, whimpering. Then he toppled off and clambered to his feet.

He staggered, blood-spattered, and stared at his victim. The man was a mass of blood, welling from his chest. Then he tried to get up. He tried to roll over and heave himself up onto his hands and knees, and the first man gave a cry and lurched back at him. The second man tried to raise his arm to defend himself, but he collapsed. The first man dropped to his knees beside him, and sawed the blade across the man's gullet.

Then he clambered to his feet, red sand sticking to him. He looked at his victim; then he turned and picked up his package. He looked for the gun, picked it up, then wiped the sand off it. He sat down with a thump, chest heaving, getting his breath back; then he put his hand in his pocket and pulled out an oilcloth bag. He cut it open with trembling fingers, and pulled out a cardboard box. It contained bullets. He opened the magazine of the gun. He pulled out the shells, and reloaded. He scooped up the empty shells, and threw them into the sea. Then he turned to his package.

It was also an oilcloth bag. He cut the stitching. Inside were two smaller bags. He stood up unsteadily, and buried one in a trouser pocket. In his other pocket was a bulky leather wallet. He pulled it out and put the other bag in its place. He then tried to stuff the wallet into the pocket beside the bag. It was too much, so he stuffed it into his breast pocket. Then he turned back to the corpse.

He took hold of the dead man's ankles and dragged him above the high-water line: then he began to scoop out a shallow grave.

He rolled the body into it. He scooped the sand back over it, then clambered to his feet. His mouth was parched. He walked unsteadily back to the sea. He washed the bloody sand off his arms and face. Then he started plodding down the burning shore. He only knew that he had to head south. That was where civilization lay. How far, he did not know.

He only got about a mile before he had to rest. It was blazing hot and he was frantic with thirst. There was a promontory of rocks. He clambered over them. On the other side, he crept into the shade of a big boulder, and sat down, the

3

gun dangling between his knees. That is how he was when the two Damara strandlopers came creeping over the rocks, following him.

The white man jerked and swung the gun on them. The two Damaras stopped, frightened.

The white man scrambled to his feet, the gun trained on them shakily. Then both Damaras turned to flee, and in a flash the man fired. Both men froze, cowered, terrified. The white man stood there, wild-eyed; then he motioned with the gun, ordering them to drop their weapons.

The Damaras laid down their bows and their slingbags. The terrifying white man held out his trembling hand. *'Wasser!'* He made a drinking motion.

Carefully one Damara opened his bag. Inside was an assortment of old bottles with wooden stoppers. He lifted one out.

The white man snatched it. He drank feverishly, his eyes never leaving them. He swallowed and swallowed, and the two men watched him fearfully. He drank the bottle dry, then threw it down. He held out his hand for another. It was given to him. He drank half of it. Then he said:

'Swakopmund!'

The Damaras understood. Neither of them had ever been to the white man's town faraway to the south, but they had heard about the extraordinary place at the mouth of the river which is almost always dry. The Damara who was called Jakob pointed down the hostile coast.

The white man picked up their bows and motioned them to start leading the way.

In less than an hour he knew it was hopeless: he had to struggle to keep up, and tonight, when he fell asleep, the two men would disappear. He could not afford to leave witnesses, and when the sun began to get low he decided to kill them so that he could throw himself down and sleep. First, however, he wanted them to make a fire.

There was plenty of driftwood. He called a halt, and

motioned them to put their slingbags at his feet, before indicating that he wanted a fire. The Damaras set to work. The
white man collapsed in the sand. He opened one of the
slingbags and found dried meat, which he began to chew
ravenously.

The two Damaras made the fire. Jakob took a straight stick,
the size of a pencil, out of his bag, and a piece of flat wood.
He put a pinch of sand on the very edge of the wood, and
some kindling underneath. Then, holding the straight stick
vertical, he rubbed it between his palms onto the sandy
wood, very hard, until the friction caused smoke. A tiny glow
fell off the wood into the kindling below. The other Damara,
called Petrus, blew on it, whilst Jakob ground the stick, and
the kindling blossomed into a little flame. They scuttled
about on their haunches, getting more kindling, crouching to
blow. Then Petrus suddenly gave a gasp and pointed down
the beach; the white man turned to look, and Jakob hit him.

Jakob seized a piece of jagged wood and swung it with all
his might and the white man flung up an arm. The wood
crashed against his wrist and gashed it to the bone, and he
sprawled. His wallet jerked out of his pocket and the gun
went flying. Jakob bounded and swiped the man's mouth,
and his lips split and his front teeth smashed off at the roots.
Jakob raised his club again and the man cried out, trying to
cover his head. Jakob threw down the stick and snatched up
his slingbag, and Petrus snatched up the bows and the man's
wallet. They ran away into the dunes, leaving one slingbag
behind in their panic.

A thousand miles down the Skeleton Coast is the Cape of
Good Hope, 'The Tavern of the Seas' on the route from
Europe to the East, with its oaks and its vineyards and its fruit
– the Fairest Cape of All, it is said. Further to the east are the
mighty Tsitsikama forests, and then come the rolling hills of
the Ciskei and the Transkei, the homelands of the Xhosa
people beneath the mountain stronghold of Lesotho, the

kingdom of the Basuto people; then come the lush green hills of Natal where the sugar cane grows, the home of the Zulu people, who were a mighty warrior nation. Then across the magnificent towering Drakensberg mountains lie the farmlands of the Orange Free State, the vast highveld and the bushveld of the Transvaal, the land of rich goldfields, the strongholds of the hard people of Dutch descent, who are called Afrikaners. They live surrounded by many tribes: the Swazis in their mountain kingdom, the Tswanas, the Vendas, the Matabele. To the west of this country is the Kalahari desert and beyond that lies the vast desert country called South West Africa-Namibia, with its Skeleton Coast, where live the Ovambo people, and the Himba and the Herero, the Damaras and the Bushmen, to name but some, as well as Germans and Afrikaners. There are many different countries in this dramatic land of southern Africa, with many different climates, and many different peoples, and many languages and many different customs, but the most dramatic country of all is the one known as The Land God Made in Anger, the desert land called South West Africa-Namibia, or more commonly simply Namibia, where this story began.

Legally, Namibia is not part of the Republic of South Africa. It is a former German colony which was handed to South Africa by the League of Nations at the end of the First World War under a mandate to govern in the best interests of the natives until such time as it was appropriate to grant the colony independence. Halfway up is the little enclave of Walvis Bay, the only deep-water harbour in the whole vast coast, which *is* legally part of South Africa. It was to this unusual part of the world that James McQuade came back forty years after Jakob and Petrus saw the two men erupt out of the sea and fight to the death on the burning shore.

James van Niekerk McQuade once served twelve months in prison for contravening the Immorality Act, but do not be too alarmed by that because it happened like this: in those days, when he was starting a trawler-fishing company in

Cape Town, he sailed to the Antarctic every year on the whaling fleets to make extra money, and down at the Ice he fell madly in love with the ship's nurse, a South African girl who happened to have some Malaysian blood. She was only one-sixteenth Malay, but that was enough to make her a Coloured under South Africa's laws in those days. When they got back from the Ice she was pregnant and he unlawfully married her. When they were charged for breaching the racial laws, he packed her off secretly to England to have her baby. The magistrate sentenced him to twelve months imprisonment with hard labour, and he never saw his wife again. She wrote to him in prison saying that she had miscarried, that she had ruined his life and that he should forget about her. There was no address. When he came out of prison he moved his fishing company to Walvis Bay to get away from his wicked past, put a skipper in charge and hurried to England to look for his wife. After six months he had given up and emigrated to Australia to start life again, an embittered man. No way was he going to go back to goddam South Africa.

Nor did he, for twelve years. He hated the place. Not the country — for it is a wonderful country — but the government with its Apartheid laws. But he still had connections with South Africa. There was his house, which returned a reasonable rent, mortgaged to pay for his trawler, and there was his fishing company, which most years showed a reasonable profit. While in Australia, he had formed Sausmarine, a small, one-freighter shipping line that plied between Australia, South Africa and Ghana, a route that became profitable when the Australian Dockworkers' Union refused to off-load South African cargo. Australian businessmen document their cargo as bound for Ghana, and your understanding Sausmarine off-loads it in Cape Town. And vice versa. You'd never believe the mistakes these shipping clerks make: South African exports get misloaded into crates bearing Ghanaian labels. (Sausmarine never went near Ghana — her

7

ship was called *Rocket* because she did the putative trip so fast.) And to make confusion more confounded, Sausmarine was registered in Panama. But, during all those years, McQuade did not sail to South Africa: Kid Childe, Tucker and L. C. Brooks ran the ship, and McQuade ran the company from a one-roomed office above a Greek café on the Adelaide waterfront. It was not bad business until sanctions against South Africa heated up and the competition with other sanction-busters became too sharp. McQuade had not the slightest compunction about beating the Dockworkers' Union at their own commie game, but he drew the line at more prison. Finally he decided to sell up Sausmarine, go back to South Africa and work the fishing company hard with a skeleton crew, then sell it and put the money into a small passenger ship to ply down the Great Barrier Reef, from Cairns to Sydney. That's a lovely part of the world, and there was a crying need for that service.

There was another good reason for getting his investments out: called 435. United Nations' Resolution 435 ordered South Africa, the polecat nation of the world, to grant independence to South West Africa-Namibia. For years South Africa had been fighting a war with SWAPO, the South West African Peoples Organization, a terrorist Marxist movement, and had no intention of handing the country over to *them*: but now SWAPO had thirty thousand Cuban soldiers to help, and McQuade saw the writing on the wall. The same writing that had spelled out the collapse of Rhodesia and the Portuguese colonies and the Congo and the rest of British Africa: you win every battle but lose the war. God knows McQuade had no love for the South African Government but he had much less love for communists, and certainly no desire to fish in their territorial waters. So – sell up whilst the going was still good, and wash his hands of goddam Africa forever.

That is how James McQuade was feeling when he walked off the tarmac into Jan Smuts Airport in Johannesburg and heard South African accents again. Ivor Nathan was there to meet him, looking as much like Groucho Marx as ever. They had been at university together. Nathan gave him a bed for the night and tried to cheer him up: South Africa wasn't as bad as it used to be, Nathan said, Apartheid was unenforced almost everywhere now, except in the rural districts where the Hairybacks still thought the world was flat. 'But it's all still on the bloody statute book,' McQuade said.

'The Sex Laws have been repealed,' Nathan said. 'The Immorality Act and the Mixed Marriages Act. The government is trying to reform but it daren't repeal them all at once, for fear of a backlash, but give them time, my boy, my life.'

'Just another decade or two?'

'Well, we've got a Coloured House of Representatives now, and an Indian House of Delegates. I tell you, things *are* changing.'

'But no Black House. It's all too little too late. And what about this right-wing AWB mob, stomping around with their bloody swastikas and armbands?'

'Lunatic fringe,' Nathan said.

'They don't sound so fringe in the overseas press! It sounds as if the whole country's turned Nazi.'

'Lunatic fringe,' Nathan insisted.

McQuade sighed. 'Anyway, what about the war on the border – that's *my* problem. What about 435? Is South Africa going to grant independence to Namibia? That's the question. If so, the fishing industry goes down the communist drain and I'm bankrupt.'

'No *way* is South Africa going to implement 435 as long as the Cubans are there, and no way is Castro going to withdraw them because he wants to go down in history as the Scourge of the Afrikaner. Independence is a hell of a long way off, so your fishing's safe for a long time.'

'Is it, hell. The fleets of the world are out there raping the Benguela current because South Africa daren't enforce

9

Namibia's two hundred-mile maritime belt because of god-dam 435.'

Nathan sighed. 'What's Australia like?'

'Australia's great,' McQuade said, 'and it's got no Black Problem.'

'Because the Aussies shot most of them. At least we were Christians.'

'*We?* You're a closet Goy, Nathan.'

'Once a South African, always a South African.' Nathan sighed. 'You can't expect too much of us.'

The next day McQuade flew to Cape Town. Even beautiful Table Mountain rising up seemed to be only a monument to Afrikanerdom, and God he was glad he was washing his hands of the lot of them. He was an Australian now. He checked his house. He felt no pangs when he saw the nice old place, and he was glad he was getting rid of it. He visited half a dozen estate agents. Then he bought an old Landrover. That afternoon he set off, driving north, out of the beautiful vineyard country with its grand old Dutch architecture, heading for the Orange River and South West Africa-Namibia beyond, the Land God Made in Anger.

You probably don't know that bridge over the Orange River. The road curves down out of the dry, stony hills at Vioolsdrift where there is a general dealer's store, a gas station and a police post. Then suddenly there is the river, the water muddy orange, a belt of green, then the flinty desert rising up beyond: hot, hard, dry as hell. McQuade saw nothing beautiful in that desolate vista, but when he was halfway over that river he felt his depression lift. Man, this was dramatic country, he had forgotten how magnificently dramatic it was. And the Republic of South Africa was officially behind him and there was a feeling of youthfulness on this side of the river, a frontier feeling of wide open spaces, as if the long arm of Pretoria had to pull its punches here because of 435, and everybody knew it. He stopped at Noordoewer, which is a little hotel on the other side. There were a score of Coloureds squatting around, doing nothing. He filled up with diesel and drank a row of cold beers, and the Afrikaans words he had not used for twelve years came flooding back to his tongue without thinking: and, by God, it was a strange but nice feeling. These were people he just naturally knew and understood, and he almost felt like an African again.

He bought a six-pack of beers and set off north again. And there was nothing beautiful in that flat, hard, grey-brown desert stretching on and on, blistering hot, and maybe it was the beer he was drinking as he drove, but he found himself almost happy, and it almost felt as if he was coming home. At Keetmanshoop he turned west, towards Lüderitz on the far-away Atlantic, and now he was driving through thorn-tree country with sparse yellow grass, and he saw wild horses and ostriches. Near Aus he turned north again, through the vast cattle country, ranches thousands of square kilometres in size. That night he slept beside his Landrover, under the stars, near the oasis called Sesriem, where the creeping sand dunes are three hundred feet high and change colour from pink to mauve to apricot to gold in the shifting light. Maybe it was because of all the beer, but it seemed there is no feeling like an African night, no stars so bright, no night sounds so intimate and significant, no smell and light of fire so true to life. And even the next afternoon, when he came grinding down out of the hot hard hills of the Namib desert onto the vast sand-duned plains, and then the distant hostile Atlantic began to show through the shimmering haze, until finally, the flat white smudge of Walvis Bay, one of the drabbest ports in this world, began to coagulate in the distance – even then he still felt better about coming back. As Nathan had said: 'Once a South African, always a South African – you cannot expect too much of us.'

11

PART ONE

1

Nowadays, beyond the cold horizon, the Atlantic is lit up like a fairy land at night with the fishing fleets from around the world raping the icy Benguela current; the Russians, the Japanese, Norwegians, Spanish, Portuguese, the South Africans, all with the most sophisticated gear, and factory ships for refrigeration. The South African boats bring their catch back to Walvis Bay, and the smell of fish hangs like a cloud. Yet it is said that you only cry twice in Walvis Bay: the day you arrive, and the day you leave. McQuade couldn't understand it: the town was an eyesore, row upon row of squat, drab dwellings with corrugated iron roofs standing in dismal plots of desert sand, stretching back from the odiferous wharfs and the railway line. The shops are aggressively unattractive, and the sand blows down the streets and banks up in the gutters. Forty kilometres up the coast, beyond the enclave's invisible borders, is the town of Swakopmund, with old Bavarian architecture, elaborate old public buildings and homes and nice hotels with *gemütliche* bars with flowering, shaded courtyards under the desert sun. Both sun-blistered towns were built at the same time, at the start of this century: the difference being (according to McQuade) that Swakopmund was built by real Germans with culture behind them, whereas Walvis Bay was built by Afrikaners who had been detribalized from Europe for three hundred years. Yet he was always happy when he saw the flat, drab port come up over the horizon and he felt an extraordinary affection for the place. Maybe that was because anybody would be happy coming back after four weeks on the heaving Atlantic, or maybe it was the steamy thighs of the Stormtrooper awaiting

15

him – ('When will you marry me, you *englisches Schwein*, you cad, you unspeakable bounder?') ('*Liebchen*, I'm still married.') (*Liar . . .*) Or maybe it was the magnificent desert. But it was more: there was a colonial youthfulness about this ancient land, a sense of optimism, a comradeship amongst its people, almost a conspiracy against the heavy hand of faraway Pretoria. He had been back two years and the company was still in debt, but although it was still the plan to sell up as soon as possible, go back to Australia and start that passenger line, till then he was glad he had come back to Africa. That is how McQuade was feeling that afternoon of the 20th April as his trawler, *Bonanza*, came churning through the oily harbour of Walvis Bay to off-load her refrigerated catch, and give the crew a few nights' shore-leave. He tied the *Bonanza* up alongside the Kuiseb wharf, where he always sold his fish, and left Potgieter in charge while he went to the bank to draw some money for the Coloured crew.

McQuade and Tucker and the Kid and Elsie went uptown in the Kid's new car. The Kid's real name was Nigel Childe and he used to be a captain-gunner in the All England Whaling Company fifteen or more years ago. His father had been chairman of the board and the Kid had come into a lot of money, but he had spent most of it before McQuade persuaded him to invest in Sausmarine. The Kid could not afford this new car, but said that he could not afford to do without it either on account of he was now forty years old, a sombre anniversary for a hedonist, and he was madly in love with his wife, Beryl the Bitch, who was always threatening to leave him; while he was at sea, she prepared long memoranda of her grievances. Today the Kid was hurrying uptown to the dentist to have his new smile fitted, which he could also ill-afford, as a surprise for Beryl: last month the dentist had filed his upper teeth down to points and fitted temporary caps while his smart permanent ones were being made, and now he wished he'd kept his own old ones. Hugo Tucker was the ship's engineer, the smallest ex-shareholder in Sausmarine,

16

and he could play the mouth organ, music as mournful as his countenance. Tucker was always worried, often about the *Bonanza*'s engines, mostly about his own money, and always about his wife. He was a South African but married to Rosie, an Australian who used to earn her very own money as a dress-maker in Adelaide – and now where was she? – broke in fucking Walvis Bay! From heaven to hell in one airline ticket, and all because of McQuade, the Kid and Elsie and their hare-brained schemes. Elsie's real name was L. C. Brooks, the ship's cook and book-keeper, who had been with McQuade and the Kid on the whalers in the old days. Elsie did not have woman-trouble because he did not like women but now that he was over fifty he had given up the other way too. 'There's nothing more pathetic than an ageing queer,' Elsie said, 'I'll just bite the bullet and grow old gracefully.'

They all got into the Kid's new car. It was a Renault and he called it Rene because it was electronically programmed to speak to him. '*Bonjour*, Rene,' the Kid said as he switched the ignition on.

Rene said: '*Fasten your seat belts please.*'

'You heard him,' Kid said, 'fasten your bleedin' seat belts before he calls the gendarmes.'

Rene said: '*Oil pressure is satisfactory.*'

'Merci, Rene,' Kid said.

'*Water pressure is satisfactory.*'

'Merci, Rene.'

'*All systems are satisfactory.*'

'Merci, Rene.' He put the car into reverse.

'*Release your handbrake,*' Rene requested.

'What happens if you actually drive off with your hand-brake on?' Tucker asked with morbid professional interest.

'He screams *Mon Dieu, mon Dieu!* and heads straight for the AA.'

They drove out of the sandy compound, into Oceana Road. There were big oil tanks and acres of container-yards on the raw desert shore, and the sand lay across the tarmac road in thick streaks and ridges. They drove past the fishing compounds and the Kid said mournfully, 'At least you'll grow old gracefully with your own teeth to bite the bullet with, Elsie.'

'But why did you *do* it?' Elsie complained.

'She wrote me this memorandum,' the Kid said, 'which went: "Nag-nag, nag-nag, and furthermore I wish you'd do something about your teeth." And that got me right here.' He tapped his heart. 'She'd never complained about my teeth before.'

'The only time she *won't* complain is when you strike an oilwell in your backyard!'

'Please,' the Kid said. 'Please, don't talk about her like that.'

'I'm very sorry,' Elsie said firmly, 'but why don't you let her go if she's always threatening to leave, instead of borrowing thousands of rand to have your perfectly good teeth filed down like a goddam Amazon headhunter. Honestly, what you boys *do* for women!'

'We don't want to grow old gracefully, Elsie,' McQuade said. 'We want to grow old shagged out.'

'I'm serious,' Elsie said seriously. 'Look at you all! You're all a mess! Kid should be a millionaire and all, but what is he? – an ageing playboy! And look at you, James, the Stormtrooper's always throwing tantrums because she's thirty-five and wants to get married so you can spend the rest of your life supporting her—'

'In be-*yoo*-tiful condition for thirty-five,' the Kid murmured.

'And look what happened to you when you *did* get married: Vicky writes you a Dear John letter while you're in prison—'

'It wasn't exactly a Dear John,' McQuade corrected mildly.

'But the state you were in when you came to England, and the *money* you spent looking for her! You were all screwed up for years, but look at you now, forty years old and with all your brains, you should be at the top of the tree, but instead you're a rolling stone who's gathered no moss. Look at Tucker – every penny he earns he gives to Rosie but does he get any gratitude? Moan, moan, moan.' He snorted. 'And now Kid and his *stupid* new teeth!'

'Please don't say they're stupid,' the Kid whined. 'It's done now.'

'Yes, Elsie,' McQuade agreed.

Elsie suddenly looked worried. 'Oh, I'm sorry. What I mean is I *worry* about you boys! Look, I'm not against women – I just wish you'd marry the right girls.'

'*You better be careful, Elsie!*' Tucker suddenly shouted. He looked close to tears.

Elsie groaned and sat back. 'Oh dear.' Then he put a hairy hand on Tucker's shoulder. 'Look, all I mean is, I do the accounts and I know every penny you earn. Remember . . . you guys are the only family I've got.'

The episode was terminated by their arrival at the municipal market. Elsie got out to do the revictualling for the ship. He leant in the window and shook the Kid's shoulder. 'I'm sorry.' He turned and lumbered off into the market. McQuade said:

'He means well, Kid. And Beryl's going to love 'em.'

The Kid groaned. '*Will you please, please, please for Christ's sake quit talking about my stupid new teeth!*'

They parted outside the dentist's surgery. They wished the Kid luck but he did not even answer, just stomped off belligerently. McQuade and Tucker walked to the bank and cashed a company cheque for the Coloureds. Tucker returned to the ship to pay them, and McQuade walked to his house in Fifth Street.

He called his house Railway Yard View, which is a pretty bloody awful name for a house, but then, as McQuade said, Walvis Bay is a pretty bloody awful town. Half the houses in Fifth Street were empty, windows broken, paint peeling, abandoned. McQuade's windows were intact and the Stormtrooper had made him some curtains ('*How you can live like*

19

this, Englisch!'), he had a coloured maid called Maria who came once a week to sweep up the dust that came in every crack when the Ostwind blew, and the second-hand furniture he had bought was not too bad. He had built the big double bed himself by knocking together stout planks, and had put in some nice lamps and indoor plants, but it was still a bloody bleak old Railways house, and the garden was desert sand, one cactus plant and a rubber bush alongside the garage and servants' room, as depressing as all get-out but what the hell, what do you expect for thirty rand a month in Walvis Bay? He was here only temporarily, he would have a proper place in Australia, next year. He let himself in the front door and walked through to the room which he used as the company office. There was no mail except a bank statement which he did not care to open. There were no messages on his telephone answering-machine. He dialled the Stormtrooper's cottage in Swakopmund. It rang and rang. He glanced at his watch. School was over and today she had no hockey practice. He went to the bathroom and ran water into the old enamel tub.

He proceeded to scrub himself up for the Stormtrooper. He washed his hair cheerfully to be beautiful for the Stormtrooper, then shaved and put on Eau de Cologne to smell nice for the Stormtrooper. Thinking about her magnificent thighs.

He still had the old Landrover he had bought two years ago in Cape Town. He drove over the railway bridge and the desert opened up, the barren coast on one side of the tarred road, yellow sand dunes towering up on the other, ridged and fluted by the wind. He was in a good mood. Twenty-five minutes later he crossed the bridge over the dry Swakop River, into the little German town that is so different to bleak Walvis Bay.

He turned down a wide sand street towards the sea and parked outside a house. He walked down to the cottage at the back, and entered the Stormtrooper's sandy garden. All the windows were closed. He tried the front door. Locked. He knocked, and waited. Then he retraced his steps. It was after five o'clock, so she could not be shopping. He drove to the Europahof Hotel.

It is built in Alpine style, with beams inlaid into the walls. There was singing in German as he walked into the bar. There were a dozen men whom he knew by sight. As he entered, the singing abruptly died away. McQuade gave them a polite nod and went to the empty end. There was a moment's hush, then conversation picked up, in German. The bartender came over. Maybe it was the way the singing had stopped but McQuade had the feeling the man's smile was frosty. 'Good afternoon, Klaus,' he said. 'A beer, please.' He put the money on the bar. 'Have you seen Helga this afternoon?'

'Not this afternoon.' Klaus took the money to the till.

McQuade was surprised. He felt distinctly unwanted. Yet he had often used this place, and the Germans had always been polite. He could only think that they knew something about Helga. They knew he dated her, but something had happened. He felt uncomfortable. He could feel them looking at his back. He thought, Well to hell with this. He lifted the glass and just then there was a shout:

'*Heil Hitler!*'

McQuade turned, astonished. A fat man stood in the door, his right arm out, his feet together, a drunken solemnity on his flushed face. There was a silence, then several men admonished him in German. The fat man dropped his arm, glanced around drunkenly and then came in, grinning unsteadily.

McQuade turned back to his beer. Jesus Christ. He drank the rest of his beer down, down. He got up and turned for the door. '*Auf Wiedersehen*,' he muttered.

He walked back to his Landrover, and sat behind the wheel, thinking about the atmosphere in that bar.

Never encountered it before, and he didn't simply mean the man giving the salute. That was just a drunken fool. No, it had something to do with Helga. Had she found herself another boyfriend? He wouldn't have credited it but he felt a stab of jealousy. Anyway, he was going to get to the bottom of this. He started the Landrover, and drove up the sand street, to Kukki's Pub.

Which is another nice bar, in an old German building, patronized by the younger South Westers. English was the language most heard in here. It was half full. McQuade got a stool at the bar, nodding greetings. Kukki came over. 'Beer, please, Kukki. Listen, have you seen Helga today?'

Kukki looked blank. 'No.' He reached under the counter for the beer.

'No idea where she might be?'

Kukki looked puzzled. 'No.'

'Would you tell me if you knew?'

Kukki looked mystified. 'Sure. Why?'

McQuade felt embarrassed saying it, but Kukki was his friend. He beckoned. Kukki leant closer. 'If she's found herself another boyfriend, I'd like to know.'

Kukki smiled patiently. 'If she had, I'd know. And I know she thinks you're the greatest thing since bratwurst and sauerkraut. Which shows there's no accounting for taste.' He moved off down the bar.

McQuade sipped his beer. All very well, but that wasn't solving his problem of getting laid. Where was the Stormtrooper? She of the magnificent Teutonic thighs goldened by the desert sun, her magnificent sweaty arse in her scanty skirt as she bullied for the ball on the hockey pitch, she of the magnificent breasts which gave him such bliss when she wasn't giving him a Teutonic hard time. ('You think I just do this for dinners, huh?') Well, he wanted to buy her the finest damn dinner, then take her back to that *gemütliche* cottage and make havoc with her well-nourished body. He went to the public telephone and dialled her again.

22

Still no reply. Well, he had better leave her a note telling her where he was, so he quaffed back his beer.

The cottage was still silent. He pinned the note to her door and walked back up the sandy lane. As he passed the window of the front house there was a tap on the glass. Annie, the neighbour, beckoned him. She opened the window.

'Hi! Helga's gone to her parents' place for the night.' Annie said.

McQuade's heart sank. Helga's parents lived on a ranch near Usakos, two hundred kilometres inland. 'She's spending the night there?'

'She said she'd be back in the morning in time for school. She'll be mad that she missed you.'

'Not as mad as I am. May I use your phone?'

He went into the house, without optimism. He dialled exchange and asked to be put through to the radio tower. He asked the operator to try the call-sign of the Schmidt ranch's two-way radio.

'Sorry, no response,' the man said.

'Oh *shit* . . .'

And he made up his mind. No way was he going another night without a screw. He thanked Annie and drove back to Kukki's Pub. He bought four cold beers, two bottles of wine and borrowed a glass. He drove out of town, onto the tarmac road for Usakos and the Schmidt ranch.

The sun was going down as he roared out into the desert, gleaming golden pink on the dunes and rocky outcrops, the big water pipeline stretching away into the darkening east. He snapped the cap off a beer, and it tasted like nectar.

2

He had finished the beers by the time he reached the farm gate shortly before Usakos. Here the desert was turning to thorn trees, scrubby low mountains. This was the start of the cattle country. McQuade closed the gate behind him and set off on the long dirt road through the Schmidt land. It was nine o'clock when he rounded the hill and saw the Schmidt homestead twinkling ahead.

He was taken aback by the number of cars. It appeared that a big party was in progress. There was a black guard with a flashlight at the gate. McQuade wondered if he was doing the right thing, showing up uninvited. The black man recognized him. '*Goeie naand, Baas* Jim.' He pointed his flashlight, indicating parking space. McQuade parked near the back of the house, and when he switched off the engine he heard orchestra music.

He felt very doubtful about this. This was a large formal party and he didn't even have a tie. But, hell, he'd just come back from sea and the old people always made him welcome. ('You come to marry my dodder, aha-ha-ha!'). He mounted the steps to the verandah and walked towards the front door. As he passed the living-room window he stopped, and stared.

The big room had been cleared of furniture and two dozen couples were waltzing. From one wall hung a massive flag, red, white and black with a huge swastika in the middle of it. On another wall hung another flag, almost identical, but the swastika was three-legged: the flag of the AWB, the Afrikaner Weerstand Beweging, the right-wing Afrikaner movement. The women wore ball gowns; half the men were

24

in military uniforms. Some wore black, some grey, with shiny black boots, and each was wearing a swastika armband. Some younger men were in smart khaki uniforms, wearing the AWB swastika armband. McQuade stood on the dark verandah an astonished moment, then suddenly a voice boomed behind him, *'Willkommen!'* He turned around. Helga's father was lumbering down the long verandah towards him.

He was a big man, with a barrel chest and a balding head with a round face wreathed in beery smiles, his big arms extended. On his arm was the swastika. McQuade took an uncertain step towards him, and the old man stopped. He stared at McQuade in surprise; then he dropped his arms. 'What are you doing here?'

McQuade said: 'Excuse me.' He made to turn and leave.

The old man cried: *'Who invited you?'*

McQuade stopped. 'Nobody. I'm sorry, I've just got back from sea.'

'Not even my stupid dodder would invite you today!'

'She didn't.'

'So can't you see today is a private party?! So what we going to do now?'

'Forget it, I'm leaving.'

McQuade strode across the verandah. The old man suddenly lumbered after him. *'Jim – Jim, I'm sorry . . .'*

'Goodnight, Herr Schmidt.'

'Jim . . .' the old man pleaded, then he bellowed: *'Helga!'*

McQuade was on the lawn when Helga burst onto the verandah. She stared at McQuade disappearing into the darkness, then she clutched up her evening gown and ran down the steps. *'Jim!'*

McQuade was halfway across the lawn when she caught up. 'Jim!' She grabbed his arm. Her blue eyes were aghast. 'What are you doing here?'

McQuade looked back at the house. Half a dozen figures had emerged onto the verandah. 'What are *you* doing in

25

there? Dancing under the Nazi flag. With gentlemen wearing uniforms and swastika armbands! And wearing this!' He pointed at a black velvet choker around her neck, from which dangled a little gold swastika.

'Didn't the guard stop you at the gate?'

'Yes but he thought I was a Nazi too.' He frowned with amazement. 'Do you do this *often*?'

She glared. 'Don't be ridiculous. Don't you know what the date is? The twentieth of April!'

'So?'

She glared at him. 'Oh, don't be dense! Whose birthday is on the twentieth of April?' She waved a hand at the homestead. 'This is just . . . a little traditional celebration. The English do the same thing on the Queen's birthday.'

'Whose birthday is the twentieth of April?'

She glared at him sullenly. 'Adolf Hitler's, you fool!'

McQuade stared at her. Absolutely amazed. He couldn't believe this. But suddenly he understood what had happened in the bar of the Europahof Hotel, and he was staggered that she was part of this. 'Jesus Christ.'

She opened her mouth but he went on in wonder: 'So every year you celebrate the Führer's birthday? With great big swastika flags and SS uniforms and Nazi armbands? And this . . .?' He flicked the little golden swastika.

She hissed. 'That is just jewellery – the swastika is an ancient international symbol of good!'

'The Nazi Party was good?'

'You drink a toast to the Queen on her birthday . . .?'

He wanted to shake her. 'The Queen of England happens to have an unblemished political record! You are celebrating the birthday of the most brutal mass-murderer the world has ever known! The man who ordered the Holocaust of six million Jews!'

Her hand flashed in the moonlight and cracked across his face. He stared at her, shocked, his face stinging, and she screamed: '*That's the hoax of the twentieth century! There was no*

26

Holocaust!' Her breasts were heaving.

McQuade took a deep breath to control his fury. 'Goodbye, Helga.' He added sarcastically: 'Heil Hitler.' He turned and strode away.

Helga stood on the lawn, her eyes bright; then she shrieked; *'Yes, Heil Hitler!'* She stamped her feet together and shot out her right arm and screamed: *'Heil Hitler!'*

A man leapt over the verandah rail and started running towards the Landrover. McQuade got in, slammed the door, and started the engine. He roared off down the gravel drive.

3

He drove hard back towards Swakopmund, the desert flashing by in his headlights. He was over the anger of the confrontation: now he was left with the shock. It made his flesh
creep. It was macabre. Not just because she had obscenely
shrieked *Heil Hitler* at him; it was the whole nine yards of the
great swastika in all its frightening glory, the arrogant
uniforms, the strutting jackboots — it evoked a legend of
dreaded times, a legend he had learnt at his mother's knee
had been brought to life before his eyes. He had just seen
ordinary, decent people ritualizing it, rejoicing at the altar,
and if ordinary people were doing this on a remote farm in
the heart of Namibia, what was happening in the rest of the
country tonight?

Almost everything in life is a coincidence, in that something happens because something else has just happened to
happen. If the good ship *Bonanza* had not come back to port a
day early so that the Kid could have his new teeth installed
for Beryl, this story would never have happened: if the
Bonanza had returned any other day, the Stormtrooper
would have been waiting for McQuade with open arms, he
would not have driven out to the ranch in his determination
to get laid, and he would not have come roaring back into the
little German town of Swakopmund, angry and determined
to get drunk, and parked outside Kukki's Pub at the moment
that the drunken Damara tribesman lurched around the corner and offered to sell him an Iron Cross.

McQuade was in no mood for drunken peddlers and he
glared at the German medal because he presumed the man
was also trying to exploit the birthday of Adolf Hitler. 'No

28

thank you.' But the drunken Damara had more to sell. He buried his hand into his pocket and laboriously extracted a piece of white paper. He thrust it at McQuade dramatically and said: 'Sell you this for only one rand!'

McQuade looked at it in the lamplight. A banknote? A *white* banknote? On the corners were the symbols £5, and the text read: *The Governor of the Bank of England promises to pay to bearer on demand the sum of five pounds sterling* ... McQuade turned it over. The other side was blank. A banknote printed on one side only? Its date of issue was 1944. An old English fiver? He looked at the Damara. 'What's your name?'

The Damara said drunkenly: 'Skellum Jagter.'

'No, man, your real name.'

'Skellum Jagter!'

McQuade half-smiled, despite himself. Jagter means hunter and Skellum is slang meaning sly. 'Where did you get this?' It was then that he saw the identification tag in the man's dirty open shirt-front, and the words stamped on it, *Seeoffizier Horst Kohler.*

He frowned. *Seeoffizier* is German. *Horst Kohler* is definitely a German name. How did this drunken Damara come into possession of such a personal thing? 'Where did you get that?'

Skellum suddenly looked alarmed. He tried to snatch the banknote back. McQuade said in Afrikaans: 'No, I'll pay for it! Just tell me where you got it.' He pointed at the identification tag. 'And that. Five rand and a bottle of wine.'

They sat in the front seats of the Landrover, outside Kukki's Pub. It was a long story, difficult to extract, because McQuade made the mistake of giving Skellum the bottle of wine immediately, and the drunken Damara got drunker.

'And where is your father now?'

Skellum waved the bottle northwards: 'Damaraland.'

McQuade said in Afrikaans, 'And are you sure he says

there was no boat? These two men just came up out of the sea?'

'No boat! They were just white wizards!'

Then they came from a submarine, McQuade reasoned. Absolutely fascinating. Forty years ago. It must have been a German submarine, with an officer named Horst Kohler, and it must have been wrecked. Why else would two men erupt out of the sea? 'And one was wounded?'

'Blood,' Skellum said happily. He wiped his hand downwards over his face. 'Blood.'

'And the first man was carrying a package.'

'*Ja.*' Skellum clutched one hand to his chest and made exaggerated swimming motions with the other.

'And then they fought on the beach?'

'Fight,' Skellum said joyfully. He punched the air aggressively. Then drew his finger across his scrawny throat cheerfully. He collapsed back onto the seat, to signify death.

McQuade thought: two submariners escape from a sunken submarine, then fight to the death when they reach the shore? Why? 'And then the man who won the fight forced your father to lead him down the coast? But your father hit him with a piece of wood?'

'*Wham,*' Skellum said joyfully, reliving the battle. '*Whok!*' He smashed one hand down on his forearm. 'Blood!' He made the clubbing motion again. '*Whok!*' He curled his arm over his head and cowered theatrically. 'Finish,' he said triumphantly as if he had laid the man low himself.

'And your father returned to the place where the other man was buried? And the jackals had dug him up? And he took this tag from him. Did he ever return to the place where he had hit the first man, to see what had happened to him?'

'Gone.' Skellum waved his hand extravagantly at the horizon. Then he fixed his eyes on McQuade's nose. He slurred conspiratorially, 'Does the Baas want to buy some more white money?' He burrowed into his pocket, and pulled out a

30

black wallet importantly. 'My father found this after the fight.'

McQuade took the wallet. It was bulky and made of leather. Some initials were imprinted on it. He switched on the cab light. The letters were in Gothic style: the initials were H.M.

The wallet was packed with white paper money. He pulled a note out. It was the same as the one he had bought. He pulled out some more. They were in good condition, though the edges of some were worn. He counted them. There were ninety-seven notes. Four hundred and eight-five pounds. He turned to Skellum. 'This is *old* English money. It is not used any more. How many of these have you managed to sell?'

'None,' Skellum proclaimed. 'Only to you.'

McQuade did not believe him. 'So this wallet did not belong to the man who was stabbed to death? The man this tag came from. It belonged to the first man?'

'*Ja.*'

Then McQuade noticed something else: the serial numbers on two notes were the same.

He flicked through a dozen notes. They all had the same serial number.

Counterfeit money . . .

He had read somewhere that during the war the Nazis had counterfeited tons of English money which they intended to flood onto the market to destroy Britain's economy. He thought, this gets curiouser and curiouser. Two men escape from a sunken German submarine over forty years ago. One, a man called Horst Kohler, is already wounded but is chasing the other man, whose initials are H.M. H.M. is carrying a package. On the beach they fight to the death. H.M. is also carrying a wallet containing a lot of *counterfeit* English money.

Where had he got that money from? And why did they fight? Over the money? The contents of the package? *Why did only two men escape from the submarine?* Why was Horst Kohler

31

chasing H.M. so furiously? H.M. was armed with both a pistol and a knife, Kohler had nothing but his fists, yet he persevered. Surely he would not have done that just for five hundred pounds. That meant H.M.'s package contained something much more valuable. Like diamonds?

Another point: H.M. was carrying the package as he swam ashore: he swam with difficulty. Only after the fight did he open the package and put the two bags into his pockets. Why did he not do that *before* he escaped from the submarine? Answer: H.M. did not have *time* to open the package inside the submarine – he only had time to snatch it up. *That suggested that he left behind more valuables.*

The more McQuade thought about it, the more convinced he became. That submarine was shipwrecked, because only two men emerged from it, in disarray, one pursuing the other. So, it was still where it sank, and inside was a hell of a lot more valuable stuff than H.M. had managed to struggle ashore with. Why? Because of the counterfeit fivers. Surely only a very senior Nazi official had access to counterfeit money *and* a submarine. McQuade had read somewhere about the vast treasures the Nazis were said to have accumulated and shipped away to South America. Well, here we have another case. To arrange a submarine you must be a very senior official, and a high-up Nazi official has more loot stashed away against the day the shit hits the fan than five hundred counterfeit English pounds and one package of diamonds.

McQuade stared down the sandy street, his excitement mounting. *God, if all that was correct, there was a fortune somewhere down there, in that submarine. Crates of the stuff.*

But why was this German submarine off the coast of South West Africa? That's a long, long way from South America where all the Nazis ran to.

McQuade stared through the windscreen, trying to think as a seaman.

Two possibilities. One: because of Allied maritime patrols

in the Atlantic, the commander decides to hug the coast of West Africa. He has navigational problems and because of treacherous currents, the submarine crashes into a sandbank off the infamous Skeleton Coast.

McQuade shook his head. All right, it was a possibility, but the Skeleton Coast was simply too far off the route to South America for it to be a credible course for even the most cautious submariner.

So, possibility two. Namibia, or South West Africa, as it was called, was a German colony until the First World War. It was then occupied by South African troops to protect the Cape sea route from German warships. At the end of the war, the colony was handed over to South Africa to govern as a trusteeship territory. But the country remained heavily pro-German. So this submarine had been heading for this vast, sympathetic, pro-German territory to unload its Nazis and their loot. However, before it could do so it came to grief on the treacherous Skeleton Coast, and H.M. escaped with some of the loot, with Kohler pursuing him to get his share . . .

This was the most likely scenario: Namibia was so vast and so German that it would be a good place for Nazis to hide, to become absorbed. This scenario presupposed that arrangements had been made with German agents in Namibia to rendezvous with the submarine, in a fishing trawler, for example, to receive the Nazis and the loot. This also explained why the submarine was so close in-shore, waiting for the rendezvous, that it came to grief on sandbanks.

But why did only two men escape? What happened to the rest?

McQuade sighed. He knew very little about submarines. Was it possible that two men were discharged, and the submarine sailed away happily? It was not *likely*. For several reasons:

Firstly, H.M. was struggling to swim with his package. Surely, if the disembarkation was planned, he would have secured his package in some way to enable him to swim properly. Secondly, Horst Kohler was injured, and he was furiously pursuing H.M. Kohler was trying to *prevent* H.M. from escaping. And thirdly, the most compelling reason of all: if the disembarkation had been planned, why would they choose the killer Skeleton Coast? Why not further south, close to Swakopmund, and why not come ashore with some kind of raft carrying some food and water?

So, it was obviously a case of shipwreck.

But why did only two men escape?

But all those questions surely did not matter. The only thing that mattered today, forty-odd years later, was that somewhere on this Skeleton Coast lay a German submarine with a lot of Nazi treasure in it. In water so shallow that two men could escape from it.

McQuade sat back. Excited. And he made up his mind. 'Have you got a job, Skellum?'

Skellum turned to him, his eyes glazed. '*Nee.*'

McQuade pulled out a fifty-rand banknote.

'You and I are going to drive up to Damaraland. To meet your father. So he can tell me this story himself.'

4

He first went back to his ship and collected the sextant, the nautical almanac, the sight-reduction tables, an Admiralty chart of the coast, a plotting sheet and parallel rulers. He grabbed some cans of food, beer, two bottles of brandy, some cooking utensils and four blankets, which he slung in the back of the Landrover. Then he drove back towards Swakopmund and the Skeleton Coast beyond. Skellum was sprawled in a drunken sleep. That was okay with McQuade: he expected no great meeting of minds on this journey and just hoped that the man had not made up the whole story.

The road north from Swakopmund was smooth, compacted sand. To the left was the moonlit Atlantic, in all other directions was only sand, hillocks and humps going on and on. At three o'clock they came to Henties Bay, a little resort for sport-fishermen, holiday houses sitting on bare sand, and McQuade swung off the coastal road, north-east, towards Uis Mine. Now they were in the dune country, hills of yellow and white in the flashing headlamps, going on and on. Then, gradually, the dunes began to turn flinty hard, impacted with the brown gravel hurled into them by the winds, and now the earth was turning into flinty rockiness, hills of rocks rising up into the starry sky, stones flying up from the wheels. Then the dry scrub began to appear. The first light came, greyness turning to pink. Outside Uis Mine he turned left, towards Khorixas, and now here and there were iron windmills. Sunrise came, red and gold fanning up behind the rocky mountains; it was early morning when McQuade drove into dusty, dry Khorixas and stopped at the service station. He shook Skellum awake.

'You must show me the way from here.'

Skellum blinked around, all hungover and horrible. Then memory dawned on him. He suddenly looked uncomfortable.

'Ah – I cannot take you to my father's kraal.'

So it was all a hoax! 'Why not?' McQuade demanded dangerously.

Skellum shifted. 'Because he will beat me.'

'Why will he beat you? Because your story is a pack of lies?'

'Because,' Skellum shifted uncomfortably, 'he does not know I took these things from his hut.'

'You stole them from your own father?'

Skellum waggled his hungover head. 'I only borrowed them . . .'

McQuade grabbed him by his shirt front theatrically. 'Last night I paid you fifty rand to take me to your father. Now get on with it! And if you're frightened he's going to beat you,' he snatched a bottle of brandy off the back seat, 'fortify yourself with this!'

It was nine o'clock when the Landrover went grinding up the stony track through the yellow brown rocky hills and came to a halt at Jakob's kraal. It consisted of three small stone huts, plastered with mud, roofed with flattened paraffin tins. A cooking fire smouldered outside the central hut. A scrawny old man and an old woman appeared in the dark doorway, astonished.

Skellum was right to be nervous. As he and McQuade climbed out of the vehicle, the old man's astonishment gave way to fury. He snatched up a thick stick and came charging at Skellum, swiping. Skellum flung his arms up and his father swiped him on the shoulders, *swipe*, *swipe*, shouting curses, and Skellum scuttled about backwards, his scrawny old father swiping after him. 'Stop!' McQuade shouted. 'Stop! I am not the police! I am a friend!' He grabbed the stick. 'I am a friend!'

*

They sat around the smoky fire, on the ground, while the old woman made tea. Skellum sat against a hut wall, malevolently nursing his bruises and his hangover. Scrawny chickens scratched in the earth and half a dozen goats wandered around. Jakob had been pacified by a present of a bottle of brandy and assurances from McQuade that he had not come to make trouble. Why did the Baas want to hear the story? Because he was interested, McQuade said, and as he already knew the story, why should not Jakob repeat it truly? The old man was sullenly impressed by these arguments and the brandy, whilst still glancing malevolently at his son.

He solemnly told the story again. McQuade had to be careful how he asked his questions lest it appear that he criticized his conduct. They spoke in Afrikaans:

'And you're absolutely sure only two men came out? Is it not possible that more emerged after the fight?'

'Not possible. I would have seen their footprints when I came back.'

'Why did you go back?'

'Because I had left my bag when I ran away. I hoped it would still be there.'

'But you only found the wallet?' He did not believe that – the old man had stolen it. 'How many bottles of water were in your bag?'

'Five.'

About five pints. A determined man could get a long way on five pints. 'And how much dried meat?'

Jakob put his finger on his wrist, indicating a piece of meat the size of his hand.

'And where is Petrus now, the other man with you?'

'He has died.'

'Have you or Petrus ever told this story to anyone else?'

Jakob shook his old head.

'Do you remember the time when the great war ended?'

'I remember hearing it was ended.'

'Did this happen before or after that?'

'After,' Jakob said.

'How long after? One month? Two? Four?'

'Maybe one month.'

Oh yes, McQuade thought.

'And was there water to be found in the river beds near the coast? If a man dug for it.'

'If he dug for it he would find some water.'

'And game?'

'Yes, there would be some game near the river beds.'

So he could have got food and water. And he had a gun. 'Why didn't you take his gun?'

Jakob said, 'I was frightened. I ran away. I did not think about the gun until afterwards.'

'And the man's front teeth were definitely broken?'

'Broken.' Jakob pointed at his own gums.

So he was in pain for a long time, McQuade thought, so the first thing he would have done when he reached civilization was go to a dentist. 'Can you describe this man? How old was he? Was he younger or older than me?'

Jakob glanced at McQuade. 'About the same age.'

'And how old am I?'

'Maybe you have forty years.'

Not bad, McQuade thought. That meant that if H.M. had survived, he would now be an old man of about eighty. 'What colour hair did he have?'

Jakob pointed at a dark rock.

'Was his hair curly or straight?'

'Straight.'

'Eyes?'

Jakob indicated his own eyes. 'Brown.'

'Anything else? Scars, for example?'

Jakob shook his head. 'I saw no scars.'

'What was his nose like? Broad, thin, straight, crooked?'

'It was straight, like yours.'

'How was his mouth?'

'He had thin lips.'

'How was his chin? Did it have a dent, like mine? Or was it round, like yours?'

Jakob thought. 'I think it had a dent.'

'How tall was he?' McQuade stood up. 'Taller than me? Or shorter?'

Jakob stood up. He compared McQuade to himself, then touched the tip of McQuade's shoulder.

That's short for a white man, McQuade thought. He himself was six foot so H.M. was about five foot three or four.

'And was he fat, thin or average?'

'He was not fat, he was not thin.'

'Did you get anything else from the *dead* man apart from the cross and the tag? A piece of paper, maybe? Another wallet?'

Jakob shook his head. 'Nothing.'

'And what did this man look like?'

Jakob said: 'He was dead. His face was covered in blood and sand. And the jackals had been eating him.'

'All right. Now please – ' he was going to say 'be honest' but changed it, ' – please think carefully. Was there anything else in the wallet apart from the white money? You can tell me without fear. Was there a card, perhaps? Some papers?'

Jakob glanced away. 'Nothing.'

McQuade thought he was lying but let it go for the moment. 'Did you ever exchange any of the white English money for our money?'

Jakob said emphatically: 'No.'

McQuade knew he was lying. Four hundred and eighty-five is an untidy number of forged English pounds. But only a few people had trusted the strange-looking money. 'Why not?'

'Because I was afraid the police may say I stole it.'

McQuade nodded. 'How many people know about this story, Jakob?'

'I told only my wife and my son.' Jakob gave a truculent glance at Skellum.

'Did Petrus keep anything taken that day?'

'He did not want anything.'

'And how did Skellum get hold of it?'

'He stole it! From my hut!' Jakob said indignantly.

'When?'

'Last month he ran away. Later I found he had stolen these things.'

Skellum was sitting against the hut wall, a big bruise on his temple, one eye swollen, looking murderous. McQuade wanted to ask him how many people he had told the story to, but didn't think he would get any truth from Skellum. Now for the all-important question.

'And can you remember the place on the shore where the white men came out of the sea? The exact place?'

Jakob glanced at him. Then looked away.

'I do not think I remember.'

'But why not? Damara people remember the eyes of a buck they shot fifty years ago!'

'Because the coast walks.'

This was true. The Skeleton Coast changes, the winds and tides slowly shifting the great expanses of sand, so that old wrecks are sometimes found buried hundreds of yards inland. McQuade burrowed his hand into his pocket. He counted off four fifty-rand banknotes elaborately. He held them out to Jakob.

'Please take me to this place.'

5

They drove back through the scrub-rock hills towards the Skeleton Coast, stones flying from the wheels, dust billowing up behind. McQuade wanted to make the coast while the sun was still high enough to use the sextant. Then the yellow-grey hills gave way to the rock mountains heaped up on the horizon, iron-brown and shimmering under the merciless blue sky. It was afternoon when they reached the ranger's post at Springbokwasser, midst a clump of reeds. McQuade got a twenty-four-hour permit.

They drove on. Slowly the iron-brown mountains gave way to the flinty dunes, grey-brown and yellow. McQuade said to Jakob:

'This man spoke in German. You understand German?'

'I understand many words.'

McQuade said: 'How was it when the Germans ruled this country?'

Jakob stared through the windscreen. '*Sleg*,' he said. Bad.

'Why?'

Jakob shook his head. 'Twenty-five lashes. And if the whip does not whistle that lash does not count.' He added: 'Blood.'

'For what offence did people get twenty-five lashes?'

'For anything.' He added: 'For falling down. Even women and children.'

McQuade frowned. 'Why did they fall down?'

'Because the loads were too heavy. When the Germans were building the harbour at Lüderitz. I was a boy then.'

'Were *you* ever lashed?'

For answer Jakob pulled up his shirt. His back was a mass of scar tissue.

McQuade was shocked. 'For what offence?'

Jakob said: 'The sickness of hunger. And the cold.'

'But did they not feed you enough?'

'There were no crops. The Germans had killed very many men in the wars, and so no crops were planted. The women and children had to build the harbour because there were no men left, but there was no food because there were no crops.'

McQuade did not believe this. The old man was repeating folklore. History was not McQuade's strong point, but nobody had taught him this at school. He knew something about the German colonial war against the Hereros, and presumed it was a pretty bloody affair, as wars of pacification were in that era. What about the Red Indians in America? What about the Aborigines in Australia? But he did not believe this story about women and children being worked and starved and lashed by the Germans of South West Africa.

The gravel-encrusted hillocks gave way to the yellow sand dunes, row after jumbled row, going on and on: then, way ahead, a haze came onto the horizon and then the mauve-black of the Atlantic.

McQuade stopped where the road joined the coastal track. He made a note of the mileage, and said to Jakob, 'Which way?'

Jakob pointed left. South.

'Are you sure?'

'Sure,' Jakob said.

But Jakob was not so sure. On his instructions McQuade drove off the road half a dozen times in the next two hours, grinding down to the shore, and then along it, while Jakob peered all around for landmarks. He said he was looking for a promontory of rocks sticking out into the sea. It was after four o'clock when he pointed with conviction.

McQuade stopped. From Jakob's description he had expected the rocks to reach much further into the sea. 'How can you tell?'

'By the shape of that rock. Like a seal.'

'So where did you first see the two men come out of the sea?'

Jakob pointed behind them.

McQuade turned the Landrover north again and drove along the sandy, hummocked shoreline. After about a mile Jakob signalled him to stop. Jakob got out, looked up the shoreline, at the pounding, seething surf, then down it. He studied the sea for a full minute, then began to trudge northwards, up the coast, with conviction.

McQuade followed him in the Landrover.

After ten minutes Jakob stopped, looked at the sea, then at the sky. He looked south, at the featureless surf. Then he looked east, inland, at the featureless sand dunes. He announced, 'Here.'

McQuade looked at the moonscape of desert and sea.

'How do you know? The coast has changed much in forty years.'

'I know.' Jakob pointed at the black Atlantic, the rows of breakers rolling in, the flatness beyond. 'There,' he said.

McQuade had to work fast. It was after five o'clock and the sun was dangerously low on the horizon: any angle approaching ten degrees had to be treated with suspicion. If he had to wait for tomorrow for the sun-sight he would have to wait until noon because the morning sun would be in the east, over the desert, and he would not have a usable horizon because of the dunes. He sat on the sand, hastily opened his notebook, put the sextant to his eye and pulled down some shades. He fiddled with the angle-adjuster, until he found the image of the sun. Then he slid the adjuster and brought the sun's image down, until the lower limb of it just touched the horizon. He rocked the sextant, so the sun just skimmed the horizon in an arc. Then he looked quickly at his digital watch. He noted down the exact hour, minute and second, allowing for reaction time. Then he read off the angle shown on the adjuster, and sighed.

The angle of the sun was eleven degrees, twenty-four minutes and about thirty seconds. That was perilously close to ten degrees. If he had been at sea, where it did not much matter if he'd been a mile or two out, he would have used the angle: but in this case, if he was a mile out in calculating where on the earth's surface he was sitting, he could waste a lot of money, and not find that submarine at all. The only sensible thing was to spend the night here and get a noon-shot tomorrow to verify his position.

Jakob had been watching him in amazement. McQuade picked up a piece of driftwood, and stuck it upright in the sand. He went to the Landrover and got out the provisions and the pots.

He poured brandy into two mugs, added a dash of water, and gave one to Jakob. He sat down.

If Jakob was telling the truth, somewhere just out there was an old German submarine. Loaded with loot. And James McQuade was going to be a rich man. He said to Jakob:

'So somewhere near here lie the bones of the man who was killed? Do you think we will see his ghost tonight?'

Jakob stared at him.

'Baas, we must not sleep here tonight! We must sleep a long way down the beach from this place!'

And McQuade knew that Jakob had been telling him the truth.

They slept two miles down the beach. McQuade was awake at sunrise, and thank God the sky was clear. He would get his sun-sights.

He built up the fire. Jakob was still asleep, curled up in his blankets; he had got drunk last night. McQuade put a pot of water on the fire. There was nothing to do but wait till noon. He went to the Landrover and got his fishing rod.

He walked along the beach, looking for bait. It was plenti-ful, in brown, spongy lumps the size of fists. He selected one and cut it open. The bait was inside little pockets – meaty, pink, like plums. He thought: H.M. could have survived on this stuff alone. He threaded a lump onto his hook. He swung the rod and cast out into the surf.

In fifteen minutes he had caught four good fish. He cleaned them and went back to the fire. Jakob was still asleep.

He made coffee. There was nothing to do but eat and wait.

At eleven-thirty they drove back to The Haunted Place. Five minutes before local noon McQuade sat down and faced north. He put the sextant to his eye, found the sun and adjusted the shades. He slid the adjuster and brought the sun down until the lower limb of it just skimmed the horizon. He looked at the angle, then at the time, but did not make any notes.

Jakob was watching him in amazement. McQuade smiled at him. He waited half a minute, then raised the sextant again, found the sun, tweaked the angle-adjuster, and skimmed the sun on the horizon again. The angle was a minute of arc higher than last time. He waited half a minute, and did it again. At noon the sun stays at its zenith for about four minutes before it begins to descend into afternoon. About five minutes later, after measuring half a dozen times the angle between the sun, his eye, and the horizon, he was satisfied about the zenith.

He noted down that angle. He allowed seven feet for Dip, and allowed for the sextant's Index Error. He then subtracted the sun's noon angle, in degrees and minutes and seconds, from ninety degrees, zero minutes, zero seconds. The final result was an exact parallel of latitude.

This piece of beach he was sitting on was exactly nineteen degrees, seventeen minutes, forty-eight seconds South. Assuming Jakob was right, somewhere out there, due west along that latitude, lay the submarine. Probably about half a mile out.

With the next part of the navigational calculation he could take his time. He had a coffee. He gave the sun an hour, then took another sight with the sextant. He noted the exact time.

He used the Landrover's flat bonnet as a table, and began his calculations. He unfolded his nautical chart of the Skeleton Coast and drew in his latitude. He read off the longitude of the point where his latitude line crossed the coast. That in itself was enough to tell him exactly where on the earth's surface he was. But, to double-check, he wanted to put in the afternoon position line as well. He calculated his Local Hour Angle, noted down his post-noon sun angle, allowed for Dip and Index Error, opened the nautical almanac to the page for that day, found the hour, did the calculations and arrived at Height Observed. He then opened the sight-reduction tables to the appropriate page, and worked out Height Calculated. He subtracted that from Height Observed and came up with a minuscule Intercept. He then drew in the position line on the chart. It intercepted at the point where his latitude line crossed the coast. He was quite satisfied about where on the earth's surface he was standing.

He took a deep breath. Okay, the first step was to verify the submarine's existence. Bring the *Bonanza* up here and sweep the ocean floor in a pattern. Her depth-sounder would show up anything as big as a submarine lying on the ocean bed.

Then dive down and have a look at it.

How do you get into a sunken submarine?

He had no idea. Worry about that later.

What were the legal ramifications? And if word got out there'd be fortune-hunters from all over the world looking for this submarine. So, consult a good maritime lawyer, and meanwhile tell absolutely nobody. He'd have to tell the Kid, Tucker, Elsie and Potgieter of course, but he'd give the Coloureds a few days leave and bring the *Bonanza* up here with a skeleton crew.

6

It was a long shot, but it was worth looking into: *had H.M. survived the Skeleton Coast?* Was he alive today? He might well have survived: he was a youngish man in 1945 and he had had Jakob's water bottles, which he could have replenished at the Ugab river by digging. He had a gun and he might have shot a buck at the Ugab. Or a seal. If he reached Swakopmund, he would have gone immediately to a dentist because he would have been in pain. And probably seen a doctor, to treat his gashed arm. Records of all this might still exist. If McQuade could uncover those records he might find out H.M.'s name.

It was two o'clock the following afternoon when McQuade drove into Swakopmund, after returning Jakob to his kraal. He parked outside the old municipal buildings, under the palms, and went into the information bureau. A coloured woman came forward. *'Guten Tag.'*

'Can you advise me please?' (People like to be asked their advice) 'I am writing about Swakopmund during the war period. Is there a municipal archive I can research in?'

The lady said, 'Only the Sam Cohen Library.' She produced a glossy brochure and opened it at the map. 'Here. And the Public Library's here.'

McQuade circled them. 'How would I find out . . .' he waved his hand, '. . . how many dentists there were in Swakopmund in 1945, for example.'

'Maybe at the library.'

'And do you happen to know what hospitals there were in 1945?'

'Only the Antonius Hospital. Across the street there.'

47

'Thank you.' He went downstairs, back into the glaring sunshine.

The Antonius Hospital was an attractive old German building. He walked into the small foyer. A number of black women were sitting on chairs with infants. On the walls were government posters about nutrition, infant care, family planning, and the smiling people depicted in them were all an attractive shade of brown. McQuade went to the door marked Reception. A black woman in a white smock was sitting at a typewriter. 'Good afternoon,' he said in Afrikaans, 'is this where all the records of patients are kept?'

'Yes, sir.'

'Do you have the records for 1945 here?'

The woman looked nonplussed. 'No. In those days this was a German missionary hospital. It was later taken over by the government.'

'Do you know where the old missionary records are?'

'The missionaries took them away.'

'And where are the missions' headquarters now?'

'In Windhoek, maybe. Or maybe in Germany.'

McQuade thanked her and left the hospital. Well, he'd drawn a blank there. He walked towards the main street, Kaiserstrasse.

The public library is in the old Woermann-Brock Shipping Line building, built in Bavarian style around a large open courtyard. McQuade asked the librarian what books she had on German history of Namibia in general and Swakopmund in particular during the war period. 'Giving me details like how many dentists and doctors the town had in those days, et cetera.'

The librarian was a cultured, elderly German lady. 'For that you must go to the Sam Cohen library. It is dedicated to the local history. Mr Cohen made a great deal of money out of Swakopmund and built the institute out of gratitude. Meanwhile, sit at a table and I'll bring you what books we have.'

48

He found a table in the reference section. The librarian arrived with a pile of books.

The topmost book was by a Professor du Passani on the constitutional history of South West Africa. McQuade flicked through it. It seemed erudite stuff, more than he needed.

The next book was written by Adolf Hitler himself, *Mein Kampf*. McQuade put it aside. The next was a large tome about the Nuremberg Trials. He resolved to read it one day but it seemed hardly relevant to Namibia. However, a chapter had been marked by a pencil line, so he speed-read it. The gist of it was that many people challenged the legality and the morality of the Nuremberg Trials. They were without precedent in history. Before these trials, there was no such crime as 'crimes against humanity', a legal concept that was invented only *after* the war, so it could not legally be applied to deeds perpetrated *before* its conception. Furthermore, it was argued, the court did not have jurisdiction to hold the trials. Only a sovereign state had such power and the Allied forces were not a sovereign state, only an occupying army: so only the state of Germany itself had the legal power to try these 'criminals'. Furthermore, was it morally right to hold these 'criminals' responsible for obeying orders? McQuade skipped the rest — he had no patience for such arguments. There were photographs, however. A photograph of the principal war criminals in the dock at Nuremberg: Hess, Göring, Dönitz, Ribbentrop, Keitel, Kaltenbrunner, Speer and others.

Some of the names he knew as legendary villains of the war, others meant nothing to him. It struck him how ordinary these notorious men looked in civilian clothes, stripped of their awesome uniforms. There was a photograph of the gallows, specially built in a gymnasium for the executions. A photograph of the hangman, Master-Sergeant Woods of the United States Army, preparing a noose. A photograph of the bodies after the execution, lying in a long row on top of their coffins: some had blood coming from the eyes and nose. A

49

macabre but interesting detail, McQuade learnt, was that the condemned were not told until a few hours beforehand that their executions were 'imminent', so each day they woke up not knowing whether it was to be their last. Furthermore, they were hanged one at a time, so once the executions started, some had a long wait before their turn came. There were photographs of concentration camps, the likes of which he had seen before, shocking pictures of emaciated people behind barbed wire, trainloads of Jews lined up on railway platforms outside concentration camps undergoing selection by SS doctors for the gas chambers and slave labour, crematoria chimneys belching smoke, emaciated corpses filling open graves.

It was shocking, but it was distant history to McQuade and had nothing to do with the modern Germans whom he knew and liked – except for what he had seen three nights ago on the Schmidt ranch on Hitler's birthday, and what Jakob had told him about the harbour at Lüderitz. If Jakob's story was true, the Second World War was not the first time the Germans had used slave labour.

The next book was a pictorial history of Hitler's rise to power. It was vaguely familiar stuff. The goose-stepping armies on parade, the gleaming jackboots, the square helmets, the phalanxes of trucks, the armadas of battleships, the skies dark with Messerschmitts with the cross emblazoned on their wings. Here were the swastikas, flying, draped dramatically on walls, and the massive crowds, right arms out rigid in the Heil Hitler salute – you could almost hear the roar coming up out of the pages. McQuade had seen such pictures before and he would not have spent time on them now, but for what he had seen on the Schmidt ranch.

God, the whole thing gave him the creeps. He thrust the book aside and picked up the last one.

It was called *The Hoax of the Twentieth Century*, by Arthur Butz. McQuade stared. These were Helga's words three nights ago when he had said that Hitler had murdered six million Jews. *'The hoax of the twentieth century!'* she had shrieked before she hit him. McQuade turned to the back cover. The publisher's blurb read:

Dr Butz gives the reader a graduate course on the subject of the Jews of World War II Europe — concluding not only that they were *not* virtually wiped out; but, what's more, that no evidence exists to date to confirm that there was ever any Hitler government attempt to do so . . . He focuses on the post-war crimes trials where the prosecution 'evidence' was falsified and secured by coercion and even torture. He re-examines the very German records so long misrepresented; he critiques the European demographics which *do not* allow for the loss of the 'Six Million'; he re-evaluates the concept and technical feasibility of the 'gas chambers' with some startling conclusions, and separates the cold facts from the sheer tonnage of myth and propaganda . . .

McQuade thought, *God* . . . This was what Helga, an educated woman, believed? He flicked open the book. Many passages had been underlined. He speed-read a page which had been flagged:

The thesis of this book has been proved conclusively. The Jews of Europe were not exterminated and there was no German attempt to exterminate them . . . The Jews of Europe suffered during the war by being deported to the East, by having had much of their property confiscated and, more importantly, by suffering cruelly in the circumstances surrounding Germany's defeat. There may even have been a million dead.

Everybody in Europe suffered during the war. The people who suffered most were the losers, the Germans and Austrians, who lost 10 million dead due to military casualties, Allied bombings, the Russian terror at the end of the war, Russian and French labour conscriptions of POWs after the war, Polish and other expulsions from their homelands, under the most brutal conditions, and the vengeful occupation policies of 1945–1948.

The 'gas chambers' were wartime propaganda fantasies . . . The factual basis of these ridiculous charges was nailed with perfect accuracy by Heinrich Himmler, in an interview with a representative of the World Jewish Congress just a few weeks before the end of the war: 'In order to put a stop to epidemics we were forced to burn the bodies of incalculable numbers of people who had been destroyed by disease. We were therefore forced to build crematoria, and on this account they are knotting a noose for us.'

It is most unfortunate that Himmler was a 'suicide' while in British captivity since, had he been a defendant at the Nuremberg Trials . . . he would have told the true story . . . But then, you see, it was not within the bounds of political possibility that Himmler live to talk at the Nuremberg Trials . . .

The author went on to describe 'holocaust' literature as 'supreme examples of total delusion and foolishness and will be referenced only in connection with the great hoaxes of history'.

McQuade soberly went back to the librarians' counter with the books. 'I'd like to take this one out please. On the constitutional history of South West Africa.'

The librarian said, 'Another book has just come back. Do you know it?' She held it out.

It was called *For Volk and Führer*. 'No.'

'Take it also, it is a true story about South Africa during the war.'

Swakopmund is a friendly town. The Sam Cohen librarian gave him a charming smile. 'Ah so, the Englishman! The public library telephoned me and I have prepared a pile of books on German history in South West.'

The books stood on a polished table. 'Thank you. May I take them home?'

'*Nein*, but you can read them here as much as you like.'

'Thank you. I'm also particularly interested in Swakopmund during the war period.' McQuade waved his hand. 'How many doctors there were.' He tried to say it casually: 'For example, can you tell me how many dentists there were in Swakopmund in 1945?'

'Yes. One. Doctor Wessels.'

This was lucky! 'Only one?'

'Yes, he died only in the last couple of years.'

McQuade's hopes sank. It sounded a strange question but he could not dress it up. 'Where are his old records now?' He added, trying to make it sound casual, 'I mean, has his old surgery been taken over by a new dentist?'

'No. We have several dentists nowadays, but they have their own surgeries. But maybe Doctor Wessels' son has his father's old stuff.'

McQuade's hopes rose again. 'His son's here?'

'He lives in his father's old house.'

'I see.' McQuade tried to conceal his eagerness. 'Well, it's after four o'clock. Can I come back tomorrow to read those books?'

'*Natürlich*.' She handed him a piece of paper. 'Here is a list of the books, in case somebody moves them.'

He walked out into the glaring desert sun, feeling lucky. *Only one dentist in 1945*.

He hurried down the Kaiserstrasse to the Hansa Hotel to telephone Doctor Wessels' son. He looked up his number in the directory. He rehearsed his story. Then dialled.

The telephone rang, and rang.

He hung up. The man might not come home for hours.

He telephoned Roger Wentland, the attorney for his fishing company, to consult him on the law of salvage.

7

There is definitely something in the Old School Tie. Roger Wentland and McQuade had hardly anything to do with each other at school. Roger had been one of those bespectacled swots who sat in the front row and always came top, whereas McQuade had sat in the back row and cribbed the homework of the likes of Roger. At university they had had even less contact, where Roger had done political philosophy, law and spent his vacations on archaeological digs, whereas McQuade did marine biology and spent his university vacations on the whaling boats. But when McQuade had returned to Walvis Bay and found that Roger Wentland had a law practice in town, they had greeted each other like long-lost buddies and McQuade had immediately given Roger all his legal business out of a vague loyalty. They only saw each other on business but it was always conducted over a row of beers and Roger hardly ever sent McQuade a bill. That afternoon they met in the bar of the Atlantic Hotel in Walvis Bay. They sat where nobody could hear them.

'This is absolutely confidential, right?'

'Of course.' Roger was a fleshy, bespectacled, untidy man with thick lips who looked like an absent-minded professor.

'I want to know my legal rights if I salvage valuables from a German submarine that was sunk off the coast of South West Africa forty-odd years ago.'

Roger looked at him. 'You've *found* such a shipwreck?'

'Not yet. But I think I know where one is.'

Roger sat back. 'Boy . . . You'd better tell me the story.'

McQuade gave him as much of the facts as he needed to know.

Roger stared pensively across the bar. 'Boy . . . Look, I'm not the best guy to consult on this. You need a maritime law specialist. I'd better write to a firm in Cape Town for an opinion.'

McQuade said: 'That's exactly what I *don't* want you to do. In case the word gets out. I don't want any of this written down for clerks to read. I'd have every treasure hunter in the world up here trying to beat me to it – they're all fucking pirates.'

The lawyer sighed. 'Well, then I'll have to do some research. But, in general principle . . . In principle, a sunken ship and its contents belong to whoever salvages it if the original owner has abandoned it. That's if the vessel is sunk in international waters. If it's sunk in a nation's territorial waters, that nation's laws apply. Now, because South Africa administers Namibia, I think you'd have to register a salvage claim with the maritime authorities.'

'Could they refuse my claim?'

Roger spread his hands. 'A submarine is a *warship*. Indeed an *enemy* warship, because Germany was South Africa's enemy at the time. And it may come under the peace treaty signed by the Allies and Germany at the end of the war.'

'Oh boy . . .'

'And if they granted your claim, I think the government would demand part of the salvage.'

'How much?' McQuade demanded.

'I don't know. Never had a case like this. It would probably depend on your effort and expense, and the risks you took.'

McQuade did not like the sound of that. 'And if they refused my claim?'

'Well, you could appeal to the courts, but that's expensive, and you may end up appealing to The Hague, the International Court of Justice, because the United Nations and Germany may get in on the act.'

'The United Nations?' McQuade said indignantly. '*Why?*'

'Because,' Roger said, 'of Resolution 435. This submarine

lies in Namibian waters. Well, Namibia is governed by South Africa as a trusteeship territory, under the Treaty of Versailles, which ended the First World War. Under that treaty Namibia was confiscated from Germany and given *temporarily* to South Africa to govern. Well, the United Nations, which is dominated by black states, passed Resolution 435 in 1978, demanding that South Africa grant independence to Namibia immediately. South Africa refuses because of the thousands of Cuban troops in Angola, et cetera, et cetera. Well, if you end up appealing to the courts, the United Nations may decide to make this a *cause célèbre*, take the opportunity to argue that the salvage belongs neither to you *nor* South Africa, but to the people of Namibia who should be independent. Et cetera, et cetera.'

McQuade sat back. 'Oh Lord . . . ' He signalled for two more beers. He waited until the barman was out of earshot again. 'And why might Germany get in on the case?'

'Look, until I've researched these points I can only outline the *potential* snags. But this submarine is technically the property of the present German government. I remember reading some years ago about a German frigate that was found off the coast of Denmark by a Dutch salvage company. The Dutchmen got inside it and found a few skeletons. They filed their salvage claim with the Danish authorities. The Danes refused because the frigate was in their territorial waters and the Danish *government* began to salvage it. Whereupon the *German* government intervened through the courts and stopped the Danes, because they said it would be the desecration of a German war grave. So? Nobody got the ship.'

'Oh God! So what might they do with a treasure trove involved?'

'Exactly. Now, if you want me to do the research, I will. But it'll be expensive.'

McQuade shook his head. 'No, you've told me enough to worry the shit out of me. Let's see if I find the submarine first.'

'And how does one look for it?'

'With my trawler's depth-sounder. The depth of the ocean bed registers on a graph. If I go over the area in a pattern, the graph will jump when I pass over something as big as a submarine. Go over it again, in the next leg of the pattern. Do it often enough and the whole outline of the submarine should show on the graph.'

'Clever. And then? Send a diver down? Who?'

'Me. If it's not too deep. It can't be very deep if two men escaped from it.'

'Can you dive? Yes, of course you can.'

'I've done a bit of scuba-diving. But only in shallow water. But Kid Childe can dive. And Tucker, if he has to. We keep a couple of scuba-kits on board for emergencies with propellers and nets and things.' He added: 'But I don't like doing it any more. Sharks and similar.'

Roger shook his head. 'Rather you than me. But then you always were one of the boys, going on the whaling ships and all that when we were students – the girls were always vastly impressed. Made the rest of us look rather wet.'

'The rest of you got nice wives and got rich.'

'And the rest of us got grey hair and paunches. You don't look a day over thirty-five. What about visibility down there?'

McQuade smiled. 'The visibility down there will depend on the current, the amount of plankton, weed, sunlight, the depth and so on. It could be clear or it could be like pea-soup.' It gave him the willies to think about it.

'And? How do you get inside?'

'Worry about that after I've seen it. Maybe there's a nice big hole in the side. I may have to get a professional diver to help me, and I'll have to read up about submarines, so I know what to expect.'

'Somebody at the naval base here should be able to advise you. But be careful, if you want to keep this a secret. Say you're writing a story. And if you employ a diver, don't go near Straghan Salvage Limited – Red Straghan is a bad bastard, he'll steal you blind. Go to Alan Louw, he's honest.'

'I hope I won't have to use any diver.' He took a tense breath. 'Okay. Send me a bill for this consultation.'

Roger smiled. 'You pay for the beers. When you crack that submarine I'll send you a whopper.' He added: 'And? You said there were *two* things you wanted to ask me about.'

McQuade nodded. He produced the book he had borrowed from the Swakopmund library.

'That looks complicated legal stuff for a marine biologist. Can you give me a run-down, in a nutshell, of the constitutional history of Namibia and how we got it off the Germans?'

Roger flipped through the book then looked at the list from the Sam Cohen library.

'Why this sudden passion for German history of this neck of the woods?' He looked over the top of his glasses. 'You're looking for a *political* reason for this submarine being off this coast?'

McQuade said: 'If there *was* a political reason – if these guys were high-up Nazis and not ordinary sailors, they probably had a stack of loot on that submarine.'

Roger looked at him over the top of his spectacles. 'Okay. Where do you want to begin?'

'Assume I know nothing.'

Roger raised his eyebrows. 'And he wants it in a nutshell. Okay . . .' He rubbed his chin. Then began like a professor delivering a lecture. 'When South Africa was colonized, this whole vast area of South West Africa was unwanted by anybody. Because it was desert. Then the Scramble for Africa began in earnest. The Germans grabbed Togoland, the Cameroons and Tanganyika. Then a young German, called Lüderitz, found a nice little shallow-water harbour and persuaded the local chief to sell it to him, plus the surrounding area in a radius of five miles. Trouble is that Lüderitz meant five German miles, which are twenty miles of ours. So local war broke out. Lüderitz asks the Kaiser for protection. Troops arrived and pacified the natives. Then Great Britain gets nervous that the Germans may threaten her Cape sea route so she seizes the only deep-water harbour, namely here at Walvis Bay. Which pisses off the Krauts. Even Queen Victoria wasn't amused because she wanted the Kaiser, who was her dear nephew, to have a bit of an empire too. So Germany officially colonizes the rest of South West Africa. Then . . .' he held up his finger, '*diamonds* were discovered. Such as the world has never seen, just lying in the sand dunes for the picking. Fortune hunters from all over the world arrive in thousands, and the German colonization of South West began in earnest.' Roger spread his hands. 'And the inevitable happened. When the natives found they were being forced off their land they rebelled. The colonists mounted punitive expeditions, and inevitably full-scale bloody wars of pacification.

'Finally, after years of intermittent warfare, the Germans were fully in control of the whole vast territory. With only the British enclave of Walvis Bay spoiling the Teutonic picture. And . . .' he shrugged, 'the Scramble for Africa was over. Great Britain had Egypt, Sudan, Uganda, Kenya, Northern and Southern Rhodesia, Nyasaland, Nigeria, Ghana, and the Union of South Africa. The French had Algeria, the Sahara and Equatorial Africa, the Portuguese had Angola and Mozambique, the Belgians had the Congo, and the Germans had the Cameroons and Togoland and Tanganyika and South West Africa – or Namibia. Everything seemed stable in the world. But . . .' he held up his finger again, 'Germany had other plans for Africa.'

He took a swallow of his beer.

'It was Germany's plan to expand from Namibia and Tanganyika, gobble up South Africa and start to strangle the British Empire. With her warships based in Namibia she would have been able to dominate the Cape sea route, and with her warships based in Tanganyika she would have dominated Suez and the Indian Ocean. Then South Africa would have fallen into their hands. It was the South African goldfields and diamonds that Germany desperately wanted. However, they jumped the gun: the First World War came a little too early. And Great Britain asked the South African Government to send troops into Namibia and Tanganyika, to save the empire. But you must know all this?'

'The First World War is distant history for me.'

'But it's not distant history to the Germans.' Roger nodded down the bar. 'These guys are more German than the Germans. Just like in the former colonies you meet people who are more devoutly British than the British. But the *Germans*?' He sighed. 'As individuals they're fine – even less offensive than the British. But together? Put a dozen Germans together and you've got a fucking regiment. They'd love this territory to revert to German rule.'

'And in 1945?'

'I'll come to that. Under the Treaty of Versailles in 1919 at the end of the war, Britain took over Tanganyika, and South Africa took over the administration of Namibia.' He glanced down the bar. 'The Germans were stripped of their colonies for two reasons. Firstly, their strategic value. Secondly, the Germans were told by the Allies that they were "Unfit to govern".' He snorted. 'And the Allies were right.'

'Meaning?'

'Meaning,' Roger said softly, 'that the Germans were *bastards* towards the natives . . .' He glanced down the bar. 'Drink up and let's go to my house. I'll lend you some books. Barbara's got people coming to dinner, but we've got time for a beer there.'

The Wentlands' house overlooked the lagoon that was always full of flamingoes and sea birds. Roger went straight to the living-room bookshelf. He looked at the list provided by the Sam Cohen library, then pulled out a book. 'This list is inadequate. You must read *German Rule in Africa* by Evans Lewin.' He pulled out another. 'And *Britain and Germany in Africa*, published by Yale. This compares the two countries' policies and behaviour.' He reached for another book. 'And *The Germans and Africa*.'

McQuade took them. 'But how were the Germans so bad?'

'In a nutshell?' Roger went to the bar in the corner and got two beers. 'British colonial policy was to maintain the tribal structures and the natives' rights as far as possible, as well as the authority of the chiefs. German policy was the *opposite*. It was to destroy the authority of the chiefs, to render the natives powerless so they could be press-ganged into labour and deprived of their land. It was even written in the *Koloniale Zeitschrift* . . .' He reached for one of the books and leafed through it. 'Here. This was written in the German press. Quote: "Our colonies are acquired, not for evangelization of the blacks, not for their well-being, but for ours. Whosoever hinders our object we must put out of the way".' He looked at McQuade. 'That was German policy, in a nutshell. When the Hereros rebelled, General von Trotha arrived from Germany with nineteen thousand soldiers and his entire purpose was extermination. He slaughtered them in their scores of thousands. He drove them into the desert where they died of thirst and starvation in the thousands, while his soldiers gleefully picked them off. Only a few thousand survived, to struggle across the desert into British Bechuanaland. Finally there was an outcry in Germany against this inhumanity and von Trotha's extermination order was cancelled.' He shook his head. 'They were the same in Tanganyika and Togoland and the Cameroons, and the result of their policies has always been ruin and chaos. Because of their extermination campaigns the Germans had no native labour! In 1898 the black population here was 300,000. Fourteen years later, in 1912, there were only 100,000 blacks! Two-thirds of the population slaughtered!'

'Jesus.'

Roger nodded. 'So when the First World War broke out and South Africa occupied this territory, we came as liberators. At least we brought law and order and Native Commissioners to look after natives' rights, et cetera.'

McQuade's schoolboy history was certainly sketchy. 'And how did the Germans take it?'

Roger snorted. 'After the war, many South Africans immigrated up here, and the Germans were bitter. When local self-government was set up by South Africa, the legislative assembly was always divided: Germans against South Africans. The Germans wanted to run it their way, but the South Africans wanted the country to become another province of South Africa. *Then* . . .' Roger held up a finger again . . . 'Herr Adolf Hitler came along . . .'

He got up and went back to his bookshelves. He plucked out three volumes.

'You must read *Germany's African Claims*. Published by the *Daily Telegraph* in the 1930s. And this, *Nazi Activities in South West Africa*, published by the Friends of Europe. But the most important book of all,' he held it up, 'is *Hitler Over Africa*, by Benjamin Bennett.'

McQuade was all attention. Roger drained his mug. He was beginning to get along with the beer. He got out two more.

'Hitler came to power on the massive wave of German bitterness after their defeat in the First World War. They had been humiliated, forced to pay reparations for the war costs, and stripped of their colonies. Germany was bankrupt. Hitler came along with his Brown Shirts and started whipping up the good old German martial spirit. *"We demand that the unjust Treaty of Versailles be scrapped! We demand our Lebensraum, space for expansion! It was international Jewish money which waged the war against us! The Jews – the Jews!"* And we know what happened to the Jews. The same that happened to the Hereros. The German Solution . . .' He sighed. 'Anyway, the Germans in South West Africa and

Tanganyika *loved* all this rhetoric ... They loved Hitler's shouting. They were smarting under South African rule. And Hitler was bellowing that the former German colonies had to be returned to Germany, to provide *Lebensraum* and raw materials to rebuild her economy which had been bled white by international Jewry. And Hitler's bully-boys were running around kicking the living shit out of any German who disagreed. Remember?'

McQuade nodded. Roger continued:

'Hitler and his Nazis created a *tyranny* – before they were even elected as the government – and they intimidated the rest of Europe as well. The Germans were on the march again, rattling their sabres and singing "Tomorrow Belongs to Me..." And all the time demanding their African colonies back. *Then* ...' Roger held up his finger again, 'Hitler was elected the Chancellor of Germany. And within weeks German democracy ceased to exist. Within weeks Hitler had suspended the German parliament, the Nazi Party *became* Germany and Adolf Hitler *became* the Nazi Party. Absolute dictator.'

Roger leant across the bar at him. 'But even *before* Hitler came to power the Nazi Party had formed branches here and in Tanganyika! Bullying, just as in Germany. They set up cells across this country ruling the German community with a rod of iron. They kept dossiers on everybody, and any uncooperative German was reported to Berlin and the SS took reprisals against their relatives in Germany.' He waved his hand. 'They set up their own courts, circumventing the local courts, and a vast local Hitler Youth, with the Ordeal of Fire ritual – kids leaping over flames to cleanse and harden themselves for the Führer. Taking the oath of undying loyalty to the Führer.' Roger snorted. 'Of course, the South African government banned the Nazi Party – these Germans were legally British subjects, because South Africa was the legal government, and owed allegiance to the King of England. So it was unlawful to swear allegiance to Hitler.' He shook his head. 'The Nazis respected no such niceties. The Hitler Youth changed their name to the Pathfinders and sent local Germans to Berlin to undergo training courses in preparation for the day when Hitler would retake the place.' He shook his head. 'Most Germans here were caught up in this fever. Every day they huddled around the radios listening to the propaganda bellowed from Berlin, listening for the joyful news of the day of liberation. "*Der Tag*" they called it, The Day, and they went around warning the South Africans to watch their step. "Nobody can stop our Führer!"' Roger smiled grimly. 'They were bloody nearly right, weren't they?'

McQuade's mind was working ahead. 'And?'

'The Berlin Colonial Office – and remember that since Germany didn't *have* any colonies, how the hell did they have the nerve to have a "Colonial Office" – anyway, they even published a celebrated map of how Africa was going to look after Hitler had got their colonies back. Did you know that?'

The door bell rang. The first dinner guest had arrived. Roger stood up. He pointed at the books.

'It's all in there. It was an improved version of the Kaiser's plan, but, in short, it was South Africa Hitler was after and from there the *whole* of Africa would crumble under the German might, with its vast reservoirs of raw materials and black slave labour to build the Thousand Year Reich.' He jabbed his finger again. '*That* was his plan.'

Roger left to go to the front door. McQuade stared out the window.

8

It was dark when McQuade got back to his house in Fifth Street. It was three days since he had been home and he was in dire need of a shower. He unlocked the peeling front door. Something scraped across the floor. It was a bulky brown envelope, which had been pushed through his letter box.

His name on it had been typed: *McQuade*. No initial, no Mr. He tore it open. Inside was a book.

It was *The Hoax of the Twentieth Century*. The very same book he had been reading that afternoon, which denied that the Holocaust had taken place. He looked inside. Passages had been underlined throughout. McQuade stared across the room.

Who had sent him this, and typed his surname only? It was insulting, almost aggressive. The Stormtrooper? But if Helga had sent it she would surely have hand-written his full name. No, it was typed because the sender wished to be anonymous. But who, apart from Helga, would worry what McQuade thought about the Holocaust? People he had seen at the Schmidt ranch? But for what reason? To explain? To tell him to keep his mouth shut?

He walked pensively through to his office, carrying Roger's books. He stood a moment, thinking; then he reached for the answering machine.

It clicked; there followed the soft hiss of the tape, and then a deep male voice said softly, 'Mind your own business, McQuade.'

Then another click as the machine cut off.

McQuade stared across the room. Then he rewound and played it again.

He could not recognize the voice. Even the accent was hard to identify. It sounded as if the speaker had disguised it. It might have been Afrikaner, but it could also have been a German accent, or even an English-speaking South African. But what was unmistakable was the menace.

McQuade frowned. What he felt was anger that some person was trying to frighten him. And, yes, he felt a twinge of fear. The bastard had succeeded! His first reaction was to snatch up the telephone and tell the Stormtrooper to tell her bloody friends to leave him alone before he reported them to the police. Just then the telephone rang.

He jerked. It shrilled in the empty house. There was a click as the answering machine took the call. McQuade stabbed the audio button. There was a moment's pause, then a softly sneering voice said: 'Did you get my message, McQuade?'

McQuade's hand reached out for the telephone, and the voice said softly: 'I know you're there, McQuade, because your lights are on and your Landrover's outside.'

McQuade snatched up the telephone. *'Who is this?'*

There was a smirk. 'Just to confirm you got the message.'

McQuade barked: *'What are you talking about, you big oaf?'*

There was a chuckle, then the voice said, 'Just forget about everything, and stay healthy.' The telephone went dead.

McQuade slammed it down.

He was furious. And shaky.

He snatched up the telephone again. Then hesitated.

And tell the police what?

He slowly sat down.

Tell them how much? 'Mind your own business,' the voice had said. 'Forget about everything.' What business? Forget about what? What you saw on the Schmidt ranch? A bunch of Germans getting sentimental about the old days? Or the submarine-business?

He stared at the wall.

But how could the voice know he had been looking into the submarine story? It was hardly possible for anyone to know he'd been sitting on the Skeleton Coast with his sextant. Somebody saw him talking to Skellum outside Kukki's Pub and put two and two together? Certainly nobody followed him to Jakob's kraal. So? So the only possibility was Skellum or Jakob had opened their mouths about the strange things McQuade had been up to. But that seemed hardly likely, in the short time since he left them.

McQuade sat. Trying to think it through.

If the voice had been referring to the submarine, it could only mean that he was trying to scare McQuade off, or was trying to hush up the story. That could only mean that there was a *political* connection. Somebody did not want it known that forty years ago a German came struggling ashore from a sunken submarine. *And if that was the case, it most likely meant that that German was still alive . . .*

McQuade sat there, thoughts cramming his head. Then he slowly returned the telephone to its cradle.

But surely it was unlikely that the voice was referring to the submarine. And the voice had doubtless delivered *The Hoax of the Twentieth Century*. So it was highly likely that the call was from somebody who was at the Schmidt ranch. Highly likely. But he wasn't going to take the chance of reporting to the police since he certainly did not want them to know what he had been doing since then.

McQuade rubbed his chin. He considered telephoning the Stormtrooper, telling her to call off her bloody bully-boys. 'Stay healthy.' *Christ, how juvenile.* No. He got up. He felt silly doing it, but he went to the front door and made sure it was locked. He switched off the living-room light, then pulled back the curtains. All he saw was the silent, empty sand-street and the railway yards.

He went to the kitchen, got a beer, then walked through to the bathroom. He turned on the taps.

He went back to his office and got the topmost book off the pile. *German Rule in Africa*, by Evans Lewin. He took it back to the bathroom.

He hesitated; and then locked the bathroom door. He had never done that before in this house.

Here again coincidence came into play. If he hadn't received that threatening telephone call he wouldn't have read Roger Wentland's books all night; and, had he not done so, it is doubtful whether he would have persevered in the long chance of trying to trace the man who landed on this coast forty years ago from a sunken German submarine. In the books he learnt about political battles of not so long ago, history of which he was sure most educated people of his generation had little idea; recent history with a relevance to the present to make his blood run cold.

That night was unreal. A fog came rolling in off the Atlantic, so dense that a man would have been invisible five paces away, and the town was completely silent: it would have been a perfect night for villainy. McQuade sat in a yellow-grey pool of light, the mist rolling in his open window, jerking every time he imagined a sound, growing hourly more appalled by Germany's colonial history. He read speeches by parliamentarians in the Reichstag denouncing their own government for maintaining German rule by the terror of the whip, calling their African territories 'The Colonies of the Twenty-five', referring to the twenty-five vicious lashes that were meted out for the most trivial offences – for failing to salute a white man, for failing to raise a hat, for collapsing when carrying heavy loads, for not being punctual with the master's dinner. 'The insensibility to the feelings of others, the disregard of native rights and the elementary principles of justice, the brutal callousness . . . and the total inability to conceive any system of administration that is not upheld by cruelty and by designed intimidation . . . stamps German administrators as on a par with the most brutal of the old Arab slave hunters'. He read a report about District Judge Rotberg in Togoland, who 'was making a journey when one of the porters, overcome by his burden, fell to the ground.

The representative of German justice knelt upon him, pummelled him in the face, and then had him flogged. The poor fellow fell again. He was again thrashed – this time with fatal effects.' He read the verbatim report of a German judge, protesting in the Reichstag in 1906 in these words:

The native, after being completely stripped, is strapped across a block of wood or barrel, so that he cannot move, and then . . . the strongest amongst the black soldiers has to wield a plaited rope, or a correspondingly thick stick, with both hands and with all his strength, and with such violence that each blow must whistle in the air. It has happened that if the blow does not whistle it has to be repeated, and, moreover, if it does not do so the soldier gets it himself.

And he read about forced labour as a substitute for taxes, about blacks being caught 'like so much game' and being driven by soldiers in chained gangs to work on the road-making and railway-building and on the colonists' farms, about women being taken as hostages if the men ran away when the soldiers came to seize them. He read:

Removal from their primitive homes to new conditions, where the food has frequently been different from what they were accustomed to, kept at strenuous labour from early morning till late at night; herded together in insanitary surroundings; goaded by the brutalities of their taskmasters; flogged for the slightest offence: the unfortunate natives frequently have died after a few months . . .

On certain plantations in the Cameroons and Tanganyika the death rate was admitted to being between fifty and seventy per cent within six months. There was an eye-witness account by a South African, describing the harbour-building at Lüderitz:

69

I have seen women and children . . . at Lüderitz dying of starvation and overwork, nothing but skin and bone, getting flogged every time they fell under their heavy loads. I have seen them picking up bits of bread and refuse thrown away outside our tents and being flogged when caught.

Another witness, writing in the *Cape Argus* newspaper in 1905, described seeing a woman, carrying an infant on her back, and a sack of grain on her head, when 'she fell . . . The corporal sjamboked her certainly for five minutes and the baby as well.' And the result of all this was depopulation, the harvests could not be reaped, or even sown, because the men had been dragooned away for forced labour and there was famine in many places. And the overall consequence of all this brutality was rebellion and thirty years of bloody warfare, punitive expedition after punitive expedition, warfare moreover that seemed to be regarded as a kind of sport. He read a verbatim report by a German soldier writing in a Strasbourg newspaper describing a battle in Tanganyika:

. . . we surprised the rebels as they were attempting to cross the river. There was a long narrow bridge, which they had to cross, so that we could pop them off comfortably. There were seventy-six dead, besides those torn to pieces by crocodiles . . . In the middle of the river was a sandbank where they wanted to rest, but here too our shots caught them. That was a sight! I stood by the river behind a felled tree and shot 120 rounds. The prisoners were always hanged!

And in the Cameroons there was a Captain Dominck who permitted his soldiers to drown fifty-two children who were survivors of a massacre of a village. The children were put into baskets and hurled into the river for sport. But the most

70

ruthless of all was the war of extermination against the Hereros of South West Africa, when General von Trotha issued this infamous proclamation in 1904:

> I, the great general of the German soldiers, send this letter to the Herero nation . . . The Herero nation must now leave the country. If the people do not do it, I will compel them with the big tube. Within the German frontier, every Herero, with or without a rifle . . . will be shot. I will not take any more women or children, but I will either drive them back to your people or have them fired on. These are my words to the nation of the Hereros.

There was no mercy: the wounded were killed, women and children were shot and hanged. There was a quotation from a book written by a German pastor who witnessed the dreadful campaign:

> We found some old water holes and near them hundreds of new ones dug by the enemy the day before . . . It was now reported that there was still a last water place about five hours further on and that great numbers of the enemy were there. It was decided that we must drive them away; and we wanted to, for if we hunted them out of that place nothing remained to them but the wilderness. From a hill we saw two mighty clouds of dust moving towards the north and north-east, towards death from thirst . . . (Later) I saw people sitting in crowds, shoulder against shoulder, quite motionless. The heads of some drooped on their breasts and their arms hung down, as if they were asleep. Others sat leaning against a bush or neighbour, breathing fast and hard, their mouths open; they regarded us with stupid eyes . . .

Punitive expedition after punitive expedition, rule by the whip and the gun and the noose, to the point where a parliamentarian called Bebcl cried out in the Reichstag:

'Gentlemen, you do not come as deliverers and educators but as conquerors, as oppressors, as exploiters . . . to rob the natives with brute power of their properties! You make helots of them, force them into strange service, into villainage for strange purposes! *That* is your colonial policy!'

McQuade read through the unreal night. He was appalled — and this was part of *his own* family history: the *van Niekerk* part of his name was his mother's maiden name, which ostensibly made him half-Afrikaner (though *not* half-Hairy-back), but *her* mother was born Kessel, of pure German immigrant stock before she married grandfather van Niekerk, making McQuade in fact one-quarter German. Yet he'd had no idea of this awful recent history, and bet that most people of his generation had equally little idea. Yet, shocking though it all was, he would have put it down to the unenlightenment of the times, had it not been for what he had seen on the Schmidt ranch — after all, had not the British, at the same time, conducted a scorched earth policy in the Boer War to starve the Afrikaners into submission, burning homesteads and crops and driving Afrikaner women and children into concentration camps where twenty-six thousand of them died of disease and malnutrition? Did not the Australians drive the Aborigines out of their traditional homelands? Were there not verified reports of hunting them down for sport? Had not the New Zealanders waged bloody war against the Maoris? Had not the Americans butchered Red Indian resistance? Was it not the American settlers who had introduced the barbaric practice of scalping so that they could claim a bounty for every Indian they killed? There was, however, that threatening telephone call echoing in his mind during that unreal fogbound night, the vivid image of the swastikas at the Schmidt ranch, and there were the photographs of the Third Reich he had seen in the library that afternoon, and it was not so easy to relegate the brutality of

72

German colonial policy to history: there was a pattern of behaviour, a national susceptibility towards aggression and domination. It was because of the coincidence of all these circumstances that he read on, despite his tiredness, and learned things that changed the course of this story; about Hitler's grand plan for Africa, which Roger Wentland had mentioned.

It was spelled out in the book published by the *Daily Telegraph*, *Germany's African Claims*, in *Britain and Germany in Africa*, published by Yale University, and in *Hitler Over Africa*, by Benjamin Bennett. Nor was Hitler's grand blueprint for Africa a new one: it was as old as the original Scramble for Africa, as old as the Boer War when German agents were planted in South Africa to stir up the Afrikaners against Great Britain. The extermination campaign that General von Trotha waged against the Herero in 1904 was part of it, for the troops that were brought out from Germany for that war were to be used against South Africa after the Herero were crushed. And after Germany lost the First World War, Hitler resurrected the grand plan for Africa: one of the first things he demanded in his sabre-rattling speeches was the return to Germany of her former colonies to provide *Lebensraum*.

But Hitler's grand plan embraced much more than that: not only would his warships based in South West Africa and Tanganyika have dominated the Indian Ocean, Suez and the Cape sea route, thus strangling the British Empire; by controlling Suez, the Persian Gulf and its oil would have come under German control and then the whole Far East would have fallen under German domination, even Japan, for they were all dependent on Persian Gulf oil – and the whole of Europe would have been held to ransom for oil; Europe would have ground to a shattered halt under one blitzkrieg. But not only that: German bombers from Tanganyika and South West Africa would be in easy reach of the South African goldfields, and South Africa would fall to Germany, and then the Rhodesias and the Congo with their copper mines would fall, until finally the whole of Africa would be one vast German colony, with a massive army of black soldiers, and the whole vast treasure-house would be Germany's, with its vast reservoir of black slave labour, with autobahns and railways connecting it all. Truly it would have become the Reich To Last A Thousand Years.

That was Hitler's grand plan for Africa, and for the world; and it all depended on his getting back South West Africa, now called Namibia, this desert land where McQuade sat reading. And there was open talk here about the 'Aryanization of South Africa', racial purification, the confiscation of Afrikaner farms and Jewish property; and all the time the talk about *Der Tag*, which would be soon because 'what our Führer demands our Führer gets.' But the Führer did not get his colonies given back. War broke out and the South African government rounded up almost every German male in Namibia and shipped them off to concentration camps to prevent them fighting for the Führer. Then Hitler launched a gun-powder plot in South Africa. It was called Operation Weissdorn and the key man was a South African called Robey Leibbrandt.

McQuade knew of Robey Leibbrandt as a legendary character, once South Africa's boxing champion, who became a Nazi spy during the war. To McQuade he was some kind of nutcase, almost as distant as Guy Fawkes: he had no idea how important Operation Weissdorn had been, or how close it came to changing the outcome of the war.

The extraordinary true story was told in a book called *For Volk and Führer*, by Hans Strydom, formerly President of the Southern African Society of Journalists. So, a big wheel. An authority. McQuade read the book through the eerie, unreal small hours, his tired mind racing, the possible significance of it in terms of today dawning on him, pieces of a jigsaw materializing out of the foggy night into his yellow pool of lamplight; as a plan Operation Weissdorn could be as valid today.

Robey Leibbrandt represented South Africa in the Olympic Games held in Germany in 1936. His family had suffered during the Boer War and he was fanatically anti-British, a detail known to the Nazis. Even before he set foot in Germany it had been decided to recruit him as the key man for the grand plan. In Germany he was fêted by the Nazi press, and became a cult-hero with his dazzling boxing in the preliminary fights. He was introduced to Hitler, who flattered him. He broke his hand but nonetheless courageously insisted on fighting in the finals, and only missed the gold medal because of his hand. Invited to return to Germany for 'further education', he became a fanatical Nazi. When war broke out he remained in Germany and was trained in sabotage and espionage. He was now invited to spearhead Operation Weissdorn, asked to return to South Africa and gain control of the Ossewa Brandwag, the faction of Afrikaners bitterly opposed to the British and to South Africa's involvement in the war, and to set up a large guerrilla infrastructure. Then he was to assassinate General Smuts, the pro-British prime minister of South Africa, seize control of the country, and order the South African troops fighting in North Africa to return home. Rommel would then have vanquished the British under Montgomery, and Germany would have dominated the Mediterranean and the Suez Canal. With the Cape sea route in Nazi hands, the British empire would have been strangled. If Operation Weissdorn had succeeded, Hitler would have won the war, and achieved the grand plan of establishing the Third Reich in Africa. From there the Persian gulf was his, and from there the world . . .

The rising sun did not penetrate the dense fog; the morning was opaque and chilly and cars drove with their headlights on. McQuade stared out his window at the hanging mist, astonished that he did not know how close his country had come to changing the world: Operation Weissdorn failed only because of the expert, hair-raising work of one dedicated Afrikaner policeman, called Jan Taljaart, who infiltrated the organization.

McQuade sat there, wide-awake tired, trying to see whether all this could reasonably have anything to do with that submarine.

Then he picked up the telephone and dialled the son of Dr Wessels, the man who, in 1945, was the only dentist for many miles around.

9

Mr Wessels' charming wife had coffee ready. She had a slight German accent. 'Of course I can tell you something about the old days of Swakopmund, and about my father-in-law, but I do not understand why you need to look at his old records of his patients. I agree, dental records are not so . . . *delicate* as medical records – teeth are only teeth, but nonetheless . . .' She trailed off.

McQuade took a breath. 'Mrs Wessels, I was not entirely frank with your husband when I telephoned him this morning.' He sighed. 'I really *am* writing a book. But I've come to do so in a roundabout way . . . I am trying to trace my father.'

'Your father?'

He nodded. 'My surname is McQuade. But that is my mother's maiden name. You see, I am illegitimate.'

Mrs Wessels looked embarrassed. 'I see . . .'

McQuade held up a palm. 'I'm quite used to the notion. But . . . naturally, I have an intense curiosity about my father. I believe that that's very normal.'

'I'm sure . . .'

McQuade said, 'I don't even know my father's name. My mother refused to tell me, and now she's dead, too. But . . . I believe that *my* father consulted *your* father-in-law shortly after the end of the war, and I believe that if I searched through your father-in-law's records for that period, I would be able to identify him. From the dental work done on him. Then I would have his *name*.'

Mrs Wessels was sympathetic. 'I see . . . But why do you think your father came to Dr Wessels?'

'Because,' McQuade said, 'it is one of the few details that

77

my mother ever told me.' He smiled: 'One of the few things I know about myself is that I was conceived in Swakopmund. In 1945. My mother happened to be here, looking for a job. Plenty of jobs, because so many Germans were interned in concentration camps. The war ends and the Germans start coming home. And out of the desert comes staggering this handsome German. That's how my mother described him.' He smiled, then went on: 'Evidently when the South Africans had started rounding up the German males, my father hid in the desert. And survived there throughout the war.'

'I see . . .'

'Evidently my father had been in a fight. He was in bad shape when my mother met him. And in pain. His front teeth had been broken. My mother took him to the dentist. And the only dentist in Swakopmund in 1945 was your father-in-law.'

'I *see* . . .'

'And,' McQuade said, 'if I could get his name, maybe I could trace him. If he's still alive.'

In the corner of the spare bedroom stood an old filing cabinet. On the floor lay the long boxes of dental cards which McQuade had already searched. Mrs Wessels came in with another mug of coffee for him. 'Any luck?'

'Your father-in-law was a busy man.'

'He used to say that his practice here extended over an area the size of Bavaria.'

'Do you know who his dental nurse was in 1945?'

'Sometimes it was my mother-in-law. But she's away at the moment. Sometimes it was Mrs Kruger. She lives in the apartments on the beach called *An der Mohle*.'

McQuade was delighted. 'Do you think she'd mind talking to me about your father-in-law's patients?'

'I'll telephone her when you're finished here.'

'Thank you very much.'

Each card showed two crescent rows of teeth: upper and

lower jaw. At the top was the patient's name, address, age. On the rows of teeth, Dr Wessels had made marks in black, indicating the dental work done before the patient came to see him: other marks, in red, indicated the work which Dr Wessels himself had done. Below were notes, describing the work. Extracted teeth were marked with a cross.

McQuade was only concerned with cards after May 1945. Females, children and males under thirty he discarded immediately.

He ran his eyes over the marks on the upper jaws. He was only concerned with the front teeth and red marks. He flipped through them, his eye racing, looking for the marks on the two front teeth.

It was afternoon when he saw them.

McQuade looked at the card joyfully. There they were: *the two front teeth crossed out.*

And below were the notes: *27.6.45. Both front teeth broken. Extracted. Denture made.*

At the top of the card was written: NAME: *Mr H. Strauss.* ADDRESS: *In transit. Cash* £10.

McQuade exulted silently. *He had found it!* He feverishly scrabbled through the remainder of the cards for 1945. Not one of them recorded such work on two front teeth.

McQuade sat back. This was the man: *Mr H. Strauss.* It was too much of a coincidence not to be true! Even the initial was right! *A man who takes on a false identity wants to keep his first name because that is how he thinks of himself!*

Of course it is the same man!

Mrs Kruger received McQuade cheerfully and offered him coffee. 'Strictly speaking, you should not have been shown those records – but it's done now.' She put on her spectacles and peered at the dental card that he showed her. She shook her head. 'No. We had a number of patients named Strauss, it's quite a common name. But no H, that I recall.'

'Mrs Kruger, you must remember the months after the war ended quite clearly? The men coming home?'

'Yes, I suppose so.'

'In fact, Doctor Wessels must have had fewer adult male patients than normal, because so many men were interned in concentration camps?'

'That's quite true.'

'About that time, don't you remember a German man coming into the surgery who was very sunburnt? And probably dirty. Probably a bit wild-looking. And hungry-looking.'

Mrs Kruger frowned. McQuade waited, then went on: 'He was in pain. An emergency. He probably said he had lost his teeth in a fight. He may have said that he had walked across the desert, to explain his condition.'

Mrs Kruger frowned into the middle distance.

McQuade said: 'Now think carefully: probably his arm was injured. Maybe it had a bandage on it, or it might have healed over, but obviously it was a recent injury.'

Mrs Kruger looked at him. 'Any other clues?'

Playing his last card, McQuade pulled out the old English five pound note. 'Have you ever seen one of these?'

She took it.

'Yes!' she exclaimed. 'And I remember now.' She looked at him earnestly. 'The injured arm! And he paid for his treatment with two notes like this!'

McQuade was exultant. He thrust the dental card back at her. 'Was it this man? If I tell you that I've been through all Doctor Wessels' records for this period and this is the only case of two front teeth being extracted, does that jog your memory?'

Mrs Kruger looked at the card again.

'If that's true, then it must be the same man.'

McQuade wanted to jump up and kiss her.

'Mrs Kruger, you've been very helpful. In helping me trace my father. I have only one further question.' He paused, for emphasis. 'Have you ever seen or heard of this man again?'

Mrs Kruger shook her head slowly. 'No.'

McQuade got back into his Landrover, and sat, trying to think. He was exhausted after his sleepless night.

So? He had found out that the man had survived, as well as the name he had used. And, it was possible that he had continued to use that name.

So? So what?

Well, was he still alive? Where was he now? McQuade sat there, dog-tired, trying to think. Tomorrow the *Bonanza* was going back to sea and he had to have his decisions made. So, where did all this get him?

Well firstly, if indeed there had been more loot aboard that submarine, it was highly likely that the man had later salvaged it himself. And McQuade was wasting his time, except for having the bastard arrested for murder.

Secondly, if the man had *not* succeeded in salvaging the loot, but was still alive, it was quite possible that he would find out about it when McQuade started sending down divers, and it was highly likely that he would try to stop him.

Was that what that threatening telephone call was about?

McQuade stared down the road. Then he shook his head. No, he'd thought this one through last night. How could H.M., or H. Strauss as we now know him, know what McQuade had been doing these last four days? Unless Skellum was slobbering around town. But how likely was that, in so short a time? No, that phone call was purely 'political'. Some Hitler-crank throwing his weight around because McQuade saw their orgy at the Schmidt ranch.

So, what do we do about Herr H. Strauss?

The answer would be to find that submarine as fast as possible, before thinking about Herr Strauss.

McQuade took a tense, weary breath. Okay. So, buy

some decent diving gear, and speak to somebody about submarines.

Almost everybody in Walvis Bay is very approachable. McQuade had briefly met Commander Ian Manning, the officer in charge of the South African naval base, only once, yet the man was only too pleased to help and he insisted on entertaining McQuade in the wardroom while he did so. McQuade had hoped for a more private place but he had no choice. He had to rush back home to put on a tie. A smart rating escorted him from the naval base gate. Half a dozen young officers were clustered respectfully around their commander in the wardroom, whilst an orderly hovered with a tray of hors d'oeuvres. Ian Manning tapped a thick book on the mahogany bar and said: 'I'm not the best chap to advise you on submarines, but I've brought *Jane's Fighting Ships* along. What's your story about?'

McQuade said: 'Well, it's about this guy who's cruising in the Mediterranean on his yacht. One day he drops anchor and when he comes to pull it up again, it won't budge. So he dives down to dislodge it. And he finds it's caught on this old German submarine. So he tries to get inside it. To see if there's anything valuable. What I want to know is what did those German submarines look like inside and how does my hero get inside it – assuming there isn't a big hole in the side? What problems is he going to encounter?'

The young officers were all rapt attention. Ian Manning said: 'Hmmm. And? Does he find anything valuable?'

'Aha. That you must read the story to find out. But, yes, he finds something very important.'

'And from there all kinds of exciting things happen?'

'Exactly.' All the young officers smiled. Everybody loves a story. McQuade asked, 'First of all, do you know the *escape* procedures from an old German submarine?'

'But what type of submarine? The Germans built various kinds.'

'I don't know. I was hoping you could tell me.'

Ian Manning reached for *Jane's Fighting Ships*. 'Make it a Type VII C.' He turned to the appropriate page. All the young officers waited attentively. Manning read aloud: '"There were 1,174 U-boats constructed in Germany between 1935 and 1945, of which 785 were lost. There was the Type XXIII, et cetera . . . Type XXI . . . et cetera. Then, Type VII C . . . This may be regarded as the standard type of German submarine, having been built in largest numbers. Displacement, 517 tons. Length 213 feet, beam 19 feet, height 13 feet. Five torpedo tubes." And here . . .' he turned over the page, 'are some diagrams.'

Everybody clustered round. The scale of the drawings was small. A confusing mass of dense detail.

'What exactly was abandon-ship procedure?'

'Well,' Manning said. He called for a sheet of paper from the barman, drew a large cigar-shape. He sketched in the conning tower. 'There's a water-tight hatch in the top of the conning tower. There's another hatch below it, in the central control room. Now, mounted in this second hatch is a telescopic escape tube, which you can pull down. Big enough for a man. Here.' He drew it in. 'So, when your submarine is wrecked, and you abandon ship, you pull down this telescopic tube until it is about two feet above the deck of the control room. So.' He drew it in. 'Now, you open valves in the hull of the submarine,' he drew a few crosses, 'and flood water *into* the submarine. The water stops entering when the air pressure inside the sub is the same as the sea pressure outside. The sub is now about half-full of water, and everybody is standing in water up to their waists. Each man has an air-bottle. Now, the *upper* hatch is opened, and water floods into the conning tower, and into this telescopic tube. But no more water enters the part where the men are because the pressure has been stabilized. Now, each man ducks under water, into the flooded tube, and swims up it, one at a time. Up through the conning tower, out into the open sea. He rises slowly to the surface.'

'I see. And every man could escape like that?'

'Every man. Provided the sub was in less than fifty metres of water. Deeper than that and the sea pressure would kill them.'

So why did only two men escape? And suddenly McQuade knew how to get into the submarine: the same way that those two men got out, but in the reverse direction.

'And after forty years, would the submarine still be half-full of air and that tube still full of water?'

'Yes.'

'So my hero could get into the submarine the same way? Go into the conning tower and swim *down* that tube?'

'Theoretically, yes.'

McQuade ran his hand over his hair. 'And what's it going to be like when he gets inside?'

'Black as ink. Stinking. The air would be unbreathable, he'd have to keep his breathing apparatus on.' He turned to one of his officers, 'Daniels, you've done a diving course?'

'Yes, sir,' Daniels said. 'We dived down on a number of wrecks, but never on a submarine.'

'What marine life is our hero likely to find down there?'

Daniels said earnestly: 'My guess, sir, is that the conning tower is likely to have a lot of fish living in it. In the lower part of the submarine the water would be pretty foul, but my guess is that there would be sufficient circulation of water down that tube to support marine life like crabs and some small fish. And possibly some octopus.'

McQuade did not like the sound of this. Black as ink. 'And skeletons? Of crew who did not manage to escape?' he asked.

'Oh yes, sir. The crabs and crayfish would have eaten them long ago. Just skeletons now.' He added cheerfully, 'Their hair would survive.'

Ian Manning said: 'Why didn't they *all* escape?'

'Ah,' McQuade said, 'part of the story.'

'The plot thickens, eh? All right, but if some chaps failed to escape they might have crawled up onto their bunks to die. Above the water line. What would their condition be? Would they be kind of mummified in that salty environment?'

'Skeletons, sir,' Daniels assured him.

'I wonder,' Manning said. 'Barman, pass me the phone please.' He dialled, then said, 'Doctor Walters, please ... Jack, this is Ian. Got a technical question for you ... These chaps have been in this sunken submarine for forty years ... Yes, of course they're dead, not just irritable ...' He gave the naval doctor the facts, grinning. He listened, then thanked him and hung up. He turned to McQuade: 'Didn't follow all that medical jargon but it's possible that the chaps on upper bunks may be mummified. Something to do with body fats hardening into a wax-like substance under certain conditions. Interesting, that.'

'Thank you very much,' McQuade said.

'What else do you want to know?'

'I need to know the entire layout of the submarine. Where the water-tight doors are, how they lock and unlock, what the different compartments hold, and so on. You haven't a bigger-scale diagram than that one in *Jane's*?'

The commander stroked his beard. 'Not in Walvis Bay. They've got a submarine in the war museum in Johannesburg. Don't know what type it is. Otherwise, you'd have to go to Germany to *their* submarine museum. In Kiel, I think it is, but that would be a ridiculous expense ...'

It was eight o'clock when McQuade got back to his house, scratchy-tired. He snapped on the telephone answering machine. A sultry female voice said:

'Jim, please come to see me urgently. This is important for both of us. I know you are not at sea, so I'm waiting. Helga.'

McQuade snorted. Important, huh? After slapping his

face and shrieking *Heil Hitler*? No way. He picked up the telephone and dialled Elsie's number. He got his answering machine.

'Elsie, please phone the Kid, Tucker and Potgieter and tell them there's to be a shareholders' meeting aboard the *Bonanza* at ten o'clock tomorrow morning. And get word to the Coloured crew that we're not going to sea because we've got repairs to do.'

He went to his bedroom, to sleep, sleep, sleep.

10

The shareholders' meeting took place on the bridge of the *Bonanza* around a case of beer McQuade had provided to jolly them along. Walvis Bay was still shrouded in thick fog. The Kid was late in arriving and everything got off to a bad start with Rosie, long-suffering Tucker's long-suffering wife, showing up with her four children at heel. She came clomping up onto the bridge in her sexless sandals, sand between her toes, her sexless dress clammy, to lay down a few laws. 'Now look here, James McQuade, I hear you're not going back to sea today, and I demand to know what this meeting's all about because if it's about another cut in salaries I'm here to tell you—'

'Rosie, this is a shareholders' meeting.'

'And *this*,' Rosie pointed dramatically at undramatic Tucker, 'happens to be *my* shareholder, my breadwinner, and *these*—' she indicated the little girls staring up at him — 'happen to be the little mouths he has to feed. I don't mean with fish, the damn freezer's full of damn fish, but four little mouths, *plus mine*, need more than fish, you know, they need ordinary, *normal* things from places like supermarkets that you wouldn't know much about but which, I assure you, *ordinary, normal, healthy* people with responsibilities *do* know about and have to spend considerable sums of money in just to stay *normal* — let alone happy! — and I know what happens at these damn shareholders' meetings, it's *money money money*, how we've got this whopping great overdraft, and we need these new nets and what about a new whatnot and the fishing isn't like it used to be so hadn't we all better tighten our belts another notch! I'm here to tell *you*, Jim

McQuade, that if one single rand comes off my housekeeping as a result of this meeting,' she held up a finger like a sword, 'one single rand, and you'll be hearing a lot more from me!'

Elsie murmured, 'Even more?'

'Yes, even more! You,' she pointed at McQuade, 'just because you're prepared to live like a gypsy in that appalling house of yours doesn't mean that you can drag everybody else down with you, and I insist on having some say in my own future. My Hugo happens to be a first-class engineer who could get a well-paid job anywhere and he hardly brings home enough to keep body and soul together except more damn fish, we got fish running out of our ears, but we need meat and shoes and clothes and Tammy needs a new bed and Gracie needs a new bicycle—'

'Please . . .' Tucker groaned. He held his head.

Rosie turned on him: '"Please"? "Please stop embarrassing me?" And will you please stop letting him—' she pointed at McQuade – 'walk all over you just because he owns fifty-one per cent of this damn company!'

'That's Company Law . . .' Tucker groaned.

'And it's also Company Law that you're entitled to your say, and if you're too much of a softie to say it you're going to transfer your shares into my name so I can say it for you!'

'Oh Lord . . .' Elsie sighed.

'Well until that happens,' McQuade said, 'this is a meeting for shareholders only.'

'Which—' Rosie continued at Tucker – 'you will report to me verbatim! Or there's no more you-know-what for you! And one penny off my housekeeping . . .' She glared at them all and left the threat unspoken. 'Good morning, gentlemen!' She turned and stomped off the bridge.

Tucker held his brow. 'Oh Lord . . .'

Then the Kid came toiling up to the bridge with a big cut on his forehead and a big hangover behind it, and all because of his fucking Bitch. Elsie demanded: 'What's her problem this time? Let's have a look at your new teeth?'

The Kid sat down in a lump and reached for a beer. Then he bared his new smile at them. His teeth were magnificent, even and white. McQuade said, 'Wasn't she pleased?'

The Kid lifted the beer and glugged it down, down, down. Then banged the bottle down. 'Now get this for a hard-luck story.' He paused, glaring; then went on dramatically: 'They wheel me into the dental surgery. They proceed to give me about *twenty-four* lethal injections, right up to the eyeballs. Then out comes the drill. And for the next three hours he re-files all these upper teeth down to needle-points. Then he glues in my beautiful new ones.' He paused and bared his new carnivorous smile again, for clarity. 'For the next two days I can't even *see* them, because of the swelling. I can't *eat* anything except baby food. But yesterday the swelling subsides. *Out* I go to the airport with my brand new smile—' (Another glare of his dental perfection) 'to meet Beryl . . .' He paused, glaring at them murderously, then swept his arm dramatically, 'And *through* the door she comes . . .' He paused again. 'And up to her I go, *beaming*—' he grimaced — 'my bee-you-tiful new smile! . . .' He paused, his face suddenly a mask; 'And she says: "There's something different about you . . ."' The Kid put on a modest smirk: 'And I said, "Well, yes, actually . . ." And' — he frowned prettily — 'she says, "It's your teeth!"' He smirked modestly again, re-living it all: 'And I said modestly, "Well, yes, actually . . ."' He paused. 'And she frowns and says, "But why . . .?"' The Kid waved his hand. 'And I said, "*Well*, remember you wrote me that memorandum . . .?"' The Kid glared at them, then he ended dramatically. 'And the bitch says: "I meant the *bottom* ones . . ."'

He dropped his head on the table and banged his fist and howled: '*She meant the bottom ones . . .*'

They were all laughing, except Tucker.

*

89

McQuade called the meeting to order.

'The proposition I am about to put to you must not be repeated to *anyone*. Got that, Hugo?—' Tucker blinked. McQuade looked at him hard, then turned to Potgieter. Pottie nodded earnestly. McQuade went on, '*If*, when everybody has had their say, there is one dissenting vote, then the subject is closed, and I will carry out my plan by myself. At my own expense, with a chartered boat.' He paused. 'In that case, all the profit will be mine.' He paused again. 'But I *don't* want to charter a vessel and hire a crew. I want to use the *Bonanza*, which has got all the gear for the job, heavy-duty winches and derricks and so forth, and I trust you guys. I'd rather share the loot with you than with a hired crew I don't know.'

The boys were listening with rapt attention.

McQuade proceeded to unfold the story. He did not tell them what he had seen at the Schmidt ranch, nor about the threatening telephone call afterwards, nor what he had learnt from the dental records. He started with his meeting Skellum, and ended with what Commander Manning and his men had told him. The boys' reaction was one of enthralled astonishment, followed by enormous enthusiasm for becoming rich. The Kid got up and did a little jig and Elsie solemnly went off to his cabin and came back with a bottle of champagne. Oh, they all wanted to be millionaires, particularly the Kid who had The Bitch to maintain and his new teeth to pay for. Only Tucker was not brimming with excitement; oh, he wanted to be a millionaire too, of course, with all his little mouths to feed, of course he did, don't be stupid, but what about the cost? 'But what about the cost?' Tucker said worriedly. 'What about our housekeeping money meanwhile?'

'Oh Jesus,' Elsie groaned.

'But I mean,' Tucker explained worriedly, 'this is going to cost a lot and we aren't going to have any fish-income while we're doing it. Are we going to be able to draw our housekeeping money and stay within our overdraft facility at the bank?'

'If you struck an oilwell in your own backyard,' Elsie sighed, 'Rosie would complain about the mess.'

'I *mean*,' Tucker said, 'we may never *find* the submarine, and we've spent all that *money* . . .'

'One week we can risk, but that's all, Hugo!' McQuade said. 'Okay, so we have to give the Coloured crew a week's paid leave, and I know we've got a bloody great overdraft at the bank, *but*,' he held up his finger, 'in one week we could all be millionaires!'

'And if it takes *two* weeks?'

'One-and-a-half days to steam up there. One-and-a-half to steam back. That gives us four days to search the area with the echo-sounder.' McQuade grabbed the chart and poked it. 'Look at that coast. It's mostly all shallow water. Absolutely perfect for using the depth-sounder. If we haven't found it inside five days the bloody thing's not there! But at least we've *tried*. You can't have a chance like this and not try!'

'Exactly,' Elsie groaned.

'And I can get my bottom ones done!' the Kid sang.

'And how many more weeks once we've found it?' Tucker complained. 'I'm only trying to be realistic and *sensible*. What special equipment do we need? What does it cost? We got to think about all that stuff—'

'We get *into* the submarine the same way as those two guys got *out*! The only extra equipment we need is a few extra airtanks, an air-compressor and some new wetsuits. We've already got the dinghy and an outboard motor.'

'But,' Tucker frowned worriedly, 'supposing we can't get in that way, supposing we've got to cut our way in and even *hire* an expert to do it, I can see this taking *months*, and all the time our overdraft's mounting up.'

'You're an engineer,' Elsie said testily, 'you know how to use an oxyacetylene torch to cut steel.'

'Not underwater I don't, I'm not going down there.'

'We can all scuba-dive, we'll all come down with you!'

'Not *me*,' Tucker said emphatically, 'I've only dived around nice shallow rocks, looking for crayfish and periwinkles, I'm not diving out there amongst the big biteys, I've got my family to consider.'

McQuade did not want to think about the big biteys either. 'No problem with sharks out there. They're too well fed.'

'And Jim knows because he's a marine biologist!' the Kid said.

'And I'm a family man, not like you guys. *And*,' Tucker continued worriedly, 'supposing when we crack the submarine there's no loot inside? And what about our insurance? Will we be covered if we have an accident on a job like this? With a skeleton crew?'

'That's a chance we'll have to take.' McQuade decided to cut through all this. 'Now, can we please have a vote? On whether we want to be millionaires. Elsie?'

'I'm in,' Elsie said.

'In,' the Kid sang: 'In, in!'

'Pottie?'

'*Got*, yes, man,' Potgieter said earnestly.

'Hugo?' McQuade said.

Tucker looked at them unhappily.

'But what do I tell Rosie?' he fretted.

'You tell her nothing! We've told the Coloureds we've got engine trouble and we're going off on sea-trials. Same for Rosie.'

Tucker looked thoroughly miserable. 'Do I have to dive?'

McQuade said flatly: 'If it becomes necessary we *all* have to dive. Except Elsie.'

'Oh Lord . . .' Tucker groaned, racked. 'And if we don't find the submarine, what happens to our cheques?'

McQuade said grimly, 'If we don't find it, we'll all have to take a cut in our cheques.'

'Oh Lord.'

'Well?' McQuade demanded. 'In? Or out?'

Tucker took an anguished breath. 'In,' he muttered. He looked as if he might burst into tears.

PART TWO

11

The *Bonanza* sailed late that night. The fog had gone. By midnight the lights of Walvis Bay were disappearing astern and a wind was blowing in off the cold Benguela current, whipping the spray across the bows. McQuade stood on the bridgewing in his foul-weather gear, on watch, the helm on autopilot, the black sea surging and smacking and flying. He did not want to go diving down into that any more than Tucker did, and oh God, no, he did not want to be opening up the charnel house of skeletons and stink of death that Commander Manning had promised, he did not want to be diving head-first down that tube of black water into that black tomb, he did not want to be putting on his new expensive wetsuit tomorrow and toppling himself into that dark deep cold water – and those lights of Walvis Bay looked awfully good.

And there was something else for him to be uptight about: Red Straghan, the diver Roger Wentland had warned him about. That morning McQuade had bought one new wetsuit from Alan Louw's shop and another second-hand tank and harness, but he had had to go to Straghan's shop for a second-hand air-compressor. Red Straghan himself had come out of the workshop when he heard McQuade's voice, his hard red face wearing his truculent smile, his hard blue eyes opaque, and said, 'An air-compressor, Jim? What d'you need one of those for? Doing a lot of crayfishing these days?'

'Just for emergencies,' McQuade had said. 'An airtank's no good if you can't refill it out there, is it?'

Red Straghan had leered, 'Well, if you need any under-

97

water work done, remember your friends, Jim . . .' leaving McQuade with the uneasy feeling that he knew something was afoot. But how could he know?

McQuade did the entire night-watch himself: he was too tense to sleep. Finally the sun came, first flaming pink, making black silhouettes of the sand dunes, then golden red, then over the horizon came the sun, big and blinding gold and setting the dunes on fire, and the shore became visible, ancient and harsh, stretching on and on. The *Bonanza* ploughed northwards up the Skeleton Coast in the early morning, and McQuade surveyed the treacherous shore through his binoculars: the seething Atlantic swells breaking in long crashing lines, and beyond the desert rose up, harsh and dry, going on and on, not a living thing to be seen. When the boys began to show up, McQuade gave orders to assemble marker-buoys out of anchors, chain and rope he had bought yesterday. He went to bed but two hours later he was still awake and he went back to the bridge. They were passing Cape Cross and the rocky shore was black with seals, the seething sea alive with them; then the lifelessness came back into the burning shores. From time to time his binoculars picked up the skeletons of shipwrecks on the shore, stark bits of hulls, sometimes high and dry, half-buried in half a century of shifting sands.

McQuade moved restlessly between the bridgewing and the satellite-navigator, plotting the co-ordinates, and the boys also moved restlessly, watching the progress on the chart, watching the echo-sounder, watching the shore. All their enthusiasm for treasure-hunting seemed to have evaporated. Tucker, who had never had much, was quietest of all, watching his dials, glumly counting the cost of each passing hour. The Kid paced about restlessly, rethinking his convictions that big biteys were too well fed in this part of the world. Only Potgieter seemed placidly unworried.

'What're you looking so cheerful about, Pottie?' Tucker complained.

Potgieter said, 'No, *Got*, man, everything's okay, hey.'

'You're not afraid of bankruptcy?' Tucker complained.

'No, *Got*, man, that's a chance you've sommer got to take, hey?' Potgieter said.

'Not afraid of big biteys?' the Kid complained.

'No, *Got*, that's a chance you sommer got to take, hey?' Potgieter explained.

'What you going to do if you meet a big bitey?' the Kid demanded. 'Stick your finger in his eye?'

'No, *Got*, you worry about that when it happens, hey?' Potgieter explained philosophically.

'There's going to be nothing to worry about, boys,' Elsie said.

'*It's all very well for you!*' Tucker cried.

Elsie held up his palms for calm. 'Think *positively*,' he said positively. 'Think about all that money. Think of that lovely passenger ship we're going to own. Think of your nice smart white uniforms, think of all those lovely girls in their short-shorts shaking their pretty arses at you . . .'

'Now you're talking,' the Kid said. 'Keep telling us how it's going to be, Elsie . . .'

The sun was going down in a riotous glow of orange and red over the cold Atlantic, and the Skeleton Coast a magnificent desolation of pink and mauve, when the *Bonanza* began to approach latitude nineteen degrees south.

McQuade stood at the sat-nav, the word *computing* flashing, waiting for it to tell him the ship's latest position. Then it appeared: *Lat 19° 18' 57" S Long 13° 12' 32" E.* McQuade gave a tense sigh. 'Okay, we've crossed our latitude. By one minute, nine seconds. Plus twenty minutes at three knots – another mile. So we've over-shot by about two point two miles. Turn her around, Pottie. Steer one seven zero.'

'One seven zero, man.' Potgieter swung the wheel.

McQuade tripped the knotlog. The *Bonanza* swung around in the setting sun. 'Stand by to throw the float over.'

The Kid and Tucker clattered down the companionway to

the fore-deck. The yellow marker-float was attached to a hundred and fifty feet of nylon rope, thirty feet of chain and a thirty-pound Danforth anchor.

McQuade watched the knotlog. It clicked off the distance run in tenths of a nautical mile. The coast was about a mile to the east, a low brooding mass in the short twilight, the crests of the breakers just visible against the gloom. He looked at the depth-sounder. The needle wriggled its way busily across the sensitized paper, showing a steady eighty to ninety feet here. He looked at the radar. The sweeping line showed the ragged coastline, but it was deceptive: the radar was not rebounding off the actual shore but off the sand dunes beyond. Many a ship had come to grief on this coast because of that.

The knotlog clicked over. 'Stand by.'

The Kid picked up the anchor and lowered it over the side until it hung just above water. Tucker picked up the heap of chain. They waited.

The knotlog clicked up two point two miles. 'Let her go!' McQuade shouted.

The Kid released the anchor into the sea, and Tucker hurled the heap of chain over. The rope went lashing after it, followed by the yellow float.

McQuade stood on the bridgewing. The float bobbed on the swells. 'Now stay there.'

He turned back to the bridgehouse. On the chart he had drawn a rectangle representing an area of sea three miles long by one mile wide: the parallel of latitude which he had calculated following Jakob's indications ran through the centre. The marker float which they had just dropped was approximately on this latitude. The eastern end of the rectangle began three hundred yards off the shore, in thirty feet of water. The western end of the rectangle was in a hundred and fifty feet of water, the maximum depth from which a submariner could reach the surface alive. Tucker said anxiously:

'We aren't going as close in as three hundred yards in the dark, are we?'

'No. We start our search pattern one thousand yards off tonight. In the morning we move in-shore.' He tripped the knotlog again and said to Potgieter: 'Steer due east.'

'Oh Lord . . .' Tucker said.

The bows came slowly round. The *Bonanza* began to churn towards the dark shore, her engines at Slow.

They stood in front of the radar, the knotlog and the depth-sounder, watching them. The *Bonanza* chugged slowly towards the shore in the big dark swells. The knotlog clicked up the first two hundred yards. Click went the knotlog: four hundred yards. Click: six hundred yards. Click: eight hundred.

'Oh, Lord . . .' Tucker breathed.

'We're still twelve hundred yards off-shore!' Elsie snapped.

The *Bonanza* ploughed on into the darkness. The Kid suddenly burst out: 'For Christ's sake, let's wait until daylight!'

'*Oh Lord yes!*' Tucker cried.

McQuade turned to him: 'Waste a whole twelve hours, Hugo? Half a day's wages?'

'*Okay!*' Tucker cried.

'Elsie?'

'You're the skipper,' Elsie said.

'Okay. Turn her around, Pottie. Two seven zero.'

Potgieter turned the wheel hard over. McQuade said:

'We'll go five hundred yards further out, then drop the anchor for the night. Two-hour anchor-watches. I'll do the first. We start at sunrise.' He sighed. 'And now, I think, we'll have a drink.'

'And I'll make a lovely dinner,' Elsie beamed at them. 'You're all being very good brave boys.'

'Then tell us some more about the pretty girls and our nice white uniforms, Elsie,' the Kid said.

12

The Skeleton Coast was born again, dark against the pink dawn, the sea running in long heavy swells. As the sun came up there was the rattle of the *Bonanza*'s anchor coming up. And her propellers churned, and she began to plough back towards the shore.

McQuade and the boys stood on the bridge, watching the depth-sounder. The needle wriggled across the sensitized paper steadily decreasing. Eighty feet . . . seventy-eight . . . seventy-five . . . seventy-three . . . McQuade said, 'Call it out, Elsie.' He went out onto the bridgewing.

'Seventy-two,' Elsie called, 'Sixty-nine . . .'

McQuade swept the shoreline with his binoculars. The waves were breaking about a hundred yards out. 'Sixty-four,' Elsie called.

'Radar says?' McQuade called.

'About seven hundred yards off-shore,' the Kid called.

'We're closer than that. We're bouncing the beam off those sand dunes,' Tucker whispered.

'Sixty feet . . .'

When McQuade estimated they were three hundred yards off-shore he called, 'Steer about three five zero.' He came back onto the bridge and looked at the compass, then at the shoreline. 'Keep parallel to the shore.'

He went to the chart. He tripped the knotlog again. He marked his estimated position on the rectangle drawn on his chart and wrote the time against it. He looked at the depth-sounder. It was registering forty-eight feet, approximately what the chart told him to expect.

'Okay, we're starting the first leg of our zig-zag pattern.

102

Three miles up on this course, then we turn around again, and return on the reciprocal course, parallel to this tack.' He traced his pencil up the rectangle, then back again. 'Three miles on the reciprocal course then tight turn-around and back for three miles. And so on until we've covered the whole rectangle. Got that, Pottie?'

'*Ja, man,*' Potgieter said.

'Sing out when we're approaching each turning point. Hugo, you don't take your eyes off that depth-sounder. You're looking for any significant decrease in depth. If we pass over the submarine, the depth should suddenly diminish by ten to fifteen feet. Got that?'

'Okay,' Tucker said unhappily.

'Scream when you see the depth suddenly decrease. It either means we're millionaires or that we're going over rocks that don't appear on this chart.'

'Oh, Lord,' Tucker said. 'How recent is that chart?'

'The latest. Kid, you watch the sat-nav. Call out each time a new fix shows up. Check our latitude constantly. Watch the radar. Keep a log of the distance run, and mark our pattern on the chart every fifteen minutes. Got it?'

'Gotcha,' the Kid said.

'Okay,' McQuade said. 'But I wish you'd all look more cheerful about it. Elsie, how about some fried egg and bacon sandwiches.'

'Anything for my boys,' Elsie said happily.

Three miles, at about three knots, takes one hour. Each leg was roughly twenty-five yards apart. Therefore it would take at least forty hours to cover the area once. If he doubled the speed, it would take about twenty hours; about two days of daylight. If the depth-sounder found nothing encouraging in the first coverage of the area, they would cover it again at right-angles to the original pattern, namely in an east-west configuration: this would take another two days.

By midmorning McQuade decided to increase the speed.

The *Bonanza* ploughed up and down the Skeleton Coast, her depth-sounder's pulses bouncing off the seabed and activating the needle across the paper. Down the coast she ploughed for three miles, then Potgieter said, 'Coming about,' and back up the coast she went on her new track, parallel to her last one, slowly working her way deeper out into the Atlantic. There was mostly silence on the bridge, only the muffled throbbing of the engine and the occasional sighs and shuffles and the sssh and slap of the sea. The boys sat at their instruments, pencils in hand, logging, plotting, occasionally calling out a new observation. McQuade paced back and forth, between the bridgewing and the instruments, peering over shoulders, everybody waiting and watching.

'How about something to eat?' Tucker complained.

'Nice hamburgers?' Elsie said brightly.

'Make mine medium-rare,' McQuade said.

'Rare, please,' the Kid said, 'but not unusual.'

When the sun began to get low, they had covered three-quarters of the area. And everybody was tired.

'All right, we're about fifteen hundred off the shore,' McQuade said. 'We've got about another five hours to finish the first pattern. Every leg we do is taking us into safe water. What do you want to do? Drop the anchor and sleep, or keep going all night?'

'Oh, drop the hook!' Tucker said.

'Another twelve hours of wasted wages?'

'Oh, fuck the wages!'

McQuade smiled. 'Kid?'

'Oh fuck my bottom ones,' the Kid said. They all laughed.

'Anything's okay by me, hey?' Potgieter said.

McQuade sighed. 'Okay. Can you bring up a case of beer, Elsie? We keep going until dark, then drop the hook. And start again at first light.'

They started again long before that. At two a.m. McQuade woke up and went onto the bridge to check that everything was all right. The Kid was on anchor-watch. Potgieter was

104

lying on the bench, wide awake. 'What's the matter, Pottie?'

'Agh, no man, I slept a bit, hey,' Potgieter said.

'He's thinking what he's going to do with his million,' the Kid said.

'Seen any lights?' McQuade looked at the log-book.

'No.'

'Last Fix?' McQuade pushed the button on the sat-nav. He compared the read-out with the log-book.

'Half an hour ago,' the Kid said. 'We're spot-on.'

'And what are you going to do with your million, Pottie?' McQuade said.

'Buy a farm, hey,' Potgieter said happily, 'and grow rabbits.'

'Rabbits, huh?'

'Bladdy good money in rabbits, hey, man,' Potgieter said, 'with all the kaffirs wanting meat.'

'But what about all those pretty Aussie girls shaking their pretty arses at you in your nice white uniform?' the Kid said.

Tucker burst onto the bridge in his underpants. *What's wrong?*

'Pottie's going to leave us and buy a farm,' McQuade said.

'And grow rabbits,' the Kid said. 'Jolly good money in rabbits.'

'Rabbits?' Tucker said. He added in a rare sign of humour, 'I'll leave with him.'

Then Elsie appeared up the companionway, in his silk dressing-gown. 'What're you boys all doing up?'

'Hunger, Elsie,' McQuade said. 'Sheer malnutrition.'

'The National Union of Seamen,' the Kid said, 'is taking up our case.'

Elsie beamed at them, his fat bristly cheeks dimpled. 'Well, we can't have that! What'll it be?'

'More of that treacle tart,' Tucker said. 'Hot, with ice cream.'

'And seeing we're all awake,' McQuade said, 'why don't we get on with the job?'

The sun was up when they finished the last leg of the north-south pattern, over a mile out to sea. The depth-sounder had shown no sudden variation in readings. And McQuade doubted that the submarine had come to grief this far out: the water was over a hundred and seventy feet deep – despite what the chart said – over the maximum depth at which escaping submariners could survive.

'All right, so now we start the east-west pattern.'

'It's not here,' Tucker whined. 'That submarine's not here.'

Potgieter swung the wheel. The bows came round, pointed towards the hostile shore.

'It's not here,' Tucker moaned. 'All those wages . . .'

But it was. It was late afternoon when Tucker hollered: '*Got it!*'

McQuade rushed in from the bridgewing. '*Time! Knotlog!*' He bounded at the throttle and rammed it to neutral. '*Radar!*' he shouted. '*Measure it off!*' He rammed the engine to Astern. '*Hold her straight!*' he shouted at Potgieter. He bounded to the depth-sounder.

And yes, there it was. The busy line had been steady at about forty feet, then suddenly it had jumped to thirty feet, then back it went to forty-odd. Tucker had scribbled down the exact time and the knotlog's read-out. The *Bonanza* was now churning sternwards towards the shore, four hundred yards away. They were all staring at the depth-sounder. 'Here it comes!' the Kid whispered.

And the needle suddenly leapt to thirty feet again before dropping back.

'*Oh yes!*' McQuade pulled the engine throttle to neutral again. 'Fifteen degrees to starboard!' He waited for the *Bonanza* to slow, then shoved the throttle to Slow Ahead again.

The bows swung slowly to starboard and the *Bonanza* began to churn forwards again. They all clustered around the depth-sounder breathlessly. The ship passed over the submerged object again from a different angle, on a line fifteen yards different from the last. And the echo-sounder's needle suddenly shot up to thirty feet again, then dropped back.

'*Stop!*' Potgieter yanked back the throttle. McQuade snapped, 'Drop a buoy.'

The Kid scrambled down the bridge companionway. Elsie followed him, to help. The Kid snatched up the anchor of a prepared float, and Elsie grabbed the chain. They heaved it over the side into the sea.

The float bobbed on the swells, marking the spot. McQuade took a deep, excited breath.

'Okay,' he called down to them. 'This is it. Go to the anchor.' He took the helm from Potgieter and pushed the engine control to Slow Ahead. The Kid ran up the deck and scrambled up onto the fo'c'sle, to the windlass. He looked back at the bridge. McQuade eased the *Bonanza* forward for two hundred yards. Then:

'*Let go!*' he shouted.

The Kid slammed his hand on the ratchet. There was a clattering, and the big anchor went crashing down into the blue-black sea. McQuade eased the throttle astern and watched the counter as the chain rattled out. One hundred feet. One-twenty. One-fifty. '*Avast!*'

'*Avast!*' the Kid bellowed. The chain stopped. McQuade put the engines harder astern. The trawler churned backwards sluggishly, dragging the chain, then suddenly it lurched as the big flukes bit into the sand. McQuade slammed the engines into neutral, and shouted: 'Everybody get kitted up. We're going to look for it before the light goes . . .'

13

Their wetsuits were on. They lifted the inflated dinghy over the rail, and dropped it overboard. Potgieter lowered a short rope ladder. McQuade clawed his way down it into the rocking dinghy. The Kid followed. Then Potgieter lowered the outboard motor, on a rope, which McQuade eased over the dinghy's transom and fastened. Tucker lowered down the airtank harnesses. Elsie lowered the fins, masks, tool-bags, floats. Last came Tucker, looking as if he were going to a funeral. He clambered into the wobbly dinghy and said: 'I'm only wearing this wetsuit in case I fall overboard.'

'Dry your eyes and start the engine.'

The marker floated about a hundred yards behind the *Bonanza*'s stern. Four hundred yards beyond it the surf thundered against the Skeleton Coast. Tucker ripped the cord and the outboard motor roared to life.

'Tank up,' McQuade said. He hefted on his airtank harness. He buckled on his weight-belt. He wrestled on the fins. The Kid was tanked up. McQuade called, 'Cast off.'

Potgieter untied the painter and threw it down to them. Tucker opened the throttle and the dinghy churned away from the hull of the *Bonanza*.

'*Good luck, darlings!*' Elsie shouted. '*Good luck.*'

Tucker eased the dinghy up to the float. McQuade grabbed it, and looked at the surging blue-black sea. God, he did not want to be going over the side into it. 'Okay,' he said soberly to the Kid. 'Goggle up.'

He spat into his mask, smeared the saliva across the glass, then rinsed it in the sea. He put it on, over his eyes and nose.

'First I'll check the visibility.' He said to Tucker: 'If we can see the bottom it'll be quicker if you tow us around the area, with the Kid and I hanging onto the dinghy.' He added: 'And nicer.' He put his regulator into his mouth.

He lay down on the fat rubber gunnel, clutching it with one arm. He buried his head under the water.

All he could see was brilliant blue, fading into misty darkness. He peered all about, then raised his arm and made a circling motion.

Tucker opened the throttle unhappily and the dinghy began to churn into a circle. McQuade kept his head under water, hanging onto the gunnel, and oh God he did not like that darkness down there, but no way was he going to see anything like this. He pulled his head out, sat upright and Tucker slowed the engine. McQuade took the regulator from his mouth. He looked for the yellow buoy to get his bearings. Then looked at his wrist-compass.

'We're both going over,' he said to the Kid: 'We follow the buoy's rope down to the anchor, where the sub should be, but the anchor may have landed way off. If we don't see the sub immediately, you go north,' he pointed, 'I'll go south. You'll have to get down at least twenty feet to see the bottom.' He looked at Tucker. 'Circle around slowly and keep both our bubbles in sight.'

And before his nerve could fail him, he put the regulator back into his mouth and clutched his mask and toppled himself over backwards, into the sea.

There was the crash about his ears, the roaring of the bubbles, the sharp bite of the cold on his face, the bitter taste of the sea. Below him, and in all directions stretched the blue gloom of the icy Atlantic, surging darkness. There was another splash, and there was the Kid, his eyes wide behind his mask. McQuade gave him a confident thumb-sign he did not feel and he thrust his head down, and he lifted his buttocks, and he kicked, and down he went, into the underworld.

*

He dived down six feet, his breath roaring, looking for the rope hanging from the marker-buoy. The Kid was swimming towards it. The rope curved away into misty darkness, and down they went together.

They swam side by side, down ten feet, twenty: still they could not see bottom. Down they went further; at twenty-five feet the bottom came mistily into view, a seething mass of waving weed and rocky sand. The rope disappeared into it. Then they saw the chain. They followed it, and there was the anchor, its flukes caught insecurely in a mass of weed. McQuade gave it a tug. The anchor shifted easily. He jabbed his finger at it, the Kid grabbed one of the flukes and McQuade grabbed the other. They lifted it. They swam with it, to a wide wedge of sand ten feet away, and dropped it. McQuade wrestled the flukes into the sand. He gave the chain a tug. It held.

They hovered, bubbles roaring, and looked in all directions for the submarine. Visibility was only about fifteen feet, fading into opaque gloom. McQuade looked at the depth gauge on his wrist: they were at about thirty-five feet. How far from the submarine had the anchor landed? A hundred feet, even two hundred, allowing for the ship's movement? McQuade tapped the Kid, pointed at his wrist-compass and then pointed north, and made a circling motion, then tapped himself on the chest and pointed south.

And, oh God, it was lonely down there, without the Kid beside him. McQuade swam hard, his breathing roaring in his ears, scanning from side to side, while ahead the seething sea faded into sinister grey-blue nothingness. There were many fish of all sorts and sizes. Now he was swimming over a large stretch of hard, ribbed sand, then ahead low rock shelves appeared out of the gloom, weed surging at him, and all the time the myriad of fish cruising about him and then darting aside. McQuade swam and swam, heart knocking, for about fifty yards, then turned into a circle towards deep-sea and began a sweep back towards the anchor, searching.

110

The seabed shelved off deeper and deeper underneath him, rock and sand and then rock again, fading off into the opaqueness. He checked his wrist-compass and swam on through his circle, scanning left and right, every minute expecting the welcome sight of the Kid to emerge out of the darkness, and the rope of the anchor-buoy. But ahead was only the shifting gloom of sand and weed and rock; he swam and he swam for another five minutes, then he was suddenly overcome with a fearful loneliness and a desperate need to confirm his position, and he turned upwards, and kicked.

He rose slowly, at the same rate as his ascending bubbles and it suddenly felt as if all the fiends of the ocean were rising up behind him with jaws agape and he had a desperate desire to thrash up to God's own air; then the surface was dancing above his head, and he burst through it. He looked for the dinghy, whirled in the water, then saw it, and the float.

He was astonished. He had overswum it by two hundred yards. He had been completely disorientated down there. Tucker sped the boat across the swells and came up beside him. McQuade grabbed the gunnel and kicked and heaved himself over. He spat out the regulator. 'Have you seen Kid?'

'No,' Tucker said worriedly. 'Should I have?'

'Take me back to the float.'

Tucker swung the boat around. 'We're doing this all wrong.' McQuade panted. 'You lose your way down there . . . Tomorrow we're all going down together . . . In a long line, about twenty feet apart so each man can still see the next . . . And we sweep the seabed in a pattern . . .'

Tucker was all eyes. 'Oh Lord . . . And now? Are you packing it in for the day?'

With all his heart McQuade wanted to pack it in, but he still had at least half an hour of air left in his tank. He looked at the sun: he still had at least an hour of useful daylight.

'No.' He rammed his regulator back into his mouth and he toppled backwards into the sea again.

*

111

He dived down on the float's line again, until he could see the anchor; then off he swam again, south-west this time.

He swam and swam, twenty-five feet below the surface, turning his head left and right, trying to keep an estimate of the distance he was covering. He knew he was breathing inefficiently in his nervousness and the air would probably last less than half the normal time. He tried to take shallow breaths. He swam and swam over waving weed and rambling rocky shelves and stretches of sand. Both the chart and his depth-sounder had told him that this part of the seabed was flat, and they were basically right, but every now and again there were ravines and grottos that faded into weedy darkness, waving, and all kinds of fish cruised and drifted amongst them. It was when he estimated that he had only about ten minutes of air left, that the submarine almost burst out of the watery gloom at him.

14

At one moment there was only gloom, the next there it was, materializing like a ghost twenty feet in front of him, and his heart lurched. For an instant he did not grasp what he was seeing: it was a long dark shape that seethed and beckoned like a mass of wraiths, giant webs reaching out to ensnare him. He recoiled, his eyes wide and his heart pounding with the roar of his bubbles, then he realized what he was looking at, and he stared at the big shrouded shape that disappeared off into the freezing darkness. Old fishing nets festooned the ghostly hulk, shrouds of nets partly supported by corks, stretching off into the gloom, great ghostly waving webs as high as a house wafting slowly back and forth and towards him like giant anemones. And behind these shrouds lay the long sleek tomb, festooned in waving weed and encrusted in barnacles, and hundreds of fish swam around like sentinels.

McQuade hung in the water, wide-eyed, his heart pounding. He felt no excitement, only a primitive fear that made him want to whirl around and flee from a haunted place, with all his pounding heart he just wanted to get the hell away from this ghastly tomb from battles long ago, thrash his way back to the surface. Then he pulled himself together.

At least he had to get a marker-float tied to this submarine . . . He looked over his shoulder, desperately hoping that the Kid would appear, but all he saw was gloom out of which anything could attack him. He hesitated, his heart knocking, and he knew that if he turned away now he might never find this dreadful machine again, and kicked himself towards it.

He was near the stern section and could just make out one rudder. It was crushed against a large shelf of rock that rose abruptly out of the swirling weed. In front of it, embedded in the sand, was part of a propeller. He swam towards it, eyes wide, pulse racing, looking for a place to tie his float onto, but quickly turned aside: it was thickly shrouded in nets. He turned and swam up the side of the submarine.

He moved fast, ten feet off the bottom and as far away from the ghostly hulk as he could, looking for a gap in the nets through which he could safely swim, in order to tie a float onto the submarine. There were fish everywhere. The hull stretched away, disappearing, encrusted with barnacles, half buried in the sand. There were many rents and gaps in the nets, but no way was he going to try any place where he might get snagged. He swam as fast as he could, desperate to get this over; then suddenly a big shape loomed up in front of him, and he recoiled again, as if he had seen a giant; then he realized he was looking at the conning tower.

It rose up above him, dark and menacing behind the seething nets, and immediately behind it bristled the gun platform, the guns pointing towards the surface. McQuade hovered in the water, staring at it; the guns wavering with weed, fish swimming amongst them: and oh, that conning tower was the ghostliest part of all, like a giant guarding the portal to the mausoleum below, the way he had to enter the dreadful tomb. With all his heart he just wanted to thrash his way to the surface and get the hell away from this haunted place. Then he swam slowly towards it, and he could just make out some numbers showing through barnacles on the side of the tower; the letter U, then 1, then part of 0 or the top part of 9, then another 9, then 3 or part of an 8. And, beckoning at him, was a gap in the nets. It was big enough, but he wanted to see if there was an easier place, and he turned and swam on.

The bow section of the submarine tapered away into mistiness, wafting in broken nets, swarming in fish. McQuade swam fast, desperate to get this over. There were no holes in the hull. He swam past the portside hydroplane; it was half-buried in sand, buckled against a wedge of rock. Then the hulk tapered into the bows, and the wafting nets ended.

McQuade swam to the bows, fearful of what might burst out at him from around the point. But only fish darted out of his way. The bows were clear of the sand, elevated slightly as if the submarine had been driven backwards into the rocks at the stern. There were the four torpedo ports encrusted in barnacles, but apparently undamaged. He peered down the long deck. It was awash in weed, the nets wafting upwards on both sides. He could not see the conning tower from here. He took a deep rasping breath and kicked, and began to swim down the deck towards it.

He swam down the avenue of waving nets, his eyes wide and darting and his heart pounding, the long barnacled foredeck a few feet beneath him; and now he could make out some planking between the weed; on he swam, on, his breathing roaring, nets wafting on either side, then his heart lurched again as the conning tower suddenly loomed up at him, dark and menacing. Closer and closer it loomed. Then he could make out a handrail, and he grabbed it.

He clung to the rail, the tower above him, the shrouds of nets surging about him. He buried his hand into his pouch and feverishly pulled out a cork float. He partly unwound the nylon line and tied the end to the rail. Then he released the float. It went disappearing upwards, trailing its tail of line.

McQuade clung there, staring fearfully about. He felt no excitement about the wealth within his grasp, only the nerve-cringing dread of what he had to do, struggle and fight his way inside, down into that terrible blackness, into a charnel house, pitch black and soupy with rotten bone and hair.

But not now. No way was he going into that submarine alone. Right now he had only one more job to do: find out if those hatches were still open. Before his nerve could fail him he kicked himself up the barnacled side of the conning tower. He clasped the rim and looked over, into the bridge.

There was the first hatch: big and circular. And it was open.

McQuade clung and all he wanted to do was to thrash away up to the surface, but his job was not over yet. He still had to check the lower hatch, inside the conning tower, that led down into the dreadful bowels of the mausoleum. He clung a moment longer, sick in his guts and his cold flesh creeping; then he took a deep breath, swam over the rim and down to the hole. He grabbed the hatch-cover, to anchor himself, and feverishly pulled out his underwater-torch. He thrust it down inside the hatch and peered.

It was a ghostly sight. He was looking into a steel oval chamber, black as death, down which a ladder led. The water was completely still. McQuade stared wide-eyed into the frightening place, his bubbles roaring, darting his torch around. There were swarms of small fish, dials and instruments, rusted and encrusted and blurred and furred with barnacle and weed. He feverishly looked for the lower hatch with its telescopic tube leading down below. He swept his torch across the weed-covered deck; and there it was. It was open, but barnacle-encrusted and half-clogged with weed and anemones.

McQuade stared at it, his torchbeam trembling. God, surely there was nothing more for him to do except get out of here . . . But there was: he had to find out whether that escape tube was damaged, or obstructed in some way. He flashed his trembling torch around once more, then before he could funk it he shoved his head down into the hatch, gripped a ladder-rung and kicked.

He surged down into the conning tower, then twisted himself upright frantically and clung to the ladder, and swung his torch onto the lower hatch feverishly. He bent and parted the weed with his torch, but he could not see properly. He let go of the ladder and pushed himself down. He hovered over the hatch and parted the weed with his free hand.

There it was, the black tube of water leading down into the

116

charnel house below. The sides were encrusted with barnacles. Up this tube H.M. and Horst Kohler had swum forty years ago leaving scores of dead men behind. Tomorrow he had to swim down it. But he still had to find out whether anything was blocking it. Grasping the hatch-cover to anchor himself, he pulled himself down to the opening. He shoved his torch down into the blackness and he peered through the weed.

For a horrified moment he did not grasp what he was looking at. All he knew was that something was blocking the tube right in front of his torch – and the same instant he saw the two devilish eyes, and the big octopus flew at him.

It came flying out of its lair and in one terrifying impact it was onto McQuade's face, its thick tentacles clutching his head and shoulders. McQuade recoiled, terrified, horrified, and dropped the torch and struggled backwards, both hands clawing at the dreadful beast, trying to tear it from his head, its fiendish suckered belly plastered to his mask. He could see nothing and all he knew was the horror of the squelchy beast in his hands, its huge tentacles lashed around his shoulders. He crashed into the ladder, and his regulator was wrenched from his mouth and he sucked in choking black water and he retched while his hands clawed into the mass of tentacles, trying to wrench the regulator from the coiling suckers. He kicked and clawed blindly. His head crashed into the edge of the hatch and he sucked in killer water again and half-screamed in choked terror. He kicked again with all his might, and his head burst through the hatch, and the octopus saw its escape and in an instant it was gone.

The octopus shot off into the gloom in a great cloud of ink and streaming tentacles two yards long. McQuade blindly flailed around his head for the regulator, choking, strangled, panic-stricken, terrified, then his desperate hand found it and he rammed it back into his mouth. He sucked and choked and gagged and sucked again. He clung to the rim of the bridge, heart pounding, gasping, shuddering, looking about wild-eyed for more dreadful fiends, then he kicked towards the surface.

He rose frantically between the waving nets, keeping pace with his own bubbles, trying to control his terror and the retch of bitter seawater in his throat. For an eternity he rose and rose, then the silver surface was heaving just above him, and he burst through it.

He spun in the water looking for the dinghy, then rammed his head under and swam wildly for it. He thrashed and thrashed, horrified of the dreadful fiends following him from behind. Tucker swung the dinghy towards him. The Kid was already aboard. McQuade thrashed up to it, and frantically heaved himself out of the water, and the Kid grabbed his belt. He crashed into the dinghy. He spat out his regulator and ripped his mask off and clutched his face.

'Oh *Jesus* . . .' he shuddered. '*Oh Jesus* . . .'

Tucker was open-mouthed. 'Did you find it?' the Kid demanded.

'Big . . . fucking octopus . . . lives in it . . .' McQuade panted.

'Oh Lord . . .' Tucker moaned.

'*He's gone now . . .*'

'Oh good,' the Kid said. 'And his wife and family have gone too?'

'*Back to the ship,*' McQuade panted at Tucker. '*Top up our tanks. And make a spear . . . Tie a big knife to a broomhandle. Then two of us are going down . . .*'

'Let's think about this,' Tucker whined.

'*We're going down again! If we stop to think about it, I'll never go back again!*'

15

It felt better having the Kid swimming beside him, but not a hell of a lot better.

They followed the float-line down. Down they swam, down into the gloom – ten feet, fifteen – then the nets came into view, wafting up to meet them, and then the long shape of the submarine, fading away, and McQuade felt his stomach contract again. He stopped, and hovered. He could not yet see the conning tower; the float's line curved away into the gloom towards it. The Kid hovered beside him, wide-eyed, his bubbles streaming up. McQuade peered downwards, desperate to get this over; then he kicked down between the waving nets.

He swam in front, Tucker's home-made spear in one hand, his satchel of tools hanging from his chest, the nets looming up on both sides of them. He swam down between their treacherous tentacles, his heart knocking above the unreal roaring of his breathing, until the conning tower loomed. And with all his fearful heart he did not want to go near the dreadful place again and he swam straight at it fiercely, and grabbed the rim, and peered over the top.

There was no octopus. McQuade pulled himself over, spear first, and surged down to the hatch.

There was a ghostly yellow glow in the conning tower, coming from the torch he had dropped. The Kid surged alongside him, peering down wide-eyed. McQuade thrust his new torch into the hatch and shakily shone it around. Then, before he lost his nerve, he grabbed the ladder and pulled.

He burst down again into the conning tower. The Kid came

surging after him in a flurry of bubbles, clung to the ladder and peered around. McQuade looked fearfully at the lower hatch: then he gripped his spear like a long dagger, surged at the hatch and stabbed down it.

He jabbed the spear down into the black hole, banging the blade against the metal sides for half a minute, then he hung back from the hatch fearfully, waiting for another awful mansize octopus to come flying out. They waited, hearts hammering, bubbles roaring, before McQuade shone his torch into the terrible opening.

The black water was cloudy with bits of barnacle and weed his spear had knocked off, but he could see to the bottom. And what he could see, at the end of the escape tube, was a seaman's boot.

It was only the sole that was visible. McQuade stared at it, and he felt sick in his guts. That boot symbolized the whole horror of the charnel house that was waiting for him down there. What was inside that boot? The bones of a seaman's foot? Would there still be rotting flesh attached to it? Toenails? A rotten, flesh-sodden sock? And ankle bones, shin bones, a whole human leg? A whole human skeleton, still in its rotting German naval uniform that would crunch apart into dreadful soupiness the moment he disturbed it? God, how many other boots and skeletons lay awaiting him down there in that dreadful hell-hole? The Kid looked back at him wide-eyed. McQuade took a deep breath, and before he lost his nerve, he pushed his head into the dreadful hatch, and kicked.

They had discussed this manoeuvre. McQuade shoved his shoulders down into the hole, and the Kid grabbed him and supported him in a vertical position. McQuade frantically jostled his shoulders and kicked again, the Kid shoved him downwards, and McQuade's hips entered the hole, and he jammed to a stop.

All he knew was the terrifying descent, then the sudden grating of his airtank against the barnacled sides, and he was stuck. *Stuck upside-down in this terrible place, both arms ahead of him helpless, his bubbles roaring in his ears and the blood pounding in his face and that boot just four feet in front of his wild eyes.* All he wanted to do was thrash and go plunging backwards up this terrifying tube, and he kicked his feet frantically, and wrestled his shoulders and beat his hands to shove himself up backwards, but up there in the conning tower the Kid shoved him down harder. And McQuade screamed, and he sucked in bitter black water around his regulator and shook his head frantically and he wrestled his shoulders furiously and beat his gloved fists upon the barnacles. All he knew was that he was going to die in this horrible hell-hole with the blood pounding in his head, *die die die in this terrible place,* and the Kid gave him another shove downwards. McQuade thrashed his legs, bashing his knees, twisting his hips and beating his hands, desperately trying to tell the Kid to pull him out, until up there the Kid got the message from his frantic movements, and McQuade felt his hand grab his belt, and heave.

The Kid crouched over the hatch and *heaved* again, and McQuade felt himself unwedge. He came grating backwards up the tube, scraping and grinding through the clouds of dislodged barnacles and weed. He came surging out backwards into the conning tower, gasping, reeling.

He lurched away from that terrible hatch and grabbed the ladder and clung, head down, bubbles roaring, gasping, his whole body shuddering. The Kid held onto the ladder, staring. McQuade clung there half a minute, getting the blood out of his pounding face and the pounding out of his heart, then he shook his head furiously and held up his finger in warning. Then he pulled off his fins and shoved himself back at the dreadful hatch. He swung his feet into the black hole. He glared at the Kid to be ready to help him, then he shoved himself into the tube, feet-first.

Down he went, his airtank bumping and scraping. He shoved himself downwards, and his head disappeared into the tube, and then he ground to a stop again. With all his heart he just wanted to kick himself upwards and get out of this horrifying place but he twisted his shoulders, felt the barnacles crumble against his tank, and he clenched his teeth and shoved downwards again; and his feet hit the deck below.

He came to a sudden stop and felt the German seaman's boot squelch under his foot in the blackness. His body was still inside the tube, but he was standing in the black water of the control room. He wanted to kick and claw upwards out of this hell-hole: and he fiercely screwed up his eyes and bent his knees and tried to shove himself downwards and backwards, out from under the end of the tube. He felt his hips clear the end, and then his airtank again jammed against the barnacles.

For a horrible moment he hung there, his back arched, his legs protruding into the blackness of the submarine's control room, the rest of him curved upwards; then he shoved again frantically, and he felt his airtank wedge tight. Panic screamed up him and he wrestled his shoulders frantically, but his tank was locked solid. He gargled in horror and grappled his hands up the barnacled tube and shoved with all his frantic might, and he felt himself grate free. He kicked his feet against the steel deck below, and went clawing up the tube like a spider. His head burst back into the conning tower. He came scrambling out of the escape-tube in a mass of bubbles and grabbed the ladder and clung.

He clutched, fighting to get the panic under control, then looked at the Kid and shook his head. The Kid pointed at McQuade's hips and chest. His new wetsuit was ripped, gaping on hips, chest and both arms, slashed by the barnacles, and seeping out of the gashes were thin tendrils of blood. McQuade stared at his torn wetsuit, then jabbed his finger upwards. He snatched up his fins and wrestled them onto his feet, then he pulled on the rung and he surged up the ladder. He bumped through the hatch and burst up onto the bridge. The Kid came through the hatch after him in a flurry of bubbles. They both kicked off, towards the surface.

They rose slowly, keeping pace with their own bubbles, rising between the waving nets midst the gloom and darting fish: then there was the surface, like a contorting mirror, and they burst through it simultaneously. McQuade twisted, looking wildly for the dinghy, then he struck out for it. He hurled himself onto the gunnel and kicked and threw up his leg, and rolled over into it.

The Kid sloshed more brandy into the glasses: 'Indulge in some more of this.' McQuade sat slumped on the bench in his underpants, his hair matted, his shredded wetsuit on the deck, while Elsie dabbed disinfectant on his cuts. 'You poor thing,' Elsie tutted, 'you poor thing.' McQuade took a big gulp of brandy and shuddered. 'You nearly killed me, Kid.'

'Sorry about that,' the Kid said.

'Ruined,' Tucker said, morbidly examining the wetsuit. 'Ruined, can't patch this. Brand new,' he added.

'I can still taste that deadly black water.' McQuade shuddered.

'Brand new,' Tucker repeated sorrowfully.

'Oh, for God's sake!' Elsie snapped.

'What I mean is—'

'We know what you mean!'

'We'll just take it out of Rosie's housekeeping,' the Kid joshed.

'Oh please be serious!'

'Serious?!' the Kid cried. 'Serious, the man says! Here we've *found* the bloody submarine while you sat in your nice warm dinghy! We've almost cracked it and we're all about to be millionaires and all you do is grizzle about a torn wetsuit!'

Tucker shouted, 'It's not just the wetsuit! I'm saying we don't know what we're doing – that's why the wetsuit's ruined! Because you should have cleared those barnacles off first—'

'*Right! So next time you go down and clear the barnacles!*'

123

'You nearly killed yourselves down there!' Tucker shouted. 'Because we don't know what we're doing! We're rushing in where angels fear to tread!' He pointed angrily at McQuade. 'You could have got stuck in that tube and never got out alive! The barnacles might have cut your air-hose!'

McQuade held up a palm, eyes closed. 'Of course we've got to clear the barnacles next time. But we've found out that we can't get down that tube with airtanks on, barnacles or no barnacles, because when you get to the bottom and try to bend at the waist—'

'So how're you going to get in,' Tucker demanded belligerently '— by osmosis?'

McQuade was surprised that Tucker knew a big word like osmosis. 'The best way is to go down the escape tube *without* an airtank on. But with the regulator in your mouth. The airtank harness is lowered down after you, on a rope. Maybe it'll even float. Then when you get to the bottom, and you're safely out of the tube, you pull the harness out after you and put it on.'

They were all looking at him. Then the Kid said, 'Of *course*. Why didn't we think of that?'

Tucker stared, then jabbed his finger, 'Because we *didn't* think first! Because,' he waved his hand, 'we *rushed* in like a bull at a gate! And so you nearly killed yourself, and ruined a brand-new wetsuit!'

'Oh, fuck the wetsuit!' Elsie shouted. 'Look at this man's wounds!'

'So the trip's been a success!' the Kid cried. 'We've found out how to think! All for the price of one wetsuit!'

There was a silence. Then: 'Now, now, boys,' Elsie murmured.

'And the rest,' Tucker glowered. 'You nearly lost your lives as well. What happens when you get inside? We don't know a thing about the layout of submarines. What about watertight doors? How do you open them? What tools do you need to take with you? What lights?'

'So what are you suggesting? That we give up?'

McQuade jerked as Elsie dabbed iodine on a new wound. 'There, there,' Elsie crooned. 'There, there . . .'

Tucker glowered at them sullenly. 'I don't know, but I do know that we're a fishing company and we can't afford to waste money trying things we know nothing about.'

McQuade banged his hand on the table angrily. 'You're absolutely right! We've got to find out about this type of submarine. *All* about it. And that means I've got to go to the submarine museum in Germany.'

They were all staring at him. Potgieter blinked. Tucker looked aghast.

'To *Germany*?' he whispered. 'How can we afford that?'

'For God's sake, did *you* nearly kill yourself down there today? No — *I* did! There's no way I'm going to try again until I know what I'm doing! And that means seeing a submarine, going over it! *Studying* it, looking for places where loot could be hidden so *we* know where to look!'

'But the *expense*,' Tucker whined.

McQuade pointed at the sea angrily. 'There's a fortune lying just down there—'

'We don't *know* that. There may be nothing inside.'

'Then all the more reason to find out more about it! I'll be able to trace that submarine through the German archives!'

'But we can't *afford* to send you to Germany—'

McQuade banged the table again. 'Then I'll go at my *own* expense! While you go back to sea and catch fish!'

PART THREE

16

Because it is so popular with German tourists, there is a Lufthansa flight direct from Namibia to Frankfurt, but Nathan had friends in the travel business who organized him a bucket-shop deal via London. It was still more than McQuade could afford, but he resolved to enjoy the trip. He had a bottle of duty-free whisky which was half-finished in a couple of hours, but he still was not enjoying himself: all he could think of was the vile blackness of that submarine, the horror of bones crunching under his feet, the stinking taste of death and the choking retch in his throat. When the cabin lights were switched out, he could not go to sleep: when he closed his eyes the dark cocoon of the aircraft became that long terrible tomb of the submarine. Was he crazy to be spending all this money so that he could dive down on that terrible thing again? It was very late when he at last fell asleep, but he awoke with a grim, hungover determination to do what he had set out to do.

It was mid-morning when he cleared customs at Heathrow airport. He found a public telephone and looked up the number of the German Embassy. He dialled and asked to speak to the Naval Attaché.

'*Guten Tag*,' a cheerful voice intoned.

'Good morning,' McQuade said. 'Can you help me, please? I'm very interested in German submarines of the World War II period. I believe you have a naval museum in Germany where I can see some?'

'In Laboe,' the officer said. 'Near Kiel.'

McQuade scribbled a note. 'Which type do they have there?'

'Type VII C. That was the standard German submarine.'

'And is there a naval archive open to the public, where I can find out details about individual submarines, and what they did during the war?'

'The U-Boat Archive, in the town of Sylt. Near the Danish border. The man in charge is Horst Bredow, he was a sub-mariner during the war. I will give you the address. Say hullo to Herr Bredow for me.'

Ten minutes later he was buying a ticket to Hamburg. The Lufthansa girl who served him was heart-achingly beautiful, and as charming as she looked. He went in search of a bar, feeling lucky. Everybody was being so nice. He was starting to enjoy himself.

It was early afternoon when he arrived in Hamburg, full of Löwenbrau beer and feeling no pain. He took a bus to the railway station. There was still plenty of time to get to Kiel before nightfall, but he thought, what the hell! He asked what times the trains ran in the morning, then he crossed the road and checked into Popp's Hotel. Then, determined to enjoy himself, he did what tourists do in Hamburg and went to the Reeperbahn.

He sat in the Glass Elephant and drank expensive whisky while he watched some of the most beautiful girls in Germany copulating on stage. The most impressive performance was by one man with two girls, who managed to do it while they all whizzed around on rollerskates. Between acts the girls circulated amongst the audience and offered hand-jobs for fifty marks. He went back to his hotel late, jet-lagged and sex-bothered.

He hadn't really enjoyed himself. He lay in bed wondering if he was crazy to be spending all this money on such a long shot.

It was freezing in Kiel. He left his bag in a locker, then asked how to get to Laboe. He bought a notebook from the newspaper kiosk, then he left the railway station and turned down to the waterfront, to the Bahnhofbrücke pier. A ferry was waiting. There was still ice floating in the harbour.

Half-an-hour later he disembarked at the village of Laboe at the mouth of Kiel's long harbour, opening onto the bleak Baltic Sea. There were snowclad woods around the mouth. He asked the way to the U-boat museum.

It looked a nice little seaside holiday town, shut down for the winter. There were pleasure yachts and fishing boats wintering, closed up. He set off briskly down the seafront road, past solid Germanic suburban houses in neat little gardens. Within a few hundred yards he saw it, half a mile ahead, the long grey shape mounted on concrete blocks on the wintry shore, and the tall red-brick memorial opposite it, the shape of a submarine's conning tower, rearing hundreds of feet up into the grey sky.

McQuade stood at the fence surrounding the submarine and stared at the long, sleek, dangerous-looking machine. All the horrors of that charnel house came flooding back to him, the dark ghostly shape materializing out of the gloom, the gaping black hatch of the conning tower, the horror of the octopus flying out at him with its suckers clawing, the stinking choke of death as he struggled upside-down in the tube, the dreadful boot lying at the bottom. He gave a tense sigh and raised his camera.

He took three photographs, of the stern, midships, and bows, then went through the gate. He paid the admission and bought the brochure on the submarine; there was a two-page drawing of the internal layout. He mounted the steps up to the doorway cut into the vessel's stern section. He stooped through, into the aft-torpedo and electrical machine room.

It was brightly lit, and very clean. He was in a narrow passage, ten metres long, lined at eye-level with metal cabinets with dials and wheels. Below these, half under the steel footplates, were the long generators. In the very stern was a torpedo tube with a circular steel door.

McQuade's heart sank. In this room alone there were a

hundred places where a man could conceal valuables. Under the steel foot-plates, behind the labyrinth of pipes . . . He raised his automatic camera, and took four photographs, from different angles. Then moved on, to make a quick familiarization tour before going over everything carefully. He went through a water-tight door into the *Dieselmotorenraum*.

He was being grimly businesslike, but again his heart sank. Again there were a myriad of places to hide things. Big diesel engines, five feet high, lined the long narrow corridor. Overhead was a mass of twisted pipes, dials, valves.

He took more photographs, then pushed on, through another door. Into the galley, where some cook had once fed fifty-two men.

It was two metres by four. There was a black oven, some cupboards, a small toilet leading off, like a pantry, and that was it. McQuade looked around. Surely nobody would hide loot in a place like this?

He ducked through the next door. Into the *Unteroffizierenraum*, the Petty Officers' Room.

There were eight bunks, four on each side. Covered in red cloth. There were two folding tables in the narrow alleyway. Above and below the bunks were wooden lockers. He tried to open one. It was locked. Then he crouched through a circular water-tight door. Into the *Zentrale*, the nerve-centre of the boat. He stood there, looking around. This was the part he had looked down into through the escape tube.

The periscope hung from the deckhead. To the right was a corner bench, and to the left, a stand-up table. All around, in a mind-boggling array, were dials, valves, more dials and more valves. Above his head, in the centre was the hatch leading up to the conning tower. This was where the telescopic escape tube came down from. It had been removed from this submarine and an iron grille prevented anybody going up to the conning tower.

He made his way forward, and stooped through another

circular water-tight door. Into the Commander's Room.

It was tiny. There was a narrow bunk, a locker and a folding table. A curtain was there for privacy, but the cabin was also a thoroughfare for the whole crew. On the other side was the radio room.

He tried the lockers and cupboard. All locked.

The next room was the officers' sleeping cabin. Three bunks, lockers, a folding table. He went through it quickly, into the next part – the petty officers' sleeping cabin: four bunks and a toilet. He passed through another water-tight door, into the main torpedo room.

This was it, the killing part of the machine.

It was fifteen paces long. In the bows lay the four big torpedo tubes. One hatch was open. Inside lay a torpedo, its propeller visible. From a rack hung a torpedo, nine metres long. There was a hatch angled into the deckhead above it, where new torpedoes were slid into the boat and onto the racks until loaded into the tubes. There were also nine bunks for the ordinary crew, and lockers. Everywhere ran pipes, valves and dials.

He closely examined the locking mechanism of the torpedo-tube hatches; they were secured by locking wheels in the centre, and locking pins. He tried to open one. The mechanism was painted over solid. He would need a crowbar to twist them open.

He looked around grimly. There were a thousand places on this boat to hide treasure.

He sighed and retraced his steps, to start going through the boat again, foot by foot, taking photographs and making notes. Until he knew every nook and cranny.

It was mid-afternoon when he finished. He had been through the U-boat four times. It felt as if he knew every corner and crevice, and he would scream if he stayed inside it a minute longer. He came out of the cold submarine into the freezing grey day.

He crossed the road towards the rest of the museum, and mounted the long path. He entered the massive memorial built in the shape of a conning tower.

He stared at the wall. It was a gigantic mural depicting thousands of ships and submarines, all in relief. Every German ship that was sunk, every submarine that went down, was represented here, to scale, in bleak grey sculpture.

McQuade stared. It was awe-inspiring. Staggering. And horrifying, that this is what men did to each other when they went to war. The horrifying waste of human life. Written in stone, in huge Gothic letters: '120,000. *Sie Starben Für Uns.*' You died for us.

McQuade turned away from it abruptly. Trying to push the shrieking image of that black soupiness out of his mind, trying to feel tough, like a fortune-hunter. He grimly crossed the courtyard to the second building.

Here was the other half of the horrifying story. There were seven maps of the world, representing seven stages of the war on the sea. Red dots indicated where every Allied ship was sunk by U-boats. Blue crosses represented sunken German submarines. In the first three maps, representing the periods up to December 1941, red dots of sunken Allied shipping were densely packed around Britain, Portugal, Gibraltar, France, West Africa and even South West Africa, and there were very few blue crosses. In the maps representing January 1942 to May 1943 these red dots were massively concentrated around the east coast of America, the Caribbean, West Africa, South Africa and the north Atlantic – but there were many more blue crosses now. The last two maps, depicting the period June 1943 to mid-1945, showed the way the war was going for Germany, the terrible price her submarines were paying: the red dots were sparse and the blue crosses were numerous. He then took the stairs that descended into a large, circular mausoleum. And he wanted to get out of the place. It was ghostly. Dull light filtered through a glass opening to the courtyard above. Laid into the walls, and on a raised dais in the centre, were coats of arms, and flags of U-boat squadrons that went down. McQuade hurried through it, to the exit staircase on the other side, almost feeling the ghosts behind him. He found himself re-entering the massive conning tower again, with its sculptured mural of sunken shipping and the inscription, *'You died for us'*.

There was an elevator leading to the very top of the memorial. McQuade had had enough; but he entered the elevator. He emerged onto a balcony at the top of the tower.

It was freezing up here. He looked down.

Hundreds of feet below him, down on the bleak beach, lay the U-boat he had just examined so carefully, long and mean and dangerous. And beyond lay the Baltic Sea, grey and icy under the leaden sky. Beneath his feet was the sculptured mural, the haunting mausoleum, the maps with all those blood-red dots and funereal-blue crosses. McQuade looked down at that grim submarine, and he saw again that ghostly shape under the freezing Atlantic off the Skeleton Coast with its pitch-black horrors. He tried to force the image from his mind, and think of the loot waiting for him. But he could not make it; all he could see and think and smell and taste and feel was that charnel house, that ocean tomb, a war grave that he was going to desecrate, the bones and soup of brave German boys he was going to wade through.

He turned abruptly, back to the elevator.

He hurried back along the freezing seafront, to catch a ferry back to Kiel. To catch a train to Sylt, where the U-boat archives are. He felt like a grave-robber all the way.

17

You drive out of the flat little town of Sylt with its solid houses, onto the airfield road, past cold, military-fenced fields, before reaching a big gate. You show your passport, and drive on through numerous, long, low red-brick buildings, past a football field, and rows of no-nonsense apartment buildings. There follow aircraft hangars and depressing buildings that look like warehouses, all painted grey under the leaden-grey sky. The taxi stopped outside one of them. '*U-Boot Archiv,*' the driver said.

McQuade opened the grey door uncertainly. There was no vast hall filled with submarines. A concrete staircase led upwards.

He mounted the stairs, his footsteps echoing. There were paintings of German submarines in stormy, wintry seas. He came to the first floor where an open door led into an office. A grey-haired man sat at a desk, in a grey tracksuit. '*Ja, guten Morgen?*'

McQuade said, in English, 'Good morning. The German Naval Attaché in London suggested I come here to see Herr Horst Bredow, the U-boat archivist.'

The man got up, his hand extended. He wore sandals and yellow socks. 'I am Horst Bredow. How is Karl?'

They sat on the carpet at the bookshelves while Horst Bredow plucked volumes off and thrust them at him. 'You must be right in your facts! The rubbish people write about submarines! You must read books like this, and this, and this. . .'

The books piled up: *Submarines of World War II, U-Boats*

136

Under the Swastika, Few Survived. 'I am one of the few who survived. So I keep this museum in memory of those who did not. It is my *own* museum. The German government does not pay me, except my war pension, but it provides this building.'

'I see.'

He crinkled his brow: 'And please don't write too much rubbish about the Nazis.'

'I won't. . .'

'The English seem to think all Germans were Nazis. No submariner was a member of the Nazi Party. We served only the state. We saluted like *this* – ' he brought his fingertips up to his brow – 'not like this – ' he gave the Heil Hitler salute. He glared, then demanded, 'What's your story about?'

McQuade said: 'My hero is trying to trace the family of a German U-boat man who was sunk. Do you have records of every U-boat of World War II?'

'Yes.' He waved his hand at the next room.

'And the crew members of each boat?'

'Yes.'

'And details of the crew's families? Wives, for example? Where they are today?'

'Sometimes. If they wish to tell me such details. If the man is alive, his family is his business. If he was killed in action, his widow is probably drawing a war pension – which is also a private matter. The details of such widows are kept by the pension office, the *Deutsche Dienststelle* in Berlin.'

'Can you write that down for me?' He handed Herr Bredow his notebook.

Bredow scribbled the name and address for him.

'Thank you. So if I gave you the name of a crew member, you could trace which U-boat he served on?'

'Yes.'

'And once we know his boat number can you also tell me where it was sunk?'

'Usually. But not necessarily.'

'Why's that?'

Bredow said, '*Passiermeldungen*. Every day the submarine commander had to radio to Berlin in code, telling his position and what he was doing, what enemy shipping was about, and so on. This is called a *Passiermeldung*. He also received any orders Berlin wanted to give him. So, if that submarine is thereafter sunk, we know approximately where, because the commander gave us his recent position. But a U-boat could go a long way in twenty-four hours, chasing a ship Berlin knew nothing about. Or, it may happen that a commander cannot radio his *Passiermeldung* on time, because of bad weather, for example. Then, if he gets sunk, we don't know where.' He paused. 'But the British Ministry of Defence may know. Or the National Archives in Washington DC.'

'How would they know?'

'Because the British and Americans deciphered our secret code used in the *Passiermeldungen*, so they knew what was being said. They then hunted that submarine and may have sunk it. So *they* know where, but we don't.'

'But won't they tell you now? The war ended forty years ago.'

Bredow sighed. 'Civil servants. The British are not very helpful. If I have a good reason to know about a specific boat – because the family want to know what happened to their loved one, for example – the British will sometimes tell me. But sometimes they will deny all knowledge. Sometimes they will even deny that a particular British ship was sunk when we *know* we sank it. The Americans are more helpful. They have all their information on microfilm now and I can soon buy it. But, of course, the Americans do not necessarily know everything the British know. All the *Passiermeldungen* we received can be found in the B.D.U., the Daily War Book. B.D.U. means the *Befehlshaber der U-Boote*, and the archive is in Freiburg. Here is the address of the British Ministry of Defence.' Bredow got up and fetched a letter off his desk. 'Naval Staff Duties, Foreign Documents Section, Ministry of Defence, Room 2606, Empress State Building, London, SW6

1TR. The address of the American National Archives is Washington DC 20408. Write to Tim Mulligan.'

McQuade scribbled it all down. 'I've looked at *Jane's Fighting Ships*, and it seems from their figures that there are a number of U-boats which are completely untraced. Missing.'

'Yes. There are twenty-eight missing U-boats. Here is a list.' Bredow went to a filing cabinet. He brought out a cyclostyled sheet. 'You can keep that.'

'Many thanks.' McQuade ran his eye down the list. A number went missing right at the end of the war, April and May 1945. His pulse slipped. One of the missing boats was U 1093. Which matched the obscured numbers he had seen on the conning tower of the sunken submarine. 'No trace at all? Didn't they send any *Passiermeldung*?'

'Not shortly before they went missing.'

McQuade took a breath. Now for the big question. He did not want Horst Bredow getting too interested. 'Does the name Horst Kohler mean anything to you? *Seeoffizier* Horst Kohler?'

Bredow shrugged. 'Kohler is a common German name.'

'Would you mind looking up his name in your files? And telling me the number of his U-boat?'

Bredow frowned. 'Why? I do not mind telling you about submarines, Herr McQuade, but I cannot give out personal information without good reason.'

McQuade sighed apologetically. 'I'm sorry.' He put his hand in his pocket and pulled out the identification tag of Horst Kohler. He said, 'I found this. I'd like to find out about this man. So I can return this tag to his family.'

Bredow stretched out his hand. 'Where did you find it?'

McQuade said: 'In London. In a stall that sells war memorabilia. That is what made me think of writing a story.'

Bredow turned it over and over.

'If you like, I will return it to his family,' he said. 'Otherwise I would like to buy it for my museum, please.'

'You can have it if the family don't want it. But I would

like to deliver it to them personally.' He added, 'For my story.'

Bredow nodded slowly, fingering the tag.

'Very well.' He went into the office beyond and returned with two files. He stood at his desk, and riffled through pages, muttering 'Kohler, Kohler ...' His finger stopped. 'Yes, Kohler, Horst. The only Horst Kohler. *Seeoffizier*. Joined in 1940 ... His U-boat was number 1093.'

McQuade's heart leapt. Herr Bredow then opened the other file and was riffling through the pages. 'And U-boat 1093 was ... It is one of the missing ones.'

Bredow sat down and looked across the desk at him pensively. McQuade concealed his elation. 'Do your files say where U-boat 1093 was last seen?'

Bredow glanced at his file. 'Yes. Near Flensberg, 1st May, 1945. She had just returned from a mission. But there is no record of her going back to sea.' He sat back and frowned at the ceiling.

Oh yes! McQuade said, 'If she *had* received orders to go back to sea, would there definitely be a record of that today?'

Bredow sighed. 'Not necessarily. This was right at the end of the war. Germany was in chaos. Hitler had committed suicide. Bombs, fires, tanks overrunning Berlin, street-by-street battles. Admiral Dönitz had taken over the government and he had just moved his headquarters near Flensberg.'

It all fitted. 'And what day did the war end?'

'The 10th of May.'

'Ten days later. So there was still time for the U-boat to receive orders to put to sea.'

'This is not so remarkable,' Bredow said pensively. 'The submarine went back to sea, obviously, but no record exists because of the chaos. It was sunk, in the British Channel most likely, at that stage. Kohler's body is washed ashore, somebody finds it and takes the tag as a souvenir. Forty years later it shows up in a shop in London.'

'Maybe the submarine wasn't sunk by the Allies, but hit a

140

rock or a sandbank. How easy is it for that to happen?'

'Unlikely. A submarine likes deep water. The asdic shows the commander the rocks – even a shoal of fish.'

'But currents and the weather could confuse him? Make him lost for a while. There was no sat-nav in those days. So the submarine had to surface to enable the navigator to see the sun and use his sextant. Well, if the sky was overcast for days he'd have to dead-reckon and that could put him miles out with a strong current? Suddenly, *bang* – he hits a sandbank.'

Herr Bredow nodded. 'It is possible.'

'If he does bang into a sandbank, or rocks, how does he get off?'

'Usually he would reverse. To pull himself off.'

'And if he reversed into more rocks behind? And damaged his rudders?'

'Then he's in big trouble.'

'He would have to abandon ship?'

'Possibly. He would try other things first.'

McQuade took a deep breath. 'Is Horst Kohler's wife listed in your file?'

Bredow shook his head. 'No. That is not unusual. If she's still alive and drawing a war pension.'

'So I'll have to find out from the pension office in Berlin?'

'Yes.'

McQuade felt he was getting places. He wanted to get going. 'Last question, Herr Bredow.' He pulled out the submarine brochure he had bought in Laboe. He opened it at the diagram of the submarine. 'A naval officer explained the Abandon Ship procedure for German submarines to me. How the submarine is partially flooded by opening valves, until the pressure inside is the same as the sea pressure outside. The conning tower hatches are then opened and the escape tube fills with water. The crew swims up it, and rises to the surface. Now I presume a diver could subsequently re-enter the submarine by the same route, but in the reverse direction?'

'Correct.'

'Is there a better way?'   .

'Only if he cuts a hole in the side. Or, if a torpedo port is open and the tube is empty.' He added: 'Submariners have been known to escape that way.'

That didn't apply to his submarine because he had seen the torpedo ports were closed. 'But *all* the crew would be able to escape up the normal escape tube, if the submarine was wrecked in less than fifty metres of water?'

Bredow nodded. 'All will escape.'

So why did only two men escape from that submarine off the Skeleton Coast?

18

It was dark when his train got back to Kiel. He bought a ticket to Berlin, then went to the station buffet and drank a bottle of wine while he chomped through a plateful of pig's knuckles and sauerkraut. He got on the train. He could not afford a couchette and bumped his way down the corridors looking for a half-empty compartment. A large, glamorous blonde of about forty gave him the eye outside her empty couchette compartment, but he was too tired to try to get laid in German. He found an empty second-class compartment, spread his bag and jacket around to make the place look heavily occupied, and switched off the lights.

He awoke to his compartment door clashing back. He sat up groggily, in harsh electric light. A man was lying on the seat opposite him. At the door stood a fierce young man in green uniform. He snapped in German, 'Your passport!'

'But I've already shown my passport . . .'

The official barked, '*Passport!*'

McQuade pulled it out. The man snatched it. The other man murmured in English: 'We are now passing through communist East Germany . . .'

The official glared at the passport as if McQuade had made it himself, compared him closely with the photograph, then, his lips tight, he stamped it and thrust it back. The door slammed after him.

McQuade sat back. 'Nice guy.'

The young man waved a finger at the dawn outside the windows. 'Soon we will see The Wall. And their dogs.'

There were farms and forests, a few small towns, all dead

quiet. No cars. Then suddenly a high brick wall was running alongside the railway on both sides, and barbed wire, and beyond were twinkling houses with many cars parked in the street, and there were supermarkets and neon signs. 'That is West Berlin other side the wall,' the young man said.

The train eased to a halt. McQuade opened the window. Green-uniformed guards with straining Alsatian dogs were patrolling the platform.

In the freezing early morning the train pulled into Berlin. The Berlin of Checkpoint Charlie, the Berlin of Spandau, the Berlin where Hitler committed suicide.

Eichborndamm is a long tree-lined street, dominated by big red-brick buildings. The *Deutsche Dienststelle*, the pension office, which had window-boxes with flowers, looked like a pleasant apartment block. There was a uniformed guard at the door. McQuade said in halting German, 'May I please speak to somebody about U-boat pensions?'

The guard took his passport and made a telephone call. After a few minutes, down the stairs came a flustered young woman. She wore a tweed skirt with black boots, and big spectacles: she looked well-bred and wholesome. She smiled uncertainly, 'I speak not much English.'

McQuade put on his most charming smile. He pulled out Horst Kohler's identification tag, and said carefully, 'I would like to trace the family of this U-boat officer, who died during the war. I want to return this to his family. I have been to the U-Boot Archiv in Sylt and found out that his U-boat was number 1093.'

The girl looked surprised. 'Please, follow me.'

They mounted some stairs to the first floor, which had rows of shelves holding thousands of files, and mounted the next flight of stairs. More shelves, more files. She led him into a spacious office with one government-looking desk with in-trays, out-trays and pending-trays, all empty. A middle-aged man in a cardigan got to his feet politely. 'Herr Wagner,' the girl introduced anxiously.

They shook hands. Herr Wagner indicated a chair. 'Please.'

They all sat and the girl began to speak rapidly in German. Herr Wagner turned the tag over. Then he excused himself, and left the room with it.

McQuade and the girl waited in self-conscious silence, until Herr Wagner came back with a green file. He opened it on the desk. Some of the documents within were partly scorched. Wagner said something and the girl interpreted, 'Bomb-damage. Fire.'

Herr Wagner flipped slowly through the file. Then spoke in German. The girl then said:

'Yes, there is a widow. She draws a war pension.'

McQuade's heart leapt. 'Can I have her address?'

Herr Wagner shook his head, and spoke in German. The girl said: 'That is forbidden. Only relatives can be told such things. Herr Wagner must write a letter to Frau Kohler. If she wishes to meet you, then we can inform you.'

'How long will that take?'

'Perhaps two weeks.'

'But isn't it possible to telephone her?'

The girl interpreted. Herr Wagner sighed. The girl reported: 'It is not regular to telephone.'

'But I've come all the way from England for this.'

'We can post the tag to Frau Kohler.'

'But it is . . . a sentimental matter to me to meet the lady who is a victim of the tragedy of war.' He lied: 'My father died in a submarine during the war, too, you see.'

'I understand,' the girl said. She interpreted it.

Herr Wagner hesitated, sighed, then gestured to McQuade to be patient. He left the room.

McQuade waited, his hopes up. 'Thank you,' he said to the girl.

'Don't mention it.'

Five minutes later Herr Wagner came back. He spoke in

German. The girl smiled. 'Frau Kohler agrees. But your visit should be short. Herr Wagner will write a letter to introduce you. She lives in Freiburg.'

19

The East German train from Berlin served no beer or wine, only Soviet whisky, pure firewater. And all the toilets were broken. In Hanover McQuade gratefully changed to a West German train to Freiburg.

It was early morning when he arrived, its tree-lined streets quiet. He sat in the station café and drank coffee restlessly, waiting for Freiburg and Frau Kohler to wake up.

It was ten o'clock when the taxi dropped him outside a small apartment block in a quiet suburb. The solid German houses were silent. Here and there smoke curled out of a chimney-pot. McQuade went through glass doors, into a warm passage, and stopped at apartment number 4. He pressed the bell.

There was a spy-hole in the door. He saw it darken. Then the door opened.

'*Guten Morgen*,' McQuade began, 'Frau Kohler? . . .'

'Are you Mr McQuade?' she said in English.

The apartment was warm and solidly furnished. It overlooked small communal gardens. On a cabinet stood a number of framed photographs. A naval officer was in several of them. Frau Kohler was about sixty and wore her grey hair pulled back into a severe bun. She had obviously once been a handsome woman. She read Herr Wagner's letter without using spectacles.

'You are kind to take such trouble.'

McQuade felt like an impostor. He took the identification tag from his pocket and held it out. 'I'm sure you'd like to have that.'

She looked at it in his hand a moment: then she took it

147

carefully. She gently rubbed her fingers over it.

'Thank you. I would like it very much.' She looked up at him. 'But I must pay you what you paid.'

'No, I would not dream of that.'

She accepted that. 'Then you must at least accept some coffee? Or the English prefer tea, perhaps?'

McQuade smiled. 'Coffee please.'

'And some scones? When Herr Wagner telephoned me yesterday I thought I must at least make some English scones for an Englishman who comes on such an errand.' She got up and turned, then stopped. 'Where exactly did you find it?'

'In Petticoat Lane. That's a—'

'I know Petticoat Lane. Every tourist to London goes to Petticoat Lane sometime. So . . .' She nodded at the tag in her palm. 'I wonder how it got there?'

She turned out of the living-room. McQuade sat there, feeling a fraud. He peered guiltily across the room at the photographs. Frau Kohler must have had everything prepared, for she returned immediately bearing a tray. She set it down. She poured black coffee into cups. She picked up a jug of cream, then abruptly put it down again, and dropped her face in her hands.

She sat completely still, holding her face. McQuade looked at her in discomfort. He did not know what to say or do. Then, as abruptly, Frau Kohler dropped her hands and sat up straight.

'I'm sorry.' Her eyes were moist, her face a little suffused. 'I'm sorry, I was thinking . . .' She shook her head. 'I was imagining the . . . terror as the submarine was sinking. The water pouring in. Then his body washing up on the shore.'

McQuade felt terrible. Frau Kohler pulled herself together. 'Cream?' She added it anyway. 'I'm sorry,' she said again. 'This must be difficult for you too, because Herr Wagner told me that your father was also killed on his submarine . . .'

Oh Lord, he could cut his tongue off for saying that. 'Yes . . .' He guiltily took the cup Frau Kohler extended. He said, to get away from himself, 'Are those photographs of your husband?'

Frau Kohler sniffed once. 'Yes.' She clearly did not want to discuss them; then she got up, as if doing a duty to her guest. She handed the biggest photograph to him. 'My husband, twenty-seven years old.'

It was a large, formal portrait. He was a handsome young man, dark hair, clean shaven, looking at McQuade with a twitch of a smile. His officer's cap on, the submarine insignia in the middle. So *this* was the man who fought H.M. to the death on the Skeleton Coast forty years ago . . . He looked a nice guy.

'And this.' Frau Kohler held out a smaller frame.

It was an enlarged snapshot. Horst Kohler in civilian clothes, his hair awry, his arm around a pretty, tall woman. Both laughing at the camera, their faces puckered by the sun. In the background was a lake. '1943,' Frau Kohler said. 'He was on leave from his U-boat.' She held out the last photograph. 'Our wedding day. 1944.'

It showed a handsome couple outside a church, the groom in uniform, the bride in a long white gown, both beaming. The bride looked radiant.

McQuade did not know what to say. 'How sad.'

'Yes.' Frau Kohler took the photographs. 'War is terribly sad. And for what?' She replaced them on the cabinet, as if closing the subject now. She returned to the tray. 'Now, your scones!'

'Thank you.' He was not hungry, but took one. He said: 'Did you not have any children, Frau Kohler?'

She did not want to talk about it any more. 'No. We were only married for a year. During that year I only saw him for about six weeks.'

McQuade did not like to persist, but this was what he was here for. 'When did you last see your husband?'

She said grimly, 'First of May, 1945, ten o'clock at night.' Suddenly she was bitter. 'Ten days before the war ended!

Why did he have to go to sea again? The war was all but over! Germany was in ruins! Adolf Hitler had already committed suicide! So why did they send him back to sea? Hadn't he fought enough? For four years a U-boat man, and he had only just returned from a mission. So why risk his life at the very end? He didn't understand it either.' She looked at him, moist-eyed. '*Why?*'

McQuade said uncomfortably: 'Where did you last see him?'

'Flensberg. I last saw him as he walked away into the base.'

'You said he didn't understand why he was being sent back to sea? Were you with him when he received his orders?'

She sighed. 'No. A message arrived at our house his first night home that he must report to base again. He came back furious that he had to go to sea the next night. He was exhausted.'

'Did he say where his submarine was going?' He added, 'I only ask because his boat is registered as missing. Unaccounted for.'

'No. Orders are secret. Not even known to him until the boat gets to sea. He was only second-in-command.' She took a deep breath. 'Yes, missing.' She sighed. 'For years I thought he may come back. Maybe he had only been wrecked on a desert island, or maybe he had reached neutral territory, or lost his memory perhaps. For years I thought he may come through the door. Or a letter arrive. Finally I realized it was a dream. Now . . .' She picked up the tag. 'This proves it.'

McQuade felt very bad. 'I'm sorry,' he murmured.

'No, I knew it already. It was very kind of you to come.' She went on abruptly: 'More coffee?'

'Thank you.' He accepted to keep her talking. There was only enough for half a cup, but she did not offer to make more. 'And did the rest of his crew have to go back to sea too?'

'I presume. Of course.'

'But they didn't all live in Flensberg, surely? Some of them must have gone out of town.'

'Maybe so.' She clearly wanted to stop talking about it now. 'Another scone, Mr McQuade? You must take these with you on your journey.'

'That's very kind of you.' He added hastily, 'I'm sorry to keep asking questions, but I am . . . very interested in your story now. Tell me, did you know most of his crew?'

Frau Kohler put her empty cup down with a certain finality. 'Some of them. They were at our wedding. As a guard of honour.' She smiled wearily, 'Mr McQuade, there is something else I baked for you when I heard you were coming. Do Englishmen like apfelstrudel?'

McQuade got the message. 'Oh yes . . .'

She smiled and got up and walked out. McQuade stood up, marshalling his last question. Frau Kohler came back with an open cardboard box. In it lay a golden apfel pie. 'You shouldn't have done this, Mrs Kohler.'

'I hope you enjoy it.' She put the box down and bent to tie string around it.

'Frau Kohler, you have been very patient with me, but I have one last question please?'

'Yes?' she asked, still tying. 'Of course.'

McQuade said: 'Do the initials H.M. mean anything to you? Was there a member of your husband's crew with the initials H.M.?'

Frau Kohler froze, bent over the box. There was a silence. McQuade watched her. She did not look up. Then her fingers continued tying the knot.

'No . . . Why do you ask this question?'

Oh yes! McQuade was convinced he was onto something very significant. He had nothing to lose by telling her half the truth now.

'Forgive me, I really did come here to return your husband's tag, but I have not been entirely frank with you.' He took a breath. 'Frau Kohler? I have evidence which

151

suggests that your husband did not die in his submarine.' He paused. 'He died on a beach, fighting a man with the initials H.M., who came from his submarine.'

There was a stunned silence. Then Frau Kohler slowly straightened up. Entranced, she looked at McQuade, her blue eyes wide. She whispered:

'How do you know this?' McQuade opened his mouth but Frau Kohler suddenly clapped her hands to her ears. *'Oh, mein Gott, nein! Oh mein Gott, es ist doch wahr . . .'*

McQuade stared at her. 'What? So what's true?'

Frau Kohler stared, her hands over her ears. She gasped again: *'Oh mein Gott . . .'* Then she turned and sat on the sofa.

McQuade crouched and put his hand on her shoulder. 'Frau Kohler? *What?* What is true?'

Then she dropped her face into her hands and burst into racking sobs.

McQuade sat down beside her. As suddenly, Frau Kohler sat up. She looked at him, her face suffused with emotion, her eyes wet. Then she held out a trembly palm, to keep his sympathy at a distance. She said,

'Tell me. Everything. The whole truth, please . . .'

20

She asked him to get a bottle of cognac from the cabinet. She sat rigidly on the sofa, her glass drained, and listened intently, while he told her half the truth. He told her Jakob's story, except he did not tell her how many times H.M. stabbed her husband, nor how he sawed his throat open; he called the two Damara strandlopers Paco and Fernando, and instead of the Skeleton Coast he placed everything off the jungled coast of Argentina.

'When Paco knocked the man down a wallet fell out of his pocket.' He took it from his jacket. 'It has the initials H.M. on it.'

Frau Kohler stared at it. Then her fists clenched on her knees, and she closed her eyes in fury. She whispered,

'Oh . . . It must be him . . .'

'Who?' McQuade said urgently.

She put her fists to her temples. 'For *him* my husband died! Murdered by *him* . . .'

'By *who?*'

Frau Kohler slowly lowered her fists to her lap. She looked at him with angry, moist eyes; then she whispered:

'I've never told anyone this. For fear . . .'

McQuade waited, pent. 'Trust me, Frau Kohler . . .'

She hesitated; then took a deep breath and hissed at him,

'*Heinrich Muller! The initials stand for Heinrich Muller! The chief of the Gestapo . . .*'

McQuade stared at her. Jesus Christ . . . The head of the Gestapo. And he wanted to jump up and throw his arms in the air – if it was Heinrich Muller, that submarine would be *bursting* with top-level loot! He said, 'But there are millions of people with the initials H.M. . .'

Frau Kohler's hands were clutching her knees. She took another deep breath, then whispered,

'I've never told this to anybody. But I've told you so much now . . . Can I trust you, Herr McQuade?'

'Yes . . .' McQuade lied desperately.

Frau Kohler looked at him, racked by hesitation. 'And I want to talk about it.'

McQuade nodded urgently.

Frau Kohler closed her eyes and sat forward, her elbows on her knees, her fists clenched. She said softly:

'When my husband received the message, he went to the base. He returned late that night. He was . . . furious. He told me they were going to go to sea with only half the crew.' She opened her eyes and whispered angrily, 'How can a submarine fight with only a . . . skeleton crew?'

McQuade nodded urgently.

'The next day he returned to his U-boat to supervise the preparations. I would meet him at the dock gates at ten o'clock that night to say goodbye. I . . .' She closed her eyes in exasperation: 'You must realize what it was like in those days. Everything chaotic. Nobody knew what was happening . . .'

McQuade nodded. Frau Kohler went on:

'Of course, I was heart-broken. And . . . *furious*. My husband had fought so much. Why don't we just hold up our hands and let the Tommies capture us? I begged my husband to do so . . .' She shook her head bitterly. 'Of course he would not. It was his duty. And so on . . .'

Frau Kohler took a trembly breath.

'So . . . I went to the docks at ten o'clock. I waited. My husband came out . . .' She closed her eyes at the memory. 'He was white with anger. He said that the U-boat only had one torpedo. So how could it fight? Then he . . .' She looked at McQuade squarely. 'He said he was *sure* they were not going on an aggressive mission because there were *civilians* on board!'

McQuade wanted to punch his palm. 'How many?'

Frau Kohler shook her head. 'There were several. But he only spoke of one. But what business does a *civilian* have on a submarine? This man was sitting in the commander's cabin. With a hat on, and dark glasses. *Why* sunglasses inside a submarine?'

McQuade waited, excited.

'So . . . My husband was so angry about everything, about the crew, about only one torpedo, about these civilians – so he had demanded to know from his commander what was happening, where they were going?' She snorted softly. 'The commander was a good friend, but they almost had a fight. Finally, to make my husband keep quiet the commander told him: "That is Heinrich Muller. We are going on an important mission for the Reich . . ."'

McQuade wanted to shout for joy. 'Did he say where?'

Frau Kohler took a weary breath.

'No. I have spent forty years wondering.'

McQuade urged: 'But did your husband recognize the man as Heinrich Muller?'

'No. He was not sure what Muller looked like. And he had glasses on. Keeping quiet. My husband detested the Gestapo.'

'Did he protest to the commander?'

'Of course! He demanded to know on whose orders they were taking this man – because he refused to accept orders from the Gestapo, only from the Admiralty. But the commander assured him the orders were . . . in order.' She looked at McQuade. 'I *begged* my husband to disobey! Outside the very gates I begged him. "Why go to sea for this man," I cried, "you hate the Nazis!"' She looked at McQuade. 'My husband detested those . . . bullies. And, by this time we had information about what they were doing to the Jews.' She shook her head. 'Terrible rumours . . . "Why risk your life for such a Nazi?" I cried.' She closed her eyes bitterly. 'But I could not persuade him to desert. "Orders are orders!"'

McQuade sat back. His heart went out to the poor woman – but he felt elated. That submarine was carrying a lot of loot for the benefit of top-Nazi Heinrich Muller. 'And that's the last you saw of your husband?'

She looked at her hands. 'We said goodbye. He told me he would be back soon. He said he would come back to me as a civilian!' She closed her eyes. 'He told me to stay in the air-raid shelter . . . "Sleep there, eat there", he said.' She sighed. '"And do your duty for the new Germany when it comes . . ."' She snorted softly: 'A man does not tell his loved one that if he expects to come back.'

McQuade was moved. He liked Horst Kohler. And he liked his poor widow. She slumped back in the sofa.

'And now I have told you everything. And now I know what his destination was – Argentina.' She snorted bitterly. 'That is not surprising. Many of those Nazis ran away to South America, while good men like my husband died for them.'

McQuade felt a bastard for having told so many untruths to this good, sad woman. 'Frau Kohler, thank you for taking me into your confidence.'

She heaved herself up straight. 'Thank *you* for coming to see an old German woman about her young husband of long ago.' She looked at him. 'He was wonderful man, Herr McQuade.'

McQuade nodded. 'And it took great courage to be a submariner.'

'Yes, but he was also a *kind* man.' She turned to him. 'So . . . I have not told anybody else, Herr McQuade. In forty years. I've only told you because you came all the way from England to give me my husband's tag. It has . . . upset me.' She looked at him intently. 'But you must please not tell anybody about Muller. Because I am afraid.'

'Of what?' McQuade said.

156

She sighed guiltily. Then: 'I am afraid that my husband's last voyage was not official – not ordered by the Admiralty. Possibly the commander lied to my husband. Possibly Muller gave the orders, to escape from Germany. In which case, I am afraid that if my husband did not die on an official mission, I will not receive my war-widow's pension.'

McQuade sat back. 'I see.' And he felt terrible doing it, but he proceeded to capitalize on her fear because he didn't want anybody else knowing the story either. 'You are quite right. You might indeed lose your pension. So you must tell *nobody* else.'

He hurried down the street, looking for a taxi, tense with excitement. *Heinrich Muller!*

The taxi dropped him at the Tourist Information Bureau. He asked the pretty Fräulein at the desk: 'Is there such a thing as a Jewish Council in Freiburg? A Jewish Cultural Committee perhaps?'

'One moment.' The girl went to the telephone directory. A minute later she came back with a note.

'Try this number. The Jewish Historical Society.'

'Thank you!'

There was a public telephone in the bureau. He hurried to it and dialled. 'Do you speak English, please?'

'*Ja*, good morning?' the voice said.

'Good morning! I'm a visitor to Germany and I'm trying to write a book about the Jews during the Second World War. About the concentration camps, and so forth. Is there anybody in Freiburg who speaks English who can give me information about war criminals. In particular, about the Gestapo?'

'The Gestapo?' the man mused. 'In the library, of course. But the libraries are mostly in German.'

'Isn't there a well-known Jewish hunter of war-criminals called Simon Wiesenthal?'

'Of course,' the man said. 'But Simon Wiesenthal is in

157

Vienna, in Austria. Not in Germany.'

'Can you give me his telephone number?'

'I do not know it,' the man said. 'But if you search in the Vienna telephone directory . . .'

'You're *sure* he's in Vienna?'

'Perfectly sure. Ask any Jew, even my little daughter. His office is called "The Documentation Centre".'

McQuade made a note, thanked him and hung up.

Vienna! Simon Wiesenthal was surely the best man to tell him about Heinrich Muller, the head of Hitler's Gestapo. He could spend days in libraries trying to learn what Wiesenthal could tell him in twenty minutes. If Wiesenthal would speak to him.

The post office was down the street. Rows of tables held the telephone directories for the whole of Europe. McQuade found the Vienna directory.

He looked up Documentation Centre. Nothing. He tried the German: Dokument-whatever Zentrum. Nothing. Zentrum Dokument-whatever? Nothing. He looked up Wiesenthal. Scores of Wiesenthals, but no Simon.

Of course – a man like Simon Wiesenthal has an unlisted number. He doesn't want cranks phoning up. McQuade feverishly looked up the number for Directory Enquiries. Vienna 08. He went to the telephone cabins.

'I am sorry,' the Viennese operator reported back, 'that number is unlisted.'

'It is vitally important that I speak to somebody in Herr Wiesenthal's office. Can you possibly connect me to some Jewish organization who will consider my request?'

'One moment, please.'

After a minute the operator came back. 'You can speak to the Israelische Kultesgemeinde. Their number is Vienna 36 16 550.'

'*Thank you, madam!*' He scribbled the number down.

He stood a minute, thinking it through. Then he dialled. 'Good morning. I am trying to write a book about Nazi-hunters and of course Simon Wiesenthal is the most famous one. Would you be so kind as to give me his telephone number so I can try to arrange an appointment?'

There was hesitation. 'Mr Wiesenthal is a very busy man.'

McQuade said earnestly: 'I know, but it's to Mr Wiesenthal's advantage that he see me. I will write about him whether he talks to me or not and I may make mistakes that will embarrass him.'

There was a sigh. 'Who is your publisher?'

He was about to lie, then changed it in his mouth in case the man checked up. 'This is my first book, I haven't got a publisher yet.'

The voice said: 'What is your number? I will speak to Mr Wiesenthal and call you back.'

Twenty minutes later he was striding back to the railway station, feeling on top of the world. He asked when the next train left for Vienna.

He had several hours to wait, so he went to the bar.

He was feverishly excited. If it was Heinrich Muller on that submarine, it was a sure bet that there was a great deal of loot on it. The commander had told Horst Kohler that the voyage was *official* 'for the Reich'. Obviously an official escape by the head of the Gestapo must have been accompanied by a lot of valuables; it was well-known that the Nazis sent shiploads of looted treasure abroad. Even if it wasn't an official mission, even if Heinrich Muller had somehow commandeered the submarine to make his private escape, it was highly likely that the head of the Gestapo had prepared himself for his new life.

McQuade ran his fingers through his hair. Okay, but was he wise going to see Simon Wiesenthal? The man might give him a lot of information but if Wiesenthal thought that McQuade was on to no less a war criminal than Heinrich Muller, he could really throw a spanner into the works: if Wiesenthal started looking for Muller in South West Africa-

Namibia, that submarine could slip right through McQuade's fingers.

He stared across the bar.

No, of course he had to go to Wiesenthal. To find out as much as possible as quickly as possible about the man whose looted treasure he was hunting. Firstly, was the man alive or dead? If he was alive he had to be very careful about that submarine. And how he disposed of the loot. But maybe it wasn't Heinrich Muller at all, maybe Simon Wiesenthal would prove that Muller died in the last days of the war, in which case there might not be any loot at all on that submarine. Or maybe Wiesenthal would tell him that Muller was alive and well somewhere in Paraguay living off the loot. Maybe anything. *You don't embark upon a costly search for sunken treasure without trying to establish the probability of its existence* . . .

But there was another reason: Heinrich Muller was probably a most-wanted Nazi war-criminal. If he was still alive, that made him a dangerous man. McQuade desperately wanted to know what he looked like: see a photograph of the man. If he was alive, McQuade wanted him brought to justice, and on an Israeli scaffold.

But, please God, not until James McQuade had cracked that submarine and got the loot out. If Muller was found before that, McQuade would not be allowed near that submarine.

21

It was eight o'clock the next morning when his train pulled into Vienna. He had a shower and shave in the station bathroom, and put on clean clothes. He put his bag in a locker.

Salztorgasse is a depressing street that leads off the broad Danube Canal, in what looks like the garment district. Number 6 is an old, four-storey office building, which also happens to be the building the Gestapo used as their Vienna headquarters in the bad old days. At the next intersection is a synagogue, guarded nowadays by a policeman with a sub-machine-gun. The Documentation Centre has an inconspicuous nameplate on the doorpost. McQuade pressed the button. He had the feeling a television eye was watching him. He said into the entry-phone: 'My name is McQuade, I telephoned you yesterday from Freiburg.'

The door clicked open. He entered a bare hallway and walked up to the second floor, where an armed policeman sat outside the door of the Documentation Centre. McQuade nodded politely and pressed the bell.

He was admitted by a polite Austrian woman in no-nonsense tweeds.

'May I see your passport, please?'

She took it into an office on her right. She returned a minute later, with a smile.

McQuade hung his coat on the rack. There were framed certificates on the walls, honorary doctorates awarded to Simon Wiesenthal. He glanced into the secretaries' office. Three women sat at desks; the walls were lined with hundreds of files and books. Suddenly a figure appeared down the passage.

A large old man was looking at him, checking him out.

'So, you want to write a book about Nazi hunters?' Simon Wiesenthal said.

The room was cluttered. A large desk covered with files, the walls lined with crammed bookshelves, two armchairs and sofa in old red velvet, and a brass Moroccan coffee table. On one wall hung a large map of central Europe with the legend *'Deutschland Unter Der Hitler Diktatur 1933 – 1945'*. Studded across it were Stars of David, indicating Nazi concentration camps. Written beneath each star were the numbers of people murdered therein; *France, 1,500,000, Holland 220,000* . . . Simon Wiesenthal sat in an armchair, a good-looking grandfather of a man with heavy eyelids. He said, as if he had given this interview many times:

'I have no police powers. I cannot order arrests. All I can do is collect the evidence. Collect, collect. Every day many letters arrive, telling me they have seen this war-criminal here, seen that criminal there, people telling me they are witnesses to their terrible crimes. Everything is carefully evaluated. I have developed a feeling in my fingers for good evidence.' He rubbed them together. 'If the evidence is good, I act.' He waved his hand at the secretaries' room. 'I have files of over one hundred and fifty thousand war-criminals I still want to bring to justice.'

McQuade was staggered at the number.

'And me over seventy already! How much time have I got left to do my work? And at least twenty thousand of them can never be caught, because forty years have passed and the witnesses to their terrible crimes have died.' He threw up his hands wearily. 'Twenty thousand brutal murderers who are living comfortable lives as businessmen where people like you spend your money. Some of them are top men in Germany today. Well respected. But I know who they are.' He tapped his old head. 'And *they* know that I know . . . They do not sleep good at night. Because *they* do not know what

162

witnesses still exist. Every time the door knocks, maybe it is Simon Wiesenthal come to say hullo.' He looked at McQuade: 'And that is good. Such people have no right to sleep.'

McQuade said, 'But the other one hundred and thirty thousand?'

Simon Wiesenthal nodded. 'I will catch as many as I can. But how many years are left to me? I pray the Lord to give me more, and health to work – *to work*. But how many can I still catch? Of course my job is difficult because I must be . . . *super*-careful never to damage an innocent person.' He turned his old blue eyes to McQuade. 'We must *never* do what the Nazis did.'

McQuade nodded earnestly. 'Presumably these Nazis have assumed new identities?'

Wiesenthal nodded wearily. 'Usually they only change their family names, because it is easier for a man to keep his first name – easier for his wife, his children, and they often change their appearances. For example, recently I have been looking for a man whose first name was Franz. I get evidence he is working in Brazil, at a German factory there. I send a man to Brazil to look at this Franz. My man must get friendly with a secretary in this company to look at the records about this Franz. Finally my man tells me there are nineteen men called Franz at this factory. So, there is much more work to do.'

'So you have men who do such dangerous work?'

Simon Wiesenthal crinkled his eyes. 'I have no police force. I don't have hired guns. I am just a detective. I only have people who do *enquiry* work, *voluntarily*. Jews and Gentiles. All over the world. For example, banks Banks often have much information about a man. His passport; his earlier passport; where his money comes from; and so on. Recently I had such a case in Milan. I went there. Sure enough it was my man. I had him arrested.'

'By whom?'

'By the public prosecutor. I have no strong young men to do my dirty work for me.'

McQuade did not believe that. 'But if the public prosecutor refuses? As must happen sometimes in countries like South America?'

Simon Wiesenthal spread his hands eloquently. 'All I can do is character assassination. Tell the press, the employer. Hopefully get him fired.'

'You don't call in Mossad? The Israeli secret service?'

Wiesenthal winced. '*Mossad?* The last time they had success was with Adolf Eichmann.' He shook his head. 'I don't work with Mossad. Or Interpol.' (McQuade certainly did not believe that. Interpol, maybe – but Mossad?) 'Something else you must understand for your book . . .' He tapped his chest. 'I am not interested in vengeance. I spent five years in five Nazi death camps, and somehow I survived. I was young. Maybe I was also smart. You can see I am a big man when I am properly fed. When I was liberated by the Americans I weighed only ninety pounds. My parents had died in the camps – I watched my mother being driven away by the SS. My own wife I believed to be dead in the camps – sent up the chimney, as the saying was. But somehow *I* survived! And somehow my wife did too, though I did not know she was also still alive until a long time afterwards.' He looked across with those old judicial eyes, and for a flash McQuade felt the incredible horror of those frightful years. 'When the Americans finally opened those terrible gates, and fed us, they asked me, "What work did you do before the war?" I told them I'd been an architect. When they said, "Well, you can go back to your people and build houses again," I said to myself: "But who will live in the houses? My people are dead, how can I build houses only for money? No, I must do my best for the people who do not need houses any more." And I resolved to try to see they got justice.' He spread his hands. 'But how do you bring justice for so much suffering? For so many dead? To so many little children who will never

164

live in a nice warm house? But I decided to start trying. I stayed in the liberated camp and went from person to person and said "Tell me what happened to you. Tell me who did it. Give me names, dates, descriptions." Because I knew that out there in the ruins of Germany these murderers, these *torturers*, these ... SS men were slipping away, they had thrown away their smart uniforms ... these hangmen were mixing with the starving refugees, saying to the Allies, "I was only an aircraft mechanic – please, I was only a private . . ." I knew that Generals in the SS and Gestapo were pretending they had nothing to do with those chimneys – with mass murder.' He looked at McQuade, 'So, with my friends, I began to write it all down. The names. The dates, the places. And I said to the Americans, "Arrest these criminals – here is the evidence . . ."'

McQuade was rapt. 'And did they?'

'When my facts were good. Because world opinion was outraged by the Nazis. They were preparing for the Nuremberg Trials. The world was finally *conscious* of the horrors.' He sighed. 'But when the Nuremberg Trials were over, and some top criminals hanged, world opinion was satisfied. The Allied troops went home, and the new ones who replaced them had not seen the horrors of the concentration camps, the survivors . . .' He shrugged. 'They were not so energetic after that, and there were plenty of pretty Fräuleins who were desperate for a pair of silk stockings or a tin of coffee. And now the Americans were more interested in catching communists than war-criminals, and even employed former SS officers to help them because they had inside knowledge of communist activities in Germany; for example Klaus Barbie, the Butcher of Lyons, even though the French wanted him for war crimes, the Americans shielded him because he was useful.' He sighed. 'So thousands upon thousands of war criminals escaped. *Murderers – mass* murderers.' He waved a hand. 'And today they live comfortable lives, all over the world, like respectable citizens. While the *Bonzen*, the Nazi bigwigs, don't even work. They live like lords on Odessa funds.'

This was what McQuade badly wanted to know about. 'Can you tell me about Odessa? Were their funds mostly Nazi plunder?'

Wiesenthal glanced at his watch.

'Haven't you read Frederick Forsyth's book, *The Odessa File*? He came to me for advice, too.'

'A long time ago,' McQuade said. 'I know Odessa was a secret organization to help Nazis—'

'*Is* a secret organization,' Wiesenthal interrupted, 'which still very much exists. It stands for *Organisation der SS-Angehörigen*, "Organization of SS Members".' He sighed wearily. 'Set up at the end of the war when the Allies were hunting SS men, Odessa helped SS members escape, paid for their defence at trials and supported their families. It pretended to be a charitable organization, but in reality it was a vast underground network between the SS members in captivity and the others outside. It had highly organized escape routes, produced perfect false documents and had safe-houses and sea-tickets and jobs and money. It even had friends in the Vatican – there was the "Monastery Route" over the Alps to Rome – and from there to Spain and South America. Also the Middle East, where the Nazis had big Arab friends also hostile to the Jews.' Simon Wiesenthal sighed again. 'Their funds were partly plunder, yes – the SS were in charge of the Final Solution, the concentration camps and confiscation of Jewish property. All the confiscated wealth was sent to the Reichsbank, the German Reserve Bank, including the gold from the teeth of the Jews sent to the gas chambers, and sure, some of it got into unauthorized hands. But most of the funds came from the big German industrialists who attended the Strasbourg Conference in 1944.' He looked at McQuade. 'Do you know about that?'

McQuade shook his head earnestly.

Wiesenthal glanced at his watch again.

'The conference of Germany's leading industrialists took place on the 10th August, 1944, at the Hotel Maison Rouge in Strasbourg. It was top secret. Hitler knew nothing about it. This was the "smart money" of Nazi Germany. They agreed that preparations must be made to safeguard Nazi assets from the Allies. They knew that the war was lost, so they must build up funds for the Third World War. They established large secret accounts and set up seven hundred and fifty companies in neutral countries for the rebuilding of the Fourth Reich. They created a network all over the world.' Wiesenthal held up a finger. 'I have seen the minutes of that meeting – the Americans found them . . .'

He got up and plucked a book off the shelves. 'This is called *The Murderers Amongst Us*. I wrote it.' He flicked through pages. 'The chairman of the conference was Dr Scheid of Herrmannsdorfwerke. He said, and I quote: "From now on Germany's industry must prepare for the economic post-war campaign. Every industrialist must seek contacts with firms abroad, without creating attention. And . . . *we must be ready to finance the Nazi Party, which will be forced to go underground for some time.*"' Wiesenthal looked at McQuade meaningfully, then ran his finger down the page. 'The minutes of the conference continue, "The Party leadership expects that some members will be convicted as war criminals. Thus preparations must be made to place less prominent leaders as 'technical experts' in various German key enterprises. The Party is ready to supply large amounts of money to industrialists who contribute to the post-war organization abroad . . ."' he paused, then continued quoting with emphasis: '"*so that after the defeat a strong new Reich can be built*".'

Wiesenthal looked at McQuade, then snapped the book closed. 'Furthermore, it is well known that the Nazis buried dozens of crates of treasure in the lakes in the Aussee region of Austria, for future use, and Hitler hid *billions* of dollars worth of plundered art treasures in a salt mine in the region –

which the Americans discovered and returned to their rightful owners. But only a fraction of the treasure in the Aussee lakes has been recovered. *Der Stern* magazine mounted a diving operation in 1959, which brought up fifteen crates, but they only contained counterfeit English five-pound notes.'

McQuade's pulse tripped. *Counterfeit fivers* . . . Wiesenthal slapped the book back on its shelf.

'So a vast economic network was set up to prepare for the Fourth Reich. And *that*'s where Odessa gets its money from, to this day.' He paused, then ended, 'And thousands upon thousands of war-criminals escaped. To South America. And to Australia, and to South Africa. Even to the United States, and England. Where they live happily to this day.' He added, 'We have given the Australian Foreign Minister, Mr Hayden, a list of two hundred Nazi criminals living in Australia – he has promised action. In 1948 the British asked the Australians to "go easy" on war-criminals, you know. In Britain itself there are over two hundred – we have complained to the Home Secretary, Douglas Hurd, and he is going to form a War Crimes Inquiry and advertise for witnesses.'

'War-criminals escaped to South Africa?' McQuade had not meant to echo that.

Wiesenthal shrugged. 'A lot. Many Afrikaners were pro-Germany during the war, and now have a big neo-Nazi organization there, that even uses a swastika-like emblem – what do they call it, the AWB?'

'But do you consider that AWB a significant force? Or lunatic fringe?'

Wiesenthal snorted. '*Any* neo-Nazi movement is significant, my friend, because Nazism is not dead – its evil is alive and well, world-wide. My information from South Africa is that the AWB is *very* powerful, and a serious threat to the government. It has direct historical parallels with the rise of the Nazi Party in Germany – decadent South Africa, public discontent, persecution of the blacks, even the Ghetto-mentality of Nazi Germany is legally enforced by the Group Areas Act, public anxiety about the future – then a lion comes out of the hills, like Adolf Hitler did, and whips the people up into a belligerent attitude. This AWB leader even demands *"Lebensraum"*, just like Hitler did – except he calls it his pure-white state.'

McQuade considered the old man was exaggerating the situation, but he again recalled the Schmidt ranch, and the three-legged swastika of the AWB. Wiesenthal went on: 'Many Nazi war-criminals are right here in Germany and Austria. As directors of big companies. Pillars of society. Some of them are even top civil servants, some even in parliament.'

McQuade was rapt. 'And are they still Nazis?'

Wiesenthal smiled grimly. 'Although the Nazi Party is banned in Germany, Mr McQuade, it is very much alive. Its economic power is enormous. There has been a resurgence of Nazism.' He waved his hand. 'I'm not talking about the ordinary suburban Germans who lived under Hitler – they got swept along because people are sheep, and the vast majority want to forget their past. No, I'm talking about serious,' he clenched his fist, '*hard-core* Nazis, who *believe* in Hitler's National Socialism, who seriously want to re-establish it.' He sighed. 'And this is world-wide, not just in Germany. Extreme right-wing politics is gaining ground.'

McQuade badly wanted to ask him about Hitler's grand plan for Africa, but thought better of it. 'And, do the governments cooperate with you?'

Wiesenthal snorted softly. 'Depends. On who I'm after. On who Mr Big is. On a lot of things.' He smiled wearily. 'For example, you've probably read in the newspapers recently that in the United Nations War Crimes Archives four hundred files have mysteriously gone "missing"?' He raised his eyebrows. '"*Missing*"? How? And it's reported that tens of thousands of documents have been stolen from the Nazi

Documentation Centre in West Berlin. How? Who would want to *steal* from the Documentation Centre?'

'Who?'

'Who indeed?' Wiesenthal shrugged. 'Certain members of the staff, perhaps? To sell, perhaps? To *"interested parties"* perhaps? To destroy evidence, perhaps?' He waved a finger. 'Of course, this is conjecture, but, for example, there is a certain politically important gentleman, not far from this building, in the heart of Vienna, who might be the kind of person to have such an *"interest"*.' He shook his face in disavowal. 'But that is only one kind of difficulty I face, Mr McQuade. And how many more can I catch before I die?' He sighed. 'But they must not sleep good – because tomorrow it may be their turn.' He shook his head. 'My wife says, "Why don't we retire and go to live in Israel near our grandchildren?" Yes, I want to do that very much. But not while I still have my health. Enough to catch some more Nazis and make them sleep badly. Such men have no right to die in peace.' He looked at McQuade, then held up an old finger earnestly. 'I repeat, I am not interested in vengeance. Once I have had a man arrested and handed my evidence to the public prosecutor, I don't care whether the court convicts him or not. I have done my duty. To all those people who died. My duty is ensure that mankind will not forget. So the Holocaust does not happen again.' He nodded grimly. 'Because mankind forgets very easily. Genocide soon becomes old history, and anti-Semitism is not dead, young man. It is *not* dead . . .'

Simon Wiesenthal had finished. He looked at his watch significantly. It was a practised gesture. McQuade said earnestly: 'Just one more question, please.'

Wiesenthal heaved himself to his feet. 'Yes?' he said.

McQuade said: 'I'm very interested in the Gestapo. In particular, in Heinrich Muller. What became of him? Is he alive or dead?'

Wiesenthal looked at him. McQuade hurried on: 'Can

you show me a recent photograph of him?'

Wiesenthal looked at him. His old face changed.

'A *recent* photograph of Heinrich Muller already?' He raised his eyebrows. 'What makes you think Heinrich Muller was still alive recently?'

McQuade said hastily: 'Maybe he isn't. But for my story, will you tell me what you know about him?'

'And what do you want to know about SS General Heinrich Muller?'

'Well, he's a war-criminal, isn't he?'

Wiesenthal had not taken his eyes off him. 'Probably *the* most-wanted war-criminal. Now that Mengele and Martin Bormann are dead. Germany was a police state and the Gestapo were the police. Heinrich Muller was the general in charge of the Gestapo. "Gestapo Muller", they called him. Adolf Eichmann came directly under him.'

'Is he still alive?'

Wiesenthal said slowly, 'Sometime after the war a grave was found in a cemetery in Germany. The tombstone had his name and details on it. But when the authorities exhumed the coffin it was found to contain the bones of *three* different people.' He looked at McQuade. 'None of those bones were Heinrich Muller's.'

'So he faked his death.'

'Or somebody did so on his behalf.'

'So where did he go? Is that known?'

Wiesenthal said slowly, 'To Russia.'

McQuade was amazed. 'Russia? . . . But the Russians were arch-enemies of the Nazis.'

Wiesenthal sat down again and said quietly, 'It is thought that after Hitler's suicide, Muller went over to the Russians in the last days of the war . . .'

McQuade knew that wasn't true. Because Horst Kohler had him aboard U-boat 1093. Why would the Russians accept the man? 'Do you believe that?'

Wiesenthal said quietly, 'Have you ever heard of the "*Rote Kapelle*"? The Red Orchestra?'

McQuade had not. 'No?' Wiesenthal said woodenly. 'It is a known fact that there was a spy in Hitler's bunker. The Gestapo knew that radio transmissions were going to the Russians. Within hours of a decision being made in Hitler's bunker, the Russians knew about it — troop movements, strategies, and so on. The Gestapo called it the Red Orchestra. They scoured Berlin, looking for the illegal radio. With their specialized equipment they narrowed the source down to the area around Hitler's chancellory itself. The only radio in Germany which the Gestapo did not control was that of Martin Bormann, Hitler's right-hand man, which was used only to keep in touch with Nazi Party offices.' Wiesenthal raised his eyebrows. 'So? So who was the best person to fool the whole Gestapo with an illegal radio? Or to use a *legal* radio for *il*legal transmission? SS General Heinrich Muller himself?'

McQuade did not believe it. Any radio operator who was left alone for ten minutes could have done it. 'But Muller and his Gestapo were responsible for hunting down communists too, weren't they?'

'Yes.'

'So why should he defect to the Russians? Did Muller have access to Hitler's bunker?'

'Yes. And through Himmler, his boss, who was chief of the entire SS, which included the Gestapo.'

'But would he have known Hitler's secret decision-making process?'

Wiesenthal hadn't taken his eyes off him. 'Probably not.'

'So if Muller was the Red Orchestra, he must have had an accomplice who *was* plugged into Hitler's decisions?' He shook his head. 'Maybe Martin Bormann himself was the Red Orchestra. He had a sacrosanct radio, you say.'

Wiesenthal said with a twitch of a smile:

'So, you are an intelligent man, Mr McQuade.' He lifted his finger. 'There is another theory, that both Bormann *and*

Muller were Russian spies. *Both* disappeared from the bunker when Berlin fell.' He paused, smiling lightly. 'But it seems even more unlikely that Martin Bormann, Hitler's right-hand man, who had made the Nazi Party his whole career and who was notorious in his persecution of Jews and communists – it is even more unlikely that *he* was the Russian spy. Most historical experts agree that Martin Bormann probably was killed whilst trying to escape with other senior officials from Hitler's bunker in the Russian bombardment of Berlin – whereas Heinrich Muller is last heard of a day *before*, disappearing from the bunker.' Wiesenthal raised his old eyebrows. 'If Bormann was the spy, why would he wait till the very end, when he could have joined his Russian friends days earlier? So that leaves Muller as the suspect. Hmm?'

McQuade was fascinated. But he did not want to believe it. If this were true there was probably no loot on that submarine. 'Do you believe it, Doctor Wiesenthal?'

The grand old man smiled at him widely for the first time. 'I am a detective, Mr McQuade. I believe nothing until I see conclusive evidence. But it is very obvious that *you* don't believe it.'

The old man was seeing through him. McQuade blundered on: 'Has he been *seen*, since those days forty-odd years ago?'

Wiesenthal did not blink. 'Mr McQuade, in my job I daily receive letters from many people saying they have seen this criminal and that. Even ones we know are long since dead.'

'And have you investigated these reports about Muller?'

Wiesenthal smiled. 'I do not have the resources of the CIA. I have investigated the reports which – ' he rubbed his fingertips together – ' give me that feeling in my fingers.'

McQuade blundered on, 'But can you tell me when you received the last report?'

Wiesenthal shrugged hopelessly and shook his head.

'Were you given the name he was using?'

Wiesenthal looked at him with a little smile.

'Unfortunately not. Can you tell me why you're so interested in my dear old friend Heinrich Muller?'

McQuade sat back. 'Just for my book.' He smiled self-consciously.

Wiesenthal nodded. 'For your book, of course . . . And is this book fact or fiction, Mr McQuade?'

'I haven't decided yet. I've only just started my research.'

Nod, nod, nod. 'And what have your researches produced? Very little has been published about my old friend Heinrich Muller.'

'That's why I've come to see you.'

'To ask for a *recent* photograph? So you *too* think Heinrich Muller is still alive?' He smiled. Then he rubbed his fingertips together. 'I have that feeling in my fingers, again.' His eyebrows went up. 'I think you know something you must tell me, Mr McQuade . . .'

McQuade insisted, 'Only what I've read.'

Simon Wiesenthal smiled. 'That feeling in my fingers, Mr McQuade . . . I am seldom wrong.' He raised his old eyebrows and smiled: 'And it is your solemn human duty to tell me what you have found out, Mr McQuade . . . Your *duty* to mankind. You must help me to do justice, Mr McQuade.'

'Of course I would.'

'*Good!* Thank you! So tell me, hmm?' He smiled.

McQuade tried to sigh. 'I have nothing to tell, Doctor.'

Wiesenthal shook his old head. Then suddenly he scowled. 'I *want* this Heinrich Muller! I want him, I *want* him!' He paused, glaring. 'So you must *tell* me what is in your head! So I can pay my friend Heinrich Muller a little visit!' He paused again. Then suddenly his scowl vanished benignly. 'Do you mind showing me your passport, please?'

McQuade was taken aback. 'Certainly.' He produced it.

The old man took it politely. He leafed through it.

'It says here your profession is marine biologist.'

'Yes, but I have my own deep-sea trawler.'

'Ah. And where do you fish?'

McQuade winced inwardly. But he had known these questions might be asked, it had been a calculated risk and there was probably no point in lying because the man could easily check up on him, but it was worth a try. 'Off the South African coast. But I have business interests in Australia and South America.'

'Ah, a businessman too.' Wiesenthal put the passport on his desk. 'You must not think me rude for asking such questions, but your request for a recent photograph of Heinrich Muller is an unusual one.' He let that hang, then he called to the secretaries' office, *'Bring me the Heinrich Muller file, please.'*

McQuade's heart leapt. He had succeeded! And obviously Muller was alive!

A pretty girl brought in a big box-file. The old man took it and sat there, apparently thinking deeply. Then he tapped the file lovingly.

'So, okay, I make a little deal with you, Captain . . .' He opened the file, and admired it. 'You tell me what you know. And I will show you a photograph of Herr Heinrich Muller.'

So the old boy was using a carrot. 'I know nothing that is not in the library.'

Wiesenthal sighed theatrically. He stood up, and called, 'Come take the Muller file, please.' He turned to McQuade. 'Pity. I have some good photographs. And other information valuable to an author.'

McQuade stood up worriedly. *He wanted that photograph!* 'Doctor Wiesenthal?'

The old man looked at his watch. 'No more questions, please.' The girl entered and Wiesenthal gave her the file.

McQuade said urgently, 'Will you tell me when the photograph was taken?'

Wiesenthal turned innocently and put his hand on McQuade's shoulder. 'And now, Captain,' he smiled, 'I must do some work. Thank you for calling.'

McQuade sighed with frustration.

'Okay, Doctor Wiesenthal. It's a deal.'

Wiesenthal smiled kindly at him.

'*Good*.' He called: 'Bring back the Muller file, please . . .'

He wasn't going to tell the old fox the whole truth. Not until he'd got the loot out of that submarine. Then he would gladly tell Simon Wiesenthal everything, do everything to catch Heinrich Muller and put him on an Israeli scaffold. He told Wiesenthal what he had told Frau Kohler, and what the good woman had told him. He stuck rigidly to his story that he was only writing a book.

Wiesenthal listened intently, without interruption but scribbling notes. When McQuade finished, he said,

'Why didn't you tell me all this at the outset?'

'Because I did not want the story getting out. Then any journalist could write about it before me.'

'Ah. A scoop.' Wiesenthal nodded understandingly. 'And where on the Argentinian coast was this supposed to have happened?'

'I don't know. I met Paco and Fernando in Rio de Janeiro. They simply said it happened in the south.'

Wiesenthal picked up the passport again. He leafed through it. 'Have you got a Brazilian immigration stamp?'

McQuade was ready for this one. 'No, I was crewing in the Cape Town to Rio yacht race. Crew didn't get stamped.'

'I see. And you could find this Paco and Fernando again?'

'I doubt it. They were off a fishing trawler.'

'Could you recognize them again?'

McQuade shook his head. 'Possibly. It was a dark bar. They wore beards. Spanish-looking.'

'And why did you buy the wallet and the tag?'

'I was fascinated by the story.'

'And why did you take the trouble to find Frau Kohler?'

'The story. And to return a sentimental souvenir.'

'Although you didn't even know if she was alive? Quite an expense?'

'It's quite a story. And I was due for a holiday.'

'But the initials H.M. meant nothing to you?'

'No. It was only *after* Frau Kohler told me her story that I decided to research into Heinrich Muller.' He sighed. 'May I please see the photograph?'

'And what have you done about the submarine?'

McQuade's heart missed a beat. He frowned. 'The submarine? I don't even know where it is.'

'It's off the coast of Argentina.'

'That's a hell of a long coast.' He paused. 'It might not have sunk. Maybe it only put two men ashore.'

'Who fought to the death, and the submarine is officially listed as missing? You're not interested?' He added hastily, suddenly disarming, 'Forgive me but I must examine your evidence carefully. That's my job.'

'Of course,' McQuade said stiffly.

'And if we have a deal, I must get my money's worth.' Wiesenthal stroked the file affectionately. 'If I was writing this story, I'd be very interested in the whereabouts of this submarine, and what else Herr Muller left behind inside it when it sank . . .'

McQuade's pulse tripped. The old boy had read him like a book. God, he'd been a fool! He forced a smile.

'But as we'll never know, maybe I should write the book as fiction.'

'Hmm, maybe so . . .' Wiesenthal stroked his chin in solemn agreement, then heaved himself to his feet, as if out of a reverie. He glanced at his watch. 'Excuse me one moment.' He walked out with the file.

McQuade picked up his passport. After a minute Wiesenthal returned, still with the file. He held out his hand. 'Well, I wish you luck with your book.'

'May I see the photograph, please.' It was not a question.

Wiesenthal held up a finger, as if remembering. 'Ah, yes . . . Oh, I'm sorry, Mr McQuade,' he said with great sincerity, 'but we have no recent photograph of SS General Heinrich Muller.'

McQuade glared at him. 'You tricked me.'

Simon Wiesenthal's shoulders rose expressively. 'Tricks, schmicks, I never said I had a recent photograph of the man. If you feel tricked, I am sorry, and can only say I do not care if I have to play little tricks to get evidence against war-criminals. As long as the evidence is trustworthy, and I'm afraid your evidence is only partly trustworthy. Indeed, you tried to trick *me*.'

'It's the truth!' McQuade said shamelessly.

Wiesenthal's old eyes were amused. 'So, what does it matter to you? You have now decided to write fiction. Why does a fiction writer need to know what an old Nazi war-criminal looks like? So' – he shrugged – 'write anything you like, and good luck to you.'

McQuade was furious. 'You old rogue.'

Wiesenthal shrugged, with a twinkle. 'Oh yes. Ask Adolf Eichmann, God rest his soul.' Then he tapped McQuade on the shoulder conspiratorially. 'You be frank with me, Captain, and I'll be frank with you . . .' He gave his old Jewish smile, waited a moment, then held out his hand, 'Well, unless you have something more to tell me . . .'

McQuade wasn't going to fall for those theatrics again. 'I've told you everything, Doctor.'

Simon Wiesenthal looked at him, then he sighed, resigned. 'Captain, you asked for a *recent* photograph? Well, I have only this.' He flicked through the box-file and pulled out a photograph.

McQuade took it, his hopes soaring.

It was a black-and-white photograph of a man in uniform. He was smiling faintly, directly at the camera. A thickset man in his late thirties? Eyes and eyebrows dark. A handsome man. A strong jaw with very thin lips.

'Thank you,' McQuade said sincerely. 'May I keep this?'

'Yes. I have copies.'

'But is this the most recent photograph you have?'

'Taken in 1943, I believe. Now, if there's anything else you can tell me about this matter, it is your duty to do so. Your duty to mankind . . .' The old blue Jewish eye held the blue Gentile eye.

'I've told you everything, Doctor.'

Wiesenthal smiled. 'Then I wish you a safe journey.'

22

McQuade hurried down the street looking for a taxi, agitated that he had let the cat out of the bag. So, he had a photograph of Heinrich Muller, but where was that going to get him? Was he going to look for him? Right now he was after the man's loot, not his odious person. He had learnt that Muller did not die in the last days of the war, so what Horst Kohler told his wife was probably correct, and so there might be a lot more loot in that submarine than Muller had swum ashore with – but so what? The loot was either there or it was not, regardless of what he had learned from Wiesenthal, and the price he had paid for the information! The old fox had seen right through him, sniffed out his intentions, tricked him, and cross-examined him into a corner like a lawyer. God, he'd been a fool! He should have thought it all through before rushing to Wiesenthal. The very thing he had been afraid of had happened! He looked back to see if he was being followed. There were people everywhere.

He came to the Danube Canal. Several taxis were approaching. He waved and ran. '*Bahnhof, bitte.*' He scrambled in and looked through the rear window. There were cars and people everywhere. He slumped back and sighed furiously.

Of course Wiesenthal would have him followed. Wiesenthal knew that *he* knew more about Muller – and Wiesenthal wanted Muller. Although Wiesenthal wasn't a treasure-hunter he'd be very interested in whatever was in that submarine: documents, evidence of Muller's intentions, evidence about other war-criminals. McQuade seethed.

For one thing Wiesenthal could now have him rolled,

waylaid by his heavies, his arm twisted until he told them the truth.

That wouldn't be Wiesenthal's style? Wiesenthal would be opposed to violence? McQuade snorted. He did not believe for one moment that the man had no 'muscle'. He was dedicated to catching the most evil bastards the world has ever seen. How could he be squeamish in that job? What are a few twisted arms compared to the suffering of five million Jews? And if he didn't have heavies, Mossad certainly did, and Mossad *certainly* wouldn't be squeamish. And Wiesenthal would certainly call in Mossad to find Heinrich Muller and that submarine. And that meant following James McQuade.

Oh, Jesus, Mossad . . .

By the time the taxi dropped him at the railway station, however, he had calmed down.

Okay, so he had made a fuck-up. Now, he must assume he was being followed. So he had to shake these people off. That was going to be hard in Vienna, a town he did not know, unable to speak the language properly.

He had to go to London to use his return air-ticket to South Africa. He retrieved his bag from the locker and went to the public telephones. He consulted the directory, then dialled Thomas Cook's, and asked about flights to London.

There were several flights, and plenty of seats. He did not make a reservation in case Wiesenthal's boys had access to airline computers. Use your goddam head for a change, McQuade.

At the airport he waited till the last moment to buy his ticket. In the departure room he went into the toilet and deliberately missed his flight. When he emerged the room was empty. He retraced his steps to the main departure lounge, told the girl at the information desk about his upset stomach and asked to be put on the next flight to London. He was the last person to enter the plane. At London's Gatwick airport he remained seated until the aircraft was empty. There was nobody lurking in the airport's corridors on the way to Immigration.

He rented a car, wincing at the cost. He drove out of the airport complex, down the highway, until he came to a roundabout. He noted the cars in his rear-view mirror, and slowly circled the roundabout. Where he came to the third exit, two cars were behind him. He passed the last exit and drove on around. He looked back. Both cars had gone. He sighed in relief, and swung back towards the airport.

He took the first road into countryside, and drove past farms, scattered houses, thickets. A woodsy pub called the Fox and Rabbit, its lights twinkling. It also had a *Bed & Breakfast* sign. There were a few cars behind him. He turned down a winding secondary road, then stopped. He waited five minutes. Only a motor cycle came and disappeared into the dusk. He drove back to the pub.

He ordered a pint of beer and went to the public telephone. He called British Airways, asked about flights to Johannesburg. Yes, there was plenty of space on all flights. He did not make a reservation.

He returned to the bar and drank his beer.

Unless he was badly mistaken, he was not being followed. So, maybe he'd misjudged Simon Wiesenthal. Maybe he had been dismissed as a total fraud. Maybe he could relax.

Wrong. The old man had got intensely interested. 'I *want* him, I *want* him . . .' 'It is your *duty* to mankind to tell me . . .' The tricks. No, Wiesenthal clearly did not think Heinrich Muller was dead, and Simon Wiesenthal would not risk letting a big fish like that slip through his fingers by failing to put a tail on Dumbo McQuade.

But how had he given them the slip so easily? Yet nobody had followed him to this pub. He had to assume that Wiesenthal's boys would be watching for him at all airports.

He ordered another beer from the barmaid, a handsome blonde Scandinavian. 'Can I have a room for the night?'

'Certainly can. What's the name?'

'McGregor,' McQuade said.

He thought of flying to South Africa under a false name, but his return ticket was in the name of McQuade. At the check-in counter they check your ticket against the reservation. Nor could he get a refund and buy a new one in a false name because they check your ticket against your passport at the check-in counter.

God, he'd been a fool to visit Wiesenthal.

Well, maybe he could turn his foolishness to advantage. Why not make a reservation to Argentina in the name of McQuade, for three days hence, to give Wiesenthal's boys plenty of time to find out about it, assuming they had access to airlines' computers. Then they'd be watching for him that day at that airline's desk. Meanwhile, slip out to South Africa!

Sheer genius. And take that one step better by making the reservation to South America via *Israel*. London to Tel Aviv – that looked as if he was doing more research on Heinrich Muller – then Tel-Aviv to Buenos Aires on El Al. Wiesenthal would definitely get that message. Mossad definitely had access to El Al's computers.

Very good, McQuade . . . Do that tomorrow.

And there was something else he would do tomorrow: go to the Imperial War Museum, and try to read up about the loot the Nazis had plundered in Europe. Maybe he'd find out what loot Muller himself plundered. Find out more about this Strasbourg Conference of German industrialists in 1944 to rebuild 'a strong Fourth Reich'. Maybe Heinrich Muller's submarine had a role in that. And find out something about Heinrich Muller himself. How old he was, for example, and what specific crimes he committed. In fact, some of the questions he had failed to ask Wiesenthal. Any clues – that was what he had come to Europe for.

23

The next morning confirmed that he had not been followed. Not a soul was to be seen on the country road. He turned onto the major road to London. There was little traffic this early. He watched his rear-mirror. Isolated cars overtook him. None appeared to be following him.

Nevertheless, he would make the fake reservation to Buenos Aires. That cost nothing. He drove into the outskirts of London, and with great difficulty found the Hertz depot. He returned the car and set off for the underground station. People were hurrying to work through the drizzle.

First he telephoned British Airways and established there was space on their flight to Johannesburg that evening. He did not make a reservation. Then he telephoned El Al airline. He made a reservation for James McQuade on their flight three days hence to Tel Aviv, and another reservation two days later from Tel Aviv to Buenos Aires.

It was probably a waste of time, but he might as well carry it one step further. He had thought this one up last night on his second bottle of wine, before talking the barmaid into bed. He telephoned the Israeli Embassy.

'My name is James McQuade. I'm flying to Tel Aviv in three days time, to do some research into the Holocaust. I'm particularly interested in Heinrich Muller, once head of the Gestapo. Now, is there a library in Israel which specializes in this information?'

'There certainly is, sir.'

Five minutes later he hung up, almost convinced that he really should go to Israel. Well, if Wiesenthal's boys enquired, they'd certainly get that message.

He consulted a map of the London underground system, then bought a ticket to Sloane Square and waited for the next Circle Line train.

The rush hour was over. Only two people got into the half-full carriage with him. He settled down to see if anybody stayed on the carriage with him, all the way round the circle, back to Sloane Square.

By the time the train was half way round all the original passengers had left, so that when the train got back to Sloane Square he was absolutely satisfied he was not being followed.

It was only eleven o'clock. He asked at the ticket office how to get to the Imperial War Museum, and was sold a ticket to Elephant and Castle. He emerged from the bleak underground into the bleak rain.

He walked up the steps into the Imperial War Museum, and asked the receptionist, 'May I use the library, please?'

'What subject are you researching, sir?'

'The Gestapo. In particular, Heinrich Muller.'

An old uniformed attendant creaked him upwards in an old elevator, then escorted him down corridors, up stairs and into the library in the big sepulchral Victorian dome. There were a dozen people researching at curved tables.

The librarian already had half a dozen books waiting for him. McQuade sat down and started reading the fly-leaves. Within ten minutes he knew he would not be catching tonight's flight.

None of the books was specifically about Heinrich Muller, but about the Gestapo and the Nazi Party. He turned to the index at the back of each and looked for Muller's name. There were many page references.

The first volume was called *The Encyclopaedia of the Third Reich* by L. L. Snyder. He found the appropriate page.

MULLER, HEINRICH. Chief of the Gestapo and leading administrator in mass killing operations. *Gruppenführer* (Lieut. Gen.) Heinrich Muller was . . . one of the fifteen top-ranking Nazi bureaucrats present at the Wannsee Conference on January 20, 1942, when the Final Solution to the Jewish question was arranged ... In 1942 Himmler decided to make his concentration camps *Judenrein* (Jew free), and delegated much of the responsibility for the task to Muller. In January 1943 Muller rounded up 45,000 Jews from the Netherlands, 3,000 from Berlin, 30,000 from Bialystok ghetto, and 10,000 from Theresienstadt, to be deported to Auschwitz for extermination. In June 1943 he was sent by Himmler to Rome to ascertain why and how Italian Jews were escaping arrest. In the summer of 1944, when the German frontiers were being breached in both east and west, Muller, at Himmler's orders, took terrible vengeance. He sent huge transports of Jews to Auschwitz and the gas chambers ...

In the final days of the Third Reich Muller was present in the *Führerbunker* (Hitler's Bunker) .... By now Muller was almost independent of Himmler, and made no secret of his ambition to succeed his superior officer. For some years after the war it was assumed that Muller had been killed when the Russians encircled Berlin. Later he was reported to be in Brazil and Argentina, where he was said to be an 'enforcer' among escaped SS criminals ... He was placed on a list of most-wanted Nazis.

McQuade felt a flash of self-satisfaction. This confirmed that Muller had not defected to the Russians. But only James McQuade knew that he had gone to South West Africa, at least in the first instance.

He turned to the next book, *Who's Who in Nazi Germany*, by Robert Wistrich. He read:

MULLER, HEINRICH. Head of the Gestapo ... Adolf Eichmann's immediate superior, responsible for implementing the 'Final Solution' ... During World War I he served as a flight leader on the eastern front and was awarded the Iron

Cross (First Class). After the war, the ambitious Muller made his career in the Bavarian police, specializing in the surveillance of Communist Party functionaries and making a special study of Soviet Russian police methods . . . The stubborn, self-opinionated Muller was highly regarded by both Himmler and Heydrich, who admired his professional competence, blind obedience and willingness to execute 'delicate missions' . . . spying on colleagues and despatching political adversaries without scruples . . . The model of the cold, dispassionate Police Chief and the bureaucratic fanatic, Muller was rapidly promoted . . .

As head of *Amt* IV (Gestapo) . . . Muller was more directly involved in the 'Final Solution of the Jewish Question' than even his superiors, Heydrich, Himmler and Kaltenbrunner . . . Until the end of the war, Heinrich Muller continued his remorseless prodding of subordinates to greater efforts in sending Jews to Auschwitz. In his hands, mass murder became an automatic administrative procedure. Muller exhibited a similar streak in his treatment of Russian prisoners of war and gave the order to shoot British officers who had escaped from detention, near Breslau, at the end of March 1944. Muller's whereabouts at the end of the war are still shrouded in mystery. He was last seen in the *Führerbunker* on 28 April, 1945, after which he disappeared. There were persistent rumours that he had defected to the East . . . either to Moscow, Albania or to East Germany. Other uncorroborated reports also placed him in Latin America.

There were several books on the Gestapo. McQuade looked for Muller's name in the indexes. He was looking for personal information about the man, his personality, habits, his family history, significant incidents in his life – anything that would give him clues about the man he might be looking for, what he might be doing now. It was not his intention to make a study of the whole history of the Gestapo and the Holocaust, but, by the time the library closed, that was what he was doing, and he knew it would be at least a week before he flew back to South Africa. At five o'clock he left the library with his bag and a big sheaf of notes and pages he had had photostatted.

He took the underground to Tottenham Court Road. He bought a cheap pocket-size tape-recorder. He went into Foyle's bookshop, asked what was available on German submarines and bought *The Type VII C U-boat*, by David Westwood. Then he took the underground to Earls Court and started looking for a cheap hotel. It took him an hour to find that there were no cheap hotels in London any more, but in a newsagent's window, amongst the cards of Monique and Miss Cane, he saw a bed-sitter advertised. He found a public telephone and rented it for one week, unseen. He bought a four-pack of beer and two bottles of wine and moved in. He settled down at the table, spread out his notes and photostats. He had to summarize his notes, to try to get a clear profile of Muller.

He picked up the pages he had photostatted from *Gestapo, Instrument of Tyranny*, by Edward Crankshaw, and re-read them.

Muller did his job, while Berlin rocked, shuddered, and disintegrated . . . and Hitler prepared himself for the end. Then . . . the chief of the Gestapo vanished – whether to die in the streets of Berlin, to escape under an assumed identity to Austria or Spain or the Argentine, or to join the Russians he admired so much, we do not know . . . For some time he had been using captured Russian agents to communicate false intelligence to the Soviet armies, using their own codes and their own wireless sets; and it would have been entirely possible for him to enter into detailed communication with the enemy by this means without anyone being the wiser. Be that as it may, like a perfect civil servant, he went, leaving not a trace, his files totally destroyed.

He turned to an earlier passage.

Muller . . . will repeatedly appear by name in these pages.
But we shall never meet him. He was the archetype of
non-political functionary, in love with personal power and
dedicated to . . . the State. He worked anonymously . . .
We find his signature on orders authorizing the most atro-
cious deeds. We glimpse him once or twice in action, and
are surprised to discover that this man without a shadow,
this office bureaucrat, could walk about and use a gun. But
we know nothing about him, neither where he came from
nor where he went. Even his subordinate, Eichmann, the
murderer of the Jews, who never on any account put his
signature to a document, left behind friends and acquain-
tances who have given us vivid glimpses of the man. Muller left nobody. We see him lunching at the Adlon Hotel
with Heydrich, Nebe, Schellenberg, later with Kaltenbrunner. They are all dead.

McQuade sighed and opened another can of beer. He sifted
through his notes, then began to dictate into his recorder:
'Heinrich Muller. Bavarian. Square head. Short, stocky,
heavy. Considered good-looking, with hard face, often
expressionless. Large forehead, piercing flickering brown
eyes. Heavy eyelids. Very thin lips. Short neat hair. Large
strong hands, fingers.
'Joined Munich police as ordinary detective. Worked his
way up to top by hard work. A good bureaucrat. Very stubborn. Self-opinionated. Expert policeman. Great energy. No
scruples. Great believer in force and fear. Highly efficient,
cold police boss. Very ambitious. Very jealous of his power.
Distrusted others. Blindly obedient to Himmler (Chief of
entire SS, which included Gestapo) and Heydrich (head of
S.D.) and Hitler. Frequently visited Hitler's bunker to see
Martin Bormann, Hitler's right-hand man. Officially Muller
was fifth in the chain of command (Hitler – Bormann –

Himmler – Heydrich – Muller): but eventually he became the second most powerful man in Germany after Himmler because Nazi Germany was a police state with Muller as its chief.'

McQuade paused. He sorted through his mosaic of notes, trying to marshal his facts.

'The SS (*Schutzstaffel* or Protective Force) duplicated every branch of the civil service and dominated every aspect of life, even the army. Gestapo was the spearhead of the SS. "Gestapo" is acronym for *Geheime Staatspolizei* (Secret Police). It was the Nazis' instrument of terror. Hitler decreed that the Gestapo was above the law. No appeal. Only the Gestapo had the power to send people to the concentration camps and death camps: therefore Heinrich Muller was ultimately responsible for the entire Holocaust. Torture always preceded interrogation. Afterwards the victim went to death camps or concentration camps. Frequent executions by shooting or hanging. Standard torture was crushing testicles: a special machine was invented. Other standard Gestapo procedures included electrocution through genitals and anus, wrist-crushing, wrist-hanging, flogging, burning, icy baths. Terror was Gestapo's standard procedure. Muller developed a spy system which made every individual feel it was impossible to trust anybody else – ordinary citizens were made honorary Gestapo members, informing on everything everybody else did. Thus giving impression that Gestapo omniscient. Giant filing system for all Europe, tabulating secrets of millions of people. This terror was typified by so-called *Nacht und Nebel* Decree of 1942 (Night and Fog Decree) in terms of which suspects were immediately executed or vanished into the "night and fog" of Germany, never to return. Vast terror and destruction. In all, Heinrich Muller and his Gestapo were responsible for the execution of eleven million people.'

It was almost midnight. He threw himself on the bed.

Good God . . . Eleven *million* people . . .

About twice the population of New Zealand. Two thirds

the population of Australia. And all their horrible deaths to be laid at the door of one man called 'Gestapo Muller'. And only James McQuade knew what had become of the bastard! And oh God, God, once he had cracked that submarine, he was going to find him if he was still alive. And see him stand on a scaffold.

24

The next three days passed in a fever of study that was much more intense than his cramming for his final university examinations, when he had lived off benzedrine for weeks in a last-ditch bid to defraud his professors. He read feverishly, and with mounting horror and astonishment, of the bestiality of man, and he was amazed that he had not been taught all this at school, that amongst his contemporaries such appalling recent history was relegated to the mists of time with no relevance to today. McQuade had come to this library to research details relevant to Nazi plunder which might be in a sunken German submarine. He ended up reading with fascinated horror about a holocaust the likes of which mankind has never seen – and his submarine was way off in the background. Each morning he was at the Imperial War Museum when it opened. Each evening he left with a stack of notes and photostatted pages, bought a four-pack of beer, a bottle of wine and a can of bully-beef, and hurried back to his bed-sitter to synthesize his notes onto his tape-recorder. But these dictations were no longer simply a quest for clues about Heinrich Muller. They became a quest for a coherent understanding of the most horrific piece of history man has ever known. He dictated, summarizing almost verbatim from *The Encyclopaedia of the Third Reich*:

'Social Darwinism had intensified anti-semitism in the nineteenth and twentieth centuries. Hitler espoused all these pseudoscientific theories in his book *Mein Kampf* (My Struggle) – sold over five million copies, made him a millionaire – which became blueprint for Nazi Party. Germany was in a bad economic state after her defeat in World War I. Hitler exploited anti-semitism for political purposes.

'Hitler said Germans were naturally superior people and must become racially pure, to fulfil their natural destiny of world supremacy as the master-race with the highest culture. Nationality and race lay in the blood, he said, not in language. A Negro may learn perfect German but could never be German because of his blood. The mixture of blood in the Germans must be corrected by weeding out the contamination of lower elements. Therefore the state must keep the race clean, enforce modern birth control so no weak or diseased people breed children, teach "racial knowledge" in schools, prepare the German nation for future leadership.

'The real chosen people was the Aryan race, Hitler said, especially the Teutonic or German. The survival of mankind depended upon the survival of the Aryan race. Hitler said history shows that every mixture between Aryan race and lower races has resulted in downfall of the Aryan. South America is weak because the Aryan settlers miscegenated with non-Aryans.

'The Aryans are the genius race and the *founders* of civilization, races such as the Japanese copied the Aryans and became *bearers* of civilization, whereas other races, such as the Jews, were *destroyers* of civilization, Hitler said. The Jews' desire for self-preservation does not go beyond the individual, Jewish clannishness was only a "very primitive instinct", "nakedly egotistic". Jews do not have a real culture, they have always only borrowed from others and have no idealism. Hence Jews are parasites, making a state within a state. The Jewish spirit was working for the ruin of Germany, Hitler said. Quote: "The black-haired Jewish youth waits for hours with satanic joy in his eyes for the unsuspecting Aryan girls, whom he shames with his blood and thereby robs the nation. He seeks to destroy the racial characteristics of the Germans with every means at his command ... to destroy the hated white races through bastardization, to tumble them from their cultural and political heights and to raise themselves to the vacant place." He said the evil of Marxism was also attributable to the Jews who wanted to destroy "the national bearers of intelligence and make slaves of the land." Therefore the elimination of the Jewish danger was a life and death struggle for Germany and the entire world . . .'

McQuade sifted through his photostatted pages, looking for another passage out of the *Encyclopaedia*. He re-read it, then dictated it almost verbatim onto his tape:

'This Nazi doctrine that the fate of a nation depends on racial purity, has no scientific basis . . . Leading anthropologists agree that the juxtaposition of races has resulted in an inextricable tangle in which it is impossible to find a pure race. World society is a melting pot composed of energetic mongrels. There never was an Aryan race, but there were Aryan languages. There was no Roman race, but there was a Roman civilization. There never was a Jewish race but there is a Jewish religion or culture. In the biological sense a race is a group of related inter-marrying individuals, a population that differs from other populations in the relative similarities of certain hereditary traits, of which colour is only one characteristic. In the political sense, race is meaningless fraud . . . In the Third Reich an entire nation was forced to accept the intuitions of a badly educated politician whose theories on racial matters actually belonged in a theatre of the absurd.

'Hitler became Chancellor in 1933 and immediately persecution of Jews began. Jews were boycotted. New laws dismissed Jews from the civil service, government, universities, hospitals, from all cultural life and they were forbidden to engage in certain industries and trades. Jewish shops were smashed and synagogues vandalized. In 1935 the Nuremberg Laws withdrew citizenship from Jews. With these laws racialism became the legal basis of a modern nation for the first time . . .'

McQuade put down his tape-recorder. He ripped the top off his last can of beer.

And the second modern nation to do it was South Africa?

He stood up and began to pace across the room.

Yes, what South Africa had done also belonged in a theatre of the absurd. Had not it espoused a similar racial doctrine when it embarked on the road of Apartheid?

McQuade gave a sigh. Yes, but no. God knew that he had no reason to argue in favour of the South African government; and God knew it was true that the South Africans had legislated that non-whites were second-class citizens, deprived of their rights to vote, not allowed to work where they liked, to live where they liked, to marry whom they liked, to educate themselves where they liked, to eat, drink, swim, picnic, forgather, visit, stroll, sit on a bus or train where they liked. True that this not only belonged in a theatre of the absurd but was appallingly unjust and cruelly humiliating. Truly it was stupid politics. But there the similarity ended. What the South Africans embarked upon was nothing like the mind-blowing madness that made the Germans follow Hitler down the horrific road to Hell.

He returned to the table and picked up his recorder.

'Hitler banned all opposition political parties, and made himself dictator, his concentration camps filled with anybody the Gestapo considered undesirable. In 1938, an official at the German embassy in Paris was assassinated by a young Jew called Grynszpan to protest Nazi treatment of Jews, to which the Nazis retaliated with the *Kristallnacht* pogrom, the "Night of the Broken Glass" when the Gestapo ordered party thugs on a rampage. They smashed and looted 7,500 Jewish shops, and destroyed 177 synagogues. Hitler publicly warned: "If international-finance Jewry . . . should succeed once more in plunging nations into another world war, the consequence will be . . . the annihilation of the Jews in Europe".

'In 1939 Hitler declared war on Poland. Britain declared war on Germany. Hitler's armies rapidly conquered Norway,

Holland, Belgium, France. In 1941, Hitler declared war on Russia. Now Hitler unfolds his "Final Solution of the Jewish Question."'

McQuade opened the wine. He had no glass, so he lifted the bottle to his mouth. Now came the really mind-blowing part of his research. And he was amazed all over again at how ignorant he had been. He sifted through his notes, getting his information in sequence, then slowly he began:

'This Final Solution had two arms of extermination. One: the *Einsatzgruppen*. Two: the Extermination Camps.

'The *Einsatzgruppen* were special commandos who followed the German army's invasion of Russia, and their sole job was to carry out genocide of the Jews. There were four *Einsatzgruppen*, A, B, C and D, a total of 3,500 men. And they were formed by our friend Heinrich Muller and were under the Gestapo. Their modus operandi was as follows:

'After the German army had successfully occupied an area, the *Einsatzgruppen* arrived. Suitable execution sites were immediately prepared. These required a killing-pit which either had to be dug by Jews, or already existed as anti-tank ditches or natural depressions in the earth. The Jews in the surrounding conquered towns and villages were then ordered to assemble, then marched or driven off to the execution site, where they were ordered to strip, place their belongings in separate piles, and then queue up naked. In batches of about twenty they were then ordered to file into the grave and lie down in a line. They were machine-gunned. A soldier then walked through the bodies, shooting anybody still alive. The next batch of Jews was then ordered to file into the grave and lie down on the bodies of the last lot. They were then shot. And so on. Day in, day out. New killing-pit graves were concurrently prepared, depending on the size of the population to be killed. When a grave was full, it was covered in earth by Jewish conscripts who were thereafter shot. However, graves were often left unfilled overnight and there are a number of cases of wounded Jews struggling out from under the bloody corpses and crawling away. Some are alive today to tell their tale.

'When the entire Jewish population in a given area was killed, the *Einsatzgruppen* packed their kitbags and moved on to the next area. With the benefit of experience, the Gestapo improved slightly on this system by devising "gas-mobiles": while most Jews were marched to their execution site, some were transported in specially designed sealed vans, into which the exhaust-fumes from the engine were pumped during the journey. This method usually took fifteen to twenty-five minutes to kill, and was only worthwhile if the drive to the execution site took that long, but had the merit that these people were dead on arrival and ready for the mass-grave except for the tedious business of stripping off their clothes. This was done by Jews who had arrived for their own execution on foot.'

McQuade searched through his papers for a photocopy of a document that had been presented at the Nuremberg trials by Sir Hartley Shawcross, for the prosecution. It was an affidavit by a German civilian called Graebe who was in charge of a building operation in Rovno.

'Shortly after ten p.m. the ghetto was encircled by a large SS detachment and Ukrainian militia. SS and militia squads entered the houses. Where the doors and windows were closed the SS men and militia broke the windows, forced the doors. Since the Jews in most cases resisted, the SS and militia applied force. They finally succeeded, with strokes of the whip, kicks, and blows from rifle butts, in clearing the houses. In the streets women cried out for their children, and children for their parents. That did not prevent the SS from driving the people along the road at running pace, and hitting them, until they reached a waiting freight train. Car after car was filled, and the screaming of women and children and the cracking of whips and rifle shots resounded unceasingly. All through the night these

197

beaten, hounded, and wounded people moved along the lighted streets. Women carried their dead children in their arms, children pulled and dragged their dead parents. I saw dozens of corpses of all ages and both sexes in the streets . . . At the corner of a house lay a baby, less than a year old, with its skull crushed. Blood and brains were spattered over the house wall . . .'

A few months later Herr Graebe witnessed a mass execution at a death-pit dug on an aerodrome where his building firm was operating. His affidavit continued:

'. . . an old woman with snow-white hair was holding this one-year-old child in her arms and singing and tickling it. The child was cooing with delight. The parents were looking on with tears in their eyes. The father was holding the hand of a boy about ten years old and speaking to him softly; the boy was fighting his tears. The father pointed towards the sky, stroked the boy's head, and seemed to explain something to him. At that moment the SS man at the pit shouted something to his comrade. The latter counted off about twenty persons and instructed them to go behind the earth mound. The family I have described was among them. I well remember the girl, slim with black hair, who, as she passed me, pointed and said, "Twenty-three years old".

'I then walked round the mound and found myself confronted by a tremendous grave. People were closely wedged together and lying on top of each other so that only their heads were visible. Nearly all had blood running over their shoulders from their heads. Some of the people shot were still moving. Some lifted their arms and turned their heads to show that they were alive. The pit was already two-thirds full. I estimated that it held a thousand people. I looked for the man who did the shooting. He was an SS man who sat at the edge of the pit, his feet dangling into it. He had a tommy-gun on his knees and was smoking a cigarette. The people – they were completely naked – went down some steps and clambered over the heads of those lying there to the place to which the SS man directed them. They lay down in front of the dead and wounded. Some caressed the living and spoke to them in a low voice. Then I heard a series of shots. I looked into the pit and saw that their bodies still twitched or that their heads lay motionless. Blood ran from their necks.

'I was surprised that I was not ordered off, but I saw that there were two or three postmen in uniform nearby. Already the next batch was approaching. They went down in the pit, lined themselves up against the previous victims and were shot. When I walked back round the mound I noticed that another truckload of people had arrived. This time it included sick and feeble people. An old, terribly thin woman was undressed by others, who were already naked, while two people held her up. The woman appeared to be paralysed. The naked people carried her round the mound. I left with my foreman. The next day, when I visited the site, I saw about thirty naked people lying near the pit . . . Some of them were still alive; they looked straight in front of them with a fixed stare and seemed to notice neither the chilliness of the morning nor the workers of my firm who stood around. A girl of about twenty spoke to me and asked me to give her clothes and help her to escape. At that moment we heard a fast car approach. I noticed that it was an SS detail. I moved away to my site. Ten minutes later we heard shots from the vicinity of the pit. Those Jews who were still alive had been ordered to throw the corpses into the pit, then they themselves had to lie down in the pit to be shot . . .'

McQuade took a deep breath. The climax of the ghastly story was the annihilation of the Warsaw Ghetto.

He rested his head in his hand. God. He had spent half the

day reading about the Warsaw Ghetto, it was such an epic horror-story, so mind-blowing in its wealth of evidence of man's dehumanization and relish of cruelty, that it was impossible to summarize briefly, but there was one detail he had to note. He found the photostatted pages he wanted, which he summarized flatly.

'The Warsaw Ghetto was established by the Nazis in 1940 as a holding place for Jews pending their transportation. The ghetto was walled off by the Nazis. It originally accommodated 400,000 Jews. Over two years, 300,000 were deported to various concentration camps for slave labour and to extermination camps. The remainder fiercely fought the SS troops. Finally Himmler ordered the SS to "clean out the ghetto with utter ruthlessness." SS General Stroop, who was in charge of the job, subsequently wrote a book called *The Warsaw Ghetto is No More*, after he had set fire to the ghetto. He wrote: "Jews ... frequently remained in the burning buildings and jumped out of the windows only when the heat became unbearable. Then they tried to crawl with broken bones across the street into buildings which were not afire ...

'"Countless numbers of Jews were liquidated in the sewers and bunkers through blasting. The longer the resistance continued ... the tougher became the members of the Waffen SS, Police and Wehrmacht, who always discharged their duties in an exemplary manner ... This action eliminated a proved total of 56,065. To that we have to add the number killed through blasting, which cannot be counted ....

'"The longer the resistance lasted the tougher the men of the Waffen SS became. They fulfilled their duty indefatigably in faithful comradeship and stood together as models and examples of soldiers. Their duty hours often lasted from early morning until late at night. At night search patrols with rags bound around their feet remained at the heels of the Jews and gave them no respite ... High credit should be given to the pluck, courage and devotion to duty which they showed

. . . Officers and men of the police, a large part of whom had already been at the front, again excelled by their dashing spirit."'

McQuade paused. Jesus: 'Dashing spirit'? 'Pluck, devotion to duty'?

He snapped off his recorder and got up. He collapsed on the bed and stared up at the ceiling.

Good God . . . And the swine he had stumbled upon was the very man who had organized these slaughter-men. The *very man* . . . And, by God, if the man was still alive, he was going to find him . . .

He was a little drunk and he had supped full of horrors. It was almost five o'clock in the morning and he was brittle with tiredness. But he could not leave this alone. He wanted to fly back to South Africa tonight if possible. He swung off the bed and returned to his table.

He grimly rearranged his notes, and began to summarize.

'In total these *Einsatzgruppen* killed two million people. Meanwhile, the other arm of the Final Solution, namely the extermination camps, had gone into operation.

'This had been formalized at the so-called Wannsee Conference, on 20th January, 1942, attended by Heinrich Muller and high-ranking Nazi officials. The "Final Solution of the Jewish Question" was that all remaining Jews would be rounded up and sent to concentration camps, to be used as slave labour in factories nearby the camps, where they would be worked to death. As they died of starvation and exhaustion they would be replaced by new arrivals who in turn would be worked to death. Those who survived this treatment would be gassed. Those Jews who were unfit for work on arrival at the camps would be gassed immediately. It was announced that "in the course of the execution of the Final Solution, Europe will be combed from west to east".

'The Gestapo were responsible for rounding up the Jews. The massive task of transporting them to the camps was given to Adolf Eichmann, with Heinrich Muller as his boss.

The chain of command for the Final Solution went: Hitler – Himmler – Muller – Eichmann.

'This extermination policy had already been in practice informally since 1941. Meanwhile, too, euthanasia schools had been established to train personnel in state-of-the-art genocide. They practised on mentally handicapped German people mostly, the theory being that if they could kill helpless fellow-Germans they would have no difficulties in mass-killing of Jews. Auschwitz-Birkenau was already in operation as a death camp. Now, in preparation for the Final Solution, the Gestapo (under Heinrich Muller) were building new extermination camps. Experiments at the euthanasia schools had shown that the best method of mass-killing was gas, but the problem was which gas was most efficient and most economical. The exhaust gas from old diesel engines was used, but this proved less than satisfactory because the diesels were often difficult to start up, despite German efficiency, which caused tiresome delays. Heinrich Muller was urged to investigate more efficient gases. Prussic acid, under the trade-name Cyclon B, was finally put into general use. These crystals, delivered by the manufacturers in convenient cans, were simply poured down vents into the gas chambers. When the victims were dead, squads of Jews, called *Sonderkommandos*, were sent in to drag the corpses out, collect gold teeth and jewellery, hose down the chamber, and take the bodies to the crematoria. Auschwitz was the most efficient of the death-camps, under the Commandant Franz Hoess; it could kill and cremate twelve thousand people a day.

'And so, the Final Solution got into top gear. Systematically German-occupied Europe was "combed from west to east" by Heinrich Muller's Gestapo, the Jews herded into ghettos pending Adolf Eichmann's trains to transport them to the extermination camps. It was a massive job. Because of the devotion to duty of Adolf Eichmann and his boss "Gestapo" Muller, the trainloads of Jews often arrived at the camps faster than the death-facilities could process them, and often the transport arrived with many of the Jews already dead.'

McQuade scratched through his photostatted pages for some vivid details of the inhuman conditions in these camps, to incorporate them into his notes. But there were so many that he gave up. How to annotate the screams of mothers for their children, the cries of children for their parents, the cracking of whips and the crashing of rifle-butts on helpless flesh and bone, the harsh 'Raus-raus', the herding of the helpless into the gas chambers, babies being thrown in on top, the slamming of the doors, the hissing of the gas, the choking, the terror? The heartbreak? McQuade gave a bitter sigh. He picked out pages containing the affidavit made by the commandant of Auschwitz, SS Colonel Hoess, which was used in evidence at the Nuremberg Trials. He shook his head. In its legal baldness it seemed to sum up the callousness better than he could.

'I, Rudolf Franz Ferdinand Hoess, being first duly sworn, depose and say as follows:

'I have been constantly associated with the administration of concentration camps since 1934 . . . I commanded Auschwitz until 1 December 1943, and estimate that at least 2,500,000 victims were executed and exterminated there by gassing and burning, and at least another half million succumbed to starvation and disease, making a total dead of about 3,000,000 . . . Included among the executed and burnt were approximately 20,000 Russian prisoners of war who were delivered at Auschwitz by regular Wehrmacht officers and men . . .

'I visited Treblinka to find out how they carried out their exterminations. The camp commandant told me that he had liquidated 80,000 in the course of one half-year . . . He used monoxide gas and I did not think that his methods were very efficient. So when I set up the extermination building at Auschwitz, I used Cyclon B, which was crystallized prussic acid, which we dropped into the death chamber from a small opening. It took from three to fifteen minutes to kill the people in the death chamber depending upon climatic conditions. We knew when the people were dead because their screaming stopped . . .

'Another improvement we made over Treblinka was that we built our gas chambers to accommodate 2,000 people at one time, whereas at Treblinka their ten gas chambers only accommodated 200 people each. The way we selected our victims was as follows: we had two SS doctors on duty at Auschwitz to examine the incoming transports of prisoners. The prisoners would be marched by one of the doctors who would make spot decisions as they walked by. Those who were fit for work were sent into the camp. Others were sent immediately to the extermination plants. Children of tender years were invariably exterminated since by reason of their youth they were unable to work. Still another improvement we made over Treblinka was that at Treblinka the victims almost always knew that they were to be exterminated and at Auschwitz we endeavoured to fool the victims into thinking that they were to go through a delousing process. Of course, frequently they realized our true intentions and we sometimes had riots and difficulties due to that fact. Very frequently women would hide their children under the clothes but of course when we found them we would send the children in to be exterminated . . .'

McQuade took a deep breath. Jesus . . . *And Jesus, Jesus, Jesus again* . . . What can you say about people like that? The mind grapples and fails. Hoess gave evidence at the Nuremberg trials and he was asked: 'Did you yourself ever feel pity with the victims, thinking of your own family and children?'

'Yes.'

'How was it possible for you to carry out these actions in spite of this?'

'. . . the strict order and the reason given for it by Reichs-führer Himmler.'

McQuade continued into his tape recorder: 'And what did Himmler say?' He ferreted through his photostatted pages. He found two passages he wanted:

'Himmler said, "Anti-semitism is exactly the same as de-lousing. Getting rid of lice is not a question of ideology, it is a matter of cleanliness . . ." Comparing the Final Solution to the Spanish Inquisition he said: "If the Catholic Church had not had the courage to do these things, it would never have survived."' McQuade searched through the photostats, then dictated: 'This is an extract of a speech made by Himmler to his Gestapo officers in charge of the *Einsatzgruppen* mass-acres. "What happens to the Russians, the Czechs, the Poles . . . interests me only in so far as we need them as slaves for our purposes. Otherwise it is of no interest to me. Whether ten thousand Russian females fall down from exhaustion while digging an anti-tank ditch . . . interests me only in so far as the anti-tank ditch for Germany is finished. Talking about the . . . extermination of the Jewish race . . . most of you know what it means when a hundred corpses are lying side by side, or five hundred or a thousand. To have stuck it out, and at the same time . . . to have remained decent fel-lows, that is what has made us hard! *This is a page of glory in our history which has never been written, and is never to be written . . .!*"'

McQuade snapped off his recorder.

God! Glory? Murder eleven million people and call it a 'delousing operation' . . . ?

'That says it all . . .'

He had not yet begun what he had really set out to do, namely summarize, in correct order, every detail of Heinrich Muller's part in this horrific story, so as to know everything possible about his man, but that would have to wait till he got back to South Africa. Right now he wanted to sleep. But there was one last piece to incorporate into his summary. He searched amongst his photostatted pages. It was a paragraph from *The History of the Gestapo* by Jacques Delarue and the author had said it so well that he dictated verbatim:

'The crimes of Nazism are not the crimes of one nation. Cruelty, a taste for violence, the religion of force, ferocious racialism, are not the prerogative of a period or of a people. They are of all ages and of all countries. They have biological and psychological bases which it is by no means certain that we shall escape again. The human being is a dangerous wild animal. In normal periods his evil instincts remain in the background, held in check by the conventions, habits, laws and criteria of civilization, but let a regime come which not only liberates these terrible impulses but makes a virtue of them, then from the depths of time the snout of the beast reappears, tears aside the slender disguise imposed by civilization and howls the death-cries of forgotten ages.'

He thought of the three-legged swastika of the AWB, '*Then from the depths of time the snout of the beast reappears . . .*'
He snapped off his recorder.

He got up and pulled off his clothes. He climbed into bed. He shut his eyes and tried to shut out the images of those killing-pits and gas-chambers.
But he could not make it. At seven o'clock he was still awake. He swung out of bed. His flight did not leave until tonight and he just wanted to get out of this room, into the free streets of London. He went down the passage to the bathroom and showered. Then he set out into the early morning.
He walked towards Fulham, taking deep breaths to purge himself of the ghosts. He found himself in the King's Road. A Number 22 bus was coming along. He boarded it: he wanted

to sit on the top of a London omnibus and watch the free early morning go by.

The bus took him to the familiar territory of Piccadilly Circus. He walked down Haymarket. It was ten o'clock when he found himself in Trafalgar Square, amongst the pigeons. The doors of South Africa House were opening. The usual anti-Apartheid demonstrators were clustered outside with their placards, demanding the release of Nelson Mandela.

He went in, to have a look at the South African newspapers: he hadn't read a newspaper in two weeks. The demonstrators jeered him. 'I'm on your side,' he murmured. He went upstairs, into the oak-panelled library.

All the recent South African newspapers were laid out. And the headline of the first cried at him: 'SA GOVERNMENT TO IMPLEMENT 435 – SWA/NAMIBIA INDEPENDENT SOON'

McQuade snatched up the newspaper. He felt the cold hand of bankruptcy on his gut.

In a dramatic announcement after years of stalemate, the South African President, Mr P. W. Botha, last night announced that his government would implement United Nations Resolution 435 soon, possibly even this year, provided certain conditions are met, thus ending over seventy years of South African colonial rule of the former German territory. It will also end almost twenty years of war against SWAPO, recognized by the United Nations as the sole lawful representative of the people of South West Africa, and many years of costly war against their allies, fifty thousand of Fidel Castro's bush-hardened Cuban soldiers.

Mr Botha's conditions are: in exchange for an immediate cease-fire and withdrawal of all South African troops from Angola, he demands immediate withdrawal of Cuban troops from the battle zones and a total withdrawal of all Cubans from Angola within seven months: lesser, but nonetheless weighty details like responsibility for South Africa's massive international loans to the territory over the years for economic development, are to be worked out later: the policing of the subsequent elections to ensure that they are fair and that there is no intimidation of voters is to be the responsibility of the United Nations.

General world reaction to the news was unreserved applause for the South African peace initiative. Informed sources say there was popping of champagne corks in SWAPO headquarters abroad; but contacted by telephone, a spokesman, while claiming victory over the 'racist Boers', darkly cautioned our reporters against undue optimism: 'We have heard promises from South Africa before. It is ridiculous to make the withdrawal of the Cuban soldiers a pre-condition. Why should Cuba withdraw from a legitimate international struggle in Angola to appease South Africa and Ronald Reagan in Washington and the Iron Lady in England?' In South Africa there was relief that the unpopular, costly war may soon be over, if mixed with anxiety for the strange godchild territory, but the Right Wing of Afrikanerdom, spearheaded by the vociferous AWB, came out with contemptuous criticism of the government's move: 'This is a sell-out of our brethren in South West Africa. If this spineless government goes ahead with its surrender there is going to be trouble. If the government can do this to the South Westers they will surely do the same to us . . .'

Resolution 435 requires the South African Government to hold free and fair elections amongst all its peoples to form a Constituent Assembly. This Assembly must then draw up a constitution for the future Namibia, which must be passed by two-thirds of the Assembly. Thereafter a further election will be held under this constitution to elect representatives to the new Namibian parliament . . .'

*

McQuade speed-read the rest of the news item. Then he sat there, staring across the library, feeling ice on his stomach.

So, at last it could be happening, goddam South Africa getting out of Namibia . . . Free. Yes, but what was going to happen to his fishing licence? What was the new Marxist SWAPO government going to do about *that*? What was going to happen to his overdraft at the bank? And suddenly the long strong arm of Pretoria over Namibia did not look like such a bad thing . . .

He got up and left South Africa House. He felt feverish, desperate to get home and get his submarine venture on the road. *That submarine was the answer to all his worries. Get that loot out and get out before the SWAPO commies take over and take everything away . . .*

He went to the nearest pub and ordered a pint of bitter. He drank it down, down; and ordered another. He was dog-tired. And scared. Too tired to think straight.

But surely that SWAPO spokesman speaking from his five-star hotel in Sweden was right: We have heard these South African offers before. And they've always been rejected by Cuba. Why *would* Fidel Castro agree to pull his troops out? Surely Castro, bent on defeating South Africa, would refuse the conditions – so surely the war would go on? And so surely James McQuade and his fishing company were safe for a good while yet? . . .

He was too tired to think anymore. About the snout of the beast or Fidel Castro and 435. He took a taxi back to his digs.

25

His landlady woke him up at four o'clock. He telephoned British Airways and confirmed there was space on their flight tonight to Johannesburg. He did not make a reservation.

At quarter to five he left his digs. He hurried through the drizzle, glad to be getting this show on the road, determined to finish the job. He was still haunted by those huge open graves filled with bloody corpses, the long lines of naked people queuing up for their turn at the killing-pit while the *Einsatzkommando* swings his legs as he cradles his machine-gun and smokes a cigarette. Haunted by the slim girl who said to Herr Graebe, 'Twenty-three years old'. The heart-break. God, God, what makes men obey their leaders and commit such brutality, follow them into such chasms of cruelty, transport them into such towering madness? Was it only the madness of those times that released the beast? Or was it in the blood, as Hitler said it was, like it's in the blood of a bull to fight. Was the fighting bloodline of a bull-mastiff in the theatre of the absurd, or is a fighting dog born a fighting dog? Were the Germans warriors only because their leaders like Adolf Hitler made them so? What about General von Trotha's proclamation to the Hereros in South West Africa? Oh God, McQuade did not know, but he did know that his whole attitude towards this submarine had changed: By God, as soon as he'd got that loot he was going to tell Simon Wiesenthal everything he knew. And that idea gripped him as much as the prospect of the treasure itself.

He walked into the first pub and ordered a double whisky, drank it down in one throw, and ordered another. He had several hours before he had to be at the airport. He had done some very good work in Europe! Money well spent. He was feeling positive, *positive*. Even going down into that dreadful submarine was not so terrifying anymore, the graveyard he was going to find down there would be nothing compared to the horrors he had been reading about. And he would be a rich man at the end of it, and then he was going to do his Duty to Mankind . . .

At seven o'clock he left the pub. Feeling just fine. He hailed a cab to take him to Heathrow airport. To hell with the expense.

It was forty minutes before the flight's departure when he dashed into the airport, side-stepping people. There were only a few passengers at his check-in counter. He appeared to be the last. 'You've got space on this flight to Johannesburg, I believe?' He produced his ticket.

'Smoking or non-smoking, sir?'

'Smoking. Drinking. Singing. Women . . .'

He hurried through Immigration, into the Duty Free Shop. No way was he going to wait for the stewardess to come down the aisle with her booze trolley. He snatched a bottle of whisky off a shelf, and a bottle of wine. He paid and hurried out into the long corridors, following the signs.

He approached his departure gate. Airline personnel were checking the last of the boarding cards as people filed out to the aircraft. It was a waste of time, but he had nothing to lose. He walked past his gate, then stopped, as if waiting for a fellow passenger to catch up with him. People hurried on past him towards other gates. The passengers inside his departure room were diminishing rapidly. When the last person was filing out he walked in.

He checked through. At the exit he glanced back. He was definitely the last passenger. He filed aboard, feeling on top of the world. He worked his way down the crowded aisles.

The seat next to his was occupied, but in the centre block there were several rows of unoccupied seats. That wouldn't last long. He passed his allocated seat, put his bag on the aisle seat of the nearest empty row, then went on down to the galley. 'May I have a glass of water? For my medicine?'

He went back to his empty row with the water, poured a stout measure of whisky into the plastic glass. He took a big sip. And it was nectar.

He settled back happily. They could take as long as they liked with their take-off procedures. James McQuade had his own bottle of Scotch.

The Boeing 747 burst through the dark clouds above England. People were claiming the empty rows. He claimed the empty seat adjacent to him, with his bag, then he put his coat on the seat beyond, hoping thereby to have three seats to lie down in later.

But the hope was short-lived. A woman took the seat at the end, and put her coat on top of his. McQuade sighed, leaned across and took his coat away. 'Thank you,' she said.

Well, if he was going to share his chaste couch, it might as well be with a pretty woman. He indicated his glass and said, 'Would you like a drink?'

'Thank you, but I'll wait for the trolley.'

'That can be quite some time.'

'But I can wait.' She sounded American; and it sounded as if she thought he should wait too. She stood up, opened the locker above her head, folded her coat and stuffed it in. McQuade took a look at her. She was pretty, all right. Thick dark hair, shoulder length, wide full mouth. Excellent body. She sat down again, opened a book, and started to read. McQuade sat back. Oh well, he had tried.

Ten minutes later the stewardesses appeared at the top of the aisle with their booze trollies. But it would take an age before they reached him. McQuade had had enough whisky; he pulled the wine from the plastic bag. He opened the corkscrew on his penknife. The cork came out with a loud pop. The girl looked up. McQuade gave her a conspiratorial wink. 'Terrified of flying.'

She gave him an amused smile and returned to her book. McQuade said, encouraged, 'You going to South Africa on holiday?'

She looked at him from under her eyebrows. 'Uh-huh. A busman's holiday anyway.' She added: 'I'm a journalist and I've got to write about it.'

'For how long?'

'A couple of months.'

'Nice life. Which newspaper?'

'If you can take the pace. The *Christian Science Monitor*.'

McQuade had heard of it. 'Can you? Take the pace?'

'I'm just whacked.' She sighed. 'Look, can we continue this conversation later? I need a little sleep.'

'Of course. I'm sorry.'

'Please ask the stewardess not to wake me for dinner.'

She raised the armrest on the adjoining seat, and packed the pillows on her aisle armrest. She pulled off her shoes, and lay down on her side, knees bent.

McQuade sat back. He had got the brush-off, loud and clear. Oh well, nothing ventured, nothing gained. He lifted his glass of wine. He glanced at her, and thought, the *Christian Science Monitor*, huh? Sounds like a barrel of fun!

PART FOUR

26

He woke up at dawn, very aware that yesterday he had drunk a good deal. The girl was not in her seat. Through the windows, a red sky was burgeoning. He went to the toilet, took out his toothbrush and brushed his teeth thoroughly. He washed his face and combed his hair before going to the galley. He considered asking the stewardess for a beer, a hair of the dog, but decided on coffee.

He returned to his seat with it. The American girl had reappeared. Looking fresh and groomed. And drinking a can of beer.

'Good morning. That's a very good idea.'

'Don't let my example corrupt you. I've been up for hours.'

He went back to the galley and returned with a beer. 'I've been up for hours too.'

'Liar.'

He took a big swallow of beer and it went down like a mountain brook. 'So, the *Christian Science Monitor*?'

'Uh-huh. And you?'

'Fishing industry. Is the *Monitor* a religious publication?'

'Ordinary newspaper, now. We're in Boston, Massachusetts.'

'And you're a columnist?'

'I do what I'm told. And right now I'm told the boss wants a series of articles when I come back from South Africa.' She made quotation marks with her fingers: '"All moral issues."'

'Well plenty of those in South Africa.'

She took a sip. 'Good stuff, beer. What do you do in the fishing industry?'

'I've got a massive fishing fleet. One trawler.'

'So, a sea captain. A girl in every port.'

'Oh yes. Irresistible, me.'

'Modest, too.'

'One of the many things I like about myself.'

She grinned and he said, 'James McQuade.'

'Hi, I'm Sarah Buckley. Where does your fishing fleet operate?'

'South West Africa. You probably know it by the name Namibia. Ever heard of Walvis Bay?'

'Sure. Know something about Namibia too: 435, and the Etosha Game Reserve, I'm going there sometime.' She added, 'I'm going to the Kruger National Park the day after tomorrow. Then Natal. I believe that's lovely? Subtropical?'

'Yes. Bananas. Sugar cane.'

'And Zulus? I've got an interview lined up with Chief Buthelezi. Then the Cape, then back to the dynamo of Johannesburg and Soweto, after I've got a feel of the place.'

'So, you can go where you like and write what you like?'

'It's *my* busman's holiday.' She gave a businesslike smile. 'So, if you'll excuse me starting work so early, tell me what you think of your country's politics.'

It is the question most South Africans are wary of. And weary of. But McQuade did not mind a bit. Not from the ravishing Ms Buckley. He imitated the public address system: '"Ladies and gentlemen, we are about to land in jolly Johannesburg. The weather is fine and the political temperature is explosive. Kindly put your watches back fifty years . . ."'

She thought that was amusing. 'Where are you staying in Johannesburg?' he asked.

'At . . .' She pulled out a notebook and flipped through it. 'The Sunnyside Park Hotel. Do you know it?'

He did. And it was far too expensive for James McQuade. In Johannesburg he always stayed with Nathan. 'Will you have lunch with me?'

'I don't think it's possible. I'm being met by our man in Johannesburg. He'll expect me to have lunch with him.'

'Dinner tonight, then?'

She sighed. 'I think I'd better take a raincheck. I'm going to be whacked tonight after two days' flying. And so will you be. Maybe tomorrow night?'

He said uncertainly, 'I should be getting on to Walvis Bay tomorrow.'

She said: 'Well, shall we play it by ear? Maybe Matt – that's our man in Jo'burg – maybe he's not expecting me for lunch. In which case, fine. But I really think dinner tonight is not on for this poor body of mine. Where are you staying?'

He thought, The things I do for a fuck! The *chance* of one. 'Funnily enough, I usually stay at the Sunnyside Park Hotel.'

'Well, this is easy. Play it by ear, huh?'

He thought, Smart work, McQuade – even if lunch isn't on she can't refuse dinner in her own hotel. He was delighted with himself.

27

He persuaded the air-hostess to sell them a bottle of champagne with breakfast, and they were feeling just fine when they arrived at Johannesburg. The *Christian Science Monitor*'s stringer, Matt Mathews, was there to meet Sarah and grudgingly offered McQuade a lift into town. 'Oh, same hotel?' and shot McQuade a dubious look. Matt and Sarah talked all the way about people she should try to interview, from P.W. Botha downwards. McQuade sat in the back, feeling very, very happy about Ms Sarah Buckley. To hell with the expense. When they reached the hotel, Matt said to Sarah, 'Can you come to dinner tonight at home?' The invitation definitely did not extend to McQuade.

'Matt, I'm really not up to dinner after two nights' flying. Any other time.'

To McQuade's intense relief Matt said, 'Can't do lunch today. How about we finish the briefing right now?'

Oh boy, McQuade's heart sang.

They checked in. Matt and Sarah adjourned to the bar to talk shop, while McQuade went up to his room, which over-looked sunlit gardens. He picked up the telephone and dialled the number of the telecommunications tower in Walvis Bay. 'I want a radio hook-up with the *Bonanza*, please, to be charged to the ship. Here is her call sign . . .'

Half a minute later Tucker's anxious voice came over the line: '*Bonanza*, over.'

'This is McQuade, when're you getting to port, over?'

'You're back! We expect to be full on Wednesday or Thursday, back about Friday.' He added worriedly, 'How did it go? Over.'

'See you on Friday then. Prepare to return to sea the next day and give the Coloured crew a week's leave. Out.'

That gave him four days to get up to Damaraland and back to show Jakob the photograph of Heinrich Muller. Good.

The next call might not be so easy, but he had to look into this in person since he did not want to leave it to the mail. He dialled again. A female voice sang: 'Nathan's Lingeries . . . More-Better-Cheaper-Faster, can we *help youuu?*'

'May I speak to Ivor Nathan, please.'

There was a tinkle of seductive music before a gravelly voice barked: 'Nathan.'

'Why are you at work, you heathen? It's the Sabbath!'

'I've *been* to synagogue, I've *been!* So why aren't you at sea already?'

'Because I've come to make you an offer you can't refuse already.'

'On the Sabbath?! Where are you? I'm there already.'

'Sunnyside Park Hotel, room 203.'

Astonishment. 'Why aren't you staying with me?'

'I've gone upmarket.' McQuade hung up, grinning.

He stripped off and headed for the shower. He gave himself a thorough scrubbing, to be nice and clean for Ms Buckley, shampooed his hair to be beautiful for Ms Buckley. He had a good shave to be smooth for Ms Buckley. He dabbed himself with after-shave to smell irresistible for Ms Buckley. Then Nathan arrived.

Nathan had graduated with McQuade from university as that rarity, a penniless Jewish marine biologist. But then he had got his cock caught in the cash-register and married one of the Cohen girls of garment industry fame. Nathan had never looked back, except to invest in Sausmarine when McQuade leaned hard on him. There was no mistaking Nathan's ancestry. He was a big, well-nourished man with a big nose over a bristly moustache. 'Painfully kosher,' his wife described him, '– why won't he have a nose-job, and my uncle a plastic surgeon already, why must he for ever continue to look like Groucho Marx?' Now Nathan sat on the edge of the bed, a beer in his hand, looking very like an astonished Groucho Marx. '*Where* exactly is this submarine?'

McQuade had not told him about Heinrich Muller. 'All I want to know is, will you bank-roll the operation? Give us a loan to cover the crew's wages for about two weeks' lay-off and the equipment we've got to buy?'

Nathan's marine-biologist's mind was locked in combat with his businessman's. 'And how much is all that?'

'Ten to twenty thousand rand. More like fifteen. Depending on how long it takes.'

'The company can't lay its hands on fifteen thousand?'

'Not if we don't catch fish for two weeks. We could negotiate a bigger overdraft, but the bank will want to know why and I'll have to tell lies because I don't want anybody knowing what we're up to. If that leaks out, we lose everything.'

Nathan blinked. 'Shit no. And if I don't lend the money to the company?'

'Then we tell lies and borrow the money elsewhere and keep *all* the loot for ourselves.' He half-closed his eyes happily. '*Millions* and *millions* . . .'

Nathan looked at him with a twinkle in his eye. 'And if we *don't* find any loot, when do I get my money back?'

McQuade had to work at it to keep a straight face. 'You don't. You get shares in the company instead.'

'But I don't *want* any shares in your fucking fishing business! And, if we do find the loot?'

'Well, *then* we're all rich! You get your money back plus ten per cent of the loot.'

'Ten per cent! I want more if I'm risking my money.'

'But you're not risking your *life*! We're providing the seamanship! And we know where the submarine is, which you don't.'

Nathan looked at him, then gave a conspiratorial wink. 'Better idea. I charter a yacht. Just you and me. We split the loot fifty-fifty. That way the *Bonanza* keeps working and earning.'

McQuade shook his head. 'The boys are already in. Anyway I need at least three divers, and you and I couldn't handle a big yacht in those seas by ourselves. And the only yachts on that coast are way down south, and we'd attract attention. I've thought it all through, Groucho.'

'I'll think about it.'

'You have to think about it right now. Because tomorrow I start. Which brings me to my second reason for being here. How do we launder the loot?'

'Launder it?'

'Sell it. Get rid of it. It is quite likely to be in the form of gold. And diamonds, jewellery maybe. But unlicensed dealing in gold is a serious offence in South Africa – IGB. So is illicit dealing in diamonds. And it wouldn't be easy to smuggle large quantities of the stuff out of this country. We can't sail away with it to Europe without knowing where we're going to launder it. So?' He raised his eyebrows. 'You're a big underwear businessman. Do you know any *real* businessmen who could help us get rid of the stuff, for a piece of the action? But he must be honest.'

Nathan stared at him.

'An honest illegal diamond buyer? Can't we do this *legally*?'

'No. As soon as we lay a legal claim to that submarine we'll be tied up in courts for months. So, who do you know? Haven't you got a brother-in-law who's a jeweller – Bloomfield, the guy who always wears a bow-tie?'

'Bloomberg,' Nathan said. 'That schmuck. He's an antique dealer, not a jeweller. He's my *cousin*-in-law.'

'Could we trust him?'

'Christ, he's so respectable he'd have a heart-attack at buying illegal gold and diamonds.'

'But he probably knows somebody who'd do it. Why is he a schmuck?'

223

'Anybody who marries my cousin is a schmuck, even though she's had a nose-job. Why can't this wait until we know whether we've found the loot?'

'Because,' McQuade said, 'we don't want security problems. We can't leave the stuff lying around on the ship for weeks. So we must be prepared. Now, can we trust Bloomberg to keep his mouth shut?'

Nathan shifted on the bed. 'He wouldn't dare drop me in the shit. The family would kick his arse all the way to Baghdad. But I can tell you now he won't touch it. He's too much of a sissy.'

'And you? Are you too much of a sissy?'

Nathan grinned at him, his nose burying into his moustache. 'If there's one thing I can't stand it's a goy smart-ass.'

'Well, are you in? Or out?'

Nathan shook his head, then said irritably, 'In.'

'And you'll ask Bloomberg today? In the strictest of confidence. I want his answer by tonight. Yes, or no. No maybes. Otherwise I look elsewhere.'

'What commission are we offering him? Or the guy he recommends?'

'Ten per cent? Negotiable.'

'Five, non-negotiable,' Nathan said aggressively. 'That arty schmuck.'

McQuade said: 'Well?'

'Well what?'

'Got your cheque-book?'

Nathan put his hand into his jacket pocket reluctantly. 'You goys are hard bastards.'

'At least I don't sell pantihose on the Sabbath!'

He was on top of the world as he made his way downstairs to the bar, Nathan's cheque for twenty thousand rand in his pocket. Sarah was sitting in the corner with Matt Mathews, scribbling notes. McQuade gave them a cheery wave and made for the bar. Sarah called, 'We're almost finished, come and join us.'

He bought a bottle of Grand Mousseaux and took it to their table. Matt gave him a sour smile, and finished up. He gave her a few more names, people to contact, subjects to consider. A minute later he took his leave with a brief handshake. McQuade said to Sarah:

'He doesn't much like me. Been pen-pals for long?'

She grinned. 'Only met him once in Boston. I think he thinks you've got designs on my untrammelled body.'

'Perish the thought!'

They adjourned to the restaurant for an early lunch. (McQuade was anxious to get the show on the road.) He ordered the best wine. She smiled, her sensuous mouth crying out to be ravished: 'Can we continue with my edification in the multi-faceted moral complexities of South Africa, to quote Matt?'

And all McQuade wanted to do was take her beautiful hands across the table and tell her he was going to make wild passionate love to her if she would only be a sport. And he felt absolutely charming and on top of the world and he had Nathan's cheque in his pocket and this time next week he was going to be a millionaire, and he continued her edification in the multi-faceted moral complexities of his troubled land. And he was very amusing whilst he was very serious and edifying, and thoroughly enjoying himself, and Sarah Buckley scribbled and thoroughly enjoyed herself too. He ended:

'But you've got to keep this fact in mind constantly: the Afrikaner – the Dutchman – has been fighting for his piece of the sun ever since the British took the Cape Colony off the Dutch. And the Great Trek set him free, and they set up their own republics, and the British conquered them all over again in the Boer War. And the Afrikaner has been fighting the Boer War ever since – and he's finally got his own beloved Afrikaner country at last, but he is still fighting – but now it's no longer just the British, it's the whole world. And he'll fight the whole world, like the Israelis will.'

She said: 'But evidently they're not going to fight for Namibia? What do you think about this bombshell of Resolution 435?'

McQuade sat back. 'I don't believe Resolution 435 will come to pass for a long time yet.'

'Why is that?'

McQuade sighed. 'Because South Africa has made it a condition that Cuba withdraws her fifty thousand troops from Angola, where the fighting is. I simply don't believe that Fidel Castro and his Russian masters will do that small thing. Because the Cuban soldiers are not only fighting the South Africans on behalf of SWAPO, they are also fighting UNITA on behalf of the communist Angola government. Do you know about UNITA?'

'Yes, they're the pro-western rebels—'

'They're *not* "rebels" – they're a perfectly legitimate political party which the communists are *illegally* trying to crush. When Portugal gave independence to Angola and held elections, the communists promptly seized power, formed a one-party Marxist government and denied the UNITA party their share of government. So UNITA took to the bush under General Savimbi and have waged *legitimate* civil war ever since for their rightful share of democracy. Of course the Russians don't want any democratic nonsense in Angola so they sent their surrogate Cubans in to fight UNITA, and so America and South Africa are jointly supporting UNITA with aid.' He shrugged. 'If the Cubans withdraw from Angola, UNITA would win and install a pro-western government. I simply don't believe the communists will permit that to happen. And anyway,' he ended, 'Angola is only part of the story – only part of Castro's ambitions. Because after he's crushed UNITA, he wants his troops to march south and "liberate" South Africa too. He wants to go down in history as the "Conquistador of the Boers". And have the Cape sea route in

226

communist hands. They've already got Suez anytime they like through their puppets in Yemen and Ethiopia. The Mediterranean is a Russian lake anytime they like. So that will only leave Panama to get. *Then* the commies will really have the world sewn up.'

She said: 'So the South African government knows its offer will be refused, so it's made an empty gesture?'

'They've made an astute diplomatic move. They've put the ball in the communist court. If the communists reject the offer, *they* are clearly the warmongers. And South Africa *would* like to be rid of an expensive border war, and in exchange for that I think they really are prepared to give independence to Namibia – South Africa can live with a SWAPO government in Namibia because they will be our economic hostage, bound to reasonably tolerable behaviour. But not if SWAPO brings their fifty thousand Cuban pals with them to shoot across the fence at South Africa.'

She smiled. 'And you? Could you live with a SWAPO government? I've gathered from everything you've said that you don't like the South African government.'

He sighed. 'Look, I hold no brief for the South African government. I hate Apartheid. But – whether your readers in Boston, Massachusetts believe it or not – things are changing. Yes, I want Namibia to be independent of South Africa. Free and multi-racial. But no, I could not live with a SWAPO government. Because they're communist. They'll ruin the economy. And so they'll ruin the fishing industry, and so they'll ruin me. Q.E.D.'

Sarah scribbled. It was mid-afternoon when she sighed: 'It's been a lovely day. But now I really must go and sleep off my jet-lag.'

It was the moment to close in on her. He took her hand across the table – then the head waiter appeared at his side. 'There's somebody to see you, Mr McQuade . . .'

He saw Nathan at the entrance, looking furtive.

'Excuse me,' he said apologetically. He held a finger out at her: 'Don't move . . .'

Nathan was in the foyer. 'Can't this wait?' McQuade complained.

Nathan slipped him a piece of paper with a number written on it. 'That's a public telephone. Call it immediately from *that* public phone' – he pointed across the foyer. 'A man called Julie will answer.'

'Julie who?'

'I don't know. Friend of Bloomberg, who's waiting at the other phone right now. The call can't be tapped, see?'

McQuade didn't like it. 'What does this Julie do?'

'Big wheeler-dealer in antiques, carpets, that sort of thing. International, Bloomberg says.'

'Bloomberg doesn't know you were asking on my behalf, does he?'

'*No*, I'm not a schmuck.'

'So this Julie doesn't know who I am?'

'How can he, schmuck, if Bloomberg doesn't know?'

'Jewish?'

'Bloomberg's pal? My boy, my life.'

McQuade wanted to get back to Sarah before she went to sleep off her jet-lag without him to comfort her, but the man was waiting. He hurried to the public telephone, and dialled. It was answered immediately. 'Yes?'

'Julie?' McQuade said.

The man said, 'I have three conditions. First, my commission will be thirty per cent. I have international outlets for these artefacts and immense expertise in the business.' The voice was soft, almost flabby and very British. 'Well?'

McQuade said tersely, 'Second condition?'

'That this whole matter be handled on the basis of complete trust. You don't cheat me on the quantities, and I won't cheat you. You must accept the prices I get without subsequent argument and acrimony. If you're going to quibble afterwards, I'm not sticking my neck out. I must know all about you, so I can satisfy myself you're not a crook, and that I'm not handling stolen goods.'

'And are you prepared to tell me who you are? So I can satisfy myself *you*'re not a crook?'

'Not yet. My third condition is that I accompany you on your expedition, so that I can see the merchandise the moment it appears.'

'And after the merchandise appears, what happens?'

'I take it away with me and dispose of it.'

'Where to?'

'That is my business at this stage. That's why you're involving me. For my expertise.'

'It's also my business. Do I accompany *you*?'

'If you wish to take those risks.' He paused. 'Well? Are those conditions accepted?'

McQuade was irritated. 'Not yet. We'll have to meet. Give me a telephone number where I can contact you.'

'Then that meeting must take place immediately.'

'The meeting.' McQuade said. 'will take place when I arrange it. Through Bloomberg. Goodbye.'

He hung up, annoyed. Yet also impressed. He looked at his watch, then said to Nathan, 'Find out all you can from Bloomberg about this Julie. I'll phone you later. Then we'll arrange a meeting.'

He hurried back into the restaurant, to Sarah. 'I'm sorry, just a bit of business.'

He paid the bill, adding an over-generous tip. *The things I do*. They walked out of the restaurant, to the staircase. She said, 'Don't bother to come up . . .'

'Oh, I'm going up to my room too.'

They mounted the stairs. He felt she had read his mind, and thought, what the hell – tomorrow I'll be gone, so it's now or never. They walked down the corridor to her room. She unlocked the door. 'Tomorrow I'm returning to Walvis Bay,' he heard himself say, 'then driving up the Skeleton Coast into Damaraland to see somebody. Why don't you join

229

me'? Leave the Kruger National Park for another time.' He paused. 'We'll have time to see the Etosha National Park too.'

She had the door open.

'That's sure worth thinking about. Thank you. Can I tell you tomorrow?'

He smiled. 'You can tell me over dinner tonight?'

She leant against the doorway. 'Dinner? Look, I'm not at my best – thanks to you.'

He stepped through the door and took her in his arms. And, oh the wonderful feel of her against him. He whispered ardently: 'Please . . . Then we can fall into a beautiful sleep together.'

She pressed her forehead into his shoulder and giggled. 'That's the corniest approach I've ever heard.'

'I'm not at my best either.' He tilted back her chin and he kissed her, and her smiling mouth was soft and warm as she pressed her belly against him, and he felt himself swell. She thrust her lips against him hard as if she wanted to bite him, then she broke the kiss.

'Let's see how we feel about this tomorrow. In our sound and sober senses.'

'I know *exactly* how I'll feel about it tomorrow!'

She grinned and turned him towards the door. 'Will you have lunch on the *Christian Science Monitor* tomorrow?'

'Lunch is going to be in the aeroplane to Walvis Bay.' He took her in his arms again, and kissed her grinning mouth and to make love to her was the most desperately important thing in the whole wide world and he pushed his loins against hers. She gave a tiny shiver and again she broke the kiss. She took a step backwards, her hair a little awry and her face smouldering. 'Wow . . .' She held up a hand to restrain him. 'Okay, dinner tonight. Fetch me at eight?'

'If you promise to be in your sound and sober senses . . .'

She bundled him out the door, grinning.

230

28

He wanted to give a little skip as he walked down the corridor. He couldn't remember when last a woman had turned him on so; and tomorrow she was surely coming away with him for five glorious days, and next week he was going to be millionaire! And he had Nathan's cheque to bankroll the expedition, and he probably had Julie to dispose of the loot. Absolutely everything was going right! But what was he going to do with this hard-on until eight o'clock?

It was probably too soon to telephone Nathan but he did so nonetheless. 'Any information?'

'Bloomers says he's reliable. A bully, gets his pound of flesh, but reliable.'

'And his business is antiques?'

'And there's a lot of money in antiques. He imports and exports all over the world. I've got his business address, so we can go and look at it from the outside this afternoon, get an idea.'

'But can we trust him receiving payment on our behalf?'

'No way. I've put up twenty grand for that merchandise and I'm going to stick with it. He's just the agent, the merchandise stays at my factory until it's sold and price received. I've got twenty-four-hour security guards, dogs, the works.'

McQuade liked that. 'But maybe he's got to export it to show it to the customer.'

'Then I go with it. The factory can survive without me.'

McQuade liked that too. 'I'll go with it, too. What about his thirty per cent? I say he gets fifteen.'

'Ten is max! Start at five! My boy, my life, leave the bargaining to your Uncle Ivor already.'

'Okay. But, he wants to come on the trip with us. I don't like that. I don't want anybody knowing the whereabouts of that machine.'

'Right. Maybe you're not such a schmuck.'

'He wants to make sure I don't steal it, and that he gets all the business, not half of it.'

Nathan mulled that over. 'Maybe we should hold back half of it to sell elsewhere, hedge our bets? And we needn't tell him we're leaving next weekend. We could just present him with a fait accompli.' He added: 'That's a fancy Yiddish expression meaning "Fuck you, Julie, I've done it".'

McQuade smiled. 'Anyway, let's take a look at his premises, then tell Bloomers to arrange a meeting this afternoon at the Turkish baths.'

'The Turkish *baths*. Why?'

'For the simple reason that it's hard to conceal a tape-recorder on your person in a Turkish bath!'

The premises of Goldstein International Limited were impressive. Gold lettering on the big windows announced the company's speciality as antiques, objets d'art, fine paintings. Subtle lights lit up piles of artistically arrayed carpets, impressive paintings and fine old furniture and pottery.

'Looks solvent,' Nathan remarked.

'But what's a guy like this doing in IGB?'

'Maybe that's how he got solvent.'

'Okay, tell Bloomers to arrange the meeting for six o'clock tonight. I'm going back to the hotel for a couple of hours sleep. But at the Turkish baths *you* are going to interview Julie. I'm just going to observe, from a distance.'

'Why am I taking all these orders?' Nathan complained.

'Because you're Uncle Ivor who knows how to do the bargaining, and because I don't want the guy to know what I look like until we've made a decision.'

Things were looking better and better. A guy with an outfit like Julie Goldstein's obviously did good business. With rich customers.

The Turkish baths had white tiles like a railway lavatory and rooms of different temperatures arranged around a small icy pool. Nathan sat in the coolest steam-room, a towel wrapped around his beefy loins, the sweat running, looking thoroughly discommoded. McQuade sat across the room, his head down, revelling in the booze oozing out of him. Julie Goldstein sat beside Nathan, sweating profusely, looking almost exactly as McQuade had imagined: large and bulbous, hairy and saggy, balding pate glistening, a fleshy, petulant face with Middle Eastern eyes. He said *sotto voce* to Nathan:

'I have no objection to Turkish baths — I do a lot of business in Istanbul — but what I find thoroughly objectionable is firstly your *insistence* that we meet in this unusual environment, and secondly the absence of your principal! If I'd known I wouldn't have come!'

Nathan wiped his sweaty brow. 'Tough, Julie.'

'What does *that* mean?'

'It means, Tough, Julie. This is where the boss wants me to meet you.'

'And where is this boss?'

Nathan shrugged his hairy, sweaty shoulders. 'Maybe I'm the boss. But then maybe I'm not.'

'You don't sound like the man who telephoned me!'

'Maybe that was me in disguise.'

'How do you know Bloomberg?' Julie demanded.

'Never heard of Bloomberg. I heard of you through Rubenstein.'

'Which Rubenstein.'

'Rubenstein, Finkelstein, Hazeltine, Valentine, what does it matter? You're here and I'm here.'

Julie stood up, his flabby pectorals hanging. 'I'm leaving.'

Nathan propped his sweaty chin in his sweaty hand.

'Goodbye, Julie. Goodbye to your five per cent.'

Julie Goldstein glared. 'Five?! I stipulated thirty!'

Nathan long-sufferingly wiped his brow, then flicked the sweat away like a martyr. Julie slowly sat down again.

'I won't take a point less than twenty-five.'

Nathan wearily flicked more sweat away. Across the steamy room, McQuade watched in admiration from under his sweaty eyebrows. 'Supposing you start by telling me what business you're in?' Julie whispered. 'At least you're Jewish, that's a point in your favour.'

Nathan rolled his big eyes at him. 'How about ninety-five percentage points in my favour? Supposing you tell me *your* business; and what makes you think I'm Jewish already so soon?'

Julie stared at him angrily. '*Wealth*,' he said fleshily. 'I deal in *wealth*. The magic and mystique of it. I sell wealth to the wealthy. And I'm the best salesman there is.'

Nathan raised his sweaty eyebrows. Julie went on pompously: 'There are three stages in material life. First comes money. Second comes riches. Thirdly, and finally, comes *wealth*.' He held up a podgy finger. 'First, we start by working for money, to feed and clothe ourselves. Secondly, after we have sufficient of that, we work to buy *riches* with our excess money: nice cars, better houses, jewellery for our women, stocks and shares to provide growth and security. But very, very few of us proceed onto the third stage, where we have *excess riches*, and can make the final, magic investment in true wealth: masterworks of art, wonderful gold ornaments, glittering ensembles of diamonds, magnificent ancient pottery, magnificent Persian carpets. Why do we do it? What is a masterwork but some paint on a canvas? What use are gold and diamonds? There is little practical application for them. What use is fragile ancient pottery – you cannot cook in it? What is a Persian carpet but knotted wool?' He looked at Nathan, then leant towards him. 'It is their *magic* that makes them pricelessly valuable! The aura of them. The beauty of them. The mystique of them! The reverence we bestow upon them . . .' He held up a fleshy finger again, his big eyes bright: 'And that magic . . . that value . . . endures. It remains when the stock market crashes and money goes through the floor. So the wealthy stay wealthy while the rich get poor . . .' He waved his hand grandiloquently, 'It endures for *centuries*! For *millennia*!' He glared at an enraptured Nathan; then ended with a Levantine whisper. 'I sell that magic . . . I advise princes and potentates and captains of industry all over the world on what magic they need, on what magic I can get for them . . . and they are happy. *That's who I am. . .'*

McQuade got up with a happy sigh and left Nathan to deal with the magician.

He took a taxi back to his hotel. He was feeling wonderful, rested and steam-cleaned. And everything was going right! He hurried into the bar and drank a cold beer, down, down, down, and it flooded his dehydrated system beautifully. Then he hurried to his room and changed into fresh clothes. He brushed his teeth thoroughly and combed his hair carefully. Just then the telephone rang.

'Nathan,' Nathan sighed.

'Well?'

'Twenty-five per cent,' Nathan sighed.

'You schmuck! You seemed to be doing so well!'

'Yeah, but the man's a magician. When he speaks flowers bloom, seas roll back, doors open onto crystal palaces, you smell frankincense and myrrh . . .'

'But how does he physically dispose of the merchandise?'

'He waves his wand. He flies his magic carpet . . . He arrives by parachute in the palaces of the mighty and flogs it to them, cash.'

'But we go with him?'

'Nothin' easier, we will be borne along on the wings of cherubs, we will sleep on beds of roses, we will wallow in perfumed womanflesh while he does the haggling in a dozen languages. Yeah, we can go with him.'

'But has he got an *organization*?'

'My friend, he has telexes and fax, computers and catalogues, he has a hundred and ten outlets in fifty-one countries and accounts in sixty banks. His name is revered from Sotheby's to the Baghdad bazaar.'

'For Christ sake, Nathan!'

Nathan sighed. 'He's a bullshitter. But he's got an organization all right.'

McQuade said emphatically, 'He's not coming with us next weekend.'

'He doesn't know we're leaving next weekend. Indeed he doesn't *want* to come – *refuses*, my dear fellow – until he's met you, brought his exquisite judgment to bear and sussed you out.'

'But he knows nothing about me?'

'Nor about me. My name is Smith.'

'And what's your assessment, Smith?'

'We'll go for him,' Nathan said. 'That guy could sell central heating in the Congo. He impressed the shit out of me.'

McQuade was feeling positive as he strode down the corridor to Sarah's room. Everything was going well and fast! He felt wonderful, and yes he also thought they'd go for Julie Wonderful, and oh my he was looking forward to Sarah Wonderful. He rapped jauntily on her door.

She was radiant, refreshed, groomed, her hair shining, her eyes bright. She wore a simple red dress that clung around her breasts and flowed away over her hips. She wore stylish red high heels. She was smiling widely, screwing an earring onto her lobe. 'Hi . . .'

'You look beautiful.'

'You look pretty good yourself. Come in.' She turned to the dressing table and picked up the other earring. The dress plunged midway down her back and her skin was golden brown. 'Are you hungry?'

'Are you?'

He thought, What lovely legs.

She asked, screwing on the other earring: 'Did you sleep?'

'Yes. Did you?'

'Like a child. Ready!'

He put his arms around her. She leant back in his arms, smiling. He looked at her ardently, and then gently kissed her.

And her wide soft mouth was sweet and her breath quivered, and he felt himself harden against her belly. She broke the kiss, and her green eyes were intent. Then she said softly:

'No . . . No, I'm not hungry . . .'

And her eyes were suddenly smouldering, and his heart seemed to turn over, and he slowly slid his hand down over her back and around her hips and up to her breast, and she took a sighing breath and closed her eyes. And, oh, the warm sweet fullness of her body, and he felt her nipple harden, and she came against him. Her arms slid around his shoulders, feeling him, and his hands were sliding over her hips and her thighs and over the warmth of her loins and the sweet soft swelling between them, and her tongue searched into his mouth, and his fingers peeled the dress down over her shoulders. She leant back in his arms again, and her fingers went to his tie and pulled the knot undone, then they were plucking at his shirt buttons, her eyes fixed smouldering on his, and he peeled the red dress away from her hips. It fell at her high-heeled feet. Her breasts stood perfect and naked, the nipples stiff with excitement, her soft flat stomach tapering out into the roundness of her hips in her scanty panties. She stood there, glorious, her lips parted, her long legs a little astride, and she took McQuade's breath away. And, oh, it was the most beautiful compelling feeling in the world, and he stooped down and took her breasts in both hands and buried his face into their full softness, the most fundamental of fulfilments, then he dropped to his knee, in a classic

237

attitude of need, and his mouth slid down over her soft belly and his fingers pulled her panties down her rounded hips.

Afterwards, lying on the bed, in the exhausted minutes of after-love, deliciously at the beginning of something new and tremendously exciting, she whispered:

'Yes . . .'

'Yes, you're hungry?'

'No. Yes, the Kruger National Park can wait . . .'

PART FIVE

29

It was fun all the way. They woke up late that Sunday, with only time for a riotously sensuous shower together ('What are we going to do with *that*, McQuade — we simply haven't got time . . .') before rushing to the airport. He had brought two bottles of champagne the night before and they drank the first one in the taxi and hurried last up into the aircraft. And to sustain them during that painful eternity before the air hostesses cranked up their trolleys, they opened the second bottle with a resounding pop and flying spume. It all seemed terribly funny. Mercifully the air hostesses reached them before the second bottle was finished and they bought a third. They changed planes in Windhoek and bought a fourth. They were feeling no pain at all when their aircraft finally bounced down on the desertous outpost of Walvis Bay. McQuade held a finger out at her: 'Remember you only cry twice in Walvis Bay. The day you arrive . . .'

The taxi drove them past the only bit of greenery of the municipal gardens, down into Fifth Street, to McQuade's house. 'And the day you see the Railway Yard View.'

There was a letter from the Stormtrooper. He shoved it in his pocket unopened. 'I'll get some blankets and things for the road.'

He put his notes about Heinrich Muller in a box under his bed, and kept only the photograph. Twenty minutes later they were on their way out of town, the Landrover loaded with bedding, cooking utensils, canned food, cold beer in an icebox, wine and other booze.

It was holiday-mood all the way. He was vastly impressed at how much she could drink: she kept pace with him, beer for beer, glass for glass as they drove. She was delighted with this unexpected adventure, she was enchanted with the Germanic quaintness of Swakopmund, enthralled with the desert beyond, the vastness, the sand dunes, the crashing Atlantic surf. He had intended spending the night at the little hotel in Henties Bay, the last watering hole until they reached Damaraland, but she protested, 'But we're in Africa. I thought we were going to camp!' At Cape Cross he drove down to the shore to show her the seal colony. This was where Bartholomew Diaz first set foot in Africa in the fifteenth century and raised a cross. As they approached, they could smell the rich ripeness of wet seals, and the air was full of their barking and bleating. 'Oh my!'

Thousands of seals basked and flopped and quarrelled on the rocky beach. Great bulls reared and flashed their jaws at each other, contesting territory; calves scampered and wrestled or howled for their mothers, cows lolled and flapped and dozed. The rocks seemed a vast mass of seething, heaving, fat furry life, and the crashing surf beyond was black with seals hunting and surfing, crashing and skidding onto the beach. Sarah was enthralled, snapping photographs, and making notes into her tape-recorder.

The sun was getting low when he pulled off the road and drove down to the sea to camp. She grinned, 'Last one in doesn't get laid!' She scrambled out and whipped her dress off over her head. She pulled her panties down her hips with a wriggle and ran for the beach. McQuade was tearing off his shirt as he ran after her, yelling *'Unfair!'* He was still hopping and wrenching his trousers over his ankles as she hit the Atlantic surf in a crash, her body gleaming gold in the sundown. He went charging in after her, the cold hitting him like a blow. She broke surface beyond him and shrieked, 'It's freezing!'

He thrashed out after her, she flailed away from him, arms flashing and lovely legs kicking. He seized her slippery body and wrenched her satiny nakedness into his arms.

'So I don't get laid, huh?'

'Nope, only I do!'

They came wading out of the crashing water, hand in hand, feeling braced, goosefleshed, happy. McQuade watched her as she wriggled fresh panties up over her thighs and he felt his heart turn over for the sheer curvaceous, athletic beauty of her. She grinned. 'Something wrong with these panties?'

'They'll have to go,' he said sadly.

They dressed up warmly, stunned almost sober and fresh by the Atlantic. He built a crackling fire out of driftwood, and they sat side by side under the stars, staring into it – sipping good Cape wine with the glow of the sea and fire, while lamb chops slowly grilled. The moon came up, lighting up the black Atlantic, silvering the silent desert and baskets of stars came out to match the lovely glow of the good wine. They ate a raft of succulent chops with their fingers, tearing the pink flesh and crispy fat off the bones, and it tasted like the best food they had ever eaten; they ate until they were both gloriously replete, then she collapsed back on the sand, her arms outflung and she smiled. 'Oh – I'm so glad I came . . .'

She scrambled into the double sleeping bag – McQuade had artfully zipped two together – with a grin of pure pleasure on her face, and her almost girlish excitement at the whole adventure was just as sensuous as the sophisticated woman he had feverishly stripped the night before. Afterwards, lying flat out on her back, her hair spreadeagled, her breasts heaving with passion spent, she smiled up at the stars and whispered:

'Oh, I'm so happy . . .'

The sun was up when they reached the lonely ranger's gate to the Skeleton Coast. They crossed the dry, caked bed of the Ugab River. She made notes into her tape-recorder. 'What magnificent desolation . . . Daunting vastness. The sun beating down, the dunes rearing up. A moonscape of blistering sand and rocks undulating. Just over there the Atlantic thundering and crashing. It is hard to imagine that there's any life here, yet gemsbok and springbok and jackals live in this desert land, feeding on the small patches of green that line the dry riverbeds, and lions sometimes come down out of the faraway hills to cross the desert to feed on the seals.'

McQuade said, 'And they're very dangerous lions because they're very hungry.'

She repeated the detail into her recorder, then sighed. 'This is so harsh yet so beautiful . . .'

Just before Torra Bay they came to the road that led east, across the desert towards Damaraland. She said into the recorder, 'We have left the sandy coastal road. Now the dunes are changing colour to crusty pinky brown – this is gravel which the wind has swept up onto them. Now the land is losing its moonscape quality and turning into a flat hard brown stoniness that shimmers in the distance. Here and there are massive sprawling plants with fleshy, tentacle-like leaves that lie on the earth – these are welwitschia, and they are over two thousand years old.'

Now, on the horizon, hills were rising up, under the mercilessly blue sky, jumbled mountains of many different shapes, carved by the winds, gleaming iron black under the searing sun, and there were shimmering mirages on the hard earth between them: it was afternoon when they came to the Springbokwasser gate. McQuade went into the ranger's office and signed out of the Skeleton Coast.

They drove into the jumbled hills of Damaraland. It was late afternoon when they reached the oasis of Palmwag. Tall palm trees rose up, and clustered around them were half a dozen thatched huts. A thatched gateway bade them welcome to the Palmwag Safari Lodge.

'Oh,' she said, 'it's delightful!'

Heavy greenery clustered under the palms. There was a thatched bar and dining hut. Amongst the palms were small swimming pools where the stream came out of the ground.

They were the only guests. The floors of the huts were raw cement, and the walls were made of cane that let daylight through. The whole place was delightfully African and tranquil. She said, 'This country *gets* to you . . .'

They plunged into the blue cool pool and he took her in his arms. They held each other, hands laced behind each other's necks, and she slipped her legs around his hips and they just grinned at each other in sheer happiness; and he slipped his hand under her bikini and felt her soft cool nakedness, and she slipped her hand inside his swimming trunks. They wallowed in the beautiful pool, sharing the excitement of each other, the sheer pleasure and anticipation of what they were going to do. She grinned at him with sparkly eyes: 'I'm having a lovely time . . .' and it seemed McQuade had never been so happy. He had lived long enough to know that these things take time, but it felt as if he was head over heels in love.

Early next morning he drove to Jakob's kraal. He left Sarah still deep asleep in their hut. He took the photograph of Heinrich Muller. An hour later he ground up the track to Jakob's cluster of stone huts. The scene was exactly the same as last time: the cooking fire smouldering, the goats wandering and the chickens scratching. Jakob came out of the dark hut, looking astonished. '*Goeie more, Jakob!*'

Jakob took the photograph in gnarled fingers. He looked at it only a second.

'*Ja.*'

McQuade felt triumphant. Oh yes! '*Ja,* what?'

'*Ja.*' Jakob nodded at the photograph. 'This is the man who came out of the sea.'

'How can you be sure? Here he is neat, his hair combed. When you saw him he was wild.'

Jakob said: 'I am sure.'

McQuade was satisfied. These natives could describe the markings of an antelope they killed ten years ago. 'Jakob, have you told anybody about this, since last I saw you?'

Jakob shook his head.

'And Skellum? Where is he?'

Jakob waved his hand eastwards. 'In the towns. Working.'

'Which town?'

'I do not know.'

McQuade didn't like that, Skellum slobbering around civilization with his big drunken mouth. And no way did he want to double the risk through Jakob. 'Jakob, I need a man to work for a month or two. If I come back to fetch you in three days, will you come to work for me? I'll pay four hundred rand a month.'

Four hundred was untold wealth to Jakob. He said emphatically, at McQuade's chest, 'Ja, Meneer.'

'Good. And don't repeat any of this to anyone . . .'

McQuade was feeling very pleased with life as he drove back to Palmwag. He had been right, he had stumbled upon something very big indeed. And it was a glorious morning and he was driving back to his glorious woman and they had four glorious days together before the *Bonanza* came back, and next week he was going to be a multi-millionaire. Then he was going to cover himself in glory by being the man to find Heinrich Muller, the most-wanted war-criminal today.

30

They had a lovely time, those four glorious days.

They had intended leaving that morning for Etosha National Park, but instead they stayed right there at Palmwag and that happened like this: she was singing in the shower when he got back and he could glimpse her nakedness through the reed partition. He stripped off his clothes and opened the door, and she took his breath away: she had her head back in the teeming water, her hands squeezing the shampoo out of her long sodden hair, her breasts uplifted, the water gushing down over her belly and her silken pubic triangle and golden legs in sensuous sheens. McQuade stood transfixed, eating her up with his eyes, then he seized her. It was a very sensuous shower, soaping each other languorously, the warm water teeming down. When they could both bear it no longer they walked to the bed, dripping, and collapsed onto it. And the soft warm deep secret of her was the most blissful thing he had ever known, and the whimperings and cries of her orgasms were the sweetest sounds he had ever heard.

Afterwards he said, 'I thought you wanted to go to Etosha to see the animals.'

'I've got my own animal today.' She rocked him. 'Very beautiful, very expensive . . .'

'I'm not expensive, I'm free.'

'Ah, no.' She sighed at the rafters. 'The price is looking higher each day. It looks like it's going to cost me my whole heart.'

'I know the feeling,' he whispered.

About noon they made it out of bed. They lay on the grass

beside the swimming pool with an ice-bucket of champagne, and talked in the first quiet time they had had. They talked about themselves, wandering through the delightful court-ship business of unfolding their lives, showing who they really were, telling their pasts, what they were going to do with their futures.

He told her about his days on the Antarctic whaling ships with the Kid and Elsie, about Australia and Sausmarine and about the passenger service they were going to start when they sold the fishing company.

'Oh, wow, that is exciting. When will this be?'

'Quite soon, I think.'

'But how can you bear to leave this country?'

'I can't bear the South African government, that's how.'

She prodded the grass with a hairpin as she told her own story. 'My father was in the US Navy, a flyer, so I lived in naval bases all over the world, such as Hawaii, the Philip-pines, Japan, Spain, and when I was a kid I wanted to join the Navy too, I *felt* part of the Navy and I longed to be one of those swashbuckling flyers. My parents wouldn't hear of it, so journalism was my next choice – see the world and write about it. But it was the *service* I really wanted – Uncle Sam, the star-spangled banner and all that. So, my desire to be a hero got channelled into other causes; Civil Rights, Save-the-Whale, Ban-the-Bomb, and other things I felt strongly about. Anyway, I won the college essay prize two years running, which got me a job on the *Washington Post*. After a few years of hard living, I packed my knapsack and set off to see the world.'

'What kind of hard living?' he said jealously.

She smiled wanly. 'Most newspapermen drink like hell, and I made my fair share of the usual mistakes, jumping into bed with the wrong people, falling in love – or so I thought – with married men. Finally I said to hell with it, and took off.'

McQuade was madly jealous, but then didn't give a damn

how many lovers she'd had as long as *he* was her last. 'Where did your knapsack take you?'

'Just about everywhere *except* South Africa, though I was such a smart-ass I knew all about the place, of course. I wrote articles about my travels and sent them home to various magazines, which paid good money. I was actually in east Africa, about to go down to South Africa when I got offered a good job on the *Monitor* – they'd published some of my stuff. I thought I'd better grab it – I'd been on the road two years – so, home I went. Now, five years later, here I am, picking up where I left off.'

He wanted to ask her if there was a lover back home, but didn't. 'What did you think of the rest of Africa?' He added: 'In one paragraph?'

She sighed. 'It's an unmentionable notion, totally unfashionable, absolute heresy, quite unacceptable to your average reader who hasn't been to Africa, but it's obvious to anyone who has that the rest of Africa is a misgoverned *mess*. Lovely country. Lovely people. But to a greater or lesser extent a corrupt, inefficient, non-democratic, bankrupt mess.' She looked at him. 'And? What do you think?'

McQuade shook his head. 'If I were a black I think I'd find just about anything is preferable to Apartheid.' He told her about his brief marriage to Victoria, his year in prison.

She was amazed, and very sympathetic. 'No wonder you haven't got much time for the South African government.'

'Goddam Hairybacks. But,' he added grudgingly, 'they are improving. Albeit at the speed of the ox-wagon.'

'Do you want to see One Man One Vote tomorrow?'

McQuade sighed. 'The big question,' he said. 'The tragedy of African politics in general, and South African in particular, is that it drives people into extremes. The solutions lie in the middle, in compromise, but the extremists don't want the middle, nor does the outside world – the world wants One Man One Vote.' He shook his head. 'I want to see *Apartheid* abolished tomorrow. Apartheid stinks. It's unjust. Every person, black, white or brown should have his dignity and the right to work, live, marry et cetera where he likes and where he can afford. But if the country is handed over to One Man One Vote at the same time, tomorrow, there is no doubt that South Africa will rapidly degenerate into a non-democratic, inter-tribal mess. So? So abolish Apartheid tomorrow, but don't bring in One Man One Vote overnight, like the British did when they pulled out of Africa. We must devise a specialized constitution to suit the particular needs of South Africa with all its different tribes and attitudes – with a Bill of Rights and elaborate checks and balances to protect minorities. Maybe something like the Swiss have, with their cantonments. Maybe we should start with a limited franchise, or proportional representation and keep that system going for a decade or two while we acclimatize the people to new political responsibility – in other words, finish the job the British abandoned when they so hastily folded their tents.'

'But will the South African government do it?'

'They'll have to soon. They can't sit on the lid of the boiling pot for ever. It's getting damn hot. Sanctions are hurting, and Apartheid is an obvious failure, it's breaking down under the weight of its own impracticability. At long last, after ruling us with a rod of iron for forty years, the Afrikaner government has realized it must reform and share power in some form.'

'But can they sit on the lid for a decade?'

McQuade sighed. 'They've got the army and police force to do the job, but how long can they *afford* the expense? Especially with sanctions?' He waved a finger northwards. 'Up there on the border the army is costing the government one million rand a day fighting the Cubans and SWAPO. How long can South Africa keep it up – winning the battles but losing the war?' He shook his head again. 'The rest of the world will never let up their sanctions until we have One Man One Vote, and the communists will never be satisfied until we have a one-party Marxist state where *no man* has a vote.'

'And the ANC?' she said pensively. 'What about Nelson Mandela? Do you think he should be freed?'

He said emphatically, 'Yes. We've got to talk realistically to the ANC some time, as a major political force, and the sooner we get down to the negotiating table the better. It's common sense to do it while we have the upper hand and can drive strong bargains with them – to ensure they renounce violence, to ensure everybody's good political behaviour and cooperation with the new constitution, et cetera.'

'And here in Namibia – ideally, what do you want to see happen?'

McQuade sloshed more champagne into their glasses. It wasn't his problem any more: in a week he'd have cracked that submarine and would be a multi-millionaire.

'I want the Cubans to go home. Then I want the South Africans to do our dirty work for us and thrash SWAPO, and impose a peace on them. And meanwhile we should work flat out towards preparing the country for democracy – as the government is belatedly trying to do – encouraging black middle-class political parties, et cetera. Then – with SWAPO disarmed and discredited as the terrorist Marxist outfit it is – give us independence on 435. *Then* I'd take my chances on a chastened SWAPO behaving in a tolerable manner.' He shrugged. 'Risky, but worth the risk in exchange for getting rid of South Africa. And that's how most of us here feel.'

She plucked at the grass pensively, the sun a sheen on her golden body.

'And how do you feel about Victoria now?'

He snorted softly.

'It's a long time ago now,' he said.

Lunch was long and very boozy. They were still the only guests. He told her about the Kid's new teeth, and when he got to the bit about 'I meant the *bottom* ones,' she threw back her head and laughed until the tears ran down her face. That established him as a raconteur and when he started telling her a story she started to giggle, just in anticipation, before he got to the funny bits, and when he got to the punchline she was convulsed. She thought he was a scream, and it is lovely to be madly in love with somebody who thinks you're a laugh-a-minute. And their lovemaking that afternoon was the happiest and wildest either of them had ever known, desperately trying to get more and more of each other until simultaneously their world exploded in a magnificent crescendo.

31

The next morning they left for Etosha, driving east through the hard rocky hills. They saw zebra and springbok and elephant and, when he stopped to let her photograph some wild ostrich, they were attacked by an angry male who leapt in the air and kicked his massive spurs against the Land-rover, before pursuing them down the road until he was satisfied he had impressed them. Sarah thought everything was terrific.

But she hadn't seen anything yet. The next two days seemed the most delightful in her life. She had never heard a lion roar or an elephant trumpet. Now, at the Okakuya rest camp in Etosha she lived and slept amongst them. On the edge of the camp is a big waterhole, where, all day and night, the animals trooped up to drink. Their first night they sat drinking wine and grilling chops over their open fire, watching the parade of animals. Sarah was enthralled. She whispered breathlessly into her tape-recorder:

'There is a strict code of priority. The zebra will not come too close when the wildebeest are drinking, the bad-tempered rhinoceros will share his waterhole with nobody . . .'

The big black rhinoceros stood up to his knees in the pool, his prehensile lip slurping, his beady eye on the other animals malevolently. A new herd of springbok appeared like yellow wraiths out of the bush beyond, then stopped when they saw the rhino. He glowered at them. McQuade pointed to where, beyond the rhino a row of heads appeared above the treetops. 'Giraffe.'

The heads swayed towards the hole, then they emerged out of the bush into the floodlit clearing, lanky and graceful.

They also stopped when they saw the rhino. He turned his massive head to glower at them, but decided their distance was respectful enough. He doggedly buried his mouth back in the water. Everybody waited, immobile in the floodlights.

Finally the rhino raised his head. He eyed the buck and giraffe challengingly. He had had enough water, but he stuck to his rights, letting everybody know who he was. The springbok and giraffe waited understandingly. 'Come on, you old meanie,' Sarah whispered. Finally the old meanie lumbered out of the water, but he had not yet finished pulling his rank. He stood on the bank truculently, immobile, his prehistoric horn curving up, telling the world there would be no nonsense. The giraffes and springbok understood perfectly. Finally, when he was satisfied that he had impressed them, he turned and lumbered off into the bush, happily bad-tempered.

'The mean old bastard!'

The giraffes unfroze and came lankily towards the water-hole. The springbok moved towards the opposite end twitching their tails. While the giraffes lined up on the edge, the springbok daintily entered the water. The giraffes planted their long spindly forelegs wide astride, and they lowered their long gentle necks to the water, their piebald rumps up in the air.

For a minute Sarah sat there, gazing at them, absolutely happy; then she marshalled her thoughts and whispered into her recorder: 'In an attitude of complete defencelessness the lofty, kindly giraffe . . .' At that moment the lofty giraffes snapped their long necks up and the springbok sprang around and started bounding out of the water. The giraffes scrambled their spread-eagled legs together and ran. They disappeared into the black bush in a loping gallop. Sarah was frantically reporting the event into her recorder. There followed an expectant silence. Not a thing moved. Then out of the blackness, into the floodlight, stalked the lions, and she gasped.

There was a big male and three tawny lionesses. They came purposefully out of the night. They sniffed the air, but disdainfully; they moved powerfully down to the water's edge. Then they crouched, their haunches bulging, and began to lap.

'*Oh,*' she breathed, 'I'm over the *moon* . . .'

The lions drank, ears back, tail-tips twitching, and their silent presence dominated the night. Sarah was transfixed, her recorder poised. Suddenly the lion jerked up his big head and his three lionesses did the same – and then Sarah saw the huge shapes wafting slowly through the treetops. '*Elephants!*'

There were six coming ponderously, silently out of the darkness, huge and grey and wrinkled, their massive ears slowly flapping and their gnarled trunks slopping. Then the big cow leader saw the lions. She froze, and the other five stopped simultaneously, their trunk tips up, sniffing the night. The four lions crouched, all heads facing the massive intruders, bulging muscles tensed, their tails flicking angrily. For a full minute the two sides glared at each other, then, suddenly, the silence was shattered by a short snarl. It came from the big-maned lion and it was very impressive. It was answered immediately by an angry trumpet from the big cow elephant, high-pitched and deep-chested, and she shook her great head and flapped her ears and swung her trunk sideways so dust flew. Behind her the others stood immobile, letting the boss handle the crisis.

This exchange of insults was followed by deep, hostile silence, attended by the flicking of the lions' tails and much mutual glaring. Finally, the lion returned his head to the water and resumed his lapping, and his lionesses followed suit. But without much relish. The big cow moved her great self and began to plod slowly towards the water. Her herd followed in slow motion. She moved resolutely into the water, twenty yards away from the lions, her ears slowly flapping and her trunk restlessly slopping. She glared at the lions once more, then gave a great contemptuous sigh and immersed her trunk tip. The lions lapped hurriedly, and then the male abruptly got up. He turned and stalked away. His lionesses glared at the elephants, then rose and followed their lord, huge muscles rippling, long tails flicking, disdaining to look back, only just satisfied that they had not lost the confrontation. The big cow sighed voluminously, then curled her gnarled trunk up to her cavernous mouth, and squirted the water into it with a great swoosh.

Sarah wanted to burst into applause. '*Oh, what a spectacular charade!*'

They went to bed late and happy. She fell asleep in his arms, her mind a tumult of gangling giraffes and bounding springboks, and sulking lions and self-satisfied she-elephants squirting great gushes of water over their backs. When he woke up at three a.m. she was not beside him. She was sitting on the verandah with her tape-recorder, terrified of missing anything.

She woke him up at sunrise whispering, '*The sun is up and the gate is open* . . .' She was in her tracksuit, her face made up.

'Come back to bed,' he complained.

'Tonight,' she bit his neck, 'tonight I'll make love till you cry out for mercy, but right now the gate is open and all my beautiful friends are out there waiting to have their photographs taken.' She bit his ear and growled loudly into it.

'But what am I going to do with *this*?'

She looked at the area in question, the white sheet thrusting upwards like an arctic encampment.

'My, you're a smooth-talking bastard.' She unzipped her tracksuit top with a grinning flourish.

They left an hour later for Namatoni rest camp, a hundred and fifty kilometres away. McQuade had been through this park half a dozen times but had never seen so many animals so close. There were great herds of wildebeest in the open plains, herds of zebra, giraffe galore browsing off the treetops whilst Sarah hung out of the Landrover photographing, vast herds of springbok turning the plains golden, great lumbering elephant gazing at them thoughtfully. On a small rise, they saw a pride of three lions, sitting bolt upright like cats, watching a line of wildebeest moving. McQuade stopped. The two lionesses suddenly left their knoll in unspoken agreement, and went racing off in opposite directions, while the male remained, his ears pricked. McQuade pointed, and Sarah picked out the hapless wildebeest which the predators had selected, straggling five hundred yards behind the rest.

One lioness raced across the plain, and came to a crouching halt three hundred yards in front of the creature's path, whilst the other halted three hundred yards behind it. Suddenly the solitary wildebeest smelt the lioness in front of it, turned and went racing away in the opposite direction, panic-stricken, and the hindmost lioness waited for it to come. The other lioness raced after the wildebeest, flashing over the veld. At the last moment the waiting lioness sprang in a tawny flash of invincible muscle and claws and jaws and she landed on the animal's neck and clung as it bucked and kicked and reared, and the other lioness hit it in an avalanche of fury. The wildebeest collapsed, the lioness's jaws buried into the terrified nostrils, clamping them shut while the other lioness's jaws sank furiously into its windpipe midst gushes of blood. Within a minute the prey's kicking stopped. All the while, the male lion sat stock-still on his knoll, watching the drama with deep military interest. Now he descended and stalked over to the kill. He swatted his females aside with his big paw, and settled down. He sank his jaws into the warm wildebeest's belly, and started to feed. After a minute or so he let his females in to share.

Sarah's camera was going clickety-click. She collapsed back with an anguished sigh. She felt she had seen all the wonders of the world.

The Namatoni rest camp is an old German fort. In far-off days this white rectangle, with its battlements and clanging gates, housed the *Schutztruppe*, the German troops sent out by Bismarck to pacify the natives. Now the barracks are bedrooms for tourists and the parade square within is a shaded garden. There is a restaurant run by the Wildlife Department but Sarah wanted a fire, the stars, Africa.

She stared into the embers, prodding the chops with a fork. McQuade said: 'Anything the matter?'

'No. I'm just so happy, that's all.' She gave a big sigh. 'I don't want it to end. And tomorrow you must go back to Walvis Bay.'

With all his heart he didn't want it to end either, he did not want her to disappear into the maelstrom of South Africa chasing newspaper stories; he desperately wanted to keep her for himself.

'Don't go back to South Africa yet. I'm only going back to sea for a few days. A week, maximum. Stay in Namibia a bit longer. You're *here* now. There's so much for you to write about – the politics, the history. You can borrow the Landrover and drive up to Windhoek.' He looked at her. 'When I come back we can drive to Ai-Ais, you must see that, and Lüderitz, where the history of this place began . . .'

She had a half smile on her lovely face. Then she sighed. 'And then you must go back to sea again.'

He wanted to laugh, because when he came back from that submarine next week he was going to be a millionaire and wild horses wouldn't get him back to sea for a long, long time. 'Let's cross the bridges as we come to them! At least we'll have had the extra time together!' He added: 'To think.' And, he just wanted to laugh out loud that he loved her. 'About each other. We can't just walk out of each other's lives on Friday, Sarah.'

Her eyes glistened a moment.

'No.' She sat staring into the coals, then she sat up straight. 'Let's think about it.' She turned to him with a bright smile. 'And now shall we stop being sad about it?!'

*

That night, lying in each other's arms in the old fort in the happy, exhausted hour after love, they heard a lion roar, a long deep-throated grunting sound, and she tensed in thrilled excitement; then she went limp and sighed at the ceiling. 'Oh, how can I live in Boston after this?'

And he kissed her neck and he made up his mind. Next week he was either going to be a millionaire or he was going to have to catch more fish, but either way he was damned if he was going to let this lovely woman go out of his life! He said:

'When I come back we'll drive to Ai-Ais and Lüderitz. And then you're coming to sea with me. You can write a wonderful story about the fishing grounds out there in the Benguela – an *important* story, about how the world is raping the seas. And you'll get fantastic photographs.'

She slowly turned to him, with a gentle smile of hopelessness. And before she could refuse he heard himself saying, 'I love you, Sarah.' And he knew with absolute certainty that he meant it.

She looked at him a long moment, then gently stroked his eyebrow with a fingertip. 'I know the feeling . . . But it's not as simple as that, is it?'

McQuade wanted to laugh. 'It is! The explosive South African situation can wait!' She grinned at that and he repeated solemnly, with all his heart: 'I *love* you, Sarah. You can't have a chance of such happiness and not see it through!'

Her lovely face went serious. Then she pressed her fingertip to his lips.

'I think you may be right. And I think you think you do. And yes, I think I do, too. And I think we better think about it.'

McQuade was completely happy. Because he knew that she would stay till he came back next week, a millionaire.

*

The next morning it was still like that, and McQuade was feeling on top of the world as they left Namatoni in the sunrise, heading back towards the faraway Skeleton Coast-.They still had a whole night and almost two more days of each other, and he was convinced that Sarah was going to stay on. She was in excellent spirits too, and her eyes had a shine. She was bursting with excitement and camera-clicking again. It was mid-morning when they passed through the formalities of the Okakuya gate, and mid-afternoon when they reached Jakob's kraal. Jakob loaded his belongings into the Landrover and bade his wife farewell. McQuade told Sarah that the old man was an old acquaintance who was coming to work for him. That night they slept on the Skeleton Coast, built a roaring fire and grilled sausages and baked potatoes. A heavy fog rolled in off the cold Atlantic, and it was cold, and the whole world was still. It was beautiful, the fairy-like mist slowly moving over them, and she felt she was in an enchanted land and the last few days seemed like a dream. They lay together deep in the big warm sleeping bag behind a hummock where Jakob could not see them. Finally she said quietly: 'I can't bear to leave you. And you're right, there is plenty to write about here. So, yes, I will stay until you come back next week, please.'

He squeezed her tight.

The dense fog lay heavy along the Skeleton Coast all the next day, making the desert look like a winter landscape. Sarah sat beside him in the glow of the instrument panel. The whole world was beautiful, and even the prospect of what he had to do when he got to that submarine did not daunt him. All that mattered was here and now, with her. When they got to Swakopmund the fog was so dense the streetlights were on, and it looked like a Bavarian skiing village. And even drab, flat Walvis Bay, smelling of fish, looked pretty and cosy with its twinkling lights.

McQuade first went to his house and installed Jakob in the servants' quarters adjoining the garage, before they drove down Oceana Road to the fishing wharf. Even the lights of the trawlers looked cosy in the fog. He pulled into the Kuiseb compound, and there was the *Bonanza*.

'Well,' he said. 'There she is.'

She was silent and ghostly in the swirly fog, her bridge lights twinkling. She must have been in for some hours because the fish weighing was over, the refrigerated containers gone. For the first time in three weeks McQuade felt the dread of where he was about to go with her, and was going to be very glad when this was over. 'Want to have a look at her?'

'I particularly want to see the captain's cabin.'

The boat was deserted. There was a note from Elsie in an envelope. It said that everybody would return at sunrise, except the Kid whose ankle was badly sprained, and the Coloured crew who had been given one week's paid leave. Nathan had arrived that afternoon and was installed at Railway Yard View; the ship was revictualled and ready to sail at any time.

Sarah had said that she was perfectly happy to spend the night in his house in Fifth Street, but he insisted on the Europahof Hotel in Swakopmund. He had a lot to do in the morning which he did not want her to know about, and he did not want her to come to the harbour and see them sail with a skeleton crew. Madly in love though he was, he wanted to be able to walk out easily in the morning. And they had had a lovely five days together, a magical five days, and he did not want to spoil it by having the last night in Railway Yard View, with Nathan.

After dinner, lying in his arms in their bed, she stroked his head and said:

'Oh yes – very expensive.'

And even the prospect of that submarine did not spoil his happiness.

PART SIX

32

The fog was still thick as smoke, and he wished that it would stay. He did not want to be diving down on that submarine tomorrow. He said goodbye to Sarah, with promises to be back in a week: he gave her the *Bonanza*'s call-sign, so she could radio-telephone him to find out exactly when he was returning. He was outside the Dive Shop when it opened.

He bought another new wetsuit to replace the one torn by barnacles, three tank-contents gauges, another harness and tank, another box of batteries for the underwater torches. When he wrote out the cheque he was very glad indeed that Nathan had come to the party. He drove back to his house, gave Jakob some money for food and gave him some chores to do around the garden, raking the sand and tidying up. He retrieved his notes from under the bed. He drove down to the wharf. The fog was still thick and all lights in the harbour were on. Oh God, he did not want to go to sea.

His humour was not improved by Tucker bursting up onto the bridge wide-eyed: *'What about this 435?'*

McQuade was in no mood for Tucker. 'Forget 435! It'll never happen!'

Tucker cried: *'It's happening! The South Africans say they're prepared to withdraw their troops from Angola! They could all be back across the river in a few days!'*

McQuade stared at him. 'South African troops are withdrawing from the war?' he said incredulously.

'Not yet but almost!' Tucker cried. 'To show they mean peace! Where've you been that you haven't heard?!' He waved his arm: 'Terrible things have been happening! What's going to happen to our housekeeping when SWAPO takes over everything?!'

McQuade stared at him. He said slowly, 'Has Cuba agreed to withdraw her troops from Africa?'

'Yes!' Tucker cried. 'And Angola's agreed! All they've got to organize now is how long it takes to get the troops out! South Africa's just throwing us to the wolves! And then what's going to happen to our housekeeping . . .?'

'*ELSIE!*' McQuade roared.

Elsie came bursting up onto the bridge in his apron. 'Yes?'

'What's this about 435 and South African troops being poised to withdraw from Angola?'

Elsie slumped his shoulders and rolled his liquid eyes. 'Oh, bullshit, bullshit, bullshit, darling! Yes, Cuba's made a *dramatic* announcement that they're prepared to withdraw their troops – over a period of time – provided South Africa withdraws *immediately* and implements 435 and provided South Africa and the US stops supporting UNITA. And so there's international jubilation, et cetera. But we've had cliff-hangers like this before, haven't we? Cuba always changes its mind – moves the goal posts. And anyway the South Africans are demanding the impossible – withdrawal of all those Cuban troops in seven months. According to the news it would logistically take two years for fifty thousand to piss off, with all their horrid tanks and all.' Elsie shook his fat face at him. 'So, it's just a smoke-screen, darling. South Africa is making a grand gesture, so Cuba does the same. The Hairybacks know full well the Cubans won't accept in the end. So when her troops roll back into Angola they'll go as martyrs, more in sorrow than in anger.' He ended, 'No way will South Africa withdraw unless the Cubans do, and they won't.'

McQuade felt immense relief. Elsie was on the ball, almost an intellectual. He glared at Tucker. 'Do you think you can remember all that, Hugo? Now dry your eyes and forget about 435!'

But it wasn't so easy to forget about it. His mood was not improved by Nathan's good spirits when he showed up on the bridge. 'At ease, men, *aha-ha-ha*!' He was thoroughly enjoying himself, wreathed in Jewish smiles. McQuade would have preferred the man to be worried sick about losing his money. 'Can I steer?'

'No, you stick to ladies' underwear and let us run the ship. Out of my way, please!' They began putting to sea. He turned on Tucker's long face.

'*Now* what's wrong with you?'

Tucker whined, 'How can we do this without the Kid?' He waved his hand at the new diving gear. 'And now this new *expense*. Now we owe Nathan *and* the bank . . .'

'Dry your eyes, you're not going down into that submarine tomorrow!'

For a moment Tucker's demeanour improved. 'You going down alone?'

'I said *into* that submarine! You're still coming with me into the conning tower. And don't count on not having to go any further, I may need you inside.'

Tucker looked aghast. 'Now look,' he said emphatically, 'let's get one thing absolutely clear: I am *not* going any further than the conning tower. I am a *father* . . . I vote we put this whole thing off until the Kid's ankle is better.'

Elsie snapped. 'We've already paid the crew off!'

Tucker cried, 'It's all right for you – *you* don't have to go down where angels fear to tread! We could go'n round up the crew—'

McQuade shouted, 'Shut up everybody! While I tell you what I found out in Germany!' He glared at Tucker: 'At my own expense . . .'

He unzipped his holdall and pulled out the book *The Type VII C U-Boat* by David Westwood, the photographs he had taken of the submarine at Laboe, and the brochure of it. He did not produce his file of research done at the Imperial War Museum because there was no need for them to know about

Heinrich Muller yet: if that was repeated ashore it could ruin all his plans. He banged the book and glared at them all, especially Tucker.

'It's all in there. Every minute detail of our submarine. To scale. We'll go through it together, page by page, drawing by drawing, until we know every step backwards. And I was right in trying to enter feet-first by the escape tube. Except I must do it without the harness on my back. It's got to be lowered down to me after I've cleared the bottom of the tube.'

'Oh Lord,' Tucker moaned.

'Now will you please start going through that book while I get some sleep. And Hugo? . . .'

'Why have I got to know what the inside looks like?' Tucker whined suspiciously. '*I'm* not going inside.'

McQuade controlled his irritation. 'I want *everybody* to study that book so *everybody* knows what's down there, in case there's an emergency and *somebody* has to stick their neck out and help me! Got that? And Hugo?'

'Oh Lord. And what else did you find out in Germany – you went to see if you could trace the submarine in the archives.'

McQuade said triumphantly, 'It is one of twenty-eight submarines officially listed as missing! Last reported in or near Flensberg at the end of April, 1945. And I traced Horst Kohler's widow. Her husband told her that the submarine was putting to sea on a *non*-aggressive mission. Because it only had one torpedo. And it was carrying a number of civilians, as passengers.' He raised his eyebrows. 'They must have been very important civilians, and very important civilians escaping in a Navy submarine must have been carrying a lot of swag. So will everybody please cheer up?'

They were all staring at him. '*Wow* . . .' Elsie breathed, 'congratulations.' Nathan was looking smug. Pottie Potgieter was open-mouthed. '*Jere*, man . . .' Only Tucker looked unimpressed. He opened his mouth but McQuade cut in.

'Wake me in two hours! And Hugo? Will you please, please for Christ's sake stop saying "Oh Lord" every time I tell you something?'

He picked up his holdall and beckoned to Nathan to follow him. Tucker cried: 'And will you please, please, please stop saying Christ when we're about to risk life and limb where angels fear to tread?'

Nathan followed him down into the saloon. McQuade said, 'Did you find out anything more about Julie Goldstein?'

'Yep,' Nathan said cheerfully. 'That he's a crook.'

'For God's sake, Nathan, be serious.'

'He's a crook. And he's just the guy for us.'

'How is he a crook?'

Nathan said, 'Oh, he's a genuine antique dealer. World-wide, et cetera. But he beats the Exchange Control Regulations for rich clients who want to get money out of the country illegally.'

'How?' McQuade demanded.

'Easy. You buy one of Julie's antique vases, from his catalogue. The vase is worth, say, ten thousand. But you pay him twenty thousand. He gives you an invoice for ten thousand. He imports your vase and delivers it to you. He then pays the equivalent of the other ten which you overpaid into a Swiss account for you, from his own Swiss account – less thirty per cent.' He spread his hands. 'And everybody's happy. Julie's happy because he sold a vase and he's made an additional thirty per cent on your other ten thousand. And you're happy because you've got a nice vase *and* you've got seven thousand out of the country.'

'I see. Bloomberg told you this?'

'Bloomers,' Nathan agreed. 'Another way is this. You sell your Ming vase to Julie. Although its real value is ten thousand, he pays you one thousand, and gives you an invoice for one thousand. He then crates it up and sends it to a rich buyer in, say, Istanbul. The Istanbul gennelman pays ten thousand for it, into Julie's Swiss account. Julie now pays you your nine thousand, less thirty per cent, into your Swiss account. Simple.'

McQuade rubbed his chin. 'Where's the catch? How come he doesn't get caught?'

Nathan spread his hands. 'What's the value of a Ming vase?' He tapped his head: 'Its value is in the mind. That's the beauty of this "wealth" he talks about. He can prove he only paid one thousand for it, because he's got the copy of the invoice he gave you. Customs can't call in experts from Sotheby's every time, and if Exchange Control asks questions he says he *paid* one thousand and *sold* it for fifteen hundred. He *imports* fifteen hundred back into South Africa to keep Exchange Control happy.'

McQuade gave a worried sigh. 'I don't like this. So, technically we're going to *sell* him the loot – at a fraction of its value. So legally it's *his*. And we've got to trust him to re-sell it for us? Is he to be trusted with millions?'

'He's got an awful lot of rich clients he doesn't want to lose.'

'If he cheats us he won't need any more rich clients. And our loot is probably in the form of gold bullion. Or diamonds. He can't say that's a Ming vase.'

'He'll export it in crates of carpets and artefacts. He's exporting stuff all the time.'

McQuade went to his cabin. He lay in his bunk, staring at the deckhead. He dreaded diving down on that submarine tomorrow. That long dark ghostly shape. And what horrors would he find in there?

He forced the image aside and thought about Sarah.

Tucker did not wake him after two hours. 'You were asleep and I thought what the hell, I'm so uptight I wouldn't be able to rest so I might as well stand your watch for you.'

McQuade said irritably, 'For God's sake, I'm the poor bastard who's got to go down that tube!'

'Don't feel obliged,' Tucker said. 'We can turn around right now if you want!'

'Yeah, and what about the money you're going to make?'

Tucker was morbidly studying the book on U-boats, the helm on auto-pilot. Elsie was in the galley preparing lunch, Potgieter was off-watch, Nathan was lying on the foredeck sunbathing.

McQuade went through the photographs with Tucker, then leafed through the book with him, page by page, explaining. 'Okay, okay,' Tucker said irritably, 'I'm not stupid, you know.'

'Just scared shitless?'

'Just scared shitless.'

He left Tucker to study and went back to his cabin. He took the recorder and tapes from his holdall and went to the galley. Elsie was making a salad, chopping up radishes with a meatcleaver. 'Mind your fingers, Elsie.'

'I've plenty of 'em. Now tell me what really happened.'

'I've met the girl I'm going to marry, Elsie.'

Elsie stopped chopping. 'Oh James! How *wonderful*! Who is she?'

McQuade grinned, 'I'll tell you later. Right now I've got work to do. And a job for you.' He handed him the tapes and recorder. 'Transcribe those tapes using the typewriter. It'll take you a couple of days, probably.'

Elsie looked surprised. 'What are they about?'

'All relevant to our submarine. You're to treat this as absolutely confidential, the boys must know nothing about it until it becomes necessary, because if one of them opens their mouths ashore, the most-wanted Nazi war-criminal of today may escape.'

Elsie was staring at him.

McQuade went to his cabin. He unpacked his file of notes and spread them out on his table. He had a jumble of facts about Muller's activities which he now intended to put into comprehensible sequence, in an effort to know everything possible about his man, in the hope that some detail would turn up which would help him find the bastard once he was finished with that submarine.

He began to make notes from notes. An hour passed before he got his facts into acceptable order. His most helpful source was the photostatted pages from the *Encyclopaedia of the Third Reich*. He began to paraphrase:

'Heinrich Muller rose through the ranks of the Munich Police by dedicated, intelligent work. Before Hitler came to power, Muller was sent to Russia to study police methods. He became a great admirer of the Soviet Secret Police spy system and terror techniques.

'When Hitler's Nazi Party began their subversive tactics, Muller energetically tried to suppress them. However, when Nazi power was climbing, Hitler murdered his niece with whom he was having an incestuous affair, and Muller, who investigated the case, was bribed by Martin Bormann to conceal evidence and hush up the case.

'When Hitler came to power in 1933 Muller promptly directed his police expertise against anti-Nazis and communists, using the terror techniques he'd learnt in Russia.

'Muller did many dirty jobs for Hitler. He masterminded the Night of the Long Knives in which the stormtroops – the Brown-Shirt thugs who had been Hitler's bodyguards – were systematically murdered. Thereafter Muller subjugated the army for Hitler by destroying the reputations of generals who did not want war.

'Meanwhile, as head of the Gestapo, Muller was ultimately responsible for deciding who would be sent to the concentration camps built for Hitler's enemies.

'To provide Hitler with an excuse to declare war on Poland in 1939, Muller faked a Polish attack on a German radio station near the border by providing condemned German prisoners who were put into Polish uniforms and shot dead in the fake radio station "attack".

'When Hitler declared war on Russia, Muller organized the

Einsatzgruppen to carry out genocide. The plan was that thirty million Slavs were to be killed to provide *Lebensraum*, living space, for Germany.

'Muller was one of the fifteen top Nazis at the Wannsee Conference in 1942 at which Hitler's Final Solution was unveiled. His Gestapo was given the job of building extermination facilities in concentration camps, of "combing Europe from west to east" for Jews. He was Adolf Eichmann's boss, responsible for all Eichmann's actions.

'In 1942, Deputy-Führer Rudolf Hess flew to England to attempt to make peace with Churchill, and has been in prison ever since. Hitler was furious and Muller conducted the murderous purge that followed to root out possible traitors. Similarly, when Heydrich, head of the Security Service, was assassinated in Prague, Muller conducted the purge. The town of Lidice was razed to the ground, all male inhabitants shot. Muller was also very impatient with the French and the Italians for failing to send sufficient Jews to Germany for extermination, and he applied pressure on both countries to improve.

'Muller issued the "Bullet Decree" ordering that certain prisoners of war were to be executed, a breach of International Law intended as a terror-deterrent to Allied parachute commandos and airmen who crashed over Germany.

'Throughout the war Muller tried desperately to suppress the "Red Orchestra", a spy's radio transmissions to Russia. He made many arrests, but the radio transmissions kept popping up again elsewhere. He failed to suppress the last one, which was coming from near Hitler's chancellory in Berlin. Some theorists suggest that the spy was Martin Bormann himself, Hitler's right-hand man, who had the only uncontrolled radio in Germany, used to send instructions to Nazi Party offices. Other theorists even suggest that the spy was Muller, who was an admirer of the Soviet Secret Police. This seems highly unlikely. Under the Nazis, Muller turned his terrible expertise on the communists in Germany, masterminded the *Einsatzgruppen* to murder millions of Russians, including communists, and furiously tried to crush the Red Orchestra. He personally ordered "special action" – the gas chamber or firing squad – for thousands of Russian prisoners of war. He made himself into an arch-war-criminal all down the line.

'Muller was a member of The Brotherhood which, as the war closed in on Germany, organized escape routes for senior Nazis, and funds to rebuild the Fourth Reich. He offered false identification documents to members of his circle, including Adolf Eichmann. Muller probably had false identification documents made for himself. Since he used the name H. Strauss at the dentist in Swakopmund, it is likely that that was the name on his false documents and that he stuck to that name.

'Throughout the war, Hitler raided the museums of Europe and stole vast quantities of works of art. When the war turned against Germany, Hitler had most of his loot transferred to a salt mine in the Aussee region. Also, many sealed crates containing treasure were dropped into lakes in the region. Some were recovered after the war and mostly contained counterfeit English bank-notes. More sunken crates containing treasure were found in Black Lake in Czechoslovakia: records prove that these crates were loaded under the supervision of Heinrich Muller.

'He directed the terror-machinery of Germany up to the end. He frequently visited Hitler's bunker, probably daily. He worked closely with Martin Bormann, Hitler's right-hand man. Hitler dictated his will and political testament the day before he committed suicide, appointing Grand Admiral Dönitz as his successor to carry on the "Heroic Age" of Nazism. Copies of the will were despatched by couriers through the conflagration of Berlin, to Dönitz at his base in northern Germany. After Hitler's body had been burned, along with his bride's, Eva Braun, in the chancellory garden, Muller helped Bormann store important documents. Both thereafter disappeared from the bunker, though not together. It is known that Bormann intended to escape from the ruins of Berlin and make his way to Admiral Dönitz to offer his services in Dönitz's new government, as did Himmler and Ribbentrop. It is highly likely, therefore, that Muller did the same thing.

'Conclusion. Because Muller arrived on the Skeleton Coast in possession of "official" Nazi loot (counterfeit banknotes), and because Frau Kohler says the submarine left on a non-aggressive mission (only one torpedo) it seems likely that Admiral Dönitz sent Muller off on the submarine to carry out the late Hitler's testament – in which case there is likely to be a great deal of treasure aboard. Alternatively, Muller pulled strings to commandeer the submarine on his own initiative – in which case he is likely to have had more treasure on board than he could swim ashore with.'

McQuade threw down his pen.

But why did only two men escape?

The sun was going down, blazing red and gold. McQuade stared out at the cold, seething Atlantic. By God, he was going to bring the bastard to justice if he was still alive . . .

33

It was a long night. The *Bonanza* ploughed northwards, gently rolling with the long Atlantic swells. Nobody showed up in the saloon for dinner: Tucker was asleep, Nathan had had too much sun, Elsie was typing and Potgieter was on watch, studying the U-boat book with furrowed brow. McQuade ate alone, then went up to the bridge and plotted their latest position. He reckoned they would reach their destination before dawn. Then Tucker showed up with his long face and McQuade disappeared back to bed to forestall any discussion.

But he had difficulty going to sleep. He tried to think of Sarah.

It was four a.m. when Potgieter woke him. 'We're there, hey, man.'

He went up to the bridge. The sky was full of stars. Half a mile away he could see the ghostly Skeleton Coast.

He checked the depth-sounder. The radar. The sat-nav. He dropped the anchor. And went back to bed. But he could not sleep. Nor could he read. He could not even concentrate on Sarah. When he could, he just wanted her here to hold his hand, to tell him it was going to be okay. To think it was exciting, to see it through journalist's eyes – a big deal, diving to retrieve the treasure of Heinrich Muller, Hitler's head of the Gestapo, no less, and maybe then he would see it through her eyes, and then he would not be so shit-scared. Maybe with Sarah watching he would dive down on it without the horror of that tomb overwhelming him, the veritable fear of God . . .

He swung out of his bunk, went to the bridge and switched

on the spreader-lights. All the equipment was laid out on the foredeck. Tucker had made an implement for clearing the barnacles off the tube, a shovel-head lashed to a pole, and had also made another spear, a carving-knife lashed to a broomstick. McQuade checked everything again: the gas-tanks, the harnesses, the regulators, the new tank-contents gauges, the toolbags, the ropes, the underwater torches.

At sunrise everybody was up. Nathan was in his busybody good spirits, rubbing his beefy hands and making jokes, Tucker looking as if he was going to a funeral and complaining he had not slept at all, *not at all*. Elsie was making breakfast. Only Pottie Potgieter looked happy, trying to be helpful, doing another check of this and having another look at that, and then fetching four more mugs of coffee. As the sun came up, glorious red and gold, the Skeleton Coast was born again, mauve-black on riotous fire.

'Okay. Everybody up on the bridge, and we go through everything one more time.'

'Oh Lord,' Tucker prayed.

McQuade had decided to leave Potgieter on board, rather than Elsie, in case the ship dragged anchor. The dinghy lay alongside the *Bonanza*. Elsie climbed down the rope ladder into it. They lowered the gear down on a rope. Then Nathan clambered down, and then McQuade, followed by Tucker, in their wetsuits. Elsie started the outboard motor. Potgieter cast the dinghy off. 'Good luck, hey!'

Nathan shouted, 'Put champagne on ice!' as the dinghy surged away.

The yellow marker-float rode over the long swells, then disappeared down into the troughs. The dinghy went churning towards it, down into the troughs and over the swells. They surged up to it and McQuade grabbed it. He tied the dinghy's painter to it. The dinghy rode on the swells, anchored now to the submarine.

Elsie tied the end of a coil of rope to the bottom of the sacks containing the spare gas tanks, while McQuade and Tucker hefted on their harnesses. Then he tied another coil to the other end of the sack. McQuade put his regulator into his mouth and tested the airflow. He took it out and said to Tucker, 'Remember to take shallow breaths.'

'Yeah, yeah, yeah.' Tucker's face was pale.

'And keep an eye on your tank-contents gauge. When the needle enters the red area you've only got about five minutes of air. Less if you breathe hard.'

'Yeah, yeah,' Tucker said miserably.

McQuade spat in his mask, smeared the saliva across the lens, then washed it off in the sea. He pulled the mask on, then his gloves, and before he could hesitate he toppled himself over backwards. There was the blow of cold sea and the roaring of bubbles. He broke surface and grabbed the dinghy. Nathan handed him his toolbag, which he slung around his neck. Elsie passed him one end of rope, with a loop tied in it. McQuade thrust his arm through it. Finally Elsie handed him one spear and the barnacle scraper. 'Good luck, darling.' McQuade buried his head beneath the water, lifted his buttocks, and he kicked.

He dived down into the gloom, following the line of the yellow float, clutching the spear and scraper, dragging the rope. Down he swam, his eyes wide, peering, then suddenly it emerged out of the gloom, the shrouds of nets, then the long, ghostly shape, fading away into greyness. His heart was knocking and he clenched the regulator and he kicked.

Down he went, his breathing roaring. Now he could see the hordes of fish, all sizes and colours, the tentacles of nets were waving above his head, the conning tower was looming at him, frosted in weed and barnacles, the guns of the wintergarten pointing ghost-like at him. He grabbed the rim of the conning tower. He pulled himself down into the bridge. He unslung the toolbag. Then he slid the rope off his arm, and tied the end to the handrail.

He looked upwards. The rope trailed away between the

278

waving nets. He gave two sharp tugs on it. Up in the dinghy, Elsie hefted the first sack up onto the gunnel. Tucker whispered, 'Help me now, Lord,' and crossed himself fervently, then toppled backwards into the sea. He reappeared with a wild-eyed gush and Nathan handed him his toolbag. Tucker slung it round his neck frantically, then Nathan passed him the spear. Tucker clutched it, crossed himself frantically one more time, then rammed his head under the water. And Elsie gripped the rope and tipped the first sack into the sea.

It crashed under water about Tucker's terrified head, and Elsie gave three tugs on the rope and down in the conning tower McQuade began to pull. Wild-eyed, Tucker began to swim down beside the sack, guiding it. Down in the conning tower McQuade pulled on the rope, peering upwards, while up in the dinghy Elsie fed the rope out on demand.

McQuade saw the shape of Tucker materialize between the waving nets, his legs kicking like a desperate frog, his spear clutched in one hand, the other desperately clutching the sack, trying to steer it clear of the nets, *heave* and kick, *heave* and kick ... McQuade pulled, watching this apparition, praying the nets didn't snag Tucker, and down Tucker came, his spear-arm frantically trying to paddle sideways away from the nets. The sack cleared the nets, and McQuade closed his eyes in relief. He heaved the sack towards him and Tucker came roaring down to him.

McQuade turned to the hatch. Tucker looked at the black opening fearfully. One small fish, a finger long, came wandering out, unperturbed by their giant shapes bubbling goggle-eyed at it. McQuade pulled out his torch. He peered down into the black chamber below.

There were a few fish swimming around amongst the weeds, and two crayfish this time. But no sign of octopus. Before his nerve failed him he surged down through the hatch, in a roar of bubbles. Tucker thrust the spear down to him. McQuade took it and approached the lower hatch slowly, then shone his torch down it.

No octopus came flying out. All he could see was the murky deck at the bottom of the tube, yellow-grey in the torchlight and the toe of the seaman's boot. He shone the torch shakily down the hole for a minute, to see if any creatures came into the light: only one crab scuttled past. He signalled up to Tucker. The sack appeared and McQuade grabbed it. Then came Tucker's spear and the scraper. Then came Tucker, surging down wide-eyed.

Tucker shone the torch down the tube. McQuade shoved the scraper into the hatch and began to knock off the barnacles.

It took twenty minutes to get all the barnacles off. The water was cloudy with particles. McQuade looked at his gauge; it was almost thirty-five minutes since he had left the dinghy. The gauge needle was in the red, so he had less than five minutes of air left in his tank. He turned to the sack. He pulled out the two spare harnesses and tanks. He unbuckled his harness and shucked it off, keeping the regulator in his mouth. Tucker feverishly unbuckled his own harness and pulled on a new one. McQuade pulled out a coil of rope and tied it onto his new harness, which had a lead weight tied to it to overcome its buoyancy. He handed the coil to Tucker, and then turned to the dreadful hatch.

He pulled his fins off his feet and put the regulator from the new harness into his mouth. He took a deep breath, and slid both feet into the fearful black hole. He gripped the rim and shoved himself down until his shoulders were level with the rim. He clung there, his heart pounding, and Tucker crouched over him, holding the new harness and the rope. McQuade scowled at him fiercely, and Tucker nodded nervously. Then McQuade closed his terrified eyes and he shoved himself downwards, and Tucker lowered the harness down after him. McQuade's feet hit the lower deck of the submarine.

He felt the seaman's boot crunch under his foot. Gargling

in horror, he bent his knees, hollowed his back, and shoved. He surged under the lower end of the tube. He burst through backwards into the pitch black water, and the harness bumped onto the deck below the tube. He scrambled frantically, groped and seized it, and burst above the water into the fetid blackness, sucking on the regulator. He fumbled blindly for the knot on the rope, pulled it apart, and swung the harness onto his back feverishly. He buckled it on, buried his hand into his toolbag, and frantically pulled out his torch. He crouched, and stared.

And, oh God, it was a frightening place. He was in the *Zentrale*, the control centre of the submarine, and his trembling torch threw leaping shadows over the fearful place. There hung the periscope, and all around were dials, valves, gauges, pipes, gear, all blackened and blurred. All around him, up to his waist, was black water, thick as broth, choked with shreds of cloth and wisps of human hair, soupy with particles of human matter. McQuade crouched there, rasping, horrified, his flesh crawling, then he retched.

In one awful instant his stomach heaved in revulsion and his regulator shot out his mouth and he retched, convulsed, and then he sucked in the fetid black atmosphere, reeking of death and he clutched his throat and gagged, horrified, aghast, and he retched again, and up his throat it erupted, coughing, shuddering. He grabbed frantically for his regulator and rammed it back into his mouth. He staggered forwards, rasping in clean air, convulsing at the taste of fetid death, and clutched at the periscope. He clung there, desperately trying to force his convulsing stomach under control; for half a minute, rasping, shuddering, then he shook his head feverishly. He opened his eyes, and made himself shine his torch all around, dreading what he might see.

He did not know what he was looking for. How would the loot be contained? In crates? In sacks? They could be submerged in this stinking water. But most probably it would not have been stored in this room, which would always have been manned. He flashed his torch all around, then shoved himself away from the periscope and made for the first forward hatch. He waded towards it, rasping, his legs trembling, his heart pounding. His feet stirred up squelchy things that crunched, and he desperately tried to force that out of his mind. The top of the circular hatch was visible above the black waterline, and in one frantic movement, before he could recoil, he sunk his head under the thick black water and ducked through. He burst into the next compartment and stood up with a gush.

He was in the commander's cabin. On the port side was the commander's bunk. Lockers were above the waterline. He waded feverishly towards them, wrenched open the nearest one and shone his torch inside.

It held mouldy clothing. He pulled it out, and rummaged through. If only he knew what he was looking for! Surely Muller would not have hidden his loot amongst the skipper's things? He waded further, opening each locker above the waterline, rummaging, feeling like a grave robber. Only clothes. Then he took a deep breath and he plunged his head under the water.

God, it was awful. His bubbles roaring and his light shining through the awful soupiness, particles of human matter suspended. He shone his torch over the bunk. Thank God, there was no dreadful relic of a human being on it. He pulled the lower lockers open, and rummaged through them frantically, desperate to get it over. He shone his torch onto the lockers underneath the bunk. His eyes widened in horror and he gagged, and he burst up out of the water, aghast. He splashed backwards and crashed against the bulkhead. He clutched it, rasping: he had just shone his torch onto a skeleton.

An entire skeleton; the rotting cloth sagging over soupy white bones, the skull staring at him. He must have trodden on a leg, for it had broken away from the rest. McQuade leant against the bulkhead, and with all his horrified heart he just wanted to get out of this terrible place. And oh God this terrible search was hopeless, with so many places to hide things and most of them under this death-laden water. It could take weeks of searching! He clenched his teeth, and reached out for the door leading to the officers' cabin, and his foot crunched on something and his nerves screamed and he wanted to retch. He waded desperately through the doorway, his heart pounding, and shone his torch around.

The lower bunks were under the black water, and the two upper bunks were partly hidden by rotting curtains. This was where Horst Kohler would have slept. McQuade shone his torch around shakily, then his stomach turned over again, as he saw a man's boot.

The foot protruded from an upper bunk, the rest of the skeleton concealed by the rotting curtain. He stood there, staring at the terrible foot; and oh God he just wanted to give up this terrifying search. He reached out and pulled back the curtain.

It came away in his hand. And he felt his heart lurch. He recoiled and stared.

He was looking at another entire skeleton. It was in a tattered uniform, and the head was turned towards him in a terrible grimace. Stretched over the skull was dried skin, wrinkled, the hair clinging in salty black curls. The eye-sockets were empty, and in the centre of the forehead was a round, ragged hole.

McQuade stared, aghast, forcing himself to keep his trembling flashlight on the dreadful face, his horrified mind fumbling. *That was a bullet hole . . . This man had been shot in the head . . . This man had been murdered . . .* He stared at the dreadful face. Then he grasped the nettle in both hands, turned to the opposite bunk, and ripped back the curtain.

He was staring, heart pounding, at another entire skeleton. It also was clothed. It lay on its back, its head partly turned away from him. Blond sparse hair clung to desiccated scalp, and in the temple was another ragged hole. McQuade looked

283

at it a horrified moment, then he lurched away from the bunk, nauseous. He blundered forward to the next doorway.

This was the *Oberfeldwebelraum*, the chief petty officers' quarters. There were four bunks. The starboard upper bunk was empty, the curtains open, but on the port upper bunk sat a man – and McQuade recoiled.

The desiccated corpse was slumped against the bulkhead. It wore a crumbling singlet over skeletal chest. From under-pants protruded two legs, the flesh shrivelled to the bone. McQuade knew before he looked at the skull what he was going to see, but this one was worse than the others; the bullet had smashed the nose-bridge away, so the eye-sockets were joined into one gaping hole.

McQuade clung to the opposite bunk. Mass murder . . . That was what he had blundered upon! A hell-hole of mass murder of German seamen committed forty years ago. McQuade clung to the bunk, eyes closed, heart pounding. Then he shoved himself off and waded frantically on, to the last section.

This was the torpedo-room. There were nine bunks, half of them under water. All the curtains were drawn back. McQuade waded desperately down the alleyway, feverishly flashing his torch over the upper bunks. He saw one skeleton glaring at him with a bullet hole in the face. His feet bumped solid things. He blundered on, trying not to feel the terrible human debris underfoot. He came to the torpedo tubes.

He stopped in front of them, wild-eyed. He flashed his torch all around, looking for crates showing above the ter-rible waterline. This was the most likely storage place if the loot was in large containers, the only part of the submarine that had a fairly large open space.

Nothing protruded above the black water. He shone his torch over the torpedo tubes; the two above the waterline were closed. He waded frantically to the nearest tube-hatch, and seized the lock-handle. It was rusted solid. He turned hurriedly to the other tube-hatch and wrenched. It did not move. He groped frantically under the water for the lower tube-hatches. They were locked solid. He shone his torch over the top of the tubes, over the mass of pipes and cables and valves and dials – a thousand places where small packages could be hidden. He turned and groped with his feet under the water, desperately feeling for containers or sacks. His feet touched things that rolled aside and he desperately tried to close his convulsing mind to what he was stirring up: he waded up and down, groping with his feet through the fetid stinking black water. Up and down he waded, his stomach heaving, and all he felt was bones and skulls crunching and rolling. He leant against the bulkhead, rasping, nauseated. Nothing! And all he wanted to do was get out of here. He shoved himself off the bulkhead and started wading frantically back towards the *Zentrale*.

He blundered down the dreadful watery alleyway between the bunks, as if he were being pursued by the hounds of hell, and burst back into the *Zentrale*, the rotten, oily water running in globules down his mask.

For a moment he clung to the periscope, trying to get the pounding out of his heart, trying to tell himself that no dreadful fiends were pursuing him. All he wanted to do was plunge into that escape tube and go surging back up to that silvery surface, and burst through into God's own glorious daylight and fresh air, but when he looked at his tank-contents gauge through the slime on his mask he saw that he had at least another fifteen minutes of air left. And, oh God, he had waded so far through horror that he should not give up now. He shoved himself off the periscope, and waded for the aft section. There was another circular hatch here. He plunged his head into that black water, burst up on the other side, and shoved up his mask.

He was in the *Unteroffizierenraum*, and his stomach lurched all over again. A broken-up skeleton was flung back in an upper bunk, grinning mouth open, and in the middle of the forehead was another jagged hole. McQuade took one horrified look, then he blundered on. He burst through a doorway, into the galley. He flashed his torch around; black water lapped at the rusted stove. On the other side was a lavatory, the bowl submerged. He waded feverishly on, into the engine room.

The two rows of big diesel engines stretched on into the dreadful blackness; between them was the avenue of black oily water that had not been disturbed for forty years. There was not a sign of a body, but he knew that there were bodies all right. He flashed his trembling torch over the bulkheads. There were another thousand places to conceal small packages, but surely a crowded engine room was not the place where somebody would store loot? He went sloshing and rasping down the avenue of black water, and his feet bumped a multitude of bones, and his nerves screamed. He went frantically wading and slipping down that dreadful avenue, until he burst into the Electrical Room. He paused and flashed his trembling torch, then plunged on down into the blackness.

He came to the aft torpedo area. As he made for the tube, his foot slipped and he grabbed for support, and the torch shot out of his hand. He crashed over sideways. His head went under the dreadful water and all he knew was the gut-wrenching horror of the terrible soup on his maskless face. He frantically struggled upright in the total blackness, snorting the water out of his nostrils, and his foot crunched on something horrible and he lurched and crashed under again. He scrambled upright and crouched there in the blackness, snorting, gasping. And under the black churning water shone the glow of his torch and he pulled his mask down over his eyes and in one whimpering, heartgasping lunge he plunged his head back underwater and in the glowing soupiness he saw hair and fragments of cloth, and his hand closed over the torch. He burst back up. He staggered sideways and banged into the bulkhead.

He leant there, rasping, shuddering, the dreadful taste of

286

death on his lips, then he lunged at that torpedo tube. He wrenched the handle, but it was rusted solid. He frantically flashed his torch over the churned-up black water, looking for containers showing through the surface. He started wading up and down, feeling with his feet, slipping and sliding – he sloshed and rasped his way up and down that terrible black space, and his feet touched nothing but bones and unspeakable matter. He leant against the bulkhead, flashing his torch around one last time, wild-eyed, nauseous, then he turned and plunged back towards the *Zentrale*.

He went floundering between the rows of machinery, pursued by all the ghosts of hell, his torch throwing jerking shadows on the bulkheads and bunks with their horrible skeletons. He plunged his head under the black water at the circular hatch, and he burst through into the *Zentrale* again. He paused, gasping, trying to wipe the dribbling slime from his mask. It was then that he saw the water move, and a gargle of horror welled in his throat.

It was at the far end of the *Zentrale*. Suddenly there was a big swirl in the black water, and then the movement went towards the escape tube. Halfway there, it stopped.

McQuade crouched, his heart pounding, horrified eyes wide. It was that octopus again! What was it doing now? Was it making for that tube also? Or was it waiting to see what he did, as frightened as he was? He had to restrain himself from scrambling up onto a bunk. He looked frantically at the tank-contents gauge – the needle was in the red. For a desperate moment he crouched there, then he took a terrified breath and charged at the escape tube, beating the water with both hands to frighten the beast away.

He blundered up to the tube, and forgot to take off his harness. He plunged under the water and twisted onto his back and shoved himself into the tube. It was only when his airtank banged against it that he remembered it and he gargled in horror, expecting to feel the dreadful tentacles close on his legs. For a terrified instant he was going to scramble out again and take the harness off, but then he kicked instead and he found himself fully inside the tube despite the harness. He looked frantically upwards and there was Tucker's torchlight. He kicked fiercely, and he rose up the tube, scraping and bumping. He burst out through the hatch and clawed himself away from it. And, oh God, this seemed the cleanest, sweetest place! He jerked his head at Tucker, grabbed the ladder and he surged up through the upper hatch, looking fearfully about at the sea out there for sharks. Tucker came bubbling through the hatch, with the sack of empty airtanks. They kicked off.

McQuade rose towards the seething surface at the same pace as his bubbles, every nerve screaming. He spun wildly looking for the dinghy, then thrashed towards it with all his frantic might. He seized the gunnel and heaved.

He collapsed into the bottom of the dinghy, gasping, and wrenched out the regulator.

'*Oh my God . . . Oh my God, mass murder . . .*'

Elsie and Nathan were staring at him. Tucker thrashed himself aboard and collapsed into the dinghy beside him. Elsie said, 'What?'

McQuade rasped, '*I'm going to find the bastard! Back to the ship!*'

Nathan stared, then erupted, 'What about my twenty grand?!'

McQuade jabbed a finger at the sea and shouted:

'*The only way we'll find the loot is to find the bastard who hid it! The same bastard who murdered the entire crew!*'

PART SEVEN

34

At noon the following day the *Bonanza* tied up at the Kuiseb wharf in Walvis Bay. The east wind was blowing hot and strong, sand flying off the dunes in furls and curls blowing down the streets and banking up in the gutters, sand peppering the trawlers.

It was a very subdued skeleton crew who disembarked. Nathan was 'pissed-off about my twenty grand', Tucker was worried sick about the company's overdraft, about Nathan's twenty grand and about what Rosie was going to say about his pay-cheque, and McQuade was tensed up about what he was committing himself to now. Even Elsie, the only one who knew the identity of the man McQuade was going to search for, thought it would be a further waste of time and money. McQuade still had the taste and stink of death in his mouth. And what was he going to do about Sarah? Everything was fucked up. He'd thought he'd return as a conquering hero, loaded with loot, with nothing but fun, fun, ahead with Sarah – at the very least he had promised to take her to Ai-Ais and Lüderitz – and now he had to tell her it was all off.

The only good news was that the Kid was fit to return to work. McQuade got rid of Nathan by telling Tucker to take him to the airport, sent Potgieter off to round up the Coloured crew, and drove Elsie to the municipal market to re-victual the ship. He wrote out the company cheque, looked at the balance and thought, God, this better pay off. He drove on to his house. It was stuffy and hot, but he could not open any windows because of the east wind. He checked the answering-machine. There was a message from Sarah, yesterday:

'Hi, I'm calling from Windhoek, I'll be back in Swakopmund tomorrow evening, staying at the Europahof Hotel, eagerly hoping for your timeous return. Bye-ee.'

He gave a sigh. What the hell was he going to tell her? He went out to Jakob's quarters. The servants' room door was ajar, letting sand blow in. Jakob lay on the bed, snoring loudly; McQuade did not wake him. He returned to the house, got a beer, went into his study, and pulled his notes out of his holdall.

He re-read them, then took out a clean sheet of paper and began the sobering business of figuring out how to trace a Nazi war-criminal who landed here forty years ago.

Where did he start? Looking amongst the German community here? Finding out who were Nazis in 1945? Who were still Nazis today? He felt daunted. Was there even any loot on that submarine?

No, he was sure that submarine had been carrying more than the world's most-wanted war-criminal. The man had been on his way to the friendly shores of South West Africa, and the loot on that submarine was not just one small package but the Nazi Party's hoard to recreate the Third Reich.

McQuade stared into the middle distance and re-examined the new facts.

That submarine had gone aground because it was hanging around waiting to rendezvous with a local boat that was going to take SS General Heinrich Muller on board. That meant that there had been an organized conspiracy, set up from Berlin, to arrange the boat, the time and place of the rendezvous, and it was not just to save Heinrich Muller's skin. *Because the conspiracy was to murder everybody on the submarine so that nobody would be alive to talk and blow the plan for the Fourth Reich!* Finding those terrible skeletons yesterday, made that irresistibly clear. Why else would the Germans on the rendezvous boat be prepared to see Muller murder the whole German crew of the submarine?

McQuade dragged his hands down his face at the memory

of those ghastly skeletons. But he was glad he had seen them because they proved he had come upon a massive and terrible conspiracy. It all fitted: the Strasbourg Conference where the Nazi industrialists had laid economic plans for the Fourth Reich, the Great Nazi Art Robbery, even Hitler's last testament . . . Here we have Nazi Germany's top policeman sailing to South West Africa, and when he's shipwrecked, he murders everybody according to plan – because no unauthorized person must know about a plan so important.

Okay, of that McQuade was certain, and it was a fact so massive, so awesome in its significance, that alone it was worth all the expense and risk so far. Against that fact the loot faded to secondary importance.

He dragged his mind back to practicalities. So? So the submarine gets wrecked and Muller tries to murder everybody and makes his escape. He eventually arrives in Swakopmund. He had English money, and probably diamonds or gold. He would probably have sold some to get quick cash. Maybe he opened a bank account?

If so, he would surely have done so in the name of Strauss, the name he had given the dentist, the identity that had been prepared for him in Berlin, and maybe he had stuck to that bank ever since.

Bought a car in that name, for example.

Or bought a railway ticket.

Bought or rented a house in that name.

So, Step One would be to find out which banks were operating in Swakopmund in 1945, then find a way to look at their records.

McQuade didn't want to incur more legal fees, but he had better consult Roger Wentland. He reached for the telephone.

'Sorry to trouble you, Roger, but is there any legal way I could get at bank records for the year 1945 and find out if a certain person opened an account?'

There was a surprised pause. Then Roger said, 'Bank records are confidential. The only legal way would be through the police in their investigation of a crime, or if you were suing somebody and you needed the evidence contained in their bank records. What's this all about?'

'Is there any illegal way?'

'*Illegal?* Plenty. Ask any good burglar.'

'I mean, do you know anybody in the banking system who could help me?'

'No bank employee would do that unless he was a crook.' He added facetiously, 'You could seduce one of their aged spinsters.'

'Tell me, would the railways still have records of who travelled in 1945?'

'Funny questions. I doubt it. Ask the Station Master.'

'Okay. Now, when you buy a vehicle, it's registered in your name in some government office, right? Where was that office in 1945?'

'The Vehicle Registration Office. It was probably attached to the Magistrate's Court in those days. Along with the registration of births, deaths, marriages, and so on.'

'And would the Magistrate's office here still have the records for 1945?'

'They're probably in the archives in Windhoek.'

'Okay. Now, what's the situation with the Passport Office? Can an ordinary person like me go in and find out if a certain person has ever been issued with a passport?'

'No, those are confidential government records, like income tax. It could only be done for some official purpose. Who is this person you're so interested in?'

McQuade sighed. 'We'd better meet. How about a beer at the Europahof when you finish work? I'm meeting somebody else there later.' He added: 'What do you think of this 435 business, by the way? Just a diplomatic tactic?'

'Personally,' Roger said, 'I think the South African government means business this time.'

McQuade's heart sank. 'But the Cubans won't withdraw!' he protested. 'That's South Africa's big condition!'

'Sure,' Roger said, 'but it's a whole new ball-game now – now they've got to talk and argue again and that re-opens possibilities for a peace deal.'

'But Cuba wants to stay on to fight UNITA!'

'I know, I know,' Roger said, 'so 435 is a good way off, don't panic about your fishing licence yet.'

He left a message at the reception desk for Sarah. He sat with Roger in the lounge, where he could see the lobby. He had brought his file of notes with him, in case he needed to refer to them.

'I've found that submarine. And I've found evidence of mass murder.'

Roger's eyes widened. McQuade told the lawyer everything he had learned since last he saw him, except Heinrich Muller's name and the name which he had got from the dental records. Roger listened with rapt attention. McQuade ended:

'So how do I go about finding this bastard?'

Roger said slowly, 'And why do you want to find him so badly?'

'Because he's a mass murderer! And a Nazi war-criminal.'

Roger looked at him. With a small twinkle in his eye. 'Then why don't you go to the police? This is an extraordinary case.' He answered himself, 'Because of the loot and legal hassles over that German frigate found off the coast of Denmark a few years ago?'

'I assure you I feel very strongly about Nazi war-criminals.'

Roger said: 'Boy, what a case it would be. And what you've been through in that submarine! I take my hat off to you. But you always were a tough guy.'

'Not so tough, I assure you. Look, first of all, I've got to find out if the man is alive. Where are deaths registered? And then, assuming he's not dead, how do I find out whether he got married, to whom, his address at that time, et cetera?'

'Deaths are recorded in the Registrar of Births and Deaths

office, which is usually attached to the local magistrate's court. If he got married in Namibia in those far-off days, the registration will be in the archives in Windhoek. If he got married more recently, you could also find it in the Magistrate's Office of the district in which he got married. In any event, because Namibia is still legally administered by South Africa, all these details will be in Pretoria. In the Population Registration computer.'

McQuade's hopes rose. 'Of course.'

Roger elaborated: 'All South Africans, which includes South Westers up 1984 when they got limited local self government, have to carry the so-called Book-of-Life. An identification document. It contains all the bearer's details, his date and place of birth, his address, his marriage, everything of an official nature that he's done in his life. Haven't you got one?'

McQuade shook his head. 'No, I'm officially Australian now, I left before these things came out. I only had a citizen's card. But, of *course* . . .' If Muller was on that computer he would find out all about him in one fell swoop! 'And is there a way to get access to that computer?'

Roger said drily, 'Sure. Bill Sikes the burglar again.' He shook his head. 'Legally, no. It's all confidential government information, like the income tax department. You'd have to get a Supreme Court order. Which means you'd have to satisfy the court that you need the evidence contained in the computer for some legal reason.' He added significantly, 'The police can do it, of course.'

McQuade sat back. No way could he go to the Supreme Court and tell the judge he wanted to find out which Mr H. Strauss was Heinrich Muller. 'Don't you know anybody in Pretoria who could help me?'

'No.'

McQuade thought out loud: 'So I'd have to find an accomplice? Who works with this computer in the Population Registration Office?'

Roger said nothing. McQuade continued, 'How do I even find out who *works* in that office?'

Roger pursed his lips, then sighed. 'You're determined to find this guy, aren't you?'

'Yes.'

Roger nodded soberly. 'And I've done my duty, as a lawyer? I've advised you to report the matter to the police? And I've done my duty as your lawyer, I've told you it's impossible to get the information you want unless you go through the courts?'

McQuade nodded earnestly. Waiting for wisdom. 'You have.'

'Let me make another point clear. As your lawyer.' Roger paused emphatically. 'It's a serious criminal offence to try to get this information *illegally*. Particularly to *bribe* an official. Or to blackmail them.'

McQuade nodded earnestly.

'That was your lawyer speaking. Never forget what I said.' Roger took a breath. 'But I'll add something else, as a lawyer. It is commendable that criminals be brought to justice. Particularly Nazi war-criminals. And now, having said that, I'll speak as your friend.' He added. 'And I'll deny I ever said it.'

McQuade nodded. Roger looked at him.

'In Pretoria you'll find the offices of the Public Servants' Association. All civil servants are registered there. You can try to get a copy of their membership list. It should tell you who works in which department. Then look up an old friend of mine called Johan Lombard. He's a freelance journalist and he knows everything that's going on in town – in South Africa, in fact. Ask him about a scandal that broke in the Population Registration Office a few years ago – resulting in a big prosecution.' He paused. 'Then go to another friend of mine called Peter Duncan. He runs a health studio, called Duncan's. Look it up in the telephone directory. Ask him about the same scandal and show him the Public Servants' Association list.'

McQuade was frowning. 'What'll Peter Duncan tell me?'

Appearing not to hear, Roger finished his drink and stood up. 'And now I really must get home. See you around.'

He walked out of the lounge, leaving McQuade staring after him.

Then Sarah came into the hotel lobby. 'Hullo! . . .'

She looked hot and wind-blown, but she was smiling all over her beautiful face. McQuade's heart missed a beat. 'Hullo! You look beautiful.'

'In this wind? Boy, is it blowing out in the desert. How was the fishing?'

'Good. What'll you have to drink?'

'Here?' she said with a twinkle in her eye. 'I've got a better venue in mind. It's just upstairs.'

She checked in at the reception desk while he bought a bottle of wine. They hurried up to her room and when he took her in his arms, she looked at him with a happy grin and her fingers went mischievously to her blouse. 'I've been thinking about this for four terrible days.'

'So have I.' He slid his hands inside her blouse, and oh the beautiful smooth soft feel of her, and she was grinning as she crushed her mouth against his and pulled his shirt off his shoulders and pressed her glorious breasts against his chest. Her hands went behind her back and she unclipped her skirt and it dropped to her feet, and she turned and collapsed onto the bed.

Afterwards they lay together, happily exhausted, sipping wine. 'Now what do we do?' she smiled.

'That was a pretty tough act to follow. Go downstairs for dinner? Tell me what you've been doing.'

'I've been to Windhoek, Gross Barmen, the Daan Viljoen Park and I came back via the Hochland Pass across the Naukluft desert today. Took lots of pictures; now all I've got to do is write the story. When do we leave for Ai-Ais and Lüderitz?' She continued, 'The boss thinks a story about my fishing-trip with you is a great idea! I phoned him.'

McQuade felt very badly about letting her down. 'That sea trip will have to wait, I'm afraid. I have to go to Pretoria on business tomorrow.'

'Oh.' She was clearly disappointed.

He went on hastily, 'But I'm driving, and Ai-Ais is on the way. So that is still on. I'll drive you back to South Africa and we'll do the sea trip another time.'

She perked up. 'How long are you going to be in Pretoria?'

He didn't have a clue how long it would take to crack the Population Bureau. 'A week. Maybe two.'

She said with a smile, 'Not a girlfriend?'

'No. Business.' He added: 'Urgent financial arrangements.'

'And when you're finished in Pretoria?'

This was tricky. He desperately wanted her to stay around, but he had things to do which she must not know about. And he didn't want to break promises. 'Depends on how things turn out. The *Bonanza* is going to sea tomorrow for about a month.' He changed the tack, 'What have you got to do?'

She waved a hand that took in the whole of southern Africa. 'I'm on holiday. In Johannesburg alone I want to spend a couple of weeks, what with the mines and Soweto and so forth. And go to the Kruger National Park. Swaziland. Sun City.' She grinned. 'What I'm getting at, in case you haven't noticed, is that I'm hoping – since I've decided I've fallen madly in lust with you whilst you were off on the high seas harassing poor pilchards – we might get together occasionally whilst you're in Pretoria and I'm languishing in nearby Johannesburg.'

'Absolutely.'

'In fact, at the risk of sounding positively obscene, I have a suggestion to make. Where are you staying in Pretoria? In some hotel?'

'Right.' He intended staying with Nathan.

'Well, I telephoned Matt while you were away and he's offered me an apartment in Johannesburg. Belonging to a friend who's away for a while. Save some hotel bills. Anyway, it occurs to me that just maybe, when you're working in Pretoria, you'd like to save some hotel bills too? With me.' She flapped her eyes tizzily.

McQuade felt on top of the world. 'Thank you. As long as you don't mind if I have to work at night.'

She held up a hand. 'See how you feel when you get there. Maybe we'll be fighting like cat and dog by the time we reach Johannesburg.' Then she pointed a finger at his nose. 'As long as it's not another woman you're seeing at night, McQuade . . .'

'No.' He grinned down at her happy face. And everything was going right again! Roger had given him a strong lead in Pretoria, the honeymoon was not over and he was wildly in love. He took her lovely nipple in his mouth, rolled on top of her and she slid her lovely thighs apart.

Just then there was a loud knock at the door. Sarah jerked, then called, 'Who is it? I'm in the bath.'

An Afrikaans voice said, 'The police, madam.'

She turned to McQuade, astonished. '*Police?*' she whispered. McQuade was equally astonished. He swung off the bed, grabbed his clothes, and went into the bathroom.

Sarah got up and pulled on a dressing gown. 'One moment.'

She waited until McQuade was dressed, then went to the door and unlocked it.

Two men in civilian clothes stood there. One flipped open an identification wallet. 'Detective Sergeant Bekker, madam. I believe Mr McQuade is with you?'

Sarah demanded, 'May I ask what all this is about?'

McQuade was amazed. 'Yes?' he said. He emerged from the bathroom. He knew Bekker by sight. 'How did you know I was here?'

'It's a small town, sir,' Bekker replied. 'And your Land-rover is parked outside. Sorry to trouble you, but would you mind coming to the police station in Walvis Bay?'

'*Why?*' Sarah demanded incredulously.

'Because,' Bekker said to McQuade, 'your house has been broken into and your boy, Jakob, has been severely assaulted. In fact, tortured.'

McQuade was thunderstruck.

35

Sarah wanted to come too, but McQuade did not want her hearing what might emerge in the police station. He followed the police car, his mind working feverishly. Who would break into his house? Only somebody who wanted to know about the submarine. The only outsider who knew about it was Roger Wentland, his lawyer, but maybe Red Straghan suspected something – he had been very inquisitive when he sold McQuade the air-compressor. Unless somebody like Potgieter had opened his mouth around town, or Tucker, snivelling to his wife. Nathan would not have opened his mouth, nor the Kid. But that bastard Red Straghan had made him uneasy. *But why was Jakob tortured?* Nobody knew about Jakob, not even the *Bonanza* crew. Jesus, this was ominous. It meant that *somebody* knew about Jakob seeing those two men come thrashing ashore forty years ago; and if that somebody was German it could mean that McQuade was up against the local Nazis already. *And what explanation had Jakob given to the police?*

He slammed the Landrover to a stop outside Walvis Bay's police station.

'Very strange, man,' Inspector Dupreez said in a heavy Afrikaans accent. He was a large man with a coarse but intelligent face. 'These two white men wearing balaclavas – so only their eyes show – they drag your boy Jakob out of bed and force him to open up your house. Then they ransack your office, going through all your papers, but they don't steal nothing and there was things to steal, like your radio. Then they start beating up Jakob. They *donnered* him something terrible, cracking his ribs, and they burned him with cigarettes.'

McQuade was shocked. 'Good God — *why?*' But he knew why, and his mind was trying to race.

'Exactly,' the inspector said. 'Obviously to tell them something. But Jakob won't tell us nothing — so maybe you can.' He sat forward, hands clasped on the desk. 'Finally they beat him so hard, Jakob loses consciousness. Just then your friend Potgieter comes to your house looking for you, because the same thing has just happened aboard your ship: while nobody was aboard, the bridge was broken into and all your papers thrown about. When Mr Potgieter arrives at your house these two guys run away. Pottie chases them but they get away in a white four-wheel drive. He couldn't get the number. Meanwhile Jakob crawls out into the street. A passing police car brings him here. We've taken him to hospital and patched him up, man, but he won't tell us anything more. Just keeps saying you must take him back to his kraal so he can die in peace, man.'

McQuade was shocked, but heaved an inward sigh of relief that Jakob had not spilt the beans. 'Where is he, I'll speak to him.'

'But can you think what they wanted to know from Jakob?'

'I've no idea. I don't keep anything valuable in the house.'

'But they mostly looked amongst your papers. Is there anything in that lot that's so important?'

McQuade knew what they were looking for: a note of the latitude and longitude of where the submarine lay. 'Only normal company accounts.'

The inspector frowned. 'How long have you known Jakob?'

McQuade knew what was coming. 'Not long. But he's a nice old man. So I offered him a job.'

The inspector looked puzzled. 'As what? He's a raw old Damara who knows nothing.'

'As a garden boy.'

'As a garden boy?' the inspector echoed. 'But there's nothing in your garden except sand.'

'Exactly – I thought it was time I did something with it. And he could clean the house.'

'But haven't you got a Coloured maid who cleans your house?' He glanced at a sheet of paper. 'Maria Booysens, your bosun's wife.'

McQuade was surprised that he knew. 'Yes, but other days the place needs supervision and cleaning.'

'How did you meet him?'

McQuade had given the possibility of these questions some thought driving over from Swakopmund. 'I met his son. I was going up to Damaraland and he asked me for a lift.' He shrugged. 'I took him to his father's kraal. Met the old man. He wanted a job. I fetched him a few weeks later after I'd taken my girlfriend to Etosha National Park.'

'Why were you going to Damaraland?'

'I like it up there. I wanted to stay at the Palmwag Safari Lodge for a couple of days after being at sea for weeks.' McQuade decided to go onto the attack. 'That's not unusual, is it?'

'No,' the inspector agreed, 'but I must try to find out all the facts. This is a serious case, hey. So, you stayed at Palmwag?'

He could not admit to camping on the Skeleton Coast while he surveyed the area Jakob had shown him. 'Yes. Then I went back to sea. When we came back, I went overseas on holiday.'

The inspector nodded. 'For how long?'

'A couple of weeks.'

'Where did you go?'

'England and Germany.'

'Germany? Any reason?'

'I like the beer. And the nightlife. Look, what's the purpose of all this questioning?'

The inspector said apologetically, 'I'm just trying to understand everything. I've got to send my men out to look for two white thugs who tortured your garden boy and I'm trying to find a motive, man.' He continued, 'Did you bring back anything from overseas, which they could be so interested in?'

McQuade's pulse tripped. 'No, it was just a holiday.'

'For two weeks? A short holiday, man.'

'It's all I wanted. Just a break.'

'And then you came back and went to sea again?'

'Yes. But first I took my girlfriend to Etosha.'

'Is that the lady staying at the Europahof Hotel in Swakopmund?' He glanced at the sheet of paper. 'Sarah Buckley, an American lady?'

McQuade was very uneasy that the man knew so much. 'Correct. She's a newspaper reporter, on holiday in South Africa.'

'How long has she been your girlfriend?'

'I met her on the plane coming back.'

The inspector twinkled. 'Holiday romance, hey? Good. And while you were at sea last time, she stayed in Namibia, waiting for you to return?'

'Yes. We're going on another trip tomorrow.'

'Does *she* know Jakob?'

'She's only met him after Etosha when we went to his kraal to pick him up. She knows nothing about him.'

'Did they talk?'

'No. Jakob can't speak English and she can't speak Afrikaans.'

'Can she speak German?'

McQuade frowned. 'German? I don't know. Why?'

'Because Jakob speaks some German, from the old days.'

'I see. But they did not converse at all.' He frowned. 'You think these two thugs may have been questioning Jakob about Sarah?'

'I'm just trying to think of every possibility, man. This is a very strange case. Jakob's frightened of something.'

305

McQuade felt feverish. 'Well, let me ask him. In private.'

The inspector asked pensively, 'Why did you go to Etosha?'

McQuade frowned. 'To show Sarah the wildlife.'

'Of course. But is that the only reason for the trip?'

McQuade's heart sank. '*Yes.*'

'And so after your short overseas holiday you had another little holiday with Sarah at Etosha?'

He knew he was being trapped. 'Not unusual. When you meet a pretty girl to invite her on a trip.'

'No,' the inspector agreed, 'but when you left Europe you did not know Sarah, and didn't know you were going to take her to Etosha. So what did you plan to do with those spare days here – *before* you met Sarah?'

The only thing to do was to act puzzled. 'I was going to go to Damaraland to fetch Jakob. Why?'

'*Ah* . . .' The inspector sat back. 'So showing Sarah the wildlife of Etosha was *not* your only reason for the trip. The other reason was to fetch Jakob?'

'Yes.' McQuade's heart was sinking. 'Nothing strange about that, is there?'

The inspector shrugged. 'What is a bit strange is that you return from a short holiday in Europe, which must have been expensive, just to drive up to Damaraland to fetch an old native, who you've only met once, to be your garden boy. You could have fetched him some other time. Especially as your garden is only sea-sand. What was the hurry?'

McQuade was angry with himself. He had walked straight into it. The man knew there must be another reason for going to see Jakob.

'Well, I'd had enough of Europe. And now, let me speak to Jakob.'

'*Ja*, okay, sir.' The inspector stood up resignedly. 'Thanks for your time, hey. This way.' Then he stopped. 'Where are you going tomorrow with your girlfriend, sir?'

'Ai-Ais. Then Johannesburg.'

The inspector smiled. '*Another* little holiday?'

'Well, a man's entitled to a little nonsense over a girl, isn't he?'

'Of course,' the inspector grinned, man to man. 'But where will you be staying?'

'In hotels. Don't know which yet.'

'Well, will you telephone me every few days or so? In case I have any questions.'

'Certainly. I'd better speak to Jakob outside the police station, if he's frightened of your people.' He was not going to risk hidden tape-recorders.

'He's frightened of *something*, all right.'

McQuade led Jakob to the Landrover. He felt terribly sorry for the old man, and very responsible. Jakob walked with difficulty, supporting his ribs. His face was swollen, his forehead stitched in two places, and dressings covered cigarette burns on the back of his hand. McQuade said in Afrikaans, 'I'm terribly sorry, Jakob.' He pulled out a fifty-rand note as a consolation. 'Tell me what happened.'

Haltingly, Jakob repeated what the inspector had already told him.

'What language were they speaking?'

'Afrikaans,' Jakob said.

'No German?'

Jakob wheezed, 'Yes, they asked me some questions in German, and in Afrikaans.'

McQuade felt feverish. 'But did they sound like real German people?'

'I do not know.'

'And you could only see their eyes?'

Jakob nodded.

'What colour were they?'

Jakob shook his head. 'I think one had blue eyes.'

'How tall were they?'

'One was your size. The other was smaller.'

'And the man my size, what colour were his eyes?'

'I think he had the blue eyes.'

Red Straghan? But he would rather deal with Red Straghan than with Heinrich Muller's bodyguards. 'Jakob, I promise I will not tell the police anything. So please tell me what questions they asked you.'

Jakob's swollen eyes went opaque. 'They asked no questions.'

'But you told me they did! In Afrikaans and in German.'

Jakob looked inscrutable, and said nothing. McQuade said: 'Why did they beat you? And burn you?'

'Because I would not answer them.'

'And why did you refuse to answer them, even though they burned you with cigarettes?'

Jakob gave a groan. 'Because I was afraid they would report me to the police.'

'Why would they report you to the police?'

'Perhaps they would say that it was I who killed the white man on the beach.'

McQuade stared. 'Did they *ask* you about that?'

'I was afraid they knew.'

'*Why* did you think they knew?'

'Because they asked me why I worked for you. They said, you are a useless old Damara, why are you now working for a white man in the city?'

'And what did you say?'

'I told them I went with you fishing from the beach, to get bait and clean the fish. But I do not think they believed me because they burned me with cigarettes.'

McQuade said desperately, 'Did you tell them you had shown me where you saw the two men swim ashore?'

'No, I only said we went fishing there,' Jakob said. 'That is when they started beating me.'

Oh God. 'But did you say *where* it was that we went fishing?'

'Yes.' Jakob wheezed painfully. 'They said I must show

them the place. Then they beat me more and I was knocked out.'

McQuade slumped back. Oh God ... So they definitely knew about the submarine. 'Did you tell them how I used the sextant?' He mimed it.

'No, they did not ask me before I was knocked out.'

Thank God. 'Jakob, do you know what a submarine is?' He said it in both Afrikaans and German.

'I have heard of such a thing. They asked me where I had seen a submarine on the coast.'

McQuade felt feverish. 'And what did you say?'

'I said I have never seen one. So they beat me more. They asked if I had seen people swimming in the sea.'

McQuade closed his eyes. 'And what did you reply?'

'I said No. Because I was frightened they would say I killed the man. Then they beat me.'

'Did they know where you lived?'

'I told them.' Jakob groaned again. 'I want to go to my kraal.'

McQuade breathed deep. 'No, Jakob, you must not go home. These men know where you live. The only reason they did not drag you away to show them the place on the beach is because somebody heard them beating you. They will come back for you.' He said with finality, 'You must stay on my ship. Where nobody can find you.' To stop any protests, he opened the door. 'I will tell the police that you are going to work for me on the ship. And you must never, never tell anybody anything more than you have. Understand?' Jakob looked at him, anguished, and McQuade felt brutal saying it: 'Or maybe they will say that it was you who killed the white man on the beach.'

36

After he had signed a formal statement to the police, and had deposited Jakob into the safe custody of Potgieter on the *Bonanza*, McQuade had returned to his house and hastily packed a bag. He had a licensed pistol, which he put in his pocket. He also had an old twelve-bore shotgun, which he locked in the metal tool-box in the back of the Landrover. He drove fast through the night, back to Swakopmund, feverishly thinking it all through.

Firstly, it was clear that Inspector Dupreez suspected that Jakob was more than a gardener. Dupreez knew that McQuade had gone to Europe for some reason other than a holiday, then returned hurriedly, specifically to find the old man and keep him under wraps. He also knew that McQuade knew why Jakob had been tortured. That interview was all very bad news. The only consolation was that Dupreez had failed to connect the case with any submarine, and had not asked why the *Bonanza*'s last trip had been so short. Thank God the *Bonanza* was sailing at dawn, with Jakob on board.

Secondly, who were these two whites who ransacked his house and tortured Jakob? This was the really bad news. Obviously they knew about a submarine. Just thank God that Potgieter had stopped them dragging Jakob away to show them the whereabouts.

Who were these bastards? Red Straghan and his boys? Straghan was a hard character, but burning an old man with cigarettes? Was Straghan that hard?

If it was Red Straghan, that would be the good news. He would only be up against a bunch of treasure-hunting pirates. The terrible news would be if they were Germans.

310

Then it was a whole different ball-game, because it meant that a German information network existed and that probably meant they were Nazis. Which probably meant that Heinrich Muller was going to be very hard to find, and very dangerous. If they were Germans, the only good news was it probably meant Heinrich Muller was alive and McQuade was not wasting his time in looking for him.

But whoever they were, what were they going to do to James McQuade?

Thirdly, what about Sarah?

He didn't want her mixed up in this, and he didn't want her knowing anything about this submarine, either. So? Tell her to catch a plane back to Johannesburg, while he drove across Africa to Pretoria?

No, he could not bear to let her down again. And what explanation could he possibly give her without hurting her? And without arousing her journalist's instincts for a story? The very last thing he wanted was to lose her, and the safest thing he could do right now was to drive her away from the Skeleton Coast. He had told Inspector Dupreez that he was driving her to South Africa. Dupreez had all the resources to find out if that was true, and he would be very inquisitive if it wasn't. So the *best* thing he could do was drive her to Johannesburg – she gave him an alibi.

It was after ten o'clock when he roared across the dry Swakop river. He parked inside the courtyard of the Europahof, rather than leave his Landrover outside for all the world to see. She came to the door in a bathrobe with worry all over her face. She closed the door behind him and said tensely, 'I've just received a threatening phone call. Or rather *you* have. Literally a minute ago.'

McQuade stared at her. 'From whom?'

'I don't know. This male voice said: "Is McQuade there?" I said, "No, who's speaking?" He snarled: "Just tell McQuade to lay off or else!" Then he hung up.'

McQuade stared at her, his heart knocking.

311

'What was his accent? English-South African, like mine. Or Afrikaans? Or German?'

'Not like yours. Afrikaans. Maybe German. They sound pretty similar out here.'

'How did they know I was here?'

She demanded, 'Who's "they"?'

'Don't know. The same guys who beat up Jakob, obviously.'

'And how *did* they know you were here?'

He shook his head. 'Like the police said, it's a small town. We've been seen together. Maybe they followed me from Walvis Bay this afternoon.'

'But you must have an idea who your enemies are. And *what* you've got to lay off from?'

Oh, this was getting tricky. 'Just a fishing dispute. With my rivals. It could be any number of guys.' He added unconvincingly, 'It's a cut-throat business.'

'And what's this dispute about?'

'It's very complicated.'

'But what would poor old Jakob know about a very complicated fishing dispute? He's an old peasant, not even a member of your crew.'

Just then the telephone rang again. Sarah looked at him. McQuade took a breath. 'Answer it.'

She picked up the receiver. 'Yes?' Pause. 'Yes, he is. Who's speaking?' Then she turned to McQuade. 'Inspector Dupreez.'

McQuade took the receiver. 'Yes, Inspector?'

Inspector Dupreez said, 'Sorry to trouble you again, hey, but I've got bad news. Your boy Jakob has just died.'

McQuade was aghast.

The inspector went on, 'Mr Potgieter has just come to report it. He went to Jakob's bunk and found him dead. Probably fractured skull and internal haemorrhage, the doctor says. Anyway there'll be a post-mortem examination tomorrow.'

'Oh God,' McQuade breathed, 'poor man . . .'

The inspector said: 'This changes the case to murder, hey.' He paused. 'So, are you quite sure you have nothing further to tell us, Mr McQuade?'

'I've told you everything.'

'Well, if you think of anything, please telephone me immediately. And we'd better record a statement from Miss Buckley. We can send a man over right away.'

'But Miss Buckley knows nothing.'

'Let me speak to her, please,' the inspector said.

McQuade handed the receiver back to Sarah.

'Hullo?' Sarah said. '*Murder?*' She listened, aghast. 'Of course. Now is better than the morning. Goodbye.'

She replaced the receiver, and turned to McQuade.

'Now it's a murder case . . .' She stared. 'Are you going to tell them about the threatening phone call?'

'No,' McQuade said grimly.

She stared. 'You don't want me to mention it?'

'Correct.'

'And why not? It seems to me to be most relevant.'

'It's my business, Sarah.'

'Like hell it's just your business! Now it's a case of murder!' She put her hands on her hips. 'Look – if I've got to withhold information from the cops I'd like to know why! I don't want any trouble. I'm a nice American on a good-behaviour tour and I don't want my editors to hear that this reporter topples into bed with a man who's covering up murder! Supposing I'm detained as an accomplice?'

McQuade sighed angrily. What he had to do had no place for a woman in it, nor for her penetrating questions. 'I'm not covering up a murder. I'm trying to *find* a murderer! So I beg you please not to mention that threatening phone call because it will complicate matters. But you're right. I don't want you involved in this. So tomorrow you fly to Johannesburg and I'll drive alone. I'll contact you when this is over.'

She narrowed her eyes. 'Just let me get one thing straight, Mr Secretive McQuade. Is this trip to Pretoria to find the murderer?'

'Yes.'

'But you were going to Pretoria *before* Jakob was murdered. So has this murderer murdered before?'

'Yes. And that's all I'll tell you.'

'And Jakob knew about this man?'

McQuade sighed. 'No. And I'm not going to explain myself.'

She glared. 'Can you just explain how you're going to find the murderer?'

'That's my business, Sarah.'

'Is it, hell! One minute I'm making mad passionate love to you, the next the cops are announcing murder! Listen, buster' – she tapped her breast – 'I like to know who I'm fucking! How do I know you're not a crook?'

'You'll just have to take my word for it.'

'Or tell the police the snippet about the threatening phone call?'

He looked at her angrily. 'If you do, it will screw everything up. Because they'll question me about what I'm supposed to lay off, and then *they*'ll try to find this guy I'm after. And they'll screw everything up. Believe me.'

She stared. Then demanded, 'And if I don't tell them, will the cops leave us alone? Or are they going to be on our backs for the rest of my jolly holiday?'

'They'll leave us alone. We haven't committed any crime, and we're not suspected of any.'

'Then, there's no reason why I shouldn't drive to Johannesburg with you!'

He said firmly, 'I don't want you involved, Sarah.'

'I *am* involved! I'm making false statements to the police! I know something about a murder which I'm withholding from them.' She looked at him. 'And I'm involved emotionally. I want to come with you . . .'

McQuade sighed. And smiled. 'Okay. I also want you to come. But I won't answer any more questions.'

She held up a hand. 'Okay. But *do* try to find it in your heart to understand that I'm worried witless about what's happening. What may happen to me . . .'

37

He had tried to think of a way of getting out of town without being followed, but it was hopeless. Whoever the bastards were, they knew he was in the Europahof, they knew his Landrover. The town was too small, the desert was too open.

He could see no evidence of being followed, however. They left Swakopmund in the dawn; the little German town was silent. They got onto the road to Windhoek, and as the sun came up, blinding gold and red over the desert, his tension began to lift. Just before the scrub-tree country began, a white Ford appeared in his rearview mirror. It cruised past them. There were two men in it. McQuade made a mental note of the number. When they passed through Usakos he saw the same vehicle at the petrol station. Thirty minutes later it overtook them again, and disappeared. It was after ten o'clock when they were driving into the hills surrounding Windhoek. He did not see the white Ford again. He drove into the city and parked near the Kalahari Sands Hotel.

He held a finger out at her. 'No questions – you agreed.' He led her into the shopping complex and up into the hotel foyer. 'I'll meet you here in about an hour. If you want to look at the shops, stay within this complex. Amongst people.'

He asked at the reception desk for the telephone directory. He found the address of the Births, Deaths and Marriages Registry. Then he hurried out into Kaiser Wilhelmstrasse. The sun beat down, people of all colours were thronging. German colonial architecture dominated the street, but there were modern buildings. Up on the hill were the government buildings, and over there was an equestrian statue of General von Leutwein, on his horse, surveying his subjects with no-nonsense forbearance.

An hour later, having told the clerk that he was trying to trace a distant relative, and having paid a search-fee, and having waited a remarkably short time for the computer's print-out, he walked back to the Kalahari Sands Hotel feeling he had got somewhere. It was not conclusive because there were many people named Strauss, but no *Heinrich* Strauss had died since 1984 when South Africa granted limited self-government to Namibia.

He took the dirt road south to the Kupferberg Pass, to show her the hill country; they would spend the night at Maltahoe and reach Ai-Ais next morning. They were ten miles into the hills when he noticed the vehicle behind.

It was a four-wheel-drive truck, probably a Toyota Landcruiser. He watched it in the rearview mirror, several hundred yards behind, in his dust, but making no attempt to overtake them. Sarah looked back. 'Worried about them?'

'Not yet. I'll give him a chance to pass on the next straight bit.'

There was no other traffic but it was difficult to overtake. Then the road straightened out, and McQuade slowed down. The Toyota slowed down also. McQuade waved the driver on impatiently. The Toyota slowed further, driving in thick dust. The straight piece of road was ending: McQuade accelerated again. 'Maybe he's just a nervous driver.' He rammed into third gear and ground into the Pass.

The Toyota dropped further behind. Now they could no longer see it. They churned on, winding round the bends and grinding down through rocky hills. Only a reckless driver would attempt to overtake them here. Finally they emerged into the flatter country below. A few minutes later the vehicle reappeared.

It surged up behind them, then it swung out to overtake, and went roaring past them with a cloud of dust. There were two men in it. 'Make a note of its number,' McQuade said.

The Toyota roared away ahead, disappearing in its own dust. 'Strange,' Sarah remarked.

Five minutes later they saw it again. They came round a bend and the vehicle was on the shoulder of the road, about to turn around, and McQuade's pulse tripped. The next moment it pulled onto the road, and slammed to a stop across it. *'Oh Christ!'*

McQuade slammed his hand on the horn and rammed the Landrover into third gear. A man got out and waved both his arms, seventy yards ahead. McQuade searched the bush frantically on both sides of the road. The Landrover was down to twenty-five miles an hour, the Toyota fifty yards ahead. *'Hold tight!'*

McQuade rammed the vehicle into second gear, trod on the accelerator and swung the wheel. The Landrover went onto the shoulder of the road, then off it, bouncing and roaring. He went roaring through the sparse scrub, bouncing and bashing over bushes and stones, then he swung the wheel and went charging back up onto the road again beyond the Toyota. He rammed the gears and trod on the accelerator, and they went roaring off in a fury of dust.

'Well done!' Sarah gasped. McQuade looked frantically in the rearview mirror. He could see nothing for dust. He kept to the middle of the road. Then a blaze of headlights appeared.

The Toyota was roaring up behind, only its headlights visible, its horn blasting. It swung out to overtake, but McQuade swung the same way to block it, there was a screech of metal and sparks flew, and the headlights dropped back. Then it swerved the other way. McQuade swung in the same direction and the vicious headlights surged up again, and there was another crash and the Landrover jolted. Then the vehicle swung off the road, and over the shoulder. It went pounding through the scrub alongside the road. It roared up parallel with the Landrover. McQuade rammed on the accelerator, desperately trying to make the old Landrover go

318

faster, and the Toyota roared and bounced along beside them; for a hundred yards they raced each other, then the Toyota got ahead and swung to remount the road and McQuade swung at it, his teeth clenched furiously, and the Toyota swerved away at the last instant. McQuade swung back into the centre of the road. He looked desperately in his mirror; the headlights were back on the road, roaring up on him again, and he swung out furiously. There was another crash of metal and the Toyota surged ahead. It went blasting past and swung in front, and then another vehicle appeared.

It was a cattle-haulage truck, bearing down on them in a cloud of dust three hundred yards ahead. McQuade swung desperately onto the shoulder, and the Toyota swung in front of him, and there was nothing in the world but the terrible cattle-vehicle screaming down on them with a howling blast and the screaming hissing of its brakes. McQuade swung wildly off the shoulder onto the verge praying *Please God, please God.* The cattle-truck went screaming past in a howl of horn and McQuade swung desperately towards the trees.

Ahead was a barbed-wire fence. He roared straight at it and hit it at thirty miles an hour, and there was the wrenching of it dragging behind him, before he broke free of it. He went racing flat out through the trees, wildly swinging left and right, skidding and churning, going any way he could, and back on the road the Toyota turned with a scream of gravel, going for the hole in the fence.

McQuade went churning through the bush, bouncing and banging. The Toyota charged at the flattened fence, following McQuade's tracks. McQuade could not see the Toyota for dust. Suddenly there was a farm track in front of them. McQuade swung wildly onto it. He could go twice as fast on this. He raced down the sand track at fifty miles an hour. Ahead another track joined his at right angles leading back towards the road. McQuade swung onto it. He looked wildly behind and he could see nothing through his dust. Then through the trees he could see the road again beyond the fence, and he desperately charged at it. There was a great crashing and jolting of barbed wire again, and they burst through. McQuade roared up the verge and onto the road, and swung towards Windhoek. He went roaring down the road.

'You're going the wrong way!'

McQuade looked feverishly behind but could see nothing through his dust. 'We're going back to Windhoek to put you on a fucking aeroplane to Johannesburg!'

'Like hell you are! Unless you're coming with me! Who are these bastards?'

'The same bastards who beat Jakob to a pulp! And I'm not having you involved!'

She cried, 'I *am* involved!'

McQuade looked in the rearview mirror. He could see no vehicle. He took a shaky breath.

'Not far from here is the turn-off to Rehoboth and the main road. Fifty miles north of that is Windhoek, which has an airport. That's where I'm taking you. You'll be in Johannesburg by tonight. Thirty-six hours from now I'll be in Johannesburg also, and I'll tell you what a wonderful trip I had through the desert!'

'*Like hell I'm flying to Johannesburg!*'

'*You'll do as I bloody well say!*'

There was something else he had to do — and he was furious with himself for not thinking of it this morning: he had to go to Jakob's kraal and tell his wife and Skellum not to breathe a word to the police or anybody about what happened forty years ago.

Dammit, why hadn't he thought of that this morning?

320

38

It was midnight when McQuade got to Outjo, after getting Sarah onto a plane. He slept for an hour at the side of the road. It was dawn when he was grinding up the track through the hills to Jakob's kraal.

The cooking fire outside was not smouldering, and the main hut's door was ajar. McQuade gave a short hoot and got out of the Landrover. *'Skellum?'* he called. *'Old lady?'* He went to the door and knocked.

There was no response. He knocked again. Nothing. Then he pushed the door open and peered into the dark interior.

At first he did not grasp what he was seeing. Skellum stood there, his back to him – but he was so tall. Then Skellum slowly turned towards him, and McQuade gasped and recoiled. Skellum was that tall because he was hanging from the rafters with a rope around his neck.

McQuade stood in the doorway, horrified. Skellum's eyes protruded bulbously, congealed blood oozed at his nostrils, his mouth gaped open and his tongue stuck out. At his feet was a chair, on its side. For a moment McQuade stared, then he bounded into the hut. He seized Skellum by the chest and heaved him upwards, to take the weight off his neck. The body was stiff and cold. He rammed his ear against Skellum's heart, but there was not a sound. He let go of the body, frantically buried his hand in his pocket and pulled out his penknife. He ripped open the blade and sawed through the rope. Skellum crashed down onto the earth floor. McQuade dropped to his knees, loosened the knot on the neck, then plunged his head down and again listened for a heartbeat. He

321

sat back on his haunches, panting shakily. It was then that he saw the old woman.

She was sprawled in the dark corner, motionless. McQuade scrambled across the hut to her, and plunged his hand onto her heart. There was no heartbeat. Then he saw the big dent in her skull, the congealed blood on her old contused face. Lying beside her on the floor was an empty brandy-bottle. And across her body lay a knob-stick.

McQuade crouched there, his horrified mind fumbling. Then he scrambled to his feet, and backed out of the door.

He turned and ran to the Landrover, scrambled in, and gunned the engine to life.

Highway One leads due south from Windhoek, a wide tarred road going straight across the flat hard desert for a thousand kilometres. It was after dark when McQuade by-passed Windhoek and got onto that highway, for he had spent most of the morning with the police in Khorixas, reporting the murder. For this was a case of *double* murder, he was sure, not suicide. The bastards had clubbed Jakob's wife to death with a knobkerrie, to make it look as if Skellum had done it, then hanged him to make it look as if he had taken his own life in remorse. The Khorixas police sergeant had thought it was just that, a family row resulting in double tragedy; McQuade had said nothing to disillusion him.

He drove feverishly hard. He was certain he was not being followed, although he tensed every time a car's headlights appeared in his rearview mirror. He drove through the night, the bleak brown desert flashing by in his headlights, feverishly trying to think it through.

Who were these bastards? And what did they intend doing to him?

He was convinced now that he was not dealing with Red Straghan and his boys. Red Straghan was a hard bad bastard, but was he capable of cold-blooded murder? Maybe he was capable of burning old Jakob with cigarettes to make him talk – but cold-blooded murder of a defenceless old woman and her harmless drunken son? No, he was absolutely convinced about two things. One, that he was dealing with the Nazis who were worried about that submarine. Two, that almost irresistibly meant that Heinrich Muller was alive and directing operations against yours truly, Jim McQuade. And, by God, he was going to find the murdering bastard . . . By God he was furiously determined now. And he was delighted that he now had the registration number of that Toyota. He would trace the bastards through the Vehicle Registration Office, and that would lead directly or indirectly to Heinrich Muller himself! That fight with the Toyota was the best thing that could have happened!

And he was frightened. He had thrown himself into the deep end. He was playing with the big boys now. Thank God he had managed to get Sarah out of this, onto that aeroplane.

He took a deep, tense breath. Think positively. Just take one day at a time. They don't know where I'm going. They have no idea I'm going to Pretoria to crack the Book-of-Life computer.

He switched on his cab-light and reached for the road map. The next place on this highway was Marienthal. Just a native store and a hotel. But at Marienthal a dirt road led off, going south-east through the desert. Via a place called Aroab, to Karasburg. From Karasburg he would rejoin the main road heading east towards Johannesburg, another thousand kilometres away.

The sun was just coming up over the desert when he pulled into the village of Karasburg, on the main road leading east to South Africa. He had not seen another vehicle since leaving the highway.

It was too early to telephone Roger Wentland and ask him to trace the owner of the Toyota. He pulled down a side road in the village and examined the damage to the Landrover briefly. It was a mess. He climbed into the back, locked him-

323

self in, lay down on the foam mattress and went straight to sleep.

He woke up early afternoon with the sun on his face. He drove to the service station and tanked up the Landrover with diesel before going to the public telephone and dialling Roger Wentland's office in Swakopmund.

Mr Wentland was out of town for three days holiday, the secretary informed him. No, she didn't know where.

'When he comes back, please ask Mr Wentland to get his associates in Windhoek, or wherever, to go to the Vehicle Registration Office and find out the owner of this vehicle . . .' He spelt out the number carefully.

He bought a meat-pie and got on the road, heading east, to drive through the night again for the bleak, dusty, western Transvaal, with the mighty dynamo of Johannesburg and the city of Pretoria beyond.

PART EIGHT

39

Pretoria – that dull-sounding citadel of South Africa's vast bureaucracy and labyrinthine Apartheid administration, that throbbing heart of Calvinistic conservatism with its massive Victorian-style Union Buildings embracing the horizon, its hundreds of modern apartment blocks for its thousands of civil servants, its ultra-modern government sky-scrapers and its huge statue of Paul Kruger telling each day there will be no nonsense – Pretoria is actually rather pretty. The streets are characterized by jacaranda trees, and pleasant green suburbs spreadeagle over a surrounding crescent of hills. It has a rather gentle, small-city atmosphere. It was eight o'clock the next morning when McQuade found his way into it, and the air was brisk and the sky was young, well-ordered traffic was starting a new day and stylish, pretty girls were on their way to work. And it was friendly:

'But *certainly*,' Johan Lombard said, with hardly a trace of South African accent, 'any friend of Roger Wentland is a friend of mine! How about a hair of the dog at lunchtime? Where are you staying?'

'Nowhere yet, I'm speaking from a public phone.'

'Stay at the Burgerspark, dear boy, best pub in town. What scandal was Roger referring to?'

'He just said I must ask you about a recent scandal in the Population Registration Department.'

'This whole government is a scandal, dear boy, I tell them so every day in the newspaper, but I know the one he means. Meet me in the German Club, in Paul Kruger Street at noon. Sort of unofficial press club. Say you're my guest, don't swear about Adolf Hitler and you'll be fine.'

'Thank you. One other thing. How can I get hold of the Civil Servants' Association membership list?'

'I'm sure I've got a copy somewhere. I'll dig it out. Why do you need it, by the way?'

'I'm trying to trace an old friend.'

'I'll find a copy. And, how is dear old Roger, haven't seen him since Pontius was a pupil Pilate . . .'

McQuade hung up a minute later, feeling extremely lucky.

He next traced Peter Duncan's health studio number in the telephone directory. 'Dun-can's,' the voice sang.

'May I speak to Peter Duncan, please.'

'It is he. In the flesh.'

Peter Duncan was also delighted to hear from Roger Wentland, and delighted to meet McQuade for a drink this afternoon. Lester's Bar at four o'clock, jolliest pub in town, old man.

Feeling things were going his way, McQuade sorted out his coins and dialled Roger Wentland's office in Swakopmund. No, Mr Wentland had not been in contact with the office yet. Yes, the secretary would remember to ask him to trace the vehicle.

McQuade hung up. He should telephone Inspector Dupreez, as promised, but he wasn't going to do so today; the Inspector would have been told by the Namibian police about the double murder by now, and McQuade was not looking forward to his new questions. He stacked up his coins in preparation for telephoning Sarah. He wasn't going to tell her about the double murder yet, since he did not want her panicky questions.

'Hullo darling!' Sarah cried. 'Thank God. I've been so worried. Where are you?'

'In Pretoria,' he grinned.

'I should never have let you bully me onto that plane. I've had nightmares about those swines catching you! When are you coming to Johannesburg?'

'Tomorrow evening, I hope. I've got meetings all today and

tonight. Have you had any contact from our friend Inspector Dupreez?'

'No. How would he know where I'm staying?'

'Right, but the police have infinite resources. Anyway, if he gets hold of you, please remember not to mention that fight with that Toyota in the bush.'

'But I wish I knew why not. It's very hard to tell these lies when you won't explain *why*. I think this is all very serious – a man's been beaten to death and the same thugs are chasing you across the country – I think the police *should* be informed, if only for your own safety.'

'Sarah, I just need a few days. To try to find out something. If I fail, I'll tell the police everything. And you.'

'Is that a solemn promise?'

He took a breath. 'Yes.'

'And if you *succeed* in these few days?'

'If I succeed I'll solve the whole mystery, and bring these bastards to justice.'

There was a pause. Then she sighed. 'Okay. Where are you staying tonight?'

'I don't know yet.' He added, to forestall further questions, 'Probably with my friend Johan Lombard. I'll telephone you tomorrow.'

'Promise?'

'Promise.'

'Okay.' She sighed. 'Jim? I think I'm madly in love with you.'

For a moment he was deliciously happy. 'I'm madly in love with you as well.'

The German Club is a solid, stolid building, the lounge in heavy furniture with potted palms, yesterday's newspapers all the way from Germany, and muted German music on the air. Johan Lombard was a jolly, portly man with curly grey hair and cherubic cheeks. 'Not kind of me at all, dear boy, always have a hair of the dog at this very hour if the slings and arrows of outrageous fortune permit, sitting on this very bar stool. Now, I presume Roger is referring to the homosexuality scandal in the Population Registration bureau?'

McQuade was relieved — he had been afraid of arousing Johan's suspicions by not even knowing what the scandal was about. 'Yes. Has there been any other scandal in that department?'

'The mere existence of the department is a scandal!' Johan said. 'Why must we have our entire official lives recorded in a single booklet? So that any passing policeman can scrutinize our personal histories from the cradle to the grave at a moment's glance.' He held up a finger. 'History has always shown that the citizen's personal freedom has been at its lowest when governmental regimentation is at its highest. It is an oppressive government which insists you have a *number*, and in this benighted country, a *racial* classification to boot! It's a cattle-brand — in black and white. And ne'er the twain shall meet. Except,' he added grudgingly, 'I detect a ray of hope in our present State President, the illustrious P. W. Botha. A measure of reform is in the air, after forty years of bloody-minded Boer rule. And I've got a feeling Botha will be replaced quite soon by a younger, more go-ahead man. However, what about this homosexuality scandal?' He peered at him. 'Not a bum-bandit, are you?'

McQuade grinned. 'No. Roger just said that you'd know all about it, being a newspaperman.'

'Forgive me asking, old chap, and as a newspaperman I'm quite accustomed to nosey-parkers, and any friend of Roger's is a friend of mine, et cetera — but what is your interest in this *sordid* piece of Pretoria history?'

McQuade was ready for the question. 'I'm an external student of the University of London, doing a degree in Political Science. Roger and I were talking about political history one day, and when he mentioned this scandal, he told me to ask you if I was ever in Pretoria. And here I am. On a few weeks holiday.'

330

Johan nodded. 'Governmental cock-up, our daily fare — except it's my unhappy lot to have to meet a dead-line every day when intellectual pursuit beckons from so many watering-holes.' He held up a finger again. 'Professor Simone Jansen. You must meet my friend Simone, teaches Political Science at the university. I'll give her a call for you. Anyway, about this scandal.' He waved a hand. 'Did you know that Pretoria has a substantial homosexual population?'

'No.'

'Something to do with all the Calvinistic red tape, I suppose. Anyway, it so happened that a few of them worked in the Population Registration Department, and one of them was having it off with some Coloured boys — by which I mean near-whites.' He rolled his eyes. 'Eventually these Coloured boys began to blackmail this hapless official to do . . . guess what? To issue them with false Books-of-Life, which said they were *whites*! He was caught out. Sent to jail. Big scandal. End of story.'

McQuade picked up his beer. His tired mind working and his heart sinking. Blackmail? That was what Roger was indirectly suggesting to him — blackmail of some homosexual official to give him the details of all the Strausses in the Population Register? How the hell did he go about that?

'I see.' He wanted to ask Johan the quickest way to find out about Nazis in South Africa. But that was too direct. Too close to the subject of Population Registration. He said conversationally, 'This is a big club. Are there a lot of Germans in Pretoria?'

'Lots, dear boy. Came flooding here after the war when this Afrikaner government got into power.'

'Are many politically active?'

Johan glanced around the bar. 'Dear fellow, this isn't exactly the place to discuss the political ambitions of the Master Race.' He glanced at his watch. 'Nor the time. I've got to get back to the grindstone before my vast readership stages a riot.' He held up a finger again. 'Professor Simone Jansen.

She's the lady to talk to about German activity in this part of the world. *And* me, but not here.'

They said goodbye outside the club. McQuade walked down the street, looking for a café where he could sit quietly and look at the Civil Servants' Association list which Johan had given him. He saw a Wimpy Bar, crowded with lunch-time traffic, black and white. It was many years since McQuade had been to Pretoria, and it was a surprise to see blacks sitting with whites in this conservative town. Things sure were changing. He ordered coffee and a hamburger.

The Civil Servants' Association list was a year out of date, but it was comprehensive. Under the Population Registration Department there were hundreds of names. He finished his lunch, walked uptown looking for a shop that did photo-copying, and had the pages relating to the Population Registration Department photo-copied. He borrowed the shop's scissors, cut the heading off the pages, and all telephone numbers, leaving only the names. He paid and asked the shop assistant the way to Lester's Bar.

What was he going to say to Peter Duncan? Roger had said he must simply show him the list of civil servants after speaking to Johan about the scandal. So obviously Duncan would know which of the people on this list were homosexual. But Duncan would surely want to know why he needed this information. And how the hell was he going to use it after he got it? How was he going to go about blackmail?

Lester's Bar is smart, modern, with leather furniture, sub-dued lights and art-nouveau pictures of muscular men, chic women and fast cars.

'And how is Roger?' Peter Duncan said. He was a thick-set, healthy, balding man of about forty, who did not look in the least bit gay. He was drinking tomato-juice.

'Very well, sends his best wishes to you.' McQuade decided to get straight on with it. 'He's my lawyer, and said you'd be able to help me.'

'Oh? Pity. I thought my luck might have changed. But how could I help you?'

The innuendo made McQuade more uncomfortable. 'Roger said you would know all the gays in this town.'

'Did he, now? But you aren't one of us, are you? I can usually spot them.'

McQuade felt relieved. This man was out of the closet. 'No,' he smiled.

Duncan shrugged. 'Well, I hardly know them *all*, old chap.' He added with a frown: 'But *why*?'

'But with your ... connections, you could find out whether a certain person is gay or not?'

Duncan frowned. 'Maybe. But what's all this about?'

McQuade pulled out his photo-copied list. 'Roger wants to find out if any of these people are gay.'

Duncan took the list, but did not look at it. 'Why didn't Roger telephone me himself?'

McQuade sighed, theatrically. 'Because it's all rather sensitive. Legal ethics and all that. As a lawyer, Roger dare not be directly involved. Suffice it to say the information is needed for a case he's handling for me.' He paused. 'Only the information. Nothing else.'

Duncan nodded slowly. 'And that's all you want to know? You won't be asking me do anything else – of an illegal nature?'

'Correct.'

'Cross your heart?'

'Cross my heart.' McQuade smiled.

'Can I telephone Roger, to verify this?'

'Yes. He'll have to be evasive, but, yes, telephone him and ask if I'm a client. And a good friend.'

Duncan turned to the bulky list. He ran his finger down the first page slowly, then looked to see how many pages there were. He folded the list, and slipped it into his jacket pocket. 'Leave it with me. Call me tomorrow.' He stopped. 'No, telephones are not to be trusted in this country. Better drop around to my health studio at about ten o'clock tomorrow morning.' He produced a card.

'Many thanks, indeed.' McQuade added earnestly, 'You'll be discreet with that list, won't you?'

Duncan smiled wryly. 'In the Fast Lane – in the intimate, *bitchy* world of homosexuality – it is very hard to be discreet. But for Roger's sake I'll do my best.'

McQuade walked back to the Landrover. Feeling a bit more encouraged. That the meeting had gone fine. No questions he couldn't answer. He was not even worried about Duncan telephoning Roger, who would verify his credentials, and he felt confident that Mr Peter Duncan would come up with the information. He felt he had done a good day's work, and right now he was going to find a cheap hotel and sleep. In a delicatessen he bought two hamburgers, in a liquor store two bottles of wine.

After asking for directions, he drove through town, looking for the Burgerspark Hotel which Johan Lombard had recommended. It looked too expensive for James McQuade, set in well-kept gardens, with a black doorman in a top hat and tails. McQuade did not even stop, but two blocks further down was the squat Assembly Hotel, a one-star establishment with neon signs advertising billiard room, beer garden and Flamingo Ladies Bar – that looked more McQuade's speed.

He checked in and carried his own bag upstairs. The floor had not been polished for a long time, the double bed had a torn headboard, the bathroom had white tiles of public lavatory persuasion, but he did not care. It was cheap and all he wanted to do was sleep. He sat down on the bed, poured a glass of wine and held his face.

After Peter Duncan came up with the names of all the queers in the department, then what? How the hell was he going to blackmail an official queer? A queer official? Without ending up in jail?

Take one problem at a time. One day at a time. You've done very well in one day . . .

You've found out the scandal, found the names of all the civil servants, broken the ice with Peter Duncan, and Johan and this Professor Simone Jansen are going to save you a lot of work by telling you about old Nazi activity in South Africa. *You have had a good day.*

Then the chilling thought came back. What about the new double murder? And Inspector Dupreez? The Khorixas police would have informed him by now. McQuade had to telephone him tomorrow. Dupreez wasn't going to be fooled. How many other natives in the area had Skellum or Jakob told about the two white demons who came struggling ashore forty years ago? How long before Dupreez discovered that motive for murder? Then that submarine would disappear out of his grasp. And so would Heinrich Muller.

And how long before those murdering bastards caught up with *him* . . .?

40

He was woken at about midnight by the thumping of a dance-band in the hotel, a gabble of voices from the beer garden below his window, and the roaring of motorcycles and screams of tyres in the street. He knew the type: the lower-class whites which this country protected with its Apartheid, the *lekker ous* with their leather lumberjackets and their zoot suits and gum-chewing chicks with their rums-an'-coke who called the blacks the bladdy kaffirs. Oh God, he wanted to get this over with and get out of this country back to Australia. Of course there were plenty of the same type in Australia but at least the law did not make white trash lords over the blacks, at least there were not many blacks in Australia to be white trash to. And where were the bloody police, with all this noise?

He lay awake, worrying about Inspector Dupreez.

At ten o'clock he arrived at Duncan's Health Studio.

It was a large suburban house in the jacaranda-lined avenues. Interior walls had been knocked down to create a number of big rooms with exercise apparatus. There was a mirror-lined hall for aerobic classes, showers, lockers, a sauna room, two jacuzzi rooms, and a lounge with a health-bar. The place was very well-kept. A healthy girl in a sky-blue leotard directed him into the weight-lifting room to find Peter Duncan.

He was instructing a woman in the use of weights. He was in sky-blue ballet-tights that showed off bulging genitals. On the walls were glossy photographs of monstrously muscled, glistening winners of body-building contests. Duncan waved and led the way into his office. He went to his jacket, pulled out the list.

'The name is marked with a tick.'

McQuade said with relief, 'Thank you very much, Peter.'

'As long as that's the only detective work I do.'

'It is. But was there any difficulty?'

'I refuse to divulge the name of my informant on the grounds it may incriminate me. By the way, I presume you know who you're dealing with? The Population Registration Office.' He tapped the list. 'Do tell Roger to be careful. There was a big scandal a few years ago, which doubtless accounts for why he wants you to do his dirty work for him.' He twiddled his fingers in farewell. 'Toodle-oo.'

'Just one thing. Do you know him?' He tapped the list.

Duncan said: 'Her.'

McQuade blinked.

'As a matter of fact, I do,' Duncan said. 'I didn't know she was one of the girls, though. A closet case. She comes to the aerobics class most days after work.'

McQuade's mind was racing. 'If I come here this afternoon will you point her out to me?'

'No, I've told you I'll do no more.' Duncan added airily: 'But rather pretty. Long blonde hair, if you like that sort of thing. But I'm afraid she won't much like you.' He twiddled his fingers again.

McQuade slowly opened the list.

The name that was ticked was: Lisa van Rensburg.

He had checked out of the Assembly Hotel but his Landrover was still parked there. He walked back, feeling discouraged. And this whole notion of blackmail was distasteful. Repugnant. Especially blackmail over homosexuality. Especially blackmail of a woman.

He passed the Burgerspark Hotel, turned back and went in. It was gracious. Quiet. A good place to think in.

He sat in the lounge and ordered coffee, and tried to think.

337

Okay, blackmail was repugnant, but he would be doing it to find the most-wanted Nazi war-criminal of today. Systematic murder of millions of Jews was infinitely more repugnant, as well as murder of the whole crew of a submarine. He would only be blackmailing her to find out which Mr Strauss was Heinrich Muller. He wasn't going to blackmail her for his personal *gain*.

Except the loot in that submarine.

Okay, but it was really Heinrich Muller he was trying to find now. The loot he'd find himself. He closed his mind to that uncomfortable distinction. And tried to weigh up the risks.

The only risk was that Lisa might denounce him to the police. Confess her homosexuality rather than be blackmailed. Then he was in very big trouble indeed. No Heinrich Muller, no loot, and a long time in jail.

But what was she *likely* to do? She was a closet gay. She would lose her job if this was found out. She was only going to make an extract from the computer of the details of a number of men of a certain age-group named H. Strauss – nothing more. Surely she was unlikely to sacrifice her job by confessing her homosexuality for such a small undertaking?

He stared across the lounge, trying to weigh the risk against the rest. And the rest was compelling. Get your priorities right!

You *know* he hasn't died to date – or you're almost sure.

You *know* the name he's likely to be using.

You *know* that all his details are on a computer a few blocks away.

You *know* a lesbian has access to that computer and you know that *she* knows she'll lose her job if her homosexuality becomes known.

And once you know the address of the right Mr H. Strauss, you become a multi-millionaire and you'll bring the most-wanted Nazi war-criminal to justice.

How can you turn down odds like that?

He sighed deeply. Okay. That decision made.

It was eleven o'clock. The cocktail bar was open. And he needed a drink.

The bar was plush, with subdued lights. He ordered a beer. He drank a third of it down, down, down.

Okay, how? How do you blackmail a closet lesbian?

Obviously, by getting evidence of her homosexuality, then putting the hard word on her. And how? Obviously, by getting another woman to seduce her. An accomplice.

Obviously, a call-girl. A bisexual hooker. So, step one: meet the right hooker.

Step two: the hooker goes to Duncan's, pals up with Lisa, takes her home to bed. That shouldn't be hard: surely lesbians are usually on the lookout for sexual partners.

Step three ...? Well, you meet Lisa and tell her you'll disclose her secret unless she gets to work on that computer.

Step four? Make yourself very scarce very fast if she refuses. And think again.

He drank the rest of his beer down in one long go, and ordered another.

He sat there. Trying to think about step three.

It was noon when he felt he had figured out all the possibilities: the what-ifs, the what-to-say-whens.

He went to the reception desk and bought a copy of the *Pretoria News*. He opened it to the classified advertisements, and was surprised at the number of advertisements for escort agencies and massage parlours. In Pretoria, the citadel of Calvinistic Afrikaner conservatism? There was Touch of Class, Discretion, Astor, Elegance, and umpteen others.

He went to the public telephones in the foyer, and dialled.

'Taste of Sugar,' a female voice crooned.

McQuade said, 'Do you service couples?'

There was a moment's hesitation. 'What is your number, sir, I'll call you back. And your name.'

'My name is van Rensburg.' He gave her the number of the public telephone and hung up.

He waited. The telephone rang. 'Van Rensburg,' he said.

'Yes, Mr van Rensburg,' the lady said. 'That can be arranged. Where are you?'

'My wife and I have just arrived in town. We'll be finding a hotel shortly, we'll call you. What are your charges, please?'

'A hundred rand an hour. But the entire night would only be five hundred.'

McQuade decided to clarify it. 'You do understand that my wife would want to be involved?'

'I understand perfectly,' the lady said.

'I'll call you back when we've settled down in a hotel.' He thanked her and hung up.

He took a tense breath. He then telephoned Roger Wentland's office. The secretary informed him that Roger had not called in, so nothing had been done about tracing the owner of the Toyota, but he would be in the office tomorrow. 'Can't you trace it for me?' McQuade demanded.

'No, Mr McQuade, the Vehicle Registration people only give that information to the police or to a lawyer because it's relevant to a case.'

McQuade hung up, frustrated. Well, before he committed himself to the dangerous game of blackmail he had better get his telephone call to Inspector Dupreez over with, and find out if anything new had turned up. He rehearsed his lines, then dialled.

The telephone was answered by Detective Sergeant Bekker. 'Inspector Dupreez is up in Khorixas assisting the Namibia police on the case, sir. Of course you know about Jakob's family.'

'Yes, I reported it. Terrible tragedy.'

'The Namibia police thought it was a family row, then a suicide, but the Inspector's convinced it's murder, hey. The same guys who did Jakob in.'

This was no surprise. 'Any clues?'

'You remember Mr Potgieter went to your house and disturbed those two bastards beating up Jakob. He chased them, but lost them. Well, two men answering their description, wearing balaclavas, were seen by somebody a few minutes later, jumping into a Toyota four-wheel-drive and rushing away.'

'A Toyota? What colour?' McQuade demanded.

'White or grey. The witness isn't sure, but he got the number. We've checked it out at Vehicle Registration, but it doesn't exist. So either it's a false number plate or the witness got it wrong.'

'And that number was?'

Bekker told him.

The same number as the Toyota which waylaid him, and he had just lost his best lead to the chief of Adolf Hitler's Gestapo!

'And how was your trip over, sir?' asked Bekker.

McQuade's pulse tripped. He was sure the question was loaded. 'Uneventful.'

Bekker said conversationally, 'Because the police in Windhoek received a report of reckless driving from a cattle-truck driver. He complained that two vehicles were approaching him, racing each other, and there was bladdy nearly a hell of a smash, hey. This second vehicle was also a white Toyota. The other was a green Landrover, like yours. I jus' thought it might be those same bastards chasing you.'

'No, nothing like that happened to me.'

There was a silence. 'Oh, well. Where can Inspector Dupreez telephone you?'

'I'm in a public phone box, I'll have to call him.'

'Well, please call him tomorrow, sir.'

McQuade said he would, and hung up. He leant against the cabin wall. Oh God. His best lead gone out the window – false number plates! That meant he had no option but to go the blackmail route. The other bad news was that Detective Sergeant Bekker clearly didn't believe him, and he still had to deal with Inspector Dupreez later.

The next call was easy to make – to Roger Wentland's office to tell the secretary not to bother about tracing that Toyota – but he hesitated over the next call to Sarah. It was going to be tricky telling her he was not going to make it to Johannesburg tonight, and staving off her questions. Put the call off until after he's sussed out the Lisa van Rensburg route? No, that could be midnight. He stacked up his coins, and rehearsed his new lines.

'Hullo, darling,' Sarah cried. 'Where the hell are you?'

'Still in Pretoria, in a public box.'

'What time do I see you? That double bed's awful lonely!'

'I don't think I'm going to make it tonight. I'm busy until at least midnight but I promise I'll be there tomorrow—'

'Oh, *Jim!*' she cried. 'You can come after midnight . . .'

McQuade closed his eyes. 'Darling, it'll be awfully late and I don't know my way around Johannesburg—'

'Nor do I, but I love you, dammit!'

'I love you too, but we're about to get cut off . . .' He broke the connection.

He stood there. God, he wished he *were* going to Johannesburg, not doing what he was about to do.

He went to the reception desk and took a double room. He was going to say his name was van Rensburg, then realized he'd have to use his bank card, and registered in his own name.

It was a nice room. He sat down to telephone the Taste of Sugar agency. He looked at his watch. Duncan's aerobics class started at five o'clock.

He reminded the lady of their previous conversation. He arranged for the girl to present herself at room 503, Burgerspark Hotel at four o'clock. 'And can you please ask her to bring a leotard or a tracksuit.'

The lady was accustomed to different requests, but she'd never heard this one. 'A *track*suit?'

'Yes, please.'

41

He had over three hours to wait. He went into the nearest liquor store and bought wine, gin, whisky, brandy, and beer. He collected his Landrover and drove into the covered parking attached to his hotel. He went back to his room.

It was not yet one o'clock. He telephoned Johan Lombard, but he was out. He telephoned the German Club and asked for him.

'Just phoned to invite you for lunch.'

'Excellent, dear boy, why don't you come and join me with the Krauts?'

'You said you'd rather not discuss certain subjects at the German Club.'

'Got you, dear boy, got you,' Johan said, 'but I'm afraid I can't leave my colleagues right now. However I've arranged with Professor Jansen for you to pop up to the university anytime. Here's her number . . .'

One of the biggest universities in the world is the University of South Africa. It has over one hundred thousand students. It is a massive complex on the hillsides outside Pretoria, set in manicured gardens. But there are few lecture rooms, no playing fields, no dormitory blocks: all the students receive their lectures by correspondence. Most of them are people whose daily responsibilities preclude attendance at an ordinary university, and the majority are non-white.

McQuade was impressed. He had lunch in the big staff dining room with Professor Jansen. She was a pale, severe, attractive woman in her forties who was quite unsurprised by McQuade's visit and his questions: she was accustomed to pilgrimages from students. She seemed to assume that McQuade knew nothing as he was a student of the University of London.

'Historically the Afrikaner and the Germans identify with one another – that is why so many Germans came here, particularly after the last war. I, for example, am almost entirely German by blood, though my family has been here for generations and I regard myself as an Afrikaner. The Afrikaners of the war period identified with the Germans because they were anti-British. Hitler's victory would have enabled the Afrikaner to get his country back which the British had stolen.' She pointed with her fork. 'It all started with the Great Trek.'

McQuade knew most of this but he did not want to interrupt the professor's flow. She went on: 'The British captured the Cape from the Dutch at the beginning of the last century. The Dutch resented British rule so they packed up their ox-wagons and trekked out. With great bitterness and suffering. They settled down legally on empty territory and established their little Boer republics. Then they struck gold. What happens? Britain comes along and annexes them. So there followed the Boer War.' She waved her fork. 'The might of the great British Empire *hurled* against these backward little republics. Three years of bitter guerrilla war, scorched earth, British concentration camps. And when the Boers were finally crushed, their republics were forced into a British-dominated Union of South Africa.' She looked at McQuade. 'And for the next *forty* years the pro-British element ruled the roost in South Africa! Politically, culturally, economically. While the Boers, the Afrikaners, were like poor-whites, backward country bumpkins who had been robbed of their country.' She shook her head at him. 'So now there was the bitterness of backwardness after the bitterness of being robbed, after the bitterness of the Great Trek.'

McQuade wanted to get back to the German content. He ventured: 'Meanwhile, in South West Africa . . .?'

'Meanwhile in South West Africa-Namibia a similar situation developed. After the First World War, Namibia had been handed to South Africa to administer, making the German residents bitter. So when Hitler went to war against Britain, both the Germans in Namibia and the bitter Afrikaners were rooting for him to win, because that would break the British yoke in southern Africa. And the *Ossewabrandwag* – which was the military wing of the Afrikaner movement – engaged in all kinds of sabotage. So many were put in concentration camps. And *again* these bitter-enders were frustrated – because Hitler lost the war. So the Afrikaners were *still* under the British yoke. But then,' she held up a finger, 'then, in the aftermath of war, came the new elections. In Britain, Winston Churchill – who had "won" the war' – she made quotation marks with her fingers – 'was defeated, and in South Africa, General Smuts, who had been in Churchill's Imperial War Cabinet, also lost the election. For the first time in one hundred years the Afrikaner was master in his own country at last! For the first time since the British occupation of the Cape.' She looked at him with bright eyes. 'Can't you imagine the rejoicing? The emotional ... *orgasm* of the Afrikaner people?'

McQuade nodded.

'And the new Afrikaner government opened its doors to the defeated Germans who had been their spiritual allies against the British. Thousands flocked here.'

'And many of them were Nazis?'

'Of course. Germany was full of Nazis who needed a new home.'

'But Nazi war-criminals?'

'What do you think? Germany was full of war-criminals who the Allies were determined to prosecute once the gates of Auschwitz and the like were opened, and they saw what had happened. Nazi war-criminals were fleeing Germany like rats, and South Africa – in particular South West Africa – was a very attractive place for them. Namibia was German

345

already, the Afrikaner was pro-German, and they were *Aryans*. Even the languages were similar, and the customs. The new Afrikaner government welcomed them as reinforcements against the British element.'

'And they rewarded the government with their political support?' McQuade asked.

'Indeed. But now, forty years later, that German connection is an embarrassment to the government, because now the failure of Apartheid has become evident. The government has finally come to realize not only that it is unworkable, it can't defy world opinion indefinitely, and there must be some form of power-sharing with the blacks. This has resulted in a split amongst the Afrikaners, between the reformists and the hardliners. This,' she held up a finger, 'is where the Nazi element comes back to haunt the government. Because the AWB, the ultra-hardliners, not only want to perpetuate Apartheid, they want their own pure-white state, a "volkstaat", in which there will be *no* blacks at all. And this volkstaat will be run on Nationalist-Socialist lines, like Hitler's Germany. Even the AWB flag has a swastika on it, with three arms instead of four, but unmistakably a swastika. And the AWB appeals widely to the old Afrikaner spirit.'

McQuade said, 'But are the AWB really Nazis?'

'No doubt about it. An examination of their manifesto makes that obvious. The *"Herrenvolk"* idea appears repeatedly, as does anti-semitism. They openly reject the parliamentary system of democracy as obsolete, calling it the *"British–Jewish"* parliamentary system, and demand an authoritarian system, with no opposition political parties. They want a centralized one-party political body with dictatorial powers. Where, in their own words, "community interests always take precedence over individual interests". And of course, they've got the same rampant racist superiority as the Nazis – the blood and soil rhetoric, the socialist and militaristic emphasis, their swastika and eagle emblem, the red-black-white colours of the Nazis, the warped religious admixture, and the leadership cult – and their leader, Eugene Terreblanche, is almost as charismatic as Hitler was, with the same powers of rhetoric. He rants and raves very effectively and drives his audiences wild. He's studied Hitler's speech-making style, and even gives Hitler's sloppy salute, and goes about surrounded by bodyguards.' She snorted. 'The laugh is that for all his racism, if he has his way South Africa will become just another tin-pot one-party African state, because he's the typical African dictator.'

'And *could* he get his way?'

The professor snorted again. 'The AWB is not to be taken lightly. They are not simply a "lunatic fringe", as people like to call them. They have a very big following indeed. Their appeal is that they claim to be the true torch-bearers of the original Afrikaner nationalism – they say the Botha government has deserted the true cause, gone soft on Apartheid, intends to share power with the blacks, the beginning of the end, et cetera. Their appeal is their directness, their return to the values of the old republics. This appeals very much to the Afrikaner with his dour Calvinistic values who expects his political leaders to be straight and rigid. Now the AWB has put its weight behind the Conservative Party, the hard-liner members of parliament who split away from the government a few years ago. And as a result the Conservative Party is now the official opposition.' She raised her eyebrows. 'So in reality the *AWB* is the official opposition! *That*'s how seriously we have to take them.' She paused. 'Now we're in the sobering situation where the Nationalist Party, which has ruled this country with its iron rod of Apartheid for forty years, is now the *moderate*, centre party defending themselves against the *right*. And,' she ended emphatically, 'they have every reason to be worried, because at the next election the Conservative Party and AWB could win.'

McQuade was thinking of Hitler's Grand Design, his blueprint for Africa. 'And these Nazis who came here after the war – they support the AWB? And the Conservative Party?'

The professor glanced at her watch. 'Most of those Germans just wanted to forget and start a new life. Indeed most of them were innocent of any wrong-doing. But the *true* Nazis?' She shook her head. 'They were the Master Race, remember. They were going to change the world into a paradise for Aryans. For this ideal they sacrificed all norms of morality, countenanced all brutality, rationalized genocide. Dehumanized themselves by deifying themselves.' She shook her head again. 'People like that don't think they were wrong, particularly in an environment like South Africa. They kept a low profile, sure, but many were active in their own groups, keeping the spirit of Hitler alive. Now they've grouped themselves behind the AWB, as a front for their own political ambitions.'

McQuade's mind was trying to race through what Wiesenthal had told him about Odessa and the Strasbourg Conference for the recreation of the Third Reich: 'And what are those ambitions? Are they different from the AWB's?'

'I am an historian, not a political journalist.' The professor smiled. 'My expertise stops here. But having said that, do you know the story of Robey Leibbrandt, the South African Olympic boxer who Hitler sent to assassinate General Smuts during the war?'

McQuade nodded earnestly.

'If Robey Leibbrandt had succeeded in assassinating General Smuts, and mounting a coup,' Professor Jansen continued, 'Hitler would have cut off Australia, New Zealand, the whole Far East, and dominated both the Indian Ocean and the South Atlantic all the way to South America, which was pro-Nazi anyway. He'd have won the war. That would have left only America to worry about.' She looked at him professorially, as if she were addressing a tutorial. 'Can you imagine how different the world would be today if he had succeeded, and Africa in particular?' She frowned. 'Autobahns from Cape Town to Cairo. Efficient railway lines streaking across the continent carrying raw materials. The natural resources of this magnificent continent *scientifically* exploited and *redeveloped*, instead of *raped*.' She waved a hand: 'The forests preserved and replanted, instead of hacked down mindlessly for firewood. The land refertilized, instead of turning into dust bowls. The wildlife *conserved* instead of butchered into extinction . . .'

McQuade waited, desperate to hear professorial evidence that his submarine was loaded with Odessa loot to recreate the Third Reich. He said earnestly: 'But the Nazis who came here after the war, who are now grouping behind the AWB – are you saying that they are doing so as part of a scheme to implement Hitler's old blueprint for Africa?' He waved his hand. 'To create the Fourth Reich, in South Africa?'

Professor Jansen smiled. Then shook her head.

'I am simply an academic, whose job it is to understand history. I'm not going to stick my neck out on a ragbag of newspaper facts.' She glanced at her watch again. 'For that you must look to Johan Lombard, the purveyor of current events . . .'

42

It was half-past three. McQuade drove fast back to his hotel feverishly excited. *Treasure for the recreation of the Third Reich* – that's what he had stumbled onto! That submarine had been carrying a top Nazi official to the fertile shores of southern Africa with the Nazi Party's treasure accumulated for the specific purpose of creating the Fourth Reich, which was why Heinrich Muller murdered the whole crew . . .

It was almost four o'clock when he got back to the Burgerspark Hotel. There was a telephone message awaiting him at the reception desk. He stared at the note. *Please call Sarah urgently.*

How had Sarah known he was staying at the Burgerspark Hotel? He'd certainly not told her. He hurried up to his room to call her. As he reached for the telephone, it rang. He snatched it up. 'Hullo?'

'Good afternoon. Mr van Rensburg?'

The Taste of Sugar girl. 'Yes!'

'I'm downstairs in the foyer. Shall I come up?'

'Oh . . . Yes, please.' He put down the telephone shakily. It was all about to happen – his first step in blackmail. He feverishly rehearsed his lines for the last time. He was suddenly very nervous again. If the girl got scared and called in the police he could come very unstuck now. There was a knock on the door. He strode across and opened it.

A good-looking woman of about thirty stood there, blonde and stylish. She carried a plastic shopping bag. She was smiling professionally. 'I'm Miss Brownlee.'

'Miss Brownlee, thank you for coming.'

He stood back as she walked in. She had a very good

figure. He closed the door and waved a hand at an armchair. 'What can I get you to drink?'

'White wine, thanks.' She had an Afrikaans accent, but a cultured one. She held out a visiting card. It read: *A Taste of Sugar*, and below, *Fiona*. 'The second number is my home phone.'

'Thank you.' McQuade put it down on the table and reached for the wine.

'May I mention the money?'

'Of course!' He burrowed into his pocket and pulled out two red fifty-rand notes.

'Only one hour, is it?'

'There'll be more.' He began to open a bottle of wine shakily.

Miss Brownlee sat down and crossed her legs elegantly. 'Well, I brought the tracksuit. Where are we running?'

McQuade smiled, despite himself. He passed her a glass of wine. 'Not far.' He sloshed a big shot of whisky into a glass and took a swallow.

Miss Brownlee said: 'Where's your wife? I was told that this was a,' she fluttered her eyelids, 'special assignment.'

'Is that all right with you?'

She was charming. 'Quite all right. It's not an unusual request, you know.'

'Isn't it?'

She smiled. 'Many wives want to try it. And *all* men. I'm unshockable. So, where's the wife?'

McQuade took a breath. 'I want to offer you a thousand rand.'

Miss Brownlee raised her eyebrows. 'Now you're talking. To do what?'

'To find out if a certain lady is a lesbian. I think she is, but I want confirmation.'

Miss Brownlee looked at him. 'Why do you want to know if she's a lesbian?'

'Because I'm very fond of her.' He paused. 'For that reason

you must not mention me to her.'

'And if she is, what'll you do?'

'That's my business. But I'll know what my problems are, and maybe I can solve them.'

Miss Brownlee nodded thoughtfully. 'And where is she? How do I meet her?'

'I'll tell you that after you've agreed.'

Just then there was a loud knock. McQuade flinched. He went to the door and opened it.

Sarah stood in the corridor. 'Thank God!' she said.

McQuade had a frozen smile on his face. *Oh shit.* 'How did you find me?'

'Phoned every hotel in Pretoria until I found Mr McQuade. I've got something important to tell you.' She looked past him and saw the girl. 'Oh!'

'*Come in!*' McQuade said hastily. He stood aside and waved a hand shakily. 'This is Miss Brownlee, who's doing some business with me. Investment. Miss Brownlee, this is Miss Buckley.'

Sarah was frosty. 'How do you do?'

'Miss Brownlee,' McQuade blustered. 'I think we'd better continue another day. I have some business to discuss with Miss Buckley, I'll be in touch tomorrow.'

Miss Brownlee stood up and picked up her shopping bag. 'Certainly.' She smiled at Sarah. 'Good afternoon.' She walked for the door.

McQuade closed it behind her. Sarah held up a hand, walked away and said:

'Okay, it's none of my business who she is. But . . .' she turned to him angrily, 'why didn't you tell me that Jakob's wife and son have also been murdered?'

McQuade stared at her grimly. 'How did you find out?'

'*Because,*' she said impatiently, 'your Inspector Dupreez has just contacted me! He phoned Matt, trying to trace you and me. Matt called me and I thought I'd better call Dupreez since

I didn't know when the hell I'd see you.'

'How did he know about Matt?'

'When I made my statement to the police, I gave Matt's number as a reference point.'

'Does he know your address? And where I am?'

'No,' Sarah said impatiently. 'I told another goddam lie for you! Said I was calling from a public box and I was meeting you later to start our wonderful scenic tour of South Africa.' Her beautiful eyes narrowed. 'Why didn't you tell me about these new murders, Jim?'

McQuade took a deep breath. 'Because I didn't want to alarm you.'

'*Alarm* me? You didn't want me thinking that you might have done it? Because that's the distinct impression I got from Inspector Dupreez!' Her eyes narrowed again. 'Why did you go back to Jakob's place after dumping me at the airport?'

McQuade's anger rose. 'For the reason I gave to the police in Khorixas. To inform the old woman of Jakob's death, and offer arrangements for his decent burial.'

'Why didn't you have such charitable thoughts before we left Swakopmund?'

'Are you suggesting I might have done it?'

She turned away. 'Of course not.'

'Why do you say Dupreez thinks so?'

She waved a hand. 'Oh, just his oily tone. How was your trip to Ai-Ais? Oh, you decided to fly back to Johannesburg instead? Probably just my guilty conscience, telling all those lies. Jim? I think I must tell the police about that threatening phone call and the Toyota chasing us.'

'I'm doing this my way,' McQuade said grimly.

'Doing *what*?' She appealed, 'If you can't tell the police you must tell me if I've got to tell lies! You owe it to me!'

'Just give me a few more days, Sarah.'

She sat down angrily in the chair Miss Brownlee had used. Then noticed the visiting card. She said dangerously, 'Will you at least tell me who Miss Brownlee is?'

'She's an investment adviser.'

Sarah said quietly: 'A hooker, I think.'

'Don't be ridiculous.'

She picked up the visiting card solemnly. '"A Taste of Sugar. Fiona".'

McQuade was furious with himself for forgetting the bloody card! Sarah carried on quietly, 'Why're you screwing expensive hookers, Jim? When you've got me, for free.' She paused. 'And telling me you're madly in love with me.'

He groaned, 'Oh God . . .'

'Oh, I understand that one can get carried along by passion and declare undying love a little prematurely – as I myself did, dumb-dumb that I am. But I didn't read you as such a shallow philanderer as to jump straight into bed with a hooker afterwards!'

'Sarah, I was not going to go to bed with her.'

'Oh, you were persuading her to invest in the fishing business?'

He said grimly, 'I'll explain everything in a few days.'

She stood up. 'I'm sorry, Jim. I'm getting deeper and deeper involved in subterfuges about an appalling case of triple murder, telling lies to the police, which is a criminal offence, and risking my life – that Toyota could have killed us. And now this.' She waved her hand contemptuously at the card. 'And you refuse to explain. Well, enough is enough. It is my common-sense duty to tell Inspector Dupreez what I know.' She looked at him squarely. 'Goodbye, Jim. It's been interesting knowing you.' She turned for the door.

McQuade closed his eyes. He sighed.

'Sarah – please sit down. And I'll explain.'

She listened with rapt attention.

He did not tell her everything. He told her about meeting Skellum, the banknotes, the wallet, but he refused to tell her the initials on it, nor did he tell her about the tag. He described how Jakob had showed him the place where the submarine lay; he told her he knew the name the man had used in Swakopmund, but he did not tell her that name nor how he had tracked it down through dental records. He told her about his trip to Germany to examine submarines but not about his visit to the submarine archives, nor about his visit to Frau Kohler nor to Simon Wiesenthal. He described the horrific evidence of mass murder inside the submarine. He told her about the scandal in the Population Registration office, about Lisa van Rensburg and what he was going to get Miss Brownlee to do.

Sarah was absolutely amazed. 'Good Lord. What a story.' She waved a hand. 'But who is this man? What name are you looking for in the population computer?'

'I'm not going to tell you, Sarah, because what you don't know you can't be forced to tell anybody else – like those bastards who were chasing us in that Toyota. The only reason I've told you this much is to explain why you must not tell Dupreez anything. Because once he knows, that submarine will slip through my fingers, and the man I'm looking for.'

'After you've got your treasure, are you really going to hand him over to the Israelis?'

'Yes,' McQuade said.

'Not to the South African police?'

'No. Because I believe this man is a wanted Nazi warcriminal. I don't want any political deals or hassles over extradition, and the Israelis have the evidence of his war crimes, not the South African government.'

'But why do you think he's a war-criminal, apart from the fact that he murdered the submarine's crew.'

'I won't tell you why yet. But I've done my homework.'

'But which war-criminal?'

'I won't tell you that either.'

'But why don't you get the Israelis to help you?' she asked earnestly. 'They're expert at that sort of thing, aren't they?'

'Because I'll probably lose the submarine in a mass of legal hassle. I don't want *anybody* knowing where it is until I've cleaned out that loot.'

'I see.' She frowned. 'But you're taking a chance using a hooker. She may tell the police.'

'I've given her a plausible story. And she wants her thousand.'

'Oh boy . . .' Sarah breathed. 'I don't like that. And if she can't get to this poor Lisa?'

McQuade sighed grimly. 'Then I use myself as bait to bring these bastards to me. They're after me like they went after Skellum. So, I let it be known I'm back in Walvis Bay. When they come for me, I'll have a bunch of guys waiting, who jump on *them*. We then force them to tell me where their boss is.'

She was staring at him. 'Oh God! Your trap fails and you're *dead*.'

'So you can understand why I don't want you around? I don't want you exposed to any risks.' He glanced at his watch. 'It's probably too late to get Miss Brownlee back, but I'll try.'

Sarah put her hand on his. 'Look, *think* about this.' She was agitated. 'I'm scared of you using a prostitute for black-mail. She may report you. Or she may blackmail *you*. Or she may bungle it, and Lisa calls the police . . .'

'Got any better ideas?'

'Yes, don't go at blackmail like a bull at a gate! You know nothing about this Lisa van Rensburg. Nothing.' She took a deep tense breath. 'So let *me* try to find out something about her. Let me go along to this aerobics class and try to meet her. Talk to her. Invite her for a drink . . . Then, when I have a better idea of your chance of success, you can send your Miss Brownlee into work.'

'But I don't want you involved.'

'I'm *already* involved! Up to my neck! I've told lies to the police. Murders have been committed, and you may be the next victim!' She gave a worried sigh. 'Anyway, I won't

356

involve myself in blackmail. I won't seduce her. I just don't want to see you rush into a terrible mistake.'

And McQuade knew absolutely loud and clear that he was in love with her.

Five minutes later she left the hotel to buy a leotard, thinking hard. She passed the Assembly Hotel, and hurried inside, to the public telephones.

She dialled a number in Johannesburg. It was answered immediately. She spoke quietly and rapidly in German.

The callee listened without interruption; then said:

'And he won't tell you that name?'

'No. And I daren't try harder.'

'And he won't tell you the name of this lesbian, either?'

She said grimly, 'No.'

The man cursed under his breath. 'Well, find out. By hook or by crook. And then do the job yourself. Don't let him use the call-girl, that's dangerous.'

'I knew you'd say that. Our contract did not mention bi-sexuality.'

'Are you capable?'

'Thanks for asking.'

'Well,' the man said, 'get on with it. And don't let him out of your sight again.'

43

At twenty-past five she parked her rented car a block away from Duncan's. She said to the healthy girl behind the desk, 'I'd like to join tonight's aerobic class?'

'An absolute pleasure. It's ten rand.'

The changing room had a long, continuous dressing-table, punctuated with ornate lights. The place was sprinkled with women disrobing, redolent with perfume and the chatter of women-talk in two languages. Sarah found her locker, unzipped her bag, and took out her new leotard.

The aerobics room was mirror-lined, reflecting female forms off into infinity, in all shapes and sizes, waiting to be instructed on what to do with their wide variety of bodies. Sarah glanced around the mass of female flesh. She identified Lisa van Rensburg immediately, by her long blonde hair.

She was wearing a bright purple leotard. Her legs were not bad, although her waist was a bit thick. Her hair was swept back and held in place by a headband. She was standing by herself, examining her fingernails.

Sarah took up the space next to her. 'Hi,' she smiled.

Lisa van Rensburg looked up. 'Hullo.'

Sarah said brightly, 'This is my first time here. Is it a tough workout?'

Lisa said, 'Not really. Depends on how fit you are, I suppose.' She had an Afrikaans accent.

'Well, I'm not. That's why I'm here, I guess.'

'Are you an American?' Lisa asked.

'Yep. I'm Sarah, by the way.'

'I'm Lisa. Are you new in town?'

'I'm new in the *country*. I'm in women's fashions. I'm

doing a market survey to see if it's worth my company's while to open here.'

'That's interesting. How do you like South Africa?'

'Pretty,' Sarah said. 'But lonely. I've hardly made any friends yet.' She paused. 'That's another reason I've come along here today.'

Just then the instructress came in. She clapped her hands cheerfully. '*Welkom terug, dames!* Welcome back, ladies!' She was a long-legged brunette in a passion-pink leotard, her hair in two stout pigtails. She went to a tape-recorder and hit a button.

'Wow,' Sarah whispered to Lisa, 'isn't she sexy?'

It was a tough workout. 'She sure gives you your money's worth,' Sarah said as they walked back to the changing room, hot and sweaty.

'Do you want to take a sauna?' Lisa said.

Sarah did not. She was quite sweaty enough. 'If you like. Or the jacuzzi?'

'Then we take a shower first.'

They entered the changing room. There were women stripping off sweaty leotards. Sarah stripped off, draped her towel around her waist, picked up her toilet bag. Lisa was waiting at the showers. 'There's three temperatures: warm, hot and freezing needlepoint.'

Sarah washed her hair, soaped herself, then turned the tap to hot. She luxuriated in it, then slammed the tap to blue. The freezing needlepoint stung her from all sides.

Lisa was waiting when she emerged from her booth.

The jacuzzi room was festooned in hanging plants, and white beach-beds were dotted around an artificial lawn. The pool, big enough for a dozen people, was made of small mosaic tiles. Steam rose off the clear, swirling water. Sarah dropped her towel and stepped in. She eased down onto the curved seat, up to her shoulders in hot water. Lisa sat a yard away from her.

'That's good, after the exercise and the needlepoint.'

Lisa agreed. Then she asked shyly, 'Are you married?'

Here we go, Sarah thought. 'No. Thank God. Are you?'

'No.'

There was a silence, before Lisa said shyly:

'You shouldn't be lonely in South Africa. You'll have men chasing you everywhere.'

Sarah rolled her eyes. 'Men? Bastards.'

Lisa looked at her. She was about to say something, then stopped herself.

'Have you got a boyfriend?' Sarah asked.

Lisa glanced at her. 'No.'

Sarah waited. The girl was looking away, as if racked with doubt. Oh, you poor kid, Sarah thought – a real closet gay. She tried to make it easier for her, without blowing it. 'Boy, am I going to be stiff, tomorrow. Who does the massage here?' She added, 'I don't like men massaging me.'

'They have both.' Lisa hesitated. Then she said. 'I'll give you a massage, if you like.'

At last, Sarah thought. She smiled at the girl.

'Thanks. That's a good idea.'

Lisa was blushing. She looked away.

Sarah sighed and pushed the jets-button. Jets of water began to pummel their backs and hips. 'Oh boy.' She closed her eyes, slithered down and half lay on the submerged seat so the jets beat her legs, and she let her foot touch Lisa's thigh. She let it linger a moment, then moved it away. And Lisa's hand came down on her ankle and gripped it against her.

Sarah opened her eyes. Blushing furiously, Lisa let go. Sarah left her foot against the girl's thigh. She smiled, 'You can do that again.'

Lisa looked at her, with utter, confused adoration. Her hand went to Sarah's knee ardently.

At that moment two women entered the room. Lisa let go

360

and Sarah sat up. She smiled at the girl. 'Let's go for a drink somewhere. Then the massage?'

She felt a bastard.

It was almost ten o'clock when Sarah parked her rented car outside the Burgerspark Hotel.

She felt saddened. She could rationalize away a sense of shame, but not her sadness about that poor, weeping girl she had just left.

She forced the feeling aside and concentrated on the story she was going to tell McQuade. No way was she going to tell him the whole truth. She sat in the dark for a few minutes. Then entered the hotel.

McQuade bounded up off the bed, relief all over his face. 'Hi,' she said brightly.

He took her in his arms. 'Oh, thank God! I was so worried.'

She squeezed him, then walked across the room with a saunter she did not feel. 'Well, I think you're going to be very pleased with me.' She turned: 'You don't need Miss Brownlee.'

He stared at her. 'You mean *you* did it? . . .'

She laughed. 'Thought that might shock you. No, I mean that she confessed it.'

'Confessed it?'

Sarah sat down on the bed. 'She invited me home, and made a heavy pass at me. I reacted indignantly. She was terribly embarrassed. She broke down and confessed she was lesbian.' She raised her eyebrows at him. 'I decided to strike whilst the iron was hot and blackmailed her. And she's agreed to give me a print-out. To save her skin.'

McQuade slumped down on the bed beside her.

'You're a genius! Tell me everything.'

She sighed convincingly. 'We had a drink. She is a very shy girl, and she was very nervous. She wanted to make a pass at me, but couldn't screw up the courage. Finally she did, and touched my breast. Very ardently. I pretended to be embar-

361

rassed and said, ''What's this, are you gay?'' She was morti-
fied.' Sarah shook her head. 'Poor girl. She broke down,
blushing and stammering, and pleaded with me to understand. Apparently there had been a big scandal in her department once and some gay men had been fired, so she begged
me not to tell anybody or she could get fired too. She's just
bought this apartment on a mortgage and desperately needs
the job. What other job could she get if she was fired on
moral grounds? Et cetera, et cetera.' She sighed. 'I really felt
terribly sorry for her.'

McQuade squeezed her knee. 'Go on.'

'I had two choices. Either report back to you, or put the
hard word on her then and there.' She paused. 'So I put the
screws on. I said I wouldn't tell anybody, provided she did
something for me. Namely, give me a print-out of all the
people in her computer with a certain name. Plus their
photographs that accompanied their original forms. I hope
you consider I did the right thing?'

'What happened then?'

'She went white. Absolutely aghast. I thought she was going
to scream. She started trembling.' Sarah closed her eyes. 'She
asked me why I wanted that information, so I made it easy
for her. Said I was trying to trace my natural father, and that I
was an adopted child and desperately needed this help. She
asked why I didn't apply through the courts to her department. I said because of the delicacy of the situation.' She
smiled mirthlessly. 'Then there was a new development.'

'What?' he demanded.

'She blurted out that I could get this information perfectly
legally by buying the Voters Roll.' She raised her eyebrows.
'You didn't think about that, did you? We could have
avoided this whole nasty business.'

'The *Voters* Roll . . .?'

'She explained that every single person eligible to vote in
South Africa – *white*, of course – is registered on the Voters
Roll whether or not they vote. Full name, citizenship num-

362

ber, address. In alphabetical order. Constituency by constituency. This Roll is updated once a month. When a voter dies, his name disappears off the Roll – the moment a juvenile turns eighteen, his name automatically appears. So if a man's name is on the Roll, you know he's alive. And his address.'

McQuade's mind was fumbling. 'But not his age?'

'Yes, that too,' she replied, 'the age is incorporated into the voter's citizenship number. For example, somebody born in 1941, on December the eleventh has a number which begins 41, for the year, 12 for the month, 11 for the day. But there's a snag. You'd have to buy the whole Voters Roll for the whole of South Africa, at so much per page – you can't merely buy the pages of Smiths or Joneses – and that costs over five thousand rand.' She raised her eyebrows. 'Expensive, but no risk of blackmail.'

McQuade felt feverish. 'But what about all the other information that's in the Population Register – date of marriage, place of birth, children, et cetera? That's not on the Voters Roll, surely?'

'No. Marriage, wife's name, yes, but no *date* of marriage. Or place of birth, no driver's licence, et cetera. I thought of all this too. So I made a snap decision to stick to the brief. I said no, the Voters Roll was not good enough, I wanted the extract from the Population Register.'

McQuade took a big breath. Oh, the Voters Roll would be the easy way out. No risk. But much less detail, no photographs, and fearfully expensive.

'You did the right thing. Then what happened?'

'Well, the poor kid capitulated . . .' Sarah lowered her eyes. 'She grabbed my hands, went down on her knees and cried. Yes she would do it, but please, please, *please*, don't tell anybody her secret. And, I felt an utter shit.'

McQuade squeezed her knee, and stood up. 'And so do I. But it had to be done.' He looked down at her sincerely. 'I'm very grateful.'

'So, she's waiting now, for me to telephone her the name,' she said flatly. 'Then she'll extract the print-out tomorrow, when everybody's gone home. It's Saturday tomorrow, only a skeleton crew works.'

'And how does she get the print-out to me?'

'She brings it to Duncan's tomorrow afternoon. She gives it to me.'

McQuade turned away and paced.

'You did very well. But *I'll* tell her the name. But not by telephone. And I'll pick it up from her at Duncan's.'

Sarah stared at him. 'I don't believe this.' McQuade sighed but she went on: 'After all I've done – putting myself on the line as a blackmailer and having myself groped by lesbians – you still don't trust me!'

'It's not a question of trust, Sarah – it's a question of security.'

'But she won't trust *you*,' she cried. 'It's *me* she's dealing with – she's almost *grateful* to me for keeping her secret! If you barge into the picture you'll terrify the poor kid! She may even call the police and make a clean breast!' She waved her hand angrily. 'Give me the name in a sealed envelope if you like – but don't make the girl suffer further!'

McQuade rubbed his chin.

'Okay, we'll do this: telephone her now and tell her to meet you in the dining-room of this hotel on her way to work. Whereupon you give her the sealed envelope. Tomorrow afternoon she delivers the print-out in a sealed envelope to you in the dining-room.'

Sarah gave him a weary smile. 'And you'll be sitting at the next table. To see I hand over the envelope unopened. . .' She raised a palm. 'Okay. But all I'd have to do if I really wanted to know the blessed name is telephone the poor kid and ask her.'

'But I don't think you'll do that. The only reason I don't want you to know—'

'Is because what I don't know I can't be forced to tell.' She sighed. 'Okay. . .'

She picked up the telephone. He bent and kissed her.

44

Seven-fifty the next morning found McQuade in the dining-room, drinking tea and reading the newspaper, while Sarah sat two tables away. At eight o'clock Lisa van Rensburg walked in, and McQuade's heart went out to the girl.

She was pale, her eyes swollen. She forced a frightened smile, made her way to Sarah, and half-sat in the chair opposite. She leant across the table urgently.

McQuade watched, above his newspaper. Sarah smiled, but he was surprised that there was no smile in her eyes. She gave the sealed envelope to Lisa, who took it fearfully and fumbled it into her gym-bag. She shook her head, refusing coffee. Sarah put her hand on Lisa's and said something. The girl replied imploringly. Then she got up and hurried out.

McQuade glanced compassionately at Sarah. She was staring sightlessly at her newspaper. He got up, and left.

She followed him a minute later. As they entered the bedroom he took her in his arms. 'Thank you.'

'We're meeting her at three o'clock. In the cocktail bar.'

'It looked as if you were a bit hard on her.'

'Theatrics. Can we now please stop talking about it?'

McQuade nodded. 'What would you like to do until we meet her this afternoon?'

'I feel like getting drunk.'

He smiled. 'The pubs aren't open yet.'

Her arms hung limp. 'I want,' she said, 'to make love.'

He put his arms around her. She did not respond.

'I want,' she said, 'you to *use* me.'

Later, while Sarah was showering, McQuade telephoned

Inspector Dupreez. He was not looking forward to this.

'Well, it's definitely murder, hey,' Dupreez said. 'The poor bastard was hanged to make it look like suicide. He was probably unconscious when he was put on the stool, because we found a bruise to the back of his head. At the post-mortem the doctor also found bruises to his back and ribs. And he'd been kicked in the balls, man. There's skin under his fingernails, so he scratched his assailant – his mother had no scratches. She was killed with a number of blows to the head.'

McQuade felt a surge of guilt for not telling Dupreez about the Toyota chasing him. 'And when does the doctor say was the time of death?'

'Between eleven p.m. Monday night and three a.m. Tuesday morning.' Dupreez drew on a cigarette. 'You left your girlfriend at Windhoek airport at five p.m. that Monday afternoon.' Pause. 'Where did you spend that night?'

McQuade felt his stomach contract. There was no mistaking that he was not above suspicion. 'I reached Outjo after midnight. I slept in the Landrover for an hour or two at the roadside and got to Jakob's kraal at sunrise.'

'That was some drive, man. What was the hurry?'

'As I explained to the Khorixas police, I felt it my duty as Jakob's employer to inform his wife of the old man's death and make funeral arrangements. Then I wanted to get to Johannesburg as fast as possible to be with my girl.' He added: 'She had urgent business and we don't have much time to be together.'

'Love will find a way, hey?' the inspector said. 'But I thought your girlfriend is on a holiday, so what's her urgent business? What happened to the trip to Ai-Ais?'

Oh God! 'Well, Jakob's death put a damper on that. We started off for Ai-Ais but then she decided to go straight to Jo'burg.'

'You started off for Ai-Ais? You see, if you were so concerned about informing Jakob's wife, why didn't you go straight to his kraal from Swakopmund, instead of starting for Ai-Ais and then changing your mind?'

Oh *Jesus*. 'We drove straight from Swakopmund to Windhoek, changed our minds on the way, and put her on a plane. I had also decided I really should go to Jakob's kraal.'

There was a silence. 'And you had no trouble with another vehicle?'

'No. I've already told Sergeant Bekker.'

Another silence. 'Why didn't you sleep at the hotel in Outjo, instead of beside the road?'

McQuade felt feverish. 'Because of the expense. And I only wanted a short sleep, to get to Jakob's kraal early and then on to my girl.'

He could almost hear the inspector nod understandingly. 'Yes, with these huge distances, I've often slept by the roadside myself. And where are you calling from now?'

'A public telephone in Pretoria.'

Dupreez said sympathetically, 'Still in Pretoria, man? When're you taking the girlfriend on her trip?'

'We're on our way now.'

'Oh, very nice. And where are you off to?'

'Spending the weekend in the country somewhere. Then Sun City, probably.'

'Very nice. Just don't lose all your money gambling, hey? Okay, jus' call me every third day, in case there's anything further you can help us with.'

McQuade hung up grimly. Dupreez knew he was lying. That bastard was onto him, too.

He went into the cocktail bar, alone. He was feverish to get this business over with. A few minutes later Sarah entered. She sat alone on a couch in the corner.

Shortly after three o'clock Lisa van Rensburg entered. She hurried over to Sarah's corner, and slumped down onto the couch beside her. Sarah smiled. 'Got it?'

Lisa whispered breathlessly, 'Yes, but I couldn't get the

photographs. There're too many files and I haven't got access to them easily.'

'Too bad. Just act naturally and hand it over as if it was a cardigan I left behind.'

Lisa implored: 'Do you swear this isn't a trap?'

Sarah felt a heel. 'Swear it. Have a drink.'

'No.' Lisa burrowed into her gym bag, and pulled out a shopping bag furtively. Her eyes darted around the bar. 'I must go now. Goodbye.'

She got up and hurried out.

Sarah finished her glass of wine. She walked out of the bar, carrying the shopping bag. McQuade swallowed his drink and followed her.

They entered the elevator. 'Congratulations!' But Sarah gave a bitter sigh.

'I know,' McQuade muttered. 'But no harm's going to come to her.'

'She couldn't get the photographs, too risky.'

'Damn!' He looked in the bag and saw a bulky sealed envelope.

They walked back to his room. He locked the door behind them, then went to the ice-bucket. 'Well, despite that unpleasantness, we have plenty to celebrate.' He added: 'And murder is a very unpleasant business.'

She waved a finger at the bag. 'Well?'

'Later.'

'Suppose there's only newspaper in it?'

He pulled the envelope out of the bag, ripped it open, and drew out a wad of computer paper. He saw the name Strauss and a mass of data. He shoved it back. 'It's there.'

She smiled. 'You mean you're only going to study it when you're alone? In case I peep over your shoulder.'

'Please, Sarah. We've been over this.'

'Okay.' She looked at him soberly. 'What happens now?'

'How about a late lunch?'

'And after that? Where do I go? I've served my purpose.

369

I've told my lies and I've blackmailed your lesbian. Now you want me to go away.'

'Sarah – this business is going to get dangerous. These bastards are after me.'

She sat up. 'Please let me come with you.'

'You've got your tour to do. And work.'

'It *is* work,' she cried. 'Good God, I'm a journalist! I've stumbled across an explosive story of triple murder, and wanted Nazi war-criminals! Any journalist would give his eye-teeth for the story; and I can help you catch these bastards! Didn't I do the job on Lisa?! Haven't I corroborated your lies to the police?' She glared, then pointed at the plastic bag. 'I can help you find your man.' McQuade started to speak, but she played her last card: 'Look – I don't even *want* to know the name on that print-out. Got that? Because I don't want that kind of bullshit to spoil our relationship. So – go and read your print-out in privacy. *But*,' she implored, 'when you know where you're going, take me with you.'

She was making it easy for him. 'I promise I will if I think it's safe,' he replied. 'I need a couple of days alone, then I'll phone you.'

She took a weary breath.

'Okay. I get the message.' She stood up. 'I don't want to feel a pest. So I'll take a powder and let you get on with it.'

He was relieved. 'Please understand.'

'I understand perfectly.'

'But let's have lunch?'

'And then drive our separate ways, into the sunset?' She shook her head. 'No, thanks.'

He said: 'I love you.'

She looked at him.

'I love you too,' she said.

45

Sarah waved, and watched him disappear down the tree-lined street in his Landrover. She sighed, and started her car. She drove through the avenues to Lisa van Rensburg's apartment block.

She knocked on the girl's door. There was no response. She knocked again. Still no response.

She looked at her watch; then drove down-town, looking for a cinema. She watched a boring matinee. At six o'clock she returned to Lisa van Rensburg's apartment and knocked. A neighbour opened a door down the corridor and told her that Lisa had gone away on holiday. No, he didn't know where to, nor for how long.

Sarah returned thoughtfully to her car. An hour later she arrived at a house in Parktown North, one of Johannesburg's best suburbs. It had a ten-foot wall around it. A sign warned of a burglar-alarm system. She put keys in the locks and walked through the pretty garden. The French windows of the living-room burst open, and Matt Mathews came out. 'What the *hell* are you doing here?' he demanded.

Sarah swept past him, into the living-room. 'The bird,' she said, 'has flown the coop.'

Matt stared. '*Why the hell didn't you go with him?*'

'Because,' she said, 'he refused to take me.'

Matt slapped his head in exasperation. 'But were you successful getting the print-out from the lesbian?!'

'I was.'

'*But have you seen that print-out?*'

'Only for an instant, from across the room.'

Matt cried incredulously, 'So you *still* don't know the name he's after?!'

'Correct.'

'Jesus!' Matt fumed. At a loss. *'But you know the lesbian's name? And where she lives?'*

'Of course.'

'Then why didn't you go back to her to get the name?!' Matt exploded. *'And arrange a copy of the print-out!'*

'I did. But she's also flown the coop. And disappeared. "On holiday".'

Matt stared. *'Where the hell to?'*

'I haven't a clue.'

Matt shouted, *'Jesus,* woman! Couldn't you have found out?'

'I tried. Nobody knew. Obviously the girl's panicked and done a runner.'

Matt stared incredulously, then bellowed: *'But why the hell didn't you follow him when he left you this afternoon?'*

'Don't,' Sarah said, 'be an ass. He knows what my rented car looks like. And he certainly knows what *I* look like. He'd spot me immediately, wouldn't he?'

'But why didn't you call me, to get somebody else onto his tail?'

'There simply wasn't time. He refused to take me and left immediately.'

'But couldn't you stall him long enough to call me to send another tail over? Make him take you to lunch?'

'No. I tried.'

Matt punched his palm and cursed. *'Gone!'* he cried to the ceiling. 'Again!' He turned on her: 'But surely he said he wanted to see you again?'

'Indeed. In a few days. When he's made his plans.'

'Where?'

'He'll telephone the apartment.'

Matt said dangerously: 'Well you get your sweet ass over to that apartment and don't *move* till he telephones! And then get to him by hook or by *crook!*' He glared at her. 'He hasn't lost interest in you, has he?'

She struck a pose. 'How could anybody?'

'Be serious! Is he in love with you?'

'But of course. And he thinks I'm a brilliant fuck.'

'*Watch your manner, lady!*' He glared at her. 'And you? You haven't gone soft on him, have you?'

She waved a hand airily. 'Oh, I just think he's a brilliant fuck, too.'

He glared at her, seething. 'Watch your step . . . Now get back to the apartment and wait for his call!'

She clicked her elegant heels and gave a Hitler salute. '*Jawohl! Zu Befehl!*'

She goose-stepped out of the room.

McQuade drove fast through the rolling countryside, heading for a small town called Hartebeestpoort. He had telephoned Nathan, to ask if he could stay with him, but the servant had informed him that her employers were in Cape Town for a week. But his roadmap showed that Hartebeestpoort was fairly close to both Pretoria and Johannesburg. He kept an eye on the rear-view mirror, although he saw nothing to make him suspicious.

Twenty minutes later he had checked into a quiet motel on the dam shore, under the name of McGregor. There seemed to be no other guests. He locked himself in his bungalow, sat at the table and pulled out the wad of computer print-out from the envelope.

His instructions to Lisa had read, '*Please supply a full extract of male persons with the surname Strauss born between the years 1900 and 1915, plus the photographs which accompanied their original forms. The photographs will be returned to you.*'

When he saw the number of persons recorded in the print-out, he understood why Lisa could not have dug out that many files and removed each photograph. But surely she could do so when he had narrowed the list down.

He began to scan the topmost sheet.

PARTICULARS OF PERSON: S.A. Citizen; IDENTITY NUMBER: 100422 5102 006; SURNAME: Strauss; FIRST NAMES: Izak Johannes; DATE OF BIRTH: 22/4/1910; SEX: male; COUNTRY OF BIRTH: South Africa; MARRIAGE CERTIFICATE EXTRACT: 691926 husband Strauss Izak Johannes and wife Viljoen Maria; DATE OF MARRIAGE: 10/3/33; PLACE: Cape Town; married by community of property; MISCELLANEOUS IMMUNIZATIONS: none recorded; BLOOD GROUP: AB; DISEASES OR DISORDERS: none recorded; DRIVER'S LICENCE NUMBER: 740763 CODE 08 DATED 14/10/27: SUSPENSION/ CANCELLATION: none recorded; LICENCE TO POSSESS FIREARM: NUMBER: A27639; DATE: 17/9/34; TYPE RIFLE: calibre 9, 3 (X62); CODE: A080; MANUFACTURER'S NUMBER: 17696; REGISTERED RESIDENTIAL ADDRESS: as from 6/7/1985 Strauss IJ, 14 Marine Drive, Shelly Beach, Natal, South Coast 0094; BIRTH ENTRY NUMBER 100422 5102 006.

McQuade was sure he could reject this man.

The most obvious reason was the marriage: 1933, in Cape Town. Heinrich Muller came to southern Africa in 1945. If he re-married at all it would have been after that date, and it was highly unlikely that he would risk having official South African records falsified in order to create the unnecessary fiction of an earlier marriage. Secondly, Muller was unlikely to have falsified records to claim South Africa as his country of birth since many naturalized South African citizens were born abroad. Thirdly, the Christian names, Izak Johannes. Wiesenthal had told him that people who assume a false identity usually stick to their first name, to make the adaptation easier. The Strauss he was looking for was likely to have Heinrich or Hendrik or even Henry amongst his Christian names.

He marked the entry with a cross.

He was hungry. He had nothing to eat in the bungalow,

although he still had all the booze he had bought to entertain the Taste of Sugar girl.

He numbered each page. He paused many times, pacing about the room, before marking an entry with a cross or a question mark, but it was almost midnight before his pulse tripped in excitement, and he was able to make his first tick. It was four o'clock in the morning when he got to the last page. The print-out lay in a serpentine heap on the floor.

He collapsed on the bed and stared at the ceiling, exhausted. God knows how many crosses and question-marks he had, *but he had twenty-seven ticks!*

He forced himself to sit up. He began to tear each page off at the perforations and stack them. He pulled out the pages marked with ticks. He spread them on the other bed. Then he sifted out the pages with question marks. He spread them in a second line.

He took a double sheet of paper and drew columns. He headed them: *Names, I.D., Birthday, Place, Address, Marriage, Blood, Wife, Allergies, Immunizations, Driver's licence, Firearms, Remarks.*

God, he was tired. But he was getting there.

He started with the questionable entries. He began to re-read, and re-think, and to fill in the columns.

The sun was up when he dropped his pen.

He had just finished his short-list. Many of the twenty-seven ticked entries now had double-ticks. That was the good news.

The bad news was that many lived in opposite ends of southern Africa. Several lived in Namibia, as did a dozen marked with question marks. Most of these men had Heinrich, Hendrik or Henry in their names, and were born in Germany around the first decade of this century. In 1945 they would have been in their late-thirties or early forties, then about Muller's age.

McQuade sat there, too tired to think any more.

He got up and stripped off his clothes and climbed into bed, even too tired to think of Sarah.

PART NINE

46

He woke up at noon. Sunday in Africa. Deafening silence. Mercilessly blue sky. What did he have to do with it?

First and foremost he had to get hold of Lisa van Rensburg, give her a copy of his short-list and tell her to extract the photographs of these men. Those photographs could lead him straight to Heinrich Muller.

Second: he had to talk to Johan Lombard again. Get as much information on modern-day South African Nazis as he could. Find a way of asking him if he had any theories about Heinrich Muller, or whether he knew any old Nazis called Strauss. Compare information with his short-list.

Three: decide how the hell he was going to get to each Strauss on his short-list. He'd had a few ideas, but probably the best method was posing as a policeman. Everybody opens the door for a policeman. But how do you get hold of a police uniform?

Four: find out what help he could get when he found Heinrich Muller. He would need tough, reliable guys to help him make the snatch, since Muller was very likely to have some impressive muscle of his own.

And five: get those dents knocked out of the Landrover tomorrow. If Dupreez found the Toyota he could match up its damage with the Landrover's.

He swung out of bed.

Ten minutes later he emerged from the shower feeling very hungry. He pulled the curtain back an inch. There was nobody to be seen. Only the dam sparkling in the noonday sun.

He drove into the pretty village, thinking about Lisa van

379

Rensburg. He found a café and ordered steak, eggs and chips, wolfed them down, then sat considering his options.

Seeing Lisa was his top priority. First he had to establish whether she was home today. Telephone her and if Lisa answers, get round there.

He didn't like this but it had to be done. He got up and went to the public telephone outside the café. A woman answered. '*Ja?*'

McQuade said, 'Lisa?'

The woman said in Afrikaans, 'No, Lisa has gone away on holiday, I'm looking after her place.'

'Gone away? For how long?'

'Three months.'

'Three *months!* Where to?'

'Well, she had all this leave accumulated and she decided to go overseas.'

'*Overseas?*'

'Can I take a message for when she comes back?'

'No,' McQuade said, 'I'm just a friend of a friend. Thank you. Goodbye.'

He hung up. *No photographs for three months! Those photos would have made it very easy for him! Damn!*

And he felt very bad about Lisa. That kid hadn't suddenly decided to take a holiday – she had fled. He thought of her wasting her money, sobbing her heart out in some London bed-sitter, and he felt a shit.

Well, maybe he could make it up to her when he was a millionaire. He sighed, and dialled Johan Lombard's home.

'Why certainly, dear boy, pop around anytime.'

Johan's house was in Waterkloof, the select suburb of Pretoria, whose leafy avenues are lined with well-kept gardens and gracious houses. But Johan's garden was overgrown, the swimming pool awash with leaves, the hedges ragged. Johan was someone whose idea of creature comforts stopped at an adequate supply of whisky, a reliable, long-suffering wife and books. Groaning bookcases lined every wall, makeshift bookcases filled any gaps, an overflowing bookcase stood in the middle of the living-room awaiting a permanent place somewhere. McQuade could see nowhere it could possibly go, except the kitchen, provided the refrigerator and oven went out into the backyard. His study was a dangerous-looking place, towers of books threatening to crush the unwary. Johan sat in his armchair, wreathed in cigar smoke, clutching his glass of whisky.

'Oh yes, dear boy – this country has plenty of Nazis. They held a big demonstration here a few years ago for the release of Rudolf Hess, Hitler's deputy, who's been in Spandau prison in Berlin for the last forty years. And when a well-known local Nazi called Dr Heusler died some years ago there was a grand Nazi funeral, swastikas, the works. The Nazi Party's been banned since before the war, but it's a happy hunting ground for them here, isn't it, with all our racialism? There're more Nazis around Pretoria than Namibia, dear boy. They call themselves the South African Nationalist Socialist Party. Not a *registered* political party, of course, but they flourish all right. Their Führer – that's what he's called – lives between here and Johannesburg, surrounded by barbed-wire and armed guards. I happen to know that they've even got a holy-of-holies in there, a sort of shrine to Hitler, with great Nazi flags and whatnot, plus their own archives. The Nazi brass gathers there regularly to have an emotional orgasm over Hitler. They're in constant touch with right-wing movements world-wide – in Germany, of course, where the Nazi underground movement is very strong again – no German or Austrian politician dare antagonize the Nazis voters, you know – and with Le Pen in France and Sir Oswald Mosley's bunch in England, and President Stroessner in Paraguay.'

McQuade was making notes. 'This local Führer, how old is he?'

'Oh, about forty. It suits their purpose to have an Afrikaner as Führer – they want to keep a lowish profile and let the right-wing Afrikaners – the AWB – do their dirty work for them. The Nazis have cells in every city and village. Under local *gauleiters*, or district leaders.'

'But what would happen if somebody showed up at the Führer's gate when the top brass were arriving and took photographs?'

'You'd be politely told to piss off. And your film rather damaged. I've tried it. Impossible, even with a telephoto lens.'

McQuade sighed in frustration. 'Why doesn't the government send the police in to raid the place?'

'The *outcry*, dear boy! The AWB would be up in arms against "government suppression" of their allies. And remember that a big percentage of the police are secret AWB members. Or sympathisers.' He waved his hand. 'Anyway, the Government knows who most of the Nazis are. The NIS – National Intelligence Service – knows everything. They know that you're visiting me right now.'

McQuade frowned. 'How?'

Johan waved a finger at the telephone. 'You phoned me. All journalists' telephones are tapped, dear boy.'

McQuade thought of his Landrover parked outside with the dents that Toyota made. If Dupreez had found that Toyota and alerted the Pretoria police to look for his vehicle . . . He decided to hurry up and get to the point: 'Do you know of any Nazi war-criminals in South Africa?'

Johan said: 'There're alleged to be a lot. But I don't know who they are, or I'd tell the Israelis to come and get 'em.'

McQuade decided to chance it. 'By the way, do you happen to know an elderly man called Heinrich Strauss? Or maybe he's called Hendrik.'

'I know a few Strausses but no Heinrich. Why?'

McQuade waved his hand. 'No, just somebody a friend of mine told me to look up, a German old-timer.' He went on: 'But what's the Nazis' overall strategy? What do they want?'

Johan sat forward.

'They want,' he said, 'what Hitler wanted. But for starters they want the AWB – which is neo-Nazi – to take over South Africa. And then, they want the whole of Africa.'

McQuade looked at him, excitement rising. What Professor Jansen refused to speculate about. Hitler's blueprint. *That submarine was loaded* . . . 'But the world wouldn't let them invade across the Limpopo . . .'

'The world didn't make a very good job of stopping Hitler invade Poland, did it? Or France, or Holland, or Russia. The only reason Hitler failed was because he bit off more than he could chew at one time.' He shook his head. 'The modern Nazis here wouldn't make the same mistake – though they wouldn't let world opinion stop them either. But they believe they won't have to do much military strong-arm stuff to get the rest of Africa – they'll get it by default. The rest of Africa is a defenceless, corrupt, inefficient, poverty-stricken mess – any fool can see that. And now Nature is going to finish off the job: AIDS is rife in the Congo, West Africa, Kenya, Tanzania. The estimates are that in ten years sixty *million* blacks will perish from AIDS. What would Hitler have said? "Good, this is Nature's cleansing process." *Sauberung* – as they called their actions against the Jews. And who is going to occupy the vast territories left largely uninhabited by AIDS? The Nazis and their Aryans. What excuse will they give the world? To stop the Chinese occupying the territories. And to bring the dreaded AIDS epidemic under control they'll doubtless put the diseased into concentration camps to die. Doubtless with a little help from malnutrition to jolly them along.' He shrugged. 'That is the "official" South African Nazi Party policy.' He raised his eyebrows. 'And from there they take over the rest of Africa.'

McQuade was rapt. 'But how realistic is all that?'

'That, dear fellow,' Johan said, 'is a *most* realistic scenario. AIDS is going to wipe out most of the blacks. No ifs about it. Only whens. And who is going to fill the vacuum left behind?

Fill the "*Lebensraum*" which Hitler demanded?'

McQuade sat back. 'And,' he said, 'if they succeed, what is life going to be like under the South African Nazis?'

Johan said flatly: 'Like Nazi Germany, but adapted to Africa's needs. Most major industries nationalized – particularly the mines. All political opposition will be liquidated.'

'And the blacks?'

Johan shook his head. 'One needs labour, doesn't one? Who's going to build the roads and work the mines and factories until the Aryans have gone forth and multiplied sufficiently? So one needs slave labour for a decade or two. One would even have to pay them for a while to keep the economy going – it's no good nationalizing a garment factory if there're no blacks to buy pants, is it? And Zulus would make good soldiers to knock the living shit out of troublesome tribes to the north who had impudently survived the fortuitous AIDS epidemic.' He waved a hand. 'Oh, blacks will be needed for some time, dear fellow, to build the autobahns, the railways, the ports, work the farms and mines.' Johan smiled at him cherubically. 'You think this far-fetched?'

McQuade was not quite sure. Not after the books Roger Wentland had lent him on German colonial history. Not after reading about Hitler's blueprint for Africa. 'But how *serious* is this Nazi threat to South Africa today?'

Johan threw an aggressive dash of whisky into his glass as if he had just noticed a troublesome new outbreak of bush-fire at his elbow. He took a swallow and marshalled his thoughts for the uninitiated.

'The Nazi threat in South Africa today –' he said slowly, 'and by that I mean the AWB with the Nazis clustered behind them, and this Conservative Party whom the AWB supports – the Nazi threat in South Africa today is as *serious* . . . and almost as *significant* as the Nazi threat was in Germany in the 1920s, when Hitler was rising to power . . .' He glared at McQuade, letting that sink in: then he elaborated slowly: 'Unless we are *very* careful . . . and *quick* and *lucky* . . . South

Africa will soon be ruled by Nazis! We will have an AWB dictatorship within the next five to ten years. And that will mean a *Nazi* dictatorship . . .'

Johan stomped off into the living-room and started ransacking his bookshelves.

He came back with a fat box file. He snapped it open and pulled out a glossy booklet and tossed it to McQuade. It was entitled *The Principles of the AWB* and it had a big crest of the German eagle, wings out, its talons clutching the three-legged swastika. 'What's the difference between that and Hitler's emblem?' Johan demanded. 'Read their official booklet and tell me the difference between their principles and Hitler's. None! Hitler demanded *Lebensraum*, living space for his pure Aryan race – the AWB demands their *Volkstaat*, living space for the pure-white race. Hitler hated Jews: in those documents' – he pointed – 'you will find seven anti-Semitic statements. Parliamentary government is rejected *fifteen* times – as a demoralizing British-Jewish political system. Twelve times they demand an "authoritative system" instead, twelve times they speak of the *"Herrenvolk"*, the master race. Freedom of speech and freedom of the press is roundly rejected four times.' He glared at him. 'All exactly the same as Hitler. Read this whole file – newspaper clippings I've collected for ten years about the AWB! They show you their whole Hitlerian history. The *footsteps* of Hitler!'

McQuade stared at him. He started to ask a question but Johan went on. 'Oh, dear fellow, I'm not talking about the rank and file membership, the good old Afrikaner farmers and housewives of Blikkiesdorp – they're just simple God-fearing folk, hangovers from the voortrekker days who believe they're God's chosen people for this Promised Land, to whom God gave victory over the blacks at Blood River and at the 1948 elections – those people aren't *Nazis*, they just believe the blacks are the sons of Ham whom God made hewers of wood and drawers of water.' He leaned forward. 'But the AWB *leadership*? They're Nazis. The organizers in every city, town, village and rural area? The secret cells in every police station and government department? The secret cells in the Army, Navy, and Air Force?' He paused to let McQuade think about all that power: then his eyes narrowed: 'And never forget about the *Youth!*' His finger shot up again. 'Hitler said: "*Give me the youth!*" And he got them! Sweet little German girls with angelic faces and strapping Germans lads thinking what fun to be in uniform. And what did Hitler's party machine do to them?' He paused, then cried: '*Turned them into little monsters!* Who grew into *big* monsters! Who were prepared to commit the hideous crime of *genocide!*' He frowned incredulously: '*Genocide* . . .? What more appalling . . . mind-blowing crime is there? Exterminating a whole race of people . . .?' He waved his hand: 'Brutally *dragging* them out of their homes, young and old, little old ladies and babes-in-arms, and herding them like cattle onto railway trucks for the gas chambers?' He frowned in wonder: 'What diabolical madness was that? A national *orgy* of insanity . . .' He shook his head. '*The Germans are perfectly decent people* . . .' He tapped his breast: 'I am part German! The Queen of England herself is part German! And half the royal families of Europe! Half the people in America and Australia and New Zealand have German origins!' He frowned at McQuade in wonder: '*So why did these decent Germans tolerate the hideous international crime of genocide . . .?*'

McQuade waited. Johan leant further forward.

'Not *just* because of Hitler, dear fellow . . . Not *just* because one of the greatest natural leaders of all time had blossomed in their midst. Not *just* because of his staggering charisma, his shattering oratory . . .' He shook his chubby cheeks. 'No, my friend. It was because of the organization he built up! Hitler was proud of saying that Nazi Germany was built by seven men. (Exactly what Terreblanche of the AWB claims!) Who recruited his first group of bodyguards – the SS!' He dropped his voice: 'Who went around breaking up the political meetings of Hitler's opponents, who escorted Hitler around with bully-boy fanfare – who gave a military, *invincible* stamp to everything he did . . .' He ended: 'Which bullied the ordinary German into submission. And all *that*' – he jabbed a finger – 'is what the AWB is doing! They have bully-boys who dress up in uniform, carry arms, who're stormtroopers to beat up anybody who heckles Terreblanche's speeches, who break up opposition meetings – even the State President's meetings! They have openly declared that no member of the government will be allowed to hold political meetings in their territory! Terreblanche has made a study of Hitler's techniques. When Terreblanche speaks, he starts off hypnotically, slowly spinning a web of nationalistic emotion through his audience, playing on their heritage and then he works himself up into a crescendo, just like Hitler did. Oh boy, what an orator . . .!' He shook his head. 'Our Foreign Minister is holding a public meeting in Pietersburg next month and the AWB has openly vowed to break it up, and hold a rival meeting instead. You must come along with me and see the fun.'

'But he's only demanding a separate white state, a *Volkstaat*—'

Johan cried, 'And what did Hitler demand? *Lebensraum!* Living space for his *Herrenvolk!* And the AWB is demanding the same! And Hitler created a one-party state, and that's exactly what the AWB want! And Hitler nationalized industry to harness their power to his one-party state, and that's exactly what the AWB say they'll do! All our massive mining, our massive industry, all our commerce will be nationalized!' He waved a hand. 'What was Hitler's first economic demand? The return of the industrial areas which Germany forfeited after the First World War. What do the AWB demand? The return of the gold mines which the Boer republics lost when they were incorporated into the Union of South Africa after the Boer War!' He shook his head. 'Officially, the AWB is only demanding their old republican territory back, but that's just the tip of the iceberg, my dear fellow. History is repeating itself. For Nazi Europe read Nazi Africa.'

History repeating itself. 'And what do the big guns of commerce think about this? And the Jews?'

Johan said wearily: 'There is an overall tendency in this troubled land to think of the AWB as a "lunatic fringe". We are so used to a strong diet of politics, so *un*accustomed to change, that there is a certain complacency. A certain numbness. But I assure you the government itself takes the threat of the AWB very seriously indeed! But the Jews? My God, *they* take it seriously! They are very aware how close Hitler came to controlling South Africa. And they're wide awake to the dangers of the AWB. As a result there is a heavy-duty Zionist movement called the Jewish Defence Organization. It is highly militarised and highly secret. Devoted to defending themselves – and the country – against the AWB and the revival of Nazism.

McQuade was thinking: *Go to the Jewish Defence Organization and ask for some muscle?* No, that was as tricky for the submarine as getting Simon Wiesenthal involved. 'But *would* the AWB start another pogrom against the Jews? Or would they just drive them out and nationalize their property?'

Johan jabbed his finger. 'Not the ordinary God-fearing Afrikaner – but the Hitler-type Youth that the AWB will spawn! The AWB is not yet in its mature form, it's still on its way up, like Hitler in 1929. But it's already the second-most powerful organization in the country! *And*' – he jabbed his finger again – '*remember* that when the AWB comes to power their policies will meet with *such* resistance that they will have to be ruthless! Just as Hitler was.' He glared, letting that sink in: 'There will be civil war! The Jewish Defence Organization will leap into action, not to mention the left wing – not to mention the blacks, the ANC.' He paused dramatically: 'The AWB will have to be *ruthless* to enforce their policies, and *that* is where the jack-boot will come in –

crushing all this opposition! All the Gestapo methods. Including . . .' he leant forward, 'the concentration camps.' He fixed McQuade with his glare. 'And once one's *got* those concentration camps, dear boy, once one's *got* all that barbed wire, what does one do with all these criminals?'

'And how do we stop them?'

Johan smiled. 'Aha – there's the rub. The irony, the paradox. Because the only way to stop them, dear fellow, is by supporting this present *distasteful* government.'

That was hard for McQuade to swallow. 'Not the Left?'

'Forget the Left, dear fellow! They've been losers for forty years, ever since General Smuts got kicked out. Maybe they'll re-organize themselves one day, but for now they've got no credible policy. And this is an *Afrikaner* country, dear fellow, the Afrikaner finally won it back after a hundred years of foreign domination and he's here to stay as long as he has powder for his gun – so the only person to lead this country to reform must be an Afrikaner bringing the Afrikaner *volk* with him. And right now, in practical terms, the only party which can do that is the reigning Nationalist Party.' He shook his head. 'God knows, I hold no brief for this government, they've fucked us up psychologically and internationally with their unjust, *stupid* Apartheid, and they've bogged us down with their over-loaded Civil Service giving jobs for the boys to ensure Afrikaner perpetuity. But . . .' he held up a finger: 'the truth has finally dawned on them that Apartheid is a failure, international opinion and sanctions are finally biting and the border war with SWAPO and the jolly Cubans is costing an arm and a leg – and at least the government is reforming, dear fellow. Apartheid is patently crumbling. They have declared a brand-new attitude, that some form of power-sharing with the blacks must be instituted—'

McQuade interrupted, 'Then why the hell don't they have the courage of their so-called convictions and *legally* abolish Apartheid – strike it off the Statute Book?'

Johan sighed patiently. 'Because of the AWB, dear fellow.

And their surrogates, the Conservative Party, who are now the Official Opposition in parliament. The outcry there would be, the AWB and Conservative Party would literally be up in arms, and the government's own rank and file membership would baulk. We Afrikaners have to be led into the twentieth century gently.' He jabbed his finger. 'And that's the terrible danger of the AWB. Don't you see? Even if the AWB don't win the next election, they will nonetheless wax in strength. Because while the government gradually pushes its reforms through parliament and drags the country into the twentieth century, the AWB will rant and rave and whip up so much conservative Afrikaner emotion that they may well win the following election. And that, my friend, is where the real Greek tragedy of the AWB will come to its terrible fruition. Because . . .' he shook his head, 'this Afrikaner government, which has ruled us for forty years, will *never* surrender power . . . And that' – he jabbed his finger – 'is when the Civil War of South Africa begins. *And the AWB will have legal right on their side because they won the election!*'

McQuade was astonished. He had never thought of this. He echoed: 'The government would not surrender power if the Conservative Party and the AWB won the next election?'

'Absolutely no doubt about it! The Broederbond was formed after the First World War with the express purpose of bringing the Nationalist Party to power and never thereafter surrendering it!' He shook his chubby cheeks. 'Never! So if the AWB won the election, the President would declare a state of emergency, suspend parliament and rule by decree . . . And then,' he raised his eyebrows, 'the shit would really hit the fan. Then the AWB would really go on the warpath. Civil war. Afrikaner against Afrikaner. And all the stops would be pulled out by both sides.' Johan glared at him. '*That* is the real tragedy of the AWB in our midst. Win or lose, they could destroy the country.'

McQuade stared at him, fascinated. 'Where would the police and Army stand in that civil war?'

'Aha!' Johan said. 'The million dollar question. About one third of our police are AWB sympathisers. But if the AWB had *won* the election the police would be legally obliged to enforce the law and give the AWB the reins of government, whether they were pro or anti. So most of the police would fight for the AWB. The Army? Most of the officer corps would stick with the President, legal or illegal. But the rank and file are mostly unsophisticated Afrikaner boys; at least half would defy their officers and go to the AWB.' He sighed. 'It would be an awful mess, dear fellow.'

'And who is going to win?'

Johan smiled. 'The Afrikaner is a tough customer. He has a very long tradition of fighting for his survival – against the British, and against the blacks. War after war.' He waved a hand. 'But, in our forthcoming *civil* war, it'll be Afrikaner fighting *Afrikaner* – to the death. And although the President's men will have superior fire-power, let me remind you, dear fellow, that the guerrilla is a very difficult man to defeat. Fidel Castro proved that. Mao Tse-tung proved that, and he was fighting not only Chang Kai-shek but the might of the USA. Even the Afghan rebels have given the Russians such a hard time that they've gone home. In Angola, Savimbi's rebels have kept the Cubans tied up in battles for years. The IRA have kept Great Britain on the hop for decades, dear fellow . . .' He shook his face: 'And don't imagine that the AWB haven't got military strategists – don't imagine that they aren't *prepared*.' He shrugged. 'The punters would put money on the President's men, I'm sure. Me, I'd put a dollar each way, on both.'

McQuade gave a sigh. 'And how will the Nazis fit into this? After the dust has settled?'

Johan snorted. 'The dust will take a long time settling, dear fellow. But, if the President's men win, we will have a long period of a Franco-type dictatorship, as they had in Spain. While the President dismantles the fortress of Apartheid brick by brick so as not to cause too many draughts and *gradually* brings the blacks into some kind of power-sharing structure. But if the AWB wins . . .? Oh, boy . . .' He looked at McQuade. 'Then it won't be just their *Volkstaat* they'll end up with. It'll be the start of the Fourth Reich.'

47

It was dark when McQuade got back to the motel at Hartebeestpoort. Exhausted from working all the previous night, he went straight to bed, but it took him a long time to go to sleep, his mind feverishly excited, turning over the importance of what he was on to.

Early next morning he checked out of the motel. He drove to a local garage and arranged for the dents to be panel-beaten out of the Landrover, the vehicle entirely resprayed. He asked where he could rent a motorcycle. He tied his handgrip onto the pillion, kicked the machine to life and got onto the by-road to Johannesburg.

He needed a hotel room with a telephone. He found the Holiday Inn in Bree Street. He checked in, locked his door, and got to work. He spread the summary and short-list on the table and dialled Directory Inquiries. 'I want the number of a subscriber in Cape Town, please.' He put his finger on the first name on his short-list.

He scribbled the number in the Remarks column of his list.

He paused, thinking through his lines again. Then he dialled.

A woman said: 'Doctor Strauss's residence.'

Doctor? 'May I speak to Doctor Strauss, please.'

'I'm afraid he's not home yet. Who's calling?'

'Allan Benson,' McQuade said. 'Thank you, madam—'

'Are you one of his students?'

'No. Thank you, I'll call back, goodbye.'

He hung up. He wrote in the Remarks column: *Doctor? Home*.

What kind of doctor has students? At age seventy-nine?

Well, it was rather unlikely that Heinrich Muller had taken a doctorate in anything.

He looked at the next Strauss on his short-list. He flicked through the Johannesburg telephone directory. Hans George Hendrik Strauss, 34, 8th Avenue, Parktown North. He dialled.

An African voice said: 'Hullo.'

'May I speak to Mr Strauss, please?'

'Yes, wait please, sir.'

McQuade returned the receiver to its cradle. He wrote in the Remarks column: *Home*.

He put his finger on the next name on his short–list. *Martin Hendrik Strauss*. He ran his finger down the directory. He noted the number down. He dialled.

A voice rasped: 'Strauss.'

McQuade said: 'Good morning, may I speak to Mr Strauss senior, please.'

'Speaking. There is no Mr Strauss junior.'

McQuade forced a grin into his voice. 'Hullo, Malcolm! This is Clive! Long time no see!'

There was a pause. 'Did you say Malcolm?'

'Yes?'

'I'm sorry, wrong number. My name is not Malcolm.'

'I'm terribly sorry – goodbye.'

He hung up. He wrote in the Remarks column: *Home*.

Two hours later he had telephoned all the people on his short-list, all over southern Africa.

He sighed tensely. Well, that was the first step. He now knew all the gentlemen on his short-list were at home. And he had provisionally shortened that list: Dr Strauss with his students in Cape Town could be written off provisionally. So could two others: one was frightfully English, the other was at the synagogue. He felt he was getting somewhere.

He looked at his watch. Then put his finger at the topmost name on the Question-mark list. He dialled Directory Inquiries again.

At one-thirty McQuade made his last entry in the Remarks column. He got up and collapsed on the bed.

All right. He now had an idea how much work he had to do. How many men he had to see long enough to have a good look at their faces. And how was he going to achieve that? He recapped his options.

Option one: Surveillance. Lie in wait outside their houses and photograph them with a telephoto lens.

No. He might have to resort to that eventually, but not now. Firstly, it would take a long time. Secondly, the surveillance could make him unconspicuous. Thirdly, he might photograph the wrong man.

Option two: find out the man's movements, the clubs he belongs to, his employment, et cetera, then think up a scheme to get a good look at him.

Again, no. Again, it would take too long. He would have to do that after he had identified his man.

Option three: Trespass and house-breaking. Climb his garden wall, shin up his drainpipe, and get a good look at him.

Obviously not. How many times could he get away with it before he was slapped in jail? Not to mention all the dogs that might bite him, the guns that might be fired. And Heinrich Muller was going to be highly security-conscious after the fate that befell his pal Adolf Eichmann.

That only left Option Four: Gain entry by a trick. In circumstances that required the man to deal with him face to face. What trick was that?

Several possibilities.

Pretend to be the man who reads the electricity meter. Or the municipal inspector come to check on his drains.

Not bad. And it wouldn't require any uniform. But it would require an identification document – especially from a security-conscious Herr Muller. And what did that look like, and how would he get one forged? But the biggest snag was that he might not set eyes on Herr Strauss – it might be Mrs Strauss or the servant who shows him the meter or the drains.

So what other tricks were there? He tried to think of an alternative, but could not: there was only one type of person he could impersonate: a policeman. Everybody opens the door for a policeman.

But how do you get hold of a policeman's uniform?

No good pretending to be a plain-clothed policeman. He would have to produce identification. And how could he get one forged? Trouble. Risk. No, he had to get hold of a uniform.

He went to the telephone and rang room-service for coffee. He opened the yellow pages directory.

There were plenty of advertisements by tailors. Men's, women's, children's, bespoke and *haute couture*, down to domestic servants' uniforms, A1 Tailors up to Zenith Tailors. He made notes of those that sounded promising. Then he turned to Costumiers.

In Johannesburg there are several costumiers, people who specialize in renting costumes to film-makers, advertising agencies, dramatic societies and for fancy dress balls. He made a note of all of them. Then he looked for Leather.

There were many leather workers, from dealers in raw hides to Olde Fashioned Shoemakers for the Hard-to-Fit and Hard-to-Please. He made his notes.

He turned to the letter B for Buttons, and ten minutes later he had finished. He thought it through, picked up the telephone and dialled.

'Backstage,' a voice sang.

'Good afternoon,' McQuade said. 'I'm a member of an amateur dramatic society. We're a new group – and we need to hire some costumes.'

'Certainly, sir. If you tell me the name of the play it would be helpful, as we've assisted in many.'

McQuade was ready for it. 'You won't have heard of this

396

one, it's just been written by a local chap. But it's a court-room drama and we need a judge's robes and two South African police uniforms.'

'No problem with the judge's robes. But I'm afraid we are not allowed to rent out police uniforms. Under the Police Act it is an offence to possess a police uniform, in case it is used to impersonate a policeman.'

McQuade closed his eyes. 'I see . . .'

'Of course,' the man went on, 'you can go to the officer in charge of your local police station and tell him your problem and he can issue you with a permit to borrow a uniform. They're usually very helpful. Now, if you want to hire an English Bobby's uniform, helmet, the lot – no problem.'

'I see. But couldn't you perhaps make me a police uniform?'

'We've got tailors who will make you anything, but not a police uniform. Phone all the costumiers in the country, they'll tell you the same. Now, when do you want these judge's robes, sir?'

'Thank you but we'll have to see the police first,' McQuade said quickly. 'I'll call you back.'

He hung up, telephoned the other costumiers, but got the same information.

What was he going to do about this?

He called Bloomberg and asked where Nathan was staying in Cape Town. He telephoned him. 'When are you coming back?' he demanded.

'Next weekend,' Nathan said.

'Listen, this is important. Have you got anybody at your lingerie factory who could make a man's suit?'

Surprise. 'Why can't you go to an ordinary tailor?'

'We,' McQuade emphasized, 'need a tailor who'll ask no questions.'

Nathan was mystified. 'Why?'

'Because, it's a policeman's uniform we want.' He paused. 'For our fancy dress ball. Remember?'

397

Understanding dawned on Nathan. 'No,' he said, 'none of my staff could do it. And I wouldn't ask anybody even if they could.'

McQuade had expected it. 'Well, you're in the rag-trade, you must know tailors you could trust?'

'Sure, but only with legal business.'

'Well *think* about it!' McQuade snapped. 'This is your investment, remember! I'll call you back in an hour.'

'But,' Nathan whined, 'why must you . . . go as a police-man?'

'Because I've thought it all through! In fact, you should come back to Johannesburg immediately and help me. I don't know this town.'

'I'm here on *business*.'

'This is your business too! You want that fancy dress prize, don't you?'

'Just give me back my twenty grand,' Nathan whined, 'and you can win the prize all by yourself. Sharon would cut me off without a penny if I walked away from this business trip.'

'Talking about money, I'm wasting it in hotels when your house is empty. Can I stay there until you come back? And use the telephone?'

'Sure,' Nathan said, relieved to be agreeable to something. He added: 'Just take it easy on the telephone.'

'Thanks. And think about a tailor.'

How was this tailor going to know what to make? He would need a real uniform to copy. A photograph? He sat, thinking. Then reached for the telephone directory. He dialled the Public Library.

Five minutes later he hung up, very relieved. There existed a large, coffee-table book called *Onse Polisie, Our Police*, with many photographs of fine policemen in all their different regalia, giving a history of the force.

Next, he turned to his notes headed Buttons. He dialled.

A cheerful voice said, 'Collectibles.'

'I believe you sell all kinds of military insignia and so forth?

I collect police buttons. Have you got a complete set of South African police buttons? Plus badges, insignia, and so forth?'

'Modern police insignia, or antiques?'

'Modern.'

'Sorry. That modern stuff isn't on the market yet. In years to come, they'll start showing up.'

McQuade's heart was sinking. 'Isn't there a shop that supplies policemen?'

'No, sir. Only Police Headquarters. Your only hope is to go to the Police Recreation Club, introduce yourself as a collector and try to meet some cops who're interested in the same thing.'

No way was he going near a policeman. 'Yes?'

'Then maybe I can sell you some insignia to swop with them. We have a big range from both world wars, British, American, South African, Australian, Italian, German, Japanese — and old police stuff. Why don't you come and have a look, sir?'

McQuade said he would, thanked him, and hung up.

He sat back. This wasn't going to be easy. If he couldn't get the buttons the uniform was useless.

He put that problem aside, and turned to his notes of tailors. He thought well before making his first choice.

An Indian voice said, 'Patel Brothers.'

McQuade put on a heavy South African accent.

'Good morning, I'm a policeman and I'm going to need two uniforms made quickly, hey. My friend and I are here on holiday, and we have to attend a formal police wedding, man. Can you make two uniforms in a hurry?'

No hesitation. 'Yes, sir. In how much of a hurry?'

'Forty-eight hours? I'll bring in a photograph for you to copy from. Look, if you can't guarantee there'll be no problems, I'll find another tailor.'

'Oh my goodness me, there'll be no problems, sir.'

'What about the material?'

'Don't worry, sir, we can find it in Jo'burg, sir.'

'And what about our caps? You can make that too, hey?'

Mr Patel hesitated. 'Your caps, sir?'

'Of course. That can't be hard, man, just some plastic covered in the right cloth? Look, there must be plenty of hat-makers in Johannesburg.'

Mr Patel said hastily, 'Oh my goodness, no problem for me to make your hats, sir.'

McQuade took a deep breath of relief.

'Okay, Mr Patel, I'll come in to your shop later, hey.'

He bade Mr Patel a no-nonsense goodbye.

Thank God for Mr Patel. He consulted his notes of leather workers.

'Leather Unlimited,' a girl said.

'Good afternoon. I want to have two belts and Sam Brownes made. You know, the leather strap that a military officer wears over his shoulders, attached to his belt.'

'Yes?' the girl said.

'If I bring a photograph, could you copy it exactly?'

'Oh, no difficulty at all.'

'Thank you,' McQuade said with relief. 'And what about buckles and revolver holsters?'

'The leather work won't be any problem. We've got all kinds of brass in stock, and we can have most things made by outside craftsmen.'

'Badges too?'

The girl hesitated. 'We haven't had this arise before. It would depend on the detail. These guys are pretty good. Or maybe they can make a mould and cast it for you. It depends on how much you're prepared to spend.'

They said their goodbyes. McQuade sat there. These buttons and badges were the only problem. The whole plan could founder on these buttons and badges.

Wide stone steps sweep up to the Johannesburg Library, massive columns support its imposing facade; the city fathers of the Golden City had spared no expense. The atrium houses bronze busts of some of them, halls of books lead off and staircases lined with magnificent old oil paintings sweep upwards to more. McQuade found his way down panelled corridors to the reference section. Many people, black and white, hunched over tomes on polished tables in sepulchral silence.

The charming librarian brought him the large pictorial book entitled *Onse Polisie, Our Police*.

He flicked through it. The text was in both English and Afrikaans, and there were photographs of policemen from all angles, front, side and rear. The front page had an excellent photograph of a policeman's cap badge.

He turned to the chapter on the Namibian police. They had a different uniform, as well as different buttons and badges.

What was Mr Patel going to say about this? Where was he going to get the Namibian buttons and badges? How was he going to explain two pairs of different police force uniforms to Mr Patel?

Answer: He couldn't. He'd have to find another Mr Patel, a Mr Naidoo or Mr Wong. More weak links in the chain; more men to convince, bribe, bully; more men to blow the whistle on him . . .

He took a weary breath, closed the book, and took it to the librarian.

'Where is the nearest shop I can buy this book?'

Patel Brothers had their premises in Diagonal Street, the old part of Johannesburg, where the shop fronts are single-storied Victorian with dirty pillars supporting galvanized iron roofs, their windows crammed with African truck, from hairpins to bicycles. The street was thronged with blacks. McQuade walked in with his new copy of *Our Police*.

The shop smelt of cloth and curry. Neon lights still left the place in half-darkness. Bolts of cloth lined the walls. There was a wooden counter, beyond which a door led onto a workroom where several blacks sat at sewing machines.

401

Another doorway led onto a steamy kitchen, a backyard beyond. Two silhouettes appeared. One was a neat Indian man with greying hair, the other a woman in a sari.

'Good afternoon,' McQuade said in a heavy South African accent. 'I telephoned you this morning about making my police uniforms, hey?'

Mr Patel's eyes flickered, and he said hastily, 'Not me, sir, my brother, sir . . .'

'Well, is he here, man?'

Mr Patel said something rapidly in dialect. The woman left, closing the kitchen door behind her. Mr Patel looked very nervous, his eyes sliding as he turned back to McQuade. 'My brother has told me to tell you he's very sorry but he cannot make your uniforms, sir.'

McQuade's heart was sinking. 'Why not?'

Mr Patel shook his head. 'We have too much work, sir, too very much work.'

'But your brother told me there'd be no problem, man!'

'My brother is crazy, sir' – he made circles around his ear – 'quite crazy, he don't know nothing, sir.' Mr Patel threw up his hands and rolled his liquid eyes. 'But he is quite innocent, sir, he does not know it is illegal to make policeman's uniforms, sir, he is quite stupid and innocent, sir—'

'But all I want is a new uniform for a wedding—'

'Oh my goodness gracious me, sir, my brother he told me, sir, but he doesn't understand about the law, sir, Patel Brothers never break the law and so I telephoned our lawyer, sir, and he said it is quite illegal to make a police uniform, sir.' He clasped his hands. 'Oh, my goodness gracious, please excuse my stupid brother, sir.'

McQuade wanted to get the hell out of here, but this was his only chance. 'Well, *Got*, man, can you tell me another tailor who is not so stupid?'

Mr Patel clutched his hands together. 'Oh my goodness gracious me, I'm sorry, sir. All my friends know the law except my stupid brother, sir.'

Oh Jesus, the word had gone around . . . With the last of his composure McQuade held a finger out at Mr Patel. 'You'll never get any more business from me, hey!'

The taxi dropped him near the shop called Collectibles. He was worried how far the story had gone from Mr Patel, and whether there was a police informer along that line. How the hell was he going to get a uniform now? He walked into Collectibles, on edge.

'Ah yes,' the man said. He went to a cabinet and pulled out a tray. 'These are old police buttons.'

McQuade had a vivid picture in his mind of the modern police buttons. And at a glance these old buttons looked almost identical! 'Have you got an entire set? Tunic, cuffs, et cetera?'

'Yes.'

'Do you have two sets?'

The man disappeared into a back room. He re-emerged with a box. He tipped buttons onto the counter, and sorted them out. McQuade watched, his hopes rising.

'All except two cuff buttons,' the man said.

'Have you got something similar?'

'Yes, but the crest will be different.' The man went off again. He came back with another box.

McQuade selected two. They bore naval crests, but they looked the same size as the police buttons.

'What are you going to do with these, sir? Swop them or what?'

'Probably just put them in my display cabinet. Can I look at your old cap badges?'

A tray came out. There were all kinds of badges, but nothing that closely resembled the police cap badge.

McQuade bought two, anyway. He would have his cap off when he came face to face with Mr Strauss.

He got back to his hotel about six o'clock, sat down and dialled Nathan in Cape Town. 'Well?'

'There's *nobody*,' Nathan complained. 'I tried one tailor friend, who just might have gone along with it, and he refused point blank. I tried Julie Wonderful, but he's in the Middle East flogging magic carpets until next week sometime. He's your best bet.'

McQuade cursed. 'Doesn't Bloomberg know anybody?'

'I asked Bloomers, and he nearly had a heart-attack.'

'Couldn't Sharon do it? All women can make dresses and things.'

There was a pause. 'Sharon?' Nathan said. 'Did you say Sharon?'

'Yes, you dope!'

'No way,' Nathan exhaled. 'No way must Sharon know about this or she'll remodel my circumcision with a blunt bread-knife.'

McQuade hung up, went to the bed and collapsed.

Okay, so he had passable buttons. Now what?

There were doubtless dozens of crooks in this town who could supply him with police uniforms. But how to find them and can you trust a crook to keep his mouth shut?

He massaged his eyelids. Not yet. No way was he about to blow his whole submarine and millions of dollars by opening his mouth to Johannesburg crooks. And how many police-informers were in that underground? No, not yet.

Unless he came up with another idea, tomorrow he would have to find a dishonest private detective, and put the problem to him.

Then he had another idea. He doubted this would work, either, but he had nothing to lose because now she knew almost everything. And he ached to see her anyway.

He got up and telephoned Sarah's apartment.

48

He arranged to meet her in the Holiday Inn's cocktail bar, but he sat in the busy foyer, pretending to read a newspaper, to see if she was being followed.

She did not see him. She hurried to the elevators, excitement on her face. And McQuade's heart turned over. He kept his eyes on the entrance. People were coming and going the whole time, but all of them seemed about their normal business.

She was sitting in the corner of the cocktail bar, and beamed as he walked in. He sat in the chair beside her. 'How're you?'

Her eyes were moist. 'All the better for seeing you! I've been worried sick.'

He held her hand tight. 'I love you, Sarah.'

She looked at him, her moist eyes steady. 'I think I love you too.' Then she grinned. 'This is just a fun trip for yours truly of the *Christian Science Monitor*. Falling in love with sea captains is simply not sensible.'

'I want to make love to you.'

'If you're seeking my acquiescence, my answer is yes, yes, *yes*. But till then, what's all this about?'

He still held her warm hand. 'Can you make your own dresses?'

She was surprised. 'Of course. Learned it at my mother's knee.'

'Could you make a man's suit?'

She was taken aback.

'I suppose so. If I had a pattern.' She added: 'It wouldn't be very good.'

'And if you didn't have a pattern? But had the man? To measure him up?'

She looked bemused. 'What's all this about?'

McQuade opened the plastic bag and pulled out the police book. He opened it at a flagged page. 'If I supply the brass-work, leather-work, could you make me a uniform like that?'

She stared at the page, then turned to him. 'Guess I could.'

He was delighted. 'You'd have to borrow a good sewing machine; or rent one. And the cap? Could you make that?'

She looked at the picture, frowning. 'Yes. If I had all the materials.'

'Wonderful! Could you make two uniforms?'

She looked at him. 'If you tell me what this is about. Who's the other one for?'

'Tucker. He's only an inch taller than me.'

'And what are you going to do with these uniforms?' She said solemnly: 'I'm not going to do this unless I know, Jim.'

'I'm going to impersonate a policeman.'

'I've figured that much myself. But why?'

McQuade sat back. 'I've made a short-list of suspects, from the print-out of Population Register. The easiest way to con-front each man, so I can compare him with a photograph I have, is to knock on the door disguised as a policeman.'

'And then what?'

'After I've identified him, I go away and make a plan to snatch him.' He elaborated, to encourage her: 'And after I've finished with him I'll hand the bastard over to the Israelis. I *promise* I'll give you the complete story. It'll be a scoop.'

She looked at him soberly, thinking.

'Okay, I'll do my best. Where do I measure you?'

He wanted to hug her.

He went down to the reception desk and borrowed a tape-measure. They took the elevator up to his room, with a bottle of wine. He locked the door and took her in his arms with a grin all over his face. 'Thank you.'

She leant back, pelvis against his loins. 'I want,' she smiled, 'to be paid in advance.'

And he crushed her against him and, oh, the glorious feel of her softness, her breasts and her belly and her thighs, and his hand slid down over her soft-hard buttocks and pulled up her skirt, and he slid his hand over her warm-cool thighs and he caught their reflection in the mirror, her long smooth legs and her skirt bunched up, and it was the most erotic and happy-making thing he had seen and he was wildly in love and he toppled her over onto the bed joyfully. 'I love you, Sarah.'

She held him tight. 'I love you too,' she whispered.

And he knew the seriousness of it when he said: 'Then, when this is over, you can't possibly go back to Boston, Massachusetts. You'll have to come and live with me.'

She had half a smile on her lovely mouth and her eyes were glistening. 'What about my work?'

But McQuade knew loud and clear what he really wanted to say and it was a wonderful feeling to say it. 'What I mean is, I want to marry you and live with you for ever.'

She looked at him with shining eyes, then she closed them, and a tear squeezed out the corners.

'I think that takes some thinking about, by both of us.'

Her taxi dropped her off at her apartment block in Hillbrow the next morning. She got into her rented car, and drove slowly through the tricky maze of one-way streets, onto Jan Smuts Highway. She arrived in the prosperous suburb of Parktown North, and parked under the trees outside the house with the high walls. She let herself in and walked through the pretty garden. The living-room door opened and Matt came out angrily. 'At last!'

'As the departmental whore I refuse to do short-times.' She strode past him into the living-room, carrying a plastic bag.

Two young men were at the breakfast table. Matt followed her in and seethed: 'You've been missing since seven o'clock last night! Why didn't you report?'

'Because I was in bed. Getting laid.'

'But why didn't you advise us where you were meeting him?! So we could tail you?!'

'Because he came to *fetch* me, unannounced. I was in his company the whole time.'

'And where the hell was that?'

'The Holiday Inn, room four-one-six, but he's already checked out.'

Matt cried, '*Jesus Christ! Again! Where's he gone?*'

'I've no idea.'

Matt slapped his head incredulously. 'You let him go *again?!* Why didn't you go with him?'

'Because he refused to take me.'

Matt held his head in furious exasperation. 'I don't believe this . . .'

'And because,' Sarah said angrily, 'I'm going to be seeing him in a few days' time when he telephones me.'

'*When he decides to telephone you?*' Matt shouted. '*Oh, dandy! ''Don't call me, I'll call you''?*'

'He'll telephone!' She pulled the police book out of the plastic bag and slapped it on the table. She opened it at the first flagged page and jabbed her finger at the photograph. 'He wants two uniforms like that! And' – she flicked to the pages on the Namibian police – 'two like that. I've promised to make them for him.' She glared at Matt. 'I presume that's not beyond the resources of Mossad?! I've got his measurements.' She thrust a note at him and turned back to the garden. 'And now, if you'll excuse me, the whore would like to perform her ablutions!'

Matt grabbed her arm excitedly. 'He's going to impersonate a policeman?'

'How very perspicacious.'

'To do what exactly?'

'To gain access to homes of his suspects. To compare them with the photograph Wiesenthal gave him of Heinrich Muller. Then make a plan to snatch him.'

'So he's finally admitted to you he's after Muller!'

'No, sir,' Sarah sighed, 'but we know that from Wiesenthal, don't we, sir?'

'No sarcasm! And you really believe he's going to hand Muller straight over to the Israelis?'

She looked him in the eye. 'Why not? He's half-suspected of murder.'

'Then why doesn't he want to hand him over to the South African police and clear his name?'

'Because the Israelis will believe him and clear his name. The South Africans may not.'

'Bullshit.' Matt turned away. 'The South African police know he was in bed with you when the first guy was assaulted. If the cops *are* after him, it's because they suspect he's after somebody big – like Muller. There's a heavy pro-Nazi element in this country, and in the police. They could be rather worried that our friend McQuade seems hot on the scent of one of them.'

'And all you care about is that James McQuade leads you to Heinrich Muller before all these Nazis get McQuade and you lose your bloodhound!'

Matt ignored the interruption. 'And I don't believe for a moment that Mr McQuade is going to hand Mr Muller over to the Israelis straight away. He wants him for another reason.'

Sarah tried not to stare at him. Her heart sinking. 'And that is?'

Matt put his fingers together as he paced.

'He told Wiesenthal a story about a submarine off the coast of South America. Bullshit. That submarine is off the coast of South Africa somewhere. Why? Because McQuade is looking for Muller in South Africa. Why? Because the two fishermen who told him the tale weren't Spanish at all – they were Namibian natives. Namely these guys who were murdered. QED.'

'Submarine?' Sarah's heart was sinking. Then she said,

with a show of indignation, 'Why wasn't I told this?'

'Because you had no need to know.' He added casually, 'Why? Has he mentioned a submarine to you?'

Sarah looked away. Her mind trying to race. 'No.' She feigned incredulity. 'So Mr McQuade wants to snatch Mr Muller to find out where that submarine is?'

'And why, already? Because he thinks there's a fortune on it.' Matt looked at her knowingly. 'Of course, that's only my guess. But it happens to be Simon Wiesenthal's guess as well.'

She blinked, then sat down. The young man called Steven said: 'Can I make a suggestion, sir?'

'Yes?' Matt said irritably.

Steven said: 'I think we're going about this the wrong way. Using McQuade as our bloodhound. Now he's disappeared again, and we're dependent on him contacting Sarah. Supposing he manages to get his uniforms elsewhere? Or if he finds Muller and makes a botch of it? Muller would go underground for ever. Or McQuade may even kill him—'

'We've been through all this! What are you suggesting?'

Steven said respectfully, 'That we take matters into our own hands now, sir. We have two options. We either find this lesbian and blackmail her into giving us the name and the print-out—'

'We've rejected that option. The girl has already panicked and disappeared on so-called holiday. The whole thing could blow up in our face!'

'I'm saying we should reconsider that option, sir.'

'Not yet. Too risky.'

'Then,' Steven said, 'I suggest that we move in on McQuade when he contacts Sarah. Sweat the name out of him, and the whole print-out. And *we* then impersonate the police and find Muller.'

Sarah said icily, 'Then you can count me out!'

Matt held a finger out at her. 'You,' he said, 'will do as you are ordered!'

'Like hell I will!' she cried. 'I refuse to be an accomplice to that guy being beaten up! And just remember that you can't do a damn *thing* without me because it's *me* he's contacting, *me* he trusts, *me* he's getting the uniforms from! And if I quit you'll never see him again!'

'I'll deal with you later—'

'You can deal with me right now! And I'm telling you right now that there's only one condition on which I'm prepared to continue! And that is that we come clean with McQuade! *Tell* him who we are and persuade him to work with us! *Persuade* him that it'll be easier and quicker because we're the experts and he's an amateur. And make a solemn *deal* with him, that he can have the so-called fortune in this submarine – if there is any.'

Matt held his tongue. Because he needed her. He turned elaborately to Steven.

'We've considered your second option of forcing the information out of him and we have rejected it. For the very good reason that it may not work, and we don't want him to know that Mossad is on his tail. We've got things working very well without him knowing, thanks to Sarah. Using strong-arm could blow things up in Mossad's face, if he created a scandal afterwards. It's not necessary yet to take those risks.'

'*Yet?*' Sarah said dangerously.

Matt ignored her insubordination and turned to her. 'As regards your "suggestion" – the same applies. Why reveal that Mossad is on his tail when we're doing fine through you? It's very likely that he would reject our offer – Wiesenthal offered him all the help and he backed off. Why? Because he thinks he'll lose the treasure. And, anyway, it's highly doubtful that he'd trust us after he finds out that you've been screwing him in the line of duty – that your whole relationship is false.' He shook his head and put an end to the discussion. 'So, the man must get his uniforms.' He picked up the police book and said to Steven, 'Find out the quickest flights to Jerusalem. Then get this book to the Israeli

411

embassy, for their diplomatic bag. With a coded letter saying we want eighteen uniforms made up immediately: nine South African police, nine Namibian. Two pairs of each for Mr McQuade, the rest for us. With fake buttons, badges, Sam Brownes, the works. Enclose the note of McQuade's measurements and find out what ours are. And we want those uniforms in the next diplomatic bag back here, even if the tailors have to work all night!'

49

McQuade rode through the rush-hour traffic to Nathan's house, getting lost several times. Dinah, the black maid, let him in. He dumped his bag in the guest room, then spread out his lists and maps of Johannesburg, Pretoria, Namibia and South Africa on the dining-room table.

He located the address of each of his suspects, and marked them on the maps. It took him over an hour. Then he transposed all the marks on the street maps onto the road maps of southern Africa, to give him a bird's-eye view. He was daunted by the task ahead. While most of his suspects in South Africa were clustered around Johannesburg and Pretoria, those in Namibia were spread across that vast territory.

It was going to be a hell of job. He folded everything up then went to the telephone and got the yellow pages directory. He looked up Detectives.

There were half a dozen listed, Executech, FM, Worldwide, Acme, BSAP, all claiming to be specialists in divorce, missing persons, security, criminal and civil investigations. Several were run by former police officers. All promised complete confidentiality. He telephoned Fidelity Detectives and made an appointment in the name of Johnson.

Fidelity Detectives had their offices in an old Victorian building in the less expensive part of town. An old grille-elevator took McQuade up to the third floor. The gloomy corridors were lit by neon strip-lights. McQuade knocked.

John Patterson was a big, earnest Englishman of about forty who had been an inspector in the Rhodesian police. The

413

certificates lined his walls, including one that declared that he was a member in good standing of the Association of British Detectives. He sat behind a large steel desk and listened encouragingly.

'This is a preliminary enquiry only,' McQuade said. 'I'm trying to find a man who came to southern Africa decades ago. I have an old photograph of him. I know the false surname he is using, and a number of addresses he may be staying at.' He paused. 'Now, how much would you charge to stake out these addresses, and find out whether or not he's the right man?'

'In principle, three hundred rand for an eight-hour day for each detective employed, which includes travelling time. Plus expenses. Night surveillance the same.'

Impossible.

'So if I'm in a hurry and want to use detectives to stake out ten different addresses it's at least three thousand rand a day — six thousand if I have two shifts a day.'

'Well,' Patterson replied, 'for such a number of detectives we'd give you a substantial discount.'

Big deal. 'And who are these detectives? You haven't got ten men on your staff?'

'No, they're freelance. All good men. Mostly ex-police or ex-army.'

'How do I know *they*'ll treat the case with confidentiality?'

Patterson tapped his chest. 'Trust my reputation. They answer to me, but you can meet them beforehand.'

McQuade had already decided he could not afford it, but he had to test the lie of the land in case he ever needed him. 'But would you never report to the police anything a client tells you? Or what you find out?'

Patterson's eyes lifted to the ceiling for a moment.

'We would not cover up a crime. Or commit a crime.'

The man had loaded the words to encourage him, while keeping his professionalism up front. McQuade continued, 'I wouldn't dream of asking you to commit a crime. But after

414

you have identified the right man, I might want you to –' he paused significantly – 'bring him to me.'

Patterson put his fingertips together. 'Bring him? You mean persuade . . .' He got up and walked slowly to the door, opened it to ensure nobody was outside, then returned to his seat. He said reasonably: 'You want to talk to the man, of course. Discuss some business with him.'

'Yes. Absolutely nothing illegal, I assure you.'

'May I ask what you want to discuss with him?'

'He's my father. I'm his illegitimate son. I simply want him to acknowledge that fact.' He added: 'It's a very emotional matter with me. And it's a matter of inheritance.'

'Oh. So all I'm doing is reuniting a family.' Patterson waved a hand. 'But for some reason, which doesn't concern me, your father denies his paternity.'

'Exactly. He would refuse to meet me if he knew what was happening. You must not mention why you are . . . approaching him.'

Patterson nodded at the ceiling. 'A trick,' he murmured. 'I'll have to think of a little trick, to reunite father and son.'

'So how much extra is that going to cost?'

Patterson brought his eyes down to his desk.

'Impossible to say, until we see the lie of the land. The place, distances, how many men for the job.'

'The minimum?' McQuade demanded quietly.

'The minimum? I'd say twenty thousand rand.'

No way. But at least McQuade knew what was possible. He stood up. 'Thank you . . .'

Patterson hurried on: 'You said you'd like to meet the men?' He scribbled a note and handed it to him. 'Pete Griffiths. He drinks at the Gold Reef Hotel every evening. I'll tell him to look out for you tonight, perhaps?'

McQuade put the note in his pocket. 'All right. I'll be in touch, after I've made my decisions.'

Patterson beamed him out the door.

*

At dusk McQuade rode back into the city. He had visited three of the leading security companies in Johannesburg, discussed their systems with salesmen, collected their brochures describing their standard lay-outs and their array of products. He felt he knew a lot about electronic surveillance, tear-gas pistols, miniature gas canisters for ladies handbags, electric stun-guns and batons, walkie-talkie radios, handcuffs, even gas masks for the hyper-cautious to protect themselves against their own tear gas. Every salesman had gladly agreed to provide him, free of obligation, with a blueprint of their recommended security lay-out when he provided them with a sketch of the house he wanted to build.

He had done some useful work, but he was depressed. The money Nathan had put up was fast dwindling: the costs to come were high – impossibly high if he had to hire help like Patterson's men. So, he would have to rely on Tucker – the Kid couldn't impersonate a South African policeman because he couldn't speak Afrikaans. And Tucker would have a heart-attack. He felt daunted – by what he was taking on, by what Johan Lombard had told him, the size and strength of the enemy – and he was worried about 435 overtaking him. And, God, was there even any loot in that submarine? Was he mad to be chasing Nazi war-criminals when he should be chasing buyers for his fishing company whilst the going was still moderately good, before 435 chased all the investors away?

He did not go to the Gold Reef Hotel to meet Patterson's man, Pete Griffiths: he knew now it was possible to hire muscle if he could afford it. He found his way back to Nathan's house. Dinah had already gone to her quarters. He got a beer from the refrigerator. He hesitated, then sat down at the telephone and called Johan Lombard.

'No bother at all, dear boy,' Johan beamed, 'just sitting here having a thoughtful hair of the Philistine's dog that bit me at lunch-time. What is it you want to know about 435?'

'Is it just diplomatic manoeuvring – another cliff-hanger – or is it really going to come off? And if so, when?'

Johan said cheerfully, 'Oh, it'll come off this time, dear boy. I know we've had similar offers from the South African government before – summit meetings with Cuba and Angola in the Cape Verde Islands, in Geneva, in Lusaka, the works – and in fact South Africa actually withdrew most of its forces from Angola in 1984 and '85, pursuant to its peace offers, but the bloody Cubans always refused to withdraw their troops at the eleventh hour because they wanted to have their cake and eat it: get rid of South African troops and then knock the living shit out of UNITA – and then fight for SWAPO. But the Cubans' tune is changing – their military leaders realize that it's a no-win war.'

McQuade felt feverish. 'So Cuba's going to give up?' (It was ridiculous that he wanted them to stay a bit longer!)

'Oh, Angola is Cuba's Vietnam, dear boy. Castro himself doesn't want to give up – he wants to be the Hero of Africa – and besides what's he going to do with fifty thousand noisy troops coming home to no jobs in his hopeless commie economy? Dirty war is about his only export. And it's kind of difficult for him to admit that the last twelve years in Angola have been in vain – especially after the Yanks trounced him out of Grenada so recently. But his military men in Angola realize they can't really win against South Africa and now Russia is getting twitchy about footing the bill: over two *billion* dollars the war has cost them – they're even pulling out of Afghanistan, dear fellow! And, of course, South Africa's finding the war too expensive too – a million rand a day it's costing us poor taxpayers – and our military men also feel Angola could be *our* Vietnam. So, South Africa's tune has also changed in the last few years. In the old days our venerable government's objectives were to prevent a SWAPO Marxist government in Namibia at *any* cost – and to avoid a local backlash of being accused of "selling out" the whites of Namibia – hence our former bluster and bravado. But bitter experience, and the cost, have brought about our present sweet reasonableness.'

'But,' McQuade protested (*protest?* – this was ridiculous) 'what about UNITA? If the Cubans pull out, UNITA will win the civil war against the Angola regime and install a pro-western government – Castro and Moscow won't risk *that*, surely?'

'Ah,' Johan said, 'there's the rub! Slice the tearful 435 onion any which way and you'll find UNITA at the core. Yes, UNITA will whip the pants off the puppet Angola regime if the Cubans pull out. So, two things are bound to happen. One, Cuba will launch an all-out offensive against UNITA while they drag out these new negotiations over 435, arguing about a timetable for withdrawal. Two, in the end result they will leave behind sufficient Cuban troops to enable the Angola regime to at least fight a *defensive* war, and to protect Angola's oil and diamond fields. Say five to ten thousand troops. And, in the end result, South Africa will accept that – South Africa can tolerate a few thousand Cuban troops way up there in the north around Luanda, especially as the United States – at least under Reagan – will continue to support UNITA in the south. In exchange for accepting that, South Africa will demand a quid pro quo, like Angola undertaking not to allow ANC military bases in the country. Which would be a blow to the ANC. It's all a question of diplomatic bargaining, dear boy. And posturing. And enduring offensive, immature Marxist platitudes and insults. But both sides will be pushed by America and Russia into giving a little here, taking a little there, and 435 will happen this time.'

'But *when*?' McQuade demanded worriedly.

'Soon, dear boy.' (McQuade's heart sank.) 'The Americans are working hard to get a deal going before the next presidential election so Ronald Reagan and his Republicans can justify his "constructive engagement" policy towards South Africa to the US electorate, going softly on sanctions, et cetera. And the South Africans are keen to clinch a deal while they can still bargain from strength, *also* before America's elections in case the Democrats win – Dukakis has darkly proclaimed he'll throw South Africa and UNITA to the communist wolves. And Britain is pushing South Africa, too, so that Maggie can justify her no-sanctions policy to *her* electorate and to the Commonwealth – which is mostly black. And Gorbachev's worried about his roubles, so he's pushing too – and Gorbie thinks that Bush-baby's going to win the US presidential election, see? Well, that all rather leaves Fidel glumly fretting over his cheque-book. No doubt he'll stall negotiations, loudly protesting it'll take *years* to remove his troops, while he waits to see if Dukakis wins the election and thus wins the war for him. All wheels within wheels, dear fellow. And, in truth, Castro could not remove all his troops in six months – it's a logistical impossibility. Eighteen months is more like it.'

'So you think we've got at least eighteen months before 435 comes in?'

'No, dear boy,' Johan said. 'I think South Africa will agree to *allowing* Castro eighteen months or two years to make a phased withdrawal. Assuming that's agreed, as soon as the Cubans are out of the danger area – away from the Namibian border – 435 could be implemented. Most likely early next year. But soon.' He ended: 'That's my view, dear boy.'

McQuade sighed grimly. Even eighteen months wasn't much time in which to sell a fishing company. 'And then what's going to happen? Once they've got independence, what do you think SWAPO's going to do to the Namibian economy?'

Johan said: 'What do *you* think they'll do, old chap?'

McQuade said angrily, 'I think they'll fuck it up! With their stupid communist economic theories – nationalizing everything! When will these people realize that communism sounds fine on paper but is a resounding failure in practice?!'

'I'm afraid I think you're right, dear boy. If I had any money – which regrettably I don't – I certainly wouldn't be investing in Namibia now. And I think Sam Nujoma and his SWAPO thugs are going to be even more tiresome than your average Marxist fuzzy-wuzzy, because they're so badly educated, dear fellow. Sam Nujoma, your future President-for-Life, has only two years of primary school education, you know. He was a teaboy in a Windhoek office before Moscow spotted his potential. And he's been living in Cloud-cuckoo-land most of his political life, courtesy of the UN and World Council of Churches, directing his "war" from five-star Scandinavian hotels – with a little help from Castro. Nice work, if you can get it. So? So one has little cause for optimism. A group of white businessmen from Namibia went to visit him in his Swedish hotel some years ago, you know, to open a dialogue and find out what their future was under a SWAPO regime. And they came back very worried about the man's economic naivety. Did you read about that?'

Indeed McQuade had. In Australia. It was one of the reasons why he had come back to sell up. 'Remind me.'

'They were worried sick that Nujoma appeared to have not a clue about how fragile the Namibian economy is. He's been living on the largesse of the World Council of Churches, Moscow, and the Scandinavian governments so long that he thought that after independence he could just continue to pass around the jolly begging bowl. Oh, he told the businessmen that they would be welcome to stay, et cetera – quite a nice chap, apparently, as long as you don't cross him –– he struck a black Namibian woman in the face when he was a guest at the European *parliament* in Strasbourg, dear boy, and shouted "You will die!" because she complained that her son had been dragooned off into a SWAPO training camp and never heard of again! How's that for a President-for-Life? But, anyway, the businessmen returned to Namibia very worried.' Johan sighed. 'These tiresome communists just don't understand the dire consequences that will ensue – to them and the world – if the Rossing uranium mine, and Consolidated Diamond Mines and Consolidated Gold Fields, et cetera, were nationalized. Oh, it all sounds lovely on Kremlin notepaper. But in practice . . .? I think they think they can just print more money. Russia hasn't shown a profit in seventy years . . .!' He ended: 'You're in the fishing industry, aren't you?'

McQuade sighed bitterly. 'Yes.'

'Well, dear boy,' Johan said, 'I know what I would do if I were you.'

McQuade thanked him, and hung up, feeling more depressed. But, also, more grimly determined because of it. That submarine solved all these problems! And delivering a Nazi war-criminal to justice was right! He had it both ways! Of course he had to continue! You can't have a chance like this and not go for it! . . .

He found pork chops in the refrigerator. He threw them into a frying pan. 'A fine Jew you are, Nathan, can't turn my back on you for a moment.'

50

The countryside around the resort area of Hartebeestpoort is sprinkled with cottages to let. On Thursday afternoon, when McQuade rode back to collect his repaired Landrover, he saw the handwritten advertisement in the garage window: *Secluded holiday cottage, three bedrooms, linen, cooking utensils, all mod cons including telephone. Apply within.*

He asked, was shown where it was on his road map and went there on the motorcycle while his bill was prepared. It was a small, unimaginative house, the furniture was cheap, the inside walls a variety of colours, but it was clean. There were a number of small-holdings in the area but it was secluded, on a hillside with a pleasant view of the valley and the distant dam. McQuade rode back, paid a week's rent and collected the Landrover.

The cottage solved a big problem: he would be going out each day dressed as a policeman and that was best not done from a public place like a motel. But the cottage was hardly the place for his reunion with Sarah after all the work she had done. He went to the public telephone and dialled the hotel in Sun City and made a reservation for Saturday night. Then he telephoned Sarah.

'Oh, *hi!*' She sounded relieved but tense. 'The job will be finished tomorrow. How do you want delivery?'

He was delighted. 'Wonderful! Is anything wrong?'

'No – no, I've been worried, that's all.'

'Well, I've booked us into Sun City for Saturday night. I'm told it's lovely. It'll only take you two or three hours to drive there. Meet me there at about six o'clock.' He gave her the room number.

'You needn't take me to an expensive place like that.'

'Yes, I must. Because I love you. And you've saved me an awful lot of money!'

He bought some beer, wine and groceries. Then he drove to the cottage. He sat down at the kitchen table, and spread out his street maps and notes.

In the past three days he had checked out almost every address of the people on his list who lived in the environs of Johannesburg and Pretoria. By tomorrow afternoon he should have finished.

Sun City (also known as Sin City), is a gambling casino in the independent black state of Bophuthatswana, a hundred and fifty miles from Johannesburg. The country used to be part of South Africa, a tribal area where the Bophuta Tswana people live, until the South African government granted it independence, whereon the new black president promptly granted South African entrepreneurs the right to build a holiday playground reminiscent of Las Vegas. The white South Africans, languishing in their Calvinistic environment, responded with glee. In their hordes they drive into the arid, eroded mini-state to the oasis of Sun City, hole up in the magnificent hotel complex, spend their money on the gaming tables, luxuriate around the artificial lakes and waterfalls and go to the naughty girlie shows, having a rip-roaring slice of un-South African life.

Sarah arrived at six o'clock. She was freshly groomed, but her face was strained. She had seen no evidence of it, but she was certain that she was being followed. Matt would not risk letting McQuade slip through her fingers again and probably already had boys in position at Sun City. She had had to tell him where she was going when she picked up the uniforms, and she had finally made up her mind what she was going to do about this business.

She drove through the big car park, looking for McQuade's Landrover. She saw it, and managed to park close to it, grabbed her holdall and the big cardboard box, then boarded the monorail train from the parking area. She was swept along towards the sky-scraper complex set amongst rolling lawns and exotic gardens, the stark bush-brown hills of Bophuthatswana beyond. The train came to a halt at the glittering hotel entrance.

She hurried to the reception desk where she was told that Mr McQuade had already arrived. She followed her porter, her long high-heeled legs clicking across the marble, her black hair shiny in a ponytail. She entered the birdcage elevator and rose up, up into the glittering beehive, like an angel.

McQuade threw open the door, a grin all over his face. His heart seemed to turn over as he clutched her in his arms. He began to hustle her into the room and she laughed, 'What about these damn uniforms I've slaved over?'

'And thank you very much!' He grabbed her bag from the corridor and slung the box on the bed and took her in his arms again.

'Try them on,' she insisted. She turned to the box and lifted the lid. She pulled out the first garment.

He was amazed. It looked the real thing. He fingered it. The stitching, shaping, was perfect. 'God, you're clever!' He examined the buttons. 'But these are real buttons!'

'No. Feel them.'

They did not feel like metal. 'Plastic?'

'Any art student could do it. Just pressed the real button you gave me into plaster of Paris to make a mould. Squirt liquid plastic into the mould. And you've got a decent imitation button. Then spray it with gold paint. Same with the cap badges. Made a plug, copying the photo, then made a mould.' She delved into the box and produced a cap.

McQuade was more amazed. 'God, you're clever!'

'Try it on.' She held the tunic out for him, and he slipped his arms into it, and turned to the mirror. 'It's perfect.'

'And this.' She pulled out a leather belt, Sam Browne and pistol holster. 'There's a shop in Hillbrow that turns out leather gear.' She delved again. 'And this.' She held up a set of shiny handcuffs. 'Got them at the security shop in Jo'burg.'

He was overwhelmed. 'You've done *marvels* . . . And saved me so much effort!'

He took her in his arms again, kissed her hard and joyfully, and his hand went to her breast. She stifled a sob in her throat, then she unplucked the buttons on her blouse as she kissed him, and then unhitched her skirt.

He lay beside her, his knee across hers, spent, happy. Her eyes were closed, her black hair across the pillow, her body pliant and replete. 'When are you going to start?'

He said against her satin shoulder, 'Monday.'

She breathed deep. 'And have you got a proper plan? With contingency plans – what to do if something goes wrong? How to get away? Where to run?'

'I've checked out all the addresses around Johannesburg and Pretoria. Monday is just the start. After I've found him I make my plan.'

'And where are you staying?'

'I've rented a good safe place.' He added gently, 'Please don't ask me where.'

'But is that damn computer print-out safe?'

'Yes.' It and all his notes were locked in the metal toolbox built into the back of the Landrover, but he wasn't going to tell her that.

She closed her eyes, then put her fingers to her eyelids. She whispered, 'Oh God, I can't bear this . . .' His arm tightened on her, but she sat up, swung her legs off the bed and sat there, her hands to her head. 'I simply can't bear this . . .'

He got up on his elbow. 'Sarah?'

She stood up and turned across the room, her hand to her forehead.

'I care for you, Jim! Isn't that obvious?'

He felt his eyes burn, and he wanted to laugh. 'I *love* you.'

She cried, 'Oh God, I'm not asking for a declaration of

love!' She thumped her palm to her head and stood there, gloriously naked, eyes closed. She whispered, 'Oh, how can anybody fall in love in so short a time . . .?' Then she pleaded, 'Oh, Jim, you don't know what you're getting yourself into!' She stared at him with anguish; then came and sat down beside him. 'Jim, I don't know what all this is really about, but I know that you're playing with *fire*.' She waved her hand. 'God, three murders have been committed, and the same swines have been chasing you. You're next, and now you're about to start impersonating a policeman to find a highly dangerous man and kidnap him.' She shook her head and pleaded, 'Jim, you need expert *help*. Look, Matt knows a hell of a lot of people. Johannesburg is a very security-conscious town, and there're security agencies everywhere. Matt would know some reliable people to help you . . .'

McQuade took her hand. 'Maybe at some stage. But all I'm doing now is reconnaissance.'

She glared at him. And made up her mind. It was all or nothing. 'Then take me with you.'

He squeezed her hand. 'No.'

'For God's sake, Jim, I'm scared!' she cried. 'For you! You come and go in my life like the Scarlet Pimpernel and I can't *contact* you, even to tell you that your bloody uniforms are ready! So what happens now? After a nice dirty weekend you disappear into the wide blue yonder and I go back to the apartment and wait for you to telephone! For God's sake, I'm in love with you and I'm worried about you! All I ask is that I be with you on this hare-brained manhunt of yours!' Her glaring eyes were moist.

He squeezed her hand. 'No, darling.'

She jumped up. 'Okay, I'm off!' She strode towards the bathroom. She stopped in the doorway, her strong body half-shadowed in the lamplight. 'I'm sorry. I simply can't bear it, Jim. I'm an all-or-nothing lady, and I was dumb to get involved in the first place.' She turned into the bathroom, and banged the door behind her.

McQuade heard the shower gush. He got up and opened the door. Steam was billowing. He said to the curtain: 'Where are you going?'

She did not answer. He could see her through the translucent curtain, her head tilted back.

'I said where the hell are you going?'

She began to soap herself vigorously. 'I don't know – and if I did I wouldn't tell you. This crazy affair is over. Because there's no future in it.'

'Why is there no future in it?'

She slammed off the shower and tore back the curtain. She grabbed a towel, and swept past him into the bedroom, swept the towel over herself, and grabbed her panties.

'There's every future in this affair, Sarah.'

'Starting when this manhunt is over? And how long is that?' She grabbed her skirt and started pulling it on.

McQuade tried to take her in his arms. 'Please wait for me.'

She stooped and pulled on her shoes. 'Wait for you to telephone? While I eat my heart out? No way.' She swept her brush once through her hair then slung it in her handbag. Her holdall stood at the door, unopened. She snatched it up. She turned to him.

'I'm sorry. For the drama. For getting angry.' She breathed. 'I would love to stay tonight, but I just couldn't bear knowing you're disappearing in the morning, without trace.' ('Without trace?' – she hated herself for saying that). 'I just couldn't bear . . . any more subterfuge—'

'There's no subterfuge!'

She wanted to cry out, *It's my subterfuge, my deceit I can't bear.* She said, 'Whatever the word is, I want to wash my hands of it. Clean break.' She took a trembly breath. 'So goodbye, darling Jim, good luck.' She turned for the door.

McQuade said desperately, 'Sarah?'

She stopped, and looked back at him. He took a deep breath and said: 'Let's get married. On Monday.'

She stared at him.

427

Suddenly he wanted to laugh with happiness. 'It's as clear as day what we've got to do! Yet we're about to go our separate ways! If we do we may never find each other again. Which is ridiculous. So – let's get married!' He went to her.

'On Monday? . . .' she said. 'And then? Where do I go, while you're off at the wars?'

'To this cottage I've rented. There're worse places for a honeymoon.' He took her in his arms. 'Then when the *Bonanza* comes in, you go and live aboard until I come back. Or you can go back to Boston and when this is over I'll come and fetch you and we'll live happily ever after!'

She looked up at him, and suddenly tears brimmed; then she buried her face against his chest. *Oh God! Oh God! How was she ever going to admit all the lies she had told him, all the deceit?* How would he ever trust her after that? He repeated: 'Live happily ever after, Sarah! And with all the money in the world! We're going to have a wonderful life!'

She took a deep anguished breath. God, how would he ever believe that she hadn't lied to him and seduced him for the money? She turned out of his arms. 'Please.'

He was astonished. 'What's all this, Sarah? Did you or did you not a few minutes ago tell me you loved me?'

She leaned her forehead against the door. She simply didn't know what to say, but had to say something, to gain time, to think. With all her heart she just wanted to make a clean breast and beg him to believe her. She heard herself say:

'The problem is I don't *know* whether I love you or not! I only *think* I do!' She stumbled on, 'Nor do I *know* that you really love me!' (That was partly true.) 'We've only known each other five fraught weeks! How do I know this isn't just some . . . *wild* infatuation?'

'It's not.' McQuade put his arms around her.

She opened her eyes.

'Please, Jim, I need to be alone for an hour.' She turned out of his arms, then looked at him with anguish. 'I need an hour, to compose myself. Please go downstairs and have a drink?'

McQuade wanted to laugh. She slumped her forehead against his shoulder.

'All right,' he whispered. He kissed her neck, then tilted her chin and kissed her moist eyes. 'Everything is going to be all right . . .'

51

She sat staring sightlessly at the window, torn between duty and love, desperately weighing the facts and probabilities for the last time.

What would happen if she walked out now? Where would she go? Back to Tel Aviv, and languish in her apartment without a job, hoping for him to call? How could she have any measure of control over events, over her man, over her life, if she did that? How long would this business take? Months, or even years? How long had it taken to find Adolf Eichmann? Klaus Barbie? How long had Mossad and Wiesenthal looked for Josef Mengele?

She heaved herself up off the bed and began to pace across the room, trying fiercely to concentrate.

She was deeply in love. So, of course she wanted to marry him. Not necessarily on Monday, she just wanted to stay with him for ever – so going back to Tel Aviv was out of the question, and so was going to live on his boat until this was over. For him she would sleep on bare boards, but no way could she languish on his boat ploughing up and down the Atlantic knowing what he was up against and waiting patiently for him to come back either triumphant or defeated. Or dead. No way could she turn her back on the case now.

And no way could she stick on the case in her 'official capacity' either; no way could she continue to deceive him. Doubtless one day she would lead him into an ambush, because *soon* Matt would get impatient and send the boys in to work him over to get Muller's assumed name out of him, as well as the print-out. In fact, she was damn sure the boys were in this hotel right now.

She gave a deep, tense sigh. And she couldn't betray her own side either. She had taken the Armed Services Oath, and a broken oath meant a court martial, and on a case as important as this to the collective heart of Israel, that meant a long, long time. No, there was no way she could betray her own side, she wanted Heinrich Muller as fervently as anyone. But she was simply not the right person for the job any more. She had disqualified herself – by falling in love.

Okay, that left only one thing to do: stay on the case *'unofficially'*. Quit the case officially and go to James McQuade with her heart in her hand and tell him the truth, tell him she was going to stick with him come hell or high water, and help him find Heinrich Muller, get the loot, then hand the bastard over to Mossad. That way she *still* did her duty to Mossad in the end. *And* to McQuade.

Okay. That only left the immediate problem of protecting him. Getting him out of this hotel before Matt and the boys closed in on him.

It took her two minutes to pack his bag. Then she telephoned the reception desk, confirmed that McQuade had paid the bill in advance, and asked for a porter to be sent up with the receipt. She gave him her car keys and told him to take their bags and the uniforms to her car. She tipped him twenty rand. Ten minutes later he returned the keys.

She looked at her watch. It was fifty minutes since McQuade had left. Just then the telephone rang. She snatched it up. 'Hullo!'

McQuade announced cheerfully, 'Your hour's up. I'll be up in five minutes.' He hung up.

She replaced the receiver. She went to the mirror and took an anxious look at herself. She was pale. She was dreading what she had to tell him now. What she said and did now could break their relationship and send him plunging off furiously into the night, never to return. She whispered fervently, 'Please help me, now, God . . .' Then the telephone rang again.

She snatched it up again. 'Hullo?'

Matt said grimly, 'Don't let him do any moonlight flits with those nice new uniforms provided by the Israeli taxpayer. Why has your baggage been taken from your room?'

She closed her eyes. So the boys *were* here. She said quietly, 'Request to be relieved of my duties immediately, sir.'

There was a stunned silence. Then: 'You will stay at your post, young lady!'

'Then I hereby resign my commission, sir.'

'Your resignation is hereby refused, woman! You will remain at your post or face court martial! You are subject to the Armed Services Act!'

'And that Act says that no officer shall be required to obey an order that is illegal or immoral!'

'There's nothing unlawful or immoral about your orders! And you accepted the assignment!'

She clenched her teeth, then said quietly, 'Circumstances have changed. I'm quitting this case. And getting married.'

She quietly but firmly put the telephone down.

McQuade rode up in the gilded elevator with four other people. He was feeling on top of the world. He was going to marry the most wonderful girl and things were going his way thanks to her. Those uniforms were masterpieces and he was going to be very rich indeed and they were going to live happily ever after. One of the women smiled at him. 'You look as if you've had a winning streak?'

He grinned at her. 'Yes, I have.'

The elevator stopped on the fifth floor and the two women got out. McQuade smiled at the two men remaining. The elevator rose and stopped on the seventh floor. They all got out.

One man turned left, the other right. He hurried down the corridor, then entered the room immediately before McQuade's. McQuade strode down the corridor behind him.

As he came abreast of the room before his, an arm reached out and grabbed his collar, the man who had gone in the other direction raced up behind him, and McQuade disappeared inside.

In one shocking jolt McQuade was wrenched out of the corridor, a hand over his mouth, and then he was crashing onto a bed. He sprawled on his side, his mouth clamped shut by a hard hand, his left arm wrenched up behind his back. He lay there, shocked, immobilized, his twisted arm in agony. Then another man was standing over him. He was big. He said in a thick South African accent: 'Sorry to do this to you, Mr McQuade.' He put his hand in his jacket pocket, pulled out a wallet, flicked it open: 'Sergeant van Tonder, South African police. Now, we'd like to make this easy for you, so if you cooperate we'll take the pressure off your arm.' He paused. 'As you probably know, you are under suspicion of murder in Namibia.' He smiled. 'As it happens, sir, I don't believe you're guilty. I personally believe that *you* are looking for the murderer of Jakob and his family. Now, all I want to do is help you – we are both after the same chap, hey.' He cocked his eyebrows encouragingly. 'But you're at a disadvantage, sir, because you are not an expert policeman, with all due respect. But, *me* . . .?' He smiled. 'Not only am I an expert, but I have the whole South African police force behind me to catch this man. For *us*.' He smiled down at McQuade. 'All I need is the name of the man you are looking for, sir.' He raised his eyebrows encouragingly again. 'So let's have it, and finish this nonsense? But,' he held up a finger, 'one peep and it's going to be unpleasant.' He said to the man holding McQuade, 'Let go his mouth.'

The man took his hand away. McQuade flexed his sore lips.

'Okay, Klaas, let him sit up.'

The pressure came off McQuade's arm, and the relief was enormous. But the man still held him half-locked. McQuade got up into a seated position. He glared. 'We're in the

433

independent state of Bophuthatswana and the South African police have no jurisdiction here!'

Sergeant van Tonder smiled. 'Absolutely correct. Except that we're collaborating with the Bophuthatswana police. And with the Namibian police.' He said to Klaas, 'Let go of him.'

The man released his wrist. McQuade massaged his bicep, his mind racing.

'Show me your warrant. If you're police you didn't need to pounce on me, you'd have arrested me normally.'

Sergeant van Tonder frowned, then appealed to his colleague, 'Mr McQuade doesn't believe us, hey? So we'll just have to take him to the police station.'

'Bullshit! Show me your warrant!'

There was a crack across his face as the man swiped him. McQuade saw stars. He sprawled on the bed, shocked, his ears ringing.

'What's the man's name?' van Tonder said softly.

McQuade scrambled up, but the hand flashed again and there was another explosion in his head. Klaas grabbed at his arm again, but McQuade whirled and swiped him blindly in the face with his elbow, and the man sprawled backwards. McQuade whirled the other way and saw the sergeant lunging at him with a karate blow. McQuade blocked it, his right fist swung with all his might into the man's guts and he gasped and staggered. Then Klaas came bounding in an avalanche of bloodied fury, and all McQuade knew was red-black stars and the breath knocked out of him. He crashed into the wall with the bloodied avalanche after him, and he butted his forehead furiously against the wild face and swung his fist with all his might again, and Klaas staggered backwards. McQuade reeled wildly for the door, bloodied, stumbling, but van Tonder seized him by the collar and slung him, and at the same moment the door shook and Sarah cried, *'Open up or I'm calling the management!'*

McQuade sprawled. Sergeant van Tonder wrenched the

door open and grabbed furiously at Sarah, but she jerked back, and squirted something from a canister. Van Tonder reeled back into the room, his hands clutching his screwed-up face. Sarah plunged into the room, slammed the door behind her, bounded at Klaas as he reached his feet, and squirted her canister. He collapsed back against the wardrobe, clutching his bloodied face.

McQuade scrambled up, shaking, astonished. Sarah stood in the middle of the room, eyes blazing, then she bounded at Klaas, grabbed his hair and wrenched back his head. He looked at her through his fingers, his eyes streaming. She snorted, '*You*.' She rammed her hand into his jacket pocket and pulled out a set of car keys, then gave him another squirt with the canister. He collapsed with a gasp, clutching his face. She turned on Sergeant van Tonder and gave him another squirt, making him gasp. She frisked him in a flash for car keys and found none. She snapped: '*Who the hell are you?*' The man clutched his face, his eyes streaming. Sarah snapped: '*Do you tell me, or do you want another dose of Mace?*'

The man turned his head away. 'Bazil Cohen,' he gasped. 'Jewish Defence Organization . . .'

She snorted: 'Better stick to your ledgers, Bazil.' She turned back to her other victim. She held the canister up and hissed: 'Just you leave him alone, huh?' She glared, then backed off across the room, her canister of Mace at her hip like a pistol. The two men were still clutching their faces. McQuade stared at them all, absolutely astonished. Sarah turned and grabbed the door handle. She flung it open and grabbed McQuade's hand.

She ran him down the corridor towards the emergency stairway.

435

52

They snatched their luggage from Sarah's car, slung it in the Landrover, and roared out onto the dark highway. He swung left, away from Johannesburg. No car was following. He roared away into the night. He was still shaky.

'Where are we going?' she asked.

'That depends on what you've got to tell me! Starting right now!'

Sarah closed her eyes. Boy, she had really fucked it up with him now. 'The whole truth, right?'

'*Right.*'

'Then I've got to trust you, James McQuade!' she cried. 'Because if you tell *them* I told you this, it's probably the firing squad for me if I ever set foot back in Israel. So trust me, and be my love, or drop me off right now and let me disappear.'

'*Israel?*'

'Please don't interrupt. I'll answer questions afterwards.' She took a shaky breath. 'Until half an hour ago I worked for Mossad. Half an hour ago I unilaterally resigned. Those two guys who rolled you – the younger one is also Mossad, the older guy is a local in the Jewish Defence Organization who was brought along today to use his accent to impersonate a South African policeman.'

'*Jesus Christ!*'

'I promise you I didn't know they were going to roll you, and swear to God I didn't lead you into an ambush. My job today was simply to hand over the uniforms to you and to stick with you. I *suspected* that I'd be followed, because that's elementary tactics, but I didn't know for sure until I heard the banging in the next room when they were working you

436

over.' She turned to him imploringly. 'I swear it! On all that's holy!'

'Go on!'

'And I swear to God I love you!'

He glared at the road furiously. *'Your assignment was to seduce me?'*

'My assignment was a hell of a lot more than that! My assignment was to follow you, cheat you, betray you, steal, lie, beat you up – even seduce poor Lisa van Rensburg! In short, absolutely everything necessary to find out what information you have on Heinrich Muller – the State of Israel doesn't give a damn what dirty tricks it plays to catch that bastard! Nor did I until I found myself falling in love with you. Now I'm in an impossible situation of divided loyalties. So I've quit!'

Jesus, he could not believe this. 'And how do I know that this confession isn't just another Mossad trick?!'

'"The punishment of the liar is that he is not believed even when he speaks the truth"?' She sighed angrily. 'The answer is, you don't! You have only my word for it.'

'And you've told Mossad that you've quit?'

'I've told my boss. Matt.'

'Jesus, Matt's your boss? And he knows that you've run off with me into the night? Well, you won't get that computer print-out from me, baby, because it's safely locked away in a bank deposit box! Did he wish you luck?'

She turned to him angrily. 'No, he did not wish me luck! He gave me a rocket and ordered me to stay at my post or face court martial! Legally, I still work for the State of Israel until my resignation is accepted. As soon as they find out I've done a moonlight flit, legally I'll be suspended from duty and a warrant will be issued for my arrest – which is unenforceable outside the State of Israel. That's the *legal* position. The *factual* position is that I've told them I'm walking off the job for reasons of conscience, and right now I'm sitting in this vehicle with my heart in my hand.'

He glared furiously through the windscreen, bemused. 'Do you really risk the firing squad? Because if so I'm taking you straight back to your post!'

'To my bed-post, huh?' She smiled mirthlessly. 'Technically, they could throw the book at me. But in practice they wouldn't dare risk the scandal that Mossad sends its agents out to screw innocent marine biologists and blackmail poor lesbians in the civil service for classified information – South Africa is a friendly state to Israel, remember. There'll probably only be a disciplinary inquiry, so I'll be dismissed from the Army, stripped of my pension and spend a year in the stockade while all this goes on.'

'The *Army?*'

'I'm only on secondment to Mossad. I'm a mere lieutenant in Signals. This assignment came up in a hurry, I was pulled off base because I've got good tits – or so they say. And I'm "unattached".' She added: 'Or was.'

McQuade was having difficulty grappling with all this. 'So is Buckley even your real *name*, for God's sake?'

'Oh, minor detail. Sarah, indeed. But Sarah Buchholz – close to Buckley. Ancestry, German. Lieutenant Sarah Buchholz, Israeli Army, at your service.'

McQuade was amazed. 'But you *sound* so American.'

'My parents are naturalized American citizens, I was born there, educated there, I only went to Israel after college.'

'Why?'

'Youth. Adventure. My father survived Hitler's holiday camps, felt it was my duty, et cetera.'

'So are you in fact Jewish?'

'You mean I don't *look* Jewish? My nose-job was *that* good?' She smiled mirthlessly. 'Go to Israel and you see them all shapes and sizes and colours, from Scandinavian to Ethiopian. I'm half Jewish – whatever that means. My mother is as Aryan as they come. But if you mean am I kosher, no.'

'But did you ever work for the *Christian Science Monitor?*'

'No. I did a BA in journalism, then went straight to Israel.

But if you had telephoned the *Monitor*, you'd have been told that Miz Sarah Buckley was somewhere in southern Africa on a busman's holiday. Mossad has friends all over. These alibis are solidly worked out.'

'But how the *hell* did you know I was going to get on that bloody plane in London?'

'I don't know. By the time I got my marching orders, all I knew was that you'd given Wiesenthal's boys the slip in Vienna. But you were picked up and followed in England. I arrived the next morning and waited on twenty-four-hour alert at Heathrow airport. Apparently, there were other girls waiting at other airports. But I was the lucky one.'

'And Matt is Mossad too? He's your boss here?'

'Yes, he got out here ahead of me. Because evidently Wiesenthal suspected you were on your way back.'

He said wonderingly, 'But those uniforms?'

'They come from Mossad's Clever Chaps Department who can produce anything from a Mozart opera to a police uniform overnight. Jetted out here by scheduled El Al.'

He said bitterly, 'And have you done other jobs for Mossad? Using your vital attributes.'

She said flatly, 'Once. To trap a nuclear scientist who was telling state secrets, but the Mossad boys nailed him before I had to drop my knickers.'

'But your come-on was so successful that when my case came up they immediately thought of Lieutenant Buchholz?'

'Okay. But can you please not say that again?'

He said sarcastically, 'Forgive me, but it's been a big day for surprises.'

'And may I again point out that I was doing my duty! In the highly important business of catching Heinrich Muller!'

'An objective you have now abandoned?'

'Of course I still want him brought to justice!' she cried. 'But I've had to quit as a matter of conscience because I've fallen in love with you and that conflicts with my duty! I've blown my cover, haven't I? I blew it when I stopped them

439

mauling you, and now I've come clean with you so I'm no further use to Mossad, am I?' She glared at him. '*But*, I now want to help *you* catch him. And you can extract your damn information from him. Hang him up by his thumbs if you like. Then when you've finished with him, give him to me, to hand over to the Israelis.'

He glared. 'So you *still* want to work *unofficially* for Mossad?'

'I want Heinrich Muller,' she cried. 'And you want Heinrich Muller to tell you where the loot is! You regard Mossad as your enemy because if they find Muller first you lose the loot, but I *want* you to have that loot! You stumbled on it first and you have the moral right.' She glared at him. 'But *don't* . . . please *don't* . . . ask if I'm after that loot too, or you can stop this Landrover right here and wave me goodbye for ever.' She looked at him, challengingly. 'I've never had any money apart from my salary and I don't *want* any more! I don't give a *shit* what you do with the money.'

McQuade started to speak but she cut in:

'Let me finish, Jim . . . And please listen carefully because this is the last time I'll mention this: so uninterested am I personally in this Nazi loot that I really want you to drive straight to the Mossad safe-house in Johannesburg, tell them everything you know, and collaborate with them. Let *Mossad* help you find the bastard . . .' She held up a finger. 'This is the last time I'll make this sales pitch, so listen to it, Jim! Mossad has three men out here this red-hot minute, trying to find out *through* me what the name is that Muller's using. They rolled you tonight because I had failed to extract the name from you with blandishments, and I'd phoned the boss and told him I was walking off the job for reasons of conscience. Now these three are only the tip of the iceberg, Jim. One phone call and there'll be a plane-load of Mossad guys out here. And believe me, those guys are *good*.' She snorted. 'Those two guys who rolled you tonight? Forget them. Only Steven, the younger one, is a professional. Tonight was a blunder. That was Panic

Action, by Matt, because I told him I was quitting. Believe me, if any of the others had tackled you, you'd have been out of that hotel without your feet touching the ground. The only reason you haven't been put through the wringer already and told everything is because Mossad hoped that I'd get it out of you politely.' She took a breath, then shook her head at him. 'But now that I've walked out and Matt's bungled it, they've got *nothing* to lose, and *everything* to gain, by doing it the easy way.'

McQuade glared at the road.

'So what are you recommending?'

Sarah took a tense breath.

'As my last official function before I am formally put on the Israeli shit-list, I am urging you to go with me to Mossad and throw your lot in with them. Make a deal with them. Tell them what you know in exchange for the use of their big battalions, but after they've found Heinrich Muller they must let you have him long enough to enable you to find that loot . . . Just think of the *work* it would save you . . . The *risk*. The time, the money.'

'And you really think they'd make a deal like that?'

She looked at him grimly. 'Your trust in me is on the line, Jim McQuade, and my answer is I don't know . . . I'm only a girlie in Signals.'

'Well I *do* know — Heinrich Muller will be out of the country without *his* feet touching the ground and the whole damn business will be out of my control. Once they've got him, Israel will play it by the book. He'll be assigned a lawyer, he'll be kept in top security pending his trial, the international press will be bellowing the whole story from the rooftops and every treasure-hunter unhung will be after my submarine. And so will the South African government, and SWAPO, and the German government — I've taken legal advice.'

'So your answer is No?'

'Right.'

She sighed. 'Okay. At least I tried.' She took an uptight breath. 'So, will you trust me? And let me come with you? Two heads are better than one, and I'm not exactly helpless.' She gripped his arm, and he was astonished at the strength of her fingers. 'So let me help you catch Heinrich Muller. And then after you've got your loot we'll hand him over to Mossad together.'

'And if I say no?'

She still held his arm.

'Tonight you asked me to marry you. And my answer to that is, I love you but I will not marry you under these circumstances. Even if I did I would not go and live on your boat until you come back from the wars. Anyway, Mossad would have me off that boat within five minutes. So? If you say No, I'm not sure yet what I'll do. All I know for sure is that I'm in contravention of the Armed Services Act and the Official Secrets Act and I've got to face that music sometime. If I face it now, it's straight into the stockade. But if I do it after you and I have caught Heinrich Muller, I'll be smelling of roses . . .'

PART TEN

53

McQuade's safe-house was not much of a place. There were only four rooms, in a line with inter-connecting doors. The centre was the kitchen and living room, divided by a formica-top counter trying to look like a bar, with a collection of swizzle-sticks and a bullfight poster. The furniture was vinyl and the floor was linoleum trying to look like red Spanish tiles.

'But what do you expect for a hundred rand a week?' Sarah said. Nor was it safe. A low barbed-wire fence surrounded the plot, the gate did not lock, the building was surrounded by bushes and trees giving ample cover to anybody approaching, and the windows were unbarred. In short, the place was indefensible.

'It's fine,' Sarah reassured him. 'If those guys find out where you are, *no* place will be defensible. This is remote and inconspicuous, that's what you want. And the view's pretty.'

Remote, yet only thirty minutes from Pretoria, forty from Johannesburg; inconspicuous, yet there were half a dozen homesteads up the valley belonging to retired people. A few miles away was a tarred road to Pretoria and beyond were the hills around Hartebeestpoort Dam, so there was substantial traffic. And the view *was* pretty. With the sunrise a mist hung over the valley and the hills of Hartebeestpoort looked on fire. That Sunday morning they lay close together in the double bed and watched the sunrise. 'It's you I'm worried about,' McQuade said. 'What they'll do to you.'

'My conscience is clear. I'm not working *against* them, am I? What I'm doing is helping you to find Heinrich Muller, which is helping *them*.' She added: 'Though they probably

445

wouldn't see it that way right now. So, let's get on with it, in a soldierly manner. In that connection I have a suggestion.'

'And so have I.'

'Well, hear mine first.' She held up a finger. 'I'm not asking for details, names, addresses, nothing. That's our deal, I don't want you to think I may tiptoe away and telephone the boys. I don't want you to tell me where your short-list and the print-out is. But I need to know your plan, your overall strategies, so I can contribute and perhaps improve on them. First of all, how fit are you? You were pretty shaky after the boys rolled you last night. You don't get much exercise on that ship, do you, and you drink a lot, like most seamen.'

'You've kept me good company.'

'But I'm *fit*. If you're going to catch this bastard, you're very likely to have to make a hell of a physical effort. Endurance. So I suggest that every day you put yourself through a strict training programme.' She flicked his chest. 'You're a strong man. Not bad shape, but not good either. So, every day before going anywhere we jog at least four miles. Every day the Five Basic Exercises for Men – lots of press-ups, leg exercises. And a high-energy diet: liver, raw vegetables, juices, cereals, pasta, potatoes, and vitamin pills.' She added, 'And I'll do it all with you.'

'But you're in be-yootiful condition.'

'You haven't got a firearm, have you?'

'Yes, a .38 revolver.'

'Oh. Do you know how to use it? Accurately?'

'Yes. I've also got a shotgun.'

'And how're you at unarmed combat? Ever learn judo?'

'No. Boxing at school.'

'So you need some coaching, pal. And coaching's what I'm good at, I was an instructor for a while. Do you know what to do if somebody goes at you with a knife? Pulls a gun on you? Puts a half-nelson on you? Or an arm-lock?'

'Not really.' He propped himself up on his elbow and smiled at her. She was beautiful and he knew with absolute certainty that she was truly trying to help him, she didn't give a damn about the money, she was only worried about him avoiding injury in his madness of trying to catch Heinrich Muller when he could invoke the entire resources of Mossad – and he knew with absolute certainty that this was the girl for him, she was putting her career on the line for him. 'So every day, while I'm off at the wars, you're going to cook up a storm, and when I come home you're going to knock the living shit out of us?'

She looked at him solemnly. 'Yep. Until the time comes when you *really* need me. To help do the dirty work. Which it will.'

'Well, I've got a better suggestion.'

'There is no better suggestion! It's *vital*. Goddammit, I'm just asking that you let me make you fit for the job! I love you and I don't want to see you made mincemeat of . . .!'

'It's a deal. But today's Sunday. And I've got no running shoes. Nor health food. But I do have a gallon of good wine. And I haven't seen you for a week. And this is a perfectly good bed? The health-kick starts tomorrow.'

She had studied the ceiling through this: then she slid her eyes to his.

'There's a perfectly good patch of lawn out there where we can do a two-hour work-out without running shoes. *Then* we'll consider your booze and bed.'

The next four days seemed the toughest of his life. On Monday they drove into the village and bought running shoes and tracksuits. They then spent an hour driving around, taking random photographs of suitable male black faces with Sarah's telephoto camera. They took the film to a chemist to have developed, then drove back to the cottage and put on their new running gear. Every one of McQuade's muscles felt stiff from the work-out she had given him yesterday.

'We take it easy the first day,' she said. 'If your heart

starts pounding, we'll slow down to a brisk walk for a while, then jog again. Take deep, regular breaths. Get into a rhythm.'

They started down the hillside track, and every muscle groaned. She jogged beside him easily, her hair in plaits. 'Okay? So now lengthen your stride, loosen up.' She lengthened her stride and his stiffness screeched. He pounded along abreast of her, but after a minute the stiffness began to go, although the knocking was now coming into his chest. She kept the pace for a quarter mile, glancing at him, then she slowed down again.

'Just shuffle along. Let your arms hang.'

She slopped along beside him, her arms loose. After another quarter mile she said, 'Okay, lengthen your stride again. If it gets too much, drop back.' She surged ahead, her long legs fluid, her arms swinging rhythmically, her plaits jouncing. He pushed himself and caught up with her. She did not pace him faster, but strode along for another minute, then slowed down to a stop. He dropped his hands on his knees.

'Good. That's two thousand paces.'

McQuade panted. 'How d'you know that's two thousand?'

'I counted. Okay, now keep walking. Briskly.'

She strode on down the track, McQuade working hard to keep up with her. 'You're in not too bad a shape. In a minute you'll feel rested,' she said.

'*Rested?*'

'Then we'll jog back. A total of five kilometres, not a bad beginning. This afternoon we'll do it again.'

'God!'

She swung around and begun to jog back up the road. 'Slow if you have to, but keep shuffling.'

He did not have to shuffle but when he reached the steep track up to the cottage, he just had to walk it. Sarah gave him a smile and ran up the hillside, disappearing into the trees. McQuade toiled up, his legs shaky. She was waiting for him on the lawn, her face shiny with sweat. She was eating an orange and had peeled one for him.

'Eat that. Lie down if you like. Knees bent, arms out. Let your exhaustion flood out into mother-earth. Then we'll do the Five Basic Exercises.'

'Oh, God.'

'That's how you get fit. By pushing yourself. Then we'll practise some of those falls again, then you can have a sleep, after lunch.'

Lunch was liver, potatoes, spinach, raw onions and yoghurt. He felt almost too exhausted to eat, but once he started he was ravenous. Afterwards, he could have fallen asleep at the counter. 'Come on.' She led him through to the double bed. He collapsed onto it. She knelt and buried her face into his sweaty neck and growled like a tigress. 'It's a pity to waste that loud smell of man. After your run tonight, and after a steaming hot bath,' she fluttered her eyelashes, 'I'll give you a *massage* . . .'

That nightfall, after another gruelling five kilometres, he sat slumped in a steaming bath, drinking his first beer, and he felt marvellous, his muscles zinging and his skin glowing. The cold beer went down into his gut like a balm and tasted like the best food he had ever eaten. She sat beside him in the bath, her legs over the rim, her face radiant with health, her black hair piled on top of her head. 'You realize that a big gun like Heinrich Muller is likely to be well guarded? And not only by bodyguards, but by all kinds of electronic gear and alarms. Do you know anything about that?'

'I've been to the major security companies and I've got their brochures. After I've identified Muller, I'll study his set-up.'

'I'll look at those brochures, security was part of my job. But once you know what kind of gear Muller's using, you must find an expert to advise you.'

'Who? I'm not trusting any of Mossad's friends.'

'Look, Jim,' she said quietly, 'I want you to succeed. I want you *alive*, not torn to pieces. So you must know absolutely everything about Muller's set-up, not rush in like a bull at a gate. I'm saying that *when* you've identified Muller and found out what security system he uses, we look for an expert in that system. He need not know whose system you're going to crack.' She paused, then went on, 'There's something else I must warn you about.'

He put his hand on her lovely knee. 'Go on.'

'Amongst the top guys in the Nazi organization here, Muller must be royalty, and they've got their ears to the ground. The worst thing you could do is ask any indiscreet questions about your man. Because it would get straight back and he'd disappear. And so would you.'

'Yes, I realize that.'

'It's one of the things Mossad is terrified you'll do, as an amateur. It could be very tempting if you think you've found somebody in the know. And there's something else you must understand fully, Jim. The Nazi or neo-Nazi organization in South Africa and Namibia is a powerful one.'

'Is that the official Mossad view?'

'Yes. I was briefed before leaving.' She went on earnestly: 'And the Nazis are ambitious. They're behind the Right Wing movement here. And it is the Right Wing which is the real threat to South Africa, because they intend to take over the country and run it on Nazi lines.' She looked at him. 'The Right Wing is fronted by the AWB. And too many people tend to regard them as "lunatic fringe". They're not – they're very powerful.' She frowned. 'The AWB is a *blatantly* Nazi movement, and Heinrich Muller must be slap bang in the middle of them. And they intend taking over this country, by hook or by crook.'

McQuade was even more impressed with Johan Lombard's views. Sarah went on soberly, 'The point of this little lecture is that a big percentage of the South African police would support an AWB takeover – legal or illegal. It therefore stands to reason that Heinrich Muller is likely to have some very important friends in the police. Who will deal very swiftly with anybody who tries to give their man trouble.' She looked at him. 'Anybody who is heard to ask indiscreet questions. Who is seen snooping around the man's property . . .'

'Old farmers' trick to keep school boys out of their fruit orchards.'

He had bought a pound of raw salt. He took a 12-bore cartridge, prised off the cardboard cap, and tipped out the lead pellets. Then he poured salt into the half-empty cartridge, on top of gun-powder. He packed the salt tight, then replaced the cardboard cap. He did the same with more cartridges. He loaded them into the pump-action shotgun. Sarah followed him outside.

He had set up an empty petrol drum on the lawn; three paces from it was a big cardboard box, three paces from that a dead, plucked chicken, bought for dinner, hung from the washing line. McQuade stood ten paces from the targets, aimed at the drum, fired, worked the pump action, fired at the box, pumped again and fired at the chicken.

The drum had been knocked over, but the paintwork was undamaged. The box had been blown five paces, the cardboard slightly pitted with salt: the chicken skin was embedded with salt but unpunctured.

'It will sting a man like hell,' McQuade said. 'Stop him in his tracks. Close up it would knock him over . . .'

She leapt at his back and flung her forearm across his throat, while her other hand swept under his armpit and around his neck and pressed hard. McQuade dropped to his knee, choking, and rolled her over his shoulder, onto her back. She grinned up at him. 'Throw me *hard*. I know how to fall. And now what?'

'I jump up and kick the hell out of you.'

451

She got to her feet lightly. 'And if you have to kill me?'

'Here.' He brought his hand down behind her ear.

'Okay.' She danced away from him, then charged at him furiously with an imaginary weapon on high; he blocked it, spun his hip into hers, grabbed her and swung her off balance, but stopped short of throwing her. She twisted out of his grasp and aimed a kick at his testicles but he twisted and took it on his thigh, and grabbed her ankle and half-flung her.

She staggered backwards. 'Okay,' she said, 'last one.'

She lunged at him and flung her left arm around his neck and wrenched him down into a head-lock. McQuade's right arm shot up over her shoulder, he twisted his hand into her face and squeezed her nose between his fingers and heaved her head back. She released him immediately, gasping. 'I'm sorry,' he said.

She rubbed her nose. 'Remember to get your fingers onto his eyes as well. So.' She got him into the same position and gouged – and sent him staggering. 'Gouging of the eyes will make anyone panic and let go. Then you finish him off.' She let go of him. 'All right, go'n have your shower and get kitted up.'

McQuade straightened his tunic and walked towards the house. He mounted the steps and knocked.

The door opened. He saluted politely and put on a strong South African accent. 'Good afternoon, madam. Are you Mrs Jones?'

Sarah frowned. 'I am.'

'Sergeant van Niekerk, madam, from the Car Theft Division. Sorry to trouble you, but can I please have a word with your husband?'

'What about?' Sarah demanded.

'Nothing to worry about, madam, this is a routine inquiry in this area because of all the recent car-thefts.'

'It *can't* be a "routine" inquiry!' Sarah said. 'It's a very

452

specific inquiry because Mr Jones' name and address is on your accused's hit-list!'

McQuade started again. 'There's no problem with your husband, madam, but we're making urgent inquiries because of all the recent car-thefts.'

'Our car hasn't been stolen, has it?'

'No, madam, but we have evidence suggesting it might be. Can we speak to your husband, please?'

Sarah gasped, '*Might* be?'

'Yes, madam, we have evidence indicating that a gang of car-thieves intend to steal your car, hey? So we better talk to your husband about it, warn him about security.'

'Goodness!' Sarah said. 'I'll call him right away! *Do* come in.'

He entered the living-room.

'Cap,' she said.

'Damn,' McQuade said. He took it off.

'Okay. Next one.'

McQuade returned to the verandah. Sarah returned to the doorway. She frowned and said, 'Does my husband know you're coming? Did you make an appointment? Did you telephone?'

'No madam, we're calling on the houses in this area as a matter of urgency because of all the recent car-thefts. We have reason to believe that your cars may be the next to be stolen.'

'You can talk to me. My husband's sick in bed.'

'I'm sorry to hear that, madam,' McQuade said, 'but I'd like to talk to you both at the same time so you're both aware of the danger. We are having tremendous trouble with car-thefts.'

'Certainly not! He's very ill indeed!'

'I'm sorry, but we *must* just see him long enough to show him certain photographs of suspects, to see if he can identify any of them. We know of a gang who are stealing cars, and we found your name and address on their list of targets, madam.'

453

'Absolutely impossible. Show *me* the photographs.'

McQuade opened the file and exhibited the photographs they had taken at random in the village. 'Have you ever seen any of these men?'

'No. And I'm sure my husband hasn't either.'

'Madam,' McQuade said sadly, 'then we'll just have to get the magistrate to issue a subpoena on your husband to assist us.' He cajoled, 'It'll only take a minute, madam.'

Sarah switched tack abruptly to confuse him. 'He's out.'

McQuade took it in his stride. 'When will he be home, madam?'

'I don't know. He's at a business meeting.'

'Okay, I'll call tomorrow.'

'Not *"call"*. That implies a phone call. And she may ask if he can call you.'

'I'll come around again tomorrow, madam.'

'I'll get him to telephone you to make an appointment.'

'No, I'm out all the time on this case and I won't get the message for twenty-four hours at least.'

'Well, give me the number of your officer-in-charge. He'll get the message to you, surely?'

'I *am* the officer in charge of this case, madam, and it's best I contact you.'

'What police station are you from?'

'Madam, I'm so busy I won't even go to the police station in the next twenty-four hours.'

'I *insist*!'

'Very well, madam,' McQuade sighed.

'Surely, "Okay"?'

'Okay, madam.' He pulled out his notebook. He scribbled the telephone number of the cottage, then said, 'Ask for Woman Sergeant Taylor. She's my assistant.'

'But you only give that number as a last resort,' Sarah said. 'All right. Now let's do Mr Jones. You've been invited into the living-room.'

'Then let's get the run over with. I need a beer.'

That night, lying in his arms, she said, 'You're tense. Psych yourself up for the role. Remember you're doing what is morally *right*. Even if you're committing a crime by impersonating a policeman. Just think of those extermination camps.' She squeezed him. 'You're well prepared. You're pretty fit, and you've got a good plan, and tomorrow's only the first day – tomorrow is just a dummy-run, so don't be tense. You're going to *catch* the bastard!'

54

Most of the commuters had already got to work when McQuade arrived in the Johannesburg suburb of Rivonia the next morning. There were the long, high, brown walls extending down the long lush tree-lined avenue, surrounding the home of Hendrik Pieter Strauss.

He stopped the Landrover outside the big wooden doors, picked up his file, opened it, pulled the photograph of Heinrich Muller out of the envelope, and studied it one more time. He thrust it back into the envelope and got out.

He walked to the big doors, and rang the bell.

A grille was opened by a black man in uniform. McQuade spoke in Afrikaans. 'Good morning. Police. Is Mr Strauss home, please?'

The black man said, 'Please wait one minute.' He disappeared. McQuade heard the guard speaking on a telephone. He reappeared and opened the gate.

McQuade walked through, into a magnificent garden of sweeping lawns, flowerbeds, trees. The drive swept up to a big, double-storied house, with colonnades and a wide portico. A Mercedes sedan was parked under it. McQuade ran his eyes over the house, trying to remember details. Beyond the house were more gardens, a row of garages. No dogs were to be seen. They came to the portico. Wide marble steps led up to the imposing front door. The guard rang the bell.

The door was opened by an elderly black maid, who showed him into a drawing room. 'The master is coming.'

The black guard had disappeared. Suddenly McQuade's nervousness was gone: this was just a practice run. An elderly man came bustling into the room with a big smile, and McQuade knew he had drawn a blank. He was tall and aristocratic, which Heinrich Muller could never be. 'Good morning!' Mr Strauss exclaimed.

'Good morning, sir,' McQuade said respectfully in an Afrikaans accent, 'sorry to trouble you, but I'm Sergeant van Niekerk of the Car-Theft Division.'

'Oh, yes?' Mr Strauss said earnestly.

'Sir, you may have heard about this recent spate of car-thefts we're having?' McQuade said. 'Anyway, our investigations have resulted in us getting hold of some documents drawn up by the thieves – a list of addresses where they intended to steal cars. Your address was on their list, so we want to warn you.'

'I *see*,' Mr Strauss said. '*Thank* you.'

McQuade opened the folder. 'Now, I see you've got a Mercedes out there. What's its number, year, model, please.'

Mr Strauss told him. 'And I also have a BMW.' He gave him those details.

McQuade noted them down. 'Well, both those cars are just the sort they steal, sir. They file off the engine serial number, respray it, and ship them off to Australia and New Zealand.'

'The swines,' Mr Strauss said in wonder.

'Have both your cars got immobilizer systems, sir? And alarms?'

'Yes.'

'Good, now, do any of these faces mean anything to you, sir?' McQuade pulled out the sheet of paper holding the mugshots of the men Sarah had photographed at random.

Five minutes later he walked back down the drive. He had drawn his first blank, but he was almost walking on air. *He had done it! The impersonation had gone off perfectly! Mr Strauss had suspected nothing!*

He got back into the Landrover, and roared off. He drove for two blocks, then pulled over to the verge.

He held his face for a moment, then fumbled his two lists out of the file and opened his street map.

He had to force himself to concentrate. The next Mr Strauss was number eleven on his list, but he lived only a few miles away.

The next three weeks were exhausting, and not because of the five-kilometre run that began and ended each day – that got easier and easier – but from the tension that built up before each knock he made on a door, which subsided into overwhelming relief as he walked back out, unsuccessful in identifying Heinrich Muller but intensely relieved at another successful impersonation of Sergeant van Niekerk. It also taught him something about human nature: everybody treats a policeman with great politeness because most people, although usually law-abiding, are disturbed at the sight of the uniform in their homes and almost gushy when they find out they are not in trouble. This gave him a great psychological advantage. Not once did he encounter the imperiousness for which Sarah had tried to prepare him, not once was he asked for further identification. In most cases he was immediately offered refreshment – one Mrs Strauss insisted he take away a fruit cake she had just baked, another Mrs Strauss asked him to lecture her housemaid on the serious view the law took of stealing sugar, while one Mr Strauss asked for legal advice on his impending divorce action. In each case McQuade was given earnest cooperation, and in four cases a Mr or Mrs Strauss solemnly identified one or more of the photographs as being of men they had seen behaving in a suspicious manner. In no case was Mr Strauss too busy to see him and only in three cases was he out. The return visits worried the hell out of McQuade lest Mr Strauss had in the meantime contacted his local police station in his desire to be cooperative: but this never happened. The houses these people lived in varied greatly; some were opulent, most were middle class in respectable suburbs, two were smallholdings and two were so unpretentious that McQuade was sure before he set eyes on Mr Strauss that he could be dismissed.

Most houses had burglar bars, and some had impressively aggressive dogs; but those that had no burglar-alarm warning-signs were unlikely to be occupied by Heinrich Muller. All these people spoke in both English and Afrikaans but only in two cases could McQuade detect a German accent and he could cross both off his list because one was squint in one eye and the other was too tall. He paid particular attention to teeth, for although patently false teeth would not be unusual, the owners of patently natural teeth could be dismissed: this was the case twice.

At the end of three weeks McQuade still considered he had reason to congratulate himself: his system was working. He could get into people's presence easily: he was daily more confident and although he had failed to identify Heinrich Muller he had eliminated sixteen of the suspects who lived in the environs of Johannesburg and Pretoria. The remaining two were both away.

And he was not so worried about 435 any more – that pressure was off him. It was the first news he looked for in the press every day: and it seemed clear that the Cubans were trying to play Clever Buggers, stall negotiations over the timetable of their troop withdrawal to give them time to wipe out UNITA. McQuade doubted they had any intention of leaving Angola at all, despite what Johan Lombard had said. SWAPO proclaimed that it was 'laughable' for South Africa to try to shift responsibility for Namibia's future onto Angola and Cuba. And so on. There were going to be more talks in Geneva and Chester Crocker, the United States Deputy Secretary of State for Africa, seemed to be running round like a dog on a tennis court, desperately trying to keep South Africa's peace-initiative alive, to persuade Russia to put pressure on Cuba to withdraw, trying to drum up support from other African leaders. It was all very confusing to your average reader like McQuade. Now Angola 'flatly rejected' South Africa's 'ridiculous offer' of peace in exchange for Cuban withdrawal and it was rumoured that she was preparing an

459

all-out offensive against UNITA by combined Cuban, Soviet and East German troops, that South Africa and America were hastily bolstering UNITA in anticipation of the onslaught. And now even Great Britain wondered whether South Africa's linkage of Cuban withdrawal to peace was not 'extraneous'. McQuade was astonished and angered. Of course Cuban withdrawal was not 'extraneous', madam – but if a no-nonsense politician like Maggie Thatcher sniffed at South Africa's offer, no way were the Marxist blacks and the Cubans going to give in. And now the South African Conservative Party and the AWB were hurrying to Namibia to drum up resistance amongst the whites, promising the 'spineless' South African government 'big trouble' if they 'sold out their kith and kin to 435 . . .'

McQuade tossed the newspaper aside. Oh, he wanted the bloody Cubans out *and* the AWB – but it was clear he had time on his side in which to sell his fishing company. And the backlash the AWB would create would slow down the government further . . .

It was Friday noon. He had had another good week. He now had to move onto those Strausses who lived in the Transvaal high veld, in the farming areas. There were five of them up there, spread over hundreds of miles. But it was not such a daunting task. Then he had to come back and look at the two remaining men in this area. Then? Then it was Namibia.

But today was Friday and surely no honest-to-God police-man would make enquiries like his on a weekend; he was going to spend two days in bed with his beautiful woman. *And no way was she going to make him run eight kilometres tonight . . .*

It was lunch-hour when he drove through the centre of Pretoria on his way home. On the corner, a black boy was selling newspapers. The board beside him cried: '*RUDOLF HESS IN HOSPITAL! CONDITION CRITICAL!*' McQuade shouted to the boy and held out a coin.

He speed-read the front page paragraphs whilst the lights were against him.

Rudolf Hess, aged 93, second-in-command to Adolf Hitler in Nazi Germany and who was sentenced to life imprisonment at the Nuremberg Trials in 1946, is critically ill. He has been removed from Spandau Prison, where he has spent the last forty-one years as the only inmate, to an intensive-care hospital in western Berlin.

In 1941 Rudolf Hess piloted a Luftwaffe aircraft alone from Germany to Scotland in a desperate bid to contact Winston Churchill and make peace between Germany and Great Britain. He had to parachute from his aircraft, was injured on descent, arrested and, his overtures rejected by Churchill, has been incarcerated ever since. At the subsequent Nuremberg Trials he was spared the gallows (the Russian judge strongly dissenting) because of his extraordinary mission. It is not clear to this day whether Hitler authorized this mission, or whether Hess, allegedly a little strange at this stage, acted on his own initiative.

The lights changed to green. McQuade drove across the intersection, through the centre of town, then swung onto the verge. He speed-read the rest of the news-item. There was a photograph of Rudolf Hess, a skinny, fatherly-looking type with thick eyebrows.

McQuade studied the photograph. It was hard to believe that this man was Adolf Hitler's deputy – a man so strong in personality that a demoniac Adolf Hitler and the rest of his brutal hierarchy approved him as Deputy Führer? This was the man who was as guilty as Adolf Hitler in his staggering crime against mankind, a mass-killer of innocent people. That picture of Hess gave him a new kind of courage. This Rudolf Hess, once deputy ruler of the strutting, war-mongering, genocidal Nazi Party, was now just a funny-looking frail man with skinny white legs and sagging singlet over a concave chest — *as was the great Heinrich Muller, former proud head of Adolf Hitler's dreadful Gestapo*.

McQuade sat there, thinking. When Rudolf Hess died, was there going to be some kind of public appearance by the Nazis in South Africa, as there had been when Dr Heusler died in the 1970s, as Johan Lombard had mentioned? Or a demonstration, like there had been in 1976, for Hess's release?

He drove off, looking for a public telephone. He called the German Club and asked if Johan Lombard was there.

'Come and have a beer, dear boy!' Johan cried. 'The boys are sulking about what the beastly Allies did to poor old Rudolf who never hurt a hair of a Jewish head!'

McQuade could not go to the club in his police uniform.

'Is there likely to be any public demonstration when he dies?'

'My dear boy, when Reichsleiter Rudolf Hess takes the dark journey to Valhalla, memorial services are going to blossom across this liberal land of ours like toadstools. The biggest will doubtless be in the Rebecca Street Cemetery right here in sunny Pretoria, where there's a big memorial to the German soldiers who died in both world wars. The Nasties will come out of the woodwork from far and wide for that, flags, Heil Hitlers, the works.'

McQuade's heart leapt. 'Will you be there?'

'You bet, dear boy, hiding behind a tombstone — so will every newspaperman. The laugh is that this German memorial is right next door to the Jewish mausoleum, we'll all probably be hiding in that to get our pictures.'

Pictures! Of course! 'Could I go with you?'

'Certainly, a cemetery is a public place.'

'Where can I rent a video camera?'

'I'll lend you mine, dear boy! Fully automatic.'

McQuade hurried back to the Landrover, grabbed the

newspaper again and opened it to the classified advertisements.

There were half a dozen firms that offered to video-film your wedding, graduation, bar-mitzvah, anything that moved. He hurried back to the telephone box.

'I want to have a video made of a funeral that's happening next week, but I don't want the cameraman to be conspicuous. That would upset people and be offensive.'

'Quite right, sir,' the man said solemnly.

'So I want the cameraman to be hidden somehow, in a nearby building or a car. Can you do that?'

'No problem, sir.'

'What are your charges?'

The man told him. McQuade telephoned two others, to compare prices. The man he liked the sound of best was a freelance, young and eager. McQuade said he would telephone again.

He felt lucky. If this worked he would have all the Nazis for miles around on film in one fell swoop! He thought; then banked up more coins and dialled Roger Wentland in Swakopmund. 'I'm in a coin-box so I must be brief. You've heard about Rudolf Hess? He's likely to die soon, and there're going to be memorial services for him all over the place. Can you find out where and when they are going to be held in Swakopmund and Windhoek?'

Roger was taken aback. 'I suppose so. Should be common knowledge.'

'Roger, can you hire some professional cameramen from a video-hire agency?' McQuade said. 'And get them to film these services for me? Trying to get every male face? Nobody must realize what's going on – so the cameraman must be *outside* the church, and film the people as they arrive and leave.'

'What's this for?' Roger demanded.

'Just believe me it's important. There's nothing illegal in

filming a memorial service, is there? So *do* it, Roger. And put the cost on the company's account.'

He returned to the Landrover, and thought excitedly: This could solve all the problems! He set off to find the Rebecca Street Cemetery.

Then he realized something. The Mossad boys would *certainly* know all about Rudolf Hess and what the Nasties in Pretoria were likely to do when he died. And if Jim McQuade had thought about being present, certainly those guys had thought about it. They wouldn't merely be looking for a man who looked like Heinrich Muller, they'd be looking for a man who looked like James McQuade, too. He would have to have some kind of disguise, and since Mossad knew his Landrover, he would have to rent a car.

He found the Rebecca Street Cemetery, on the outskirts of town. He found the German war memorial. He drew a map. There were many places to hide, but the best feature was the gateway to the cemetery. The car park was outside and everybody had to enter and leave on foot. A cameraman in a vehicle at the gate would film every face with ease. But a cameraman sitting in a car would be too conspicuous. He needed a covered van.

It was late afternoon when he got onto the road to the cottage, with four important new jobs done. Firstly, he had found a place that rented suitable panel-vans; secondly, he had telephoned the young freelance cameraman, who was called Oosthuizen, and hired him: he had been employed by attorneys for divorce cases and swore confidentiality, although McQuade had given him no reasons for his assignment. Thirdly, he had found out where to rent a television set and video-cassette player; and, fourthly, he had acquired some elementary disguise: from an optician called Frames he had bought his first-ever pair of spectacles, near-enough window-pane. From a chemist he had bought black hairdye.

But it might be weeks, months before Rudolf Hess died, so

there was no alternative but to keep going, looking for Mr Strauss.

But not till Monday. He was going to spend the weekend in bed, bed, bed, with his lovely woman.

PART ELEVEN

55

If Pretoria is the head of Afrikanerdom, the Transvaal is its throbbing heart. Out there, in the vast fertile high veld, live the real Afrikaner *volk*, the no-nonsense people for whom every word in the Bible is the pure word of God, who regard themselves as the chosen ones to whom He gave this promised land. They are a kindly if dour people who believe it is their God-given right and duty to govern the black man paternalistically, who is the son of Ham, intended to be hewers of wood and drawers of water. God delivered the Afrikaners from their enemies, first the glistening black hordes with their spears, then the brutal British soldiers with their scorched earth and concentration camps, and surely He will deliver them again from the raging godlessness of black communism, if only they stick to their guns and their holy bibles.

Early that Monday morning McQuade kissed Sarah goodbye and set out into the heartland of Afrikanerdom on the Great North Road. He had to work at it to maintain the self-confidence he had generated over the last weeks because now he was going into a different ball-game. If suburbanites hardly know any of the local policemen by sight, in the rural districts each Mr Strauss was quite likely to be on personal terms with the local police.

But by sunset he had his confidence back. He had visited the first Mr Strauss, been entertained to coffee and cake without the slightest suspicion, had solemnly inspected the security set-up, had discussed at length the immorality of this weak-kneed government who was selling the country down the river to the kaffirs, and had scratched another Hendrik

Strauss off his list. He stopped at the roadside, pulled on civilian clothes, spent that night in a small hotel in Nyl-stroom, and slept as if he had been pole-axed. On Tuesday he set off on the long journey to the next Mr Strauss. That afternoon he arrived in Pietersburg, with a large jar of home-made jam for his children and another Mr Strauss crossed off his list. He checked into a motel on the outskirts, then drove into town to look for a bar. He saw many posters announcing that tonight the Foreign Minister, Mr Pik Botha, would address a rally of government supporters in the Jack Botes Hall, and almost every poster had been defaced with the word *Veraaier*: 'traitor'. He realized that this was the meeting Johan Lombard had mentioned weeks ago, the meeting the AWB had vowed to break up. He parked his Landrover and went in search of the Jack Botes Hall.

He heard the noise from several blocks away.

The Foreign Minister had not yet arrived but the hall was packed and a crowd of about a thousand white people heaved and surged outside it, midst waving banners. They seemed to be divided into two camps, roaring at each other in Afrikaans, waving fists and hurling insults. There was a furious group of women in voortrekker costume waving banners which read 'Yankee Pik Botha Go Home'. There were many banners bearing the AWB colours and the big three-legged swastika. On the other side were the banners of the ruling government party. There were a lot of pressmen, and numerous uniformed policemen stood by while beyond, at a respectful distance, a thousand or more blacks watched the heaving, shoving, furious mob of their lords. And above all the noise rose the roaring chant from the AWB ranks: '*'n Kaffir is 'n kaffir en hy stink! 'n Kaffir is 'n kaffir en hy stink!*' (a kaffir is a kaffir and he stinks), their faces furiously contorted, spittle flying and fists waving, and hate rising up to the sky.

McQuade stared at this spectacle of Afrikanerdom tearing itself apart. He would never have believed this – Afrikaner hating Afrikaner, the Afrikaner government which had ruled this country for forty years under this siege of hate from Afrikaners. He began to try to make his way through the rear of the mob, to try to get inside. He kept to the government supporters' ranks. He pushed and squeezed his way between surging yelling people, until he came to the big doors. He peered over the heads. The stage was decked in the government party colours, but still empty, awaiting the arrival of the Foreign Minister and his local party dignitaries. Just then a new roar went up outside as the leader of the AWB, Eugene Terreblanche, arrived to break up the meeting.

His car pulled up outside the hall with its uniformed outriders on motorcycles, and policemen came forward to escort him. He shoved his way towards the steps surrounded by his armed brown-shirted bodyguards, in a roaring shoving screaming blaze of glory and hate, his bodyguards thrusting people aside; then, on cue, his bodyguards hefted him up onto their shoulders. Inside the hall people were now standing and shouting at each other, and suddenly all hell broke loose. On cue AWB supporters inside the hall started surging towards the stage to seize it for their leader, and roaring government supporters surged to stop them, and the fists started flying. In a moment half the hall was a screaming mass of fists and kicks and smashing chairs, Afrikaner fighting Afrikaner midst the shrieks of women and the whack and crunch of flesh and bone. And the first AWB thugs made it up onto the stage with wild fighting, government supporters charging and leaping furiously after them, fists and kicks and bodies flying, Afrikaner trying to hurl and drag and kick and punch Afrikaner off the stage midst the smashing crashing of furniture and the roaring and the screaming. Then Eugene Terreblanche burst into the madness, carried shoulder-high, and a greater roar went up.

It was the first time McQuade had seen the man in the flesh. He was about fifty, bearded and beefy and handsome, but it was the eyes that impressed: blue and piercing, blowtorches of eyes. But it was the bodyguards who made McQuade's blood run cold: uniformed beefy toughs in brown with the swastikas on their sleeves, armed with holstered pistols, invincibly bulldozing a path through the fighting mob towards the stage for their leader. McQuade stood jammed just inside the doorway, staring amazed at the spectacle; then he turned and began to squeeze his way out of the hall.

He made his way down the steps. The crowd was still furiously yelling at itself. He jostled his way around the edge of it. He saw Johan Lombard. *'Dear boy,'* Johan shouted, *'see what I mean?'*

'What's happened to the Foreign Minister?'

'I guess the dear fellow's hiding somewhere!'

'Why aren't the cops putting a stop to this?'

'Well we can tell whose side those cops are on, can't we?'

McQuade headed back to his Landrover. He ducked into a liquor store and bought a six-pack of cold beer – he was in no mood for bars any more. He drove back to his motel, opened a beer and lay back on the bed.

''n Kaffir is 'n kaffir en hy stink . . .' God . . . He saw again the heaving flags and swastikas, and remembered the words, *'. . . but let a regime come which not only liberates these instincts but makes a virtue of them, then the snout of the beast appears . . .'*

It was the middle of Wednesday afternoon when he left the farm of the second-last Mr Strauss on his list, with a gift of a bag of oranges. As he drove into the pretty mountain town of Tzaneen to find a cheap hotel, he saw the black boy selling newspapers beside a billboard which read, *'RUDOLF HESS DOOD!'*

McQuade slammed on his brakes, causing a screech of tyres and an angry blast behind him. He thrust a coin to the boy, and snatched the newspaper. It read in Afrikaans:

Rudolf Hess, Deputy-Führer of the Third Reich, Hitler's

right-hand man in Nazi Germany, died today in West Berlin, aged 93, after forty-one years in prison for war crimes . . .

McQuade parked the Landrover and went hurrying down the street looking for a public telephone. He banked up his coins and telephoned Johan Lombard's home. The maid said he was out. He dialled the German Club and asked for him. He could hear mournful German music in the background.

'Johan! I see Hess is dead?'

'Hullo, dear boy! Yes, at last and very much so. Come and join the party!'

'Is there going to be a formal service?'

'You bet. All the Nasty brass are gathering tomorrow at noon in the Rebecca Street Cemetery. I'll be in the Jewish mausoleum from eleven o'clock onwards, if you want to join me. I'll bring my video camera for you . . .'

McQuade thanked him and hung up. He pulled out his notebook, feverishly flicked through it, and dialled Oosthuizen, the young video-cameraman. He arranged to meet him at the cemetery at eleven o'clock tomorrow morning. Then he telephoned the vehicle rental company to reserve two panel-vans. Finally he telephoned Roger Wentland.

'Okay,' Roger said, 'I received the news and I've got people covering two memorial services for you tomorrow. One in Windhoek, the other in Swakopmund. I've heard of a couple of other get-togethers, but they're on private farms.'

'Many thanks, Roger! Can you possibly get the tapes sent to me by special delivery on the late afternoon flight to Johannesburg? I'll pick them up at the airport.'

McQuade thanked him profusely and hung up. He hurried up the street, looking for a shop that sold fabric.

He bought ten yards of cheap, blue cotton cloth. From a hardware store he bought adhesive tape, super-glue, string. He hurried back to the Landrover. He drove fast out of town, heading south, for Pretoria. At nine o'clock he stopped at a motel. He dyed his hair and had an early night, to be fit for tomorrow.

56

At seven-thirty the next morning McQuade arrived in Pretoria. He was wearing a hat and his new spectacles. It was a brilliant day, the sun shafting fresh and bright through the jacarandas. He left the Landrover in a multi-storey car park and set off through the rush-hour to the van rental company.

He arranged for one to be driven to the cemetery, while he followed in the other, then drove the man back to his garage. He returned to the cemetery. He parked one van directly outside the gates. He then parked the other one at a point where, through the cypress trees, he could clearly see the German war memorial. He returned to the first van, at the gate, and climbed into the back.

He cut the cloth he had bought to the correct sizes, then strung them as curtains, suspended on adhesive tape and string, across the windows and the back of the driver's compartment. He fixed the string at the corners with super-glue. He returned to the second van, and did the same job on that.

It was nine o'clock. His were the only vehicles here at this hour.

He entered the gate. Tarred paths ran between avenues of trees that divided the cemetery into religious and racial zones. He walked up towards the German burial zone. He came to the first part of the Jewish zone, many tombstones inscribed in Hebrew. Ahead was the single-storied Jewish mausoleum which had a yellow Star of David over the door. A man stood in the doorway, wearing a skullcap, a banner hung from the ceiling within: Charity Delivereth From Death. Sepulchral music wafted out. The German zone was divided from the Jewish by only a narrow path. On the corner of the pathway stood the big German war memorial.

It is a square block of grey granite, as tall as a man. On top stands a black steel dish to hold a flame. Engraved in the granite are the words: *Gefallen und Gestorben für Deutschland*. On the left side is *1914–1918*; on the other, *1939–1945*. There is a large black steel wreath.

McQuade glanced around. There were many funereal trees and shrubs, and many large tombstones to provide cover. But the ideal place was inside the Jewish building, filming through the window.

He returned to his panel-van.

From the front seat, through the trees, he could see the Jewish mausoleum and the German memorial. A trickle of people made visits to graves. The cemetery was waking up. Shortly before eleven o'clock he saw Johan Lombard arrive with a cameraman.

He was wearing a trout fisherman's hat. They disappeared inside the cemetery gates, and reappeared at the Jewish building. Johan looked around the area, as McQuade had done. Then the Jewish caretaker emerged from the building, Johan shook hands with him, and they disappeared inside.

McQuade pulled his hat down a little more, got out of the van and went towards the cemetery gates.

He walked up to the Jewish mausoleum, and went in uncertainly. 'Dear boy!' Johan cried. 'We have the perfect set-up! I've brought my video for you! Meet the gentleman who's so kindly given us permission . . .'

McQuade shook hands with the caretaker. 'Can my cameraman come inside to film?'

'Of course.'

'And you can have copies of my photographs too,' Johan said. 'Fetch them at the house at about three.'

McQuade thanked them, collected Johan's video camera and hurried back to his van.

Minutes later he saw his own cameraman arrive. He hurried over to his car. 'Mr Oosthuizen?'

They went back to McQuade's van. He pointed through the cypress trees at the memorial and the Jewish building, and explained it to him. 'When you've filmed every face from inside that mausoleum, go out the back door into the graveyard behind the building. There's a thick hedge around it. I want you to get more film, from that angle. Okay?'

'Okay, sir,' the earnest young cameraman said.

'Meanwhile, I'll be filming from here. Now, when you've filmed all the faces — and before the ceremony ends — dash across the back of the Jewish cemetery, climb over the fence, and get back to that van over there at the gate.'

They went to the second van, and climbed into the back. McQuade parted the front curtains.

'You set up your camera back here, poking through the curtain, and film through the windscreen as the people come out of the cemetery gates. They'll be walking straight towards you, so you should get everybody, full-face.'

Ten minutes later Mr Oosthuizen was installed in the Jewish mausoleum alongside the benevolent Johan Lombard and a dozen other pressmen.

McQuade returned to his van, and climbed into the back. He picked up Johan's video camera, switched it on, poked it through the curtains, and focused on the German memorial. He had a good image.

He settled down to wait.

57

Fifteen minutes before noon the convoy of cars appeared, driving down Rebecca Street at funeral pace.

They turned slowly into the car park, following a black Mercedes. They pulled into parking places. People began to get out. They were all ages, sombrely dressed. There were a number of pretty little girls in khaki uniforms. A dozen or more people were holding wreaths.

McQuade crouched in the back of his van, filming. He slowly panned the camera over every man's face he could get. The people milled about, forgathering, then began to move towards the cemetery gate.

A tape recorder was playing Beethoven. A huge swastika had been draped from a metal pole erected beside the memorial. It had been unfurled by one of the little girls. There were other Nazi flags. At least a hundred people were gathered around the memorial. Many of them wore swastika badges. The music came to an end; then a man stepped forward and began to make a speech.

From where he was, McQuade could not hear. Inside the Jewish building the pressmen had a perfect view through the chinks in the curtain. Johan whispered into his pocket tape-recorder:

'Koos Vermeulen making the speech. Führer of the Afrikaner National-Socialist Party ...' He paused and listened. 'He's saying the death of Rudolf Hess has initiated a new phase in the struggle for righteousness ... Jesus – "*righteousness*" ...?' Mr Oosthuizen scuttled across to the other end of the window and poked his camera through the chink again. Johan continued into his tape-recorder: 'At least twelve right-wing organizations are represented out there. There's Mynhardt Peters, executive member of the HNP, there's Professor Johan Schabort, leader of the Blanke Bevrydigings Beweging, and there's that arch-*verkrampte* Robert van Tonder ... But the most significant is the representation by the AWB ...'

There were two representatives, top lieutenants of the movement, wearing their sinister armbands, holding wreaths draped in ribbons with the Nazi colours of red, white and black. Johan dictated:

'And ain't that just great, folks? Here we have it in red, black and white: the AWB, which for practical purposes is now the official opposition in parliament – here they are in their true colours, in full official mourning for Adolf Hitler's deputy, flaunting their support of Nazi ideals and policies! *And these are the guys behind the official opposition in our parliament!* Christ, how's this going to look overseas?!'

The speech came to an end. Johan watched

'Now the wreath-laying begins ...'

One by one the people stepped forward slowly and laid their wreaths, then stood back, heads bowed for a moment, then stepped back into the ranks.

'Looks very nice. Very touching. Now here comes the well-known German scientist, Dr Helm ...'

The distinguished-looking, white-haired man in a black suit stepped forward with his wreath. He stood before the monument a moment, head bowed, then stepped forward again and laid the wreath. He stepped back. For a moment he stood at solemn attention; then his right arm came up in the dramatic Heil Hitler salute.

'*Snap that!*' Johan hissed at his photographer. 'Oh my, ain't that beautiful?'

McQuade filmed the Heil Hitler salute from thirty yards off through the cypress trees. The white-haired man returned to the ranks.

The last wreaths were laid. Then the singing started.

McQuade could hear it from the van, the haunting words of *Der Gute Kamerad*.

When the song came to an end the mourners slowly broke ranks and began talking. McQuade saw Oosthuizen duck through the cypress fence behind the Jewish building, and come into the car park. He hurried to his van at the gate and he scrambled in.

Five minutes later the first mourners appeared at the gate. McQuade was now filming through the side window of his van.

Half an hour later it was all over.

The last mourners had filed through the gate, said their farewells and driven off, while Johan and the other pressmen had hurried back to their offices to write their stories. McQuade went to the other van, thanked Oosthuizen, paid him and took delivery of the tapes, leaving Oosthuizen to drive away in his own car.

McQuade drove the first van back into town and returned it to the hire company, took a taxi back to the cemetery for the second van. Then he found a bar and sat drinking beer while he waited for Johan's photographer to develop his pictures.

There had been several men at the cemetery who were about the age and build of Heinrich Muller. From a distance any of them could have been his man. He just hoped like hell the film told him which.

And if the film did not?

Well, then it was back on the road, Sergeant van Niekerk again, and when he had finished with all the Strausses in South Africa, go to Namibia and start again.

And if he still had not found the right Mr Strauss?

He sighed. Cross the bridges as you come to them, but if he did not find Heinrich Muller after a few more weeks, then it was time to think about cutting a deal with Mossad. Play his cards right and drive a hard bargain, but how do you do that with the big boys? 'I'll give you the name, you find him, I get the loot'? And if they won't agree?

At three o'clock he drove to Johan Lombard's house. The maid handed him a manila envelope containing copies of all the photographs taken at the cemetery. 'The Baas is at the German Club,' the maid said.

McQuade drove back to the covered car park, then walked to the German Club. As he turned into its solid entrance the martial strains of *Der Gute Kamerad* enveloped him.

Der Gute Kamerad ... It sent shivers through him. The singing welled up out of the bar in the far corner. It was full, the air blue with smoke, suits and short sleeves and heads yards deep. Voices raised to make themselves heard, and over them the song rose up. McQuade peered and he could not see Johan. He began to make his way in, then he spotted him through the smoke, sitting at the end of the bar. The men around him had their mouths working in song. Johan had his head back, his grey locks hanging, the veins standing out as he sang *Der Gute Kamerad*. At that moment he saw McQuade, a smile crossed his beery face and he jerked his head, telling him to join them.

But this was not the time for talk. McQuade held up a thumb in thanks for the photographs and he made his way out of the bar.

He walked back to the car park. He had about four hours to kill before the flight came in from Windhoek with his video-tapes from Namibia. He got into his Landrover, and sat considering what to do.

Go and have another row of beers until it was time to drive to the airport? Or drive out to the cottage, to the waiting arms of Sarah and topple her into bed for an hour?

There was no contest. He had not seen her for four solid days. He started the engine, excited about seeing her. But he was overshadowed by a sense of evil, from the things he had seen today, the things he had seen in Pietersburg; the same feeling he'd had when he witnessed the celebrations of Hitler's birthday at the Schmidt ranch. The snout of the beast . . .

The feeling lasted all the way to the valley. Then, as he went grinding up the dirt track, he saw her come running down the track to meet him, a grin all over her beautiful face, and he felt wonderful.

58

They were at the airport at eight o'clock. He collected the package of tapes from the South African Airways freight department. It was almost ten o'clock when they got back to the cottage.

That night was feverish with frustration. They had already studied the pile of photographs which Johan had given him, and had seen nobody who looked like Heinrich Muller. Now they started on the videos.

They began with the video-films made in Namibia. For almost three hours they watched people arriving at the ceremonial sites, getting out of cars, filing past the camera, standing around talking. McQuade and Sarah's eyes darted, desperately searching the parade of faces, their hearts leaping and then sinking again. They saw several people who possibly could have fitted the description of Heinrich Muller, but on replaying the scenes they decided they were wrong. It was after two o'clock in the morning when they began the cassette which McQuade had made. He groaned.

It was so obviously the work of an amateur. The film shook and in his anxiety to cover every male, he had moved too quickly from one to the other, getting poor angles, not waiting long enough, or waiting too long for a head to turn. Nor had he managed to film every male face: around the memorial were people he had failed to catch in the car park. Moreover, although he'd thought he had a good field of vision from the van, he'd had too little light and wisps of the hedge got in the way. He stopped the tape with disgust, and turned to Oosthuizen's cassettes, filmed from inside the Jewish mausoleum.

This was infinitely better. The focus was perfect, the light was right, and the camera did not shake.

It panned slowly and steadily from the extreme left of the gathering. It stopped briefly on every male face. As he had instructed, if a man was looking down or away, Oosthuizen had waited until he got him clearly. Slowly the camera coursed to the extreme right, and McQuade's heart sank. Nobody looked like Heinrich Muller. The camera panned slowly back again. There were a good number of faces in the rear which were obscured by people in the front.

'Get those guys at the back!'

He sighed. Watching the same faces for the second time. And yet, several of them *could* have looked like Heinrich Muller. But what did Heinrich Muller look like *now*? His photograph was forty years old.

This was so hit and miss . . .

Now the wreath-laying was beginning, and his hopes rose a bit. People were craning their necks, and those in the rear were more visible. For an instant McQuade thought he saw a likely face.

'Back! Go back!'

McQuade sat with bated breath as the cameraman began to pan back again. Spaces were being made by people stepping out with their wreaths. More craning of necks. McQuade's hopes rose as the camera returned to the area where he had glimpsed the face, and his pulse tripped as the face reappeared. Then, the same instant, the man raised his hand to his cheek.

McQuade got up with a curse. He hit the Rewind button, then hit the Play button again. Then he cried, *'There!'* And the hand-covered face slid by.

He snapped the machine to stop. Then rewound, then hit Play again. The face came into view again. *'Freeze!'* he cried, and hit the Stop button. He looked at the picture, and groaned.

The picture was jagged, grainy, flickering. Sarah said: 'Videos always do that on frame-hold.'

'Oh God.' He hit Play again and the face slid past. He turned to her. 'What do you think?'

She shook her head. 'It was so brief.'

Suddenly the perspective changed. Now the cameraman was filming from outside, in the rear graveyard. McQuade leant forward earnestly, then muttered, 'This angle is no better . . .'

They grimly watched the ceremony to the end; then *Der Gute Kamerad* rose up. McQuade wanted to switch the damn machine off.

The song finally came to its end, and suddenly the scene changed entirely. The camera was filming an empty gateway. 'Now, he's back inside the van,' McQuade said.

They watched. McQuade felt his nerves stretching. Then the first persons began to appear on the screen.

'Excellent! He's got the focus perfect!'

These were excellent pictures. The sun was in the ideal position, and the people were walking straight towards the camera. McQuade waited, pent, the photograph of Heinrich Muller in his hand.

Through the gate they slowly came, in twos and threes, talking. 'This is more like it . . .' They were coming in bigger groups now. Men talking. Women. The little girls. 'Forty-three,' McQuade counted '. . . forty-five, fifty . . . fifty-four . . .' He breathed, '*Please God* . . . Sixty-five, sixty-eight, seventy-one . . .' And his heart began to sink again. The odds against him were widening every moment. *Please God he's here* . . .

At eighty-five McQuade's hopes began to go into a nosedive. There had only been about a hundred people at the ceremony. Eighty-eight, ninety . . .

At ninety-three McQuade gave a shout: '*There he is!*'

They stared excitedly at the man walking towards them on

the screen. He was the right height, about five foot seven, had iron-white hair, and a military bearing. He was talking earnestly to one of the men who had laid a wreath; he listened to the reply, and looked straight at the camera as he did so. On the other side of him walked a statuesque blonde woman and a young man. He was tall, heavy, strong, with sunglasses. McQuade's heart was pounding.

'*That's him!*' He bounded at the machine, hit the Stop button, and turned to Sarah excitedly, '*Don't you think so?*'

Her fists were clenched on her knees. 'God, I think it is! And that looked like a bodyguard . . .'

'Exactly what you'd expect! And the line of the face – the square chin! The nose—'

'But the hair? That was thick hair.'

'It could be a wig!' He snatched up the photograph of Muller. 'Yes! The eyebrows. The thin mouth. And the chin . . .'

'Play it again.'

Joyfully, McQuade hit the Rewind button.

The man appeared on the screen again. 'Hullo-oh . . .' McQuade said maliciously.

They watched him, making frantic mental notes.

The man walked off the screen again.

McQuade punched his palm joyfully. 'Okay Herr Muller! Now, which car did you go to from here?' He shot up a finger. 'The show isn't over yet, madam! Because meanwhile, back in *his* van, what was James McQuade, our real hero, doing?'

He snapped the Eject button with a flourish and picked up the cassette he had made from his van as the people emerged from the gate into the car park. He rammed it into the machine.

And his handiwork surpassed his wildest dreams.

Not only was the camera almost steady this time, but when his man came through the gate with the statuesque blonde it stayed trained on him all the way. McQuade sat on the edge of his chair, praying that he hadn't swung his camera off him. The trio walked towards a car, their backs now turned to the camera. McQuade prayed out loud, 'Don't move the camera! Which car did he go to?'

And the camera moved.

It swung back to the cemetery gate, causing McQuade to clutch his head. 'Oh Lord.' His camera religiously followed the new arrivals into the car park. Into the avenue between the cars. They too turned their backs, and the camera began to move from them, then suddenly they all turned and faced the camera again because somebody came into the frame, calling them. And for ten seconds McQuade's camera held them, and in the background was Herr Muller and his companions at their car. 'Oh yes! See that?! It's a white car.'

Sarah whispered, 'It looks like a Nissan.'

'Stay,' McQuade prayed, 'Stay on that car . . .'

They saw the bodyguard go to the driver's door, then the camera swung away again. 'No!' McQuade cried.

The camera dutifully swung back to the cemetery gates, and McQuade held his head.

The camera painstakingly followed the last people through the gates, taking an eternity. McQuade whispered: 'Please God! . . .'

And maybe God had helped him, for the people he had been filming stopped, and there, in the background, the white car reversed out, and slowly swung its tail towards the camera. Slowly the tail turned, as the people in the foreground began to move off-screen. Then the camera began turning away and McQuade clutched his head and cried 'Oh please no!' And the camera stopped.

The camera stopped because a man in the foreground had turned again, and in the background the rear of the white car swung out, large as life, right towards the camera. And there was the number plate, in the middle of the television screen. McQuade gave a whoop:

'There!'

The car moved off the screen and McQuade jumped up joyfully: *'I've done it!'*

Sarah cried, 'What was that number? Play it again!'

McQuade snapped the Eject button and snatched out the cassette.

'I've got the man and the car!'

Later, lying in his arms, she squeezed him and said quietly,

'I don't mind you refusing to tell me that car's number. But *please* don't make me feel you don't trust me.'

He began, 'It's only because—'

'I understand. What I don't know I can't be forced to divulge. But please, *please* take me with you from now on . . .'

59

They slept late, and did not go into Pretoria that day, but McQuade telephoned Roger Wentland to ask him how to trace the name and address of a vehicle's owner.

They got into Pretoria early the next morning, all the video-tapes locked in the metal toolbox with the computer print-out. The pretty secretaries were on their way to work. The newspaper-vendors' billboards shouted, *'JEWISH MAUSOLEUM DESECRATED!'*

McQuade pulled up, and Sarah ran into a café and bought four newspapers. She scrambled back in and McQuade drove on, looking for a parking place. Sarah looked at the topmost newspaper. 'God, they blasted the Jewish shrine with a shotgun!'

'What . . .? Read it aloud.'

'After a bizarre ceremony held at the German war memorial in Pretoria's cemetery to honour Rudolf Hess, which was attended by representatives of twelve ultra-right-wing organizations, the Jewish mausoleum, which is a few paces away from the site of the ceremony, was last night desecrated with shotgun blasts, and daubed with swastikas and graffiti. The words "Jewish Liars" and other obscenities were spray-painted in red on the walls, windows and pavings, including the words *"Das Unrecht an Hess wird geracht werden"* ("The injustice to Hess will be revenged")—'

'Good God.'

'The police are combing the area looking for clues. The

489

desecration was viewed with disgust by the Jewish Community today. The chairman of the Pretoria Council of Jewish Deputies, Mr Selwyn Zwick, said that the despicable act was "viewed as a physical attack on the whole Jewish community of South Africa." Rabbi Sidney Katz of the Great Synagogue declined comment except to say "I am so disgusted."'

McQuade swung into the first parking space under the jacaranda trees, and Sarah snatched up the next newspaper. 'Here's a front-page picture of the German memorial with a great swastika and that man giving the Nazi salute!' McQuade looked at the shocking picture while Sarah read aloud:

'A large group of Adolf Hitler's Nazi Party supporters . . . gathered in Pretoria's cemetery, et cetera . . . The group, openly carrying Nazi flags and wearing Nazi Party armbands and lapel badges, was joined by top officials of the AWB who wore their insignia consisting of the three-legged swastika. About fifteen wreaths were ceremoniously laid. Most of them bore the red, black and white colours of the Nazi Party, while several were adorned with swastikas. Amongst the wreaths were those from the AWB, the Blanke Bevrydigings Beweging (BBB or White Freedom Movement), the "German Farming Community" and the RSA Front.'

Her finger sped down the column, then she continued,

'The man giving the Nazi salute at the memorial has now been identified as Dr Erik Helm, eighty years old, who was one of Adolf Hitler's chief information officers and chief broadcaster of Nazi propaganda to South Africa during the war. As a German South African he was extradited back to South Africa after the war, charged with High Treason, and sentenced to ten years imprisonment. He served only three years before being released when the Nationalist Party came to power in 1948. Dr Helm said that the people attending the ceremony had only been "honouring a Nazi leader who strove for peace during the War. Rudolf Hess never touched a hair on the head of any Jew," said Dr Helm, "it would have been beneath him. It is the Jews who have refused to declare peace. Rudolf Hess flew to Britain during the war to negotiate peace, and was betrayed by Churchill. The Jews and the British were afraid of him – that is why he was locked up in such an inhuman way until death at age ninety-three."'

'*Inhuman?*' McQuade echoed.
Sarah ran her finger down the column.

'The leader of the AWB, Mr Eugene Terreblanche, has strongly defended the role played by the AWB officers at the Hess ceremony. "I was on my way to Natal and could not personally pay my last respects to the late German Nazi leader," he said. He hit out at the Jewish reaction to the ceremony. "The Zionists should not bring the feuds of their past into South African politics. They are going to make life very difficult for themselves." Hess, he said, had tried to make peace with the British "yet the Jews plead for the release of a man such as Nelson Mandela whose ANC is responsible for murdering hundreds of innocent victims through terrorism." Challenged to comment on the death of six million Jews at the hands of the Nazis, of which Hess was a fanatical leader, Mr Terreblanche said, "I do not get involved in overseas feuds. This has nothing to do with me." He went on: "Just as the British generals, who were responsible for the death of twenty-seven thousand Afrikaner women and children in the Boer War, were honoured in South Africa for their bravery, so the Germans in South Africa and the Afrikaners have the right to do the same." Referring to the possible disciplinary action against the little girls from the Voortrekker organization who unfurled the swastika at the ceremony ... Mr Terreblanche lashed out at the organization saying "They will be in deep trouble if those little girls are punished."'

'God ...' McQuade murmured.

'Meanwhile, the leader of the Conservative Party, which is the official opposition in Parliament, Dr Andries Treurnicht, refused to condemn the presence of the AWB at the swastika-bedecked Hess ceremony.'

McQuade breathed, 'Bloody frightening ...' He picked up the remaining newspaper. The headline read: 'NAZISM SLATED BY STATE PRESIDENT'. He read the article aloud:

'In an unequivocal statement in all three Houses of Parliament, the State President, Mr P. W. Botha, made it clear that no form of racism or religious persecution would be tolerated by the government ... He reminded Parliament that he had expressed his views on the matter in April 1982 when he said: "There is no room in South Africa for Communists and there is no room for neo-Nazis either."

'President Botha pointed out that many of our ancestors came to South Africa in the pursuit of religious freedom. "The South African Government stands irrevocably for religious freedom and protection of communities and minorities."' (Sarah snorted) '"We believe irrevocably in the dignity of man as a creation of God. We recognize the diversity of God's creation and believe we can live together in this diversity, and tolerate each other in a way that will be to the glory of God. We believe that in this diversity we can complement each other and work together to ensure the progress of all communities. We respect individuality and accept participation in matters of common concern.

But we reject racial superiority. We reject religious coercion. As long as this Government is in power, there will be no hesitation to act against any elements which threaten or defame any of our communities or minority groups. Against this background, I want to tell the Jewish community of South Africa: We appreciate your contribution to the economic, cultural and technological achievements of our fatherland. Any organization which wants to start an anti-Jewish campaign will be acting in conflict with the law and convictions of this country, and I, and the Government, will not hesitate to oppose such actions."'

Sarah snorted. 'Fine words, from the boss-man of Apartheid.'

McQuade tossed the newspaper aside and gunned the engine to life. 'But it's true. That's the irony.' He drove off down the street to return the hired television set, then to find the Vehicle Registration Office.

Roger Wentland had warned him that the Vehicle Registration Office would not divulge who was the owner of a motor car without a good legal reason, or unless it was 'to the owner's advantage' that the information be divulged. McQuade left Sarah in the Landrover and walked into the building, telling himself this was going to be a piece of cake but feeling as tense as the first time he had impersonated Sergeant van Niekerk. He followed directions, and found himself entering an office with a counter and half a dozen clerks sitting at computers. A girl came to attend to him, chewing gum.

'Can I please trace the owner of this vehicle?' McQuade produced a slip of paper with the number on it. 'I owe the man a big favour.'

The girl looked at the number as if it had deeply treasonous significance. 'Why?'

'Well,' McQuade said, 'yesterday I was in the country rushing my wife to hospital to have our first baby, and I got a flat tyre and I had no spare. This car comes along, and the driver not only rushes my wife to hospital – *just* in time to catch the baby – but he then actually drives me back to my car to replace the tyre. Sixty kilometres! He gave me his card, but in all the excitement I lost it. So now I want to pay for his petrol and send *his* wife a bunch of flowers and a nice box of chocolates, from my wife.'

The girl had stopped chewing, her head cocked on one side.

'Agh, *shame* . . .'

Three minutes later, after payment of a search-fee, he left the office with a slip of computer print-out. He looked at it in the corridor, and his heart sank.

He went back to the Landrover, and got in.

'The owner is Hertz Rent-a-Car.'

Sarah looked at him. '*Damn!*'

'I'm not sure that car-rental companies divulge the names of their clients.'

'No, they don't. In most countries.'

'So what do I do?' He cursed. 'Sergeant van Niekerk again? Investigating a traffic accident?' He sighed and shook his head. 'I hate to risk it. A big company like that probably has a lot of dealings with the police over traffic accidents. Probably know the higher officers by name.'

'And there's special procedures you know nothing about. Like accident-report forms.'

He rubbed his chin. 'So? Pull the same story? My wife had a baby? Or say I want to know the name of the man who rented their car because I want to *sue* him over an accident?'

She shook her head. 'Not the wife had a baby. They may phone him up and say, "We believe you were a good Samaritan yesterday, so do you mind if?" And you can't say he caused an accident, because they'll know there's no damage to their car.'

'I could say he caused me to swerve violently and damage my car.'

'"Report it to the police, sir, and let them ask us."'

'Well, he gave me a lift and I think I lost something in his car. A gold pendant.'

'"Nothing has been handed in to us, sir. But write us a letter and we'll forward it to him."'

McQuade sat there, thinking grimly. Then he slapped the steering wheel. 'I'm going to try it, anyway.' He twisted the ignition.

'Remember you can only play this trick once,' Sarah said earnestly. 'Once you've given the car's details, if they refuse to help you, you can't come back with another trick about the same car.'

He drove to the Burgerspark Hotel. He left Sarah in the Landrover, went to the public telephones in the foyer, and looked up the Hertz number in the directory. He took a tense breath, mentally rehearsing his lines, then he dialled.

'Good morning,' he said in Afrikaans. 'I wish to find out the address of the person who rented a car of yours, please?'

There was a pause. 'I'm sorry, sir, but we cannot give out that information.'

'I understand, but this happens to be very important. You see, this man gave me a lift yesterday, from a meeting that we both attended. He gave me his visiting card and asked me to give him a call to discuss a business deal we're interested in. And I've lost his card.'

'Well, sir, if you'd like to write a letter—'

'No, madam. You must understand that I promised to telephone him *today*.'

The girl wavered. 'What is his name, sir?'

'I was only introduced by his nickname. I'm not certain about the surname, I think it was Strauss, but I'm not sure.'

'And the car number was?'

He gave it to her.

The girl said reluctantly: 'One moment, sir.'

She was away for several minutes. McQuade waited with bated breath. The girl came back.

'Sir, my supervisor says we can't give out that information; but if you come into the office maybe we can sort something out with our manager in Johannesburg. Because I've looked on the computer and that car was rented by our airport office at Jan Smuts.'

So the man was from out of town.

'I see. Well, I suppose I should see your airport office?'

'You can try,' the girl said, relieved to be rid of the problem.

He hurried back to the Landrover, and punched his palm.

'You're right. They won't divulge clients' details, but we know our man comes from out of town because he rented it at the airport!'

'Aha! So, how're we going to crack the airport office?'

He shook his head. 'Not their airport office, because when Muller returns the car the desk-girl may say, "Oh, there was a man asking for you." The safest way is the Hertz central office in Johannesburg.'

'And say what? "I've lost his visiting card"?'

'Not good enough.' He shook his head again. 'God, I hate the risk, but the best way is Sergeant van Niekerk again.'

They thrashed out his lines as they drove to Johannesburg. By the time the sky-scrapers started rising up he felt they had anticipated all the possibilities, but he was very tense. This was not like taking a law-abiding housewife by surprise with his impressive uniform – he was about to walk into a busy office of people who were quite accustomed to policemen. Sarah warned: 'If you're uptight don't do it now – we haven't thought through other tactics yet. Don't blow your cover with lack of preparation.'

'What other tactic is there? The guy's rented a car, and he's probably about to leave town.'

He parked in a multi-storey car park. He stripped off in the Landrover, and struggled into the police uniform, combed his hair and put on his cap. He looked at Sarah questioningly.

She was as tense as he was. She kissed her finger and put it on his lips.

'Fine. If I was a Hertz girl . . .'

It was also the first time he had worn the uniform in a commercial part of town. It felt as if the eyes of the world were on him. He dreaded a traffic accident or robbers bursting out of a shop, requiring him to act as a policeman, but most of all he dreaded meeting another policeman. The ten blocks to the Hertz office seemed the longest of his life. It was with intense relief that he reached the building without even being asked the time. He walked in, taking off his cap.

There was a reception desk. Beyond it women worked at office machinery. 'Good morning,' the receptionist said.

McQuade put on an Afrikaans accent. 'Good morning. Sergeant van Niekerk, madam. I'm investigating a traffic accident, and I need to know the name and address of the person who rented one of your cars yesterday.' He pulled out a slip of paper with the number on it. 'This car was *not* involved in the accident, but we think the driver may be a *witness*.'

The girl took the paper. 'One moment, please.'

McQuade waited, his heart knocking, his hopes rising.

The girl made her lissom way between the desks and consulted an older woman. Then she went to a desk, and McQuade's hopes rose. She began to punch computer keys, waited, then made a note. She went to a cabinet, extracted a file and went into a glass office.

McQuade gave a tense sigh. Then a man appeared at the office doorway. He came to the reception desk, smiling. 'Good morning, Sergeant. What exactly is the problem?'

McQuade had straightened up. 'No problem for you, sir, only for me. I need to trace the person who rented that car of yours, sir.'

'Would you care to come into my office?'

Sarah had advised him on this. *Hurry them.* McQuade glanced at his watch. 'I must be quick, sir.' He followed the man into the glass office.

'I'm sorry about this, Sergeant, but you see it's company policy not to divulge clients' details . . .'

'Sir, your client is in no trouble whatsoever, but we believe he is an important witness. I presume you have received no report of any accident?'

'No?'

'And I presume the car has not yet been returned?'

'It has. Last night.'

'Last night? Where was it returned?'

'At Jan Smuts airport.'

McQuade opened his notebook. 'At what time?'

The man glanced at his file. 'Five past five.'

McQuade scrawled a note. 'That's two hours after the accident—' 'What accident?'

'Your client's not guilty of anything,' he said reassuringly, 'but our information is that a car with your numberplate was near the scene when an accident occurred in Pretoria yesterday. All we want to do, sir, is ask your client what he saw. Maybe he saw nothing, maybe he wasn't even in the car, maybe the car wasn't even there – witnesses often make mistakes.'

'I see,' the manager said. 'But it's interesting that this is the second enquiry about this car today.'

McQuade's pulse tripped, but Sarah had rehearsed him for this one also. 'Not surprising. There was quite a row between the two drivers. What's the name of the person who asked?'

'He didn't give a name. But he claimed our client had given him a business card which he lost.'

'Sounds like the chap who came forward to us. Said the driver of your car gave him a card, then drove off. I *think*,' he added, 'that he was the one who gave us the number.'

'But he said he wanted to discuss a business deal.'

McQuade shrugged again. 'Typical. People often hesitate to involve other people as witnesses at first. Now, sir, can I have the name and address, please?'

The manager looked at his file. 'Very well.' And McQuade

prayed, *please God the name is Strauss*.

'The name,' the manager said, 'is R. W. Diedrichs.'

McQuade's hand poised over his notebook.

Diedrichs?! Then he held out his hand for the form. 'Spelling?'

The manager handed it over.

McQuade shot his eye over it. He saw the address, and also the form of payment: an American Express card.

He noted down the card number first. Then the name. Then the address.

'Schloss Namib,' he repeated slowly, 'Outjo, South West Africa-Namibia.'

He felt feverish with excitement as he headed back through the streets for the car park. At last he had a hard lead!

He was not dismayed that the name was not Strauss – maybe the car was rented in the name of the bodyguard. He went into a shopping arcade looking for a public telephone. He snatched up the telephone book and feverishly searched for the number of American Express Travel. He fumbled for a coin. He dialled. A voice sang:

'*Besprekings*, Reservations, *goeie middag*, good afternoon?'

'Good day! What time is the flight from Johannesburg to Namibia in the afternoon, please?'

The girl said: 'Six o'clock or five-forty-five, sir, depending on which day. To Windhoek. On South African Airways. That's the only airline that does it.'

The car had been returned to the airport at five minutes past five – so Muller had probably gone to Windhoek on the six o'clock flight.

'And does SAA have a connecting flight to Outjo? That's up in the north.'

'No, sir, SAA only flies to Windhoek. Namibair do local flights a few times a week, I believe.'

McQuade thanked her and hung up.

But maybe Diedrichs and Muller had not flown to Namibia at all after the Hess ceremony. What other flights left Jan

Smuts airport after five-fifteen on a Thursday afternoon? Maybe they'd flown out to goddam Paraguay . . .

He didn't like making calls like this in such a public place. Not in uniform. He turned and strode away officiously.

He came to Bree Street. He hurried into the Holiday Inn. He went to the public telephones.

He dialled South African Airways.

'This is the police. Can I please speak to someone who can tell me about the passenger list for your afternoon flight yesterday to Windhoek.'

There was a click, then another female voice said: 'Can I help you?'

'Good afternoon,' McQuade said briskly, 'this is Sergeant van Niekerk speaking. We're trying to trace two passengers – maybe three – who we think flew to Windhoek with you yesterday on your six p.m. flight. They're witnesses to a traffic accident. We just need to record a statement from them.'

'Sergeant, would you mind coming into the office? We don't usually give out this information on the phone.'

McQuade dreaded going through the impersonation again. 'Madam, I'm phoning from the Pretoria area. All I need to know is whether they were on the flight or not. If they were, I'll telephone the police in Windhoek and ask them to record statements. If they weren't, then I've got to start phoning all the hotels in Johannesburg, hey.'

The woman hesitated. 'What are the names?'

He said gratefully: 'The first name is R. W. Diedrichs.'

There was a silence, as the woman worked her computer. 'Yes. Mr Diedrichs was on the flight.'

McQuade wanted to shout with relief. The woman said: 'The other name?'

This was the million dollar question. *Please God he was right.* 'We think it was Strauss.'

There was a pause. He waited, his heart knocking. Then the woman said: 'Mr H. Strauss?'

And McQuade wanted to shout with joy. *He had been right*

all along! 'We're not sure of the initial. Is there another Strauss?'

Silence. 'No.'

He wanted to gush his gratitude. *Not only the name but the initial!* He said soberly, 'Thank you very much, madam. You've saved us a great deal of trouble, hey.'

He wanted to jump and punch his palm in excitement.

He strode back though the crowded streets to the multi-storey car park. He hurried up to the Landrover, to Sarah's window. 'I've got him!' He hurried to the back and unlocked the doors. He scrambled in, to the toolbox, unlocked it and pulled out his short-list. Yes, a Mr Heinrich Strauss lived in the Outjo area with a post office box address! And *yes* he was born in Germany!

He scrambled out and got into the driver's seat.

'I've got him! We're off to Namibia! With a hey nonny-nonny and a hotcha-cha . . .'

But first they went to Sandton City, a suburb of Johannesburg. They rode up on the escalators into the glittering shopping arcades. He led the way to the shop called Security Centre.

He bought five stun-batons. He chose the best, the 'Multi-Force', which combined an electric shock-power of thirty-one thousand volts with a tear-gas capability. They cost a hundred and eighty rand each. He bought five more sets of handcuffs at twenty-five rand each, five large canisters of 'Spraysafe Multi-shot' tear gas, five little Spraysafe plastic pistols, five 'Stoppem' canisters of tear gas of the sort women keep in their handbags as protection against rape, five 'Achilles-less' gas masks designed to protect the home-owner against his own tear gas artillery, and four walkie-talkie radios.

When he wrote out the cheque he could almost hear Nathan and Tucker wailing.

PART TWELVE

60

There is a short cut from Johannesburg to Windhoek, over a thousand miles shorter, but it travels across the Kalahari Desert, on sandy tracks, through vast, flat scrubland, across dry stream beds, through vast sand-lands and places with names like Moshaneng and Morwamusa and Phuduhudu and Lone Tree and Okwa, just trading stores and maybe a petrol pump shimmering under the mercilessly blue sky. However, you may bog down for ever in the sand, and it takes much longer than the long hard drive down south through Kimberley, and then west through Upington and Grunau, which only takes two days of very hard driving.

They left the cottage at sunset, returned the keys, and headed south. At two a.m. McQuade pulled off the road. Sarah was slumped against her window, and he laid his head on her lap and fell asleep instantly. The following night they slept at the little hotel at Grunau, the bleak railway-siding on the eastern edge of the Namibian desert, and set off again at dawn. By mid-morning the Ostwind was blowing.

It comes rushing hot and dry over the vast desert towards the faraway Atlantic, sucking up the heat as it goes. Before its coming the earth is still, and feeling a little mad, and the sweat dries salty on you; then suddenly the waiting is over and out of the east it comes like a blast furnace, rushing and swirling and beating so scrub bends and dust goes flying in great furls and curls, stinging and blinding. Now the whole world is dirty flying yellow and the sun is darkened and the dust comes gushing in through door frames and window joints; so that after the wind is gone the roads are banked and streaked in sand and the world is snowy with dust.

The Ostwind was blowing full blast as they drove through Windhoek that afternoon, heading north for Outjo, into the vast flat scrub cattle-country, the grit swirling across the road and beating the Landrover. In the late afternoon the wind began to die down; they came to Otjiwarongo, and the hot earth was still and quiet. They turned onto the road for Etosha in a hazy sunset. At eight o'clock they pulled into the little town of Outjo.

It is a pleasant town, with single-storied Victorian shops, with gravel roads between neat, unimaginative homes. There are Herero women in their Victorian dresses and horned head-scarves, a police station, a circuit magistrate's court, a post office, and the Grand Hotel, two stars.

It was in questionable taste, but the proprietor had gone to great lengths to make it modern and out-of-keeping with the vast surrounding bushland. The doors were plate glass, emblazoned with credit-card insignia, the smart reception furniture was yellow vinyl, but there was no receptionist. After calling 'Hullo?' McQuade went to the corner and found himself putting his head into the cocktail bar attached to the Jade Grill Room, which was well supported by the sweaty, short-trousered clients. He called to the barman, 'Can I have a double room please?'

The barman shouted with a German accent: *'Double rum coming up – aha-ha-ha!'* Everybody laughed with him. He came to the reception desk jovially. McQuade signed in as Mr and Mrs Akkerman. He hesitated, then decided to chance it – the man was friendly and must know everybody.

'We're going to Etosha tomorrow. Is Mr Strauss's place on the way?'

'Schloss Namib, sir? No, Schloss Namib is about fifty kilometres down on the Khorixas road.' He pointed. 'To the west. Etosha is north.'

McQuade was elated. *It had worked.*

'"Schloss"? That means castle, doesn't it? Is it really a castle?'

'Oh yes, beautiful place. Though I haven't seen it myself.'

'But is it easy to find? Can I see it from the road?' He paused. 'He once invited us to drop in.'

'No. It's way back in the hills, about five kilometres off the road.'

'But is there a signpost or a gate, or something?'

'Just an ordinary farm gate. Maybe there's something written on it. Hang on, I'll ask in the bar.'

The barman bustled out. Sarah glared at McQuade, who whispered, 'It's worth it. Getting a bar-full of advice without asking for it.'

'No more questions!' She turned to glare at some photographs on the wall.

The barman came back into the foyer. He had his finger up. 'Nothing on the gate. What you must do is shout.'

'Shout?'

'*Jawohl*. Behind some rocks is a guardhouse. Shout and the guard will telephone the schloss and then open the gate.'

'Well, maybe we'll try,' McQuade said. 'Of course, he may be away.' He almost felt Sarah seethe.

'No,' the barman said, 'I saw his wife in town this morning, and his pilot, so he must be here.'

Pilot? 'Well, thank you, we'll get along to our room and freshen up for dinner.'

'Hope to see you in the bar first, sir, aha-ha-ha.'

They walked across the back garden to their room. Sarah closed the door behind them, and leant against it.

'Do you realize something?' She jerked her thumb at the reception area. 'In your anxiety to get that information, you have divulged to me the name of the man we're all looking for. Mr Strauss. Of Schloss Namib.'

McQuade was piqued at her choice of words. 'I realized that, but now we're here, you have to know, and I took a calculated risk with that guy. I got good information cheaply.'

'You did, and I mean it when I say I'm pleased to be taken into your confidence at last. But take my advice, Jim. You went at that like a bull at a gate. You've drawn attention to yourself as a stranger in town looking for the big Mr Strauss. Now, don't go back to the bar. In a town like this you'll soon be talking to everybody and you'll be remembered. And it'll soon get back to Mr Muller!'

'They must be used to tourists going to Etosha.'

'You've learned a lot,' she said emphatically. 'Where he is , that he's here, that he's got a castle with a guard on the gate. That he's got an aeroplane.' She held up a warning hand. 'Good. And maybe you got away with it. But *don't* go'n screw it up by asking more questions in a crowded bar tonight.'

McQuade was grateful for her advice, but piqued at her tone. 'If there's a guard on the gate there're likely to be more. A castle is likely to have a big imposing gate somewhere, with more guards, right?'

'Right. And you need to know his habits, his movements. Does he come into town? To go to the bank, do some shopping, just to have a beer? It would probably be a hell of a lot easier to snatch him on his way to town than to crack his castle. Before you do anything you've got to be absolutely sure he's the right man. See him close up, compare him with the old photographs. So far all we've seen is your video. I agree the evidence is stacking up, but the worst possible thing you could do is jump the gun and snatch the wrong man. Not only would that be a terrible injustice, it could land you in tremendous trouble, *and* your whole submarine would be blown. But,' she held up a warning hand, 'no more questions tonight.'

They dined in the Jade Grill Room. A busload of German tourists trooped into dinner en masse and sat at two long tables, quaffing steins of beer and talking loudly. The bar was crowded with sunburnt men and everybody seemed to be jolly, all talking at once in German. Then suddenly everybody at the bar went quiet and appeared to listen.

McQuade could hear a radio, a woman's voice reading a news item. He strained to listen, but could not catch it. He looked at Sarah questioningly, but she couldn't hear properly either. Then suddenly the bar erupted in noise.

Suddenly everybody seemed to be talking at once, angrily, incredulously. Expletives. McQuade's German wasn't good enough. 'What're they saying?' he demanded of Sarah.

She frowned. 'Something to do with Resolution 435 . . .'

McQuade's heart was sinking. 'But *what?*'

Sarah shook her head. The friendly barman came bustling out from behind the noisy counter. He made his way through the tables to the German tourists to tell them the news. McQuade grabbed his arm as he passed. 'What's happened?'

The jovial barman did not look so jovial.

'Independence!' he blustered. '435!'

'But what's happened?' McQuade demanded.

'They have reached agreement!' the barman cried indignantly. 'South Africa and Cuba and Angola are going to sign an agreement tomorrow! For immediate ceasefire! There is to be a Joint Military Commission to supervise the peace — everything!'

McQuade stared. '*But,*' he protested incredulously, 'Cuba hasn't actually *agreed* to withdraw her troops from Angola, has she?!'

'*Ja!*' the barman cried, '*Ja! Ja!* Exactly! The only question is how long it will take them to withdraw! But they have agreed to do it! And South Africa says it will start withdrawing its troops immediately! South Africa says that on November the first there will be 435! The United Nations are arriving here immediately!'

'*November the first?* But that's *impossible* . . .'

'Nothing is impossible for South Africa! They think they can do what they like with our country! They will sell us down the river to SWAPO when they like! So South Africa will withdraw and so SWAPO will come pouring across the river into Namibia next week! And all thanks to South Africa! And America! Because they want peace with Cuba they throw us to SWAPO . . .!'

McQuade stared. 'Good *God* . . .'

'*Ja*, we need God to help us now with Sam Nujoma as dictator!' The barman turned and bustled on to the tourists' table.

McQuade slowly put his knife and fork together midst the uproar. He felt the cold hand of bankruptcy on his stomach again. Sarah put her hand on his sympathetically. Suddenly a big German at the bar was bellowing across the restaurant at Sarah:

'It's all America's fault! America thinks all the gods live in Washington DC!'

Sarah turned to McQuade. 'Me . . .?'

'Yes, you!' the German shouted. 'America has forced South Africa to sell us down the river to the Cubans and SWAPO! Your Chester Crocker thinks he is Davy Crockett, King of the Wild Frontier! Your Mr Crocker thinks that what is good for General Motors is good for Namibia!'

McQuade murmured angrily, 'Let's get out of here, we're becoming conspicuous.'

'Agreed.' Sarah began to stand up.

The German shouted: 'Do you stupid Americans really believe the Cubans will go home when the South African troops leave? Do you really believe the Cubans won't come back when Sam Nujoma is dictator of Namibia? Do you really believe there will be democracy in Namibia?'

Sarah turned for the door. The barman was hurrying across the restaurant. He grabbed the angry German's arm. '*Wolfgang . . .*'

Wolfgang shook him off and bellowed at Sarah's back, 'You Americans are so naive you don't realise that One Man One Vote in Africa means One Man One Vote Once! And you – ' he shouted at McQuade, 'you bastards will be next when you've got Sam Nujoma's Cuban pals on your South African borders!' He yelled again at Sarah, the veins standing out on his neck: *'One Man One Vote ONCE! End of story . . .!'*

'And it'll also be the end of James McQuade if there's no loot in that submarine,' he said angrily. 'Because not only will there be a dictatorship but SWAPO will nationalize the fishing industry. Or sell all our licences to Moscow.'

They were sitting in their room, with the bottle of wine salvaged from their unfinished dinner. Sarah tried to be encouraging. 'But will SWAPO really be so bad? So *stupid?*'

'Oh God . . .' McQuade sighed. He gave up. *'Yes.'*

'But,' Sarah said, *'will* they necessarily win the elections?'

McQuade waved an angry finger in the direction of the bar: 'That bad-mannered Kraut in there is right, Sarah, in Africa democracy means that the biggest tribe wins the election. In Africa might is right. Might means the biggest tribe with the most spears. And the biggest tribe here is the Ovambos. Sam Nujoma and his SWAPO boys are Ovambos, so SWAPO will win.'

She controlled her pique at his tone. 'Then why do you want to see democracy come to South Africa itself?'

McQuade took a deep breath; then explained slowly.

'Sarah, I *don't* want democracy in South Africa if it means that the biggest tribe, namely the Zulus, dominate us all with yet another one-party African state. Because that's not democracy. What I do want, however, is a true democracy, with a specialized constitution – not a simple unitary system like Westminster's – a true democracy where every minority tribe has its proper, lawful, democratic representation and say in parliament – something like Switzerland, where all minority groups are *respected,* and legally *protected.* So there's no oppression. No dictatorship by one big black chief of the biggest black tribe with the most spears or AK 47s.' He sighed angrily. 'But, alas, that is not the African way of doing things.'

'But you think South Africa can achieve that kind of true,

just democracy. So why can't it happen here in Namibia too?'

He sighed. 'Sarah, South Africa can achieve that because our Hairyback South African government understands Africa – which Britain did not when it pulled out of Africa in such starry-eyed haste, and which the rest of the world *still* doesn't. And South Africa has the physical strength and is at last showing signs of having the political savvy to do it. South Africa has the wherewithal to finish off the job which Great Mother Britain abandoned with cowardly haste decades ago . . .' He glared at her, then said: 'That's why true democracy is possible in South Africa. But overnight in Namibia?' He snorted. 'Forget it.'

She suppressed her own snort. He went on: 'Forget it, in Namibia, Sarah. Because in jolly Namibia, South Africa – who's its own worst enemy because of its ridiculous Apartheid – South Africa has painted itself into the stupid corner of being *forced* by economic considerations to abandon its "colony" of Namibia, just like Britain was forced by economic considerations to abandon her African colonies. In other words, it's *cheaper* to give up gracefully than to fight the Cuban bandits . . . If South Africa had not had Apartheid, 435 probably wouldn't have happened: Namibia would have legally become part of South Africa years ago, as quietly and naturally as Hawaii became part of America, or Wales became part of England. But, there was Apartheid: so, there was 435. And so we will have the United Nations and their troops supervising the 435 elections in Namibia, not the South Africans – in other words the South Africans have destroyed their credibility as an election police force. So, the milk-and-water UN troops will police the elections – and they won't have a fucking clue about African politics and its big-tribe tactics and its bully-boy intimidation – they'll fondly imagine it will all be nice and wholesome like it is in Stockholm.' He sighed. 'So when the South African troops withdraw down across the border the SWAPO troops who've been sheltering behind the big battalions of Cuba will gleefully come down, filling the vacuum, and they'll come swaggering across the border with their Kalashnikov rifles and landmines and start blowing up old ladies in supermarkets and shooting up defenceless people taking their cattle to the water-hole, just to impress upon them that they better vote SWAPO or else. Because that is the African way. And South Africa with its Africa-know-how won't be able to stop them because the United Nations will be so-called policing the show.' He ended grimly, 'Yes, SWAPO will win the election, Sarah.'

She was silent a moment, then persisted optimistically: 'But will they be so stupid as to take over all the industries?'

McQuade snorted. 'Yes, Sarah. They're communists. And they're mostly uneducated.' He looked at her, then leant forward: 'Please grasp that. They're people from the bush who are going to be handed a sophisticated but fragile economy. To *own*. With their heads stuffed with propaganda from Moscow. They're under-educated, Sarah. They're not like your sophisticated blacks in America. Please *grasp* that, Sarah . . .'

61

McQuade was desperate now to get the show on the road. By seven o'clock the next morning they had checked out of the hotel to go and find Schloss Namib. The world was beautiful in the morning light, as only Africa can be beautiful, the yellow-grey trees still, the yellow grass soft in the early sun – but it all looked like dust and ashes to McQuade.

The bushland on both sides of the road was fenced with barbed wire. From time to time there were farm gates, dirt tracks leading off into the vastness, but they glimpsed no faraway homesteads, no sign of life. About fifty kilometres from Outjo, they saw the gate.

McQuade slowed. It was an ordinary farm entrance, differing from the others only in that the supporting pillars were stout columns of rock. There was a plaque on it saying: 'Geen Ingang, Eintritt Verboten, No Entry.' A chain locked the gate. There was a hillock of iron-brown rock fifty metres beyond, with smoke from a cooking fire rising up, but they could not see the guardhouse. A dirt road disappeared into the yellow-grey bush beyond, into a jumble of rising hills. Telephone poles followed the road. They passed the gate. Sarah looked back. 'Yes, I just glimpsed the guardhouse. Stone. Thatch roof.'

'You can't see anything on those hills? Any buildings?'

'No.'

McQuade was looking for a dividing fence, indicating the end of Muller's land.

Ten kilometres later they saw it. 'It's a big spread.'

Almost immediately they saw another gate. It was a large, whitewashed archway, adorned with mounted cattle horns.

A wrought-iron sign read, 'Mopani Guest Farm'. A track led off, disappearing into the hills.

McQuade pulled up opposite the entrance.

'Guest farm, huh? Next door to Muller's land? Right, this is where we spend tonight.' He swung the wheel towards the gate.

They ground up the track into the hard scrub hills. But for their engine, the world was completely silent. The track wound over the hills, then suddenly, at the top of a rise, there was an open gate. They drove through, past neat, empty cowsheds and outbuildings. Ahead was a burst of colour, bougainvillaea and trees shrouding a thatched house, which had three cars outside it. A row of round, thatched rondavels led off into the trees.

They walked down the side of the main house, and came into a mature garden, with lawns and a pretty swimming pool. The main house had a long verandah under thatch, with dining tables. Two couples were having breakfast. There was a magnificent view over a vast valley, with a range of mountains on the horizon, mauve and hazy. A white woman came out onto the verandah.

'*Bitte, mein Herr?*'

'Can we have a room please?'

The manager brought the guest-registration book to the table as they were finishing breakfast. He was a dour middle-aged German, with pale blue eyes. 'For how long will you be staying?' He had a slow German accent.

'We don't know yet.' McQuade signed the register as Mr and Mrs Peterson from Australia. The manager prepared to leave, but McQuade wanted to get him talking so he could ask about Schloss Namib. 'What do you think of this sudden independence business?'

The German sighed. '*Ja, ja, ja* . . .' He said it as if he had warned them all before. 'We never thought it would happen but at last South Africa is listening to the world. The war has got too expensive, too many of her boys are dying up there, and now it is an unpopular war. For me, I do not care as long as I can run my business in peace but I doubt it.'

'But,' Sarah said, 'the new government is still going to need tourists, for foreign exchange?'

'*Ja, ja, ja,*' the manager said, 'and so does Cuba need tourists, and so does Russia, but how many go there, and who runs the hotels? The people who know how, or the nice SWAPO government? And how many people will want to come to Namibia when they cannot drive safely any more, and the Cubans are pushing us off the streets of Windhoek? Tourists like to feel safe, you know, on their holidays.'

'So you don't believe the Cubans will go home after the South Africans pull out?'

The manager sighed. '*Ja, ja, ja* – and *nein, nein, nein.* Of course not. Some of them Fidel Castro will bring home, of course, because the South Africans will insist, but they can always come back once Namibia is independent, *nein*, and of course, they will come back again to help the communist Angolans fight UNITA and then they will invite themselves into Namibia because the next place for the clever Fidel Castro to liberate is South Africa. Anyway he has too many soldiers and no jobs for them, so he must depend on Russia, *nein*, and we all know what Russia wants, *nein*?' He shook his head. '*Ja, ja, ja . . .*'

It made McQuade feel feverish again. 'Well, we're just tourists and we're into game-viewing. Have you got much game on your farm which we can go and look at?'

'*Ja*, we have some species of buck and warthog and sometimes elephant and even some lion. There is a water-hole, I will give you a map.' He went to the end of the verandah, into an office. He returned with a hand-drawn sketch.

'Thank you,' McQuade said. 'And tell me, I believe there's a beautiful castle somewhere around here?'

Sarah kicked him under the table. The manager said, '*Ja*,

Schloss Namib. About ten kilometres that way.' He pointed east.

'Is it a real castle, with towers and all?'

'*Ja*, but in the German style of a fort for the *schutztruppe* in the old days, like the one at Namatoni in Etosha.' He turned and took a framed photograph off the wall. 'This is Namatoni, now converted into accommodation for tourists.'

The photograph showed the white, oblong fort where McQuade and Sarah spent the night two months ago. The manager said, 'Schloss Namib is the same but a bit bigger and inside the courtyard he has beautiful palms and gardens.'

'Fascinating.' McQuade studied the photograph. 'He must be an interesting man?'

'Very nice.' The manager shrugged. 'I don't know him well. Sometimes he comes here for dinner. He was here last week to celebrate his wedding anniversary.'

A black waiter appeared and said something in German.

'Excuse me,' the German said. He turned and left.

Sarah whispered, 'You did it *again* . . .'

McQuade was staring at her. Then he softly banged the table. 'I've got it!'

'What?'

'Herr Strauss is definitely Heinrich Muller!' He grabbed their room keys and stood up. 'Let's go.'

He hurried back to the Landrover, unlocked the toolbox and grabbed all his notes. They hurried to their rondavel.

It was airy, the thatch bound to raw beams, and had a magnificent view of the valley. McQuade excitedly spread out his notes on Heinrich Muller on the double bed. Then he smacked them triumphantly.

'Yes!' He turned to her. 'Herr Strauss – this Mr Heinrich Strauss at Schloss Namib – married his wife in *January* 1949, in Windhoek! But the manager has just told us that he celebrated his wedding anniversary here last week! Early *August*! Why?' He jabbed his notes. 'Because Heinrich Muller married his wife in Germany on the second of August 1938!

So what happened? At the end of the war Muller escapes from Germany, leaving his wife behind. After he's settled down here as Herr Strauss, he sends for her, and for the sake of preserving his new identity he remarries her! In January 1949 in Windhoek. But the date they celebrate as their *real* wedding anniversary is August!'

'God!' Sarah was staring at him. 'We've proved it!'

McQuade punched his palm.

'Right! First we follow this map over this guest farm and see what we can see of Muller's land. Then I'm going over the fence to case the joint while you go back into Outjo to see what you can sniff out.'

62

He did not go over the fence that day. They spent the morning grinding around the huge guest farm in the Landrover, following the manager's map, trying to determine the lie of the land the other side of the fence. The track descended to a huge plain studded with isolated hills, until, on the horizon, another hazy line of hills rose up. There was complete silence. The track meandered down, sometimes following the fence. The heat shimmered up from the mauve-grey, unmoving plain. Sometimes they got a clear view of Muller's land, and several times they glimpsed a track on the other side of the fence. McQuade stopped and peered at it, looking for signs of vehicle tracks, a sign of life. Yes, there were faint tyre marks.

In the middle of the plain they encountered a dry stream bed, marked on the map as the northern border of the guest farm. They had come over twenty kilometres from the farmhouse. They climbed a rocky hillock and looked through binoculars. Muller's land did not end here, but appeared to stretch on, beyond the stream bed, towards the distant hills. Here and there they could make out the track, but there was no sign of a dwelling, just the vast, silent, shimmering bush. For half an hour they sat on the hilltop, waiting for something to happen, something to move, dust to rise up. But, nothing.

'He sure lives in the middle of nowhere.'

They drove back to the guesthouse via the waterhole, so they could tell the proprietor they had seen it. They saw no game but plenty of spoor. It was mid afternoon when they got back; the manager let them have cold meat and salad.

They had it at a table under a tree, with beer.

'All right. How would Mossad do it?'

'Not on a bellyful of beer.'

'It's too late, anyway. It'd take three hours at least to cover ten kilometres on foot in those hills. So I'll have to go tomorrow.'

'First Mossad would do an aerial reconnaissance. Send up a man with a camera, and make enlargements of the photographs, then enlargements of enlargements, until they could see the whites of Muller's eyes. *Then* they'd go over the fence to confirm their information. Then they'd build a model of the castle. *Then* they'd make a plan.'

'I can't afford an aerial survey.'

'Why not? A lot of money is at stake. There must be literally hundreds of private planes you could hire in this vast country. Like in Australia.'

'The difficulty would be finding a pilot we could trust.'

'In Otjiwarongo there must be a flying club where you can rent a plane and a pilot. Say you're a geologist. Or an archaeologist, looking for evidence of ancient ruins. Alternatively, there are probably aerial survey photographs of most of this country on file in some government office, and detailed survey maps. You can probably get them perfectly legitimately.' She leant forward. 'What I'm saying, Jim, is that you've achieved wonders in *finding* your target. Now is the time to sit and do some clever thinking.'

'Some *fast* clever thinking: 435 is just around the corner and the country's going to be swarming with United Nations troops and officials.' He rubbed his chin. 'Tomorrow you go back to Outjo, and see what you can find out. While I go over the fence, to see what I can see. *Then* we think about aerial surveys.'

At breakfast the next morning, they told the manager they were going to look for game. At eight o'clock Sarah stopped the Landrover amongst the hills, five hundred metres from the main road. McQuade got out, holding a small bag containing her telephoto camera, his binoculars and notebook, hurried to the barbed-wire fence, climbed over it, and dropped onto Muller's property. He strode away. Within thirty paces he had disappeared into the scrub. Sarah drove on down the winding track, for the main road.

McQuade worked his way up to the crest of the nearest hill, and crouched behind a rocky outcrop.

But all he could see were more yellow-brown hilltops stretching on and on. No sign of life, no road. Only the ringing silence of the bush. He checked his watch, and the position of the sun, then set off into the jumble of hills, heading north-east.

It was about eleven o'clock when he came across the track, winding through the hills. He presumed it to be the same he had seen yesterday when reconnoitring. He crouched and examined the surface.

It was flinty. He crept along, looking for soft ground that would show a vehicle tyre. He found a patch which showed an indistinct imprint of a broad tyre. He could not judge how old the spoor was. The track twisted away, into the hills. His guess was that it joined up with the road from the gate. He started following it, avoiding any soft patches so as not to leave footprints. He followed it for twenty minutes. Now he was working his way up a big hill. He came up to the crest, and crouched down.

Below him, the hills gently flattened out into the plain. Cut through it was the brown stripe of an airstrip. Beside it was a hangar.

McQuade crept along the crest of the hill, looking for the best cover with the best view, stopped behind an outcrop of rocks, and pulled the binoculars from the bag.

He could see everything clearly, even the heatwaves shimmering off the galvanized-iron hangar.

McQuade did not know much about aeroplanes, but the airstrip looked a big one to him. The doors of the hangar were open, but from this angle he could not see an aeroplane. There was no vehicle, though some might have been parked behind the hangar, or inside it.

He swung the binoculars as far west as his field of vision would permit, then slowly swept them back, searching the distant scrub. He saw no signs of habitation. He swept as far east as he could see, and slowly swung the binoculars back, checking again. He reached the western end of his field of vision, and he saw it.

It was just a flash amongst the distant trees beyond the airstrip, a glimpse of a vehicle and a suspicion of dust in the air; then it was gone.

A patrol vehicle? He waited, searching the distance for more movement. If it was a patrol vehicle, it was possibly coming this way, very likely on the perimeter track they had seen yesterday alongside the fence, and very likely that track linked up with this one he was following.

Crouched beside his rocks, about fifty yards from the track, he did the arithmetic. That vehicle must have been three or four kilometres from him, as the crow flies, say ten kilometres via the winding track. If it hadn't shown in half an hour he could risk moving.

He sat down. He turned his binoculars back to the hangar. In the next half hour nothing happened. The only movement was heatwaves shimmering, his sweat trickling, his uncomfortable shifting. After thirty-five minutes he got to his feet with relief.

He started creeping down the hill, peering through the scrub for the continuation of the track. He saw it when he was almost upon it. It ran down around the side of the hill, heading east again. He decided not to risk walking along it. He crept through the bushes, keeping parallel with it.

After ten minutes he paused and listened. Nothing. Then he cautiously descended, down onto the track. He hadn't walked ten paces when he heard the vehicle breasting the hill, and his heart lurched.

522

He flung himself into the bush and scrambled frantically up the hill. He scrambled six, seven, eight, frantic yards, desperately looking for cover, then he flung himself flat. He looked wildly back at the track, and the Landrover burst into view around the bend.

He lay there, heart pounding, eyes wide. He glimpsed three men in the vehicle, two blacks and a white, and at least two Doberman dogs. The men were in khaki uniforms. McQuade stared, desperately praying that they would not look up the hillside. The Landrover ground slowly down the track, its engine roaring above the knocking of his heart, until it was almost level with him. If they did not look now they would not see him. He screwed his eyes up, and he heard the vehicle grind past him. He lay there, not daring to turn his head.

The noise of the vehicle diminished, and he went limp.

He got up and scrambled further up the hillside. He looked down at the track, panting. He could not see it any more, but that didn't mean that somebody down there would not see him.

He climbed to the top of the hill. Now he could see the airstrip again. He went over the crest, then began to make his way carefully along, heading east.

Fifteen minutes later he heard the aeroplane.

He scrambled to a vantage point where he could see the airstrip clearly. He crouched down and searched the sky.

A white aircraft was coming in from the south-east. He put the binoculars to his eyes.

It appeared to be a six-seater, and had two engines. He could read the markings, and memorized them. The aeroplane was descending in a slow circle; then a vehicle appeared, approaching the airfield.

It was coming down a track which McQuade could not see. His pulse tripped. It was a white, four-wheel drive vehicle and it could have been a Landcruiser, the same kind of vehicle that had chased him in the desert. It was coming from the east, so Schloss Namib was that way. It emerged from the bush, and drove across open ground towards the hangar. The aircraft was commencing its approach.

The vehicle pulled up at the hangar. A white man got out. A black man was emerging from the hangar. The aircraft touched down with a puff of dust.

It went careering down the airstrip, then came trundling to a halt opposite the hangar. The black man ran for it. The pilot's door opened, he got out onto the wing and the black man opened the door on the other side.

Four men climbed out. They were wearing dark suits. The driver of the vehicle came to attention, then he raised his right arm in the Hitler salute.

The four men responded. Then there were handshakes. They began to walk towards the vehicle. They all climbed in and the vehicle drove off the way it had come.

McQuade watched it go through the binoculars. It disappeared. He got up and began to scramble through the bush along the hillside.

Ten minutes later he saw the castle. Suddenly it burst into view, a few kilometres away. He scrambled for better cover, heart knocking.

He studied it through the binoculars. It was a large oblong building similar to the fort at Namatoni, gleaming white in the noon sun. The walls were as high as a double-storied building. The top was lined with battlements. In each corner rose a squat tower. In two stood flag poles: from one hung the red, white, and black flag of Germany of World War II, and from the other hung the Vierkleur, the flag of the Republic of the Transvaal before the Boer War. From within the courtyard rose the tops of tall palm trees. No windows broke the white walls, only what appeared to be gun slits. A large black double door was the only entrance. A gravel drive swept up to it. The area surrounding the schloss had been cleared of most of the trees. Lawns extended for about fifty yards, then there was a large paddock and a number of horses were grazing in it. Beyond was a long row of stables, and beyond that were rows of huts. McQuade thought he could make out a fence at the treeline behind the huts.

He looked uphill. He could get about thirty feet higher. He started scrambling upwards.

63

The afternoon sun beat down. The sweat was running off McQuade, his mouth dry, and he cursed himself for not bringing a bottle of water.

He was three kilometres further along the range of hills, sitting amongst a pile of rocks in the notional shade of a skeletal thorn tree. He had been there half an hour, and he intended to stay there till sunset, to find out how many times the Landrover patrolled the ranch.

He had found the track branching up from the main road into the hills towards the schloss. He had crept through the bush beside it until he had seen the guardhouse at the main road. He had lain waiting to find out how many guards there were. In ten minutes, only a woman emerged to tend a cooking pot, followed by two small children. He decided he should not wait any longer; the guard himself might be prowling the area. He carefully made his way back into the hills.

He had emerged on the top of the range. There, below, was the schloss again, the track going across the plain towards it. The whole area around the schloss, a rectangle of maybe thirty acres, was enclosed by a diamond-mesh fence, ten or twelve feet high and topped by barbed wire, mostly obscured by trees and scrub. But there were few trees inside the fence, and they provided little or no obstruction to a clear field of vision from the battlements. In the western corner was a large orchard, and some fields of lucerne. In the eastern corner were the stables adjoining the big paddock, and there was also a small grandstand under a thatched roof. Beyond the stables, back into the trees, were the thatched huts, in neat rows, obviously a labour compound. The road from the main gate wound down to the high fence, followed it to the west, up to a big main guardhouse, which McQuade had been unable to see before. This was the main entrance he had been expecting. It was like a small fort in itself. It had a big arch and the outer walls had gunslits.

He studied the guardhouse through his binoculars. There was no movement, but it was big enough to be a barracks for the guards. He took a photograph of it, and more photographs of the schloss and its surroundings. Then he drew a rough sketch plan, estimated the distances and marked them in.

He sat there, waiting for something to happen.

Three times the Landrover had driven through the hills in the time he had been here, at approximately two-hour intervals, but he had only glimpsed it through the trees and had been unable to see where it disappeared to. From here he should be able to see.

In the middle of the afternoon he heard a different vehicle. He scrambled down onto his stomach and peered.

Suddenly, coming from the direction of the main road, a grey Mercedes ground down the track past him. He just had time to make out that a white man was driving, a blonde woman was beside him, and another person in the back. It disappeared in the direction of the schloss. A few minutes later it reappeared on the plain below, alongside the fence. It drove up to the guardhouse. It did not stop. It swept up the drive and disappeared into the schloss.

Almost immediately he heard the Landrover again. A few minutes later it came into view on the track immediately below him; he glimpsed three black men. Then it was gone.

He waited for it to reappear on the plain below. It did not.

So, it had driven off down another track that he could not see. Obviously, around the eastern perimeter of the property. Was there another entrance to the enclosure in the east? Another guardhouse?

Was there a back door to the schloss? Or one on the far side? Just then the question was answered: two men emerged from the back of the schloss and began walking slowly towards the stables. McQuade shot the binoculars up to his eyes.

He could not make out faces. One was short and had white hair. They were walking slowly, heads down, talking. They stopped and faced each other; then slowly continued. They disappeared inside the stables.

McQuade waited.

Almost twenty minutes passed. Then, in the far distance, beyond the schloss, a vehicle flashed between the trees for an instant. He was sure it was the Landrover. Just then the two men emerged from the stables. They were walking briskly this time. They disappeared into the back of the schloss.

Then things started happening rapidly.

Suddenly the Landrover reappeared on the far side of the plain. It was driving down a track towards the guardhouse. At the same time, seven uniformed black men emerged from the labour compound behind the stable and walked briskly towards the guardhouse, a kilometre away. They were all armed with rifles. McQuade looked at his watch. Five minutes before five p.m. Now two black guards emerged from the guardhouse. The Landrover appeared at the guardhouse, drove through, stopped, and three black men got out. A uniformed white man emerged from the guardhouse.

The black men formed two ranks, the seven newcomers in one line, five in the other. They stood at ease, the white man strolling amongst them. Suddenly they all snapped to attention. Then two of the newcomers did a smart left turn and marched off in the direction of the schloss. They disappeared inside. Half a minute later, two black men emerged, marching smartly. They marched to the guardhouse, and snapped to a halt in the ranks. Then that line did a left turn, marched three paces, and fell out. They started walking in the direction of the compound. The rank of newcomers marched off.

Three climbed into the Landrover. It drove off towards the far side of the plain.

So, McQuade thought. Seven men to a guard-watch. Two in the schloss itself, two in the guardhouse, three in the patrol vehicle. Plus one at the entrance at the main road. At least fifteen armed men in all. Plus the white officer, sixteen. Plus the pilot, who was doubtless armed. Plus the man who had driven the car. A total of eighteen at least.

Just then, the white Toyota emerged from the schloss. It drove to the guardhouse, and disappeared out of McQuade's field of vision, in the direction of the airstrip.

He waited. The sun was getting low now.

Five minutes later he heard a soft distant roar. Then the aeroplane appeared, climbing into the sky. It turned due east, still climbing, and disappeared.

McQuade cautiously got up. He started threading his way between the trees, in the direction of the guest farm.

There was only one thing more he could learn today, and that was whether the area around the schloss was floodlit at night. It would be dark soon and that detail he could learn from his first vantage point, closer to home.

It was after nine o'clock when he toiled up the track to the guest farm. To his relief, his Landrover was there. There were several other cars. He hurried to his rondavel. The door was locked, but opened immediately when he knocked. Sarah was wreathed in smiles. She flung her arms around him. 'Oh thank God! Did anybody see you come in?'

'Don't think so.' He hugged her.

'Because you dine promptly at seven in this German establishment, or not at all. I said you were resting and ordered dinner to be sent in.' She waved her hand at a tray. 'And booze,' she added.

'Sheer genius!' He snapped the cap off a beer and drank it down, down, down. It was nectar. He sat on the bed in a heap.

'Tell me. But first tell me you love me.'

64

He told her what he had seen while he swilled down more beer. Then she told him her day while he wolfed down the food.

'It's a very friendly little town. The lady in the café would talk the hind legs off a donkey. I had to have three cups of coffee and a Coca-Cola I didn't want while she yakked—'

'I'd have given my eye-teeth for a Coca-Cola.'

'"Are you an American?" Yes, by golly-gosh, I am, going up to Etosha. Alone? No, I'm killing time whilst my husband talks boring business all day. What business is your husband in? Life insurance and pension schemes, got clients all over southern Africa – dead boring. Me, I'm keen on wildlife and photography, I believe there's a fabulous old German castle round here, brought stone by stone from Germany? That's Schloss Namib, she said, belongs to Herr Strauss, but it's built of local stone. I said, I've heard of him, is it true that he's an old eccentric who never leaves the place? No, he's a prominent man in these parts, he comes to church every Sunday—'

'Church?'

'And he drops into the café for an apfelstrudel with his wife after they've finished their business in town.'

'What days?'

'She didn't say, and I could hardly ask her outright. So I said, is he a farmer? She said, a cheque-book farmer, he breeds magnificent horses and prize cattle, he always wins prizes at the agricultural shows.'

'I saw the stables.'

'I've got some ideas on that, but let me finish. At this juncture I saw the big blonde girl we saw on the video,

530

walking down the street. I made my escape from the café. The blonde was walking towards the service station. There was a grey Mercedes getting petrol, and a man signing a chit. There was somebody in the back seat. I hurried to our Landrover, they drove out of the garage, I followed them. They stopped at Barclays Bank, and out of the back climbed an elderly lady. But sprightly. The guy and the old lady went into the bank, the blonde crossed the road to the post office.'

'It fits,' McQuade said. 'The four men arrive in Muller's aeroplane — which he sent to collect them — to talk Nazi business, so he sends his wife and flunkies to town to get them out of the way.'

'They may have been horse-buyers.'

'Then why the Nazi salute at the airstrip? Anyway, what happened next?'

'Nazi horse-buyers, perhaps? Anyway, I followed the blonde. She was clearing a postbox as I walked in. There's a public telephone there. I went to a phone, pretended to look for coins, then pulled out a two-rand note and said to her, "Can you change this for coins?" "Certainly," she said. She was very nice.'

'There are many nice Germans.'

'But not many of them work for Heinrich Muller. Anyway, I hoped to engage her in conversation to try to find out when her boss came to town, but it was no go. She went off to join a queue at the counters. I pretended to dial a number. I had a bullshit conversation with nobody, then I joined the queue behind the blonde. To buy stamps for five non-existent postcards. I got talking to her again. "Thanks for the coins." "Pleasure." "Wow it's hot, do you live round here?" She's really a good-looker. "Yes, I live on a ranch." "Really, where?" "Schloss Namib." "Is that the grand castle I've heard about?" She says, "It's more like a fortress." "Not for damsels in distress?" said I. "Aha-ha- ha! . . ."'

McQuade grinned. 'Tell it straight.'

'I am. "No" she says, "but it's lonely." But she likes the

horse-riding and the bush, et cetera, et cetera. "And your husband?" I said. "No," she said, "I'm not married, I'm the house-keeper." At that stage her turn came at the counter. The post-mistress said "Hullo, Fräulein Beyers." When she turned back I said, "Can you tell me where I can buy avocado pears?"'

'"*Avocado pears?*"'

'If I invited her for coffee she may say, "Thanks, but sorry." But for avocado pears she's got to stop and think. She says, "I'll show you the grocery store." So I bought my stamps and we left together. I said, "Do you get to town often in your job?" She said, "Once a week the old lady and I come to do some shopping."' Sarah snapped her fingers: 'Then she said, "That day we meet girlfriends for lunch at the hotel." And it was obvious that Muller does *not* come to town that day because it's girlie-lunch-day! So *that's* the day to snatch him, when the womenfolk are out of the way!'

'Brilliant!' McQuade said. 'And what day is that?'

'Wait. I couldn't ask her – we'd reached the store. And sure enough, there were avocados.' She pointed. 'Hope you eat them. I hung about politely, while she bought a few things, then as we left I said, "How about a coffee?" But she had to join the old lady. So all I could say was "Well, might bump into you on our way back from Etosha, we'll probably be stopping here." I was hoping she'd say "Well, do come to lunch with the girls." But she just said "Good, have a nice trip, *auf Wiedersehen*." And off she went. Leaving me looking a bit lost in Main Street, Outjo, clutching my two avocados and five postage stamps.'

He smiled. 'Where did she go?'

'It was now lunchtime. She went into the hotel. The Mercedes was parked there. I got its number, of course. But I couldn't go into the hotel myself because the barman would remember our asking after the Strauss family and may try to introduce me. That would have looked suspicious to the girl – Heidi's her name, by the way. And I was scared to go back

532

to my fountain of information in the café, in case Heidi took the old lady there for a nice apfelstrudel. I'd run out of places to loiter, so I made myself scarce. Thought you might be back soon, so I came back here. *But*, at six o'clock I telephoned the manager of the hotel in Outjo from here. Didn't say who I was but said that I was hoping to see Heidi Beyers at lunch at his hotel next week, but I'd forgotten what day it was.'

'*Very* good.'

'And the manager said ... "Saturday, madam"!' She cocked her eyebrows at him. 'It's a start,' she said.

'Sheer *genius*,' McQuade said.

He paced across the rondavel. 'There're four basic options.'

Sarah sat with a glass of wine, all attention.

'One,' he said, 'go in there with a bunch of mercenaries and snatch him in a military-style operation.' He shook his head. 'This is the option I like least, because it will involve knocking out the guards, blasting our way in, finding Muller, knocking him out, getting him out into the escape vehicle. There're plenty of snags with that plan.'

'I'll say,' she murmured.

'You can't do that without expecting shots to be fired, and I don't want murder on my conscience. So — Option two, and without yet having thought it through properly, this is the option I like best. Namely, get into the schloss dressed as policemen.' He added: 'My Landrover looks like a police vehicle.'

She said to her fingernails: 'And how do you get him out of the schloss?'

'I had considerable time to give this some thought today, as I lay up in the hilltops dying of thirst. I either have to *lure* him out, with some pretext — like coming back to the police station to identify someone. Or ... I have to take a bold course, and arrest him.'

'*Arrest* him?' She looked up. 'But on what charge?'

'We'll have to think. But how about something that would

really upset him? Embarrass him. Make him protest his innocence. Like indecent exposure.'

'Indecent *exposure*?'

'Imagine. If the cops knocked on my door and said they'd received a complaint from . . . some waitress, that I'd unzipped my fly and flashed man's best friend at her, I'd be *horrified*. Outraged. What absolute nonsense! *What* waitress? *Show* her to me – this is all some ghastly mistake! *Certainly* I'll come with you to the police station to prove this is nonsense – the girl's talking about somebody else!' He raised his eyebrows. 'Wouldn't I?'

Sarah stared at him thoughtfully. 'He'd say, "I want to telephone my lawyer."'

'Would he? Particularly if the policeman says, "I believe, sir, that this must be a terrible case of mistaken identity, so just come to the station to straighten it out, please." Anyway, his telephone line would be cut. By us. "Never mind, sir, you can call your lawyer from the police station."' He raised his eyebrows again. 'And even if he does phone his lawyer, he's still got to come out to the police station with us.'

She nodded slowly. 'Worth thinking about.'

McQuade turned and paced. 'Option Three, we snatch him in town, or on the way into town. But there're big problems. In town there're likely to be witnesses, and there's likely to be a fight. If we're caught, the cops are right there.'

She nodded. 'Not in town. On the road.'

'The problem there is that he's likely to be in the car with his bodyguard and wife – and Heidi too. Not only are they witnesses, there could be a nasty fight and the women could get hurt. Furthermore they'd give chase afterwards. Okay, we could immobilize his car, but it won't be long before another car comes along, so within a very short time the cops would be throwing up roadblocks all over the country. They'd know what direction we'd taken.'

'Not if they're unconscious.' She got up and went to her handbag. She took out a perfume bottle. 'Standard Mossad issue. Anaesthetic. Same stuff doctors use to put a patient out for an operation. All we have to buy is the syringe, from any chemist.'

McQuade looked at it. Its label claimed it was eau de cologne. 'Bloody marvellous.'

'Trouble is it only gives us a short start.'

'Any more tricks like that in your bag?'

'Another one of those, and knock-out pills you put in people's drinks.' She produced a plastic phial which proclaimed the contents to be Saccharin, artificial sweetener. 'Just the usual stuff.'

'*Excellent* stuff.'

'Option Four?' she said.

McQuade took a gulp of wine. 'We somehow lure him to meet us somewhere, where we can snatch him safely. This would probably be the ideal solution if we had plenty of time. We'd need time to find out what would lure him out to our meeting place. A sick relative, maybe? An important business meeting? Something to do with horses? Or politics?' He shook his head. 'But we don't know enough about him. It could take months. So, on the face of it, it's the second option. Go in as a policeman. Once we've got him under arrest, we've got to get him across the country to Walvis Bay. Onto the ship.' He waved his hand. 'We must assume that within a couple of hours somebody at the schloss will smell a rat when he fails to return, and the alarm will be raised. So, they'll be looking for our Landrover. We'll change the number plates, and we can quickly spray-paint it another colour after the snatch. Or transfer to another vehicle.' He held up a finger. 'A truck. With a crate on the back – and in that crate is our friend, Herr Muller. Sedated.'

She looked at him. 'Carry on.'

'Of course, we time our snatch of Muller to coincide with the *Bonanza* being in port. We winch the crate on board and put to sea. Throw a bucket of water over Muller, and get the story out of him.' He spread his hands and raised his eyebrows.

'We're forgetting one thing,' she said. 'If that white Toyota you saw *is* the same vehicle that chased us in the desert, the guys in it are likely to recognize you when you show up dressed as a policeman.'

'So, I'll have to have a disguise. The Landrover's had a new paint-job. We'll work out those details. And I'll have to go back to Muller's place and have another look at it from the other side before we finally decide.' He turned and paced, thinking out loud: 'But we've got a lot of things to get. Like a large wooden crate. A truck. Unless we spray-paint the Landrover another colour after we've snatched him. In which case we need a safe place off the road to do the job.'

'A coffin,' Sarah said pensively, 'not a crate. Nobody likes to open a coffin. And ideally you need something that looks like a hearse. Plus the necessary papers — all forged.'

McQuade turned to her. 'That's a good idea! We can buy a cheap coffin at any native store.'

'A *good* coffin, you need. And the phoney number plates? A wrecker's yard — but where?'

'And who do we get as muscle? Mr Patterson and his boys from the Gold Reef Hotel will be expensive. Or do I radio-telephone the *Bonanza* now and tell Tucker and the Kid to get up here?'

'For God's sake don't go in for hired guns like a bull at a gate! You don't know anything about them. How good they are, whether they can keep their mouths shut. Before you go for hired guns you have your plan down to the last detail and then you hand-pick them!' She shook her head. 'But listen, darling Jim . . .'

Sarah paused and looked at him earnestly. 'I know I've promised not to say this again, but I must. Jim, you've *found* Heinrich Muller, where all others have failed — even Mossad with all their know-how and manpower! You really are to be congratulated! You're going to be a world hero. You could sell your story for a fortune.' She looked at him earnestly. 'So now, for the last time, let me urge you to hand the rest of the job over to Mossad? With all their money and expertise.' He started to speak but she hurried on: 'Hear me out! Mossad will fly a whole team of experts out here, study the scene, make a hundred per cent plan to snatch Muller, and they'll *do* it.' She breathed. 'You and me? We stand only a fifty per cent chance. That also means a fifty per cent chance of ending up in jail or getting ourselves killed . . .'

McQuade said quietly, 'And once Mossad has snatched him, what do they do with him?'

'You bargain with Mossad *now* about that!' she cried. 'From a position of strength. You've *found* the man, only *you* know who and where he is—'

'And once Mossad snatches him, he disappears on an El Al jet for Jerusalem.' McQuade shook his head. 'No bargain I make with the State of Israel is worth the breath – and they certainly won't put it in writing! Heinrich Muller is so important they wouldn't care how many solemn bargains they broke. Once they've snatched him, would they take him to my trawler and let me twist his arm to find out where the loot is? Would they *hell*!' He snorted. 'Anyway, once Muller opens his mouth to them, that submarine disappears from my grasp in a morass of legal hassle.' He shook his head again. 'Thanks for offering, but I've come this far on my own.'

She gave a deep sigh.

'Okay. I've tried. Now what?'

McQuade looked at his watch. 'I'm going to radio-telephone the *Bonanza* to tell the boys to get back to port and get up here.' He looked at the date dial. 'Monday. That gives us four clear days to prepare before next Saturday, when Heidi goes for this lunch.'

Sarah cried, 'For God's sake – you're not going to attempt this job in four days! You need more time to plan! Saturday *after* next could be the earliest!'

He said tersely, 'The *Bonanza*'s due back any time now. *We're* here now. And *Muller*'s here now. In ten days time he may be anywhere. Or dead of old age.'

65

They were four tense, hectic days. Sarah did her best to dissuade him from rushing the planning, but McQuade would hear none of it: the *Bonanza* was back in port, 435 was about to happen, and his blood and nerve was up. 'If I wait another week I'll get stage-fright.'

He instructed the Kid to drive up from Walvis Bay to the guest farm on Tuesday to be briefed, since he did not dare do so on the telephone. He sent Sarah to Otjiwarongo that day to buy spray-painting gear, emulsion paint, brushes, sponges, buckets, turpentine, adhesive tape, rope, a large roll of brown paper, hypodermic syringes, chloroform, an aluminium step-ladder and bolt-cutters. They needed these things for the job, but he wanted to get her out of the way because he did not want to add the Kid's anxieties to her own; nor was there any need for her to know yet all the details he had to discuss with the Kid. As instructed, the Kid brought an admiralty chart of Walvis Bay, showing the lagoon, and the long sand spit that stretches out to remote Pelican Point, forming the outer perimeter of the natural harbour. He instructed the Kid to move the *Bonanza* from her normal berth at the Kuiseb jetty, as if putting to sea, and to anchor near the far edge of the lagoon, out of sight of the harbour and town.

'Then you and Tucker drive up to Etosha and meet us there in the rest camp on Thursday afternoon for the final briefing. Meanwhile Pottie waits aboard the *Bonanza* with Elsie. On Friday evening he meets Nathan and Julie Wonderful in the Atlantic Hotel and takes them out to the *Bonanza* to await our arrival – I've already phoned Nathan. We snatch Muller on Saturday morning and arrive in Walvis Bay that evening.

Pottie is waiting for us with the dinghy on the sandspit. We load Muller in and speed back to the *Bonanza* and put to sea.' McQuade picked up one of the walkie-talkie radios he had bought in Johannesburg. 'Give this to Pottie. He's got to listen to it all the time. If there're any snags or changes of plan I'll warn him to get his arse home to his telephone so I can tell him without using radio-waves. I'll simply say "Go home, Pottie".'

The Kid mused unhappily: 'This is going to worry Tucker sick. And dressing up as a cop? He's already worried sick about what 435 is going to do to his housekeeping.'

'Tell Tucker to dry his eyes! Tell him we can't afford to mess about getting somebody else because the country will soon be swarming with United Nations personnel so he'll lose the submarine *and* his housekeeping! Tell him to be bloody grateful you're diving down with me on that submarine and not him! *You* can't be the other cop because you can't speak Afrikaans and you sound like a bloody Pommie. Just kick Tucker's tearful arse, and he's not to breathe a word of this to Rosie. He tells Rosie he's going back to sea as usual tomorrow. And you give the Coloured crew a week's leave. Okay? Any more questions?'

'Why are we meeting at Etosha?' the Kid asked. 'Why not here?'

'Because I want to do a disappearing trick. We're conspicuous in this small hotel, and it's too close to the scene of the crime. Etosha is ideal because the gate closes at sunset and Mossad can't get in without a reservation. Which I've made for us. Not even Sarah knows we're meeting you in Etosha; not because I don't trust her but because there's no need for her to know yet, in case Mossad catches up with her.'

'Mossad . . .' The Kid didn't want to have anything to do with Mossad.

'They're the good guys. It's Muller's bunch we have to worry about.'

'I thought *we* were the good guys. Where exactly *is* Muller's place?'

'No need for you to know yet. Tell you on Thursday. Now, we'll go through the plan one more time, then you get your arse back to Walvis Bay and brief Tucker . . .'

McQuade and Sarah spent another two nights at the guest farm. On Wednesday he checked out the Muller ranch again. He learned that there was no other gate in the fence surrounding the schloss. On this reconnaissance he saw Heidi and Muller go horse-riding, and it was clear that Heidi was not just the house-keeper. Muller was very attentive and gallant; he showed off, galloping furiously and jumping obstacles. His horse was a huge fiery animal and Muller dominated it with zest. He appeared extraordinarily fit and agile for a man of his age: he could have been in his fifties. While McQuade was doing this, Sarah drove towards the Skeleton Coast to look for a suitable place to pull off the road after snatching Muller in order to spray-paint the vehicles different colours. She found an excellent place, down a lonely farm track, off behind a hillock. Early on Thursday morning McQuade went with her to check it out. It was ideal, and Sarah seemed less anxious about him rushing the job now. They drove back to the guest farm and McQuade surprised her by loading their bags and checking out. 'Where are we sleeping tonight?' she demanded.

'Surprise. You'll like it.'

'Good thinking,' she said. 'Though I wish you'd take me into your confidence. I'm in this too.'

They drove to Otjiwarongo and found Rietman and Sons, Funeral Directors. The funeral parlour was a squat building on an overgrown plot on the outskirts of town, with a cow grazing in the yard. The parlour had mournful olive-green carpet, with numerous stains, plaster doves and crucifixes on the wall. There was nobody manning the desk. McQuade rang the bell. Nothing happened. '*Hullo?*'

A fat middle-aged man appeared, wearing braces. He had

flour up to his wrists and was perspiring and smiling. 'Sorry, sir,' he said in Afrikaans. 'I'm making bread.'

'I'd like to buy a coffin, please. For my aunt.'

The undertaker was pleased. 'Sir, we'll take care of all the arrangements for your auntie.'

'She hasn't died yet, but we expect her to go any day. We'd like to bury her ourselves, it's her wish. On her farm.'

The undertaker looked very solemn. 'Sir, you can't jus' bury your auntie just like that, hey. You've got to have a proper Burial Order, an' you've got to bury her in an Authorized Burial Ground. But I'll take care of all that for you.'

'She wants to be buried in the family burial ground on her farm in the south—'

'Sir,' the undertaker said, 'you can't jus' drive your dead auntie around the country without proper documents, hey. You've got to have a Removal Burial Order from the Magistrate's Court, hey, an' first you've got to have a Death Certificate signed by the doctor – like this.' He produced a book of blank forms. 'Then you've got to register her death with the magistrate on a form B17 – like this.' He produced more forms. '*Then*, you ask for your Removal Burial Order. So, I can take care of all this complicated business for you, an' it's no problem for me to drive your auntie anywhere she wants, sir.'

'Thank you, but it's her express wish that we do it ourselves, so can I just choose a coffin for her, please? There's nothing illegal in that, is there?'

'No,' the undertaker said regretfully. 'Follow me, hey.'

They went into a back room. On one side was a washing machine and an old wood-burning stove. A large basin of half-kneaded dough stood on the sink. On the other side, coffins lined the wall. There was a stone mortuary slab with a drain, a tap and piece of garden hose. 'Now here's a nice coffin, sir. And,' he opened the lid, 'lined in nice satin.'

'How much?'

'This one, sir,' the undertaker said brightly, 'this one is five hundred rand.'

'What's cheaper?'

'For your auntie, sir? Well, this one is four hundred. Also nice, but cheaper handles.'

'And that one?' McQuade pointed.

'That one,' the undertaker said sadly, 'has no satin, sir. I'm sure Auntie would like some nice satin.'

'How much?'

'That one? Well, that one is only three hundred and twenty. The cheapest,' he added.

'I'll take it,' McQuade said.

'Okay, sir,' the undertaker said, saddened at the parsimony of his fellow man. 'But what about a nice headstone?'

'She wants no frills, and she's paying. Can I have a blank Death Certificate form for her doctor and the other one, B17?'

He bought a drill and bored a row of small breathing holes in the sides of the coffin. The lid also had a smaller, hinged lid that could be opened over the face of the deceased.

Late that afternoon they got back to Outjo, the coffin in the back of the Landrover, covered in cardboard cartons and a blanket. When he took the road to Etosha, Sarah said, 'Aha. What a pity we're not going to have time to enjoy it.'

'When this is over,' McQuade promised her, 'I'll buy you your own game park.'

Shortly before sunset they reached the gate. Nobody was on the road behind them. They checked through, and the gate closed for the night.

66

Beyond the low stone wall seven elephants were drinking at the waterhole. Along the wall the tourists were clustered silently. Inside rondavel 17 the curtains were drawn, the door locked.

On the wall McQuade had taped three maps. One was a large hand-drawn sketch of Heinrich Muller's ranch. The second was the admiralty chart of Walvis Bay harbour, showing the fishing compounds, wharves, the lagoon and the long sandspit out to Pelican Point. The third was a large-scale road map covering the area from Outjo to Walvis Bay. Sarah sat silently attentive as McQuade pointed at his hand-drawn map and said:

'We arrive back at Muller's gate, on the main road. Point A. With Muller as our indignant passenger, ostensibly en route to the police station. We turn towards Outjo, so that the guard at the gate sees us going in that direction—'

Tucker interrupted worriedly, 'But these guys chased you in the desert, so they know your number plates. And the guard on the gate probably notes down number plates . . .'

'Good point, Hugo,' McQuade said encouragingly. 'We have to change the number plates of my Landrover. Nothing simpler than swapping my Landrover's number plates for those on the Kid's station-wagon.'

Tucker blinked, trying unsuccessfully to find fault with this idea. The Kid said cheerfully, 'Fine!'

'Okay, but supposing the guard smells a rat when we show up at the gate? Or even worse, *Muller* smells a rat.'

The Kid groaned, 'You'll be in uniform, for Christ's sake!' He pointed at the sofa where the uniforms lay resplendent.

'It's all right for you, you don't have to go into the lion's den saying you're a policeman!'

McQuade said, 'It's highly unlikely but if there's any trouble at the gate then it's a fight, Hugo. With this kit here.' He indicated the stun-batons and tear-gas canisters on the table. 'We'll come back to this and practise it, but let's get on with the general outline—'

'How does it work?' Tucker picked up a stun-baton suspiciously.

McQuade did not want to discourage him. 'Called the Multi-Force. Guaranteed to neutralize anybody. It's made of poly-carb, so you can also use it like an ordinary baton. But see that little hole in the end, and that little button where your thumb is? If you push that button forward, tear gas squirts into the face of your attacker. And see those two little metal prongs each side of the hole? If you push the button backwards sparks jump across.'

Tucker pushed the button backwards and blue sparks crackled between the two points. McQuade said, 'All you do is touch your man with the baton – preferably on the chest or head – and he gets a terrible shock.'

'You mean just like this?' Tucker leant out and touched the Kid on the arm.

'AAAAAR!' the Kid screamed. He crashed sideways off his chair, and outside the elephants scrambled out of the water-hole and fled into the night. The Kid sprawled on the floor, shocked, face screwed up in agony. 'For Christ's sake Hugo!' McQuade cried. Sarah dashed over to the Kid.

Tucker looked at the baton and then at his victim, in wonder. McQuade snatched the baton from him. 'God, haven't you got any brains?'

'No,' the Kid writhed, 'no fucking brains . . .'

Sarah helped him up. The Kid crouched, clutching his arm, then collapsed back in his chair, shuddering. 'Prick!' he glowered at Tucker. 'Have you got piles or are you a *perfect* asshole?'

'I see . . .' Tucker said, admiring the baton, almost looking pleased with himself, 'wonderful thing . . .'

'Prick . . .' the Kid moaned, clutching himself. He elaborated: 'Prick, *prick*, PRICK . . .!'

Finally McQuade managed to revert to his map. 'Having driven through the gate with Muller, we turn left on the main road, so the guard thinks we're going to Outjo. We drive for two kilometres, until we're well out of sight, and there we meet Sarah, and you, Kid. You are parked on the opposite side of the road, in your station-wagon. With the hood up, as if you've got engine trouble. Here . . .' he pointed at the map, 'Point E. And concealed under a blanket in the back is a coffin.'

'A *coffin?*' Tucker gawked.

'Sarah flags us down. As good policemen, we stop to help a lady in distress. Then we turn on Muller. And knock him out. First with chloroform, then with this . . .' He held up a syringe. 'We then load him into the coffin in the back of the station-wagon. We then jump back into our vehicles and drive off like hell. But towards the Skeleton Coast this time, *not* Outjo. We drive to here . . .' He pointed at the map. 'Point F. It is a farm turn-off. Four hundred yards down that, we swing into the bush. There's a hillock there. We stop behind the hill. And we quickly spray-paint the station-wagon black, and my Landrover white. And then we race on for the coast.'

The Kid could not believe his ears. 'Spray-paint . . . Rene . . . *black?*' he echoed, still clutching his shocked arm.

For the second time Tucker half-brightened. 'Good idea,' he muttered. McQuade said to the Kid: 'Can we please get this briefing over and then rehash it incorporating any *sensible* ideas you may have! Tomorrow's Friday, and we've got to practise and think of *everything*. Everything except whether you like your nice new Rene painted black, Nigel! For God's sake get it into your head that we're talking about *millions*!'

There was a silence. Then Sarah said soberly:

'I'd like to add to that.' She turned to Tucker. 'Jim has

worked very hard on this case. In my opinion, for what it's worth, he has thought of everything. Short of storming Muller's schloss with fifty mercenaries, it's the best plan. And it should succeed.' She amended that: 'It's *going* to succeed. But what we need from you guys is self-confidence and high morale. No more of this pessimism! No more Oh Lord, and Oh dear poor me! For God's sake remember that when you've pulled this trick off you're not only going to be rich, you'll have brought the most wanted Nazi war-criminal in the world to justice!'

There was a sober silence. Tucker was looking at his feet. Then the Kid groaned,

'*And*, I can have my *bottom* ones done . . .'

67

The sky was cloudless blue, the sun shafting through the thorn trees, casting long shadows, and the world was young and old and beautiful, as only Africa can be.

They were up and packed before dawn on Saturday. When the gate opened at sunrise they left Etosha. Sarah was with the Kid in Rene, the coffin in the back, covered, while McQuade and Tucker drove ahead in the Landrover, the step-ladder in the back. They were all in civilian clothes. It was half-past seven when they reached the turn-off to the Skeleton Coast, just outside Outjo. Sarah and the Kid pulled up. McQuade turned towards the coast. He drove for about a mile, then he pulled onto the verge. He got out and opened the bonnet. They settled down to wait.

Tucker breathed, 'Oh Lord . . .'

McQuade turned to him. 'You're word-perfect, Hugo. We've practised every combination. Now let's have some *positive* thinking.'

'And if they open fire?'

'They won't open fire on the *police*. Anyway, your insurance premiums are paid up, aren't they?'

Shortly before nine o'clock they saw a car come over the horizon, dust billowing up behind it. They got out of the Landrover and busied themselves at the open bonnet.

'It's a Mercedes,' Tucker whispered.

It roared past them on its way to Outjo. McQuade glimpsed Heidi in the front, an elderly lady in the back. A man was driving. 'That's them.' He slammed the bonnet closed.

They scrambled back into the Landrover, and started stripping off and pulling on the police uniforms. Sarah's voice came over the walkie-talkie radio, 'Paging Mr Swanepoel, please come to the telephone.'

McQuade snatched up the radio. 'Take the number, I'll phone back.'

He looked at Tucker. 'You look fine,' he said. 'Let's go.'

McQuade had played the role of policeman many times now, but his mouth was dry and his hands felt shaky on the wheel. Tucker's face looked waxen. As the Landrover turned in at the gate to the Muller ranch, McQuade whispered, 'You're a *cop*!'

He gave a sharp toot on the horn, then got out to show his uniform. 'Guard?' he shouted.

A black man emerged from behind the rocks. He was carrying an FN rifle. He seemed surprised at seeing a policeman. He came hurrying. '*Goeie môre, Baas.*'

McQuade said in Afrikaans, 'We've come to see Mr Strauss, please.'

He had expected that the police uniform would be enough, but evidently the guard's orders were explicit. He gave a quick salute, said, 'Wait a little, please,' and ran back to the guardhouse.

McQuade took a deep breath. Was there a television eye hidden amongst the rocks? He tried to look impatient. A minute passed, before the guard came running back, holding a clipboard. McQuade got back into the Landrover, took the clipboard and scribbled in the time and his vehicle's number.

The guard unlocked the chain and swung the gate open. He touched his cap in a salute.

They drove through, and started up the track towards the hills. 'Lord . . .' Tucker groaned.

'*You're a cop!*' McQuade hissed.

They wound up into the jumble of hills. Now they were out of sight of the gate. McQuade braked to a halt. They both scrambled out. They flung open the Landrover's back door, and heaved out the extension ladder. They ran through the bush to the telephone pole. They pulled the ladder's extension out. McQuade's breath was quivering, Tucker was fumbling. They heaved the ladder up against the pole. '*Go!*'

Tucker clambered frantically up it. He pulled wire-cutters from his pocket, and cut the telephone line tremblingly.

He scrambled back to the ground. McQuade snatched the ladder away and collapsed it. He ran with it further into the bush, and flung it down in the scrub. They ran back to the Landrover and scrambled in shakily.

'*Well done.*' McQuade rammed the gear lever.

They ground on. Around and up and over the hills. Then the plain beyond came into view.

'Oh Lord,' Tucker whispered.

'You're doing fine, for Chrissake!'

They ground down, onto the plain, in shaky silence. They drove along the high fence towards the main guardhouse. McQuade took a deep, tense breath.

'Okay, Hugo. Just think of those millions . . .'

The big double gates of the guardhouse were open: they were expected. Two black guards stood on either side, holding rifles. McQuade pulled up. The white officer emerged.

He was about forty, with greying hair and blue eyes. McQuade's hands felt trembly on the wheel. The officer came to the driver's door. 'Good morning,' he said in Afrikaans.

'Good morning. We've come to see Herr Strauss, please.'

The man looked at them. 'I don't know you, Sergeant. Or you,' he said to Tucker. 'I know all the police in Outjo.'

'No, we're from the Otjiwarongo station.'

The officer frowned. 'And what's this all about?'

McQuade said with an impatience he did not feel, 'I'd rather discuss it with Mr Strauss, if you don't mind.'

The officer said, 'I'll come with you.'

Oh Jesus. 'Certainly.' The man opened the rear passenger door and got in.

The white schloss loomed ahead like a colossus. It looked

bigger than the Namatoni fort in Etosha. A guard was staring down at them from the battlements.

'Fantastic place.'

The officer did not respond.

The big wooden doors of the schloss were closed. A smaller doorway was cut in them. There was a large, gravelled parking area in front. McQuade swung the Landrover into a semi-circle, so that it was parked in the right direction for a get-away. He stopped.

The officer led the way. The door was opened by a black guard, from inside. The officer stood back and indicated it with his hand.

McQuade walked through, into a flagstoned archway. His legs felt shaky. There was another guardroom on the left, an armoury on the right. A young man in a dark suit appeared in the courtyard beyond. Unlike the officer, he was smiling professionally. 'Good morning. Follow me, please.' He turned and led the way.

They followed him, McQuade's footsteps sounding loud in his ears, Tucker behind him, the officer behind both. McQuade's eyes darted everywhere, feverishly trying to take everything in: the towering palms, the lawns, the tinkling fountains. There were three cars parked. The young man led the way down the courtyard, to a door at the southern end. He knocked, then opened it.

He walked in, announcing something in German.

It was a book-lined study, dominated by a large desk. A swastika flag hung on one wall. A bronze, lifesize bust of Adolf Hitler stood in one corner, a big world-globe in the other. There were a number of framed photographs. Behind the desk sat Heinrich Muller.

He was looking very annoyed. McQuade walked in. And for the first time he looked his man in the eye. And what he saw made his blood run cold. This was no Rudolf Hess with a pathetic old face: this was a strong, grim man, a hard old man in good health, a proud little man accustomed to command, who knew with certainty he was superior to others. McQuade could identify him with the photograph taken forty-odd years ago. The thin, lipless slash of the mouth. The jaw. The piercing eyes. He did not greet McQuade; just looked at him imperiously.

McQuade cleared his throat. He said in Afrikaans:

'Good morning, sir. Sergeant van Niekerk, Otjiwarongo station. And this is Sergeant Myburgh.'

Muller snapped, 'Don't you speak German?'

'No, I don't, sir, not sufficiently.'

'Why not?'

'I was brought up in the Cape, sir.'

Muller looked at him witheringly. 'Then speak to me in English! And isn't it a common courtesy to telephone for an appointment before calling on members of the public? The Outjo police know my number!'

Suddenly McQuade stopped feeling nervous. He had done his best and he had come this far, further than anyone else, and if he was not good enough then so be it – he was going to talk his way out of here and hand the case over to Mossad. *Fuck the submarine – this was the bastard who had sent millions of people into gas chambers!* He said quietly, 'We didn't want to involve the Outjo police, sir. We thought it best to speak to you off the record.'

The man stared at him. 'What're you talking about?'

McQuade said: 'We believe this is an embarrassing case of mistaken identity, sir. Or malicious prosecution.' He glanced significantly at the white officer and the young man. 'Can we discuss this with you in private?'

The German looked amazed. 'Mistaken *identity?*'

McQuade repeated grimly, 'Can we have a word with you in private, sir? In your own interests.'

Muller was dumbfounded. For an instant he was about to refuse. Then he snapped at his men in German, 'Leave us!'

The two men withdrew. They closed the door. Muller glared. 'Well?'

McQuade took a breath. He put on a relieved expression.

'I'm sorry, but this is embarrassing. A complaint has been laid against you in Otjiwarongo, sir.' He paused, apologetically. 'A complaint of Statutory Rape. Alternatively Indecent Assault. Sexual contact with a girl under the age of sixteen years.'

Heinrich Muller stared at him. Absolutely dumbfounded. He opened his mouth to protest but McQuade went on resolutely, 'Now, sir, we believe this is a case of mistaken identity. Or downright malicious complaint. So we've brought the girl up from Otjiwarongo, to save you the trouble of going all the way there. Her name is Maria Klaasens. A Coloured of fifteen who works as a cleaning girl at the Brumme Hotel.'

Incredulous fury had built up on the man's face. 'Statutory *rape* . . .?'

McQuade said, 'We don't believe it, sir. For one thing, there is the matter of your age. However, there remains the possibility of Indecent Assault, sir, assuming the girl is exaggerating the degree of . . . intimacy, sir.' He held up a palm. 'We don't believe that either. The girl already has two previous convictions for theft. However her parents are kicking up a fuss, so we have to investigate it.' Muller was aghast. McQuade went on, 'But if you wouldn't mind just coming with us we can straighten this out, sir. Otherwise we've got to bring the girl *and* her parents out here, which would be even more embarrassing.'

Heinrich Muller cried, *'I've never heard of such malicious nonsense!'* He groped for words. 'Do I *look* like a man who would do such a thing?!'

McQuade held up both palms. 'No sir, and that's why we wanted your staff out of the room.'

Heinrich Muller suddenly stood up furiously, with astonishing agility. 'I am absolutely . . . *outraged* . . . And if I refuse to have anything to do with this . . . *scurrilous* accusation?'

'Sir, we're trying to avoid embarrassment—'

'I demand to have my lawyer present!'

McQuade said, 'Of course, sir. But we don't believe that will be necessary. Once you face the girl, she'll back down or say it was somebody else.'

'I've never heard of the girl! I haven't *been* to Otjiwarongo for three months, and then I was with my wife!' He snatched up his telephone. 'I'm calling my lawyer!' He furiously stabbed the buttons. McQuade slipped his mini-canister of Mace out of his pocket. Muller slammed the telephone down. '*Klaus!*' he roared.

The door opened immediately. 'Telephone my lawyer to get to the Outjo police station immediately!' He turned to the other man, 'Heinz — get the car!' He strode for the corner and snatched up his hat. McQuade said hastily,

'We'll drive you there and back, sir, no trouble.'

'I don't want to be driven by police like a suspect!' Muller rammed his hat on his head. He glared at McQuade furiously, his eyes gleaming. 'Statutory *rape*...' he hissed venomously. He turned and strode from the room.

Klaus had picked up the desk telephone. But he was staring at McQuade, his face a mask of dawning comprehension. McQuade stared back at him, his mind racing, clutching the canister of Mace. Then Klaus raised his hand and pointed.

'*You!*' he rasped. '*You're not police!*'

There was an instant's shocked silence; then Tucker dashed to lock the door. Klaus slammed down the telephone, his hand scrambling for his holster and McQuade bounded at him, and squirted his canister in the man's face. Klaus gasped and reeled backwards, eyes screwed up, clutching his face, and McQuade hit him. He swung his fist with all his might at the man's guts and Klaus staggered and crashed against the wall. McQuade's hand came down on his neck in a karate chop and he crashed to the floor. McQuade wrenched him away from the gas and slapped his hand over the man's mouth. '*Elastoplast!*' Tucker came scrambling, pulling a roll out of his pocket. McQuade fumbled for the handcuffs, then heaved Klaus over and wrenched his wrists behind his back. He looked wildly around, then wrenched Klaus's wrists around the foot of the desk and snapped on the handcuffs. Tucker ripped a pre-cut length of elastoplast off the roll and McQuade snatched it and wrapped it tight around Klaus's mouth and the back of his head. 'Rope!' Tucker pulled a length of nylon cord out of his pocket. McQuade lashed it feverishly round Klaus's ankles, then lashed them to the other leg of the desk.

'*Stand ready at the door!*'

Tucker dashed to it. McQuade scrambled to his feet. He shakily composed himself. 'Let's go,' he breathed.

He strode out into the courtyard, praying Muller had not noticed the closed door. Tucker closed the door behind them, the catch down, then hurried after him, white-faced.

Heinrich Muller was nowhere to be seen. A black Mercedes now stood in the archway, with Heinz behind the wheel. McQuade and Tucker walked towards it. Then Muller appeared, slamming a Gothic-arched door behind him. McQuade prayed, *Please God he doesn't go back to his study* . . . Muller glared at him, then made for the Mercedes.

McQuade prayed, *Thank you God*. He turned into the archway. Muller got into the Mercedes. McQuade hurried through the door and scrambled into the front passenger seat of the Landrover. Tucker got feverishly behind the wheel. McQuade whispered, '*Go! For God's sake don't let him get ahead of you.*'

68

They drove up the track towards the hills, the Mercedes a hundred yards behind. McQuade was feverishly elated. *They had done it! They'd got Heinrich Muller out of his castle ...* Tucker looked waxen, wide-eyed. 'How long before that guy breaks out?'

'He's gagged and tied up! And the telephone line's cut! For God's sake think positively!'

Tucker's eyes were darting to the rearview mirror as if he expected the Mercedes to open fire. 'You should have insisted on Muller coming with us – this bodyguard really screws things up –'

'We half-expected him to bring his bodyguard! So we knock him out with an eight-hour jab! In eight hours we'll be at sea!'

They were climbing up into the hills now. They crested the first hill; the others rose up. They ground on into them. There seemed more than before. Christ, it was a long way. Past the cut telephone wire. They came over the last hill and the mauve valley beyond came into view. *Please God ...* They ground down into the flat land. McQuade's nerves were stretched tight. The guardhouse came into view. The guard emerged, carrying a clipboard. Tucker rolled the Landrover up to the gate. Muller's car stopped behind them.

The guard ran to McQuade's side. He handed the clipboard through the window. McQuade scribbled in the time, and a signature.

The guard took the board, saluted, and ran to the gate. Tucker let out a sigh. The guard unpadlocked the chain, and swung the gate open. Tucker revved the engine and the

Landrover roared through. He swung onto the main road to Outjo.

'*Oh thank God . . .*'

The black Mercedes was invisible in the cloud of dust behind them.

The road was straight, rising to a crest. They came over it and there, three hundred yards ahead was the station-wagon, facing them, on the opposite side of the road, with its bonnet up. Both Sarah and the Kid leaning under it. Sarah straightened and waved frantically.

'Stop in the middle of the road,' McQuade rasped.

Tucker put on the brakes, his leg muscles trembly. He pulled to a stop alongside Sarah, blocking the whole road. Sarah came to the driver's window.

McQuade got out of the Landrover shakily. He walked with Sarah to the station-wagon. He whispered, 'There's the bodyguard as well. Two syringes. Two chloroform pads.' Tucker got out and followed. He peered into the engine with McQuade. The Mercedes was slowing. McQuade turned. It came to a stop. McQuade turned and walked towards the driver's side, looking apologetic. Heinz was winding down his window. McQuade called:

'Can I come in your car to the police station, sir? Sergeant Myburgh's just going to help this lady. Or do you mind waiting a few minutes?'

Muller rasped in German, 'It's a trick!'

Heinz rammed the car into reverse and McQuade bounded at the driver's door as Muller tried to wrench out a gun. He squirted tear gas at Heinz's furious face, and flung himself aside as Muller fired. The shot crashed through the windscreen as Heinz clutched his face and the car stalled. Muller was also clutching his face, gasping and McQuade plunged the canister inside and squirted again. The Kid came rushing up. McQuade flung open the driver's door and the edge of his hand chopped down on Heinz's ear and his head crashed onto the steering wheel. The Kid wrenched open the back door, grabbed at Muller and slapped a wad of chloroform in his face. McQuade wrenched Heinz's head back, and Tucker slapped the other wad on his face. In the back seat Muller was unconscious, groaning. The limousine reeked of chloroform. McQuade rasped to Tucker, 'Get him into the back seat!' He ran around the car to the other rear door. He flung it open, frantically got his hands under Muller's armpits, and heaved. Tucker was desperately unshackling Heinz from his seat belt. McQuade heaved with all his frantic might, and Muller came out of the car. McQuade looked desperately up and down the road for traffic. Tucker and the Kid had hauled Heinz out. They staggered with him to the rear door. Sarah came running and seized Muller's ankles. They staggered him across the road. The Kid scrambled into the back seat of the Mercedes and heaved the deadweight of Heinz inside. McQuade and Sarah lugged Muller to the rear of the station-wagon. McQuade looked frantically for traffic and yelled, 'Hurry up!' The Kid and Tucker came running, grabbed the coffin, pulled it out of the station-wagon and laid it on the road. The lid was off. McQuade and Sarah dumped Muller into it. They all grabbed handles, and heaved it up and shoved it into the station-wagon.

Sarah ran to her bag in the front seat. She already had her syringes full. She looked frantically up the road, held the syringe up to the light and squirted it, then came running around to the back of the vehicle. McQuade was wrenching Muller's jacket sleeve up, Tucker feverishly undoing the cuff buttons. He pulled back the sleeve to expose the skin. Sarah frantically rubbed an antiseptic wad on it. 'Go for it!' McQuade snapped. She sank the needle into a vein in the white flesh.

For an eternity her thumb slowly went down on the plunger. Then she whipped the needle out, and McQuade scrambled inside and slammed the lid on top of the coffin and began to screw it down. Sarah ran back to the front seat, snatched up another syringe and ran for the Mercedes. The Kid already had Heinz's sleeve pulled up. She rubbed the antiseptic over the vein, then sank the needle in.

McQuade turned down the last screw on the coffin lid and scrambled out. He slammed the door closed, then ran for the driver's seat. Sarah pulled the needle out of Heinz, ran for the station-wagon and scrambled in. The Kid got into the driver's seat of the Mercedes and Tucker ran for the Landrover.

Maybe the whole thing had taken just less than four minutes.

They roared down the road towards the Skeleton Coast, the station-wagon in the lead, followed by the Mercedes and the Landrover. They roared past the gate to Schloss Namib and disappeared in three clouds of dust. Seven minutes later Sarah pointed urgently, *'There's the turn-off!'*

McQuade was going a hundred and twenty kilometres an hour. He jerked his foot off the accelerator, jammed his foot on the brake, the tyres bit the gravel and the vehicle went into a swaying skid and his heart lurched. He corrected the vehicle and the gate flashed past at a hundred kilometres an hour. He looked wildly in his mirror for the Mercedes but he could see nothing through his dust. He jammed on his brakes again and he felt the vehicle go into another skid. He jerked his foot off and corrected, then trod on the accelerator again.

'What are you doing?!' Sarah cried.

'Too late, we'll have to find another place.'

'But we've got to get rid of the bodyguard! And change out of uniform—'

'To turn around will take too long now! Look for another gate!'

'Oh God!' Sarah slumped back and closed her eyes. *'You're changing the plan – that's the way disasters happen!'*

'It's too late now!'

'In that coffin you have the most-wanted war-criminal in the world!'

'Look for another gate!'

The gate to the guest farm flashed past. McQuade snapped, 'About a mile ahead there's another gate. On the left.'

He saw it in sufficient time, braked without skidding and swung into the open gateway in a cloud of dust. He slammed to a stop and looked feverishly back the way he had come.

His dust hung in a pall. He expected the Mercedes to be half a mile behind him. He waited feverishly. Sarah was just as tense, staring back down the road. The dust began to drift away. McQuade's leg muscles were trembly. 'Come on, Kid . . .' he whispered. 'Use the time!' He scrambled out of the car and ripped off his police shirt. He pulled his civilian clothes from under the seat, flung on a shirt, then tore the trousers off and pulled on his suit trousers. He chucked on his suit jacket, and stuffed the handcuffs in his pocket. Well over a minute had passed. *'Oh Jesus, come on.'* He could bear it no longer and strode back onto the road as he put on a tie. Sarah scrambled out, anxiety all over her face, and hurried to join him. Then suddenly they saw the new cloud of dust coming.

'Thank God! Get back to the car. Behind the wheel.'

McQuade peered down the road at the approaching dust. Then his heart lurched. 'It's the Landrover, not the Mercedes!' He stepped out into the road and waved frantically. Dust shot up from the wheels as Tucker slammed on the brakes. McQuade pointed frantically at the gate. The Landrover started screeching to a halt and McQuade saw that its right front bumper was buckled. Tucker swung to a grinding halt in the gateway. *'They've got the Kid!'*

McQuade's mind fumbled. *'Who?'*

Tucker was wild-eyed. 'You overshot the gate but the Kid didn't see because of the dust, so he turned in and I followed. We went bashing through the bush looking for you, then suddenly I see another car and four guys with guns out. I just swung aside but they shot the Kid's tyres out. The other car started to cut me off so I bashed into it and smashed its radiator and got away.'

McQuade stared. 'Get back on the road!'

He turned and ran to the station-wagon. He flung open the driver's door. '*Out! I'm driving.*'

Sarah scrambled out and McQuade grabbed her.

In one movement he had her right arm twisted behind her back fiercely and the handcuffs snapped on her wrist. She swung her free elbow at him, then cried out as he wrenched her bent arm higher. He grabbed her other wrist and snapped the cuffs on. '*You bitch!*'

He grabbed her by the collar and shoved her to the passenger side. He flung open the door and shoved her inside. He ran to the driver's side and scrambled in, rammed the gears and roared backwards up onto the road. He skidded to a halt, then roared off, with Tucker following. He turned to her furiously:

'You bitch! So you still work for Mossad! How else did those guys know where to wait for us?'

Sarah looked at him. Her hair was awry and she was sitting awkwardly, her hands manacled behind her back, but her voice was calm. 'James McQuade, you have caught the most-wanted war-criminal in the world and Israel wants him brought to justice! And so do I.'

'*You lied to me, you bitch! All the time you were pretending to help me you were reporting back to Mossad!*'

'Yes. I lied in the course of duty.'

'*And fucked me in the course of duty! And told me you loved me in the course of duty!*'

'Yes. However I *do* love you.'

'*I don't believe you! I can't believe anything you say!*'

'Then why don't you stop and throw me out?'

'*Because you're the goddam hostage from now on!*'

'Believe me, Mossad knows you haven't got it in you to hurt me so I'm not much value as a hostage.'

'*Don't bet on it!*'

'I love you, Jim.'

He wanted to shout *Bullshit!* but he took a fierce breath and tried to force calm on himself.

'So rescuing me at Sun City, and your so-called confession were just more of your dirty Mossad tricks!'

'No. I really did try to quit the case and I really did rescue you. But when you didn't throw me out after I'd confessed I decided I had to stay on the case. Duty. After we'd settled down in the safe-house I telephoned Matt and told him I was staying on, but on my own terms, namely that no harm came to you. He was very relieved because he thought we'd both done a runner. He accepted my conditions and gave me four weeks in which to get Muller's false name out of you. Or find the computer print-out, or your short-list. You'd told me you'd put it all in a bank safety-deposit box. I searched high and low while you were out in case you'd lied to me, but I didn't have a chance to get at the tool-box because you always had the Landrover.'

He seethed. 'Why didn't Matt just come out to the safe-house, roll me and get the name out of me?'

'Because I refused to tell them where we were in case they did just that. That was the deal, and I held all the cards so he had to swallow it.' She looked at him. '*That* proves I love you.' McQuade snorted furiously, and she went on: 'Then the Hess service happened and things started jumping.'

'So you told them about the Hess service!' He seethed. 'And they followed us to Namibia! Right to the guest farm and Schloss Namib! And once they had the name of Strauss, what were your new orders? Apart from continuing to fuck me.'

'To stick with you, cooperate with you and report your intentions. By telephone.'

'Where to?'

'I don't know. A number in Otjiwarongo.'

McQuade was furiously grappling with all this. 'But once I'd led them to Schloss Namib why didn't they snatch Muller themselves?'

'I wasn't told their plans. I presume they were still casing the place, double-checking on Muller's identity, et cetera. It would be terrible if Mossad snatched the wrong man. They were hoping I'd persuade you to hold off long enough for them to carry out their own plan.'

'But today I forced their hand by going ahead?! So they fell back on a contingency plan, namely to snatch Muller from me!'

'Obviously.'

'At the place in the bush where you and I had decided to respray the vehicles! Which you told them about!'

'Yes.' She paused. 'My guess is that that was just a contingency plan for a contingency plan: they intended to forcibly prevent you from snatching Muller yourself — although they considered your plan a very good one — by jumping on you on Thursday night at the guest farm. But you foxed us all by moving to Etosha unexpectedly.'

'Why didn't you report to them on Friday where we were?'

'I tried. But there's *one* public telephone there, only available during office hours and there was a queue. I didn't have another chance because I was with you guys all the time.' She added, 'And, you mightn't believe this, but I didn't *want* another chance. I could have got to that telephone again somehow, but I didn't want to . . . betray you further. I'd done my duty, and now it was up to the gods.'

'The gods?' He snorted. 'Why didn't Mossad forcibly stop us on the road before we got to Muller's gate this morning?'

'My guess is they didn't dare tackle you on the open road, risk a big fight in a public place right near Muller's hideaway. As you'd given them the slip, it was better to let you get on with it and then snatch Muller from you in the bush.'

'*I'd have given him to you after I'd finished with him!*'

'I know that, but Mossad considers he's too important to take chances over.'

McQuade seethed. 'And what would you have done with me if you'd snatched Muller from me back there?'

'Apologized. And tried to make you understand that I really do love you.'

McQuade snorted. 'And what about that loot I've risked life and bankruptcy for?'

'I was going to try to get that information from Muller for you. I want you to have that loot. It's morally yours.'

He snorted furiously again. 'And what other surprises have you got for me? Why weren't you told Mossad's plan? Don't they trust you either?'

'Not much. They know I'm in love with you. That's why I wanted to be taken off the case. Conflict of duty. They refused. And here I am.' She added, 'In handcuffs.'

Just then they came over a rise and they saw the police ahead. McQuade's stomach lurched.

'Oh God . . .' Sarah gasped.

69

The police car was three hundred yards ahead, on the verge. Beside it was a big metal stop-sign. A policeman was walking out into the road waving his hand, another was beside the open door, talking into a radio transmitter. McQuade stared at the roadblock looming ahead, his mind racing through the lines they had rehearsed for this eventuality.

Sarah said grimly, 'You'll have to take these handcuffs off.' McQuade feverishly pulled the key from his pocket. Sarah twisted her back to him, he unlocked the first cuff. She frantically unlocked the other one and shoved the cuffs under the seat.

McQuade looked in the mirror: the Landrover was a hundred yards behind, slowing up also. McQuade coasted towards the roadblock. He came to a stop twenty paces from it, to give himself space to get away. He rolled his window down partially and called:

'We're going to a funeral, officer . . .'

Suddenly both policemen were running flat out towards them, and McQuade recognized Matt Mathews. He frantically wound up the window and slammed down the doorlock, rammed the gearlever and the vehicle leapt forward, and it stalled. Matt wrenched on the door shouting, *'Police!'* The Landrover skidded to a halt beside them and Tucker came scrambling out, wild-eyed, his stun-baton clutched like a lance. He ran at the other man and nervously jabbed the baton. The man gasped and recoiled, and Tucker jabbed him again with gusto and the man screamed and sprawled. McQuade snatched up his stun-baton, flung open his door and Matt's fist crashed down on his head. He staggered, and

565

Matt hit him again. He crashed backwards and his baton went flying and rolled under the car. Matt leapt at him, his boot swinging, and then Tucker jabbed him on the back with the baton and the man cried out and lurched. McQuade scrambled up frantically. Tucker was prancing around Matt ready to jab him again. Then the other man was trying to struggle back to his feet and McQuade charged at him and hit him with all his might in the solar plexus. The man lurched backwards, and McQuade bounded after him and hit him again so he sprawled, then suddenly Sarah was in front of him, dashing to the defence of her colleague. And there she was, feet apart, knees bent, both hands ready in a karate stance, and McQuade stopped in his tracks.

'For Christ's sake give him to Mossad, Jim!'

McQuade crouched in front of her, rasping, chest heaving, for an instant unable to do what he had to, then his eyes blazed and his brain reeled red-black in fury and he wanted to give the bitch the hiding of her life. She hissed, *'Jim, I can wipe the floor with you . . .'* and he charged. He charged at her furiously, to get an armlock on her and twist it until she screamed for mercy. She side-stepped him and her elbow smashed into his ribs and her foot flashed out and the next thing he knew he was reeling across the road. He sprawled beside the Mossad man. He lay there, winded, shocked. She stood over him, crouched: *'Jim, don't make me do it,'* and then the Mossad man was scrambling up, and in his hand was a pistol. Sarah whirled on him furiously yelling, *'No guns!'* and she grabbed his wrist. Then Tucker appeared like a guardian angel with his deadly baton and jabbed him, and both Sarah and the Mossad man screeched. The gun clattered to the ground, Sarah clutched her shocked hands to her bosom and McQuade scrambled up and he lunged at her. He got her from behind into a savage armlock and Tucker snapped his handcuffs on the Mossad man. Matt was sprawled unconscious, blood on his head from Tucker's kick. McQuade clung fiercely to Sarah and shouted,

'*Pull the distributor cap off their engine. And the transmitter!*'

Tucker ran at the Mossad car, and ripped the transmitter from the radio. He flung open the bonnet and ripped out the distributor cap. McQuade was shoving Sarah back to the station-wagon. He shouted, '*Come and help me!*' Tucker came running, '*Get those handcuffs from under the seat and get them on her!*' Tucker snatched out the cuffs and fumbled them onto her wrists.

Sarah looked at McQuade. She was dishevelled and shocked and in pain. 'Well done. Now what?'

'*Go and find some shade, Sarah Buchholz!*'

She said wanly, '*Go for it. Good luck.*'

He roared at her, '*Bitch!*' Then bellowed at Tucker: '*Get going!*' He ran around to the driver's door. He scrambled in and gunned the engine to life. '*BITCH!*' He let out the clutch and the wheels spun and he roared off.

He furiously looked in the rearview mirror. Sarah was staring after him, her wrists manacled in front of her. Then she was gone, in the dust.

He drove feverishly, the bush flying past, the dust flying up behind him, his mind racing through the same things over and over. He tried to thrust Sarah out of his mind and concentrate, *concentrate, concentrate.*

How far behind him were they?

He was pretty sure there were no more Mossad roadblocks ahead. The last one was undermanned, just Matt and a Jewish Defence Organization amateur — which proved they expected the first ambush to be successful . . .

Concentrate. So? So the roadblock was just a goalkeeper position, a contingency plan, so it was unlikely they had another goalkeeper. So if he met any more police roadblocks they were likely to be *real* police. Which would mean that Klaus had escaped from his bonds.

So don't take any chances. From Uis Mine don't take the short route to the Skeleton Coast — because that's the original plan that bitch reported to her employers. So from Uis Mine you swing south for Omaruru. From Omaruru to Karibib. At Karibib you swing for the coast again, and you'll be on the tarred highway. Mossad is unlikely to set up phoney road-blocks on the main highway . . .

But how far behind him were they now? Tucker had smashed in the radiator of the first car and ripped out the distributor cap of their second car, but they must have had another roadblock at the Outjo-end of the road, in case he changed plan and went that way. The other roadblock team would come to investigate when Matt didn't show up . . .

Oh that fucking bitch!

He took a deep, fierce breath to try to control his fury, to try to think straight.

And another Mossad team would be waiting for him somewhere on the edge of the lagoon, on the sandspit to Pelican Point. So he had to radio Potgieter on the *Bonanza* and give him a change of rendezvous.

Okay, where?

There was only the beach beyond the north end of town, or somewhere in the harbour itself. The beach was out, he didn't know what the waves would be doing. So that left the harbour.

Where in the harbour?

Basically he only had a choice of anchoring near the Kuiseb area, the wharf where the *Bonanza* usually tied up, or near Cato's wharf, where she tied up when Kuiseb was full. No, not Kuiseb – they'd be watching that because they knew he always used it. And Kuiseb had an all-night watchman – he didn't want any watchmen seeing him load coffins into dinghies. So, that left Cato. No night-watchmen, and he had a key for the main gate of the Cato compound.

So he had to radio-telephone Potgieter from Omaruru and tell him the change of rendezvous. He took a deep furious breath, furious about this change of plan that the bitch had forced on him, furious with himself for falling for her, furious

568

with himself for not making a contingency plan. Then he realized something else and he was even more furious: he couldn't use the dinghy at any of the fishing wharves because the wharves were at least six feet above the water and it was too risky to lower a loaded coffin down into a dinghy without a crane – if they dropped the coffin it would capsize the dinghy and Heinrich Muller would drown! *Oh Jesus!* Another reason he couldn't use the dinghy: thanks to the bitch, sure as eggs Mossad also had a dinghy standing by to chase him if all else failed, to snatch Muller before they reached the *Bonanza*. So that meant that the *Bonanza herself* would have to be waiting alongside at the Cato wharf to take on the coffin – Mossad couldn't stop the *Bonanza* from a dinghy . . .

He filled his lungs and bellowed to the desert: '*OH YOU BITCH!*'

And it felt as if his heart had been stabbed.

Isolated mountains rose up into the heat-haze, sprinkled scrub growing between hot slabs of rock weathered sharp and pock-riddled by the winds of aeons; the white road sweeping, the two columns of dust billowing up: in the early afternoon the white, flat-topped dumps of the Uis Mine emerged on the horizon. They raced towards them, the gravel flying up from their wheels; then ahead was the T-junction of desert roads, one leading straight west to the Skeleton Coast, the other leading south. McQuade swung left, gravel flying like grapeshot, and he roared off down the road to Omaruru, Tucker screaming after him in the Landrover.

It was three o'clock when they reached the tarred road outside Omaruru. McQuade dropped speed, twisted in his seat and slapped down the face-lid on Muller's coffin. He screwed it down. Then he drove carefully into the little green town on the banks of the wide dry river. This was it: if Frau Muller or Klaus had raised the alarm, this was one of the places the police would be waiting for him. He drove tensely through the little village, then saw the single-storied Central

Hotel. He turned into the side street and stopped. Tucker pulled up behind him.

McQuade locked the station-wagon and walked to Tucker's window. His legs were shaky. Not a soul was in sight. His mouth was dry.

'There's a change of plan. I'm going to radio-telephone Potgieter now from the hotel and tell him to get ashore to his house. Then we'll drive on to Karibib and I'll phone him again and explain the new plan. And it is this. Just listen and don't ask any stupid questions . . .'

The scrub-lands of Karibib flashed by in the late afternoon; McQuade drove hard, thanking God that Potgieter had made it from the *Bonanza* to his house in time. The town of Usakos emerged out of the hot hard dry-scrub hills. McQuade drove moderately through it, then rammed his foot flat again. He went flashing past the gate to the Stormtrooper's ranch. The scrubland began to give way to the vast bare desert again, long rolling plains of sand, sand, sand with outcrops of stony hillocks and dunes. It was sunset when the Atlantic came into view, and the twinkling lights of Swakopmund.

70

The flat glow of Walvis Bay came up on the horizon.

There is a railway bridge on the very outskirts of town, and then a big lamplit traffic circle. There are often Coloureds at the circle, thumbing lifts to Swakopmund, but not thumbing lifts into Walvis Bay, which is a few minutes walk away. However there was one tonight, at the start of the circle, standing under a lamplight with a hat on. McQuade slowed down to enter the traffic circle, got a look at the shadowed face and was sure he was a disguised Mossad lookout-man. He swept past him. He had intended swinging right around the circle and tearing down 18th Road straight to the fishing wharves but he turned the other way, towards the centre of town and the lagoon beyond. He looked in his rear mirror, but the man was out of view.

He drove fast into the town centre, Tucker behind him, then swung towards the lagoon, roared off down the street for three blocks, then swung right. He drove through the deserted shopping district. He feverishly watched his mirror, but there was only the Landrover. He roared down to 6th Street, then swung back towards the fishing wharves. There was not a moving vehicle except the Landrover. He came to 18th Road. He pulled up at the stop-sign. The bleak road was deserted, the desert around the industrial area completely still in his headlights. He swung left, towards the wharves, and stepped on the accelerator.

Tucker roared behind him. They crossed the railway tracks, then there was the start of Oceana Road and the concrete walls of the fish-factory compounds. McQuade swung right into it. This was really it. If he had fooled that lookout-man at the circle he had a good start on the Mossad bastards waiting at the lagoon. Oceana Road was deserted. He sped down it, the fishing compounds flashing past, then swung onto the sand track leading down to the Cato wharf, a hundred yards away. Potgieter appeared in his headlights, frantically unlocking the gate's chain. He swung the gate open and McQuade roared through it, the Landrover behind him. Potgieter swung the gates closed again. McQuade roared across the sandy compound, then swung the station-wagon alongside the *Bonanza*. He scrambled out, ran to the back and unlocked the doors.

Julie Goldstein was on the bridge, Nathan was on the foredeck with Elsie. Potgieter was running flat out from the gate. He had spread a cargo-net on the jetty, ready for the coffin. The derrick was already swung out over the jetty, its hook hanging. Potgieter leapt onto the deck and ran for the winch. McQuade and Tucker each grabbed a handle on the coffin. '*Heave!*' The coffin slid halfway out. They heaved again, and lugged it to the net and lowered it. There was a rattle as Potgieter slackened off the derrick's cable. McQuade grabbed the hook and Tucker pulled the net over the coffin, and rammed it over the hook. '*Take it away.*'

The coffin rose off the quay. It swung through the air towards the middle of the ship. The midships hatch was open. Elsie had disappeared down into the hold to receive the coffin. Potgieter swung it over the hatch and lowered it. McQuade rasped: '*Single up to the bow-spring.*' He scrambled into the back of the Landrover, unlocked the toolbox and snatched out the shotgun, cartridges, notes, cassettes, print-out, his bag, Sarah's and the defence gear. He leapt onto the *Bonanza*, ran for the bridge. Tucker was on the quay, throwing the stern line off the bollard. Potgieter threw off the bowline, then leapt onto the fo'c'sle to slip the bow-spring. McQuade clattered up onto the bridge. '*Out of the way!*' he rasped at Julie Wonderful. He dropped everything and seized the wheel and turned it hard to starboard.

At that moment he saw the police car. He yelled to Potgieter, *'Engine slow ahead!'* and rammed the throttle.

It looked like a real police vehicle, but he wasn't going to be fooled again. It slammed to a halt outside the gate and a man in civilian clothes scrambled out. He ran to the gate and shook it. *'Stop! Police! Stop!'* The ship was surging forward, the spring-line taking the strain, the stern swinging out. The policeman started clambering up the gate. *'Stop! Police!'* Tucker came clattering up onto the bridge. 'Take the wheel!' Tucker grabbed it. The stern was swinging away from the quay. McQuade dashed to the bridgewing and looked frantically astern as the policeman dropped to the ground from the gate and started racing across the compound. The stern was four yards off the quay now, the bows hard against it. *'Slip her!'* McQuade roared down to Potgieter. *'Full astern and hard to port!'* he roared at Tucker.

Potgieter let go and the rope whistled out, and the *Bonanza* churned backwards, her stern pointing for the open harbour. The policeman was running flat out across the compound. The bows were now a yard off the quay. The man raced at the widening gap, and leapt. He crashed onto the dark deck.

Potgieter went racing for the fo'c'sle and disappeared inside. McQuade roared furiously, *'Get off my bloody ship!'*

The man had picked himself up. He had a gun out. He dashed for cover behind a winch. He shouted hoarsely in English, *'You're under arrest!'*

McQuade shouted down: *'You bastards're a bit late, Matt! And you're on your way to sea, so come out with your hands up and have a drink!'*

There was a moment's silence. The bows were ten yards off the quay now. McQuade snapped. *'Take her away!'* Tucker shoved the throttle lever to forward and swung the wheel. Then the voice came up:

'James McQuade, return this ship to the quay! This is Inspector Dupreez of the South African Police!'

*

573

For a moment McQuade was speechless. *That was Inspector Dupreez's voice.* 'Oh Lord,' Tucker groaned. God this was trouble ... The ship was churning towards the harbour mouth. Dupreez shouted from the dark fo'c'sle:

'I'm arresting you for the kidnap of Heinrich Strauss! And for the murder of Skellum and his mother!'

McQuade was thunderstruck, and his stomach contracted. *Murder!*

'The man I've arrested murdered Skellum and his name is not Strauss it's Heinrich Muller!' he shouted. 'And you're not police, you're Mossad!'

There was a moment's silence. McQuade could just make him out, crouched behind the forward machinery. He snatched up the salt-loaded shotgun. The *Bonanza* was churning towards the end of the breakwater, the engines going doem-doem-doem. Dupreez shouted:

'Why do you say I'm Mossad?'

'Because Heinrich Muller is a Nazi war-criminal! And I've caught him, and you want him!'

There was an astonished pause.

'And what you want to do with him, man?'

'Persuade him to confess to his crimes, then hand him over to the Israeli Government so they can hang him!'

There was another silence. Longer this time. Elsie came puffing wide-eyed up onto the bridge from the hold, via the engine room. Then Dupreez shouted, 'McQuade, this is your last chance, hey. Surrender in the name of the Law or I open fire!'

At that moment McQuade saw Potgieter at the fo'c'sle doorway behind Dupreez, and his heart leapt. He shouted, to keep Dupreez's attention:

'How do I know you're police?'

'Switch on the decklights and you'll see my face, McQuade!' Dupreez shouted and at that moment Potgieter hit him.

In one bound Potgieter was through the fo'c'sle door and

he hit Dupreez on the back of the head with his fist and the man sprawled. McQuade bellowed, '*Use his handcuffs!*' And at the same moment he saw the dinghy come roaring out of the night at them. He roared, '*Lock him up in the fo'c'sle cabin, Pottie! Take the wheel, Elsie!*'

71

The dinghy was roaring along the outside of the breakwater out of the blackness. It was thirty yards off when McQuade saw it, bows up, streaking across the water. He bounded to the throttle and rammed it up to Full Ahead. The dinghy swung into a broadside against the *Bonanza*'s bow-section and two grappling hooks flew up and gripped the rail and in another instant two men were swinging expertly hand over hand up the ropes. McQuade snapped on the deck floodlights and two men in gas masks leapt aboard and raced for each end of the bridge. They disappeared under the wings and McQuade shouted, '*Gas masks! And guard that door!*' Tucker dashed out onto the port side bridgewing with his stun-baton. McQuade snatched up his gas mask and bounded out onto the starboard side, chest heaving. He fumbled his mask on and crouched at the top of the companionway, ready, heart pounding.

Nothing happened.

No man came bursting out to fight his way up the ladder up to the bridge. And there was no sound, only his rasping and the doem-doem-doem of the engine. Then a voice shouted from the foredeck: '*McQuade!*'

He whirled around, astonished. Another man was leaping over the rail onto the foredeck into the floodlights. He had pulled his gas mask off his face to show himself.

'*Jim – this is Matt Mathews. Look at me!*'

McQuade stared at him, his chest heaving. Then he lowered his gas mask and bellowed furiously: '*Get off my ship, Mossad! This is fucking piracy!*'

Matt shouted, 'We're already in control of your ship, Jim! But we want to make a deal with you!'

McQuade shouted furiously, *'I'm armed and I'm going to use it against pirates!'*

Matt stood there confidently, out in the open. 'Jim, you haven't got a chance! Not only are we better armed but we've got reinforcements on the way who can do thirty knots to your twelve! Not to mention the helicopter! So listen to our offer, Jim!'

McQuade crouched on the bridgewing. *Reinforcements?* Inside the bridge Elsie crouched at the wheel, blue-jowled and wide-eyed. McQuade looked astern for another dinghy but could see none. *'So what's your big deal?'*

'Now you're talking, Jim! Now listen! . . . We offer you everything you want out of our mutual friend! We'll interrogate him for you and find out everything you want to know and we'll pass every detail on to you to do what you want with it!'

McQuade crouched in the shelter of the bridgewing, his mind trying to race. And of course the bastard was lying – no way would Israel mess up the confession of Heinrich Muller about the murder of six million Jews by interrogating him about sunken treasure on behalf of James McQuade. He shouted: 'And how do you get him off this ship?'

'Just keep going up the coast till you're outside radar range of Walvis Bay. Then we take him ashore in the dinghy and radio the rest of our team where to pick us up. And it'll be all over. As soon as he's in Jerusalem we'll get your information, tell the world we've got him and James McQuade will not only be an international hero, he'll be off the hook with the South African police!'

McQuade crouched there. Willing Potgieter to come bursting out of the fo'c'sle door again and take the Mossad bastard from behind. He hesitated then shouted:

'First call your goons off! Tell these two shit-hot Mossad men under the bridgewings to take their gas masks off and come out with their hands up! Then you come up to the bridge unarmed to talk about it!'

There was a moment's hesitation. 'It's a deal if you throw your guns onto the foredeck first!'

McQuade felt the flood of battle rush to his face. *'Tell me another one, Matt! Do you take me for such a fool that I'd disarm myself on my own boat?! Throw your weapons first!'*

Matt shouted: 'Do you take *me* for a fool, Jim? And remember we already control your boat! Now be a good chap and let's get on with the deal!'

And McQuade's mind reeled black with fury at the image of that bitch. *'And remember how Horatio held the bridge!'* he bellowed. *'There's only one way to get up to this bridge and that's by getting your head blown off first!'*

'Now be a good chap, Jim! Mossad doesn't want to hurt anybody but if you give us any more trouble we're going to make an exception! You've got five seconds to throw down your guns.' He lifted his gas mask in readiness. 'I'm starting to count! . . . One! . . . Two! . . . Three! . . . Four! . . .'

The rest was very confused. On the *four* Potgieter came charging out of the fo'c'sle door again, and Matt never knew what hit him. And McQuade gave a bloodcurdling bellow, rammed on his gas mask, leapt down the companionway and the gas-masked figure beneath never knew what hit him either. All he saw was McQuade's shotgun at his hip then a blast of salt hit his chest like a baseball bat and he was flying backwards across the deck, senseless. There was suddenly the blinding stink of tear gas from the other side of the ship and up on the bridge Elsie was gasping, and McQuade swung his shotgun blindly and fired and the other Mossad man staggered backwards under the blast of salt. Potgieter had snatched off Matt's gas mask and was pulling it on as he ran murderously at the other Mossad man. He was struggling to get up, clutching his chest, his body an enflamed mass of stinging flesh, and Potgieter slugged him on the back of the neck and he sprawled again. Potgieter ripped off the man's gas mask and snatched up his gun. McQuade ripped off his gas mask sufficiently to bellow: '*Lock them up in the fo'c'sle, Pottie!*' Tucker ran to help Potgieter and McQuade pulled the gas mask on again. He bounded feverishly up the ladder and burst up into the bridge. The canister of tear gas was still hissing inside the doorway. Elsie had fled into McQuade's cabin. McQuade snatched up the canister and hurled it out into the sea. He looked at the compass and slapped the steering onto automatic.

It was then that he saw the reinforcements approaching. '*OH SHIT!*'

The dinghy was about two hundred yards off, coming from the direction of the lagoon, screaming across the water with about six men in it. McQuade bounded at the switch-box and snapped off the lights. The ship was plunged into darkness. He snatched up his pistol and dashed back to the bridgewing. The boat was fifty yards off now, screaming up on his port side.

Suddenly McQuade felt exultantly calm. He had done his best, he had beaten the bastards at their own bloody game! They thought that Matt Mathews was now in command of this ship but in fact *he* had *them* under the gun! Calmly, without a scrap of conscience, he raised his pistol in both hands and rested his elbows on the rim of the bridgewing. He sighted down the barrel at the sleek fat rubber bows.

The boat was screaming up alongside the *Bonanza*, twenty yards off. The men in it appeared grotesque in their gas masks. He followed the speedboat as it roared up alongside, took careful aim at the bulbous bows, and fired.

There was the shocking crack and instantaneously the rubber bows burst and the dinghy nose-dived to a halt and there was a mad scrambling and crashing, and the *Bonanza* creamed away from them.

McQuade calmly made his way up to the funnel deck, above the bridge, untied a life-raft, and heaved it overboard.

PART THIRTEEN

72

The lights of Walvis Bay were disappearing astern. The *Bonanza* ploughed into the black Atlantic swells, the bows rising up, *up*, then sinking down, *down*, heading north-west, getting the hell away from South African waters and the coast.

McQuade paced between the bridgewings and the radar screen. The radar's circling light told him that there were numerous ships about, but there were no blips of vessels putting to sea from Walvis Bay. Each time he looked he felt more elated, but still he kept the bows north-west; then, way ahead, the radar began to show a rash of blips. They were the international fishing fleets raping the Benguela current. After 435 came into effect, those lights would be everywhere, right inshore, when SWAPO sold her birthright of fish for a mess of communist pottage. McQuade ploughed on, heading straight for them, to lose the *Bonanza* in the mass of trawlers out there before turning north and creeping back to the Skeleton Coast. He was outside territorial waters when Elsie appeared up the companionway from the crew's quarters. 'He's come around, James.'

'Put him in the showers. Get him completely awake. Then keep him warm, lock him back in the saloon, and call me.' He turned to Potgieter and Nathan. 'Okay, bring up Matt Mathews. Alone. Keep his handcuffs on.'

Potgieter lumbered out onto the bridgewing, and disappeared down the ladderway. Nathan followed obediently, eager to please. Julie Wonderful sat subdued in the corner, eyes still red from the tear gas, evidently very impressed by how rough big boys can play. And a little seasick. Potgieter and Nathan reappeared, with Matt Mathews. They came clambering up onto the bridge.

Matt was sullen, ashen. He looked as if he was still in shock from the haymaker Potgieter had given him. McQuade demanded, 'What's happened to the Kid? Nigel Childe?'

Matt glowered. 'Nothing. He's of no use to us, Mossad doesn't throw its weight around unnecessarily.'

'And Sarah Buchholz?' McQuade said grimly.

Matt smiled maliciously. 'Love, is it? Forget it. If it's a character reference on her you want, I'm not the guy to ask.'

McQuade wanted to leap at the bastard and shake him. He controlled it and said grimly,

'Now let me make a few things abundantly clear, Matt! We also want Heinrich Muller on trial for his war crimes, and as soon as this little trip is finished I'm going to hand him over to you. So I want your cooperation. First, it may happen that we haven't seen the last of Muller's henchmen. They may show up in a fast boat to rescue him. Now, if that happens, I presume you're going to fight on my side?'

Matt glowered. 'You presume correctly, Admiral.'

McQuade ignored the sarcasm. 'But it may be the police who show up in that fast boat. Now, I'm not prepared to shoot it out with the police in order to get Heinrich Muller out to Israel, and I won't permit you to shoot it out with them either. So if the police show up, we try every trick *except* shooting. Got that, Matt?'

'Go'n teach your grandmother to suck eggs. Mossad doesn't want to shoot policemen of a friendly country either.' Matt glared witheringly. 'But what makes you think the police on that fast boat will be innocent? What makes you think that cop you've got locked up with us in there is innocent?'

McQuade was taken aback. 'That's Inspector Dupreez, I know him.'

'And *we*'ve got to know him in the last hour.' Matt snorted. 'And he knows we're Mossad, and he's terrified shitless of us.

Why? Because he's known for twenty years that Mr Strauss is Heinrich Muller! He's in Muller's pay! He's a Nazi himself! About a third of the police in this country are neo-Nazis!'

'Dupreez admitted to you that he's a Nazi?'

Matt looked at him witheringly. 'Nobody tells Mossad that they're Nazi, do they? But we haven't let the grass grow under our feet up there in the fo'c'sle, Mr McQuade. We wanted to know if there was going to be a police boat pursuing us, didn't we? And we have our little ways of finding out. He admitted that he was protecting Muller but insisted it was only for the money – a minor case of police corruption.'

McQuade was astonished. 'But how did he know to come down to the wharf?'

Matt said, 'Exactly, my amateur friend – why does Inspector Dupreez show up at the wharf *all by himself* to try to rescue Herr Heinrich Muller? Why doesn't he rush down there with the whole Riot Squad? Because he was tipped off about the emergency *un*officially! Not by a nation-wide police alert, because Heinrich Muller's henchmen don't want *official* involvement. So Dupreez receives the bad news *unofficially*, through the cell network. He jumps into his car and arrives at your jetty just in time to get taken for a nice ride.' Matt glared at him. 'So it figures that any police boat that shows up brandishing the name of the Law is *not* what it looks like, and I'm prepared to shoot the living shit out of it.'

McQuade was bemused. He ran a hand through his hair. He said: 'And I may need your advice on how to make Muller talk.'

Matt looked at his amateur adversary. 'Call me when you need me, chum.'

McQuade said, 'But we don't want to give him a heart-attack, we want him alive and well afterwards.'

'Got any laxative on this ship? And plastic tubing, as thick as your finger?'

'Yes?'

Matt said, 'Easiest thing in the world. Give him a laxative, tape a tube into his arse, lie him on his side and tape the other end into his mouth. Works every time. A man can only take so much shit.'

McQuade felt sick. He rubbed his hand through his hair again.

'Well, meanwhile keep talking to Dupreez. Let's find out about these Nazi cells.'

'Go'n teach your grandmother to suck eggs . . .'

He had had many weeks in which to prepare himself for his confrontation with Heinrich Muller; above all he wanted the man to spill the beans without duress or stress that might give him a heart-attack. He thought he had prepared himself for all Muller's possible responses, but he was unprepared for the man's arrogance. Heinrich Muller was standing, erect, his legs a little astride, his manacled hands casually clasped as if at ease, his white hair crisply combed, every inch an old SS general accustomed to unchallenged command. His eyes were steely, his lipless mouth a furious gash. He glared at his captor with contempt. Before McQuade had closed the saloon door behind himself Muller demanded:

'*Well?*'

For an instant McQuade felt that he was out of his league with this man. For a moment he had to remind himself who this was – a brutal murderer of millions of helpless people. He snapped: 'You are SS General Heinrich Muller. And you know why you're here.'

Muller's eyes did not flicker. He said contemptuously:

'I am Rolf Heinrich Strauss. You are some kind of a desperate treasure-hunter. A nobody. And I have numerous friends in high places and you will never get away with this outrage. You are in very big trouble indeed.' His steely eyes did not waver. 'You are evidently trying to intimidate me by alleging that I am somebody else – a so-called war-criminal. But I am Rolf Heinrich Strauss and I am in South West Africa perfectly legally, my friend! And for your information there is *no* extradition treaty between South Africa and Israel for so-called "war crimes" which were allegedly committed before the state of Israel even came into existence, and before so-called war crimes were even "invented".'

McQuade didn't know whether to believe that. 'That argument won't help you when you're in the court-room in Jerusalem – if I decide to take you there – any more than it helped Adolf Eichmann! Nor would it help you when you are tried in a South African court for the murder of Seeoffizier Horst Kohler. Murder is murder–'

Muller interrupted imperiously, 'Never heard of the man. Any witnesses to this so-called murder?'

McQuade put his hand in his pocket. 'This is your wallet.' He tossed it on the table. 'With your initials on it. Containing forged English banknotes. You ordered the witness at gunpoint to lead you to civilization – he hit you with a stick and broke your front teeth, snatched up the wallet and ran away.'

Not a flicker crossed Heinrich Muller's face. 'Never seen the wallet before. And where is this wonderful witness?'

'You had him beaten up and he died of his injuries. You then had his wife and son murdered too.' McQuade wasn't going to lose the initiative by arguing. He went on resolutely, 'And the government of West Germany could easily have you extradited to face trial for the cold-blooded murder of the entire crew of the submarine that brought you here, because that submarine has been found!'

For the first time Muller's expression changed. But not to alarm: it was almost tentative excitement for a moment. Then he said,

'Many German submarines were sunk around the southern African coast, Mr McQuade.'

'Yes, and in the German Submarine Archives there are meticulous records of where and when each submarine was sunk. But there is no record of whatever happened to U-boat

1093. Nobody knows where it is. Except me. Because I've found it!'

Muller's arrogance had not gone, but his defiance had been replaced with something approaching earnestness. 'You've found a U-boat?'

McQuade furiously played his trump card. 'I've been inside it, and I've seen the skeletons of the crew. With bullet holes in their skulls!'

Muller was not the slightest concerned about that evidence. He said, almost pensively,

'And what is it you want from me, if you have already found the submarine?'

McQuade's mind reeled red-black. *'Why did you murder the entire crew?!'*

Muller did not even blink. He said calmly, 'I wasn't even there. But I repeat. What do you want with me?' He added: 'And I also repeat: I have many friends in high places. And not only in this country, but worldwide.'

McQuade wanted to grab the bastard by his shirt. He said, 'Let me make a few things abundantly clear, Herr Muller.' He glared at him. 'First of all, you are not in "this country", you are on the high seas, and nobody knows where you are. Secondly, your numerous friends in high places will not help you one jot when you're standing on the gallows in Jerusalem!' Muller looked back unflinchingly. *'Because that's where you're going after I've finished, unless you cooperate with me!'*

Heinrich Muller's eyes gave away nothing. He murmured: 'I am Rolf Heinrich Strauss. And thirdly?'

McQuade wanted to leap at the little murderous bastard and strangle him. 'But I am not working for the Israelis, Mr Muller.' He looked for a sign of relief in those eyes but none showed. 'My interest in you is purely mercenary. As you said at the beginning, I am just a treasure-hunter. All I want is the spoils of the sea. It's got nothing to do with you being a top Nazi. In fact, I admire the Nazis. I admire Hitler, and I don't like Jews either. In fact, if you want the truth, I think it's a tragedy of history that Hitler did not win the war. The world would be run properly today, not be in the mess it's in.'

Muller's arrogance was back. His eyes were slightly amused. McQuade continued, 'Now, *I* know where your old submarine is, Herr Muller. *You* don't. And I've been inside it. But what I couldn't find was all that loot that you had stowed on board.' He raised his angry eyebrows. 'Now, here's the deal I'll make with you.' He paused, and Muller waited, his eyes serpentine. 'You tell me where the loot is, and we'll share it. Fifty-fifty. And I'll return you safely to Walvis Bay afterwards. But . . .' He held up a menacing finger. 'If you don't cooperate, Herr Muller, I'll hand you over to the Israeli authorities. I'll be a hero and you'll end up on the gallows.'

There was a silence. Heinrich Muller stared back at him unwaveringly. He seemed quite unperturbed by the threat of the Israelis, and for a moment McQuade glimpsed the sheer power and brutality of the vast organization this man used to control. Then he took McQuade by surprise by murmuring,

'How deep is the water where this submarine is lying?'

McQuade wanted to blink, but controlled it. 'About thirty feet at low tide. But you won't find it, Herr Muller, unless you know the exact latitude and longitude.'

Muller looked like a man calmly weighing his options. 'How do I know you'll keep your bargain?'

McQuade concealed his furious elation.

'Mr Muller, I do not wish to spend the rest of my life hiding from your numerous friends in high places for breaking a bargain.'

Muller looked at him. Then amusement came into his eyes for a moment.

'Please disabuse your mind of the notion that I am afraid of your threat to hand me over to the Jews. Because I am not Heinrich Muller. But I do happen to know where the treasure is on that submarine.' McQuade's pulse leapt, and Muller turned and began to pace across the saloon, his hands manacled behind his back. 'I was responsible for meeting the submarine and taking delivery. But the submarine failed to show up, and I've been looking for it ever since.' He stopped and turned to McQuade with a wisp of a sneer. 'Now you have kindly found it for me. Thank you. So I will make the deal you want, Mr McQuade.' He smiled thinly at him. 'Indeed I will improve on it. I will not only tell you where the goods are, I will show you.'

McQuade was completely taken aback.

'*Show* me? Come down into the submarine with me?'

'Yes,' Muller said.

'But you're an old man for Chrissake! I don't want to kill you!'

Muller smiled. 'It's only thirty feet down at low tide. That's no strain on anybody. And I'm an experienced diver. I've been diving this coast for forty years looking for this submarine.'

In a flash McQuade saw Heinrich Muller in that hellhole, driving a knife into his back. He frowned theatrically. 'But you can just tell me.'

A glint of triumph came into the eyes for a moment. 'No, Mr McQuade. You see, I don't care if you blow yourself to small pieces, but we have a deal: fifty-fifty. And I don't want you blowing my fifty per cent to small pieces also.'

McQuade stared at him, and for a moment he was almost grateful to the bastard for warning him. 'We're dealing with explosives?'

Heinrich Muller stood there, his legs a little astride. He answered with a little smile:

'Torpedoes, Mr McQuade. Torpedoes.'

McQuade stared at him. 'The goods are inside the torpedo tubes?'

Muller smiled at him.

'Inside *torpedoes*, Mr McQuade.' He paused for effect. '*Dummy* torpedoes. But alas there are also *live* torpedoes, and I won't know which is which until I see them . . .'

73

McQuade stared at Muller. His mind fumbling, his heart sinking. *And he knew there was a trick in this.* He tried to say it calmly,

'How many dummy torpedoes?'

'Alas, I don't know. At least one.' He added: 'Of course, more may have been included in the shipment at the last moment.'

'And how many live torpedoes?'

'At least one.' He added with a slight shrug. 'My instructions were that extreme caution had to be used in identifying the cargo as one torpedo will be aboard for defensive purposes. Of course, more may have been added.'

McQuade's heart sank. *Horst Kohler had complained bitterly to his wife that he was going to sea with only one torpedo.* 'And how were you going to identify the dummy torpedoes?'

Muller gave his wisp of a smile. 'The *live* torpedo, Mr McQuade. That's the one to worry about, isn't it? I was going to rely on the submarine's crew to deliver the correct torpedo or torpedoes up to me on my trawler. But I would have checked, of course. The live torpedo has a special mark on it.'

McQuade demanded, 'Where? What kind of mark?'

'On the propeller section.'

'*What* kind of mark?'

Muller looked at him with a glint of triumph.

'Ah . . .' he said, 'that's the tricky bit. Alas, I don't know and I won't know until I examine them myself. You see, the commander was to point out the identifying mark to me. Thereafter I was to accept only the *un*marked torpedoes.

Only the commander knew the mark. And, alas, he is dead . . .'

McQuade stared at him. His mind trying to race. Of course the bastard was lying – of course he knew the mark! And he wanted to grab the bastard and throttle the truth out of him! But, oh, the diabolical cleverness of the bastard – planting the fear! Of course the man was lying, but who would dare to disbelieve him and play Russian roulette with a live torpedo?! Muller held his eye knowingly, then turned away and began to pace again, as if in his own boardroom.

'So I'll now make you an offer, Mr McQuade. An offer you can't refuse. Fifty-fifty split, but I'll make it easier for all of us. Tomorrow we dive down on the submarine. We open the torpedo tubes, verify that the torpedoes are there, and we look for the identifying mark on the live one. It should be fairly conspicuous. But we should not attempt to remove any of the torpedoes in case we are mistaken. We don't want to blow ourselves to bits, do we? So we should then adjourn and get an expert to remove the dummies for us, and open them up for us in perfect safety.' He raised his eyebrows. 'And I have such an expert.'

McQuade stared at the man. What an irresistible offer! No Russian roulette. And he wanted to shout in rage because of the trick in it. 'And how does the expert open up the dummy torpedoes?'

'I was told the propeller section is false. Unscrew it and it comes away.'

'And how do you happen to have a torpedo expert at your disposal?'

Muller shook his head in amusement. 'Oh, Mr McQuade, I don't go at things like a bull at a gate, like you. I've been looking for this submarine for forty years! For forty years I've known that the cargo is in dummy torpedoes with at least one live torpedo amongst them. Not only have I read just about everything on torpedoes and consulted umpteen experts, but I've always had one on my permanent staff.

592

Klaus, the man who's in charge of my guards. I recruited him because he was an expert diver and salvage man, and I then had him trained in Germany in torpedoes. The man now is an overall bomb-disposal expert. Before Klaus, I had a genuine World War II expert.' He shook his head dismissively. 'I'm prepared, Mr McQuade. You are not.'

McQuade didn't know whether he wanted to bellow with laughter at the naked trickery of the clever little bastard or be grateful, strangle him or grab his hand and shake on the deal. *And the expert arrives with stormtroops, rescues Muller, murders the whole Bonanza crew and gets the whole submarine...* Jesus, the diabolical cleverness of this trump card of the live torpedo – how could he take a chance on that being a lie? It even made sense – Horst Kohler told his wife there was one torpedo! But he wanted to bellow in rage – *the bastard had frightened him!*

'And what is the value of this treasure?'

'I don't know. Except it is immense.'

'And what *is* it – this treasure?'

'Again, I've no idea. I was only instructed to receive it.'

Suddenly McQuade hardly cared any more, hardly cared about wealth. What he wanted was to punish this diabolical swine, prove him a liar and see him grovel and cry out for mercy.

'And what were you to do with this treasure? Who were you receiving it *for*?'

'I was to keep it safe until I received further instructions from the Berlin authorities.'

He was so plausible that McQuade had to remind himself that it was a pack of lies, and he felt a surge of elation that these lies were the man's weakness because he was afraid of admitting he was Heinrich Muller. 'But there *were* no more Berlin authorities.'

'When Berlin fell, the Reich government continued in Flensberg under Admiral Dönitz until the tenth of May, 1945, by which time the submarine was half-way here.'

'But who could send you instructions after the tenth of May when Germany finally surrendered?'

Muller said smoothly, 'After I'd heard of Germany's surrender, I expected the submarine commander would hand me written instructions when he delivered the consignment.'

'And you would obey them? Even though the German authorities who sent them had ceased to exist? You would never have used the treasure for yourself?'

'Certainly not. There is such a thing as honour. And what is the purpose of this cross-examination? I committed no crime.'

Committed no crime! 'I presume you do not intend to use the treasure for yourself *now*, as there is this matter of honour. So I presume that in the last forty years your instructions have shown up?'

Muller saw the trap. He said with a faint smile:

'What you do with your share is no concern of mine, Mr McQuade, and what becomes of my fifty per cent is no concern of yours. I repeat, what is the purpose of this impertinent cross-examination?'

Impertinent! McQuade rasped, 'And the Jews? What became of them? And are they no concern of mine?'

For the first time Muller looked taken aback.

'The Jews? What have they got to do with this?' Then he sighed wearily. 'We're not going to rake over those old coals, are we? I thought you said you admired the Nazis?' He frowned theatrically. 'Anyway, do you know how many Jews perished in the war? A mere one hundred and fifty thousand.'

'And they all died of old age?'

Muller smiled: 'Everybody suffered during the war, Mr McQuade. There were food shortages and disease and air-raids and the hard labour for the war effort. Millions of Germans perished.'

McQuade almost felt his mind reel red-black again. 'The Hoax of the Twentieth Century, huh?'

Muller dismissed the sarcasm with his theatrical frown: 'Let's stick to business, Mr McQuade — you're about to become a very rich man. What's the purpose of all this?'

McQuade didn't give a shit about the treasure any more! 'The purpose is to demonstrate that I'm not the simple fisherman you take me for! The purpose is to demonstrate that you're a liar! The purpose is to show up the improbabilities in your story! The purpose is to show that you are SS General Heinrich Muller of the late Adolf Hitler's Gestapo!' Muller opened his mouth to protest but McQuade rasped on: 'The purpose is to demonstrate that you were on that submarine coming out to South West Africa with complete instructions! And those instructions were so important to your masters in Nazi Germany that the entire crew of the submarine had to be murdered after you'd transferred the torpedoes so that nobody was left alive to know where Heinrich Muller had gone on Hitler's business!' He glared at the man furiously. 'And the purpose is to find out what that business was!'

If Muller had lost his composure, he had recovered it. He looked at McQuade with a touch of amusement. 'All very interesting. But, Mr McQuade, I am not Heinrich Muller.'

'*Your instructions were to use the money to rebuild the Nazi Party in southern Africa, weren't they, Herr Muller?!*'

'I am Rolf Heinrich Strauss.'

McQuade bellowed, 'Pottie!'

The door burst open and Potgieter came in, wide-eyed.

'Bring the Mossad man here!' Potgieter blinked and disappeared. McQuade turned to Muller furiously. The man had astonishment on his face. McQuade rasped venomously: 'Very well, Mr Muller, you are about to meet the man from Mossad! You will see from his handcuffs that he is my prisoner too. They tried to snatch you from me while you were unconscious but fortunately they lost the fight. *Fortunate* for you, because had they won you would be on a plane to Jerusalem now! And *fortunate* for me because if they had won I wouldn't be able to find out where that loot is!' He paused dramatically. 'Now, it was not my intention to hand you over to the tender mercies of Mossad, Herr Muller: I am not a vindictive man and I do not think the Nuremberg Trials were fair, I do not think men should be jailed and hanged for doing their duty in times of war, and I do not think so-called war-criminals should be hounded into their old age by snot-nosed young Jews who weren't even born when the so-called crimes were committed!' He paused again. 'What I was going to do after we'd got the treasure was dump these three Mossad men – who are trying to kidnap you quite illegally in terms of the laws of this country – I was going to chuck them back in their dinghy and turn them loose on the Skeleton Coast and I was going to take you back to Walvis Bay to make your own way home. But since you *refuse* to tell me the truth, Herr Muller, I am now going to hand you over to the Mossad men! They are not only going to get the truth out of you, they're going to take you back to Jerusalem to stand on the gallows!'

Muller seemed to have forced the momentary fear out of his eyes and they were opaque again. He opened his mouth to speak and McQuade bellowed, '*Shut up!*' He strode for the door. '*Pottie!*' he roared.

'Here.' Potgieter was coming down from the bridge, Matt in front of him, his hands manacled. They came filing into the saloon. Muller stared at the two men. His face was suddenly ashen. Matt had a malicious smile in his eyes. McQuade rasped at Matt, 'Show the bastard your identification!'

Matt fumbled his manacled hand into his pocket. He produced a card and thrust it at Muller.

'And who is this man?' McQuade pointed at Muller.

Matt said slowly: 'He is Heinrich Muller. Formerly SS General, head of the Gestapo in Nazi Germany.'

Muller was staring, ashen. Then his legs seemed to give way suddenly. He sat down heavily on the edge of the table.

McQuade looked at Matt in triumph. Then he jerked his head at the door.

74

Muller was trying to compose himself, his eyes closed. McQuade shut the saloon door and glared at him. 'Heinrich Muller?'

The man opened his eyes. 'You will keep your bargain?'

McQuade's blood surged. The head of the Gestapo was pleading for mercy! 'If you keep yours.' He added, for credibility, 'I want to enjoy my money, not spend the rest of my life hiding from your people. So, you are Heinrich Muller? And you sailed on the submarine all the way from Germany with the cargo.' It was not a question.

But McQuade was wrong. The man suddenly seemed to have recovered his composure: he was again the military man. He said: 'Yes, yes, yes! Perfectly legally! On the orders of Martin Bormann!'

McQuade was taken aback.

'And you murdered the entire crew "perfectly legally" after the submarine got wrecked? As you would have done after you'd met the trawler, so that nobody was left alive to tell where Heinrich Muller had gone with the Nazi loot?'

No flicker of anxiety crossed Muller's face, only weariness. 'No, Mr McQuade. There was a riot on board. A mutiny, if you like, and some of the crew started to attack me and my SS bodyguards. My guards opened fire in panic, and the whole thing got out of control.'

McQuade wanted to bellow in rage. The man felt safe in lying on this detail! He didn't intend wasting time arguing but he snapped, 'Why did they mutiny?'

'Half-way down the Atlantic we got the news on the radio that the war was finally over, and the crew was overjoyed.

Some wanted to surrender in Walvis Bay. Others wanted to turn around and run for home or surrender in Gibraltar. But the commander refused all their pleas. There were tremendous arguments, and all their resentment was finally directed at me and my two men, the passengers, and the cargo. They didn't know about treasure, but some of them said we were carrying valuables. So when the submarine went aground, and they had to risk their lives further, they mutinied. One man charged at me and then the whole lot were at us.' He ended wearily. 'It was forty-odd years ago, but that's roughly how it was. And my guards opened fire.'

McQuade was smiling maliciously. No way did he believe any crew would mutiny during Abandon-ship. But he let it go for the moment. 'And then?'

Muller shook his head impatiently. 'The commander had already ordered the submarine to be flooded. I was in the *Zentrale*. I knew what to do. I got into the escape tube with my air-bottle, rose up out of the submarine, and eventually to the surface. I inflated my life-jacket and swam for the shore for dear life.' He ended, 'Fortunately I'm a strong swimmer.'

'But unfortunately Seeoffizier Horst Kohler was pursuing you.'

Heinrich Muller clicked his tongue in dismissal. 'Was that the madman's name? Yes, I had no idea the man was behind me. I was desperately struggling in the breakers. Finally I was thrown ashore. Then saw this madman coming at me.'

'Covered in blood. And with murder in his heart.'

Muller looked at him; and McQuade knew he was dealing with a practised actor. Muller's eyes took on an exasperated expression. '*Yes*, Mr McQuade – with *murder* in his heart! Doubtless because he blamed me for the mutiny. I don't know how he got the blood. Doubtless in the mutiny.'

'And you tried to shoot him,' McQuade murmured. 'But your gun failed you. So you stabbed him and killed him.'

'You over-simplify. But yes, I killed him in self-defence.'

McQuade frowned. 'Amazing. That a senior and responsible naval officer attacks his very important official passenger after a shipwreck. What a waste of valuable energy in a crisis. Anyway, you buried Horst Kohler then set off down the coast. You had a wallet. This.' He held it up. 'You also had a bag of valuables. What was it?'

Muller looked mildly surprised that McQuade knew this last detail. 'Gem stones. Why?'

'Where did you get them?'

Muller said: 'None of your business. I bought them. I converted my personal savings into hard assets I could re-sell one day.'

'And where did you get the counterfeit English fivers?'

Muller said simply, 'Operation Birkenbaum. That was an official operation which counterfeited English currency. Those,' he nodded at the wallet, 'were part of our first production. I took them to Martin Bormann, to show him.'

'And you hung onto them. For a rainy day.'

'Yes. Who wouldn't?'

'Was that legal?'

'No. So what?'

'In fact Jews were shot on the spot for possessing as little as one foreign banknote.'

'I didn't make the laws.'

Jesus, McQuade hated him. 'How did you survive the Skeleton Coast?'

'With difficulty. What's the purpose of this questioning? I'm here, aren't I? But, to satisfy your curiosity, I had one of the strandlopers' bags containing water-bottles, and I had a pistol. I dug for water in the Ugab river bed. I stayed a week at the Ugab, getting my strength back. Later I shot a buck and drank its blood. I was in a bad way when I reached Swakopmund.'

McQuade took a deep angry breath 'So you got your teeth fixed. And you established contact with the Germans who were supposed to meet the submarine in the trawler.'

'No. I knew nothing about them – who they were or where

they were. I managed to get some local money by selling some gemstones. I bought some clothes and a train ticket and disappeared inland. In Windhoek I sold most of my diamonds. Land was dirt cheap in those days, so I bought a farm and settled down to my new life.'

'And you *never* found the people who were supposed to meet you. Through the German community?'

'No. All I knew was the codename: Swordfish. I wasn't told any more for security reasons, and for the same reason Swordfish didn't know who I was. I couldn't start asking around town who Swordfish was, could I?'

McQuade did not know whether to believe this. But he let it go for the time being. And moved on to the all-important question. 'But Reichsleiter Martin Bormann did give you detailed instructions as to what to do with the cargo contained in the dummy torpedoes.' It was not a question.

Heinrich Muller looked at him. And the eyes took on a glint of triumph again. 'Correct.'

'And those instructions were to use the money for the re-creation of the Nazi Party in South Africa! To resurrect the Third Reich!'

Heinrich Muller slowly smiled. 'No, Mr McQuade. That would have been illegal. The Nazi Party was banned under South African law.'

McQuade could not believe his ears. Illegal? . . . And he wanted to guffaw in rage and leap at the bastard and strangle the truth out of him. He shouted; *'Illegal! Suddenly the Nazis, who had broken every law in the book of mankind, wanted to do things legally?'*

Heinrich Muller smiled, and played his trump card.

'Yes, Mr McQuade. Absolutely legally. Because, you see, my instructions were to use the money to get the *Afrikaners* into power in South Africa.' He paused and then pointed at the deck. *'This very same government which is now in power and has been since 1948.'* He smiled. 'And we succeeded. Even without the money.' He smiled at McQuade again. 'All I was told to do was to rally support and help the Afrikaner people

600

into political power, legally, at the polls.' He raised his eyebrows. 'We played it by the book. There's nothing illegal in that, is there? I doubt the Attorney General or P.W. Botha would think there is . . .'

McQuade stared at him. Of course . . . That was the best way of resurrecting the Third Reich – and perfectly legally. By taking in, being absorbed into, an existing compatible political organization, namely the Afrikaner's Nationalist Party. The Nats hated the British and wanted South Africa for themselves. Many supported Hitler during the war because they hated the British so much. When the Nats got into power, they would open the door to the Germans, and then the way would be open for them to take over the Nationalist Party, from the inside. Then Hitler's blueprint for Africa, his Grand Design would be a reality! He said: 'Infiltrate the Nationalist Party? And take it over. And did you succeed in that, too?'

Muller said with weary exasperation: 'You know we did not. The German momentum was lost. For the next forty years the Afrikaners were far too self-centredly consolidating their power and their Apartheid apparatus, as well as turning themselves into a middle-class nation of civil servants and bourgeois farmers and businessmen, to let *anybody* but an Afrikaner into their privileged circle.' He shrugged. 'Oh, they opened the immigration doors and Germans flooded into the country. But the *original* German momentum was lost. Over the years they largely became Afrikaners themselves, and lost their original identity. To the point where today over half the Afrikaners are of German descent.'

McQuade glared at him. 'And so Martin Bormann's instructions are now a dead letter? So what are you going to do with your share of the loot?'

Muller shrugged. 'Keep it for myself.'

'And the Nazi movement has got nothing to do with it?'

Muller snorted softly. 'What Nazi movement?'

McQuade snapped, 'The AWB! And the Nazis behind it!'

'The AWB?' Muller said with surprise. 'A bunch of Afrikaners who want to turn back the clock?'

'You're not a member of the AWB?'

'No!'

McQuade strode to the door and flung it open. 'Pottie!' he yelled up to the bridge. 'Bring down Inspector Dupreez!'

Heinrich Muller looked taken aback. 'Dupreez?'

There was a clatter on the companionway and Inspector Dupreez appeared, his hands manacled in front of him. His hair was dishevelled and his heavy face was bruised and anxious. McQuade grabbed his arm and pulled him into the saloon. He pointed at Muller furiously. 'You know this man!'

Muller was ashen. Inspector Dupreez looked at him imploringly, then blurted to McQuade, 'I swear to God I never knew he was Heinrich Muller! I know nothing about war-criminals! I swear to God I just thought he was our regional leader!'

McQuade snapped, 'Regional leader of what?'

Dupreez said imploringly, 'Of the AWB. And that is a perfectly legal organization, Mr McQuade—'

'Is it legal for a policeman to be a member of the AWB?'

Dupreez implored, 'No, but hell, man, I was only being patriotic. I don't want to see this country handed over to the kaffirs—'

'And how do the AWB propose stopping that?'

'*Got*, man, we've got to fight, hey?'

'And when does the fighting start?'

'*Got*, man, Mr McQuade, I'm not a politician, hey. I'm just an honest-to-God policeman with a wife and three children who wants to see law and order, not the streets unsafe to walk in because communists are ruining the country like every other bladdy African country—'

McQuade interrupted, 'So you, as a policeman, will mount an armed revolution against your own legal government because it starts dismantling Apartheid and starts some power-sharing with the blacks—'

'*RUBBISH!*' Heinrich Muller suddenly bellowed.

McQuade and Dupreez both turned, astonished.

Heinrich Muller's face was suffused, his eyes ablaze. Gone was the surprised man of a few minutes ago; the arrogant Nazi was back. He glared witheringly at McQuade, then at Dupreez; then he said softly: 'You're both ignorant fools! *Fools!*' He shook his grey head at them. 'Don't you realize that there will be no reason for *illegal* armed revolution? Don't you stupid people understand that we will win this country absolutely *legally*?' Then the blood seemed to rush to his face. 'Because this South African government is going to make itself illegal! And I mean in terms of International Law! In terms of South African Law!' He glared at them. '*The South African government is about to make itself an outlaw! And the AWB will then take power absolutely legally!*'

McQuade stared at the man. Inspector Dupreez's astonished face was flushed with emotion. Muller glared at them; and he was no longer a war-criminal making a deal, he did not give a damn any more for all that; here was an angry political man who was sick and tired of fools. He turned his back in contempt and then whirled around again.

'What you fools don't realize is that we have never been so strong! And we're going to get stronger! We've never had it so good and it's going to get better! And the South African government has never been so weak and it's going to get weaker!' He shook his head at them. 'The South African government which has ruled this magnificent country for forty years is coming apart at the seams like Ancient Rome! And like Ancient Rome it will collapse in a shambles and the AWB will have to come to the rescue and pick up the pieces and restore order – *perfectly legally* . . .'

Dupreez was hanging on his words. Muller sneered at them, then rasped venomously. '*Think* about it – if you can. Think how the Afrikaner people are split down the middle with dissension because their government is making reforms. And realize that whereas the Nazi Party has been banned for sixty years it is now almost the official opposition in parliament for practical purposes.' He glared at them, then went on softly: 'For God's sake understand that this government will only weaken itself with its so-called reforms because they will please nobody! Neither the left nor right, neither so-called world opinion, nor the Afrikaner backbone of this country. The party will be split even further as more and more Afrikaners flock to the AWB banner and as more members cross the floor of Parliament to our Conservative ranks leaving the government further weakened.' He smiled at them. 'Think what will happen then – when the government's made a proper mess of it, when there're riots in the streets and the Afrikaner nation is even more frightened of the future and really rallying to the banner of the Conservative Party and the AWB. Think about the fact that the government must continue to try pushing through these muddle-headed reforms they're promising and in order to recover their numerical strength they must move even more to the *left*! So even more Afrikaners will flock to the right and make us stronger still! Now, even if the government doesn't collapse like Ancient Rome, *think* what is going to happen at the next election . . .' He paused, then shook his head at them angrily. 'Only two things can happen . . .'

He glared, then held up both manacled hands and a finger. '*One*. The government, despite its chaotic troubles, *just* manages to win the election. But with such a reduced majority, the party so compromised by deals it's had to make with the left, the people so split and the opposition so strong, so many people crossing the floor, *that it cannot govern!*' He waved his manacled hands. 'With riots in the streets and terrorists planting bombs and our soldiers fighting on the border trying to hold back the ANC . . .' He paused, then shook his head at them. 'And the AWB will have to come to the rescue and take over . . . *Perfectly legally!* Because a government which ceases to govern has no more legal or moral mandate!'

Dupreez was mesmerized. Muller was glaring at McQuade. Then he held up two fingers.

'Or *two* . . . The AWB and the Conservative Party wins the election . . .' He raised his eyebrows, then leant towards them. 'The Nationalist Party would refuse to surrender power!' He glared, then jabbed his finger at them: 'They would refuse to accept defeat!' He waved his hands. 'The Nationalist Party has not the slightest intention of giving up the power it has held for forty years! The power it lost at such cost during the Boer War! The power it struggled for all those years against the English-speaking South Africans afterwards! The Broederbond was formed so that the Afrikaner could get power, and when they got it they prepared military plans to enable them to hang onto that power forever!' His eyes were bright. He leant forward again. 'No, my fine friends . . . If they lost the election they would declare a state of emergency and try to rule by decree!' He looked at them triumphantly. 'And then there will be your armed rebellion from the AWB . . . Then there will be big trouble. Fighting street by street, city by city, town by town, hill-top by hill-top, valley by valley across the land. And the AWB will be fighting *legally!* And we will have most of the police on our side! And at least sixty per cent of the entire Afrikaner nation. And then most of the army will follow . . .'

McQuade was staring at him. Exactly as Johan Lombard had said! Muller paused, his cold-blooded eyes afire: then he went on maliciously: 'And that day is much closer than you think, my fine friends. Because this government has just brought disaster upon itself by selling Namibia down the river for thirty pieces of silver. By bowing to the tin-pot black states in the United Nations and shamelessly selling us out to SWAPO and its Cuban bandits, by selling us out to a bunch of black communists who're going to turn this country into yet another one-party, corrupt, African basket-case!' He glared at them with withering triumph. '*Just* like the British did in the rest of Africa . . . And why? Why are they doing it when they know full well what the consequences will be, when they know full well they're handing this well-run country over to corrupt, inefficient Marxist despots who're going to ruin it? Why? For the same reason the despicable British did it – because it's *cheaper*, my fine friends.' He paused and shook his head: 'And that weak-kneed surrender is going to be their downfall. Because the AWB is not going to take this treachery lying down! They're going to fight! For justice! They're going to *refuse* to hand themselves over to a black Marxist dictatorship . . .'

Dupreez was a mesmerized man. McQuade said grimly: 'And that's what you're going to use your share of the loot for?'

Heinrich Muller ignored the question. 'We may not win that battle, gentlemen, for the simple reason that we will be fighting thousands of United Nations soldiers, and the SWAPO terrorists and probably the South African army itself . . . And it will be a tragedy, a travesty of justice that we lose. But that battle will only be the first round! The decisive battle will be the second one, and it will be fought in South Africa, and the prize will be South Africa itself . . . And that battle we *will* win! Because the Afrikaner people – the whole South African people – will see how their precious government failed their kith and kin in Namibia and realize that if the government can sell us down the river they'll do the same in South Africa . . .!' He glared at them triumphantly, then hissed: 'And the people will *really* flock to the AWB banner, and there will be riots. And the Conservative Party will *win* the next election – or the next after that. And then this government will refuse to surrender power and the civil war will follow. And that battle we *will* win . . .'

Dupreez's eyes were alight with emotion. Muller's cold-blooded eyes were blazing. He ended witheringly:

'So don't talk to me about legalities, Mr McQuade.' He looked at him with contempt. 'What you stupid people don't realize is that this Afrikaner government are the *typical, true*

606

Africans! Because, like the African, if they cannot rule by the ballot box they will rule by the sword!' He glared, then he leaned forward and hissed: '"And he who lives by the sword will *die* by the sword" . . .!'

PART FOURTEEN

75

That night McQuade did not sleep. He ordered Matt to be brought up to his cabin. He reported what Muller had said. 'What's Mossad's opinion about that?'

'No doubt about it,' Matt replied sullenly. 'The AWB intends trying to make Namibia ungovernable to resist the independence. They can't succeed but it will be a *Götterdämmerung*, out of the ruins of which will arise the purified strength for the new order in South Africa itself, with the *volk* flocking to the impregnable AWB laager. From that laager they will storm forth with their jackboots and sjamboks and swastikas. That's my prognosis.'

'And if the AWB and Conservative Party were to legally win the next election?'

'The government would refuse to surrender power and then you'll have the Boer War all over again, except this time the Boers will be fighting an Afrikaner government. And this time the Boers will probably win.'

'Then we'll have a Nazi government?'

'Then you'll have big trouble, my friend. And Hitler will have finally won the war.'

McQuade did not have time to dwell on it. He spent the next two hours feverishly poring over Westwood's book, *The Type VII C U-Boat*, studying the diagrams of the torpedo tubes and locking mechanisms with Tucker.

'Oh Lord,' moaned Tucker. 'Shouldn't we take him up on his offer of an expert?'

'It's a trick!' McQuade shouted.

'But how do we get the torpedoes out?'

'We don't, you asshole! Muller says the propeller casing just comes away on the dummies!'

'And if it doesn't? If it goes bang?'

McQuade sent for Matt again: 'Do you or your men know anything about torpedoes?'

'Piss off,' Matt said.

It was three a.m. when he went to his bunk, desperate to sleep, to unwind so he would be fit for the frightening things he had to do today. But he could not, his nerves stretched from weeks of tension, from the action-packed events of yesterday, his mind a turmoil of submarines and torpedo tubes and what Muller had told him; and his furious heart breaking over Sarah Buchholz. With the dawn he gave up and swung out of his bunk angrily. He pulled on his tracksuit and went to the bridge. Tucker was there with Elsie.

'Why the hell aren't you asleep! I said Pottie had to do the whole night watch — I need you fit today!'

Tucker moaned, 'I couldn't sleep so I took over and sent Pottie to bed.'

'Well go to bed now!'

'Jim, I've got a suggestion,' Tucker pleaded. 'You haven't slept either. When we get there let's try to get a night's sleep before we go down—'

'Yes, darlings,' Elsie said with big eyes, 'you're *pushing* yourselves so.'

'We're going down today!' McQuade snapped. 'We're going to get this over with!'

He went to the chart table, looked at the sat-nav, scribbled down the Last Fix. He snatched up the parallel rulers and measured off the latitude and longitude of the fix. He slid the parallel rulers across the chart to the compass rose. He allowed for magnetic variation. 'What are we steering?'

'Zero zero seven.'

'Steer zero zero three.'

His heart was breaking.

With the sunrise Nathan showed up on the bridge, beefily

ubiquitous. 'At ease, men, aha-ha-ha! Julie Wonderful's terribly seasick.'

'Good.' McQuade wished Nathan was seasick too. 'Out of my way, please.'

It was almost eleven o'clock that morning when his binoculars picked up the yellow float. Beyond, the waves crashed onto the Skeleton Coast.

The *Bonanza* rode at anchor on the long swells, her engines thudding in neutral. Matt Mathews and his men, together with Inspector Dupreez, were locked in the fo'c'sle cabin. Heinrich Muller was in the saloon, one hand manacled to a stanchion. Julie Goldstein was still in his bunk. McQuade had cut the electric power from the sat-nav at source in the engine room and hidden the chart and sextant: if any of his prisoners broke out they could not find out the exact latitude and longitude. On the deck all the gear was laid out.

McQuade and Tucker were in their wetsuits. Both their faces were drawn. Potgieter and Elsie began to lower the dinghy down to the water. Suddenly there was a shout from the saloon, 'McQuade!'

He looked up. Heinrich Muller was at the porthole. *'What about me?! I'm going down with you!'*

McQuade turned away and picked up his airtank harness.

Muller bellowed, *'You're a lying swine! And you're going to blow yourself up!'*

McQuade hefted on his tank and did up the buckle. Muller screamed, *'You're going to die if I don't show you!'*

McQuade swung over the gunnel, onto the rope ladder. *'You're going to die!'* Muller screamed. McQuade clambered down into the dinghy. Potgieter lowered down the outboard-motor and McQuade hefted it onto the transom. *'You're going to die!'*

Tucker clambered down the ladder. 'Oh Lord . . .'

McQuade bellowed up at Nathan: 'Go'n wrap elastoplast on that bastard's mouth!'

Two minutes later all the gear was in the dinghy. Muller had been silenced. Potgieter clambered down. McQuade ripped the cord and started the outboard-motor. Elsie untied the painter and threw it down. He gave a smile and wave of encouragement. McQuade swung the tiller and the dinghy surged away from the ship. They went churning towards the crashing shore, looking for the yellow float. They surged towards it, slowing. McQuade handed over the tiller to Potgieter. 'Circle around it!' He spat into his mask, washed it off in the sea, and pulled it on. He turned to Tucker and put his hand on his shoulder. 'Nothing to it, Hugo. Just keep calm.' He put the regulator into his mouth, clasped his mask and toppled backwards into the sea.

He broke surface and clutched the gunnel, his head under the water. Potgieter opened the throttle and began to turn in an arc, while McQuade scanned the seabed.

Within a minute he saw it. There it was, long and ghostly in the noon light, the bows disappearing into the gloom, the nets wafting above it, the conning tower like a dreadful mouth. McQuade felt his stomach contract all over again.

He lifted his head and spat out the regulator and shouted above the outboard noise, 'Throw out the anchor, then lower the gear over.'

Down they dived into the ghostly gloom, and up came the waving shrouds of nets to meet them. They manoeuvred between them, then down they went, the guns of the wintergarten pointing up at them. They grabbed the muzzles of the guns, then pulled themselves towards the conning tower. And there was the dreadful black hatch leading down into the charnel house.

McQuade pulled himself over the rim. Tucker followed, wide-eyed, bubbles roaring. McQuade pulled out his torch and shone it into the hole.

Nothing happened. He leaned closer, pushed the torch through the hole and peered down into the dark cavern.

And the dreadful fiend of a octopus came flying out.

It came flying up at them in a massive streaking blur of evil eyes and head; they lurched backwards in a shocked flurry of bubbles, and the beast shot past them in a cloud of black ink. And it was gone.

They clung, hearts pounding, waiting for the ink to disperse. Then McQuade clawed and kicked his way into the hole. He burst through into the chamber in a roar of bubbles, and there was the hatch leading down into the awful tomb.

He did not look at it. Tucker lowered the toolbags and sack containing two spare gas-tanks. Then he came surging down. McQuade looked at him, nodded, then, before his nerve failed him, he pulled off his fins and shoved himself feet-first into the terrible hole. He sank up to his shoulders. Then he shoved, and down he went until his feet reached the bottom. He bent his knees and shoved and he burst backwards out of the tube into the black water. He scrambled desperately to his feet in blackness, snatched the torch out of his pouch and switched it on.

He did not shine it around the dreadful place but waited desperately for the toolbags to arrive. He could hear them banging against the side of the tube as Tucker lowered them. He plunged his head under the water and pulled them out, he fumbled the knot undone, and tugged on the rope. Then there was a scraping noise as Tucker came down. His feet hit the bottom. He crouched and wriggled and burst up out of the tube in a big black gush.

He looked at McQuade, wild-eyed, in the ghastly torchlight. McQuade thrust a toolbag at him, then turned and started through the black water towards the bows.

He waded as fast as he could, trying not to feel the ghastly things under his feet. He ducked through the circular hatch into the commander's cabin. He looked neither left nor right. Through into the officers' cabin, the terrible skeleton grinning at him from the upper bunk. Through into the petty officers' cabin. More skeletons. Bones crunching and bumping underfoot. He plunged through the last door, into the crew's quarters, and there at the bows were the torpedo tubes.

They worked feverishly. McQuade pulled out a big steel mallet and a chisel. He thrust the chisel against a spoke on the locking wheel of the torpedo-hatch. Tucker held it there and shone his torch on it, and McQuade swung the mallet at it.

It did not budge. He swung the mallet again, much harder. Still it did not move. He stood back and swung again. There was a clang, and the locking wheel shifted. He grabbed the wheel in both hands and twisted with all his might. Slowly, stickily, it unwound.

He turned to the locking pin at the bottom of the hatch, pulled out a shifting spanner, fitted the jaws over the nut. He heaved anti-clockwise. It did not move. He snatched up the mallet again, gave the spanner a hard hit, and the nut shifted. He gave it another blow, and the nut turned free.

He feverishly undid it. He got the pliers onto the locking pin and wrestled it out. He looked at Tucker triumphantly, then he grabbed the handle, and heaved.

It did not budge. He heaved again; then he snatched up the mallet again. He stood back and swiped.

The clang resounded through the submarine. McQuade grabbed the handle, and the hatch swung stiffly open. He wanted to shout in triumph.

They peered inside, hearts knocking.

They were looking at the four-bladed propeller of a torpedo. And the thing had a dreadful menace about it.

McQuade crouched and peered closely. He flashed his torch shakily over the weapon. And he felt his pulse trip in excitement. *There, on one of the propeller blades, was a dab of red paint.*

He jabbed his finger at it in triumph and flung his arm around Tucker's shoulder and hugged him. *So that swine had told the truth!* Even Tucker managed a grin around his regulator. This was the one live torpedo that both Frau Kohler and Muller said was aboard! So the other tubes contained the dummies!

He lunged at the other torpedo hatch that was above the water line. He snatched the chisel out of the pouch and Tucker held it against the spoke of the wheel. McQuade swung the mallet. It did not budge. He swiped again. Then he snatched a crowbar out of the toolbag. He inserted it between the spokes and heaved with all his might.

Two minutes later they had the hatch creaking open. McQuade shone the torch inside excitedly. And his heart leapt.

Yes, this was the first dummy torpedo! There was no red mark on it!

He punched Tucker joyfully on the arm. Then snatched up the crowbar again, and pointed at the lower torpedo hatch. Tucker plunged the torch under the water and shone it on the locking wheel. McQuade groped with the crowbar and got it between the spokes. They both took a grip on it and heaved.

This one came undone more easily. McQuade crouched until the black water lapped at his chin. He felt for the locking nut. He got the shifting spanner onto it and heaved. It also came undone more easily. Then he groped for the locking pin with the pliers. After a minute it came out. Then they both got a grip on the wheel. On their third frantic heave it gave way, and there was a sucking noise as the hatch swung open.

They wrestled the last hatch open. Then McQuade dropped to his knees again and he buried his head under the water.

He shone his torch, his bubbles roaring in his ears. There, through the soupiness of suspended human debris, was the propeller.

McQuade hung under the water, and stared. He could not believe his eyes. He wanted to bellow. He frantically shone his torch over the blades and peered again, as though, if he looked harder it would disappear: there, on the grey propeller blade, was a dab of red paint. McQuade hung under the filthy water a long heart-pounding moment, his mind fumbling. *But there's only one live torpedo – that's what the bastard said, that's what Frau Kohler said . . .*

And then his mind reeled in fury, he twisted in the water and rammed his torch into the last hatch. And his furious heart lurched.

There it was on the blade, another dab of red paint. He hung there, staring at it, trying to unsee what he was seeing: *three red marks, three live torpedos, not one live torpedo and three unmarked dummies . . .* He hung there a moment longer, then his mind reeled red-black in fury and he thrashed his legs and scrambled up, gushing filthy water. He glared furiously at Tucker as if it was all his fault, then he turned and began to plunge his way back to the escape tube.

The dinghy roared up to the *Bonanza*. Elsie and Nathan were staring down at them. McQuade shouted, *'The bastard's lied to us!'*

He scrambled furiously up the ladder, onto the deck. He snapped to Potgieter: 'Get our airtanks topped up! And get out a suit for our friend Heinrich Muller!' He started striding to the fo'c'sle. 'Come with me!' he shouted back at Nathan. He unlocked Matt's cabin and flung open the door.

'Come with me! I've got a few questions to ask Herr Muller! And then the bastard's coming down into that submarine with me!'

He slammed the door and locked it and turned furiously towards the bridge. Matt hurried after him, guarded by a worried Nathan. *'For Christ's sake.'* Matt grabbed McQuade's arm. 'For Christ's sake, man, you can't take Muller down there – you could kill him! I want him *alive* in Jerusalem!'

'The deal is that I find that loot and *then* you get him alive in Jerusalem!' He scrambled up the companionway to the bridge.

Matt hurried after him. He grabbed his arm again. 'Let me give him the shit-treatment—'

'And if he lies again?' McQuade jabbed his finger at Matt's chest. 'I'm going down into that hellhole just one more time! And I'm coming out with the loot!'

He clattered down the stairs to the saloon. He unlocked the door and flung it open. Muller was sitting at the porthole, one hand manacled to the stanchion. McQuade ripped the elastoplast from his mouth, grabbed him by his shirt and yanked him to his feet. He rasped:

'You said there was one live torpedo?! And that had a mark on it to identify it?! And the dummies were unmarked?!'

'I said at *least* one live torpedo.'

McQuade shook him. 'Well there's only *one* unmarked torpedo! And three with marks on them!' He shook him again. He wanted to strangle the bastard. 'You wanted me to blow myself to bits pulling out the live torpedo!'

Muller said quietly: 'Then why did I offer to dive down with you? I'd have got blown up at the same time.'

'Because you intended to escape first! Stab us in the backs and swim ashore!'

'But how could a man my age survive the Skeleton Coast?'

'There's a road nowadays, Mr Muller! However, you're not going to have a chance to hitch-hike on it because I'm going to be very careful you don't stab me in the back! And you're going to show me which are the dummy torpedoes and which is the live bastard!'

Matt shouted, *'You can't do that to him! Let me give him the treatment!'*

'Hear that, Mr Muller?' McQuade said maliciously. 'Mossad wants you alive and well in Jerusalem! And that's where you're going if you don't tell me the truth! Now, which are the dummy torpedoes? The ones with the mark? Or the unmarked one?'

For a moment Muller's tongue moistened his thin lips. 'Mr McQuade, I am repeating verbal instructions I received over forty years ago. So let me also repeat my other offer: let's go and get my torpedo expert, under conditions that involve no risk to you, and let him sort this out for us in perfect safety.'

McQuade screwed his fist into the man's shirt and shook him. 'And we open the torpedoes by unscrewing the propeller and its casing?!'

'That's what I was told.'

McQuade gave the man a shove, so he collapsed on the seat. 'You'll be the expert, Mr Muller! You're going to stand right beside me when I remove it!' He grabbed the man's wrist and unlocked the handcuff.

Matt shouted, '*Madness . . . !*'

Matt was locked up in the fo'c'sle again. Everything was ready: the airtanks were topped up, but there were only three wetsuits, and Heinrich Muller had to go down in one of them. There was Tucker, stripped down to his baggy underpants hopefully, his eyes haunted: 'Pottie says he'll go down in my place . . .'

'You're coming down, Hugo! You've done it and you're an engineer and know what to do!' He turned to Elsie. 'Go'n fetch Muller. Take Nathan with you.'

Heinrich Muller was clearly very tense, but under control. McQuade pointed at the wetsuit. 'Get into that. You say you're experienced?' He pointed to the tank-contents gauge. 'Do you know what that is?'

'Yes.'

McQuade took an angry breath. 'Now let me make one thing abundantly clear, Herr Muller. Technically you've got sixty minutes of air in that tank of yours. But because you'll be working, it's more like forty minutes. If you do not show us immediately where that loot is hidden, you will die after forty minutes, of asphyxiation.' He glared at the man. 'Now, both Tucker and I are armed.' He pointed at the knife-sheaths strapped to their calves. 'We're taking down a pair of handcuffs for you, and we're going to tie a nice long rope to you, Herr Muller, with the knot behind your shoulders, so you can't get at it. Tucker is going to dive down first, make the rope fast to the submarine, to anchor you. And then you and I are going to swim down together, Herr Muller. All you have to do is kick your nice flippers and Mr Tucker will pull you down gently.' He raised his eyebrows. 'If you *don't* do that, Mr Tucker is going to *pull* you down very roughly and rapidly, Herr Muller, easy as winking. And I'll be behind you, to jolly you along. Like pulling the regulator out of your mouth.'

Muller looked totally self-controlled. 'Save your breath, Mr McQuade. I'm as keen to get this over as you are.'

'And when we get down into the conning tower, Herr Muller, we do the same again. Mr Tucker will go down the tube first, with your rope. Anchor the end. Then down you go . . . Feet first, and when you're safely inside, Mr Tucker will put handcuffs on you. And I follow . . .' He spread his hands. 'Simple, Herr Muller. If you just take it easy, there's nothing to be afraid of. It's only thirty feet of water.' He glared at him. 'Once we're *inside*, you had better show us the dummy torpedoes immediately, Herr Muller. Because you'll be handcuffed and have less than forty minutes of air, and you're not going to come out until we've found the loot.' He glared at him. 'Do you get all that?'

76

Muller sat in the dinghy, his airtank on. Around his chest was the rope. The man's face was stony calm. Tucker took the end of the rope, crossed himself, then rolled worriedly off the dinghy with a splash. He disappeared in a hump of airtank and flippers.

A minute later there was a tug on the rope.

'All right,' McQuade said grimly. 'Regulator in. Mask on. And over you go, Herr Muller.'

They swam down to the submarine. Heinrich Muller in front, McQuade behind him. Down in the conning tower Tucker pulled the rope in, hand over hand.

They descended on the long ghostly shape, between the waving shrouds of nets, down to the conning tower. Tucker untied his end of the rope, gave McQuade a look, then he manoeuvred into the hatch in a flurry of bubbles, pulling the rope behind him. McQuade looked at Muller. The man seemed in total control. McQuade jabbed his shoulder, pointed, and down through the hatch Heinrich Muller went efficiently. Immediately after him came McQuade.

The three hung in the water in the ghostly torchlight, their bubbles erupting. Muller's eyes were big behind his mask but he seemed fearless. Tucker looked at McQuade pleadingly, then pointed at him, asking him to go first. McQuade angrily jabbed his finger at the hatch, and pulled out the handcuffs and handed them to Tucker. Tucker crossed himself fervently, then took off his fins. He pushed his feet into the black hatch. He shot McQuade a last anguished look, then shoved himself downwards, and disappeared in a flurry of bubbles, dragging the rope.

The bubbles and the torchglow disappeared from the tube. Half a minute passed, then came the tug on Muller's rope. He did not hesitate. He pulled off his fins obediently and lowered his legs into the hatch.

McQuade shone his torch down the tube. He saw Muller's head disappear as he wriggled out the bottom. He gave them ten seconds to get clear, then he lowered himself into the hatch.

McQuade's feet touched the deck at the bottom, and in one practised movement he bent his knees, and thrust himself out. He pushed himself clear, then burst up out of the soupiness, black water gushing off him, and Heinrich Muller hit him.

All McQuade knew as he burst up into the torchlight was the glimpse of the arm coming down on him, one handcuff on the wrist and the other clutched in the fist like a knuckle-duster, then the shocking blow of steel, and he crashed backwards. There was nothing in the world but the desperate trying to scramble up midst the roaring bubbles and the taste of foul water, and the lunging weight on top of him. He kicked with all his might and frantically grabbed his knife from his sheath and scrambled up, and steel crashed against his cheekbone again and he lashed out blindly in the blackness. He felt the man crash against him and he again collapsed into the water. He scrambled up frantically and staggered away. He saw his torch glow under the water and he plunged under and snatched it up, gasping, shaking, and swung it, looking for Muller.

And there was Heinrich Muller, tethered by his rope, crouched, clutching his throat with both hands, his body contorted with choking. His airhose hung in the water, slashed by McQuade's knife. McQuade frantically looked for Tucker. He was clinging to the periscope, his head hanging, bloody. McQuade frantically swung the torch back on Muller. The man was choking to death, sucking in the fetid atmosphere, reeling, his face contorted in terror. McQuade rammed his knife back in the sheath and lunged at him from behind and slung one arm around his chest. He ripped the regulator from his own mouth and he plunged it into Muller's.

McQuade held his breath, his heart pounding, his hand clasped over Muller's face, and he felt the man's chest heave, sucking in air, then he retched and coughed, then he sucked in air again. '*Hugo!*' McQuade bellowed, and he ripped the regulator away from Muller and plunged it into his own mouth and filled his lungs, then rammed it back into Muller's. Tucker shoved himself off the periscope, casting about drunkenly for his torch. He plunged his arm underwater, found it and came staggering desperately towards them, blood running down his face. McQuade bellowed, '*Handcuffs!*' and he pulled the regulator from Muller's mouth and rammed it into his own. Tucker frantically grabbed Muller's wrist and rammed the other handcuff onto it. Then he fumbled desperately for the valve on Muller's airtank and turned it off. He grabbed for the end of Muller's airhose, shone his trembling torch onto it, and McQuade rammed his regulator back into Muller's mouth.

Muller's hose gaped, slashed almost clean through at the regulator. McQuade looked frantically at it, holding his breath and made a snap decision: it was impossible to bind up the cut. He snatched the knife from Tucker and cut right through the slashed hose. Then he furiously rammed the end up to Muller's face, yanked the regulator from his mouth and shoved the end of the hose in. He re-opened the valve on the tank and air gushed into Muller's mouth again.

But it gushed through into Muller's mouth at high pressure without the regulator to control its flow. Muller crouched there, both manacled hands clutching the airhose, trying to breathe by the side of his mouth. He filled his lungs, exhaled, inhaled again and gagged as he sucked some fetid atmosphere in; he snorted it out, and gasped on the hose again.

McQuade clutched his regulator to his mouth, trying to get

624

the thudding out of his heart, then cast about desperately for the sack. He wrestled the spare airtank out, and hefted it under his armpit. He seized Muller furiously by the shoulder, turned him towards the bows and gave him a shove.

They went wading through the black tomb in the flashing torchlight, Muller lurching, clutching his hose, his eyes wild with fear. They burst into the crew's quarters, and there were the open torpedo tubes.

McQuade pointed at them, then ripped Muller's hose from his mouth. The man's face contorted; and McQuade rammed the hose back at him. Muller grabbed it, crouched, and sucked on it, then McQuade snatched it away again. Muller gave a strangled cry and he pointed his manacled hands at the marked torpedo in the top left tube, and then at the two tubes under the water. McQuade thrust the airhose back and Muller snatched it. He sucked, head hanging, shuddering. McQuade stared at Tucker, then grabbed Muller's hood and pulled his head up. He pointed furiously at the unmarked torpedo in the top right tube and Muller shook his head desperately, *no, no, no*, his hands clutching the hose to his mouth.

McQuade stared, his mind tumbling. *So it was the one unmarked torpedo that was live, and the marked ones were the dummies, not vice versa! It figured because Frau Kohler told him that there was only one torpedo on board. So the bastard had tried to trick them! But Jesus Christ, if this was a double trick!* . . . He snatched the airhose out of Muller's mouth again, and pointed furiously at the unmarked torpedo questioningly. Muller's hands clapped over his mouth, his eyes wild, and he desperately shook his head *no no no*. He lunged wildly to the top left tube and pointed at the nut holding the marked propeller and made desperate unscrewing motions. Then he grabbed the propeller shaft, pretending to wrench it sideways, then he grabbed the airhose again.

McQuade let him have it, staring at the nut. Then Tucker

turned and plunged to the bunk, and pulled down his toolbag. He pulled out a shifting spanner and pliers and he plunged back to the propeller. He thrust the spanner at the nut, made turning motions, and looked wildly at Muller. And Muller nodded desperately, *yes, yes, yes.*

McQuade and Tucker looked at each other. *If the bastard was prepared to let them start dismantling the fucking thing it must be a dummy!*

McQuade made his decision. He grabbed Muller and shoved him to the nearest bunk. He fumbled out the hand-cuff key, unlocked one side, wrenched Muller's arm around the stanchion and snapped the cuffs on his free wrist again.

He turned and blundered back to the torpedo tube.

77

They feverishly examined the torpedo in the torchlight, the joints in the casing behind the propellers, where the shaft emerged. The casing appeared to be welded onto the cylindrical body of the torpedo, but that could be glue, painted over. Theoretically the propeller-shaft went through the casing to the electric motor beyond but if it was a dummy there was no motor. *So if this was a dummy, just take off the propellers, get a lever on the shaft and the whole casing should break away.*

McQuade looked at his watch. He only had about thirty minutes of air left, but Muller had less, because a lot of his had been wasted. He jabbed Tucker, then pointed at the locking pin on the end of the shaft.

Tucker snatched a pair of pliers from his toolbag, snapped them over the ends of the pin and frantically squeezed, then snapped the pliers to the head. He heaved, and it came out. He thrust the pliers at McQuade, grabbed a shifting spanner and jammed it onto the big nut. He heaved on it, but it did not shift. He got his weight under it and heaved again. Then it shifted. He heaved again, and he felt it give further. He heaved again, heart pounding: and the whole casing beyond it broke away, including the propeller and the shaft.

McQuade stared at their handiwork, overjoyed. Removing the locking pin and trying to undo the nut had been unnecessary! He grabbed the propeller blades and gave it a tug. And another. And another – and the whole ensemble came grating out. He wrestled it right out triumphantly, dropped it in the water and Tucker shone his torch inside. They peered, hearts pounding; and McQuade gave an inward whoop.

Gleaming at them in the torchlight was a cylindrical metal container, fractionally smaller in diameter than the torpedo. It was covered in heavy grease. There was a handle in the centre of it. McQuade grabbed it joyfully and tugged.

It shifted. He put both hands to the handle, heaved, and out of the torpedo it stickily came, sliding on the grease that had been coating it for forty years.

Tucker got his arms underneath it and McQuade heaved it right out, his heart singing. It parted from the torpedo's stern with a sucking sound. McQuade shot his arms under it, to help Tucker. It was about three feet long. Behind, inside the torpedo, was another canister. They staggered it over to the nearest bunk, and hefted it up onto it.

McQuade flashed his torch feverishly over it, his heart joyful. It shone through the grease. At the handle-end was a screw-top cap, heavily covered in some kind of glue. The whole thing seemed in perfect condition. There was no corrosion. He winked a shining eye at Tucker, then jerked his head back at the torpedo tube.

They plunged back to it. McQuade buried his arm into the torpedo shell, reaching for the second canister, but could not reach it. He snatched the long-nosed pliers from his toolbag and reached into the shell again. He gripped the handle and pulled. The second cylinder came slowly sliding out. They lugged it over to the bunk. It was also in perfect condition.

McQuade looked feverishly at his watch, then at Muller. The man was slumped against the stanchion to which he was manacled, sucking on his hose. McQuade snatched up Muller's tank-contents gauge. It was in the red already because of the wastage. He feverishly unclipped the tank on Muller's harness. Tucker picked up the new tank in readiness. McQuade jabbed Muller's arm to warn him, then shut off the valve and frantically unscrewed it off the empty tank. He slapped it onto the new tank, screwed it down, then re-opened the valve. Air gushed into Muller's mouth again. Tucker clipped the new tank onto the harness. McQuade dashed back to the tubes and scrambled down onto his knees. They started on the submerged torpedoes.

Ten minutes later they had all six canisters out of the tubes. McQuade looked frantically at his gauge. They had approximately thirteen minutes of air left. Muller's gauge showed that the tank was half-empty already, without the regulator to control the flow. McQuade picked up a canister, and started staggering with it through the black submarine, making for the escape tube. Tucker hefted up another and blundered after him.

It took them five minutes to get all six canisters to the escape tube, and the toolbags. McQuade snatched up a coil of nylon cord, and slashed it into six lengths. They tied one piece to each of the handles on the canisters. He thrust all six ends to Tucker and pointed upwards. Tucker scrambled underwater, wriggled and disappeared. He surged up the escape tube with the six pieces of cord. McQuade feverishly jostled the first canister under the mouth. The rope went tight, and Tucker began to haul. The canister went scraping and clanging up the tube. McQuade feverishly jostled the second canister under the mouth. In the conning tower Tucker frantically hauled.

Three minutes later all the canisters were up in the conning tower. McQuade had less than six minutes of air left. He turned and went plunging back through the submarine to fetch Heinrich Muller.

The man slumped against the bunk, half hanging, his chest heaving, his manacled hands clasping the airhose to the side of his mouth. McQuade rammed his key into the handcuffs and snapped them open. Muller's head lifted, but McQuade did not see the mad look in the eyes. He grabbed the man's armpit and shoved him towards the control room.

They went blundering through the black water, splashing, stumbling, lurching past the skeletons, through the different cabins. They blundered up to the circular hatchway to the

Zentrale. McQuade shoved the Nazi's neck down and Muller took a frantic breath before he ducked his head under the stinking water. He struggled into the hole, sucked on the hose again, and he sucked on nothing. His airtank was empty. In terrified panic Muller struggled through the hatch. McQuade plunged after him, and burst through the hatch, and Muller lunged wildly at him.

All McQuade knew as he burst above the water was the wild flurry as Muller threw himself desperately at his airhose, his lungs empty and his eyes bulging wild, flinging himself at the source of life. McQuade crashed backwards under the frantic weight, and Muller's wild hands clawed the regulator from his mouth and thrust it into his own. McQuade scrambled up desperately, seized the regulator and rammed it into his mouth, and he grabbed the man's neck and shoved him towards the escape tube. Muller clawed at him again like a wild cat, his face contorted in a strangled scream, his fingers like talons. McQuade swung his flat hand at the man's head, and Muller reeled.

He reeled across the control room and crashed wildly in the water without any air in his lungs. He gasped in the vile black water and choked. McQuade blundered at him and heaved him up and stuffed the regulator into the man's contorted mouth. Muller rasped and coughed and retched, trying to suck the air down into his lungs, and McQuade shook him and bellowed, *'Dive into that tube!'* He let the wild man take another rasping breath, then he snatched the regulator and plunged it into his own mouth and shoved him towards the tube, and Muller whirled around and lunged at him again. Like a madman, his hands flailing, his contorted mouth agape, and McQuade swiped him across the head again. And Muller staggered and crashed into the water again, wild-eyed and McQuade lunged after him and wrenched him up by his harness frantically and he rammed the regulator into the bastard's mouth. He bellowed, *'Breathe deep!'* and pointed furiously with his torch at the escape tube. He snatched back the regulator and stuck it into his own mouth, he tried to ram the bastard's head under the water to get him into that tube whilst he still had air in him to fight his way up it. McQuade shoved the man's head down with all his frantic might, and Muller twisted and his fist swung wildly.

The wild punch hit McQuade in the chest, the air gushed out of him, and he staggered backwards against the escape tube. Then Muller was clawing furiously at him again, and McQuade swung up his fist with all his desperate might. It got Heinrich Muller's solar plexus. The German gasped in agony and he reeled and sprawled across the navigation desk, rasping in the stinking atmosphere, his hands clutched to his throat, his eyes full of shocked agony. McQuade looked wildly at his gauge and he knew there was no way. No way could he get this vile man out of this terrible submarine to face the gallows in Jerusalem with only one minute of air left between them. Heinrich Muller struggled up and lurched at him desperately, his mouth contorted in a strangled plea, and McQuade plunged under the water, and he was gone into the tube.

He wrestled himself into it and kicked with all his might, and up he bumped and surged. He burst up out of the hatch into the conning tower. Tucker was gone. McQuade snatched up his fins and wrestled them on, then he clawed desperately for the ladder and kicked. He burst through the upper hatch. The canisters were on the barnacled bridge. McQuade kicked again and he began to rise, and his airtank gave out.

Suddenly there was no more air. He sucked on nothing, and his heart lurched and he just wanted to kick with all his desperate might and fight his way back up to God's own sweet air. But he held his panicked breath, his lungs screaming, and there was nothing in the world but the eternity of rising, rising, rising . . . then the silvery surface was just there and his head broke through it, and he spat out the regulator and frantically rasped in beautiful air.

And down in the pitch-black submarine, Heinrich Muller staggered, his hands clutched to his throat, his eyes wild, desperately trying not to suck in the stinking black atmosphere, then his screaming lungs heaved and into his gaping mouth it went like a blow, solid and sharp, and he choked and gagged and retched, and then gasped in more solid stink, and he convulsed and choked and retched again, staggering, lurching, and he heaved in more. His head was reeling and he collapsed in the water with a crash. He wildly struggled up again and choked and retched again. And again, and again. But there was some oxygen in that stinking black atmosphere, and it took him a long time to die.

78

It took half an hour to get the canisters out of the conning tower and up into the dinghy. McQuade had to go down alone to do it because there was only one spare airtank – and anyway there was no way Tucker was going to go near the water ever, ever again.

McQuade sprawled in the bottom of the dinghy, trembly, manic, exhausted, shuddery with the horror of what had happened down there. There was no compassion, only reckless frustration that he hadn't brought the swine out alive. The dinghy bumped against the *Bonanza*. Elsie and Nathan were at the rail, wide-eyed. '*Yabbadabbadoo!*' Nathan shouted when he saw the canisters. Evidently Julie Goldstein had recovered, for he appeared excitedly on the bridgewing in a silk dressing gown. Potgieter threw the painter up to Nathan. 'Where's Muller?' Elsie called.

'We'll need a net to lift this lot!'

Elsie disappeared. He swung the derrick outboard and the hook came rattling down with a cargo-net dangling. Potgieter and Tucker loaded the canisters into it. 'Take it away!' The winch rattled again and the canisters lifted off the dinghy. They rose up to the rail, and Nathan grabbed the net eagerly and guided them down onto the deck, beaming. Julie Wonderful was also beaming, big-eyed. McQuade clambered up the ladder onto the deck.

'Where's Muller?' Elsie demanded again.

'Well, he had a little trouble.' He walked to the fo'c'sle cabin, unlocked the door and jerked his head at Matt.

Matt emerged. 'And Muller?' he demanded.

'Dead,' McQuade said. 'Sorry about that.' He didn't let the

other Mossad men out, nor Inspector Dupreez. He relocked the cabin and started towards the bridge.

Matt stared after him. '*Dead . . .?*' he whispered, aghast. Then he shouted: '*Fucking amateurs!*' He strode after him.

McQuade called down to Tucker, 'Get the dinghy aboard, then it's up anchor.'

Matt grabbed his arm. '*I told you you'd give him a heart-attack!*'

McQuade stopped.

'He didn't die of a heart-attack. He died of asphyxiation. And I didn't do it to him – he did it to himself, by trying to kill me, and Tucker. And I nearly killed myself trying to save the bastard!' He pulled his arm free and started walking again.

Matt shouted furiously, '*He should have died on the gallows!*'

McQuade stopped again. 'I'm sorry you're not going to be a hero, Matt. And I'm sorry for the whole Jewish people. But if it's any consolation he died a much slower and more horrible death than he would have on the gallows.' He added: 'Even worse than the gas-chambers.'

He turned and walked on. Feeling numb, feeling elated, feeling nauseous. Shaky. Potgieter and Nathan were lugging the first of the canisters up to the bridge, followed by beaming Julie. '*Yabbadabbadoo!*' Nathan shouted. Elsie was helping Tucker winch the dinghy on board.

McQuade climbed up onto the bridge. And, oh, it was a lovely wheelhouse, shiny and varnished and clean, it was a lovely day, and he was alive, alive . . . And oh God he felt sick in his guts about Sarah. That bitch! Where was she, to witness his triumph? Today was supposed to be *his* day, the day he had worked so hard for, but the bitch had turned out to be a fraud, working for his undoing. Well, she had failed! Mossad had failed – he'd beaten the whole lot of them. And, goddammit, *he* had failed – failed to deliver Heinrich Muller up to justice, and, oh God, he felt sick in his guts about that too! Suddenly it wasn't such a triumphant day any more. He hated the mendacious bitch for breaking his heart, he hated himself for killing Heinrich Muller and he hardly cared what was in those canisters any more. He went to the cabinet and snatched out the brandy bottle and sloshed some into a tumbler. Tucker hollered: 'Dinghy aboard!'

For a moment McQuade smelt the deathly black stink of that submarine again and he gagged, then he took a gulp of brandy and it burned down into his gut, scouring the taste of death out of his mouth. He shuddered, then shouted, 'Weigh anchor!' He shoved the throttle to Dead Slow and hit the windlass button. The rattle of the chain rose up as the *Bonanza* churned forward, helping the windlass. There was a slight lurch as the anchor broke out of the sand. Then Potgieter shouted from the bows:

'Anchor aweighed!' There was a clank.

McQuade shoved the throttle to Slow Ahead. He lifted the glass and took the rest of the brandy in one swallow. 'All hands on the bridge! We're splicing the main brace!'

Then he dropped his head and stifled a sob. Because Sarah wasn't there. Because Heinrich Muller wasn't there.

The *Bonanza* ploughed steadily, her engines thudding *doem* ... *doem* ... *doem* ... Matt Mathews sat alone in the bows, staring furiously at the sea. The entire crew were on the bridge, glasses in hand, brandy, whisky and beer on the chart table, smoke and excitement in the air. Even Tucker and the ever-placid Potgieter were looking excited. The steel canisters stood in a row, gleaming; Potgieter and Tucker were cleaning the grease off the last two. The sealing had been carefully cleared away from the big screw-top lids. It was going to take a strap-lever, strong language and some time to unscrew them. That was okay with McQuade. Everything was okay with McQuade right now, and nothing was okay, because the love of his life was a fraudulent bitch, and he felt no impatience to get those canisters open, he almost did not care any more what was inside, he didn't care about anything in thc whole wide world except that they had done it, *done it*, and they were alive and the world was beautiful and it was dust and ashes because he had *failed – he had killed the most important bastard in the world and the most beautiful girl in the world was a bitch*. Then Elsie was calling for silence, his round blue-beard face jolly and his big brown eyes moist. He held up his glass.

'Gentlemen, before we open up the goodies I have a toast to propose.' He beamed around at them all. 'And it is to our intrepid skipper and managing director, without whose high-class detective work and fearlessness all this would not have come to pass, like.' He beamed at McQuade with moist eyes. 'Jim darling – here's to you!'

'*Yeah!*' Tucker said enthusiastically, probably for the first time in his life.

'Here's to Jim!' Nathan shouted.

'*Got*, yes, man, hey!' Potgieter mumbled happily.

McQuade grinned at them and his eyes burned because he loved every one of them. All he could think of to say was, 'Okay, let's open these cans . . .'

Potgieter got down onto his belly like a wrestler and gripped the first canister. Tucker wound the strap-lever around the lid. He adjusted the tension. Everybody crowded round.

McQuade took his glass and walked out onto the bridge-wing. He leant on the rail and took a deep suck of brandy. And he wanted to bellow *OH SHIT!* Elsie came waddling out after him. He leant on the rail beside him.

'Cheer up. It may still come right with her.'

'I don't want it to come right! She's a liar. A cheat!'

Elsie said, 'She was only doing her duty.'

'And her duty was to be a whore!'

Elsie shook his fat head at the horizon. 'Not really. She was doing it for her country, like.'

McQuade breathed deep. 'For her country she pulls every sexy trick in the book? For her country she cries *I love you* and tells you she wants to marry you?'

Elsie was looking at him with spaniel eyes. 'Maybe she meant it, Jimmy.'

McQuade seethed. 'Like hell she meant it! She's a professional agent with big tits and long legs and a luscious arse who was given the assignment of screwing me! And you say maybe I can make it right with her?' He pointed furiously into the wheelhouse. 'Of course I can make it right with her, Elsie! There's millions of dollars in there! All a fucking millionaire has to do is tell a whore he's a millionaire and he'll have her doing backward somersaults from the chandelier.' He snorted furiously, but he wanted to sob.

Just then Tucker shouted: 'She's moved!'

Elsie looked into the wheelhouse. Potgieter was spread-eagled, clutching the canister, Tucker was crouched over the lid, strap-lever in hand, flushed effort on his face. Julie Wonderful and Nathan were agog. The lid had shifted a fraction of an inch under his heaving. 'Go for it!' Julie urged. Elsie put his hairy hand on McQuade's shoulder.

'Come on. Let's look. It'll seem different in the morning when you're a millionaire.'

McQuade heard Sarah say, I don't give a shit about the treasure. 'You go'n look and tell me what it's worth.'

'Nothing like what it's worth being *alive*.'

Elsie turned and waddled into the wheelhouse. McQuade gave a big sigh and sucked on his brandy. Then Tucker shouted, 'She's open!'

He unwound the lid and there was a sucking noise as air squeezed past the threads into the sealed container. McQuade tilted back his glass and drained it. Then he whispered, '*Go to Hell, Sarah Buchholz*' and hurled the glass with all his might out into the Atlantic.

Then Nathan shouted, '*Whoopee!*'

The lid was off, and Tucker was pulling out an oil-cloth sack, stitched at the top. Tucker squeezed it with awe and whispered, 'Money!' McQuade grabbed it and squeezed. It was obviously packed with tight wads of notes. 'Open it!'

Tucker snatched up a knife and slit open the top. They all crowded round. Yes, it was packed with coloured banknotes, in tight bundles. Tucker up-ended the sack, and out they came. They tumbled onto the wheelhouse deck in a heap.

They stared. 'Oh *no!*' Julie said.

McQuade snatched up a wad. They all did.

'*Oh no!*' Julie cried again.

McQuade stared. The notes were crisp, in mint condition, and they were all the same. They all bore the mark £20, with the image of Jan van Riebeck, the founder of the Cape colony and the legend read, *The Reserve Bank of the Union of South Africa promises to pay bearer on demand the sum of twenty pounds.* It was dated 1944.

McQuade stared numbly at the topmost note. He had not seen one of these for over twenty years. When South Africa was still part of the British Commonwealth. Before South Africa changed its currency from pounds to rands. '*Oh no!*' Julie cried again. '*These are no longer legal tender!*'

Tucker and Nathan were looking aghast. Potgieter was scowling numbly at a wad in his hand. Tucker whispered, 'Out of date . . .?'

'About twenty-five years out of date!' Julie cried. He sat in a heap and held his head.

'*But* . . .' Tucker appealed, 'can't we somehow take them to a bank . . .?'

'No,' McQuade said, 'they're not valid any more, Hugo! They're not worth the paper they're printed on! And' – suddenly it seemed funny – 'and they're doubtless counterfeit . . .'

'*Counterfeit?*' Tucker echoed.

And suddenly it all seemed terribly funny. 'Operation Birkenbaum! Run by the Gestapo to counterfeit money to ruin the Allied war effort!'

'But . . .' Tucker protested weakly. He was flipping through a wad. 'But the serial numbers are all different—'

'So, the Gestapo did things well!'

'Oh Christ . . .' Julie wailed. He had both hands clasped to his fat face, peering wetly through his fingers at the pile. Nathan was looking like an aghast Groucho Marx.

McQuade was grinning tearfully. Oh God, this was funny. After all they'd been through. 'Open the rest – they'll all be full of old counterfeit South African currency. Because Heinrich Muller was coming to South Africa to resurrect the Third Reich by bank-rolling the Afrikaners against the English!' He dropped his head and laughed.

'What's funny?!' Julie wept. Nathan was staring like a tearful Groucho Marx. Tucker lunged at the next canister with his strap-lever.

'Hold it, Pottie!' he whimpered.

McQuade sloshed more brandy into his glass, and hung his head, then he turned and walked out onto the bridge. Elsie waddled out after him. 'Oh Jimmy,' he appealed, 'so what? You're all alive and well and healthy.'

McQuade hung his head and sob-laughed, 'The bitch made herself a whore in vain . . .'

'She was only doing her duty, James,' Elsie said. 'Aren't we all whores in some way or another?'

'How am I a whore?'

Elsie said earnestly, 'You used your body, your strength, your guts to try to make a fast buck—'

'Open!' Potgieter called anxiously.

'Oh no! . . .' Tucker wailed.

One after the other the lids came off. One after another the wads came tumbling out. The wheelhouse deck was piled in bundles of crisp, useless money. Julie Wonderful had stopped weeping. Now he just sat, his chin cupped in both hands, his face suffused, staring out to sea. The tears were running down Nathan's face. 'My twenty grand . . .' he kept repeating. Tucker had stopped whimpering: he was openly sobbing as he slugged and wrenched his way through those canister lids with the resolution of a madman with an axe. Only Pottie Potgieter seemed scowlingly untearful, resolutely clutching each canister as Tucker applied the strap-lever. The only surprise was in the fifth canister: out came tumbling bundles of white English five-pound notes, also dated 1944, printed on one side only. McQuade held up a wad. 'Good stuff in 1945 – Muller got a set of false teeth from Doctor Wessels with a couple of these.'

Tucker took a trembly breath and approached the last canister furiously as if he could intimidate it into yielding gold.

Out on the bridgewing McQuade quaffed back the brandy, and felt a retch but he stifled it with a shudder. He hung his head over the rail, and with all his sick heart he just wanted to vomit it all up, all the brandy and the stinking blackness of that submarine and the terror of fighting Heinrich Muller for a gulp of air and the heartbreak of Sarah Buchholz and the heartbreak of those piles of useless banknotes, then suddenly he heard Julie shout:

'*Oh yes . . .!*'

He whirled around, back into the wheelhouse. '*Yes what?*'

The sixth canister stood open. Everybody was gathered, open-mouthed, staring. There was Julie Wonderful, his big face alight with delight, and in his hands he held up a crescent-shaped piece of canvas.

McQuade stared. Canvas? A picture? '*What?!*' he demanded again. And Julie turned to him with shining eyes.

'*Toulouse-Lautrec . . . "The Woman in White" . . .!*'

McQuade stared at the canvas. Everybody was staring at it, open-mouthed. Nathan couldn't believe his tear-filled eyes.

'Paintings?' McQuade whispered.

There was a silence. Then Julie snickered, '*Paintings?!*' then he threw back his head and guffawed.

'*Paintings, the man says? Do you realize what we've got here? Do you realize what this is?*' He swept his shining eyes over them, then shook his fat trembly finger at the canvas in delight and cried: 'Here we have Toulouse-Lautrec's

"Woman in White"! Never seen since it disappeared from the private collection of the Duke of Somebody! Perfectly removed from its frame by an absolute expert – of which Germany had many – and expertly preserved in this hitherto hermetically sealed container . . .!'

They all stared at the painting. Awed. Then McQuade whispered, 'Toulouse-Lautrec? Jesus Christ . . .' Nathan leapt in the air and bellowed: '*Yabbadabbadoo!*' Tucker demanded, 'Who's Toulouse-Lautrec?' Potgieter was open-mouthed. Elsie sat down in an astonished heap. 'My Gawd . . .' he whispered.

McQuade tore his eyes off the painting and peered into the canister. 'Anything else?'

Julie reverently pulled out the next canvas. He stared at it, then gave a cry of girlish delight. 'Gentlemen . . . who do we have here?' He turned to them with moist-eyed excitement. 'I'll bet my last shekel that this is a Monet. Look at that style.' He peered in the bottom right hand corner. '*Yes – Monet!* One of the leading Impressionists!' He appealed to them joyfully: 'Gentlemen, do you know what we've stumbled on? Part of Adolf Hitler's personal art treasure, part of the stuff he looted from the art galleries of Europe for the massive museum he was going to build in Linz!' He blinked at them with shining eyes. '*Do you realize what this is worth? . . .*'

Tucker was beaming. Potgieter was grappling with all this. Elsie was open-mouthed. McQuade peered into the canister. 'Anything else? Like diamonds . . .?'

Julie cried, 'Who needs diamonds when we've got all this! Do you realize what the contents of this canister are worth? Tens of millions!'

McQuade said faintly, 'But they belong to other people. And to galleries. The owners can be traced . . .'

There was a short silence, as everybody grappled with this detail. Then Julie cried, 'We'll sell them to private collectors in the Middle East – *absolutely* no problem!'

'But the owners can be *traced*,' McQuade whispered. He

waved a bemused hand. 'All the art treasures the Nazis stole are registered, surely, and if the registered owners are dead it belongs to their heirs. Anyway no collector will buy a famous stolen painting because he can't display it . . .'

'You're not listening!' Julie cried. 'We'll sell these on the black market secretly! To Arab oil sheiks and South American millionaires who make their own laws! There are dealers for this kind of thing, and *dozens* of millionaires who would give their right testicle for a Monet or a Lautrec!' He turned back to the canister joyfully. 'Who *else* have we here . . .?'

Suddenly it all seemed even funnier to McQuade. 'It's *you* who's not listening Julie, my boy, my life! *I'm* telling you that these things *belong to other people!* We can't *sell* them, because that would be stealing!'

Astonished silence. Then Julie snorted, 'It's sunken treasure!'

McQuade wanted to laugh. 'Pieces of eight and gold bars and precious stones are entirely different! The owners can't be identified! But *these* . . .' He pointed at the canister and shook his head in wonder. 'These paintings belong to the galleries they came from! They belong to the *world*.' He shook his head again and grinned at them. 'We've got to give them back. Maybe we'll get a reward of some kind but we've got to tell the world what we've found and give them *back*.'

Tucker and Potgieter were following the exchange open-mouthed. Nathan looked about to burst into tears again. Elsie had his eyes closed. Julie cried, 'Bull-*SHIT* . . .'

McQuade slapped his head and turned away. 'Oh God, this is funny!' He pointed at the ocean floor. *'After all we've been through, all the blood, sweat and tears – and we've got to give it back . . .!'*

Julie cried, *'You're not giving my share back!'*

McQuade turned to him, his eyes wet.

'You don't understand, Julius. You don't have a share. This fishing company does not deal in stolen property. I own fifty-one per cent of this company and I'm telling you, Julie

Wonderful, that this company is going to give these priceless paintings *back!* All you're entitled to is a share in any reward we get, but I assure you it's not going to add up to millions of dollars.'

They were all staring at him. Julie was bulging-eyed. Then he shook his fat face and shouted:

'*I'll sue you . . .!*' He turned furiously and lumbered for the door. He shouted back: '*Don't think you can lay down the law to me!*' He turned and clattered fatly down the steps. '*I'll sue you . . .!*' he bellowed.

McQuade thought it was hilarious. 'Sue me . . .?' He hung his head and sob-laughed. '*He's* going to sue me . . .? Tell the judge how he feels entitled to sell these things on the black market . . .? This is getting funnier . . .'

He turned and walked out onto the bridgewing, and, oh, he was suddenly ridiculously happy. The whole world was ridiculous and it was wonderful just to be alive, *alive*, breathing God's beautiful air with the engines going gently *doem doem doem*, he was happy that it was all over, all over, he did not have to go down into that dreadful submarine again, it was gone, *gone*, out of his life and he did not care about not being rich after all, he was ridiculously rich in just being alive after that hellhole.

He turned back to the boys. They were all looking at him as if they had just been whipped. He stifled a laugh and smiled:

'It's all right gentlemen . . . We'll make some money out of this, I promise you! Rewards. Insurance companies.' He suppressed a laugh. 'Fame . . . It won't be a fortune, but at least it'll pay off the hire purchase on Rene and get Rosie a new deep-freeze. Maybe even a down-payment for Pottie's farm. And the Kid will be able to get his *bottom* ones done . . .'

PART FIFTEEN

79

Of course a lot of other things happened that day. An Ovambo child trod on a SWAPO landmine and got blown to bits. Up on the Angolan border the first South African troops came trundling back across the river, hot and dirty and battle-weary. An Ovambo woman committed suicide because the witch doctor said she rode on hyenas in the night. A gang of SWAPO terrorists shot up a headman's kraal because he refused to let them take his son for training. Tobias fell off his bicycle because of strong drink. A pride of lions chased a tourist's car in Etosha. An Ostwind raged across Namibia and blew the Finger of God down and the AWB claimed it was because of 435. Lizzie was raped and so were Rebecca, Rachel, Maria and many others. Sixpence slew his grandmother to get her liver for medicine. A Himba man trod on another SWAPO landmine when taking his cattle to drink. James McQuade got drunk. So did Hugo Tucker, L. C. Brooks and Ivor Nathan. James McQuade radio-telephoned Roger Wentland and made an appointment for eight o'clock the following morning. Beryl the Bitch said *Fuck you* and punched the Kid and knocked one of his new teeth out. Rosie Tucker said *Fuckemall* and bought herself a new deep-freeze on the never-never, a new pair of shoes for Tammy and a new bicycle for Gracie. Inspector Dupreez sang like a canary to Matt Mathews. SWAPO began filling the vacuum left behind in the bush by the South African troops. The Kid went back to his dentist. James McQuade got drunker. So did Hugo Tucker, L. C. Brooks and Ivor Leave-it-to-me Nathan. Julie Wonderful reappeared and threatened to shoot McQuade, but fortunately didn't have a gun. Julie Wonderful burst into tears, and so did Ivor Nathan and Hugo Tucker. In Pietersburg Frikkie van der Merwe said *To hell with it* and spent the day in bed. In Pretoria a young white man dressed himself in police fatigues and ran through the city centre calmly shooting seventeen blacks at point-blank range before he was overpowered. On the bridge of the *Bonanza* they got the shocking story on the evening news broadcast, and McQuade radio-telephoned Johan Lombard.

'Absolutely frightful, dear fellow,' Johan shouted, 'he just fired, ran, reloaded, fired again, bang bang bang and reloaded again, absolute bloodbath! He was eventually overpowered by a black man who distracted his attention by saying "Excuse me, Baas, but that Baas over there wants to speak to you, Baas"! And it worked! Because he called the swine "*Baas*"! Christ, this is Africa for you!'

'Was he AWB?'

'Don't know yet but what d'you think, dear fellow? And what did the leader of the AWB say? He said – whilst piously condemning violence of course – he said it was all the fault of the government for making reforms and making whites feel insecure . . .'

McQuade furiously sent for Matt Mathews, thrust his tape-recorder at him and rasped, 'I want a full statement from Inspector Dupreez on everything he knows about the AWB! Or else both of you are going to get the Mossad Treatment!'

That unreal night the Ostwind dropped and a fog came in, rolling over the Atlantic like a wall, swallowing everything. It was dawn when the *Bonanza* closed with Walvis Bay. You could not make out the lights until almost inside the harbour. The mist hung dense, motionless, as they chugged up towards the fishing wharves, the trawlers ghostly shapes in the suffused glow of the street lamps in Oceana Road. There was a space at Cato's jetty. McQuade manoeuvred the *Bonanza* up to it. Tucker and Potgieter got up onto the wharf with the mooring lines and made her fast.

The first thing McQuade did was get rid of Matt and his boys. He unlocked their cabin and said, 'Okay, piss off.'

They came filing out sullenly. Matt glared at him, about to speak, and McQuade shouted, 'Back to Jerusalem, Matt! And one word of complaint out of you and I'll have the whole Israeli embassy thrown out for undiplomatic conduct, *persona non grata* and all that jazz! And the press will make Mossad a laughing-stock!'

Matt glowered. 'Fucking amateurs . . .!' He turned and clambered up onto the jetty.

The last to come out was Inspector Dupreez. His eyes were red, two days' growth of beard on his cheeks; he came shuffling out, uncertainly blinking. He appealed to McQuade: 'What are you going to do?'

McQuade wanted to grab him by the shirt-front. 'What am I going to do to your wife and three children and your twenty years of faithful service and your pension rights?'

Inspector Dupreez blinked his red-rimmed eyes. 'Yes?'

McQuade pulled his tape recorder out of his pocket and held it up to him. 'Inspector Dupreez, do I understand correctly that you are a secret member of the AWB, even though it's illegal for a policeman to be a member?'

Inspector Dupreez blinked. Then he croaked, 'Yes.'

'And do I also understand correctly that you only joined the AWB as an undercover agent in order to penetrate the organization so that you could report fully to your superiors on their nefarious activities?'

Inspector Dupreez blinked rapidly. 'Yes,' he whispered. 'Except I'm not sure about the word nefarious whatchacallit, hey.'

'Nefarious means wicked, Inspector Dupreez. Immoral. Criminal. Treasonous. And in your capacity as an underground agent penetrating the AWB, you have a host of information about other policemen who are also members, and you also know many of the people who are members of the South African Nazi Party? Who are sheltering behind the

AWB as their public front? And you've given all this information to Mr Mathews of Mossad?'

Inspector Dupreez swallowed. 'Yes.'

'And of course you are now going to your superior officers to report your successful penetration of the AWB, and name all those policemen who are working for them, and break the whole ring.' McQuade glared at him. '*Aren't you*, Inspector Dupreez?'

Dupreez looked at him. 'Yes,' he whispered.

McQuade patted him heavily on the shoulder and clicked the tape recorder off. 'Good, Inspector Dupreez . . . Because if you *don't* I've got the tapes made by Mossad, which I'll give to the Minister of Police and you'll lose your pension.' He glared at the man, then jerked his head. 'Now, *piss off.*'

The rest was dazed. McQuade had been up all night drinking and he was completely sober. The world seemed unreal. The fog was so thick you could not see twenty yards. Julie Wonderful left, balefully repeating one last threat to sue him. Elsie and Tucker left together to drive to Swakopmund. The loot had been stored in the engine room, locked behind the steel door. Potgieter and Nathan gloomily volunteered to stay aboard to guard it until McQuade found out from Roger Wentland what to do with it. McQuade went up to his cabin to pack. He looked at himself in the mirror. He hadn't shaved for three days, since the morning he had snatched Muller. God, was that all it was, only three days ago? It seemed as if he had not slept for a month. So, it was all over. No riches. No Heinrich Muller. And no Sarah bloody Buchholz, either. And he thought his angry heart would break.

He walked across the sandy compound to the Landrover. He twisted the ignition. Nothing happened. The battery was flat because Tucker had left the cab-light on. He cursed, got out and started walking. He reached the gate. A car was parked in the fog outside. He started walking up the sand track towards Oceana Road. He heard the car start. It swung around and followed him. It cruised up alongside him.

'Hullo,' Sarah said.

For an instant the world seemed to stand still. Then he was walking again. 'You're out of luck, lieutenant. You're not going to be rich!'

She cruised beside him. 'Why are you walking?'

'Because my battery's flat!' He added, 'Even flatter than my bank account.'

'Can I offer you a lift?'

He didn't answer. She drove beside him. 'I know about the treasure. Matt's just told me. I'm terribly sorry.'

'I bet you are. Now piss off to sunny Jerusalem.'

'I mean, for you. You deserved it.'

He snorted.

She said, 'I only did my duty, Jim.'

'You sure did! *Beyond* the call of duty. I hope they give you another pip for it. Now go back to Jerusalem and collect.'

'I don't want another pip. And I'm not going back to Jerusalem.'

'Go to Hell, then!'

She said, 'I will, and back. For you. I'm staying here in sunny Walvis Bay.'

McQuade almost stopped. Then kept walking. '*Oh* no you're not!'

'*Oh* yes I am! I've already resigned. I'm going to see this thing through. Because I love you, Jim.'

'I've heard *that* before.' He snorted.

'And I meant it, then! As I mean it now! Why do you think I got myself into such a mess?'

'You seemed to do pretty well!'

'*Goddammit!*' She slammed on her brakes and flung open the door. McQuade kept walking. She scrambled out and ran after him. She grabbed him by the shirt front and he stopped.

She glared up at him. '*Goddammit*, how do you think I felt being madly in love with you and knowing I was deceiving you?! *Knowing* I was going to lose you when you found out! *Knowing* that all your hard work was probably for nothing! *Knowing* that any day Matt might change his plan and jump on you and hurt you! *Knowing* that any day I might lead you into an ambush!'

'You led me into an ambush in Sun City!' He started walking again.

'No! I didn't know they were going to roll you. I didn't know their plan, and I was so shocked that you were being hurt that I lost my cool and blew my cover!'

'You then deceived me further! You told me you had quit Mossad and were going to help me find Muller! But you were *still* working for them! And you tried to lead me into another ambush after I'd snatched Muller!'

She grabbed him and made him stop. 'Yes! Because that was my god-awful duty! Because I wanted Muller on trial in Jerusalem! But I told Matt that if they hurt you I'd scream blue murder, and I was going to do my best to get the information out of Muller for you!'

'But all that help – all that training was just bullshit, to deceive me!'

She cried, 'No! I wanted to get you fit for the job you were hell-bent on doing! Because I loved you. I wanted you to be able to defend yourself! Didn't I teach you to defend yourself? *Didn't* I?'

He turned and walked on down Oceana Road in the fog. She hurried after him. 'Jim, I'm not deceiving you now, am I? What can I possibly deceive you about? Not your money because you haven't got any.'

He kept on walking. She put her arm around him. He tried to shrug it off him but she clung and said, 'Jim, I'm staying. Because I love you.'

He kept on walking. She walked beside him, holding tight. 'Please put your arm around me. *Feel* me. *Feel* how much I love you . . .'

And, oh, he longed to and he felt his eyes burn, but he

didn't put his arm around her. She strode beside him a moment longer, then took a resolute breath and soldiered on. 'What're you going to do from here?'

McQuade strode along. 'Going *fishing*.'

'Not Australia? The passenger line down the Great Barrier Reef?'

'With what money?' He snorted and strode on. 'No, I'm going to see this through.'

'See what through?'

He wanted to shout it. 'This Nazi business! See they're blown out! God knows I've got no love for this government but at least they're slowly re-joining the Human Race, and they're the only bastards who can drag this Afrikaner country into the twentieth century!' He snorted furiously again. 'God! Who would ever have thought it?'

She strode beside him through the fog. 'Good.' She squeezed him again and soldiered on, 'I've a confession to make.'

Nothing would surprise him. 'Nothing would surprise me,' he said bitterly.

'Jim, not only am I staying, I've already moved into your house.'

He stopped.

'How the hell did you get in?'

'I picked the lock.'

He glared at her. 'Of all the dirty Mossad cheek!'

'*Ex*-Mossad. Please, please, *ex*-Mossad!' Then she grabbed his shirtfront in both hands and then plunged her mouth fiercely onto his. She buried her tongue once into his mouth and then whispered, 'You're right. I'm *staying*! And you *know* I am! Because you *know* I love you! And you *know* you love me!' She shook him once. 'Admit it!'

He looked down at her and he could still taste her sweet mouth, and suddenly his eyes were burning with tears.

'What am I right about?'

She shook him. 'About remaining in this crazy mixed-up

653

country! You love it. And I love you and you love me!' She shook him again. '*Admit* it!'

He looked at her, and, oh, he wanted to weep and then laugh. He fought it back.

Her eyes lit up with joy and her wide smile spread over her face and she shook him once more and shouted '*Yippee!*' She plunged her hot mouth onto his again fiercely, then turned and began to run back through the fog to her car. '*Then why aren't we hurrying home?!*'

She ran off into the fog, and she gave a little jump and thrust her fist up into the air like a runner winning a race. She raced up to her rented car and scrambled in, then she leant out the window. He could not see her through the fog. She put both hands to her lovely mouth and bellowed:

'*I love you, James van Niekerk McQuade!*'

It seemed to echo over fog-bound Walvis Bay. He had visions of people being woken at the lagoon-end of town, the flamingoes rising up in alarm. The tears were burning in his eyes, and oh God he was happy.

AUTHOR'S NOTE

This book was completed in May, 1989. Since then, a number of dramatic things have happened in the world. None of these events, however, gainsay the political premise of this story: namely the serious threat posed by the right wing in South Africa.

United Nations Resolution 435 has been implemented and Namibia has been granted its independence from South Africa. It was his anxiety about this possibility that made the hero of this book, James McQuade, return to southern Africa. The South West African Peoples Organization (SWAPO), which represents the largest tribe, the Ovambos, won the election as McQuade predicted, and Mr Sam Nujoma is the country's president. Whilst preparations for Namibia's independence were in progress, Mr P. W. Botha was succeeded as state president of South Africa by Mr F. W. de Klerk, who immediately embarked on a bold programme of reform.

Then, completely unpredictably, the Berlin Wall came tumbling down almost overnight, followed rapidly by the collapse of most of the communist governments in the Eastern Bloc, effectively proving the failure of Marxism and the effectiveness of People Power.

While the erstwhile state president, Mr P. W. Botha, may legitimately be said to have initiated the first cautious steps towards reforms in South Africa – the 'glimmers of hope' grudgingly mentioned by characters in this book, reforms that gave rise to the right-wing backlash in the shape of the neo-Nazi AWB and similar movements – the new state presidcnt, Mr F. W. de Klerk, has initiated reforms with breathtaking speed.

The ANC and all other political movements have been unbanned, including the South African Communist Party; Nelson Mandela has been released from a life sentence imposed for treason, and most political prisoners have been released; the demolition of the Apartheid Wall and its repressive legislation has begun; a new constitutional dispensation has been promised; and formal negotiations between the government, the ANC and other political organizations have commenced to hammer out the details of this constitution. These negotiations will be protracted, probably covering years, and they will involve considerable posturing, walk-outs, 'card-playing' and 'horse-trading', and finally, it is to be hoped, hard-won concessions by both sides.

The basic bone of contention is likely to be whether, under the new constitution, 'winner takes all' in a unitary state, as the ANC demands, or whether 'minority group rights', in addition to an *individual*'s rights, will be protected, as the government demands. This the government sees as a necessary guarantee against black domination of whites, while the ANC sees it as a form of continuation of Apartheid.

Whatever the merits of either argument, all this is regarded by the right-wing organizations as an outrageous, perfidious sell-out by the government to the forces of darkness, and they vow to fight to the bitter end for the preservation of a white South Africa with Verwoerdian Apartheid or, at the very least, for a pure-white state within South Africa.

These right-wing groups, notably the AWB and the Boerestaat Party, are well-armed, well-trained and well-organized for the civil war they swear is coming (or will provoke), and they intend to derail the negotiation process. Like Heinrich Muller in this book, they vociferously declare that in the chaos that will ensue from the reforms – chaos which the government will be unable to contain – whites will see the error of Mr de Klerk's ways and flock to the laager under right-wing banners, whence the right-wing commandos will storm forth and restore Verwoerdian law and order in the land.

The chaos the right-wing clamorously forecasts is rumbling in the wings. Black-versus-black civil war is raging in Natal between the Zulu impis of Inkatha and the black ANC/UDF, with both groups trying to impose their political will on the other. Neither government forces nor the pleas of Mr Nelson Mandela to 'throw your pangas into the sea' have had any effect – indeed, apart from the many thousands rendered homeless, the fighting has already caused more deaths and injuries than did the seventeen years of South Africa's border war against SWAPO and its Cuban allies. The 'independent' homeland of Ciskei has erupted in mayhem and nihilism as the people ousted their black president, and a similar attempted coup in the 'independent' black statelet of Bophuthatswana was crushed. Demonstrations within South Africa have turned into riotous assemblies, resulting in police dispersals (whether justifiable or not) and more deaths.

The ANC is itself divided between the official representatives who are negotiating with the government on the one hand, and their own hardliners on the other, who want to bring the government to its knees. AZAPO (the Azanian Peoples Organization) condemns the ANC for 'illusory goals', and the PAC (Pan African Congress), with its motto of 'One Settler One Bullet', accuses the ANC of 'selling out' to the government and absolutely refuses to come to the negotiating table, proclaiming that power can only be won from the barrel of a gun. All this divisiveness is compounded by the age-old African tradition that political opposition is not to be tolerated, that it is the chief's natural right to rule without challengers.

Another complication is that throughout this land, which is bigger than France, Spain and Great Britain combined, there is the disturbing problem of 'the Youth': the vast masses who are unemployed and unemployable largely because they

657

chose to follow the slogan 'Liberation Before Education'; the volatile, immature legions whose expectations have been raised by all these recent heady events and who are demanding action and rewards *now*.

Most — though not all — of this witches' brew of trouble is the legacy of the failed, repressive system of Apartheid, and perhaps the violence we are seeing, and will see, is but a purging stage that the country has to go through, an evacuation of steam, now that Mr de Klerk has let the genie of freedom and political expression out of the bottle — nonetheless a witches' brew it is. It is this potential chaos, along with the 'failure' of the rest of Africa, that the sabre-rattling right wing realistically points to as their *raison d'être*. The threat they pose is very dangerous indeed. They could, and certainly want to, stop everything and drive South Africa back into the laager, whereupon the Bloodbath, so long expected of this country, is likely to ensue.

The right wing could not defeat the government in a straight fight — that is not how the battles would be fought. However, the right wing's capability to wear down the government's forces in a 'Boer War' of attrition is beyond doubt, especially as the loyalty of a substantial percentage of the police and army is questionable. Their ability to derail the negotiations by confrontations with blacks is obvious — 'a single spark can start a prairie fire', as Mao Tse-tung said. The threat they pose to peace and the new South Africa is frightening, and it is taken very seriously indeed.

As Heinrich Muller says in this book, for the right wing things have never looked better. They have never been so strong, and they are likely to get stronger in the anxious years of transition ahead.

JGD
May 1990

Hold My Hand
I'm Dying
John Gordon Davis

'This is the best novel coming out of Africa that I have read for a number of years. *It is Africa today.* It has the inevitability of a Greek tragedy . . . both moving emotionally and full of adventure.'
Stuart Cloete

The great heart of old Africa is dying. Joseph Mahoney, the last colonial commissioner in the spectacular Kariba Gorge, is there to witness the death throes. Somehow, he must also ease the birth pangs of the new Africa that will take its place. His companions are Samson, his Matabele servant, and Suzie, the girl he loves.

But Mahoney and Suzie are drifting apart, and now Samson has been accused of murder. And all too quickly, it seems, the country is heading towards a bloodbath of revenge.

Hold My Hand I'm Dying – a compelling story of freedom, friendship and love in the face of hatred, violence and death.

'A great, compassionate and deeply moving book. I did not know how to put it down.'
Marguerite Steen

FONTANA PAPERBACKS

The Other Side of Midnight
Sidney Sheldon

The magnificent novel of scorching sensation and shimmering evil that became a triumphant screen sensation.

A beautiful French actress whose craving for passion and vengeance took her from the gutters of Paris to the bedroom of a millionaire . . . a dynamic Greek tycoon who never forgot an insult, never forgave an injury . . . a handsome war hero drawn from his wife to a woman none could resist . . . and a girl whose dream of love was transformed into a nightmare of fear . . .

THE OTHER SIDE OF MIDNIGIIT

Paris and Washington, Hollywood and the islands of Greece are the settings for a dramatic narrative of four star-crossed lives enmeshed in a deadly ritual of passion, intrigue and corruption where the punishment will always exceed the crime . . .

'Gripping, glamorous, memorable, heart-stopping.'

Irving Wallace

FONTANA PAPERBACKS

Fontana Paperbacks: Fiction

Fontana is a leading paperback publisher of fiction. Below are some recent titles.

- ☐ ULTIMATE PRIZES Susan Howarth £3.99
- ☐ THE CLONING OF JOANNA MAY Fay Weldon £3.50
- ☐ HOME RUN Gerald Seymour £3.99
- ☐ HOT TYPE Kristy Daniels £3.99
- ☐ BLACK RAIN Masuji Ibuse £3.99
- ☐ HOSTAGE TOWER John Denis £2.99
- ☐ PHOTO FINISH Ngaio Marsh £2.99

You can buy Fontana paperbacks at your local bookshop or newsagent. Or you can order them from Fontana Paperbacks, Cash Sales Department, Box 29, Douglas, Isle of Man. Please send a cheque, postal or money order (not currency) worth the purchase price plus 22p per book for postage (maximum postage required is £3.00 for orders within the UK).

NAME (Block letters)_____

ADDRESS_____

_____